El Rey:
*A Novel of Renais*___*eria*

Ginger Myrick

ISBN:1481909975
ISBN-13: 978-1481909976

This book is dedicated to…

… my husband and soulmate, Terry. You have been a constant source of encouragement and inspiration and have provided me with the freedom and support to see this to completion. You are the other half of me and truly El Rey of my heart, my life, and my world.

… and my mother, Jerri Lynn Myrick. Without your patient guidance and gentle discipline, I would have never developed the confidence to attempt such an ambitious undertaking. Thank you for providing me with the vision to never focus on life's limitations, only on its possibilities.

Special thanks to ...

... my dear friend, Caren Cassidy, who was my very first reader and sounding board.

... my daughter-in-law, Jessi, who was my emotional gauge.

... my two sons, Cristian and Ian, who appear throughout the work in various incarnations.

... Andrew W. M. Beierle, author of *First Person Plural* and *The Winter of Our Discotheque*, who was my personal style guide.

... internationally acclaimed artist, John Kirthian Court, and his wife, Manuela, who provided me with the authentic perspective of the Portuguese people.

... Professors Harvey L. Sharrer, Eduardo P. Raposo, and Carlos Pio at the Center for Portuguese Studies at UCSB for their assistance with the Portuguese language.

"... with God all things are possible."- Matthew 19:26

CONTENTS

That being said, I have done my best to get the facts right and authentically depict the events of the time. I want my readers to be transported to a different age and to connect with the characters, to laugh a little and cry a little, and most of all, to be entertained. I want to leave them thinking not *did* it occur that way or *would* it have occurred that way, but *could* it have occurred that way.

Prologue
1581

The alarming boom of cannon fire resounded across the rolling green plains of the island, shattering the quiet of the peaceful summer morning. The old woman sat in her chair next to a roaring fire. It was the last week of July, the sun already blazing in the midmorning sky, but that made no difference to her tired old body. Nothing she did lately seemed to warm it.

Her great-granddaughter sat next to her. The girl's charcoal-colored eyes, a darker version of her own, stared up at her seeking reassurance. The child's pale face was surrounded by an abundance of reddish-brown curls streaked with coppery highlights. The old woman imagined that she had looked very much like this at ten, only her great-granddaughter was much prettier than she had ever been.

"Don't be frightened, *Baixinha*," she said, using the Portuguese term of endearment meaning 'little one'. "The conflict will never reach this far inland. We are very, very safe."

"But my father is not," the girl answered, crinkling up her nose in consternation. "He plans to go back down to the harbor to fight the Spanish. That is why he and my mother are arguing right now."

The old woman lovingly ran her hand over the unruly strands of her great-granddaughter's hair. Childhood came to an end much too quickly. It was not fair for a young girl to spend even a moment of this precious time in fear. She cupped the child's chin in her blue-veined hand, and with a smile she said, "Why don't you run up and fetch my box."

The little girl's face immediately brightened. She jumped

from her seat and hurried up the stairs to do her grandmama's bidding. A few minutes later, she reappeared and skipped down the steps, her cares forgotten and her eyes shining with anticipation. She had seen the maple wood box and the contents within on numerous occasions, but she still looked forward to the prospect as if it were the first time. She stood in front of the fire and ran her hand over the flowers and the bird on its intricately carved surface, mesmerized by the glassy finish.

She carefully handed over the box and bent to unlock it with the tiny key, which pended from a delicate gold chain around her neck. Her grandmama had given it to her for her tenth birthday and had promised that someday the box would also be hers. She situated herself at the foot of the old woman's chair and waited for the story to begin.

"I was not always this old," the woman said in familiar preamble. "Believe it or not, I was once a young girl with a young girl's hopes and dreams, just like you. I was not much older than you are now the first time I met *El Rey*."

Her great-granddaughter smiled up at her, a dreamy look coming into her dark gray eyes. "The King," the girl said, recalling every detail of her favorite story. It was like a fairytale, and she could never hear it too often. "What was it like, Grandmama, that day when you met the king?" she asked, taking her great-grandmother's hand and gently prodding her to continue.

The old woman smiled down at the pretty little girl. Had she ever really been this young? It was hard to believe that she had. It was so long ago. She had met El Rey the first time when she was eleven and had even asked to see his crown. She chuckled to herself, marveling at the ignorance of youth. She was now very old, and the only thing that brought her any pleasure was to remember.

BOOK 1: First Love
1509
Chapter 1: Preparation for the King

The entire household was in a dither. El Rey was coming tonight and everything must be perfect. The clash of pots and pans clanged through the kitchen, and the tantalizing aroma of fresh-baked bread hung on the air. The cooks, spurred on to unheard of feats of culinary creativity, baited each other with boasts that their own dish would be the one favored by their auspicious guest. All of the furniture had been polished to a brilliant shine, and fresh rushes were strewn about the floor mixed with lavender and thyme to add a fragrant freshness to the air. The tableware gleamed on the spotless linen, and candles were scattered about the room ready for lighting at the first shades of dusk.

Joanna García stood ramrod straight, overseeing all of the last minute details. She was a formidable woman who ruled over the household with an iron fist. As a result, her supper parties were always a success and the most envied invitation one could receive. She had been a stunning, carefree girl in her youth, but time and responsibility had changed that. Although now grown stout and showing her age, she was still a handsome woman at forty-seven.

Seeing the expression on her mother's face, Inez decided to avoid the great room. Instead, she sneaked through the kitchen, stealing an *empañada* as she went. She bit into the crusty little meat pie and made her way to the other side of the house. Though outwardly unaffected, she was just as excited as everyone else. In an attempt to maintain her decorous façade, she sang a tune to herself as she mounted the stairs to the room that she shared with her sister. Opening the door, she found the older girl seated in front of the mirror arranging her hair and putting the finishing touches on her already beautiful face. Inez never ceased to be moved by her sister's beauty. Serafina was eighteen years old and the most beautiful woman in Vigo. She was tall and slender with a tiny waist that could be encircled by a large man's hands. Her deep honey-colored hair fell in thick waves to her waist, and her skin was the golden color of a sun-kissed peach. The eyes that peered out of her heart-shaped face were the blue-green of the sea that was so much a part of their home, and her perfectly formed lips, slightly full and utterly kissable, were topped by a small straight nose.

Inez looked down at her dirty hands and ragged fingernails, crumbs of the empañada clinging to every crease. She was never more conscious of her own shortcomings as when she was in the presence of her sister's beauty, so she turned to the only thing she had to rival it...her wit.

"Serafina, why do you simper so and play the feather-headed ninny when there are men around?" asked Inez. "You are so smart. Why not show it?"

Serafina considered the question thoughtfully for a moment, her index finger placed just so on her delicately pointed chin, then answered, "Because, little sister, I want to marry well."

Without missing a beat Inez responded, "When I marry, I want my husband to respect me for my intellect and my spirit rather than fawn over me because of my feminine charms."

"You have no feminine charms," answered the older girl.

"Not yet, but someday I will. And when that day arrives, I vow that my intellect will be as well-developed!"

"You have strange ideas for one so young, little sister. I am glad that I am the great beauty in the family and shall not have to compete with you for a husband. That would be daunting indeed."

Turning away, Inez said under her breath, "We would never have to compete for the same man."

At that moment, their mother swept into their room like a winter gale. "Girls! Why are you not ready yet? Inez! You have not even put on your new dress!"

"Mama, why can't I just wear this one?"

"Because I don't want El Rey to think we are allowing street urchins to dine with us on our most special occasions!" Joanna snapped. "This supper is very important to your father. Now get dressed, and please try to keep the impertinence to a minimum."

"My dearest mother, always trying to stifle any stimulating conversation."

Turning her eyes skyward as if petitioning the heavens to give her patience, Joanna said, "Honestly, Inez, where do you learn to speak so? I never had this trouble with your sister."

"As you well know, dear lady, I learned it from my father. He is the only other person in this house who has a mind of his own."

"Then maybe I should beat him as well!"

Serafina, always the peacemaker, cut in, "Mama, you know very well that you won't beat anyone. Besides, how can you punish her for speaking the truth? Inez is only eleven. Let her be a child while she can. When she becomes a woman, her husband can beat her."

"You are right, but for the life of me I can't imagine anyone who would want to marry her. Very well, Inez, no beating tonight, but you must wear your new dress! You will at least *look* like a young lady."

As their mother breezed from their room, Inez crinkled up her nose, shuffled over to the bed where her dress was laid out, and began to undress. Green again. Why was it that Serafina always got the pretty colors? She paused for a moment, a mischievous idea dawning in her mind. Maybe she would defy her mother and not wear the new dress. After all, her mother had never beaten her in her life. Then she thought how disappointed her father would be, and it brought an almost physical pain to her.

Determined to be a credit to him, Inez stripped down to her shift and began to loosen the lacings on the new dress. Sorry for their mother's hurtful comments, Serafina softened and began to help her little sister. She dipped a cloth in the still-warm basin of rose water and washed Inez's face and hands. Then she helped her into her dress and began to brush her hair. The long, soothing strokes brought out the coppery highlights and lustrous shine, and when she was done, Inez looked quite the young lady.

"Well, little sister, you look very pretty," Serafina said as she stepped back to survey her handiwork. "You should wash your face and brush your hair more often. Maybe then our father would get complimented on his *two* lovely daughters rather than his beautiful daughter and the young hoyden who shares her room."

Inez only gave her a pinch on the arm and darted out the door.

Iñigo García was a tall, bookish man with a kindly face and soft-spoken mien. Although he had made his name as a merchant, he had the demeanor of an absent-minded parish priest. Some people took his placid, bumbling manner as weakness but soon learned different when attempting to turn business to their advantage. His church mouse exterior belied a keen mind that, like a steel trap, never let go of anything useful. He had spent his life in his trade working the most menial of jobs and could be the toughest of negotiators when required. His only weakness was his family.

He loved his women to distraction, and Inez was his favorite. In her he had found the kindred spirit he had sought his entire life. Funny that it should come through a daughter. From the moment he'd held the red wrinkly newborn, she'd stolen a place in his heart he didn't know existed. He'd insisted she be named after his mother. She was not as beautiful as Serafina, but her mind was a masterpiece. She had a thirst for learning that could never be slaked, and she understood him. What a son she would have made! He rued the fact that she had not been born a boy and wrestled with the idea that someday she would have to submit to a husband, and her amazing intellect would be squelched.

As he approached the stairs, he saw a small figure appear at the top. Inez. He was immediately filled with love and affection at the sight of her. Surprisingly, he noticed that she looked more polished than he had ever seen her. *Must be Serafina's doing*, he grumbled to himself. He didn't know why he should feel resentment at his youngest looking so pretty, but he did. Perhaps it brought him that much closer to the day when he would have to let her go.

"I came in here looking for my Mynah, and all I find is a pretty little girl looking very lost. Can I help you find your parents, little girl?"

Inez grinned as she ran down the stairs and threw herself into her father's arms. "Oh Papa, you know it's me!" she said as she squeezed his neck.

"What did Serafina do to you? You look like a different person," he said as he lowered her to the ground.

"It isn't too terrible, is it?" she asked, scrunching up her nose.

"Only when you make that face, Mynah."

'Mynah' was the pet name he had used for her since she had begun talking. She had repeated everything she heard, even songs, until she got them perfect. Iñigo smiled at the memory of his tiny daughter toddling through the house, singing the songs learned during her forays into the forbidden kitchen. How Joanna had fumed! That her daughter should sing the traditional songs of the Portuguese servants was unthinkable. He was wrenched out of his reverie by that same strident voice.

"Iñigo! If you are not doing something useful, at least take your daughter somewhere she won't be in the way! And make sure she doesn't ruin her dress!"

"Yes, dear," he said. He smiled at her and patted her affectionately on the cheek. Turning to Inez he said, "Come along, Mynah. Let's find out what we can see from the knoll."

Hand in hand, father and daughter left the house and made their way up the gentle incline, both happy to be out in the open away from the frantic preparations. The well-worn path led them past the remains of a prehistoric Celtiberian fort that had been Inez's private playground for most of her young life. Just as the heat of the cloudless summer afternoon became unbearable, they reached the welcoming shade of the ancient olive tree at the top of the hill, and the panorama opened to them.

The sea below glittered like diamonds scattered across azure velvet. Iñigo and Inez looked out at the Ria de Vigo. The large estuary stretched east farther than the eye could see to receive the water that rushed into it from the many rivers cutting through mainland Galicia. To the north, the cities of Canga and Moana stared back at them from the uneven finger of land on the other side. To the west lay the Illas Cies and beyond, the vast expanse of the Atlantic Ocean.

Although the day was clear and the sea calm, the port of Vigo was bustling with vitality. A slight breeze wafted the clean scent of the ocean inland. Fishing boats scudded into the harbor ahead of the wind after a full day at work on the waves. Seagulls wheeled and screamed greedily, watching for any dropped morsel. From their vantage point on the knoll, father and daughter could almost hear the fishmongers hawking their freshly caught goods and the townspeople haggling for a better price.

They stood for a moment, mesmerized by the activity below, each of them lost in their own thoughts. Finally Inez started to fidget, breaking the spell. She skipped over to the swing her father had lovingly carved so many years ago and plopped down. Iñigo followed her example and found his way to the bench a few feet away. Like magic he produced his pocketknife and one of the little chunks of wood that he always seemed to have with him and began to whittle. They sat in companionable silence as the late afternoon sun slanted through the silvery leaves of the sheltering olive tree. Every once in a while, one of them cast a glance down at the port to see if anything new had developed. Time passed, and eventually the sun began its descent into the ocean, the last of its rays fading before the coming of night. The sea breeze now carried a slight chill and was no longer so welcome.

Iñigo rose from the bench and stretched. "Well, Mynah, I think we should head back. It's starting to get cool, and your mother would never let me hear the end of it if you got sick." He thought for a moment then added, "Perhaps El Rey found his way up the back road." He turned and walked a few steps in the direction of the house.

Inez sighed and slid down from the swing. As she began to drag her feet toward her father, out of the corner of her eye she caught a movement on the road below. She turned to get a better view and, clapping her hands, began to jump up and down. "Look! Look, Papa!" she cried, pointing. "Is that El Rey?! Is it him?"

Iñigo came back to the crest of the hill and looked down. In the dimming light of dusk, he made out a procession galloping up the main thoroughfare. The man on the lead horse rode with the regal grace and easy seat of many years spent in the saddle. His long dark hair streamed out behind him, and the banner carried by the standard-bearer displayed the falcon crest, the trademark of El Rey.

"Yes, Mynah, it is El Rey," Iñigo answered, reaching for her hand. "Let's hurry to the house to give your mother fair warning."

Hands clasped, they dashed down the hill. When they reached the house, they pulled up short. Dark had fallen and all of the candles and lanterns were lit. Their snug, solid home looked like an enchanted cottage in a fairytale. The flickering light of the candles danced like pixies, and the clean wood smoke from the fireplace floated up to the sky like a cloud of magical dust hovering after the casting of a spell.

"Oh papa! Look how beautiful!" Inez exclaimed.

Iñigo looked down at his daughter's shining face and smiled. Because she was so intelligent, so precocious, sometimes he forgot she was still a child. In that moment, something twisted inside him, and he wished she could remain like this forever. Feeling like a sentimental old fool, he squeezed her shoulder and said, "Your mother will be waiting. Let's get inside."

They entered the house through the kitchen. The atmosphere that had seemed so oppressive before now embraced them like an old friend. Platters of food stood ready to go to the table at a moment's notice. A suckling pig, its crackling skin browned to perfection, waited alongside dishes heaped with seafood plentiful and fresh from the ocean. Steaming bowls of rice cooked with sausage, chicken, and shellfish made up the savory *paellas* that were a staple of coastal Spain. A mountain of crusty loaves was piled next to pitchers of decanted wine. Inviting desserts encased in their flaky golden crusts were just being taken from the ovens. The warmth and scents of the kitchen reminded Inez how long it had been since she had eaten a meal but excitement won out, and she scurried through to the dining room, Iñigo a few steps behind. They found Joanna supervising the placement of the chairs, scowling at the slowness with which the servants complied to her demands.

"Mama!" exhaled Inez. "We were up on the knoll and ..."

"There you are! Where have you two been? Inez! Look at your shoes! Iñigo, how could you let her get her shoes so dirty? El Rey will soon be here, and then ..."

"Mama! That's what I'm trying to tell you!" Inez burst out, cutting her mother off. "He's coming! He's almost here!"

Joanna's eyes flew wide open. Caught by surprise, she let the insolence slide. Hurriedly telling the servants to leave the chairs where they were, she whipped off the apron that covered her stately black dress and threw it into the kitchen. Then she checked her reflection in a nearby mirror, fussily smoothing and re-pinning a few stray wisps of hair. Taking a long cleansing breath, she regained her composure and became the picture of supreme poise. With her most winning smile in place she said, "Well then, shall we go greet our guests?"

"What about Serafina?" asked Inez. "Shouldn't we go get her, too?"

"Your sister is resting. You know how delicate her health is," replied Joanna. With a twinkle in her eye she added, "I'm sure our guests won't mind if she comes down a little later." With that she took her husband's arm and proceeded to the front door. Inez followed eagerly at their heels.

As they stepped outside, they saw El Rey swinging down from his mount. He casually tossed the reins to a waiting groom, and as he flipped his hair back over his shoulder, his face was revealed. Striding toward them in his cool, self-assured manner was the most beautiful man Inez had ever seen. Her head swam, and she found it difficult to breathe. In an attempt to keep her pounding heart a secret, she dropped her gaze and inconspicuously inched behind her mother. From there she peeked out to get a better look.

Inez had expected 'The King' to be a giant of a man, but that was not the case. The confidence that radiated from him added to his stature, but in reality he was only slightly taller than the average man. His long tenure as a sea captain had left him well-muscled and broad-shouldered yet still slender. His hair fell to the middle of his back and was dark and glossy as a raven's wing. The dark eyes that peered from his sculpted face sparkled with intelligence and humor, and their slight almond shape lent an exotic cast to his extraordinary visage. He had a prominent Roman nose, which on another might have been a distraction but on him was not uncomely and suited his face. As he drew closer, his face broke into a smile showing strong white teeth, and Inez had to catch her breath.

"*Senhor* García," began El Rey in Portuguese, bending slightly at the waist. "At last we meet, and what a pleasure it is. And this enchanting creature?" he asked, turning to Joanna. "Your daughter I presume?"

She giggled like a young girl as he bowed over her hand with a courtly flourish and grazed it with his lips. "*Por favor, Señor*," she stressed in Castilian, "Your flattery is well-intended, but I am far past the age to believe it. Welcome to our home. May I present our daughter," she said and pushed Inez to the fore.

Inez, feeling completely exposed, kept her head down and dropped a curtsey. "Pleased to meet you, Señor," she mumbled. She tried but could not bring herself to look him in the face, fearing that if she did, he would read her thoughts.

Finally, to her relief her father said, "Well then, shall we go inside?"

Chapter 2: The Supper Party

The party filed into the house, mingling with a few guests who had just arrived. They divided into smaller groups and made polite talk about business and the weather and what a wonderful job their hostess had done putting everything together. Laughter and the hum of human chatter filled the room to every corner. Servants circulated unobtrusively, making sure that no one suffered an empty wineglass or undue hunger before the meal. Logs blazed in the fireplace, and minstrels lent their music to the cozy ambience of the pleasantly full room.

On another night Inez would have reveled in the fact that she was the only child present. She would have discreetly eavesdropped on conversations, furtively listening to educated— and not so educated—opinions on the state of government, trade, and of course, the local gossip. Whose stable boy had been caught kissing someone else's cook, whose scullery maid was with child—mysteriously without a husband? Tonight that was not the case. She felt that her will was no longer hers to control. All she wanted to do was to be near *him* and hear the sound of *his* voice, be a part of *his* conversation and listen to *his* opinion. She situated herself in an out of the way chair just outside the kitchen where she could observe the entire room and not be seen to do so. She pretended to enjoy the festive scene, and every few minutes she stole a glance at El Rey and her heart raced anew.

Paulina, the housekeeper who had been like a second mother to her, was passing by with an empty tray to be refilled when she spotted Inez on the chair. She saw the fever-bright eyes and slightly pained expression on the little girl's face and was immediately concerned.

"Baixinha!"

Inez jumped in her seat. She had been so intent upon remaining undetected in her observation that she hadn't heard Paulina approach. Now jolted back to reality, she looked up, her dreamy eyes gradually focusing on Paulina's worried face. With an attempt to seem normal, she pasted a grin on her face and smoothed her dress across her lap.

"Hello, Paulina," she sighed. "It's a nice party, isn't it?"

Paulina knew her too well to be fooled. "Baixinha, you look feverish," she said, kneeling in front of her. Putting a hand to Inez's forehead, she was surprised to feel only cool skin beneath, so she asked, "Are you feeling all right?"

Inez nodded slowly, her smile slipping slightly to one side. "Yes, I'm fine," she said without any conviction.

Paulina took in the flushed face and over bright eyes, the listless sighing and guarded, stolen glances. "If I didn't know better, I'd say you look ..." she started with sudden realization, "lovesick."

Embarrassed to hear it out loud, Inez stammered an excuse. "No, uh ... I was just ... um, feeling a little warm, so I came to sit down and cool off."

"You came to sit next to the kitchen? To cool off?" Paulina asked, unconvinced.

Inez swallowed hard and nodded her head, unwilling to incriminate herself further.

"Well, Baixinha, I can see you don't want to talk about this now, so I will leave you alone. But when you want to talk," Paulina said, smiling and gently squeezing her hand, "remember that I too had a first love, and sometimes it helps to share with someone who cares for you very much."

Again Inez nodded and tried to smile. "Thank you, Paulina," she whispered and squeezed back.

At that instant a hush settled over the room. The occupants stopped what they were doing and looked toward the top of the staircase. It seemed that even the musicians played more softly to lend drama to the moment. The pause was followed by a collective intake of breath. Paulina and Inez looked around, bewildered by the silence, and followed the gaze of the guests. There at the landing on top of the stairs stood Serafina. Tall and proud, she was dressed in a gold gown that hugged her slender figure, showing off her graceful curves and impossibly small waist. Her honey-colored hair cascaded past her shoulders, and around her neck she wore her mother's prized aquamarine necklace. The jewels caught the light and brought out the color of her spectacular eyes. She seemed to glow from within, and she looked like a fairy queen. Even Inez, who usually sought to downplay her sister's beauty, was so stunned that she could only gape.

With practiced smoothness and a feigned look of surprise Joanna said, "Ah, Serafina. I'm so glad you are feeling better, my love. Please come down and join the party."

"Thank you, Mama," Serafina answered and descended the stairs, a golden feather floating down from the heights. By the time she reached the bottom, half a dozen male guests stepped up to offer their arms. She smiled graciously and moved forward with one admirer on each side, the rest hovering around her like bees drawn to a fragrant blossom. She made her way to a chair by the fire and proceeded to charm them all. She listened to them attentively, laughed when it was expected, and acted properly impressed when the conversation required.

Joanna surveyed the crowd around her daughter and smiled with self-satisfaction at the potential suitors. She recognized a couple of the wealthy inland merchants with whom Iñigo did business. Two *grandees,* an *hidalgo,* and a well-to-do *escudero* completed the group. They all wore the hangdog look of the completely infatuated. Men were so easy. Present them with a pretty face and a look of rapt fascination, and they were like putty in the hand. All the years of social grooming and preparation were about to pay off.

Across the room Inez itched to know if El Rey had been smitten, too. She shot a glance in his direction and was not disappointed. He was conversing with a group of the local gentry, and although he occasionally looked in Serafina's direction, his attention soon turned back to the discussion at hand. His eyes had an amused light to them and a slightly sardonic smile played about his lips. Certainly this was not the same love-struck look of the others. *I knew he was above all that*, Inez thought to herself. She smiled at her small, imagined victory over her sister.

A short time later, supper was announced and the guests made their way to the enormous trestle table. El Rey was given a place of honor next to the host, and Inez was seated across from him a few spots down where she could covertly study his every gesture. Serafina with her crowd of new conquests sat toward the other end of the table close enough to her mother so that Joanna could keep track of her daughter's progress. The feast was laid before them, and the small talk soon lapsed into the distinctive sounds of diners enjoying the meal. Utensils clinked against plates, wineglasses came together in the ringing bell tones of toasted good health, and satisfied grunts and belches bore testament to the deliciousness of the food.

As the guests ate and drank their fill, the soporific effects of the victuals made themselves felt. Chairs were pushed back from the table to accommodate expanding waistlines, chins were propped on hands to hold up heads that had become suddenly heavy, and wives leaned against husbands for support. Although the conversation dwindled, they were all loath to leave the comforting atmosphere surrounding the table. Seeking to liven the mood, one of the guests shouted, "*Capitán* Rey! A song!" Others joined in until the entire table chanted in unison.

El Rey was renowned for his ability to entertain. He was adored for his singing and songwriting talents and was reputed to be one of the most outstanding singers in all of Iberia. Some touted his voice as a gift from God. Although he made the pretense of merely fulfilling an obligation, he lived to perform.

With a resigned smile, he turned to Iñigo to beg pardon. "With your permission, Señor García." Iñigo inclined his head to indicate his acquiescence. Turning to one of the minstrels El Rey asked, "May I borrow your guitar, Senhor?" The musician passed it to him. "*Obrigado*, my friend," he said and strummed a plaintive minor chord. He began a ballad of his own composition about his first voyage when at sixteen he had sailed to India with Vasco da Gama.

Some of the guests had started to nod off with the conclusion of the meal, but as El Rey sang the first notes of the song, all heads came to attention and eyes opened wide, astonished at the purity of his flawless tenor voice. They were held rapt by the rich velvet tones and marveled at the ease of control with which he hit each note then soared on to the next. His voice was so expressive it was as if he poured his soul into each tone, giving it a life of its own. His artistry was such that each nuance, each shade of emotion, was not heard but felt. He held the table enthralled. They gasped as one at the dangers that he faced and cheered at his triumphs.

Lulled by his melodic voice, Inez closed her eyes and the scenes played out before her. She felt the jolting of the ship as it battled through heavy seas around the Cape of Good Hope, the captain shouting orders and the crew scurrying to comply. She shared the pride of the sailors as they sailed beyond the Great Fish River, the farthest point ever attained by a previous expedition. She saw the natives with their brown skin and colorful garb shouting fearsome hostilities in their foreign tongue, and she felt despair as only two of the four ships and 44 of the original 168 men limped back into the harbor at Lisbon.

Inez ventured a peek at her mother and saw that even Joanna was absorbed in the tale. She silently thanked the heavens that she had been overlooked and allowed to remain at the table to experience the retelling of such an important episode in the life of El Rey. She realized what an extraordinary man he was and ached to be a part of his life, no matter how small.

When he finished, there was a polite smattering of applause, and many of the guests were discreetly wiping tears from their eyes. "Well," El Rey said with a wry smile, "this will definitely not do for a party. How about something a little more rousing?" And he launched into a rollicking rendition of a Portuguese folk song known by most of the population in the region.

Most of the guests began singing along, and those who did not know the words clapped to keep time. Inez recognized the song and, throwing all pretense of maturity aside, joined in with all the gusto her small body could muster. Her voice rang out clear and true like the peal of a bell, and those sitting close to her stopped singing just to listen. As the song progressed, more and more of the guests began to realize that something magical was happening and stopped to listen as well. Eventually Inez and El Rey were the only ones singing, his rich tenor taking the melody and Inez naturally chiming out the upper harmony she had learned as a child. Their voices combined and, like alchemy, produced something beautiful and bright yet completely different.

The song ended and the room erupted into applause and shouts of, "Brava! Brava!" Suddenly aware of what had happened, Inez blanched then flushed from the roots of her hair down to her toes. She looked down at her lap, and when she worked up the courage to venture a look at El Rey, it was the final insult.

In all his years he had found very few people to compare with him in this arena, and here in this unexpected setting, he had found someone with a talent approaching his own. In this tiny young girl he heard a voice that complemented his like no other. The excitement bubbled up inside of him, and he threw back his head and gave out a hearty laugh of sheer joy and appreciation.

Inez was mortified. He was laughing at her! All she wanted was to be a part of his celebration, and now she was the object of his disdain. Her nose crinkled up in an attempt to stop the tears from coming, but it was too much. With a tearing sob, she jumped up from the table and ran out the door.

Iñigo started out of his chair to go after her, but El Rey put a gentling hand on his sleeve and said, "Please Señor, allow me." He left his place at the table and hurried out after her.

As he left the house, El Rey grabbed one of the lanterns hanging outside the door. Not that he needed it. A full moon bloomed low in an indigo sky, illuminating the countryside with an eerie blue light. Sizing up his options, his eyes were drawn to the worn path leading up to the olive tree on the knoll. He nodded to himself and started up the trail, the lantern swinging at his side. As he walked, he replayed the moments leading up to the girl's sudden flight.

He recalled that he had been presented with a small child when he first arrived, but there had been nothing memorable about her. In fact, he'd only seen the top of her head, and the only thing that set her apart from any other child of the region were the strands of coppery color running through her otherwise unremarkable hair. From that moment, he had not noticed her again until he'd heard her voice commingling with his at the table. When she'd been lost in song, her face had transformed into that of an angel. Her little girl's features had been suffused with an ethereal light, her eyes shining bright with something approaching rapture. In that moment she had surpassed even her sister in beauty.

As he neared the crest of the hill, he saw the olive tree clearly outlined in the moonlight. Beneath it, he could just make out a small figure in a heap on the ground. She was hunched over the bench with her head in her hands, her body shaking with the violence of her sobs. He drew up to her with as much delicacy as he possessed and sat down. He put a comforting hand on her shoulder and waited for her anguish to subside.

When her tears finally ran out, Inez let go a long, ragged breath, sniffled once, and looked up to see who had come to take her back. As her eyes focused her mouth fell open and she stared uncomprehendingly at the man sitting on the bench looking out at the sea. She blinked two or three times to make sure her eyes were not betraying her. She had expected her father, but this was far beyond anything she could have imagined. Her mind reeled with confusion, and forgetting her manners, only one question repeated in her mind.

"Why did you come?" she asked in a small, strangled voice.

"The air inside was getting a bit close," he answered, still not looking at her. "I also heard that the view from here was impressive. Just look at that moon. It looks as if you could reach out and touch it!"

His ploy worked to distract her from her misery, and she turned around to contemplate the night sky. Still looking at the moon, she asked the question for which she needed an answer. "Why did you laugh at me? Was my singing so horrible?"

He looked down at her profile, and his face softened. "Little one, I think you need to learn when someone is laughing *with* you and not *at* you. There is a vast difference. Take it from one who knows."

"Why would anyone laugh at *you*?" she asked, finally looking up at him.

"Because of this," he said, turning to the side and tapping the end of his substantial nose with his finger.

"I don't see anything wrong with it. In fact to me it looks very distinguished and lends strength to your face. Besides, you would look very silly with a nose like mine," she said, scrunching up her own.

He smiled at her endearing habit. "Ah, little one, you make much sense for one so young. But children can be cruel."

Inez usually resented when anyone made reference to her size or youth, but she let it slip, hoping he wouldn't mention it again. Then an idea occurred to her. "When those children were making fun of you, why didn't you just have them punished?" He looked at her with his eyebrows raised, a quizzical look on his face. "Well, you are the king, are you not?" she asked innocently then added, "I would dearly love to see your crown. Would you show it to me?"

He tried hard not to laugh at her sincerity and said gently, "El Rey is merely a nickname made up by those same cruel children. It is supposed to be a slur on my heritage, but to me it has become a constant reminder of the things I have overcome and those I still hope to achieve," he finished, looking up at the moon. "But that is a story for another time and too harsh for one of such a tender age."

This time it was too much. She bridled at his comment and drew up in an unconscious imitation of her mother. "I'll have you know, Señor, that I shall celebrate my twelfth birthday in five weeks! That is not so very young!"

"Not so young indeed, but it leaves plenty of time in the future for more stories." After a short pause he added, "We should be heading back."

She wrinkled up her nose at the thought of facing all those people again after her childish behavior. To him she looked like an adorable little rabbit, and before he could stop himself, the words just slipped out.

"Here, *Coelhinha*, let me help you tidy up your face," he said, putting his hand under her chin and pulling a square of silk from his pocket. "We don't want the others to think you have been crying."

He looked down at the pale oval of her face and really saw it for the first time. She had a high forehead framed prettily by an abundance of wavy reddish-brown hair. High arched eyebrows and long dusky lashes were all he could see of her downcast eyes. She had a funny little nose with a handful of freckles sprinkled across the bridge, and her mouth was wide and full-lipped and would one day be temptingly sensuous. She was pretty in a childlike way but for the most part, ordinary. Then she opened her eyes.

He could see them clearly in the lantern light, and they took his breath away. Her eyes were large and round, shimmering with a few still unshed tears. The irises were the same silvery color of the leaves above them, tinged with a muted green, but that was not the thing that shocked him. The circumference of the pupil was surrounded by flecks of pure gold, and the look behind them was one of wisdom beyond her years. *A man could drown in those eyes*, he thought to himself and shuddered inside.

Inez also felt a shock at that moment. When she looked up at him she had expected to find pity in his eyes, but what she saw was a combined look of understanding and affection. She felt his desire to protect her, and she knew she would never love anyone else. She allowed him to smooth away the remnants of her outburst and shivered at the closeness of him.

He mistook the spasm for a chill, removed his jacket, and dropped it around her shoulders. She felt his warmth and breathed in his scent. An aroma of soap and wood smoke mixed with his natural male musk made her head spin and her heart beat faster. He put his hand on her back in a possessive gesture, and they retraced the steps she had covered earlier that evening with her father.

Upon reaching the house, El Rey suggested entering through the kitchen to give Inez a bit more time to collect herself. Though not wanting to break the bond that had forged between them and the closeness she felt while wearing his jacket, she reluctantly removed the garment and handed it to him. She made a move to return the handkerchief also, but he stopped her. Putting up a hand he said, "You can keep that." She smiled a little realizing that he was making a joke then looked down at her hands, nervously twisting the cloth between her fingers.

Sensing her anxiety, El Rey laid an encouraging hand on her shoulder. "What's the matter, Coelhinha? What is causing you so much trouble?"

She looked up at him with those unsettling eyes and said, "It's just that … I don't know how to thank you." Then she swallowed hard and looked back down at her hands. "I suppose to you it was nothing, but to me it meant the world."

"I'm only happy that I could be the one to help," he said, tenderly fingering a tress of her hair.

She stifled a yawn and was instantly aware of the late hour. She had been up since dawn, and the emotion and the cold of being outside had only added to her weariness. Suddenly, all she wanted was the familiarity and comfort of her warm bed. As if in a dream she said, "I think I shall retire."

El Rey nodded and said, "That is a good idea. I think I will remain here for a few minutes to warm up. Good night, Coelhinha."

"Good night, Senhor," she said and disappeared through the kitchen door.

Chapter 3: The Pact

The next morning when Inez awoke, she was surprised she had slept so late. The sun was already peeking through her window, and the birds chirped outside, deciding which of the insects buzzing about in the warm summer air would be breakfast. Serafina slept peacefully on the other side of the room, her beautiful golden hair spilling over her pillow like a molten river.

Inez stretched and yawned, luxuriating in the coziness of her bed, and began to replay last night's events in her mind. *Perhaps it was all a dream*, she thought to herself. Then her eyes chanced upon the square of silk El Rey had used to dry her tears. She picked it up and held it to her nose, closing her eyes and breathing deeply of its scent. His scent. He had carried this piece of cloth next to his heart, and so would she. In her child's mind she felt that in some small way it would tie them together, and she tucked it into her bodice.

Not wanting to wake her sister, she slipped quietly from her nest and donned an everyday dress of russet-colored linen. She tiptoed across the cool floor to the dresser and sluiced her face and neck with rosewater from the ewer. She ran a comb through her hair, deftly plaiting it and tying it off with a ribbon to match her dress. Then, shoes in hand, she edged silently through the door and closed it gently behind her.

Descending the stairs, Inez noticed the dining table had been set for breakfast buffet-style. This meant that some of the guests had stayed over. A little thrill ran through her at the thought. *Oh, please let him still be here*, she silently prayed. She contemplated the food spread before her, stowed two apples in her pockets, and picked up a hardboiled egg to quiet her grumbling belly. Then she headed to her father's study to find out what opinions he had to offer about the previous night's gathering.

Absorbed in her thoughts and the task of eating her egg, she opened the door to Iñigo's workroom, swinging it wide the way she always did, and stopped short. There, seated across from her father, was El Rey. They were deep in discussion about business matters, and when the door opened, they both looked up at her expectantly. He looked exactly as he had the evening before. She had imagined none of his attractiveness. In fact, his looks were even more striking exposed to the light of day. She quickly swallowed what was in her mouth, murmured an apology, and left the room.

As she walked from the house, Inez berated herself for her lack of manners. How many times had her mother impressed upon her that she must knock before entering a room? She hoped El Rey would forgive the intrusion and not think she was a low-class peasant with no sense of etiquette. For some reason when she was in his presence, her normal confidence gave way to a flustered, helpless feeling. Perhaps this was what love did. Heaven knew she had seen enough of the male population surrounding Vigo reduced to stuttering fools at the sight of her sister. She laughed at the thought that, although she could speak four languages, one day she might not be able to form one simple sentence. Cheered by the ridiculous image, she skipped the rest of the way to the stable.

She entered the building, breathing in the sweet scent of hay mixed with the earthy aroma of horseflesh. She stopped in front of the stall that held her Spanish Jennet and said brightly, "Good morning, Neblina!" The little grey horse nickered in answer, and Inez slid under the half-door. Pulling one of the apples out of her pocket, she bit off a chunk and gave it to the animal. While Neblina munched on her treat, Inez found the stiff-bristled brush and began the grooming that was a part of their daily routine. She sang while she worked, and soon the animal's coat was shining and tangle-free.

"Papa is busy right now, so we will have to postpone our

morning ride," she told the creature, giving her another chunk of apple. The horse bobbed her head as if in acknowledgement, and Inez planted a kiss on her soft warm muzzle before slipping out under the door.

She was greeted by the sight of El Rey leaning casually against a support beam. "*Bom dia*, Coelhinha. It seems we had the same idea," he said, showing her the apple in his hand. "Although I don't typically serenade my horses while I groom them."

Inez blushed a little and wrinkled up her nose. "Bom dia, Senhor," she said, dropping a curtsey.

"Such formality!" he said with mock-sincerity. "I would have thought that after last night we would be on more familiar terms."

"I would like that," she answered, "but what should I call you?"

"Yes, I see your dilemma," he said, pretending to think hard. "I have told you that I am not a king, so you can't very well call me El Rey. How about plain Estêvão? It is my given name, used only by my family and closest friends."

"I would feel very honored ..." she paused before adding, "Estêvão."

"Excellent! Now let me present you with another honor." He led her over to a neighboring stall and clicked his tongue at the occupant. A dark head peeked over the top of the half-door and nosed his master gently but insistently. "He smells the fruit. Would you like to give it to him?"

"Yes," said Inez nodding slowly, a look of wonder on her face. She had never seen such a horse. Though they were a necessity of her family's everyday life, the horses kept by her father were mostly the large draft animals used for hauling wagons of merchandise. Of course Iñigo had a fine Andalusian that he used for riding, and Inez had her little Neblina, but this horse was different from any of them.

He looked black in the shadow of the stable, but where the light fell on his coat she could see the brown undertones. From what she could tell, he was more compact in height and musculature than her father's sturdily built horse. He had a small head with a dished-in face and intelligent black eyes. His neck was sinewy and beautifully arched, and he had a wide chest that tapered down to a graceful pair of fine-boned legs. He snorted and pawed the ground in anticipation of the treat, and Inez sensed the fire that burned in this magnificent animal.

"Where did you get him?" she asked, taking the piece of apple Estêvão had cut and feeding it to the horse.

"My travels often take me to lands inhabited by Arab tribes, and one day when we put into port, there was a Bedouin chieftain hoping to do some trading. He had this horse on a lead, and I knew that I had to have him. I offered the man a few sacks of wheat and some pieces of armor, and the horse was mine. I named him *Tesouro*, because to me he is a treasure."

"He is very beautiful," Inez said, meaning every word.

"He is," Estêvão agreed. "These Arab horses are legendary for their speed and stamina. They are very willing to please and lovely to look at, but for me it is their intelligence and spirit that hold the attraction."

"Fine qualities to admire in anyone," Inez said enigmatically, recalling the words spoken to her sister just the day before.

They talked for a long time about their mutual love for animals then moved on to other subjects. They discovered that they had much in common, and eventually Inez began to feel more natural in his presence. Though there was a vast difference in their ages, Estêvão, twenty-eight, found that he enjoyed her company and often forgot that he was talking with an eleven-year-old girl. He asked her opinion on various subjects and realized he was considering her answer the way he would from one of his peers. He began to view her in a different light, and he appreciated her astuteness and direct manner of speaking. Time flew by and the hour for his departure drew near.

"Well, Coelhinha," he said, looking up at the sun, "I should walk up to the knoll to see if my ship has arrived. Would you like to accompany me?"

She nodded eagerly, and they started up the path. She was silent for a while then she gave him a sidelong look and asked,

"Why do you call me Coelhinha?"

He smiled at her question. "I have the peculiar habit of giving nicknames based on a person's resemblance to an animal, and you, little one, look like a rabbit."

"How do I look like a rabbit?" she asked, bunching up her nose and twitching it to one side.

"You are small and plump, and when you make that face," he said, gently tapping her nose, "you look just like a bunny sniffing her food."

She thought his comment over and decided to take it as a compliment. "My father says it is a bad habit, and someday my face will stay that way."

"I find it endearing," he assured her.

"What is your nickname?"

"Well, I am descended from the House of Avis, so my father named the people in my family for birds. My parents likened me to a falcon from the time I was a baby, so I am called *Falcão*. My mother says it is because I can see what I want and am determined to get it, but I suspect it may have something to do with my profile," he said self-deprecatingly.

"No, I think your mother is right," Inez said seriously then asked, "Is that why you have a falcon on your standard?"

"Yes it is, and it is set on a background of cobalt blue, my favorite color."

"I have a bird name too. My father calls me Mynah, though my mother abhors it. Perhaps you should marry me to make me part of your family."

He laughed heartily at that. "Is that a proposal?" he asked, looking at her with surprise.

She mulled over his question for a moment then replied thoughtfully, "I think I would like being married to you. You sing well and have a logical mind, and we have much in common."

"So we do," he said, smiling at her young girl's reasoning. She was so adult about other matters, but in this she was still innocent. Not wanting to hurt her feelings and getting swept away in the moment he added, "I'll tell you what. I shall make you not a proposal but a promise. Someday when you are old enough if we are both still unattached, I shall come and make a proper proposal of marriage to you."

She stopped in her tracks. She looked up into his hazel-green eyes and saw no hint of a joke in them. In that moment, she realized that if he had been jesting it would have not made a difference. She would never love anyone else. Her heart would forever belong to him, even though he may never reciprocate her love. This might be the only thing that would ever bind them together, so she solemnly nodded her assent and the pact was made.

Chapter 4: Companionship

Upon reaching the knoll, Inez and Estêvão saw the port lying empty below, so they sat on the bench and chatted like old friends. She asked him where he was headed next, and he told her of his plans to stop at his home on the island of Terceira. He needed to check on his business holdings and provision his ship before sailing back to northern Africa in the continued struggle to subdue the Moors. She asked about his home, so he described the large cattle ranch and wheat farming operation his family had built up in the Azores. During his trips the entire venture was left in the hands of his very capable mother, María.

"Why doesn't your father oversee the business?" Inez asked.

"My father was killed when I was three years old," he replied, looking out at the sea. Reflexively his right hand dropped to his lap and began to twist an ornate garnet ring around the smallest finger on his left hand.

"Oh," she said not knowing what else to say. She could see the hurt in his eyes and was reluctant to cause him any more pain, so she let the subject drop. The tension hung in the air between them.

He let out a long sigh and patted her hand on the bench. "That is another long story not fit for tender ears. Someday when we have time to fill, I shall tell you the whole sordid tale."

Instead, he told her all about his mother, an incredible woman who had flouted accepted custom and raised him by her own standards. With keen foresight she had parlayed her intelligence and steely determination into the establishment of the cattle ranch that had become such a success. In the face of all tradition and the

28

conventions of society, she had turned a dire situation into a thriving business and security for herself and her family.

"She is really quite remarkable," he said with clear admiration. "She is a small, trim woman who looks sweet, yet she can be very stubborn and very opinionated. She can speak and read four languages and keeps the accounts accurate to the last *real*. She has always been my staunchest supporter and my biggest source of inspiration."

"She sounds like me," replied Inez. "The only difference is that when my family tells me that I am stubborn and opinionated, they usually mean it as a reprimand."

He laughed at that. "Perhaps my thinking is a bit backward, but I admire a bit of stubbornness. To me it shows a spirit that will never truly be broken. Maybe that is why you seem familiar to me."

She smiled with the compliment and added, "I would one day like to meet your mother. It would be nice to know a woman who saw the value in doing things for herself rather than trying to attract a man to do them for her. I think we would get along quite well."

"I think you would," he agreed.

With still no sign of his ship, Inez asked about his song from the night before. She was eager to know what had inspired it and how many others he had written. He told her that he could be inspired by any small thing, and as a result, he had boxes filled with his scribblings too numerous to count. She shyly confessed to him that she also made up ditties about everyday happenings. She sang to her horse about the chickens scratching in the yard. She sang of the pigeons nesting in the rafters of the stables while she practiced embroidery with her sister. She sang of her mother browbeating the servants while she sat in her swing.

She began a song about last night's pre-dinner preparations. Estêvão laughed at her perfect caricature of the haughty Joanna, indignant over the mix-up of which wine would be served with the evening meal. At the same time, he was again stuck by the clarity of her voice and her angelic expression. Getting a feel for the melody, he began adding the lower harmonies here and there. Once more their voices combined to recreate the special magic from the previous night.

They were so absorbed in their creative efforts that they failed to notice Serafina approaching from the path. She stood silently for a moment, astonished at their companionability. With her placid nature she could not imagine how any two people who had met just the day before, let alone a grown man and her eleven-year-old sister, could already be so attuned to each other. It seemed that they were encapsulated in a bubble of their own unconscious design, and any disruption would be an unwelcome intrusion. That and the fact that she was used to being the center of attention made her a bit jealous. She waited until there was a break in their song then applauded loudly.

Inez and Estêvão jumped on the bench, startled out of their pleasant diversion by the unexpected noise. Inez colored instantly fearing that her innermost feelings would be laid bare before her sister who knew her so well. Estêvão immediately rose, instinctively reacting with the manners that had been drilled into him since he was a young boy. "Bom dia, Senhorita," he said and bowed low.

"Bom dia, Senhor," replied Serafina, beaming at him with her most alluring smile. She continued on in Castilian. "Please excuse me, Señor Rey, but my Portuguese is not very good."

"Of course," said Estêvão, switching effortlessly into Castilian.

Inez sat on the bench, itching to expose her sister's deception, but she stayed her tongue pacified a bit by the fact that Estêvão had not invited Serafina to use his given name. She held her seat and waited to see what would happen next.

"Please Señorita, do sit down. You must be hot after your climb up the path," he said formally.

"Thank you," she said, lowering her eyes demurely. "I'm afraid I am overly delicate, and the walk from the house does wear me out so." She looked up at him as she walked past and fluttered her lashes prettily.

He ignored the attempt at flirtation, pretending not to notice. He had seen this type of girl before. She would have been raised by her mother to believe that any man could be taken in by her feminine wiles. She was very beautiful, but instead of using her intelligence to cultivate an interesting personality, her every energy would be concentrated on trying to win a man to provide her with the lifestyle to which she was accustomed. Although outwardly polite, he racked his brain for a way to extricate himself. He was hugely relieved when he heard Inez say, "Look! I think I see your ship."

As soon as chivalry would allow, he turned to the sea to confirm that it was indeed his ship. Sailing toward the port from the east came his precious *María Vencedora,* defiantly flying the falcon crest. She was a sleek little three-masted caravel named for his mother's triumph over the trials life had set in her path. Every time he saw the sturdy little vessel he was reminded of all that he and his mother had accomplished, and his heart swelled with pride.

Turning back to the sisters he made his excuses. "If you will pardon me ladies, I must collect my things and prepare for my voyage. It has been a pleasure." He made a sweeping bow then turned and strode purposefully toward the house.

When Estêvão had gone, Inez turned to her sister to confront her. She noticed that Serafina was dressed in a silk brocade gown of turquoise blue, one of her best. She also noticed that her sister's beautiful golden hair was unbound and flowing freely down her back instead of plaited for everyday practicality. This meant that she had been entertaining suitors, and Inez wondered why Serafina had climbed the mount dressed in this fashion.

Instead of phrasing her question in the polite manner that their mother always encouraged, Inez was so perturbed by her sister's manipulations that she could only think to ask her directly. "Why did you come up here?"

Serafina remained coolly unaffected. She yawned and turned to look Inez full in the face. "I have been cooped up in the house receiving visitors all morning. I needed some fresh air, so I came up here," she said with a shrug of her shoulders.

"I wonder that you didn't collapse on the path being so *overly delicate*," Inez said sarcastically. "And why did you lie about not speaking Portuguese? You speak it almost as fluently as I do."

"Dear little sister. You have much to learn. Haven't you heard our mother say never to let a man know how intelligent you are? He will be happier and more eager to please if you make him feel superior. He will also be more attentive if he thinks you are physically weak, and it will make him feel like more of a man."

"Este ... El Rey is different," Inez said, softening just to think of him. "He says he admires intelligence."

Serafina looked at her sister, her eyes opening wide in dawning comprehension. "I think you have been smitten, little sister." Inez flushed a deep red and looked down at her lap, confirming her sister's suspicions. Serafina put an arm around her shoulder and said gently, "Don't worry. Your secret is safe with me. I am not interested in him at all. In fact, I find him quite ugly."

Inez opened her mouth to object then snapped it shut, thinking it wiser not to say anything. Serafina rose from the bench and held out her hand. "Come along, little sister. Let's head back to the house. The sun is strong at this time of day, and if you stay out in it for too long, you will spoil your complexion."

Hand in hand, the sisters made their way down the hill, friends once more.

Chapter 5: The Sampler

During their walk down the path, Inez was struck with the need to speak with Estêvão one final time. She and Serafina were quickly approaching the house, and once inside her mother would put her to task working on some useless project like embroidering an altar cloth for the local church or sewing garments for the poor. She desperately searched her mind for a valid reason not to enter the house, one that did not seem obvious. She felt the remaining apple swinging gently in the pocket at her hip, and her excuse was born.

Showing the piece of fruit to Serafina she said, "Oh, look! I forgot to give Neblina her treat!" Turning toward the stable she shouted, "It will only take a moment. Tell Mother I will be right there."

Serafina only shrugged her shoulders and smiled at her sister's doting affection for the silly pony. She continued home alone, never imagining that Inez had any other reason to visit the stable.

Inez hurried away from the house, counting on Estêvão's love for his horse and his desire to see the spirited Arabian properly handled. When she reached the entrance to the stable, she heard the muted sounds of male voices coming from within. Estêvão stood chatting with the stable boy while the youth gathered the specially made tack. When the boy saw Inez, he bowed and greeted her as he always did.

"Bom dia, Senhorita Inez. Shall I get Neblina ready for a ride?"

"Thank you, Alfonso, but I won't be riding now," she said,

shaking her head. "My father is busy, so I just came out to give Neblina a treat." She showed him the apple and flushed deeply with the half-truth.

Estêvão raised his eyebrows at the attempted deception. He noted the too-direct stare, the half-smile twitching insistently at the corner of her mouth, the neck and ears that had turned a bright shade of pink, and he knew she would never be able to lie convincingly. It made him feel more dearly toward her, but he wondered what she was trying to conceal. He didn't want to embarrass her in front of the servant, so he waited to see what she would do next.

She turned to him as if she had just noticed him and said, "Capitán Rey, since you are here, may I have a moment of your time?"

"Of course," he said formally. He turned and flipped a silver coin to Alfonso and thanked him for taking such good care of his horse. Then he turned back to Inez and said, "I hope you don't mind if we talk on the way to my room. I need to ready my things for departure."

Forgetting all about the excuse she'd made to explain her presence, she happily fell into step with him as they quitted the stables and made their way toward the house. He watched her expectantly, and when she had not yet begun, he decided to help her out. "So, Coelhinha, will you eat the apple or go back later to give Neblina a second treat?"

Her ears grew hot and again turned a pretty shade of pink. She raised her head and looked up at him, her nose twitching to one side in the expression of which he was growing so fond. "I didn't mean to lie," she said miserably. "My father says that honesty is a measure of a person's integrity and one's most prized possession."

Estêvão looked at her sympathetically. "As you get older I think you will find that few people share your father's views or his integrity, but I think he is a very wise man." He saw the anxiety in her face lessen the slightest bit. Sensing her reluctance to begin the conversation, he decided to make it easier for her. "I'm glad that I found you before I left."

She stopped in her tracks and looked up at him, a look of stunned incredulity in her magnificent eyes. "You are?" she asked. He nodded, smiling down at her. "You see, I thought this invitation would wind up being just another boring supper party, the same way most of them do, but I've thoroughly enjoyed my time here, and it's all because of you."

She stood there gaping at him, not knowing how to answer. Suddenly remembering why she had sought him out, she smiled shyly and said, "That is what I wanted to tell you, but I was afraid you would think I was just a silly child," she dropped her gaze to the ground, "the way everyone else does."

He looked at her tenderly then lifted her chin with his hand so that he could see her face. "You will not always be a child, and I find you far from silly."

His closeness made her giddy, and again, she marveled at the beauty and strength in his face. She shook her head to clear it and to avoid the intensity of his gaze. She took a deep breath and, wringing her hands together, proceeded to tell him what was foremost in her heart. "You have made these last two days the most memorable of my life," she began with great dignity. "I will always remember your kindness where another would not have spared me a second thought. I wanted to give you something to remind you of me as well." She pulled a worn piece of linen from her pocket and handed it to him.

Estêvão took it from her hand with gravity and unfolded the crumpled square of cloth to examine it. There was a primitive representation of a tree in the center with some uneven shapes done in green underneath. He guessed they were supposed to be leaves. He made out some chickens—a couple of reddish-brown shapes on yellow stick legs with orange beaks. There were spots where she had practiced a few random stitches, and her name in a sloppy, uneven hand filled one corner. He wondered at the tiny rusty-colored smudges along the edge.

"I made this a few years ago when I was first learning to embroider," Inez explained in a rushed, breathless voice. "I put my heart and soul into it and worked so hard to get it right. I even pricked my fingers with the needle several times and left little blood spots that won't come out. I was so happy when I was done because I thought it was perfect. Then I showed it to my mother," here she took in a long, trembling breath then continued, "and she laughed. Afterward she said it was very good for a beginner, but I already knew she thought it was terrible. Since then I have worked very hard at it, and now I am as good as Serafina, but I've never shown this to anyone else, not even my father. I thought you would appreciate it and not laugh because you told me the story about how you keep your nickname, El Rey, as a reminder to push yourself to achieve. This is sort of the same thing to me," she finished. Her heart was pounding, and she could not look up at him for fear of seeing ridicule or, worse yet, pity in his face.

"I will cherish it," he said seriously. "I will carry it here with my other important possessions, that way you will always be close to me." He tucked it into his pocket then smiled and said, "Now, I truly must be moving. I will have to hurry so that my ship can take advantage of the tide and the favorable winds. Be a good girl, Coelhinha. Maybe in a couple of years I can come back to see you." On impulse he bent down and kissed her swiftly on the top of the head, turned, and strode toward the house.

She was so surprised that for a moment her only reaction was a stunned silence. Then she slowly regained her senses. "I will keep you in my prayers," she shouted after him. "And in my heart," she whispered quietly to herself.

Chapter 6: The Offering

When Inez could no longer see Estêvão on the path, she remembered the apple in her hand and bit into it with relish. The tangy, sweet taste was welcome and familiar, and it worked to calm and refresh her at the same time. As she chewed, she reflected on the memorable day she had just spent and knew that the course of her life had been altered forever. She took another bite of the apple and thought about what to do next. If she entered the house now, her mother would find some mundane chore for her, and that would be a disappointing end to an otherwise glorious day. An idea occurred to her, and she took another bite of the apple and headed back up to the knoll.

As she climbed the gentle slope, Inez replayed pieces of her conversation with Estêvão and tried to analyze them as objectively as her eleven-year-old mind would allow. Surely he felt more for her than just simple acquaintance, some sort of kinship or affection. He had told her things that he wouldn't have revealed to just anyone. He said he admired her spirit and she felt familiar to him. That had to mean something. Then there were the two most exciting parts.

He had promised that one day he would ask for her hand in marriage. Of course there were other conditions, but it was a promise of marriage nonetheless. She paused on the path recalling the sincerity in his hazel-green eyes at that moment. He had not been making fun of her, of that she was certain. He was a man who valued honesty and integrity, and it would be beneath his honor to toy with her affections. She took another bite of the apple and continued up the hill, her mind wandering back to the events leading up to their parting.

Though the main purpose of his visit had been to do business with her father, Estêvão had chosen to spend his free time with her. He had attributed his enjoyment of the visit to her presence and had treated her as an equal, not in the patronizing, condescending manner of most adults. He had accepted her gift in the vein she had intended and clearly valued it as she did. Then there was the kiss.

She pressed her hand to the spot on top of her head trying to recapture the thrill of the one brief second when his lips had rested there. The excitement blossomed inside her and her heart fluttered within her chest. He had kissed her the way her father would, but for the short amount of time they had known each other and the difference in their ages, any other kiss would have been beyond the bounds of propriety. It wasn't the romantic kiss a young girl dreamed about with the hero sweeping her off of her feet and taking her breath away, but it had been unexpected and sweet and had sent her soul soaring with joy. He had kissed her when a handshake or a bow would have done just as well, and if she never saw him again, she would always have this.

As Inez reached the bench, she finished the last bite of apple and tossed the core into some bushes. She glanced down at the port and saw the *María Vencedora*. Her industrious crew had already taken down the lateen sails designed to give her greater speed and maneuverability in the Ria de Vigo and rigged her out in the big, square *redonda* sails for their trip to the island of Terceira. The standard bearing Estêvão's falcon rippled and snapped in the stiff westerly wind that blew out toward the open ocean.

Her eye caught movement on the road below, and Inez turned to see Estêvão riding Tesouro toward the waiting ship. This was the reason she had made the trip back up to the mount. From here she would be free to observe the last moments of his time in Vigo without the scrutiny of outside influence causing her to check her emotions. It was one more thing that she could share with him, one more thing that she could secret away with the other memories of this precious day.

She watched as Estêvão reined his horse to a stop just before the wooden pier. He dismounted with a graceful leap and led Tesouro to the gangway. He gently coaxed the high-spirited animal onto the vessel then disappeared from view. A short time later, he emerged to untether the mooring ropes that stabilized the vessel while it was anchored at port. Inez watched as he quickly and efficiently gathered the heavy coils and carried them aboard to stow them away for their next use. The whole time she said a little prayer, repeating it over and over in her mind, a silent litany. *Please let him look up at me. Please let him look up at me.* She stood breathlessly, waiting for it to have the desired effect.

As he scooped up the last rope, Estêvão paused for a moment, raised his hand to shade his eyes from the bright afternoon sunlight, and looked up in the direction of the knoll. It had worked! Inez jumped up and down waving the square of silk he had given her like her own tiny banner, trying to make herself more visible. With his free hand he waved her a final farewell before boarding his ship and pulling up the gangplank. Overjoyed, she watched as the vessel slipped gracefully out of port to the west, heading toward the vast Atlantic.

As the caravel slowly faded from view, Inez contemplated the reality of the situation. Estêvão had said he would one day come back to see her. He was returning to a life, which was normal for him, but in all actuality it was a very dangerous existence. The sea was unpredictable and unforgiving. Any mistake could prove to be fatal. There were diseases that could strike at any time. He was strong and healthy, but even the hardiest of men could be brought low by the most trifling ailment. Last but not least, there were the Moors.

This ancient race had thwarted the Christians at every turn. For centuries they had staunchly held their ground in southern Iberia until the Spanish army ousted them from their last stronghold of Granada in 1492. They no longer occupied the lands of this southernmost part of Europe, but they were by no means conquered. They had simply moved across the Strait of Gibraltar and there continued to hinder Christian holdings in Northern

Africa. They were reputed to be fierce and cunning fighters, willing to die to defend their families, land, and way of life. These were the people Estêvão would be attempting to subdue.

Inez shivered inwardly at the realization that Estêvão would be placing his life in jeopardy, not once or twice but nearly every day of their separation. Unaware of what she was doing, she dropped to her knees with the bench in front of her and began to pray. This spot, which had been the sight of so many important happenings in her young life, now took on the new role of altar.

She didn't know before which saint to lay her petition, so she prayed directly to God. After all, He was the Father. Couldn't one speak directly to a father without the intercession of someone else? She asked for safety and protection for Estêvão, she asked for patience and understanding for herself, and she asked for the time between now and his return to pass quickly. At the end of her prayer she thought that she should offer up a sacrifice of her own as testament to her sincerity and to seal the covenant.

What would be important enough to persuade God to agree to her requests? The only thing that came to mind was her continual disobedience and insolence toward her mother. Hadn't Estêvão told her to be a good girl? She promised to be the best daughter she could if it would only bring him safely back to her. She quickly finished her prayer, stood up, and brushed the dirt from the front of her dress. She started back to the house with a smile on her face, confident that she had done the right thing, never doubting that her prayers would be answered.

It was getting close to suppertime, and she had been gone for most of the day. Her mother would most likely be angry and take the opportunity to chastise her for her waywardness, but now that she had made her deal with God, she would have to suffer the consequences. She would just think of her punishment as bringing her one step closer to Estêvão's return.

Inez entered the house in a blissful fog. As she passed through the kitchen, she greeted the servants as she always did. Though none of them could say exactly what it was, they all saw the change in her at a glance. Knowing the reason, Paulina smiled to herself, remembering what it was like to be in love for the first time.

When Inez reached the dining room, as she had suspected her mother was in a foul temper over some household calamity. When she saw Inez, she immediately began her inquisition. "Inez! Where have you been all day? I needed your help a while ago and you were no where to be found!"

Normally her temper would have flared and Inez would have answered back in a disrespectful manner, but there was too much at stake. The thought of Estêvão's safety at risk because she broke her promise to God forced her to check her tongue. She took a deep breath and answered in her most subdued manner. "I'm sorry, Mama. I lost track of the time. It won't happen again."

Anticipating a pert answer, Joanna had already opened her mouth to continue her harangue, but now she only gaped in shock. She slowly closed her mouth then formed an appropriate response. "Very well then. Go wash up and fetch your sister for supper. We should have eaten an hour ago."

Inez only replied, "Yes, Mama," then headed up the stairs.

Joanna stood looking after her youngest daughter in puzzlement. *I guess she's finally growing up,* she thought to herself with a pleased smile.

That night as Inez lay in her bed she mulled over the evening spent with her family. After supper, they had moved to the parlor to sit in chairs around the fire. Normally she would have joined her father in a game of chess or cards or just reading quietly by his side while her mother and Serafina sewed and chatted amiably. Tonight had been different. As penance for her misbehavior, she asked her mother if there was any needlework with which she could help. All three members of the family had looked up at Inez as if she were a complete stranger. If Joanna had been surprised at her daughter before supper, now she fell into a state of profound astonishment. For a few moments she could only stare silently, trying to process the question. When she finally recovered, she put Inez to work on some linens for Serafina's bridal chest.

Before her promise Inez would have thought an evening spent

41

in this manner to be sheer torture, but as she worked the tiny decorative stitches she found a certain satisfaction and small amount of pride in her accomplishment. Not only was she fulfilling her part of the bargain, she felt the patience and understanding she had asked for begin to make their mark. To help her get through it, she began to think of her stitches as passing moments of time, each one bringing her a step closer to a reunion with Estêvão.

As she closed her eyes, she reflected that it had not been so bad to behave, and the end result would be well worth it. She smiled as she drifted off to sleep, her last thought for Estêvão. She had not yet had time to dwell on his departure and let herself become melancholy. The remnants of his presence were still too fresh in her mind. She could only keep up her end of the pact, pray for his well-being, and dream about his return.

Chapter 7: Twelfth Birthday

As the last days of summer faded into fall, Inez fell into a routine. Her mornings took on the sanctity and devotional quality of a religious ceremony. When she awoke, her first thought was of Estêvão. She took the handkerchief he had given her and held it to her nose, breathing deeply of his scent as she said a little prayer for his safety. Then, so she would not forget any detail, she relived every moment that had passed between them from their awkward meeting at his arrival to the wave of his final farewell. This sacred ritual always put her in a good mood and reminded her of her vow to be a good daughter. When she was done, she felt she could face any obstacle life threw her way.

She also began to pay more attention to her appearance. She didn't know if this fell under the category of being a good daughter, but it pleased her mother, and it couldn't hurt for her to become more ladylike. Besides, she would be twelve soon, and womanhood would not be far behind. Every morning she washed her face, dressed with care, and arranged her hair neatly before heading downstairs to breakfast.

Inez found that her new attitude softened her relationship with her mother. As long as she dedicated a certain amount of time doing the things her mother deemed important, the rest of her day could be spent as she wished. As a result, their confrontations grew less and less frequent, and Joanna began to recognize and appreciate the talents of her younger daughter. Satisfied that Inez was making more of an effort, Joanna began to compromise on things that had caused contention just a short time before.

She no longer made a fuss over the daily horseback rides that had been a general practice from the time Inez was old enough to sit in the saddle with her father. After all, hadn't it always been a favorite pastime of the nobility regardless of gender? How many royal romances had begun while in pursuit of some insignificant fox or stag? Joanna herself had been an excellent horsewoman in her youth. Although she had always ridden sidesaddle because it had been the traditional fashion, she supposed it could not hurt Inez to sit astride as she was still a child.

Because there was no male heir to follow in Iñigo's footsteps, Joanna also began to see the wisdom of training their daughter to run the business, and she stopped trying to keep Inez from going with him to check on proceedings at the shop. From her father Inez had inherited a penchant for the meticulous and orderly nature of the business, and in no time she began to understand how to catalog the incoming and outgoing goods. With her organized, logical mind, she quickly comprehended the reconciliation of accounts, and she even suggested a new way of organizing them in a color-coded master log, which impressed everyone.

Before her transformation, Joanna had begrudged Inez the time spent in the kitchen with the servants, especially Paulina. She had always sensed the closeness between her daughter and the housekeeper and was jealous. Of course Paulina was a faithful worker and had never caused a problem, but Joanna was unable to overcome her class prejudice or her mistrust of the Portuguese. Having been raised in a privileged house of nobility, she could not understand how anyone could prefer the uncomfortable closeness and oppressive atmosphere of the kitchen to the cozy familiarity of a fire-warmed parlor. Though she did not understand it, Joanna stopped berating Inez over her fascination with the kitchen and even praised her for some of the imaginative and delectable dishes Inez was learning to create.

As she grew accustomed to the change, Joanna threw herself into the task of finding a suitable husband for Serafina. It seemed that all of her available time was spent planning, preparing, and chaperoning the visits of the eligible bachelors who had shown a serious interest in courting the beautiful Serafina, daughter of the

richest merchant in the region. This was the job for which she had
been born. She thoroughly evaluated the assets and drawbacks to
each match, and because she was content with the progress Inez
had made, the old misgivings about whether her younger,
opinionated daughter would ever fall into line took second place to
the immediate need of restoring her family's respectability by
finding a son-in-law with an impeccable lineage and of course, his
own source of wealth.

Inez was left to her own devices, and her days became so
carefree she wondered why she had not thought of this before. As
a child she had understood the concept of compromise to mean
that the parties involved each gave up something of their own
desire to settle on a mutual, grudging coexistence, but that had not
been the case. It seemed that she had ceded little and got much in
return. It had not been difficult. All it had taken was a well-timed
offer of assistance here and there and a show of consideration, and
it seemed that her mother had become flexible and understanding
overnight. Inez had not had to change a bit. On the inside she was
still the same stubborn, independent person she had always been.
All she had done was institute a little thoughtfulness and a bit of
charm, and with a minimum of patience, the rest had happened on
its own. It was her first experience with sacrifice and humility, but
it would not be her last.

With the new easiness and routine, the days seemed to slip by
like clouds hastening before a storm. Before Inez knew it five
weeks had passed, and her twelfth birthday was at hand. On the
morning of October 13th she awoke with a sense of excitement and
a feeling that something extraordinary would occur. In a buoyant
mood, she mulled over her choice of ribbon. She impishly selected
a pink one and quickly tied off her hair. Pink was one of the pretty
colors reserved for Serafina's use, because Joanna ruled it
unsuitable for Inez's reddish-brown hair. This morning Inez did
not care. She had behaved herself for over a month, and today was
her birthday. She was entitled to a little self-indulgence, and pink
was her favorite color. Satisfied with her reflection in the mirror,

she turned to exit the room.

Awakened by the sounds of her sister at her morning toilette, Serafina rolled over in her bed, yawned lazily, and blinked her beautiful blue-green eyes a few times to chase away the remnants of sleep. "Good morning, little sister. You seem to be in a chipper mood. Why all the excitement?" she asked teasingly.

"You know why, slug-a-bed," Inez replied saucily. "Today is my twelfth birthday, and in no time I will become a young woman."

"And then you can marry your ugly Portuguese," needled the elder sister.

Looking alarmed, Inez glanced toward the door. "Shh, Serafina! What if Mama hears," she said, her eyes pleading. "You haven't said anything, have you? You promised!"

"Calm down, calm down. I gave you my word, didn't I? Not even Torquemada could roast it out of me," Serafina answered flippantly. "I was only joking."

"You should not joke about such things. When one gives his word, it should be as binding as a sacred oath," said Inez, recalling other promises made weeks ago.

"Well haven't you become serious in your old age?" Serafina remarked with eyebrows raised. Then she went on in a mock-wounded tone, "As it so happens, I remembered your birthday and bought a fitting present to betoken such a momentous transition, but if you are not civil to me, I shall have it sent back. Now come over here and allow your elder sister to give you a birthday hug, or have you become too mature and dignified for that?"

Sufficiently cowed, Inez scrunched up her nose, shuffled over to the bed, and sat down. She allowed herself to be cosseted for a moment then she looked up at her sister and insisted, "But you won't tell a soul, will you?"

"I would sooner marry a sheep farmer and cook my own meals than betray your confidence, little sister," Serafina said with feeling. "Now go enjoy your birthday, and tell Mama that I will be down in a trice," she said with a gentle push.

Inez laughed out loud at the picture of her coolly elegant

sister sweating over a boiling kettle of mutton stew, and she knew her secret was safe. She gave Serafina a quick peck on the cheek and skipped happily from the room.

Breakfast was enjoyable, and for once Inez was the center of attention. Everyone from her parents to the servants made a show of wishing her a happy birthday. Joanna, whose eyes never missed a thing, espied the pink ribbon at the end of Inez's thick coppery braid, and though she grunted audibly into her porridge to mark her disapproval, she did not say a thing. Pleased with this small triumph, Inez finished her meal then asked to be excused. As she passed Joanna, on impulse she bent and gave her a smacking kiss on the cheek and raced out the door. Surprised, Joanna only put a hand to her face then shook her head at the strange behavior. She never ceased to wonder at the change that had happened seemingly overnight.

In a high-spirited mood, Inez could not shake the electric tingle of excitement. Maybe it was just that although she was making the symbolic leap into maturity, she still retained the partial mindset of the child she had not quite left behind. The enthusiasm for her birthday had not yet lost its savor and novelty. As she made her way up to olive tree on the hill, she allowed her mind to wander freely, speculating about the gifts she would receive.

This pilgrimage to the knoll had become another of her daily habits. Although Estêvão had said that it would be years before he returned, there was always the possibility that his plans would change, and if he came back ahead of schedule, Inez wanted to be the first to know. Of course his ship could slip into port while she was busy elsewhere, but the morning reconnaissance made her feel like she had done all that she could to look out for his arrival.

When Inez reached the crest of the hill and looked down, she saw nothing out of the ordinary. There was a French trader with a cargo of wines and textiles that had put into port yesterday. Iñigo had done a walk-through to evaluate how much of the merchandise he could manage and had given the order for purchase. Knowing that the next day would be his daughter's birthday, he had taken care of the paperwork and left the off-loading to be handled by his trusted staff.

Seeing nothing more of interest, Inez started to the stables. Her mother had asked Iñigo to remain at the house for a few minutes after breakfast. She had given an excuse of needing to speak to him about some household issue. Inez supposed it was just a pretext to work out last minute details of her birthday celebration. Their morning ride would be delayed until her mother had her say, but she would have time to give Neblina a good brushing before her father arrived.

When Inez arrived at the stables, Alfonso greeted her cheerfully, bowing low as he always did. "Bom dia, Senhorita Inez, and happy birthday to you! How old are you today?"

"Thank you, Alfonso. Today is my twelfth birthday," she replied, holding her head high.

"Ah, I could tell that you looked much more mature this morning, practically a grown woman overnight," he said with a smile. "Well, it seems I have a little something that has been waiting for this day." He turned and headed for the small room used to store tack and various tools for the care of the equine stock and their surroundings. He returned with a small paper package bound with a length of simple twine and unceremoniously pressed it into her hand.

Inez was so surprised that she just stood there. After a few seconds, she remembered how her mother had told her that she should never take gifts from the servants. It seemed ungrateful, but she knew that this was one rule on which her mother would not compromise. Sadly she looked up at him and said, "I'm very touched that you are so thoughtful, but I'm afraid I cannot accept it."

Alfonso looked at her blankly for a moment, not understanding. Then suddenly grasping her meaning, he choked back a laugh and shook his head. "I'm sorry, Senhorita Inez. Though I would like to take credit for being so considerate, I cannot. This was left for you by El Rey. He asked that I put it in a safe place and deliver it on the appropriate date. He also tipped me quite handsomely, I might add."

Now knowing that the gift came from Estêvão, Inez was even more stunned than before. Forgetting her manners, she turned from Alfonso without a word and made her way to a quiet corner of the stable where she sat down on an old wooden stool. Having completed his task, Alfonso shrugged at the girl's strange behavior and went back to what he had been doing before she came in.

With shaking hands, Inez untied the string holding the small packet together. She opened each crease slowly trying to prolong the suspense and make the moment last as long as possible. Finally she was down to the last fold. She spread the paper bit by bit until she could no longer obscure what was inside. She looked down and had to catch her breath.

There, nesting in the center of the wrinkled paper, was one of the silken tassels from the custom-made tack of Estêvão's prized Arabian, Tesouro. It was a deep wine-red interspersed with the cobalt blue he had professed to be his favorite color. Inez picked up the exquisite trinket and held it to her chest as she read the brief note written in Estêvão's educated hand. In the letter he begged pardon for not having a left a proper gift for her, and again he thanked her for having made his stay entertaining and memorable. He said he would look back on the two days they spent together with fondness, and he concluded with best wishes for her birthday and prayers for her well-being.

Inez sat for a few moments just letting the reality of the situation sink in. Estêvão cared enough for her to leave a gift and plan for it to be delivered on her birthday. This had to mean that everything she felt—their strong compatibility, their mutual affection—had not been something manufactured by her imagination. It was real. Perhaps this epiphany was more precious to her than the gift itself.

She folded the paper neatly before stowing it in her pocket. She would put the letter away where it would not get ruined, but she was not sure what to do with the tassel. She held up the beautiful glossy bauble and admired it again. Maybe she would attach it to Neblina's bridle. That would be the most logical place for it, but if she did that and the tassel somehow fell off, it would be lost forever. She shuddered at the thought. Somehow in her mind she equated the safekeeping of his gift with the security of Estêvão himself. She quickly pocketed the ornament and crossed to Neblina's stall to groom her before their ride.

Iñigo and Inez had a pleasant but uneventful ride, and the remainder of her day was the same. Finally, when she thought she would die of the wait, the time came to get ready for supper. She washed her face and hands, combed her hair neatly, and donned the green dress she had worn to the supper party five weeks before. While still in her room, she fussed over what to do with her new treasures. She could put them in the bottom of one of her drawers, but what if her mother discovered them? How could she explain their presence without divulging the entire story? There was nowhere safe enough, so she left them in her pocket and resolved to settle the dilemma later.

As she descended the stairs, she saw all of her favorite dishes staged invitingly on the table. There were crusty loaves of bread and dishes of sweet cream butter that she loved so well. An impressive array of cheeses, sliced and fanned out on a sparkling serving tray, waited next to piles of fresh fruit and vegetables cut into bite-sized pieces. A chicken, stuffed with a mixture of rice, peas, and her favorite shrimp, sat on a platter in the center, roasted to a delicious golden crispness, just waiting to be carved into savory servings. Of course no collection of her favorite food would be complete without the empañadas. The flaky little meat pies were stacked neatly in a wooden serving bowl placed conveniently near her seat.

The supper was exactly what she would have planned for herself. The mixed aromas of the food made her stomach growl and her mouth water, but instead of attacking it with her usual child's gusto, she daintily tasted each dish with a reserve that she hoped would reflect her blossoming maturity. By the time she had cleaned her plate, the other members of her family were also replete and ready to repair to the sitting room where a fire blazed to chase away the chill.

They situated themselves comfortably, but instead of taking up their usual activities, her parents and sister joined together in a traditional song to celebrate her birthday. As the serenade came to its conclusion, Inez realized how fortunate she was to have such a loving family, and she inwardly chastised herself for her previous contentiousness.

Her father interrupted her thoughts by saying, "So, my little Mynah, now that you are twelve, I suppose you will be flying off to be married in no time." Alarmed, Inez quickly cut her eyes to Serafina, but her sister simply looked back at her with a smilingly blank look. Then her father went on, "But until that blessed occasion, I believe we have some gifts that will make your remaining stay at home a bit more tolerable. Serafina, you may present yours first."

"Thank you, Papa," said Serafina and brought forth a little package beautifully wrapped in a small piece of gold silk and bound with a red velvet ribbon. "Here you go, little sister."

Inez carefully undid the ribbon, and the silk fell away to reveal a small vial in the center. She was so amazed that her mouth fell open. It was her first bottle of perfume. Up until now when she had asked to wear some, her mother had always replied that she was too young. She could not believe that Joanna had allowed it.

As if reading her mind, Serafina offered a few words of explanation. "It's pear blossom. Mama said it would be all right as long as you use it sparingly and only on special occasions."

"Oh, I will," Inez answered. "Thank you, Serafina."

Her mother was next. Out of nowhere Joanna produced a small ornate bag and handed it succinctly to her daughter. Inez disregarded her mother's brusque manner and looked closely at the exquisitely made purse. She saw that it was hand-beaded with a complicated geometric design in brilliant jewel tones. Recognizing how much covert work had gone into such a labor-intensive creation, she was immediately filled with emotion. "Oh, Mama, it's beautiful," she gushed.

Joanna smiled, pleased with her daughter's reaction. "I

thought you would like it. If you look inside, I think you might find something else that will please you."

Inez carefully loosened the drawstring holding the purse closed and stuck her hand inside. Withdrawing her closed fist, she pulled out a handful of new ribbons. Of course they were all in the colors that Joanna deemed suitable, but there were varying shades and pastels that made the mix interesting and more appealing to Inez's color palate.

"I noticed that your ribbons had grown a little shabby, and this morning you seemed to have run out of your own and were wearing one of your sister's," Joanna said arching an eyebrow, an unspoken reprimand in her tone. "There are no pink ones, but I believe there are some lavender and plum-colored ones that will look very pretty in your hair."

"Thank you, Mama," Inez said in concession. "They are all lovely." Putting the ribbons back into the little bag, she looked up at her father expectantly.

"Oh yes. I suppose I am next," Iñigo said, seeming to have forgotten. "Here you go, Mynah. I hope you like it," he said, handing her a box roughly the dimensions of the old-fashioned wooden trenchers that her mother now used as small serving trays.

Made of a high-quality maple, it was intricately carved, the edges festooned with the twining flowered vines of a morning glory, which was a specialty motif of her father's design. In the center a mynah bird perched on an olive branch paid tribute to her favorite spot and the nickname with which Iñigo had christened her so long ago. The box was fitted with a tiny brass lock with an even tinier key that he had strung on a fine gold chain. The whole thing had been smoothed and burnished to a high-gloss finish so delicate that it looked like it had been dipped in glass.

Inez immediately looked up at him, tears filling her eyes and a lump rising in her throat at the sudden appreciation of her father's artistry and the realization of how much she loved him. She could not find the words to thank him. It was the first time she had ever been truly speechless.

Seeing that his daughter was overcome, Iñigo filled the

painfully long pause by saying, "I'm afraid the chain may be overly fragile, so you must take care that it does not break. There is only one key, and it must be guarded diligently."

"Yes, Papa," Inez managed to squeak out.

Thinking that this part of her birthday was concluded, she started to rise from her chair to thank each of her family members with a hugs and kisses, but her mother put a restraining hand on her shoulder, and in a weary but insistent voice said, "Iñigo! What about the other thing I asked you to take care of?"

"Oh, yes!" he said, snapping his fingers and tapping his forehead. "I almost forgot!" In a flash he was gone from the room, and in the next moment he reappeared in the doorway with one hand held behind his back, a sheepish grin on his kindly face.

Inez was completely mystified. Never had she received more than one gift from any member of her family. Why had her mother relaxed the rule this year, and what could it possibly be? Her heart raced with excitement and anticipation.

Joanna rose from her seat and crossed to where Iñigo stood waiting. "Close your eyes, and I will put your gift into your hands, but you must be *very* careful not to drop it," she admonished. "It is very dear and cannot be replaced."

Inez nodded her head and closed her eyes, her curiosity piqued more than ever by her mother's mysterious behavior. She heard her mother's footsteps retracing their path across the room until Joanna stood in front of her. She felt something cold and heavy placed into her hands. Her mother exhaled and said, "All right, Inez. You may look now."

Inez was grateful she had been warned, because she almost fainted with the shock. There in her lap sat her mother's treasured lute. Through the retelling of countless stories, it had become the stuff of legend. It had made the journey with Joanna's great-grandmother, and namesake, from England over a hundred years before. From that time the lute had been passed down from mother to daughter only after the daughter had proven responsible and always with great ceremony and reverence. Inez could only recall a few occasions when she had seen her mother actually take it down from its place of storage high up on a dusty shelf and cradle it lovingly for a few moments before relegating it to the shadows. She didn't know if her mother could even play it, and the secrecy only added to the mythos surrounding the lute.

Inez had always been fascinated with the antique instrument but had never thought to possess it. In the past it had gone to the eldest daughter. "Mama," she breathed, "shouldn't it go to Serafina?"

"I thought about that for a long time," Joanna said pensively. "After all, I will be breaking with tradition, but I discussed it with your sister, and she agreed that you have more aptitude for things musical. At the supper party you demonstrated your talent, which seems to be the one thing Serafina did not inherit from me."

Although casually stated, this was high praise indeed for her mother to admit that Inez had an ability that Serafina did not. She smiled with the compliment, but a sudden thought occurred to her. "How will I learn to play it?" she asked.

"I shall teach you of course!" Joanna replied in her usual prickly manner. Then softening a bit she added, "It will require practice and dedication, but I'm sure you will pick it up quickly."

Inez rose from her chair, set the lute down where it was secure, and beginning with her mother hugged and kissed each member of her family in turn. They had all been generous and thoughtful and had made her feel loved. This birthday had been special in so many ways, and she would never forget the year she turned twelve.

That night as Inez readied herself for bed, she found a place for each of her new possessions. She stood the lute in a corner of the room where it would not be disturbed by everyday activities. She set her new purse with the ribbons on the dresser she shared with Serafina. Her mother had done such a beautiful job that it made sense to leave it out where it would brighten up the room. Next to it, she set down the box her father had so lovingly crafted. She opened the lock with the key and slipped the gold chain around her neck. She set the bottle of pear blossom perfume inside then reached into her pocket to retrieve her other treasures.

As she pulled out the exotic silken tassel, she was again struck by its brilliance. If she fastened it to Neblina's bridle, it would be vulnerable to sunshine and moisture. One day it would grow shabby, the fibers would weaken, and it would fall and be lost forever. In addition, there would be questions that required explanations she was not willing to give. Locked here in the box it would be protected from the elements and would never suffer the ravages of time. She could take it out to look at it any time she wished and not run the risk of exposure.

Next came Estêvão's letter. Inez opened it and read it again, her fingertips lovingly tracing the words written by his own hand. Once more she marveled that he had been thoughtful enough to not only leave her something, but to plan for it to be given to her on her birthday. He definitely felt more for her than just a passing acquaintance. With a soaring heart and high hopes for the future, she kissed the piece of paper that had rested within his grasp, refolded it, and placed it in the box, which she now thought of as her treasure chest. *Dear God, please keep him safe*, she prayed to herself as she locked the box and dropped the key inside her bodice.

Fatigued from the excitement of the day, Inez crossed the room to her cozy bed and dropped in half asleep. As her head hit the pillow and she began to drift off, her last conscious thoughts were of Estêvão. She fantasized about their reunion and looked forward to it with sweet anticipation, her imagination rekindled by the simple thoughtful note written five weeks before. It was almost as if he had shown up in person, and she was once again filled with warm feelings that thinking about him always inspired. She dreamily wondered when he would next send word and fell asleep, a secret smile on her lips, certain that it would not be long.

She would not hear from him again for two and a half years.

Chapter 8: The Talk

After the festive atmosphere surrounding Inez's birthday, the ensuing days and weeks assumed a more somber uniformity that befitted her determined attitude toward the long wait ahead. Inez continued with her ritualistic adulation of Estêvão, but he faded into a distant and idealized conception of a man, more an idol than an actual person. The silk square that had rested next to his heart, and now resided close to her own, only retained a faint trace of his scent, more imagined than actually perceived. She persisted in her nightly review of the treasures in the carved maple box to assure herself that it had not all been a dream.

The sameness of the days added to the sense that they were one long unbroken expanse of time, just another inconvenience to be endured. Once Inez adopted this mindset, they seemed to whip past. Fall rushed headlong into winter, and the change in the weather added to the tedium. As the rainy season began— providing the means by which Galicia had earned the epithet of 'Green Spain'—there were fewer days suitable for outdoor activities.

Inez rode with her father only on rare mornings when a break in the clouds provided relative assurance of a few dry hours. Her daily reconnaissance to the knoll was also subject to the weather. The thought that her reduced vigilance might result in Estêvão's slipping into port unnoticed did not occur to her. She knew he was a consummate seaman and would never chance a journey in the perilous winter seas. At this time of year the Atlantic was at its most treacherous. Many traders chose to do business in more tranquil waters rather than battling the weather and risk losing their prized ships to reach the small port of Vigo. Because this was the least busy season in the northern ports, she was not needed at the mercantile.

To compensate for the lack of outdoor activity, Inez found projects in the house to occupy her time. It seemed fitting that, as she was on the verge of womanhood, her time should be passed among female companions. If asked just a few months before, she would have likened this to some form of torture or penance for a very great offense, but surprisingly she found it much less distasteful than she would have guessed. She loved spending time in the kitchen with Paulina, the lute lessons with her mother were interesting and appealed to her musical aptitude, and there was always Serafina's trousseau to be augmented and provide busy work for idle hands.

Although the visits of suitors had dwindled, which was attributed to the disagreeable weather, sooner or later an appropriate match for Serafina would be found. Inez no longer resented having to help out with the needlework that a short time ago she had thought menial and degrading. She found the creativity relaxing, and she began to feel a certain pride in the completion of each piece. With practice she became extremely proficient, and her deft fingers acquired a skill approaching her mother's. Joanna was pleased and as a reward, instead of giving her busy work like embroidering flowered borders on bed linens, she began to entrust Inez with more complicated items.

The one piece in which Inez took excessive pride was a dressing robe she designed from the first stitch to the last. She cut it in a loose Moorish style from a bolt of sage green silk. She finished the edges with tiny, even stitching so that there were no puckers, and the garment had an easy flowing feel to it. The draping fell gracefully from the shoulders, and Inez embroidered an arabesque geometric border around the hem, cuffs, and neckline in cobalt blue paired with a deep wine red, the same colors in the tassel Estêvão had left her. She had never seen Serafina don clothing in this palette before, but her sister was so beautiful anything would be becoming. On a whim she included her initial entwined with that of her beloved in one corner of the edging. It was a lovely garment and would commemorate her feelings for Estêvão forever. Joanna made much over the completed robe and Inez's exquisite workmanship. She was all praise, and this softened the tensions between them even more.

The increased amount of time spent with her mother led to the discovery that there was more to Joanna than Inez had ever dreamed. The lute lessons thrust her into a situation where there was no alternative but to give her mother complete reign over this exclusive area of expertise or forfeit vital instruction in something which Inez so desperately desired. She finally became an eager recipient of her mother's tutelage, and this pleased Joanna to no end.

In the golden glow of Inez's newfound appreciation, Joanna began to see her daughter in a gentler light. What she had previously called willful disobedience, under closer examination she realized was a well-adjusted self-confidence. The battle of wills in which they had engaged on a daily basis she now understood were just an outward manifestation of Inez's inability to suppress her independent spirit. Having spent time with her daughter minus the prior contention, Joanna began to see the similarities in their personalities. She felt a well-disguised pleasure in the way Inez absorbed her instruction, and spurred on by the conviction that her daughter was following in her footsteps, the closeness between them continued to grow with every lesson.

Although Iñigo missed having his little Mynah with him everywhere he went, he couldn't help but be pleased with the developing friendship between his wife and daughter. The conflict between them had been a constant concern of his since Inez had first learned to speak and used her newfound talent to defy and dispute Joanna's authority at every turn. He had been secretly amused with his daughter's indomitability, but deep inside he felt a niggling certainty that one day they would have only each other to turn to for solace.

Even Iñigo with his keen foresight would not realize the depth of that need.

Along with the changes in behavior that Inez effected, she began to discern physical changes as well. Little aches and pains drew attention to parts of her anatomy relatively unnoticed until now. She felt a tenderness in her bosom, which seemed to swell appreciably. The chubby belly no longer jutted out in front but flattened and curved gently down to a narrowing waist. The hips below grew rounded and wider in comparison. With the aches in her legs came a few inches of added height, and she began to take on the appearance of a young woman. Her face elongated and lost its child's plumpness. High cheekbones and a defined chin emerged, seemingly out of nowhere, giving her a slightly more oval version of the heart-shaped face long envied in Serafina.

Joanna noticed the changes too. This was another area in which Inez would follow in her footsteps. Joanna had had the fully formed body of a voluptuous woman by the age of fourteen. Her curvaceous figure and confident manner had drawn male attention before she was emotionally equipped to deal with it, and disaster had followed quickly after. She desperately hoped to spare Inez the same fate.

Although Serafina had taken after her mother in looks, in stature she resembled the women on Iñigo's side of the family. Tall and slight, she had been fourteen before her body had shown any signs of development. This late blooming paired with Serafina's complacent disposition had delayed the necessary explanations of love and the nature of its physical expression. Serafina did not possess the same precocious, inquisitive spirit of her sister. She simply accepted the explanations and did what she was told. Inez would be a different matter.

Joanna knew that with new feelings and urges would come questions. If those questions were not answered satisfactorily, Inez would be tempted to find her own answers. This is what Joanna feared. It is what had led to her own disgrace so many years before. Her old-fashioned mother had thought to postpone the fundamentals of wifely duty until right before Joanna's wedding night, but Joanna, being hot-blooded and thinking she knew better, had decided to explore for herself. No matter how uncomfortable, parts of this episode would have to be related to Inez for her own good, and the sooner the better. Joanna would not be able to divulge the entire story—no one knew that except for Iñigo, her Aunt Margaret, and her mother, long in the grave—but there would be enough to use as a cautionary tale. She made up her mind to tackle the task at the first opportunity.

The next day dawned grey and misty. It was mid-March, five months after Inez's twelfth birthday, and a steady drizzling rain fell making the day just damp enough to preclude her morning ride. Resigned to the idea of spending the day indoors, Iñigo was cloistered in his study among his books and paperwork. The dank weather was deemed unhealthful for Serafina's delicate constitution, and she had been sent to spend a few weeks with Joanna's rich old dowager aunt who lived in a distinguished residence just outside of Santiago de Compostela. Joanna would have relative assurance of being alone with Inez without interruption. It would be the perfect time for their mother-daughter talk.

Joanna sat in the parlor, where a fire had been built to keep the dampness at bay, and waited for Inez to arrive for her lute lesson. Having a few minutes to herself, she went over the things she wished to discuss with her daughter. She tried to organize her thoughts in a manner that would seem casual enough not to sound as if Joanna were preaching, yet urgent enough for Inez to realize that this was an important lesson best taken to heart. Her musings were cut short when Inez entered the room, lute in hand.

"Good morning, Mama," she said as Joanna turned her face up to receive her kiss of greeting.

"Good morning, dear," Joanna replied, eyeing her daughter's ripening figure and thinking that the talk would be coming at just the right time.

Inez sat down in her chair and looked up expectantly. Joanna nodded, the signal for her to begin the composition learned the week before. Inez proceeded to play the complicated piece flawlessly. Joanna had a few suggestions about phrasing and fingering, and Inez ran through the piece again instituting the changes. The lesson went on as usual and about an hour later was concluded.

Inez made a move to rise from her chair, and Joanna put a gentle restraining hand on her arm. "Please sit down, Inez. There is something I would like to talk to you about," she said with a barely perceptible quaver in her voice. Inez relaxed back into her chair, her interest piqued by her mother's slightly flustered manner. With a deep breath Joanna began. "I'm sure you have noticed that in the last six months there have been many changes happening within your body."

"Yes, Mama," Inez replied, looking her mother squarely in the eye then adding with a somewhat defiant toss of her head, "I am on my way to becoming a woman."

"So you are, and that is the reason I wanted to talk to you. There are some things that will not be as evident to you as the outward changes, and I would like to help prepare you for them. Will you listen?"

Her attitude softening, Inez nodded her head, and the explanations began. Joanna laid out the basics of human development and reproduction, and informed Inez of what she could expect in the coming years. She assured her daughter that everything she was feeling was completely normal and something all young ladies went through on their journey to womanhood. She then related some of her own experiences and left Inez with an admonition against getting involved with someone just to find things out for herself.

"It is a very dangerous undertaking. Many young women have been left with a child whom they cannot care for by themselves, just because they thought they were in love," Joanna concluded.

"That won't happen to me," Inez said reflectively. "I am saving myself for my husband."

Joanna looked up at her daughter, surprised by the naturalness of her comment. This was an attitude associated most commonly with a devout religious upbringing, and as both she and Iñigo had parted ways with the church many years ago, she could not fathom how her daughter had come by it.

Inez saw the question in her mother's look and with a tolerant smile offered an explanation. "You see, Mama, those things you described sound far too intimate to be done with just anybody. I would never want to do them with anyone but ..." here she hesitated, catching herself just in time, "the man I marry."

Joanna smiled back at her, patting her hand. "That is a very grown up way to look at it. I know it is a lot to take in, so if you have questions, please come to me first."

"I will," Inez said as she rose from her chair and hugged her mother before leaving the room.

Inez found her way to the kitchen with her lute still in her hand, the conversation with her mother fresh in her mind. It was a lot to take in, and when Inez had thinking to do, she went to the kitchen to do it. The reassuring warmth of the ovens and the redolent aroma of cooking food always calmed her and made it easier for her to think through new ideas. She found a chair in an out-of-the-way corner and sat down.

She strummed the lute a little as she went back over the talk. Some of the things her mother had told her were beyond imagination. Not so much the general facts, but the idea that her mother had once been a young woman like herself and had perhaps loved someone besides her father shook Inez to the core. Maybe this had something to do with those faraway looks her mother sometimes got while Inez practiced her lessons.

She began to view her mother in a different light. The realization that her mother was a flesh and blood person with feelings and desires just like everybody else made Inez soften toward her even more. Suddenly it dawned on her that most of what Joanna did was for the good of the family, done because she loved them and wanted to spare them any sort of strife, not simply to impose her iron will over every situation. As she continued her contemplation, Inez laughed at herself for not recognizing that her mother had not always been the stout authoritarian she was now. Strumming the lute, she pictured a fair-haired child, a miniature version of Joanna complete with keys and apron, harassing the staff in a high lisping voice in the manor where she had grown up. This made Inez laugh out loud, and she added an intricate run to the picture in her mind, which made it even more comical. Her actions drew curious looks from the kitchen staff, and Paulina smiled indulgently, never surprised by the exuberance of youth.

When Inez had regained her composure, she rose from her chair, sedately smoothed down her dress, and left the room as if nothing had happened.

Chapter 9: Curiosity

Three days later, the weather had still not improved, and the rain came down in hissing gray sheets. The winds that accompanied the storm were so strong that the shapeless clouds were strewn across the sky in great muddy-colored smudges, and the sideways-falling rain pelted the windows like pebbles thrown by a protesting mob. The intensity with which the rain fell and the necessity of being indoors filled Inez with a mild case of cabin fever and a restiveness that could not be quelled. Used to doing some sort of physical activity every day, the practice sessions on her lute and needlework were not enough to dispel the anxious feeling building inside her. As usual when she was in need of solace, she found her way to the kitchen and Paulina.

Since the day of the talk with her mother, Inez had thought much about the subject matter, and many questions had arisen in her mind. There were things she wanted to know that would be far too embarrassing to ever discuss with her mother, and Serafina—never having experienced physical love—would not know anything about it, so Inez decided to talk to Paulina. She always felt that she could voice her innermost thoughts to Paulina without worry of being judged or reproached, and she knew that whatever they discussed would be kept in the strictest confidence.

Entering the kitchen, Inez saw that Paulina was just taking out the large bowls used for making bread. This would be perfect. The mixing and kneading of the bread dough required a measure of physical exertion that would provide a welcome release to Inez in her keyed-up state. That and the uninhibited conversation between the two women always left her in a more serene mood when they had done. Besides, she was working on perfecting a recipe for Portuguese sweet bread, and she could use the practice.

"Bom dia, Baixinha," said Paulina, turning at the sound of Inez's footsteps. "I was just getting ready to make some bread, and you were foremost in my thoughts." Paulina looked her over with the critical eye of a doctor assessing a patient and knew there was something on her mind. "How are you this morning?"

"I'm fine," Inez said noncommittally.

Paulina grunted to herself. She knew this child so well, as if she were her own. Inez was so stubborn that sometimes though she wanted to talk, the issue could not be forced. Paulina would have to pretend there was nothing out of the ordinary and go about her normal actions until Inez opened up on her own. She tossed the girl an apron and began to beat the eggs in one of the bowls.

Inez tied on her apron and began to stir the dry ingredients in the other bowl. She cast a speculative glance at Paulina, appraising the soft-spoken Portuguese woman who was like a second mother to her. If there was one word that described Paulina's looks, it was 'Grecian'. She had a profile the type of which graced the ancient Greek coins Inez had seen in pictures. Her black hair and fine dark eyes made her skin look creamy and translucent in comparison. With her regal bearing and swanlike neck, she evoked a certain otherworldliness, as if she were above the pettiness of mere mortals. Tall and slender, if dressed in a long flowing gown, she would look as Inez imagined Penelope had looked at her loom, waiting faithfully for Odysseus to return home from his adventures.

The two of them worked side by side for some minutes in comfortable silence. Finally when the dough was stiff enough to begin the task of kneading, Paulina turned it out on the floured surface of the kitchen table and divided it into two parts. Inez dusted her hands and attacked her portion with fervor. After a few minutes of beating the dough into submission, she gave out a long sigh and pushed a stray wisp of hair out of her face, leaving a white streak of flour in its place. With a melodic chuckle, Paulina wiped away the smear with a damp towel she had lying near.

"Thank you," Inez said, looking up into Paulina's dark eyes. Although she had matured in behavior and in body, she still had some habits that would stay with her until the end of her days. With the twitch of her nose that was as much a part of her as her opinionated personality, mustering up her courage, she decided it was now or never. "Paulina, what was it like to be married?"

With a sharp intake of breath, Paulina, who thought that nothing this child said would ever surprise her, was caught off-guard. She dropped her gaze and pretended to wipe her hands with the wet towel. After a few moments, she cleared her throat and said in a low voice, "What do you mean, Baixinha?"

Inez sensed the caution in Paulina's voice, but she knew that if she didn't pursue the conversation, she would never have the courage to bring it up again, so she pressed forward. "I mean did you like it? Were you happy?"

Paulina looked straight into Inez's eyes, and with great sincerity replied, "It was the happiest time of my life ... and the saddest."

Inez knew that Paulina had been married in her youth before she came to be part of the García household, but she knew none of the details. In fact, it had never even occurred to her to ask about it until today. With her insatiable curiosity piqued and unable to let the subject drop, she asked the question that she knew would either provoke an answer or Paulina's refusal to continue. "Did you love him?"

Paulina fixed her gaze on Inez, a poignant look of infinite sorrow on her refined face. "No, I did not love him," she said quietly and proceeded to tell Inez her story from beginning to end.

Chapter 10: Paulina

Paulina was born in 1479 in Ponte de Lima, a small town on the south bank of the river Lima in northern Portugal. Named for the bridge built by the Romans, it was one of the oldest settlements in Portugal, becoming an official town in 1125. It was also one of the chief resting places of penitents making their pilgrimages to Santiago de Compostela.

Fernão León was an innkeeper, an enormous but good-natured man, excessively proud of his inn and his Roman heritage. The inn had reputedly been established by a male ancestor about the same time as the town itself and named *The Silver Eagle* in honor of the standard of the Roman legions. That it had endured for so long attested to the fact that it had been sturdily built by his forebear. He took great satisfaction in this and kept the establishment immaculate and free from refuse, both the household and the human variety, so that the inn would stand the test of time and provide a livelihood for future generations.

As far as his lineage was concerned, Fernão delighted in telling people that he was descended from a man who had served in the legions of Julius Caesar. The legionary had been in the frontlines of the army while in pursuit of the wily Celts. He had fought like a lion and had earned the name, which had eventually become León, the name the family still bore fifteen centuries later. Of course other than Fernão's aquiline nose and patrician profile, there was no proof of his claims, but one only had to utter a syllable of disbelief, and the congenial expression on the face of this massive man would contort into a livid mask of barely-contained rage, enough to strike terror into the stoutest of hearts.

Usually upon reaching this point, the dissenter realized that it would be wiser to hold his tongue rather than lose it, and Fernão, having faced down the enemy, would quickly forgive the transgressor and continue on as before.

It was while running the inn that he met Paulina's mother. The soft-spoken, raven-haired beauty was named Leila, Arabic for 'night', as much for her coloring as to commemorate the hour of her arrival—at midnight in the dead of winter. Born to a Greek physician and a Moroccan apothecary, she had picked up substantial skill in the healing arts through accompanying her parents on their calls.

Although her mother was Muslim and raised Leila in a like manner, to her it was more a lifestyle than a religion. She had clear Christian tendencies and always felt a little guilty for not having the courage to bring her daughter up in the belief, which was a minority in their homeland. She unexpectedly took ill when Leila was seventeen, and in her final moments she poured out the misgivings of her heart and extracted a promise that Leila would make the long pilgrimage to Santiago de Compostela to atone for the grave error, which had always gnawed at her conscience.

Tradition held that the remains of the disciple St. James had been transported from Jerusalem and were buried at the shrine in the remote, northwestern corner of Castile. Rather than suffer the stain of sin on one's immortal soul, a faithful Christian could make the journey and the Catholic Church would grant expiation at the end of it. She asked that Leila now go in her stead. She gave her daughter a purse of gold for expenses along the way and a large emerald received as payment from a rich patron to give as a donation at the terminus of her journey.

After her mother's funeral, Leila said goodbye to her father, kissed him on the cheek, and set off on her mission. She crossed the Strait of Gibraltar, made her way along the southern coast of Spain into Portugal, and started the long journey north toward Galicia and her goal. To add an element of safety and to pass the time more quickly, she joined in with other groups of wayfarers en route to the same destination. All was well and she had covered three quarters of the distance when suddenly she ran a high fever and collapsed—as fortune would have it—outside of *The Silver Eagle*. Fernão carried her to a bed, tended to her needs, and fell in love.

When Leila awoke she felt an immediate attraction to the jovial innkeeper, who she later found out had taken care of her during her illness, and she went no farther. She reasoned that as she had been so blessed to have found love on her way to make atonement, God must have forgiven her mother by rewarding the daughter. She put the emerald and the remainder of the gold into safekeeping and promptly forgot them. A few days later, she married Fernão and began a happily uneventful life.

The blessings kept coming. The inn continued to thrive and became an officially sanctioned point of refuge on the Camino de Santiago. Leila set up a profitable business of midwifery and healing potions and eventually gave birth to their beloved Paulina.

In a time of unhealthful conditions and rampant disease, Paulina grew up as normally as an only child with an overprotective mother could. Because both of her parents were busy with their respective trades, she did much of the cooking and kept their snug home tidy. She spent the remainder of her time assisting her mother to make potions to cure every ailment. On occasion, if Leila deemed a residence sufficiently sanitary, Paulina went with her mother to assist in a birth. By the time she was fifteen she knew all that her mother could teach her.

One day at the local market while buying some butter for that evening's supper, Paulina got the distinct impression she was being watched. Try though she might, she could not single out the culprit, but the feeling of being observed persisted. She moved on to the produce stand, and while testing the ripeness of some peaches, she heard an unfamiliar voice address her.

"Those peaches are guaranteed to be the freshest and tastiest you can buy, *minha doçura*, but nowhere near as sweet as you, I'll wager."

Paulina looked up into the bluest eyes she had ever seen sparkling with humor. She tried to disguise her amusement by attempting as stern a look as she could conjure and replied, "They could not possibly be as fresh as the vendor!" She quickly set down the peach in her hand, curtly wished him a good day, and turned on her heel toward home.

That night Paulina tossed and turned in her bed. She could not stop herself from thinking about the tall handsome stranger. He was about the same height as her father but of a more slender build. His unruly hair was probably a light chestnut color in its natural state but had been bleached blond by the sun. He had a quick charming smile, and his eyes were that particular shade of intense blue only seen in a late autumn sky. She went over the scene again, and as impertinent and inappropriate as his behavior had been, she could not get those piercing blue eyes out of her mind. She finally fell asleep a few hours before dawn, reasoning that she had never seen him before and would probably never see him again.

The next morning while Paulina helped her mother replenish the supply of preparations most in demand, a customer entered the shop. As her mother was in the midst of boiling a tricky concoction that required full attention, Paulina hurried to the counter to attend to the person waiting. In her preoccupation she did not look up at the man until she stood directly in front of him. When their gazes met they both started at the unexpectedness of the encounter, and he laughed out loud. It was the produce vendor.

He explained that his father was laid up with the grippe and needed something to still his cough. Paulina said that she had just the thing, and if he would wait a few moments, she would put it together for him. She indicated a chair where he could sit and went about gathering the various ingredients needed to mix up the medication. While he sat in the chair, he watched her at her task. He admired her graceful movements and the sureness with which she accomplished the job. When she had done, he paid her, thanked her, and went on his way.

That evening as mother and daughter exited the apothecary they found him waiting outside. He was sitting under an old gnarled oak tree with a bag of peaches for Paulina. He rose and brushed the dirt off and formally introduced himself to both women. He asked if he could escort them home and on the way made a good account of himself with some very intelligent conversation. Leila sneaked a look at her daughter's face and saw that she had been smitten. Nuno Ribeira was asked to stay for supper, and from then on he and Paulina saw each other every day without fail.

Their courtship proceeded smoothly with the blessing of both families, and Paulina and Nuno were married a few months later. They lived in a state of unadulterated bliss, each of them wondering how they had ever existed without the other. They were supremely happy. There was only one thing that could make their union more complete, a baby.

Paulina longed to be a mother. In her line of work she helped bring newborns into the world on a regular basis. If there was one job other than midwife that she was perfectly suited for, it was motherhood. She and Nuno had been married for a year, yet there was still no sign of a pregnancy. Her mother explained to her that often when a woman brooded over the situation, her body made it more difficult to conceive. Leila gave her daughter a relaxing blend of steeped herbs and told her to sit back and let nature take its course. Paulina took her mother's advice, and two months later, she suspected that she was with child.

She was overjoyed. She knew that it was still too soon to be certain, so she kept her hopes to herself and prayed for it to be true. Another two weeks passed and the signs were unmistakable. She and Nuno would be parents before the end of the year. Now that she was sure of it, she would tell him that night while he was at his bath.

Nuno had the peculiar habit of bathing every evening. He said that working the produce stand was a pleasant change of pace from doing the heavy work of harvesting and packing crates on the family farm, but at the end of a day standing in the hot sun, he felt grimy and sweaty. A bath was the only way to wash away the dust of the streets and help him to sleep through the night. Besides, with the crowds of people on their way to Compostela—many of whom denied themselves bathing privileges as an additional form of penance—he never knew what sort of newfound guests of the six-legged class he would bring home.

That evening as Paulina washed Nuno's hair and scrubbed his back, she broached the subject in a playful manner. "You know, husband, in a few months you may be left to do this on your own."

Nuno looked up at her, the lather slowly running down his handsome face. "Don't tell me you are already tired of being married to me," he said seriously. "You promised to love me unto death, and we have a long life ahead of us."

Paulina gently pushed his head down so he would not get soap in his eyes. "It's not that. I may just have more important matters to attend to."

"More important matters? What could be more important than attending to your loving husband who has spent *all* day in the hot sun, *slaving* away to eke out a meager living to keep his beautiful wife in the manner to which she is accustomed?"

Paulina giggled at his melodramatic depiction of their lives. "I don't suppose taking care of his newborn son would take priority over seeing to his own comfort," she said with mock-exasperation, her sudsy hands on her hips.

Not grasping her meaning, Nuno continued his self-pitying rant. "More important, she says. Hah! That a son's needs should outweigh those of his father, the *breadwinner* ..." his rant trailed off, and he looked up at her with his blue eyes open wide, finally comprehending the gist of her conversation. "Paulina, minha doçura, are you saying that you are expecting?"

She nodded, eyes brimming with tears, barely able to contain her joy. Nuno let out a loud whoop of celebration as he jumped out of his bath, flinging soapy water in every direction in his zeal to embrace her. They stood clasped to each other, Paulina's clothes now sopping wet as he covered her face with kisses.

"A child! I'm going to be a father! Oh, minha doçura, could our life be any more perfect?" he asked, looking lovingly into her soulful eyes.

"No," she agreed, returning his adoring gaze. "This life is everything I have ever dreamed."

The next day Paulina and Nuno told their families the happy news. Their relatives were ecstatic. This would be the first grandchild on both sides. Fernão magnanimously ordered that the wine should flow freely at the inn that evening—of course at his own expense—in celebration of his future grandson. To be on the safe side, Leila prepared every concoction reputed to aid with a successful pregnancy and childbirth, just so she would have them on hand in case of any circumstance. Nuno's father dug out the cradle that had served his own offspring so well and undertook the task of cleaning and refurbishing it for his first grandchild. Nuno's mother and sister immediately set about sewing and knitting every type of garment or accoutrement that Paulina might need for the new life she was carrying, and his brothers began carving an impressive array of toys any child would be happy to own. Everyone was atwitter with excitement, but none more so than the prospective father.

If Nuno had not been the star of the marketplace before, he became so now. His open friendly manner and rugged good looks had made him a favorite of customers and vendors alike. Because of his loquacious nature, most of the regulars knew of the seemingly charmed life he and Paulina had begun to build. With the news of his beautiful young wife's pregnancy, he received countless blessings from well-wishers and many small items supposed to bring good luck from random patrons in the *praça*. Every evening he brought home a new surprise for Paulina, a new talisman with a new story.

Paulina's pregnancy proceeded smoothly, all of the little inconveniences taken in stride, because she knew exactly what to expect and how to alleviate each discomfort. She wanted for nothing. At any sudden urge or craving, Nuno was there to see to her desire. Several times she had to explain to him that it was good for her to do things for herself as long as she was able and that she would need his help more toward the end of her term, but this did not keep him from jumping to her aid if there was the slightest indication that she lacked for anything. He was a typical doting husband.

One evening when she was about six and a half months along, Paulina sat at the small table where she and Nuno took their meals together and stared at the bathwater, now cooled to room temperature. It was two hours later than he normally arrived from the marketplace, and she was starting to get worried. Where could he be? If there was ever a doubt about him arriving on time, he gave one of the local children a small piece of silver to run home and tell her the news. This was completely out of character for him, especially now that she was with child.

Paulina waited a couple more hours, and just as she was about to walk to the inn to ask her father to go search for her wayward husband, she heard a shuffling step outside the door. She reached the door before Nuno could open it and flung it wide to see for herself that he was intact. He stumbled heavily against her, and when he righted himself, he landed a sloppy wet kiss on her cheek. She could smell the wine on his breath, and as soon as she saw that he was unhurt and actually quite pleased with himself, her concern for him quickly turned to anger.

"Nuno!" she exclaimed, barely able to control her rising fury, spots of hot red flushing her cheeks. "Where have you been? I have been worried sick about you! Why didn't you send word? Your bath was ready hours ago, and your dinner is ruined! I didn't even eat myself because I was so ..."

A rattling snore interrupted her tirade. Nuno had fallen asleep in his chair, his shaggy blond head resting easily on his forearms on the table. This was the final indignity. Paulina resolutely strode over to him, lifted his head by the chin, and lightly slapped his cheek.

Nuno drowsily opened his eyes, and when he realized that he was in his own home, he smiled drunkenly and tried to pull Paulina into his lap. "Oh, minha doçura, you mean the world to me. Give me a little kiss to show that you still love me."

"Oh, it is hopeless to try to speak to you in this state!" she exhaled, exasperated, her defenses melting at his intoxicated yet sincere declaration of love for her. "Come, let's get you into bed."

With much effort she got him to his feet and helped him cover the distance to their bed where he flopped bonelessly, instantly snoring once more. Grudgingly she smiled down at him with affection, slowly shaking her head at the realization of how difficult it was to stay mad at him. She removed his shoes and through much maneuvering was able to get him under the covers. She thought about removing his clothing and washing him down with a soapy cloth, but she knew she should not strain herself physically at this point in her pregnancy. Just the struggle to get him into bed had been tiring enough, and the time spent worrying about him was beginning to take its toll. She got into bed, curled up beside him, and soon she was sound asleep.

The next morning Paulina awoke first, absent-mindedly scratching at a line of bites on her arm. She got up and began to prepare a mixture of orange juice, honey, milk, and an egg. To this she added some extract of willow bark and beat the entire concoction until it was well blended and foamy.

At the sound of her activity Nuno began to show signs of life. He rolled over in the bed and groaned loudly. He gingerly made his way to the edge of the bed and sat there with his hands holding up his head that felt as if it were about to burst. Paulina crossed over to him and held out the cup. "Here," she said gently. "This will help with the headache and nausea, but an apology would go much further in repairing your relationship with your wife."

He looked up, relieved to see that she was smiling, and as he took the cup from her he said, "Forgive me, minha doçura, for my thoughtless behavior. Believe me, it will *never* happen again."

She chuckled softly at his truly penitent and somewhat defeated posture and said, "I believe you, and I forgive you."

While he cautiously nursed the drink she had made for him, he told her the story of the man whom he had helped a few months before. The man passed through Ponte de Lima on his way to Compostela begging alms, as some pilgrims did, confident that God would provide for him. Nuno often had imperfect fruit and vegetables that nobody would buy, and these he put aside for just such an occasion. He had given the traveler some of the seconds, and the old man, with tears in his eyes, promised that he would someday repay Nuno for his kindness. Yesterday he had come into town and sought Nuno out to thank him again. When he discovered that Nuno was about to become a father, the old man had insisted that the two of them go somewhere to toast the blessed event. The man had some money remaining from odd jobs he had done along the way but not enough to squander unwisely in any of the 'fancy' establishments, so they had gone to the cheapest in the town, which also happened to be the dirtiest. Nuno found himself the object of much goodwill, and soon the wine was flowing faster than he could drink it. He forgot to send word, and only when others started passing out did he realize it must be very late, and he should head for home.

Paulina giggled under her breath, but when he began to scratch at his legs, with mock-sternness she remarked, "Well, you may have made it home safely but perhaps not unscathed. I think you've brought home more than a story to share with your wife." She lifted her sleeve to show him the bites there.

"Oh, minha doçura, how can I make it up to you?"

"You can start by helping me strip the bedding, and later you can help with my bath to make sure our little guests have vacated the premises."

Happy to get off with such a light punishment, Nuno jumped to his feet and began to clean with gusto.

About a week after Nuno's celebratory night out, he began to feel out of sorts. He awoke in the morning with a flushed face, a slight headache, and itchy eyes. Paulina again made him a drink with fresh fruit, honey, milk, and an egg, and dosed it with willow bark. She laid her hand on his forehead to check his temperature and found him a little warm. "Maybe you should stay home today," she suggested.

"It is already too late to send word to my father," he said, shaking his head. "Besides, it will probably improve with a bit of exercise and some fresh air."

"Your cure for everything," she smiled affectionately. "Just promise me that if you feel worse, you will come home. Your temperature concerns me."

"I promise, minha doçura," Nuno said as he kissed her on the cheek and headed off to the marketplace.

After he had gone, Paulina realized that she was not feeling her best either. She felt a slight pressure behind her eyes and was a little unsteady on her feet. She thought to call on her mother to get her opinion but reasoned that it was probably just the result of the insomnia she had experienced of late. Instead she made herself some of the same medicinal drink she had given to Nuno and lay down for a short rest. She drifted off to sleep instinctively cradling her expanding belly as if to protect the growing child inside.

A few hours later, Paulina was startled awake by the crash of the front door against the wall. Immediately she knew there was something terribly wrong. As she sat up, a searing pain tore through her head, and for a moment she could not open her eyes. The panic rose within her as she fought to clear her vision and investigate the cause of the confusion that was making her head spin. Finally the red haze lifted enough for her to see Nuno sprawled out on the floor just inside the doorway of their little house. With her heart in her throat, she half stumbled, half crawled to his form lying inert on the floor.

She placed her hand on the side of his face and immediately pulled it back in shock and terror. He was burning up! Even with the fever raging inside her own body she could feel the extreme heat radiating from his. She had to get him to the bed. She tried to rouse him, but all she got in response was a stream of rambling incoherent mumblings.

Without a thought for herself or her unborn child, Paulina grabbed both of Nuno's massive hands and began to pull him toward the bed. He was so heavy, and in her weakened state it was all she could do to keep from passing out. Only her determination and her love for him kept her going.

Inch by painful inch, she dragged him across the room and

finally got him to the foot of the bed. She frantically racked her fevered brain for a way to get him onto it when he suddenly revived enough to claw his way up while she pushed from behind. With the final heave, she felt a tearing pain shoot from the bottom of her protruding belly around to the small of her back, and she let out a little involuntary cry of pain. This roused Nuno out of his torpor for a moment of clarity.

"What is it, minha doçura?" he croaked, his throat parched from fever and dehydration.

"Nothing to concern yourself with, my love. Just one of the little aches of childbearing," she lied, smiling through the pain. "Listen, husband. You are very ill. You need to rest quietly here while I run to get my mother. She will know exactly what medicine you need and what course of treatment to pursue. I will be back so quickly that you won't even know I have gone."

"Paulina," he rasped, unwilling to let go of her hand. He fixed her gaze with those sky blue eyes that had etched his place so deeply into her heart from their first meeting and swallowed hard. "My fate is in God's hands now. Whatever He decides, I want you to know that I love you more than life itself. Our time together has been paradise, and if I have to burn in hell for eternity because I love you more than God, I go willingly to my fate."

She squeezed his hand tightly, tears streaming down her beautiful face. "Hush, my love. You know not what you are saying. You are going to be just fine. My mother will know what to do."

"I love you, Paulina," he exhaled as his blue eyes closed, and he drifted off into unconsciousness.

"I love you too," she said to her now oblivious husband on the bed, placing a kiss on his hot forehead and letting his hand drop to his side.

She turned from the bed and nearly swooned with the fever and the pain. She stood still for a moment to catch her balance then took a tentative step. The room swam before her, and she closed her eyes tightly against the nausea. She attempted another step and had to steady herself with a nearby chair. She pulled her way along the edge of the table and, with a final unreality, slid slowly to the floor.

Her last thought before blacking out was the irony and unfairness of the situation. She had spent her entire adult life seeing to the health and well-being of others, and when it had counted, she had been able to do nothing to protect the one she loved the most.

Paulina would later recall very little of the week that followed. As she drifted in and out of consciousness, she was aware of impressions more than actual events happening around her. The knowing, efficient hands of her mother applying soothing cool compresses to her face and body, a salty sweet liquid held to her lips and the gentle blooming relief that followed, and a sense of overwhelming sadness—these were the only things to convince her that she still lived. Her mother's concerned face was the only constant as she wandered in her dreamlike state of delirium.

One morning Paulina awoke to find Leila dozing in a chair next to the bed. It was the first day she had felt anything resembling clarity of mind and the first time her mother had not been at the ready with some sort of potion to put her back to sleep. She looked around to get her bearings and saw that she was in the room she had occupied as a child. Her throat was raw and dry, and she felt an unbearable thirst. She espied a pitcher on the table next to her bed and reached for it to pour herself a drink. She was shocked when her body failed to respond to the simple request for action. There was no pain, only an overpowering weakness in her leaden limbs, and she wondered how long she had lain there in this helpless state.

Paulina tried desperately to remember how she had come to be there, and ever so slowly the memories started to register. Being awakened from her nap by the crash of the door, Nuno collapsed on the floor of their little house, the struggle to get him to the bed, and his intense blue gaze communicating everything he had not been able to voice—every painful moment came flooding back to her now. She concentrated all of her will and commanded her body to obey. Gritting her teeth in determination, she forced her hands up from her sides where they lay to her belly. She had to make sure her child was safe.

As her hands reached their destination, Paulina was struck with a new source of grief. The flesh, which had been so firm and full with the new life it had harbored, was now soft and spongy and deflated with the loss of the child. Hot tears sprang to her eyes and she let out a mournful sob that awakened her mother.

"Paulina, my daughter, are you in pain?" Leila asked, wiping the sleep from her eyes and anxiously trying to ascertain the reason for her daughter's suffering.

Paulina shook her head weakly and tried to speak. "The baby?" she was finally able to get out, just above a whisper.

Immediately Leila lowered her eyes and shook her head from side to side. "I'm sorry, *querida,* I could not save her." She watched helplessly while the tears coursed down Paulina's beautiful face, knowing that she could do nothing to alleviate the emotional pain and knowing that when all was told, she would only add to it. She attempted to avoid her daughter's gaze, dreading the question that she knew would come next. She smoothed her daughter's glossy black hair back from her forehead and said, "You should sleep, Paulina. It is the best thing for you right now."

Paulina stared intently into her mother's eyes, trying to convey the question without having to ask the words aloud. Leila, reluctant to cause her daughter further heartache, could not bear to utter the phase, which would be her undoing. Finally she took Paulina's hand and looked into her expectant, tear-stained face and again shook her head slowly. Paulina let go her mother's hand, closed her eyes, and turned her head to the wall. Fighting hard to keep her own tears in check, Leila stood up, kissed her daughter on the top of the head, and left the room.

As the stark reality of the disaster that had befallen her started to sink in, Paulina struggled to understand how her perfect life had taken such a drastic turn. Had it all been a dream, fleeting and beautiful and destined to disappear? Why had God decided to punish her? Perhaps He had been jealous, because she and Nuno had loved each other too much. Why had He left her to suffer this loss and make her way through life alone?

Paulina thought that the end to her own existence would be the answer to all of her problems. At least it would stop the anguish she felt every moment of every day without Nuno. She tried to refuse all sustenance, but her mother was a constant presence and watched vigilantly to make sure she ate every meal and took all of her medicine. Leila also tried to get Paulina to talk about her grief in hopes that getting things out in the open would give her some sort of closure and let her move on, but Paulina stubbornly refused to discuss the subject. Perhaps if she avoided that particular conversation, she could pretend none of it had ever happened.

There were also other reasons Leila wanted to discuss the calamity that had taken place. She felt a certain responsibility and a considerable amount of blame for the devastating events that were the source of her daughter's suffering. She thought that if her role in this tragedy were brought out into the open, it might lessen the dark stain on her own conscience, and if Paulina could find a way to forgive her, she could be absolved of the heavy burden of guilt she was now trying to shoulder by herself. She resolved to bring it up at the next opportunity.

That afternoon Leila set up a chair in the herb garden and helped Paulina out to sit in the warm afternoon sunshine. She thought that the change in scenery would do her daughter good and lighten her mood. Paulina was getting stronger every day, and physically there was nothing wrong with her except for the lingering weakness from the fever and the trauma of losing her child. Leila was more concerned with her emotional well-being and the state of her soul.

"Paulina," she began firmly, determined not to be put off again, "you cannot live the rest of your life ignoring this terrible thing that has happened. There are some things that need to be faced, no matter how painful, so you can move past them and begin anew."

Paulina regarded her with those dark soulful eyes that could be so unsettling and stated plainly, "I had a husband whom I loved more than life, we were going to have a child who would have made our union complete, and I lost them both because of God's whim. I don't want to move past it, and I don't want to begin anew. I just want to understand why. There is nothing left to discuss, Mama, unless you can tell me why." She sat looking implacably at her mother and waited for a response.

Leila nearly wavered under the emotionless gaze of her daughter whom she barely recognized in that moment. She cleared her throat and took a deep breath. "Perhaps I *can* tell you why," she said and told the story of the sacred pact she had made with her dying mother down to the smallest detail. When she had finished, Leila searched Paulina's impassive face for a reaction.

Paulina finally shrugged her shoulders and said, "It is a sad story, but I do not understand how it relates to me."

"Don't you see how the sins of my mother have been passed down through two generations and have visited themselves on a third? I claim full responsibility, because *I* am the one who broke a vow, which was sacrosanct. In my youthful ignorance I presumed to understand the will of God. As a result I have lost my granddaughter, and with every day that passes I am losing my daughter too."

Paulina, unwilling to let go of her resentment, looked at her mother with a challenge in her eyes and said, "I still do not understand what you want from me."

Seeing the spark of irritation in Paulina's eyes, Leila unballed her hands, which she had clenched into fists in her frustration. She had not wanted to cause her daughter further distress, but any emotion, even anger, was preferable to the apathy that had transformed her into a person whom she did not know anymore. Leila knew they were at a breaking point. The next exchange would either bring her daughter back to her or lose her forever. She grasped Paulina's hands in her own, looked straight into her eyes, and said, "You must go to Compostela."

In the days that followed, Paulina grappled with the feelings brought to the surface by the conversation with her mother. Her sentiments ranged from outrage and disbelief that her mother should have kept secret something so important, to acceptance and relief that maybe there was a way Paulina could gain understanding and find some peace. The grudge she harbored against her mother and God was eating away at her soul and turning her into a person she did not want to be—bitter and hateful and unable to find any joy in the world. Finally, after much inner turmoil and many hours of prayer, she made her decision.

Paulina approached her mother, humbled by the amount of patience and wisdom possessed in her familiar form, and informed her upon which course of action she had settled. She would finish the journey Leila had begun so many years before, and at the end of it she would enter the Convent of Belvis. She would pledge her life to God that she might seek His forgiveness and at least attain a measure of tranquility, if not enlightenment.

Leila would be sad to see her go, but deep down she knew that she could never offer any of the things Paulina needed to move forward with her life. Reluctantly she admitted to herself that she had done the best she could for her daughter, and any small happiness Paulina could hope to achieve thereafter would have to come through her own efforts.

Leila helped Paulina pack a bag with articles that would be useful along the way. She dug out the purse originally given to her by her own mother containing the remainder of the gold and the emerald. She made Paulina tuck it away in a secret pocket hidden from the eyes of would-be thieves. In a final attempt to nurture and protect her daughter, Leila put together a small cache of medications and fortifications to keep up her daughter's still recuperating strength.

The next morning after a hearty breakfast, Paulina bade a tearful goodbye to her mother and father and set off north toward Galicia, resuming the journey toward expiation where her mother had left off. She did not know what the future would bring, but she now had a purpose and had made up her mind to accept whatever destiny God had in store. As she made her first steps in the direction of Santiago de Compostela, a calmness of mind settled over her, and she knew she had made the right decision.

Chapter 11: The Bond

The only sound that could be heard was the intermittent hiss of rain blown against the house by the gusting winds. With the conclusion of her tale, Paulina sat quietly waiting for Inez to comment on the story she had just been told. Inez sat in her chair lost in thought, digesting the new information. Finally she came back to the present and, true to her inquisitive nature, had a question at the ready.

"What happened next?" she asked, crinkling up her nose at Paulina's obviously unfinished narration.

"I made my way to Compostela, gave the remainder of gold and the emerald as donations, and asked to be accepted into the convent," Paulina stated simply, shrugging her shoulders.

"But you did not become a nun," Inez said, still pressing. "How did you end up here?"

Paulina inhaled deeply and filled in the missing details.

When she reached the shrine of St. James, Paulina gave her donations and declared her desire to enter the convent. Of course it was necessary for her to give a confession, and after hearing her history, the abbot deemed her unready to enter the order. He opined that her talents would be more beneficial doing God's work in the secular world than confined to the small cloistered sphere of the Convent of Belvis. She tried to argue the point, but he reasoned that by her refusal to accept the judgement of God's agent, she was not yet ready to submit fully to His will thus not ready to enter into His service. The abbot then charged her with a final mission to prove her obedience and true penitence.

There was a patron of the shrine who had a relative near to her time of confinement. The pregnant woman was known to be a bit demanding and very particular about the way things were done in her home. The abbot thought the situation would provide the perfect opportunity for Paulina to demonstrate her suitability for convent life and her readiness to accept God's plan. She could use her midwife's skills in the name of the Church, and the job would be an accurate measure of the subservience she would be expected to exhibit in her life as a nun. Paulina agreed to this final test, packed her bag one last time, and headed to Vigo.

Upon arriving at her destination, Paulina found the García household in a state of utter confusion. She learned that not only was the mistress expected to deliver within the next few days, but the six-year-old daughter of the house had suddenly fallen ill with a fever, and not even the doctor was sure which course of treatment to pursue. After learning that Paulina had been sent by the church because of her healing ability, she was immediately taken to the daughter's room.

Paulina entered the room and quietly approached the bed. The little girl listlessly opened her eyes to see who stood over her now, and Paulina was struck by the beauty of the child. Even with the angry flush brought on by the fever, Paulina could see the peachy undertones of the heart-shaped face surrounded by a profusion of golden hair. The little rosebud mouth hung open in dehydration, and the blue-green eyes beseeched Paulina with a silent plea for help. She immediately set to work.

She checked Serafina's chest for the telltale rash and found what she expected. Typhus. The same affliction that had deprived Paulina of her husband and child such a short time ago now threatened the life of the beautiful little girl before her. She ordered cold compresses made to bring down the fever, and with the medicines that her far-seeing mother had insisted she take with her, Paulina put together the life-saving preparation, which would combat the dehydration and alleviate discomfort enough to allow for the healing sleep necessary for recovery. She kept a constant vigil throughout the night. By morning the fever had abated, and

Serafina slept easily. Paulina explained that the little girl was no longer contagious and gave detailed instructions on how to proceed. One of the household servants attended her while Paulina went to assess the condition of the mistress.

After knocking lightly on the door to the Señora García's room, Paulina heard an imperious voice bid her to enter. Inside the room she was met by the haughty gaze of the lady of the house, which matched the voice absolutely. Physically the woman was a more mature version of the golden-haired child Paulina was already growing fond of, but the arrogant manner and overbearing speech left no place for sympathetic feelings. Adopting her most businesslike tone, Paulina established a timeline and determined that the woman would have a few hours before the most crucial stage of her labor began. She ordered a brew made of chamomile to ease any discomfort and told the attending maid to alert her at any sudden change. She was then shown to a room where she could wash up and rest until she was needed. A tray was sent to her with a generous meal, and a few hours later the call came for her to return to the Señora's chamber.

The birth went quickly and easily. Having been through the process before, Joanna merely waited for the nod of approval before stoically delivering her second child into the world. Paulina was present mostly to oversee the servants, catch the child as it came, and cut the umbilical cord. After clearing the newborn's airways, she gave it a smack on the backside to make sure the lungs worked properly and inspected it to make sure it was healthy and determine the sex. She announced that it was a hearty baby girl and offered the child to her mother who swept a cursory glance over her new daughter, noting the red hair and odd-colored eyes, then declined to take her claiming exhaustion. To her surprise, Paulina saw the mother attempt to disguise a fleeting look of disappointment. It was something she would never divulge to anyone else, but it added to the feeling of uneasiness developing between the women. It also made her feel even more protective toward the baby in her arms. Instead, Paulina took the snugly wrapped infant out to the father pacing anxiously in the hallway.

The tall kindly merchant took the proffered bundle with trembling hands. Paulina could see that he was as captivated as his wife had been dissatisfied. He spoke to the tiny red scrap of the plans he had for the two of them, and Paulina saw unshed tears of happiness gleaming in his dark eyes as he went on about their future. She turned away from the familial scene as much to give father and daughter their privacy as to hide the secret pain within herself, and she reentered the birth chamber to supervise the cleanup.

Some time later, the master of the house returned with his precious cargo now sleeping soundly. He approached the woman who until the day before had been a complete stranger. He now thought of her as a guardian angel and could not find sufficient words to convey his thanks. Tongue-tied, he stumbled through an ineloquent declaration of gratitude, and he made the proposal that would change the course of Paulina's life. Would she consider staying on permanently? Their current housekeeper would be leaving in a week to get married, and none of the applicants interviewed thus far had proven satisfactory. She took the baby girl from him, thanked him for his offer, and replied that she would think it over.

On the way to the nursery, Paulina glanced down at the child she carried and found herself being solemnly regarded by a pair of serious silver eyes, eyes that suggested a knowledge beyond their experience. In contrast to most newborns, the eyes seemed focused and penetrating, as if examining the countenance and conscience of the person now entrusted with her well-being. In dealing with babies, this was the first time Paulina had thought of one as an individual, and she felt an immediate bond forged with this strange child whom she had helped to bring into the world. In that moment all thoughts of the convent ceased, and she knew she would make her life here with the family about which she had already begun to care so deeply.

Paulina looked over at Inez to see what her reaction would be this time. Inez sat watching the runnels of rainwater drip down the windowpane, a dreamy, enigmatic look on her face. Paulina smiled to herself, wondering when the next battery of questions would begin. She decided to end the suspense by asking the first question herself. "So, Baixinha, is that enough storytelling for one day?"

Inez turned to face her. "Yes, the story was one I had not heard before. It explains a lot. I never understood why my mother was always so cautious about Serafina's health, but I suppose that if I had almost lost a child to illness, I would be cautious too." Inez looked back out the window contemplatively. "Was it difficult to care for me when you had so recently lost your own baby girl?"

Paulina sat quietly for a moment, seriously considering the question. "I suppose it was at first, but you were so much like my own child that after a while, I never even gave it a second thought."

Inez smiled at this. She knew what Paulina meant. There had always been a special bond between them that defied definition, a sort of tacit understanding that they belonged to one another. Although she and her mother had grown closer of late—Joanna had even stated that Inez in many ways reminded her of herself in her youth—there was always that subtle feeling that she had somehow disappointed her. With Paulina there was only love and support and a deep mutual compatibility.

Suddenly Inez remembered the original reason for Paulina's story. She shifted uncomfortably in her seat. Knowing that this would be the most painful question to pose, but unable to stop herself she asked, "Why did you say that you did not love your husband?"

Paulina looked at her with a sad little smile. She was not surprised at the question. Inez rarely forgot anything. She sighed wistfully and said, "The thing I felt for Nuno could not rightly be called love. That word is not enough to describe what we shared with one another. We were like two halves of one creature, utterly dependent on the other to exist. Until I met him I did not know what it was to really live, and without him I have never been truly complete. He was my heart, my soul, and my life, and I will never love another in that way."

Realizing the uniqueness of the mood so uncharacteristic of the usually reticent Paulina, Inez tried to keep the conversation going in the direction in which she was really interested. "And when you love somebody like that, what is it like? You know, the physical part?"

Paulina looked at Inez, her eyes narrowing warily. "How much has your mother told you about this subject?"

Wanting to seem off-hand, Inez nonchalantly said, "Oh, she told me all about the mechanics of reproduction, but I know there has to be more to it than just wifely duty. Why else would there be so many girls out there big with child and no husband to speak of? I would have asked my mother about it, but it felt a little strange. Besides, I wanted to know about an all-consuming, passionate love, and my parents can hardly be said to have *that* kind of relationship."

The truth of this struck Paulina as humorous, and she laughed a little despite the girl's lack of decorum. Leave it to Inez to state things plainly. She thought intently about how to proceed, and choosing her words carefully she began. "Well, if you think about it, some of the things your mother explained may sound a bit strange and uncomfortable, but if you do them with the person you truly love, they become an expression of that love. Your heart beats faster and you become breathless. You forget all of the strangeness and surrender yourself to the passion. Soon you cannot tell where one of you ends and the other begins. You want to give your entire self to this person and take all that he has to offer. You think about everything and nothing, and just when you think you will die of the pleasure, you experience a sweet release of emotion that leaves you satisfied and replete with love for your husband." She paused, a little surprised at herself for sharing such intimate feelings with anyone. She wasn't sure if she had told Inez what she wanted to know, but when Paulina looked at Inez's rapt face, she knew she had conveyed the excitement and delight of true love. "Well, that's how it was for me," she finished up a little self-consciously.

"Thank you, Paulina," Inez said, seeing the older woman with a newfound respect. To have loved a man so much and to have lost him put Paulina in a new role, the one of romantic, long-suffering heroine, now more like Penelope than ever. She only hoped that one day she would experience the same sort of love with Estêvão.

Chapter 12: Ceuta

While Inez was involved in the business of growing up, Estêvão was busy waging a crusade against the Moors for greater glory of God and country. During the reign of Manuel I, interest in Morocco increased, and a series of eight Portuguese fortresses was erected and garrisoned along the Atlantic coast of northern Africa. Previous occupants, some of them military aristocracy, had chosen to raid the countryside to enhance their personal wealth instead of engaging in legitimate commerce with the locals. This left the native population with a bad impression of the Portuguese altogether, and made existence doubly difficult for the honest few, such as Estêvão and his crew, who followed. They were plagued by almost daily retaliations and seemingly unprovoked assaults.

Everyday life was extremely dangerous, and there was always some perplexing task, which demanded his attention, yet Estêvão often found his thoughts returning to Inez and the two days he had spent in Vigo. He knew it could be a matter of life or death to be distracted in such a manner, but no matter how hard he tried, he could not get her bewitching eyes out of his mind. He reasoned with himself that she was just a child and should not hold such a prominent place in his affections. He attempted to fill every waking hour with the problems at hand. He berated himself for not doing his job to his utmost ability, but still the image of the upturned pale oval of her face and those magnificent silver and gold eyes shimmering in the moonlight would not leave his thoughts.

His crew also noticed the change. Though he had confided in no one, they all concurred that their captain had not been his same focused self since their visit to Galicia. Normally, though the job at hand took priority over any type of diversion, El Rey was not averse to a little entertainment and celebration with his men when business was concluded. On this trip that had not been the case. While crossing the Atlantic on their way to Morocco, most of the time not spent running the ship he had ensconced himself in his cabin, only summoning his first mate and stepbrother, João, when he needed to relay orders that did not require his personal attention. The loss of appetite, the sleepless nights spent pacing the deck, and the uncharacteristic impatience with everyday matters were symptoms of a malaise most of the crew had seen or experienced firsthand. They smiled behind his back and whispered to each other knowledgeably when their captain was safely out of earshot. It could only be one thing, a woman.

Most of them, having spent a good deal of their lives away from stable homes, knew only one reliable remedy for this ailment. A bout of hard drinking and female companionship were usually enough to draw anyone out of his melancholy state. Heaven knew that both were readily available in most port cities, but their commander was not such a simple creature. They had all served with El Rey long enough to know he was a fastidious man with a deep respect for women, not given to light affairs of the heart or the use of the fair sex as a tool to rid himself of his primal urges. Understanding him so well, they recognized that his condition must be serious indeed. Having nothing but the well-being of their captain in mind, as a group they decided they would approach João, the second-in-command. Though he openly declared himself to be neutral and usually tried to keep out of other people's business, he had a way of jollying his brother out of whichever demon was destroying the harmony of the ship at the moment. Perhaps he would be able to find out what was eating at their leader and ease the concerns of the crew.

João was a tall man with a quick mind and a biting wit. His curling dark hair framed a good-looking face dominated by a pair of brooding eyes—nearly black in color—juxtaposed paradoxically by an easy smile with a slight gap between the front teeth. His long limbs and wide shoulders made him a force to be contended with on the battlefield, and he regularly placed his own life in jeopardy in defense of his comrades. He gave the impression of not caring much about the rest of the human race—his nonchalance drove any females in range to compete for his favors—but he was fiercely loyal to his shipmates and his family, especially his brother.

When the crew came to him with their petition, he eagerly agreed to the task, stating that his brother's recently gloomy disposition had been gnawing away at his own peace of mind. In most matters he was not known to be overly tactful, but this time he realized that he needed to wait for the opportune time. He would not have long to wait.

Of all the Portuguese forts in northern Africa where Estêvão and his men could have been stationed, the one at Ceuta had in the past proven to be the most lucrative. Ceuta had always been one of Morocco's chief points of trade, and the multiple shifts from one system of rule to another had not changed that. One of the objectives of Portuguese occupation was to curtail piracy along the African coast. The fort was positioned in such a manner that a lookout could keep an eye on the incoming ships from both the Atlantic and the Mediterranean to assess any potential threats from pirates or privateers. It was a formidable assignment, but the promise of first pick of the spoils from any secured vessel was enough to override any uneasiness about being stationed there.

The other aim of the Portuguese garrison was to keep the peace between the ruling government and the subjugated local population. Among the required duties of being stationed at this profitable location were the dangerous twice-daily patrols of the area immediately surrounding and inland of the fort to scout out and capture any agitators. The heat of the sun this close to the equator dictated that these horseback rounds be made in the early morning just after sunup and in the evening just before dusk. These were the times when an attack was most likely, as a group of dissidents could easily move into an advantageous position under cover of darkness to await the passage of an unsuspecting squadron.

One day while Estêvão and his men were out on patrol, they were ambushed by a small band of Moors just inland from their home base. The day started out much the same as any other. The soldiers assembled in the courtyard of the fort just after dawn and headed out toward the west to do their routine reconnaissance. The first part of their tour was uneventful, but as they headed east, back to their home base and safety, the rising sun blazed directly into their faces, blinding them momentarily, and they were caught off-guard.

Their plan having succeeded, the rebels rushed down from their hiding places to make the most of the temporary vulnerability of the superior fighting force. The combat was fierce, and although the natives were not as well equipped, they were fighting for their homeland and in passionate defense of their religion. Not wanting to inflict loss of life and further fan the flames of insurrection, the Portuguese soon found themselves being forced to retreat. Estêvão, being the commander, brought up the rear to make sure all of his men returned to their post unharmed.

While swiftly making his way back to the fort, Estêvão looked back over his shoulder to assess the position of their pursuers. He was so focused on the safety of his men that he forgot that his mount was just one of the ordinary horses assigned to the fort—trained in the standard manner—and not his sure-footed, intuitive Tesouro. He checked the distance one last time, and satisfied that the nearest assailant was too far behind to present a threat, he turned to guide his horse through the open gateway of the fort to safety. In that moment, the unfortunate creature stumbled on an outcropping of rock in the otherwise smooth trail and slammed to the ground taking his rider with him, just fifty feet short of their goal.

As Estêvão realized what was happening, time seemed to slow down, and three distinct and unrelated thoughts ran through his mind. The first thing to occur to him was that he was glad he had left Tesouro at home. What a waste of fine horseflesh it would have been to put that magnificent beast down because of his own carelessness. Next came the thought of how sad his mother would be if he should be killed. She would be devastated to lose her only son, and everything she had slaved for her entire life would be forfeit to the Portuguese crown for lack of a male heir. Finally he thought of Inez. He would never have the chance to see her one last time or sort out his true feelings for the one person, besides his mother, who he felt really understood him. *Farewell, my Coelhinha,* he thought as the image of her compelling eyes swam before his own.

These thoughts sped through his mind in a split second, and just before he hit the ground, Estêvão's head cleared and his survival instincts took over. All of the years spent training, drilling, and defending himself from his enemies had left their memories engrained on his core. His body seemed to act of its own accord as he leapt clear of the tumbling, kicking, half-ton animal, drew his sword from its scabbard, and sprang to his feet in one smooth movement, and none too soon.

The Moor at the head of his pack, who just a few moments ago had been safely outdistanced, was down off of his own horse and upon him in a flash. He swung his scimitar down with deadly precision as Estêvão brought his sword up to parry the blow mere inches in front of his face. The clash of steel on steel could be heard by all as the heated battle raged before their eyes. The archers in the fort did their best holding the rest of the frustrated insurgents at bay, but they could not get a clean shot at El Rey's attacker without risking injury to their leader. They could do nothing but watch helplessly while their captain fought on.

The native was a taller, heavier man, and he slashed and hacked at El Rey as if possessed by the devil himself. His brute strength was terrifying, and he pushed mercilessly forward as if driven by some inner demon. The man was so close that Estêvão could hear him grunting as he rained down blow after crushing blow, could feel his hot, dank breath on his skin. He knew he was weakening under the onslaught, but the fury of the man's attack left no room for Estêvão to use his agility or the polished fighting skills, which were his strong suit. The assault thundered on and on, and El Rey could only bide his time and wait for an opening, hoping he would survive the storm of the man's hate-fueled rage. With aching arms and quivering legs, just as Estêvão knew he could take no more, miraculously his assailant began to tire, and the barrage began to slow. Estêvão saw his opportunity and mustered all of his strength for a final bid. He made a small, quick, circular movement with the tip of his weapon and unbelievably unarmed his exhausted opponent. Relief flooded through him as he watched the man sink to his knees in front of him, clearly defeated.

He held the man at sword's length and prepared to bind him and take him captive. That's when he caught a glimpse of the man's eyes framed dramatically by the headscarf wrapped loosely around his face. They were a soft grey with fawn-colored flecks around the iris. Not as stunning as Inez's eyes, but similar enough to make Estêvão hesitate a second too long and leave himself vulnerable once more. He sensed more than saw the man make a vicious upward thrust with his arm, and as he jumped back to avoid the impact, he felt a slicing pain high up on his inner right thigh. His enemy scrambled forward like a desperate wild animal, and Estêvão knew he would never get his sword around in time to defend himself. This was the end.

The crazed man quickly closed the distance, and just as he drew his arm back to strike anew, Estêvão was shoved roughly out of harm's way from behind by a large, fast-moving body. João appeared out of nowhere and, with lightening speed, ran the man through with a powerful thrust of flashing steel. Blood slowly bloomed around the fatal wound in the man's chest and consciousness began to fade from the eyes that had so distracted Estêvão in that life-or-death moment. He stared motionless, seemingly hypnotized by the dying man before him. João yanked him forcefully to his feet and shook him back to reality. "Are you injured, Brother?" he asked in his brusque manner.

"I don't think so," replied Estêvão, shaking his head.

"Then if you are finished with your playmate here, I suggest we head inside the gate before his friends turn us into human pincushions."

They turned and sprinted the last fifty feet through the safety of the gate, and as it closed securely behind them, they heard the arrows thudding harmlessly off of the heavy wooden doors. They looked at each other and burst out in nervous laughter over the precarious situation they had just survived. Estêvão clapped João on the back, and when he finally caught his breath he said, "Thank you, Brother. You saved my life again. I owe you one."

"Actually, I think that makes us even," João replied. "Your quick words saved me from that innkeeper in Soutomaior."

"That hardly qualifies as saving your life. He only reached as high as your chest," Estêvão countered.

"Yes, but I believe he would have liked to cut my head off even if he had to climb up on a chair to do it." João paused for a moment, a leering, mischievous gleam in his eyes. "But what a woman," he added. "She was almost worth it."

"She was his *wife*," Estêvão chided.

"Yes, but sometimes wives make the best partners, e*specially* if they belong to someone else."

"You, João, are a scoundrel."

"A scoundrel who loves his brother." Changing the subject, João pointed at Estêvão's wound. "I would love to continue this conversation, but you are bleeding. You should get the doctor to look at that. Sometimes these Moors poison the tips of their daggers."

Nodding in agreement, Estêvão took leave of his brother and limped off toward his quarters to get medical attention and wash off the grime of his narrow escape.

A little later while Estêvão was putting on some clean clothing, there was a knock at his door. He hobbled over to open it and found himself looking up into João's dark laughing eyes. His brother had brought him a plate piled with fruit, cheese, and bread, and a pitcher of wine. Estêvão motioned for him to enter and teetered back over to finish getting dressed.

João set the food and wine down on the table, pulled up a

chair, and stretched out his long legs. He plucked a stem of grapes from the plate and munched lazily on them as he slouched back in the chair, utterly at ease. It always amazed Estêvão that his brother could relax so completely one moment, and in the next, with the slightest provocation, he could be out the door with weapons in hand ready for battle. He had the languid grace and mercurial temperament of a cat, and for that reason Estêvão had dubbed him *Gato* from the time they were boys.

"What did the doctor say about your leg?" João asked through a mouthful of grapes.

"He cleaned out the wound, put in a few stitches, and said to stay off of a horse until it is healed," Estêvão answered with a grimace. "It's not a deep wound, and it's not too painful. It's just in a ... um ... delicate spot."

"That's putting it lightly. From what I saw, a little bit higher and you would have been singing *castrato* in God's own choir."

"Yes," Estêvão nodded, "I suppose I was lucky. What brings you here, Gato? I can tell you have something on your mind."

"You know me well," João said and took a deep breath. "Well, there's no easy way to put this, so I'll just say it. The crew and I have noticed that you have been a little ... how do I say this ... *out of sorts* since we left Galicia, and today you were not yourself either. There was that hesitation, slight, but it could have cost you your life. You know I wouldn't say anything, but it is starting to affect your work. What is going on?"

Estêvão looked at the floor to avoid his brother's direct gaze. He shrugged his shoulders in a tired gesture and said, "I'm sorry, João. I didn't realize anyone had noticed."

His brother's manner was as good as a confession. "I knew it was a woman," João said with a snap of his fingers. "I'll bet it was that merchant's daughter in Vigo. What was her name?"

"Inez," Estêvão replied without thinking.

"Inez?" João asked, a confused look wrinkling his brow. "I thought it was Sarita or Selena, something starting with an 'S'. Who is Inez? Have you been holding out on me, Brother?"

"Well if I didn't hold out on you, there would be no

untouched female flesh from Portugal to India and a string of fatherless babies all curiously with the same long legs and mocking black eyes," Estêvão said with obvious affection. "By the way, the merchant's daughter was named Serafina."

"Serafina! That's it! Well, Brother, there is really only one solution for your problem, and since you won't just take the woman and have done with it," João said matter-of-factly, "you will probably have to get married."

Estêvão thought this over for a moment then said, "You may be right."

"Well I'm glad we got your, uh, *situation* out in the open," João said, rising from his chair. He paused long enough to squeeze Estêvão's shoulder in a show of camaraderie. "You know, Brother, even if I don't harbor your same tender attitude toward women, I've still gleaned some valuable experience from them, and I am here if you ever need to talk. I promise I won't laugh at you," he added wickedly as he left the room.

With a little chuckle, Estêvão shook his head at João's backside as it disappeared through the closing door. Somehow these maddening conversations with his brother always put things into perspective and relieved his anxious mind. João was incorrigible, but possibly he had a point. After this morning's brush with death and being so rudely reminded of his own mortality, matrimony might be a wise idea. There was no way he could marry Inez. She was not much more than a child, but perhaps if he married someone else, his foolish heart could be made to stop this unrealistic fixation. Yes, maybe it was time for him to take a wife.

BOOK 2: Courtship
1512
Chapter 1: Reunion

The sun shone down on the waters of the Ria de Vigo, winking off the crests of the waves and bursting into a million dancing points of light. It was a fine clear April morning and time to bid farewell to the stormy season until next year. The port of Vigo was once again a beehive of activity after the long boring months of winter. With the burgeoning spring came a resurgence of life, a return to the cheerful, frenetic pace of the trade industry that was the town's lifeblood. Everything seemed in a rush to welcome the change. The white fluffy clouds scrambled hurriedly across the calm blue sky. The seagulls soared and dipped and cried out in a song of pure joy to be alive. The ships anchored in the harbor bobbed jauntily up and down, waiting to unload the treasures, which would bring fortune to their owners.

Inez stood under the olive tree on the hill and squinted to make out the banners rippling in the stiff breeze. After two and a half years, she still kept her daily vigil in hopes that El Rey would soon return, fulfilling his promise to come back to her. She knew that some men made promises with no intention of keeping them, but not Estêvão. During their time apart, she had exalted him to the status of hero. Her imagination had endued him with all of the best qualities the human race had to offer and none of its failings. She felt with her entire being that he was honest and sincere and that he meant every word he had said to her so long ago on this very spot.

Two and a half years. Much had changed in that time. On the

inside she was still the same opinionated, impertinent girl she had ever been, but she had matured enough to know that not every situation called for blatant honesty and that compromise was sometimes a better strategy for a harmonious existence with the rest of the world. She had learned the wisdom of holding her tongue and wording her point of view in a manner that would not offend. She liked to think that she had *gentled*. Yes, gentle was a term with a positive connotation. Any woman would be happy to be described as such, no matter how strong-minded.

Inez had changed much outwardly as well. She was only fourteen, but standing there on the knoll with the wind molding her dress to the exaggerated curves of her fully-developed body, one could have easily mistaken her for a full-grown woman, a sailor's wife awaiting her husband's arrival from sea. Although she was aware of her physical transformation, she never gave a thought to how others saw her. She was blithely ignorant of her affect on the opposite sex and the lingering looks of appraisal from some of the customers at her father's mercantile. As far as she was concerned, the only thing that her physical maturity had brought was inconvenience. It was inconvenient to have been fitted for a new wardrobe. It was inconvenient to have to bind her chest every morning. It was inconvenient to suffer the little aches and pains every month that were a woman's lot, but she gladly tolerated all of it. In her mind it brought her that much closer to her destiny.

Not seeing the cobalt blue of El Rey's falcon standard, Inez turned and started back toward the house. From the looks of the harbor she would have a long day ahead of her. She would have just enough time to pack a lunch for her father and herself before setting out to the mercantile. The birds cheeped in the trees, and the bees buzzed merrily among the wildflowers at the side of the path. The mood was contagious, and Inez skipped a little as she made her way down the gentle slope, unable to contain the delight that came with the change in the weather. She knew that she should try to exhibit a little more restraint, but she couldn't help it. On a day like this, the range of possibilities was endless. On a day like this, anything could happen.

The bells mounted on the front door tinkled a sprightly welcome as Inez entered her father's shop. She espied old Pedro Torres with a customer and nodded in greeting as she made her way around the counter to the small back room Iñigo used as an office. From the state of the desk, Inez could see that she had been correct to assume it would be a busy day. With a sigh she set down the basket that held their lunch and started to straighten the disaster her father had left behind.

Inez gathered the haphazardly strewn sheets of paper, stacked them neatly, and placed them in the box with some other receipts and invoices, which had yet to be entered into the master log. She set a rock that she used as a paperweight on top, so that the papers would not be disturbed by the draft from her father's comings and goings throughout the day. As she was doing this, Pedro finished with his customer and came in to help her.

"Good morning, Señorita Inez," he began in a rush to explain. "I tried to get things sorted out before you got here, and just as I was finished your father came in with another handful of paperwork. Then Señor Guzman showed up and needed assistance, and well, I guess the wind blew the receipts out of the box, and that's how you found them."

Inez smiled at him as she pulled her canvas work apron down over her head and tied it around her waist. "Don't worry, Don Pedro. I'll take care of it. I just wish Papa would remember to use the paperweight. It's such a simple thing, and it is right there next to the box."

He shrugged his shoulders in a gesture of long-suffering acceptance and added, "You know how your father is. He means well, but sometimes he forgets things. Not that he would ever forget the slightest detail about an account," he chuckled.

"That is part of the problem," Inez said thoughtfully. "Because he recalls every detail, he believes everyone else can do the same. I wish I could impress upon him how much easier it is this way. If it is written down where everyone can read it, *he* doesn't have to be here every minute of every day. Perhaps he could even take a vacation."

Don Pedro uttered a sound that was half laugh and half grunt, as if to say, *Good luck with that*, but he only said, "Perhaps." He paused for a moment and then motioned at the newly organized desk. "Well, Señorita Inez, it looks as if you have things under control here. Your father will probably want my help out on the dock. If you need me for anything, please call," he said, putting his worn cap on his head and exiting through the back door.

"I will, Don Pedro. Thank you."

Inez sighed again as she pulled her chair up to the desk and took the top receipt out of the box. She dipped her quill into the inkwell and, quickly and neatly, began to copy the information into the master log, her nose scrunching up in the unconscious habit that was so much a part of her. Again, she tried to understand how Iñigo, a man with genius enough to keep all of this information complete and separate in his mind, could forget something as logical and uncomplicated as a paperweight. The thought was incomprehensible. How had they ever managed without her? She shook her head to clear it and continued on to the next account.

Inez made her way steadily through the sheaf of paperwork, only stopping when a customer needed assistance. Before she knew it, half of the day had passed, and her grumbling belly told her that it was time to stop for lunch. As if on cue, her father came in from the dock with another handful of receipts and tried to set them on the desk and sneak back out the door without drawing attention.

"Papa!" Inez said sharply, just as he reached for the door. "I don't understand why it is so difficult for you to remember the paperweight! When I got here this morning, there were documents scattered all over the place," she scolded with her hands on her hips, looking and sounding remarkably like her mother. "What are you going to do if you lose something important?" she asked.

"Oh, Mynah, don't scowl so," Iñigo said in the placating voice he used so often with Joanna. Tapping his temple with his finger, he added, "Don't worry. I never forget an account."

"That is true," she said with a grudging smile. Her father's demeanor was so sheepish it was impossible to stay mad at him. "But you often forget to eat. Please sit down and have lunch with me. You can hardly afford to be any thinner, and I cannot eat all of this food by myself."

He grinned at Inez in his boyish manner, and all thought of returning to the dock left his mind. Happy to have an excuse, he crossed the room and pulled up a chair. He had never placed much importance on food, but the opportunity to pass a few quiet moments with his daughter was incentive enough to take a break. Iñigo loved his business, but more than that he loved spending time with his daughter. She was his favorite person in the world and the only thing that could distract him from his work.

Realizing that he was famished, he tore a chunk off of a loaf of soft sweet bread and bit into it with relish. "Mmm," he said closing his eyes and chewing with pleasure. "Did you make this?" Inez nodded, delighted with his unsolicited reaction. "It is delicious," he said, a little surprised yet clearly enjoying the result of his daughter's efforts in the kitchen. He fell silent for a moment, regarding Inez solemnly with his intelligent brown eyes. It was as if he was really seeing her for the first time after a prolonged absence. He swallowed hard and squeezed her hand. "One day, Mynah," he said sincerely, "you will make a wonderful wife for some lucky man."

Tears unexpectedly sprang up in her eyes at the heartfelt comment, and she quickly looked down at her lap. "Thank you, Papa," she managed to whisper, and she squeezed his hand back.

With so much work to keep her busy, Inez hardly noticed the hour. The last time Iñigo had come in to deliver a batch of receipts, he said they would be the final ones of the day. He had then gone back out to the dock to oversee the tasks that remained and supervise the clean up before they could head for home. This usually took about an hour. Inez quickened her pace in a bid to finish all of the paperwork so they could start with a clean slate the next morning.

Her back aching from sitting at the desk, Inez moved to a place at the end of the counter, so she could stand in a more comfortable position while she entered the accounts in the master log. She was so absorbed in the task that when the bells on the door jingled to announce the arrival of a new customer, she didn't even look up from the book. "Please let me know if you need assistance," she said automatically and continued writing, focusing all of her concentration on the paperwork in front of her.

A few minutes passed while the customer browsed the array of goods, walking casually from one spot to the next. Inez had nearly finished all of her entries when she heard him come to a stop in front of the counter. She was just summing up the final tally for the day when he cleared his throat and said, "Well, Coelhinha, this is not exactly the welcome I'd hoped for after being gone for two and a half years."

That voice was unmistakable. She had heard it in her dreams every night during the two and a half years of which he spoke. Her heart raced and her hand trembled, speckling the immaculate sheet of paper before her with a few random dots of ink. She felt her ears go hot with embarrassment at the awkward pause. It filled the space between them and grew more conspicuous with each passing moment, yet she could not bring herself to look up at him lest the spell be broken. She was afraid he would prove to be some hallucination conjured by her dreaming mind and would disappear if she cast her waking gaze upon him.

Estêvão waited patiently. He saw her hand tremble and her ears grow pink in her consternation. Her nose began to twitch in the endearing tic that he associated with Inez every time he thought of her. No matter how much she would change throughout her life, that adorable habit would most likely never leave her, and she *had* changed. He would hardly have recognized the young woman in front of him had it not been for her trademark quirk, the sprinkling of freckles across her funny little nose, and the distinctive color of her hair. Of course he would know her dazzling eyes anywhere, but she had not even looked up at him yet. Perhaps his memory had exaggerated their magnificence.

In an effort to put her at ease, on impulse he reached out and gently covered her hand with his own. He had just opened his mouth to tell her how happy he was to see her when the back door creaked open. They both jumped at the sudden intrusion on their reunion, and Estêvão let go her hand as Inez pulled it discreetly back across the counter. Her skin tingled with excitement where his hand had contacted hers, and she was overjoyed with his obvious pleasure in their meeting.

Iñigo strode quickly over to shake hands with Estêvão, and with uncharacteristic enthusiasm declared, "Capitán Rey! What a delight it is to see you!"

The men exchanged niceties and small talk while Inez locked the front door and put away the giant account book. She was grateful for her father's interruption. This gave her the chance to regain her composure and to reassure herself that Estêvão was not a dream, but a man of flesh and blood and all that she remembered. She stole a few covert looks at him from under lowered lashes while he conversed animatedly with her father, and she was satisfied that her mind had played no trick on her recollection. She was just taking off her apron when she heard her father say, "Well, Capitán Rey, you must come home with us for supper. My Joanna would be extremely upset if she were to be deprived of the pleasure of your company."

At this the three of them burst into good-natured laughter, bound conspiratorially together by the knowledge of the obvious untruth of the statement. The mood was transformed into one of warm camaraderie, and Inez was again thankful for the talent her father had of relieving the tension in any situation.

Chapter 2: The Silver Rabbit

On the way home from the mercantile Inez sat on one side of her father on the wagon seat while Estêvão, on the other side, related his most recent adventures. Iñigo was an avid student of the world's cultures, so any opportunity to learn something new about a foreign people interested him completely. Inez also suspected that he would have loved to lead the life of El Rey had circumstances been different, but for now he could only live vicariously through the younger man. With rapt attention he listened intently and asked incisive questions when he desired further illumination.

Inez was content just to listen to Estêvão's voice and to be able to look upon him without feeling suspect. She took full advantage of the opportunity and unabashedly observed him with an appraising eye. Outwardly he had not changed during his time away. He had maintained his slender, muscular physique. His hair was still the sleek, nearly black mane she remembered. His skin was more bronzed than when she had last seen him, but this just emphasized the flashing white teeth revealed by his easy, open smile. His familiar face still retained the strong, distinctive features she had thought so beautiful at their first meeting, and that face had grown even dearer to her after the enforced estrangement. The only difference that she could discern was in his eyes.

His hazel-green eyes had the telltale creases at the corners, which spoke of his time spent out of doors. This was to be expected, but it was not the major change. There was a sort of peace in his eyes now where before had burned an ambitious fire. The ambition was still there, but now it was tempered with something else, perhaps resolution. It was as if he had reached a milestone or made a life-changing decision. She wondered what it meant.

The wagon pulled up to the stately García home and was greeted by a couple of efficient servants who hurried to their task. Iñigo instructed them what to do with the supplies in the bed of the dray then turned to lead his daughter and his guest to the house. Upon opening the door he was met by his visibly upset wife.

Joanna stood just inside the door with her hands on her hips, the stance which had been so accurately mimicked by her daughter earlier in the day. Her eyes had a smoldering look in them, like a barely dampered fire that could burst into flames at a moment's notice. This never failed to unnerve the subject of their observation. Iñigo saw the look and knew he would have to tread carefully.

"Iñigo!" Joanna exclaimed. "Where have you been? I expected you an hour ago! Your supper has been ruined! I don't know how many times I have asked you to send a message if you are going to be *so* late. Well, why do you not answer? What do you have to say for yourself?"

Iñigo was never so glad that he had brought home company. It was a welcome stroke of luck. He knew that no matter how incensed she was, Joanna's pride and sense of duty would never permit her to be ungracious in front of a guest.

"Calm yourself, *mi reina*," he began. "I have good reason for the delay. I have..."

"*Reina* is it?" she cut in. "What have you done now? Come on. Out with it. Why do you not *speak?*"

Inez looked up at Estêvão. She saw the amusement sparkle in his eyes, and she had to clap a hand over her mouth to stifle her own laughter, a sure guarantee to land her father in even deeper trouble and perhaps herself as well.

Iñigo took a deep breath, and with superhuman patience and gentleness, he reached for his formidable wife's hand and said, "I have brought home company, dearest." Then he opened the door wide enough to reveal Inez and Estêvão standing silently behind him.

Joanna's eyes widened in embarrassment, and clearly subdued, she grumbled, "Well why didn't you say so in the first place?"

Ever the tactician, Iñigo replied, "I'm sorry, dear. I should have spoken earlier."

With a final withering look at her husband, Joanna turned to Estêvão, her most charming smile fixed on her face, and said smoothly, "Señor Rey, what an unexpected surprise it is to see you again. Please come in. As it happens supper is just coming ready. It would be a pleasure if you would join us."

Estêvão stepped over the threshold, his courtier's smile on his lips, and bowed low. "The pleasure, Señora García, is all mine," he said.

The supper was a complete success. The main course was an *estofado de carne*, a rich beef stew, which Inez knew only grew more savory and tender the longer it cooked. It had not been such a big inconvenience to put on hold as Joanna made out. The only reason Inez could figure that her mother had made such a fuss was that she was just being herself, frustrated because she could not exert her iron will over the situation. To her credit, after her initial irritation, Joanna quickly settled into her role of congenial hostess, mollified to some extent by the earnest appreciation of her guest.

The evening was not like any Inez could remember. Because her father always kept his business dealings so separate from his personal life, the large parties that Joanna often threw seemed more public relations events than social affairs. They were opportunities to bring together the other members of society with wealth and status comparable to that of the García household. For the most part, Inez supposed these gatherings were her mother's way of inferring the desirability of a union with their family and drumming up business for her father. This night had not been the least bit like that.

The setting was much like any other family supper. As there was no time for Joanna to break out the formal tableware or set the scene for the display of ostentation that was synonymous with her supper parties, she had to settle for a cozy and inviting atmosphere, which added to the singularity of the occasion. Estêvão entertained them all with excerpts from his latest tour of duty in Ceuta, and he had such a natural affinity for storytelling Inez noticed that even Joanna displayed a genuine interest, asking the odd question from time to time.

Serafina sat quietly at the table and tried not to draw too much notice to her person. Her golden presence was like an entity in itself and could never really be ignored, but tonight she willingly faded to the background, relieved for a change not to be the focus of attention. She knew how much this meant to her sister, and of late she had begun to withdraw into herself, her confidence shaken by the dwindling number of suitors and the lack of bona fide offers of marriage. She was now twenty years old and, though in the prime of her beauty, still unmarried and certain to be dubbed an old maid if a husband could not be found in the near future. She laughed and exhibited all of the appropriate emotions, but mostly it was a part she played to satisfy those around her.

Inez noted the reticence of her sister and was grateful. If Serafina decided to turn on her beguiling charm, there was no member of the opposite sex who could resist it. Inez recalled that previous occasion so long ago, when Estêvão had seemed somewhat immune if not completely put off by her sister's attempt at flirtation. But having grown up so much in the ensuing months and years, she recognized that a child's perception was not always accurate. She hoped and prayed that her initial impressions of Estêvão's interest and affection for herself would prove to be true ones.

After the meal, for which Estêvão thanked his hostess profusely and assured her it had been the best he'd eaten in weeks, Joanna and Serafina retired to the parlor to chat and work on Serafina's ever-expanding trousseau. Not wanting to be banished to needlework and local gossip, Inez glanced up at her father, a pleading look in her eyes. Catching his daughter's meaning, Iñigo suggested a walk outside to take advantage of the view from the knoll and perhaps hear a few more tales of adventure if El Rey would oblige. Estêvão readily agreed, and the three of them climbed the gentle slope, the two men walking ahead while Inez tagged along in their wake.

Gaining the crest of the mount, the view of the harbor gradually unveiled itself like a dark shimmering mirage. Dominating the upper portion, the giant half-moon rode in an inky blue-black swath of cosmos sequined with a myriad of twinkling white stars. The celestial display faded in and out of sight, obscured from time to time by the passage of eerie, tattered grey clouds. The ghostly profiles of the ships anchored at port—their sails furled, their portholes glowing with pale yellow lantern light—where like revenants from a bygone age. The scene emitted a strong otherworldly ambiance, and the trio, drawn together by their mutual attraction to the sea, collectively exhaled, awestruck by her ever-changing mood.

"It never ceases to amaze me, this view," Iñigo said with clear appreciation.

"I can see why you love it here," Estêvão answered, nodding his agreement.

Inez made her way to the swing, leaving the bench to be occupied by the two men. She listened to them discuss the difficulties of trying to maintain an empire in a foreign land so far from the seat of the ruling body. From there they moved on to the trade business and bandied ideas back and forth about changes they would make if they were in charge. Then they talked over some thoughts each of them had concerning their dealings with one another, and how perhaps they could come up with a new plan to attract a wider market by offering some new product, acquiring some communal land, or starting up a new mercantile at a previously untapped location.

It was all business talk, and Inez had heard most of it before. Iñigo occasionally argued hypothetical points with himself in moments of extreme frustration, but the fact that he was openly airing his views with someone whom he clearly respected changed everything. Just the idea that her father was beginning to regard

Estêvão as more than a business associate was a major milestone. Iñigo had very high standards and did not give his friendship lightly. For him to even speak in confidence to someone outside of the family was high praise indeed.

In a slight daze, a mood of utter contentment settled over her. These were the two men in the world who meant the most to Inez, so it pleased her that they should exhibit a mutual liking for one another. This fact in itself was reason enough to rejoice. Then, suddenly another thought occurred to her that almost caused her heart to stop.

If her father was considering entering into a more formal partnership with Estêvão, might he not wish to cement the deal somewhere down the line with a union of a more intimate nature? Perhaps a marriage? Her head swam, and excitement began to build within her as Inez recognized what this might mean to her personally. In her wildest dreams she had never imagined that her little girl's hopes might be realized in such a serendipitous fashion. She knew that she should not dare to raise her expectations lest they be dashed by reality, but she could not help herself.

Inez was lost in her own wild fantasies when she heard her father say, "Well, it has been a long day, and tomorrow will most likely prove equally so." He rose from the bench, stretching his lanky frame to its fullest height, and offered his hand to Estêvão in a gesture of partnership and newfound amity. "Goodnight, my friend," he said warmly. "I look forward to continuing this conversation another time." He walked over to Inez on the swing and kissed her on the top of the head. "Goodnight, Mynah. Do not stay out here too much longer, or your mother will have my head on a platter," he joked. With a smile he turned and made his way back down toward the house.

Inez and Estêvão sat for a moment looking out at the sea, the awkward silence building between them once more. Finally Estêvão cleared his throat, looked over at her in the swing, and asked, "Do you remember that other night like this, so long ago?"

She nodded with an enigmatic smile, an oddly mature expression in her adolescent face. "I made such a fool of myself that night, yet you made me feel as if I had nothing to be embarrassed about. It seems a lifetime ago, but I remember every detail." She was glad he was not close enough to see her blush.

"That was the night I christened you 'Coelhinha', and that is how I've thought of you ever since." He reached into his pocket and pulled out a tiny paper-wrapped parcel then walked over to where she sat on the swing. "It occurs to me that I have missed a couple of important birthdays, and I wanted to gift you with something more than a piece of frippery taken from a horse's bridle," he said and handed her the package.

Inez smiled up at him, and as she took his offering her hand brushed his, and she blushed anew. She brought the present down to her lap, so he could not see the shaking of her hands, and clumsily began to unwrap it. Her sharp intake of breath was audible as her stumbling fingers removed the final flap of paper hiding the treasure inside. There in her lap was the most delightful thing she had ever seen. It was a beautiful representation of a fluffy sweet-faced rabbit, exquisitely wrought and glowing up at her with the distinctive soft patina of high-quality silver.

Her mouth dropped open in surprise, and as Inez looked up at him, Estêvão saw that his original impression of her eyes had been no fluke. They were as bewitching as he had originally judged them to be, and the realization left him a little light-headed. He saw her mouth moving, and he had to concentrate hard to decipher what she was saying.

"It is very, very dear, but I cannot accept it," she said, still a little stunned. "It is too expensive, and my mother would never allow it."

Recovering his composure, he said, "I thought that might be the case, so I spoke to your father first."

"What did he say?" Inez asked, curious to know what had been her father's reaction.

"He said, 'What excellent craftsmanship. I wonder if the artist used a mold or if he shaped the details by hand after it was cast.' He was quite taken with it."

Inez laughed at Estêvão's comically accurate impersonation

of her father. "That sounds like him. Well, if he said it was all right, I suppose it would be rude of me to refuse it when you were so thoughtful. It is lovely," she said dreamily, caressing it with the tip of her index finger.

"Here, let me help you put it on," Estêvão said, taking the leather thong from which the rabbit pended and moving around behind her.

She lifted the heavy mass of her hair for him to tie the charm around her neck, and when he had done, it fell to a comfortable position on her chest a few inches below the base of her throat. The silver, which at first felt cool against her skin, quickly warmed to her body temperature so that she could no longer feel its silky metal consistency unless she thought hard about it. Estêvão came back in front of her to admire the fit, and Inez arched her neck and turned a little from side to side to set the necklace off to its best advantage. The radiant smile on her face far outshone the jewelry, and it was the best reward he could have imagined. He caught himself getting lost in her eyes again.

"Well," he said a little gruffly, "we should be getting back. Now that I've started to win your mother over a bit, I don't want to spoil it by keeping you out too late."

Inez didn't want that either, so she eagerly hopped down from the swing, and side-by-side they started back toward the house. In her young life she had never been so happy. She felt like she was walking on clouds. She recalled all of the times she'd had to bite her tongue and suppress her true feelings to honor the long ago vow she had made to keep her beloved safe. All of the frustration, all of the deprivation, all of the compromise, all of it had been worth the sacrifice to reach this one, precious moment.

Chapter 3: The Courier

The next morning Inez awoke at the first light of dawn. She had a keen sense of anticipation only previously experienced on the mornings of holidays like Christmas or her birthday. She hurriedly dressed, grateful not to have to take pains to be quiet. Her mother had set her up in her own room since she had begun to work at the mercantile so not to disturb Serafina's sleep unnecessarily. She checked her reflection in the mirror to make sure she looked presentable, noting with satisfaction how prettily the pendant on her chest was displayed, and slipped out her door with the highest of hopes.

Descending the stairs, Inez was more than a little disappointed not to find her father and Estêvão sitting at the table having breakfast, and there was nothing to indicate that they had recently occupied the spot. Iñigo was a notoriously early riser, but she could not imagine him being so rude as to head for work and leave his guest to his own devices. She wondered where they could have gone. Paulina would know. Inez went to the kitchen to find her.

Opening the door, Inez was greeted by the familiar warmth and the enticing aromas that made her feel so at home here. She breathed in deeply, relaxing a little, and took a look around. The scullery maid was just rinsing a small stack of plates, and Paulina was sitting at the worktable inspecting some fresh eggs. She looked up at Inez and smiled, her beautiful Grecian face looking patently incongruous in these domestic surroundings.

"Bom dia, Baixinha. What brings you here so early?" Paulina asked as she continued with her task.

"I was wondering if you know where my father has gone," Inez asked, plucking a cooling empañada off of a nearby rack.

"And his distinguished guest?" Paulina prodded, arching an eyebrow and enjoying the opportunity to discomfit Inez with a bit of good-natured teasing.

"Well I suppose his guest would perforce be included," Inez countered in an effort to sound nonchalant. She broke a little piece off of the pastry and popped it into her mouth trying to complete the ruse, but her ears betrayed her true feelings by turning pink.

Paulina shook her head, chuckling to herself over Inez's telltale flush of color. Then she caught the imploring look underlying the calm façade of the younger woman's face, and she didn't have the heart to continue teasing. "Your father and Capitán Rey left in the wagon about half an hour ago," Paulina said softly.

"But why?" Inez blurted out, her pretense falling by the wayside, the distress evident in her voice.

"They did not say, and it is not my place to ask," Paulina said gently. "Perhaps they had some business at the mercantile, and you will see them there," she suggested, patting Inez's hand.

Upon arriving in town, Inez frantically searched the harbor for the signature blue falcon banner of the *María Vencedora*, but it was nowhere to be seen. Crestfallen, she entered her father's shop and dispiritedly found her way to the back room. She pulled her apron on over her dress, plopped down into the chair, and held her head in her hands. She was on the verge of tears when her father entered through the back door.

Iñigo was a bit surprised but very happy to see that she was earlier than usual. "Mynah, I'm glad you're here so soon," he said in a rush. "I was right about it being as busy as yesterday. This is already my second batch of receipts. You'll see that I remembered the paperweight today," he said, obviously pleased with himself. He paused for a moment, just then noticing that she was not her normally cheerful self. "What's wrong, Mynah? Do you not feel well?" he asked, immediately concerned.

"I'm fine, Papa," she said in a small voice. "I just didn't sleep very well last night," she offered, praying he would leave it at that.

"Phew!" he said with relief. "For a moment I thought you might have come down with something. It would be a shame if you got sick and your mother had no one to blame but me ... or Capitán Rey."

"Is he still here?" Inez asked, hoping her father would not hear the eagerness in her voice.

"Who?" he asked absentmindedly. Then remembering he went on, "Oh, yes. Capitán Rey. No, he and his crew sailed this morning. He said he had some business to discuss with his uncle."

"Will he be back?" Inez prodded expectantly.

"Well I suppose he will," Iñigo said thoughtfully. He drifted off, lost in his own thoughts.

"When, Papa?" Inez asked, trying not to lose patience. Sometimes talking to her father was maddening.

"When? ... Oh, yes, Capitán Rey," he said, reminding himself. "Well, we discussed some business of our own last night, and it sounds like there are a few encouraging prospects, but he did not say when he would return."

There it was, the news she dreaded. He was gone again. Inez sighed, a bit disheartened yet not completely crushed. She knew that if someday they were married, it would be just like this. This was the lot of a sea captain's wife. The thing that most saddened her was the fact that he had not said goodbye. She supposed there had been no opportunity, but it would have been nice. Well, she had been patient before, and she could be patient again. She reached up and fingered the silver rabbit on her chest, a tangible reminder that she held a place in his thoughts while he was away. She smiled and thought to herself, *At least now I have this.*

The day was busy enough that Inez had no time to dwell on her romantic troubles. The morning flew by. Before she knew it lunchtime had passed, and her day was more than half over. Because of her early arrival and her concerted effort to enter the paperwork as it came in, there was no backlog, and with the late afternoon came a substantial lull in the action. To keep herself busy, she decided to dust off the displays and restock the shelves.

Armed with a damp rag, she dove into her task with alacrity.

Inez was done with all of the central bins and was just getting ready to attack the shelves when the bells on the front door heralded a new arrival. She turned to find that a young man dressed in an unfamiliar livery had entered the shop. He scanned the room to find the person in charge, and his eyes lighted upon Inez. He smiled a greeting as he approached her.

"*Buenas tardes*, Señorita," he said formally. "I have a message for Señor Iñigo García. Is he available?"

"He is out on the dock at the moment receiving merchandise," Inez explained. "Perhaps you can leave the message with me," she suggested, her curiosity piqued.

"May I have your name please?"

The question left her even more intrigued by all the mystery. Usually business communiqués came addressed to the mercantile, and the couriers rarely asked for specific names. Most personal mail came to their home, so this was uncommon indeed.

"I am his daughter, Inez," she replied.

Her name sparked recognition into his eyes, and he nodded as he withdrew the letter from his vest. "Here you go, Señorita Inez. I was told I could leave this in your care if your father was otherwise occupied."

"Thank you," she said as the messenger bowed then left the building. After he had gone, she turned the letter over in her hand to examine the seal on the back. *Interesting,* she thought to herself, trying to figure out just why the wax impression looked so familiar. Then it hit her. The image was almost an exact replica of the falcon crest on the banner of Estêvão's ship! She flipped the message back to the front to look at the writing there. She would recognize that writing anywhere. She had read the note he wrote to her for her twelfth birthday nearly every night during his absence.

Her hands itched to rip open the wax and reveal the message inside, but she knew that propriety would not allow it. Although the letter had been left in her care, it was not addressed to her. To open it would be completely unforgivable. With a frustrated sigh, she quelled the temptation rising inside her and tucked the missive into her apron.

She attempted to distract herself by continuing with her cleaning, but it was no good. She resignedly put the shelf back to rights and returned to the office. She pulled the note out of her apron and sat down at the desk. She looked at one side and then the other, turning it over and over again. Had it been any other piece of correspondence she would have felt no qualms about opening it immediately, but because it came from Estêvão, she felt she would be violating a trust.

Just as she had almost convinced herself that it would be appropriate for her to break the seal, Iñigo came through the back door with the final receipts of the day. She jumped a little as if she were a child caught doing something naughty.

"What do you have there, Mynah?" her father asked, espying the letter in her hand.

"A message came for you while you were outside," she said, handing it to him. "I think it's from Capitán Rey," she added, looking up at him expectantly.

He took the note from her hand and cracked the seal open. He quickly perused the paper, and a smile formed on his long dark face. "Hmm ... what an interesting idea," he said more to himself than to his daughter.

"What is it, Papa?" Inez asked, nearly wild from the suspense.

"Well, I shall have to discuss it with your mother before I can tell you, but it will be quite a surprise," he said with eyes twinkling. "For now you will just have to wonder."

Inez did not know if one could actually die from curiosity, but if it was possible, she knew she would not survive the night.

As soon as Estêvão had dispatched the messenger, he experienced a few minor misgivings. Why had he sent such an impetuous invitation? It was completely out of character for him to be so impulsive, but lately he had felt a little bit reckless. Since his narrow brush with mortality, he had begun to see the futility of overplanning one's life and had started to live more in the moment, but what was his true intention behind this latest whim?

He tried to justify the invitation by telling himself that the business proposition with Iñigo was the reason for the attention he was paying to the García family, but he could have easily begun this venture without any outside investors. What was the real reason he had made the offer to the merchant? Was it just an excuse to stay close to the daughter? Was he starting to develop feelings for Inez that went beyond friendship? At this point he could not say, because he wasn't sure himself. Anything beyond a platonic relationship with the girl would be unseemly. She was only fourteen years old, and he was a man in the prime of life. What was it about her that kept her in his thoughts even though he could come up with no acceptable reason for her to be there? It was those eyes.

Her eyes disturbed him. They reached down into his very soul and communicated, no, *communed* with him on a level that transcended the thoughts and words of human devising. When he looked into her eyes, he felt all manner of sentiments stirred up within him, some of which he could not name. He already felt affection and a possessiveness that he equated with a desire to protect her, somewhat like an uncle, but he was reluctant to admit that what Inez aroused in him bore a striking similarity to a schoolboy infatuation. It was like reliving his adolescence, the thrill of anticipation when they were together and the yearning while they were apart. It was driving him to do unthinkable things, like the incident with the messenger.

When Estêvão dispatched the man to Vigo, he knew it would be a couple of hours before he returned. He was loath to leave the house lest the courier should arrive when he was out, delaying an answer reaching his ears at the first possible instant. Time crept by, and he found himself pacing the floor with an abundance of excess energy. He tried to find something to distract him, but it was no good. He looked out the window. He sat in a chair. He picked at a loose thread on his sleeve. He even attempted to play with the fat old housecat—notorious for her bad temper—who was napping in the afternoon sun, but any effort to read or go over his business books or even to hold a conversation with anyone failed miserably. And so he paced.

It seemed a lifetime until the man came galloping up the lane at last. Estêvão restrained himself from running out to interrogate him as he was dismounting from his horse, because it would have been completely indecorous and would have raised eyebrows indeed. He satisfied himself by waiting just inside the servants' entrance where he could receive the news straightaway and not draw undue scrutiny. He had expected the man's immediate appearance, so when the courier did not step through the door, Estêvão moved closer to investigate.

Just outside the door the messenger had been stopped by one of his cronies and could not resist a little good-natured boasting. He was telling his co-worker about the gorgeous young woman at the mercantile in Vigo who had received the delivery with which he had been charged. He described her abundance of thick coppery hair, and her striking silver eyes, and from there he launched into a lasciviously accurate account of the señorita's most outstanding feminine assets.

Estêvão was overcome by an insane jealousy, rage boiling up hotly inside of him. He was seized with the sudden need to throttle the vulgar man and smash him repeatedly in the face until nothing remained of his filthy, lecherous mouth. He reached for the door handle, fully intending to thrash the man, and came to his senses just in time.

If he did anything untoward to his uncle's servant, there would be questions, and eventually everyone would know that he had been eavesdropping. How could he explain this without looking like a churl? He took a deep breath, got his anger under control, and strode back to the sitting room to wait for his reply. The man soon entered to deliver the news, and nobody was the wiser.

Looking back at it, Estêvão could hardly believe that it had happened. He was having trouble coming to terms with the emotion this young girl dredged up in him. He would have to watch himself carefully in the future and try to come up with a way to put her out of his mind. Maybe during her visit to Terceira she would do something to reveal her true personality, and it would make him realize that she was human with ordinary human flaws, just like everyone else. Perhaps then he could move past this ridiculous obsession and settle down to a proper married life.

Chapter 4: The Invitation

For the remainder of the evening, Iñigo was more animated than Inez had seen him in a very long time. There was a mischievous gleam behind his dark eyes that bespoke his secret, and his behavior exhibited the same playful tenor. Joanna and Serafina were baffled and shot questioning looks at each other when he was not paying attention. Inez knew more than her mother and sister, but because she did not know enough to dispel the mystery, she said nothing. Besides, her father was clearly enjoying the rare opportunity of having his women at a disadvantage for a change, instead of the other way around. Let him have his fun. They would learn the surprise soon enough.

Aside from Iñigo's strange conduct, the evening proceeded more or less in the usual manner. The family supped together then moved to the parlor to unwind and talk about their day. Joanna was plainly distracted by her husband's mood, but not willing to admit his victory over her, she suppressed the urge to ask him outright about it. Inez noticed the signs of her mother's discomfiture and savored the moment, taking consolation in the fact that she was not the only one being kept in the dark. The idea that she knew at least part of the story made her feel like a co-conspirator and brought her a small measure of satisfaction.

The time passed more quickly than Inez would have believed, and before she knew it, it was time for bed. This put her in a cheerful mood because most of the excruciating wait was behind her. If she could sleep tonight, in the morning the riddle would be solved. The family bid each other good night and headed off to their respective bedrooms.

Joanna had reached her breaking point, and no sooner had the door to their bedroom closed behind her than she laid into her husband with a vengeance. "Iñigo! What is going on with you?" she wailed, pushed far beyond the boundary of her already limited patience.

Iñigo was sitting on a chair pulling off his boots. He looked up at her and smiled broadly. "I was wondering how long it would take for you to break down and ask me," he said, tickled that he had finally forced her to do it. He continued to undress, the smile still on his face.

"Well ..." she said, trying to lead him to divulge the rest of the mystery and account for his perplexing behavior.

He looked up at her as he got into his side of the bed and luxuriantly settled his considerable length under the covers, taking the time to fold his hands comfortably behind his head. He was enjoying this opportunity to its utmost. It wasn't often that he was in the position to make his wife a slave to his whim, and this time she seemed frantic to discover his secret. For fun, he decided to prolong the suspense as long as he could.

"Why don't you get ready for bed, dear," he said, the teasing look still in his eyes.

He had prepared himself for a full-blown fit of rage, so he was completely surprised and a little bit shaken when Joanna burst into tears. He immediately jumped out of bed and ran over to where she stood, doing everything he could to stem the flood.

"Joanna, my dear," he stammered. "Hush, mi reina. Oh, shhh, shhh. Why are you crying?" he asked tenderly while he held her close and rocked her like a child.

Her sobs finally diminished into a few hitching whimpers. She brought out her handkerchief, blew her nose and wiped her eyes, and looked up at him with her tear-stained face. "I'm sorry," she apologized, still sniffling. "I don't know what came over me. It's just that ..." she could not finish the thought, and another fat tear oozed out of the corner of her eye and slid slowly down her cheek.

Iñigo was used to Joanna's histrionics when she was

displeased or could not get her way, but this genuine display of emotion was something he had not seen for a very long time. It made him sorry he had toyed with her at all. He held her close and patiently waited until she was ready to go on.

"I'm sorry," she began again. "It's just that today I was thinking about the girls and how it seems that we are running out of time with them. Serafina has not yet found a suitable husband, and it will soon be time to find one for Inez, and ..."

"Inez is only fourteen," Iñigo cut in, unable to restrain himself.

"She is fourteen and a half," Joanna snapped, some of her forceful self beginning to return. She looked up at him, a hard edge in her still beautiful blue-green eyes, and saw the hurt in his. Her heart thawed a bit, and she said gently, "She is only a few months younger than I was the first time I ... fell in love. Oh, Iñigo. It seems so *long* ago. This morning I looked into the mirror and saw an old woman looking back at me ... and ..." she dissolved into tears once more.

"And then I teased you, and it was too much," Iñigo finished up for her. Joanna nodded her head pathetically, and he stroked her grey-streaked hair and squeezed her tight. "Well, Reina, it sounds to me as if you could use a break from the everyday," he started in a cheerful voice. "It just so happens that today I received an invitation that will provide a welcome diversion."

Joanna looked up at him, the delight shining clearly in her red-rimmed eyes. "Really, Iñigo?" she asked like a disbelieving child. "Is that what has you so smug?"

He nodded, pleased with the change in her attitude. "Yes. Capitán Rey sent word that he would like us to be his guests at his ranch on Terceira." When he looked down at her, he was shocked to see that the stubborn set had come back into her face. "What is it, Joanna?" he asked, instantly wary.

"Iñigo, he is *Portuguese*. You know how I feel about *those* people," she spat out.

"Oh, Joanna, *please* don't start that," he begged her. "His mother is Castilian and comes from an aristocratic family like yours. He is a respectful, dignified young man, and he has royal blood."

"He is a royal *bastard*," she insisted.

"I believe his parents were married. It was simply not sanctioned by the Portuguese court. Besides, his uncle is the King of Portugal. He also shares blood ties with the King of England, our own late Queen Isabella, and with your original Joanna's patroness, Catalina of Lancaster," Iñigo said firmly. He looked down at her and saw her stormy face, her pouting bottom lip jutting out in defiance. "Reina," he said gently, "you of all people should know that a person's quality does not depend upon whether his parents went through a ceremony of marriage."

With this last comment, Joanna's stubbornness began to crumble, and Iñigo felt her cling more tightly to him. At this point he knew he had won, but he also knew it would be best to make it seem like her decision.

"I know you would not want him to think us so ungracious as to refuse, so I shall send word to Capitán Rey to let him know we have accepted." He said this last with a slight question in his voice to give his wife the final say.

Joanna nodded her head wearily, reluctantly giving her stamp of approval. Then with a tired sigh, to no one in particular, she asked, "Why does everything have to be so difficult?"

Iñigo smiled down at her, his eyes glowing with real love and affection. "Such is life, mi reina. We have been through difficult times before, and we will get through them again as long as we have each other."

The next morning Inez came downstairs to find her parents chatting amiably as they ate their breakfast. She was surprised to see that her father had not yet left for the mercantile and astonished to realize that it seemed the furthest thing from his mind. Her mother was more chipper than Inez had seen her for ages, and this extraordinary, joyful mood was absolutely contagious. Inez went round to her parents and gave them each a smacking kiss on the cheek to bid them good morning.

Serafina soon joined them, and the scene was complete. The family sat companionably around the table, and not one of them mentioned the rarity of such an occasion. It was as if there were a tacit understanding between them that by calling attention to the uniqueness of the mood, the fragility and specialness of it would be broken. It would be a veritable tragedy, and none of them wanted to be the cause of it.

When they had all finished eating, Iñigo cleared his throat to draw his women's attention. The three of them looked up at him expectantly and waited for him to speak. He saw the anticipation gleaming in their eyes, and the thought occurred to him that he should have done something like this years ago. He loved them all so much. He paused, caught momentarily off-guard by the sudden rush of emotion, and had to clear his throat a second time.

"Well, ladies," he began, only just keeping his feelings in check, "as you may know, I have a surprise for you." He went on to tell them about the invitation extended by El Rey. He explained to them that Joanna and he had discussed it and decided that it would be a golden opportunity to take a small vacation. The girls looked at each other and then at their mother in amazement, wondering if this could really be happening. When Iñigo finished, there was a barely perceptible pause then both girls bounced on their seats and clapped their hands, clearly excited about the prospect.

Suddenly a thought occurred to Inez. "Papa, what about the mercantile?"

"I knew you would ask that. I've already sent word to Don Pedro," Iñigo said with a smile. "He has been with me from the very beginning, and he knows everything about the business. His oldest boy used to do your job before he had his own family, and he has agreed to fill in for the time we are away. He only needs for you to go over the new accounting system with him." He looked at Inez with a mock-stern look on his face. Waving an admonishing finger at her he said, "It will mean some extra work today, but everything will be under control when we leave in two days' time."

She could stand it no more. Inez hopped up from her seat, ran around the table, and hugged her father as tightly as she could. "Oh, Papa!" she gushed. "Thank you so, so much!"

That day and the next proved to be a whirlwind. There was as much extra work at the mercantile as Iñigo had predicted. There was also the chore of deciding what to pack then the actual packing itself. Joanna looked forward to the adventure with as much enthusiasm as the rest of the family, and she channeled all of her considerable energy into making sure her instructions were followed to the letter by those who were going on the trip, as well as those staying behind.

Serafina surprised herself by realizing that she actually welcomed the change of scenery the voyage offered. She had felt so apathetic of late that she thought she would have to feign interest in this venture, as she had for many other recent undertakings. She was exhausted by the ongoing, all-consuming task of finding a suitable husband, and it seemed as though no one was ever quite good enough to satisfy her mother.

Joanna had rejected every one of the prospective suitors in the last three years for one reason or another. This one was too poor. This one's family was not respectable enough. This one was too old, and the other was too fat. Then, there had been those for whom Serafina was not good enough.

She had visited Joanna's old dowager aunt outside of Compostela a number of times. Serafina was sent there when the weather in Vigo was overly damp, supposedly for her health, but everyone knew it was to broaden her marriage prospects. The grande dame was the last surviving relic of Joanna's distinguished family and the last one to still bear a title. Aunt Margaret was officially known as the Vizcondesa de San Marcos, the title she had acquired when she married her husband, dead long since. She still ruled the social circles in that area, and many mothers of eligible high-ranking young men regularly frequented her sitting room.

During her last trip, Serafina was smitten by one such

gentleman. The dashing, elegant youth seemed to have fallen under her spell as well. They spent many hours walking the grounds of the Vizcondesa's estate, admiring the gardens. They sat quietly and watched the swans float serenely on the pond, or simply gazed into one another's eyes, making plans for their future together. All proceeded as nature would have it, until one day he ceased to come.

Serafina was crushed and bewildered. She knew it was against the rules of etiquette to inquire—a young woman of quality never questioned the disappointments life brought her way. She simply accepted them with grace and dignity then moved on—but she needed to know what had happened. She summoned all of her courage and decided to approach her great-aunt.

When she arrived at the sitting room, the man's mother was having tea with the Vizcondesa. Serafina did not possess the audacity to enter the room while her aunt was entertaining company, but her overwhelming curiosity made her desperate enough to do a thing beyond the bounds of propriety. She had to know why her love no longer came to visit, so she pressed herself to the wall outside the door and listened in the hopes she would learn the cause.

"No, no," she heard the man's mother say. "There is absolutely nothing wrong with the girl. She has perfect manners, she has obviously been raised by a skilled hand, and she is *very* beautiful, but there is that one little thing."

"And what is that?" the Vizcondesa asked.

The woman hesitated slightly, searching for a delicate way to put it. "Well, you know. Her father ..." the sentenced trailed off unfinished.

"Her father is quite a successful businessman. He is very wealthy and highly educated," the Vizcondesa retorted with obvious pride in her voice, an unspoken challenge.

"Yes, but he is ... a Jew," the woman whispered.

Serafina could listen no longer. With as much stealth as she could manage, she made her way down the hall then fled to her room in tears. She wept for some time, trying to make sense of the woman's duplicitous behavior. She had been so kind to Serafina when her son had been present, all compliments and good wishes, but when she had thought she had an audience of like mind, her true colors had shown.

Suddenly things began to fall into place. Serafina recalled all of the times when suitors had simply stopped coming. Did they share the same reasoning as this narrow-minded, high-society, gossiping old harridan? For how long had the García family been the object of this disdain? She shuddered at the thought. It infuriated her that outsiders should refuse to acknowledge her father's outstanding attributes simply because of some accident of birth. Thinking about it was exhausting. From that point on, her future seemed so far out of her own control that she no longer cared one way or the other about it. She was almost willing to marry anyone, no matter how unappealing, just to have done with it.

Perhaps the trip would break up the monotony and give her a respite from the constant pressure of her mother's mission. What bliss it would be to sit down and just be herself for a change and not some bargaining chip in Joanna's quest to regain some of her family's lost respectability. And maybe, just maybe, there would be someone in the far off place who would see the merit of Serafina's own person, and her father's heritage would not matter.

Chapter 5: The Crossing

The next morning the García family rose early. None of them had slept much the night before, tossing and turning, kept awake by the excitement of the sea voyage, which would be a new experience for them all. They had as much breakfast as they could eat then they were out the door to assemble themselves in the waiting wagon. Their luggage had been arranged the previous evening with Joanna supervising the loading, and all that remained was for them to climb into their seats and head toward the port and the waiting vessel. They rode in companionable silence down the well-worn path to town, each lost in their own thoughts.

As the wagon approached the village, Iñigo pointed out a sleek little caravel with its blue falcon banner flapping gently in the breeze. This was the *María Vencedora*, the ship that Capitán Rey was so proud of, and the one that would carry them safely across the Atlantic to the ranch his family had so intrepidly built up from nothing on a foreign island. Joanna was surprised and a little irritated at the clear admiration in her husband's voice, but she did not want to add to an already stressful situation. She knew that starting a voyage with an argument would not bode well for the rest of the trip. Besides, she had promised Iñigo that she would try to suppress her aversion to the Portuguese and keep an open mind, so she held her tongue.

Inez could hardly contain her exhilaration, and she felt as if she would burst. This port had been a part of her life for as long as she could remember, but never had it held so much significance as it did today. In her mind this trip was as much a symbolic passage as an actual one. The moment that she stepped onto the boat would be the moment her life began its journey toward completion. She felt a sense of destiny about her. After today, her life would be changed forever. When the wagon finally stopped, she had to force herself to keep her seat until her father came around to give her a hand down. She would be a married woman in the not too distant future, so she might as well begin acting like one now. That was when she saw Estêvão.

He came striding down the gangplank in his friendly, confident manner, laughing at some offhand comment from a crewmember, and Inez could no longer contain herself. Her excitement overwhelmed her, and she hopped down from her place on the wagon seat and ran to meet him, all pretense of maturity thrown to the wayside. When he saw her, he smiled broadly, his eyes shining with delight, and he squeezed her shoulder in greeting.

"Bom dia, Coelhinha," he said warmly. "Are you excited about our trip?"

"Oh, yes," she said breathlessly, gazing up at him.

Estêvão noticed that the little golden flecks around the pupils of her eyes danced and sparkled with a life of their own, like a fire fanned by a bellows. He wondered if it was the rare quality of the early morning sunlight or some other optical illusion. The strange impression occurred to him that it happened for him alone, but that was surely his imagination. His musings were cut short when Iñigo clapped him on the back in greeting.

"Bom dia, Capitán Rey," he said in a friendly manner, and they began to discuss the loading procedure.

Between the man from the García household and the members of El Rey's crew, the travel trunks and various pieces of luggage were stowed in less than an hour. All that remained was for the passengers to board. Iñigo walked with his wife, offering his arm for support, João found a way to escort Serafina, and Inez made her way on her own, falling far enough behind to keep an eye on Estêvão who was the last to come aboard. João showed the family to their quarters while the rest of the crew dealt with the task of setting sail. Soon they were under way, and the adventure had begun.

The ship made its way carefully out of the Ria de Vigo into open sea and was given full sail. Though there was a steady wind, the water's surface this far out was not as choppy as it was closer to land. The sun ruled the sky and a few fluffy white clouds provided a welcome bit of shade from time to time. They would have smooth sailing. Estêvão had planned the trip during these ideal conditions so that the crossing would be as easy as possible for the unseasoned travelers. He had even given them his captain's quarters to maximize their comfort. He had been teased mercilessly by João and the rest of the crew, but he did not mind.

He gave over command to his stepbrother and went to see if his guests lacked for anything. He was met by Iñigo and Inez strolling the main deck. They had come up from their cabin immediately after shoving off, both of them curious and glad for the opportunity to be out in the open. Joanna had stubbornly refused to accompany them on the offhand chance she might have to associate with any of the crew. She used Serafina as an excuse to remain below.

Estêvão was surprised to see that neither father nor daughter seemed to be affected by any signs of seasickness. Inez was proving to be a good sailor, and it tickled him to no end. "I see you two are acquiring your sea legs in rapid fashion," he said as they turned to greet him.

"Yes," Iñigo replied. "Isn't it funny? I have lived near the ocean for most of my life, yet I've never been on a ship except to receive merchandise. Maybe that counts, or perhaps I've gained my equilibrium through association with so many sailors."

"Well," added Inez, scrunching up her nose, "even if I were feeling ill, I don't think it would be any better to be trapped in a cabin. The wind and the ocean spray feel so much better than being in a stuffy room. Poor Serafina."

"I shall have the cook make her some tea and perhaps some broth with biscuits," Estêvão said with a slight grimace, unable to hide his disdain. He didn't know why, but a person afflicted with seasickness always frustrated him. In this case, it just confirmed his perception of Serafina as a spoiled, shallow, society girl with no pluck. He called over a passing crewmember to relay the message.

As he was giving the order for tea and broth to be sent to his ailing passenger, a black and white bundle of curls bounded up to them with just barely contained exuberance. The dog barked once then sat down to wait for his master to take notice. His pink tongue and wet black button nose were the only distinguishable features in the faceful of ringlets. Estêvão finished up with the man and turned to give his attention to the patiently waiting canine. He got down on one knee and ruffled the dog's fur, murmuring all manner of endearment to the clearly adoring creature. He looked up to see Inez staring down at them, a glazed expression of bliss in her eyes.

"This is *Tubarão*," Estêvão said. "He is a *cão de agua*."

"A water dog," Inez repeated, the rapt look still on her face. "Why do they call him that?"

"He is the ship's dog, and he's a terrific swimmer," Estêvão explained. "Part of his job is to carry messages between vessels and to keep watch when we are in a foreign port."

"And that's why you named him 'Shark'," Inez said kneeling down beside him and running her fingers through the soft curly hair. The dog turned to look at her and gave her a slurping wet lick on the cheek. She laughed and pressed her face closer into his fur, breathing in his clean animal scent.

"Perhaps you'll have the chance to see him in action. That is my uncle's ship there," Estêvão said, pointing at a vessel a short way off.

He went on to explain about his idea of starting a vineyard on a piece of property he had lying fallow. His uncle was a vintner of some renown in Soutomaior, and he was making the trip to assay the soil and determine whether it would be conducive to a species of grape he had imported from France. If the grapes thrived, his uncle would eventually establish the new vineyard. His son, Christophe, Estêvão's cousin, would be in charge of the operation.

Estêvão was just answering a question Iñigo had regarding the size of the property in question when the crewman he had dispatched earlier returned with a battered straw hat in his hand. Estêvão took the hat and thanked him. He then turned to Inez and plopped the floppy thing on top of her head. She laughed when it sank down over her eyes. She put her hand up to adjust it so she could see and to keep the wind from taking it.

"The sun out here can be brutal," Estêvão explained. "It may not seem so, because of the cool breeze and the cloud cover, but fair skin needs to be protected. Sunburn is no laughing matter. I apologize for the condition of the hat, but it will serve its purpose."

Inez crinkled up her nose in her trademark gesture, "Maybe it would stay on better if I sewed some ribbons to it," she suggested.

"Do what you like. It is yours now," he said, thinking how adorable she looked in the oversized, tatty, old hat. Tubarão barked his approval, and the three humans laughed at the appropriateness of his comment.

The rest of the day was spent exploring the ship. Iñigo, in his constant quest for knowledge, besieged Estêvão, and any other crewmember at hand, with a continual barrage of questions about each and every task being performed. As the weather conditions were ideal and the ship was being run with a minimum of effort, the men were happy to oblige, pleased that their passenger was taking such an interest in their livelihood. He took a short turn at the wheel, he thoroughly examined the navigational instruments, and he even learned how to set and haul a net to catch fresh fish to supplement their food reserves.

Inez tagged along behind her father and Estêvão, making sure to stay out of the way of the working sailors. The running of the ship was very interesting, but it would not have mattered if they had been discussing the origin of beans as long as she could be close to Estêvão. She contributed to the conversation from time to time, but she did not feel the need to monopolize his attention. Just to be near him was enough.

To listen to his voice and see the look of pride in his eyes as he talked about the virtues of his ship warmed her to her very core. To be in his presence and learn about this part of his life, which had undoubtedly played a major role in shaping him into the person he was, made her feel closer to him, and she began to understand his complex personality all the more. She became more and more certain that they were a perfect match for one another, and it only confirmed what she had felt from the very beginning. She would never love anyone else.

It also became clear to Inez that Estêvão inspired a fierce loyalty in all those who came into contact with him. Every time he spoke to his men, the admiration and respect in their eyes was evident. Most of them had been with him for many years, on land as well as at sea, and had profited immensely from his wide range of talents. They trusted him with their lives and, in return, would give theirs for his without being asked. From his stepbrother and first mate, João, down to the lowliest scullery boy in the galley, they loved him. Out here the moniker 'El Rey', The King, was not just a nickname. He was the king of his ship, and his entire crew would eagerly do homage to him as their sovereign lord. Even Tubarão had fallen victim to his magnetism.

Throughout the day the devoted canine followed Estêvão about the ship, showing a casual interest in random happenings from time to time, sniffing at this or that, but never letting his master out of his sight. Without thinking Estêvão often reached down to ruffle the dog's fur or give him a pat on the head, and Tubarão basked in the glow of his owner's unconscious attention, wagging his tail or licking Estêvão's hand in obvious adoration. The dog looked sweet and friendly with all of those bouncing curls and his jaunty black and white markings, but Inez was sure that if he were to perceive someone as a threat or menace to his beloved master, he would die in the effort to protect him.

The day was long and exciting, and the sun and wind eventually took their toll. As the afternoon faded into night, Inez and her father reluctantly headed for their quarters, drained from the sensory overload and the previous night's restless sleep. Serafina had finally succumbed to a deep slumber after a day spent miserably in the throes of severe seasickness, and Joanna was exhausted from the worry of it all. They fell wordlessly into their beds and were all soon fast asleep, except for Inez.

She folded up the scruffy old hat Estêvão had given her and placed it beneath her pillow. It was yet another treasure, a symbol of the affection he felt for her. First thing in the morning she would sew the ribbons onto it so that it would stay put, and she would not run the risk of losing it to some wayward gust of wind. She lay there in the bed she shared with Serafina and reflected on what a dream the day had been. It was more than she had ever dared to wish, and she could not believe her hopes were finally on their way to being realized. With a smile on her lips, she stroked the silky metal surface of her rabbit with the tip of her finger. Eventually she drifted off, rocked to sleep by the gentle motion of the waves.

The next few days passed in a like manner. Although the tea, soup, and biscuits helped alleviate Serafina's nausea and prevented her from becoming dehydrated, she kept to her cabin, and Joanna stayed there to nurse her. This did not seem to faze any of the crew. In fact, it relieved most of them from the anxiety that had gnawed at them since they first learned that their passengers would include three women. Sailors were notoriously superstitious, and women aboard meant bad luck. The two mature women stayed below deck, and Inez, regardless of her shapely exterior, was still technically a child and conscientious enough to stay out of the way so not to become a distraction. Because of this, they would trust El Rey's judgement in the matter and simply do their jobs. Besides, the fine weather and easy sailing were an indication that the gods were not unhappy with the situation, so the crew went about their work the same as they ever did, satisfied to be making such good time.

Inez and Iñigo spent their days on deck, delighting in the many interesting things to see. There were schools of fish, sharks, and one day they were lucky enough to be escorted by a pod of dolphins. This was a good sign and yet further proof that they were traveling under the aegis of a higher power. Dolphins were regarded as sacred protectors of seafarers with the good fortune of man in mind. They kept pace with the caravel propelled by their powerful tail fins, from time to time leaping over the waves generated by the bow cutting through the ocean's surface. They seemed to smile as they frolicked, completely attuned to their aquatic environs. Inez watched them for the entire time they graced the vessel with their presence. She was fascinated by their antics and the sheer joy that emanated from their sleek, streamlined bodies as they streaked through the water alongside the ship.

Iñigo always found pleasure in expanding his knowledge of the world. He was determined to prove himself an asset to his most recent acquaintances, instead of just someone along for the ride. Despite his bookish appearance and tall, wiry frame, he was quite strong and physically adept. He enjoyed the challenge of acquiring a new set of skills and increasing his understanding of the trade industry. He lent a hand where he could, rapidly picking up the jargon, and by the end of the second day, he could have easily passed muster as a seasoned veteran. He was extremely pleased with this accomplishment, and although he went to bed that night sore from the unaccustomed physical exertion, he looked forward to honing his newfound talent the next morning.

Inez never got to see Tubarão do the job for which he had been bred, but she did discover what a wonderful companion he was. He was always happy to see her, and his fuzzy face and perky ears gave him a wide range of almost human expressions. He was intelligent and intuitive. Sometimes when she spoke to him, he would cock his curly head to one side, and she was certain that he understood. He looked as if he were formulating an opinion, which he would share with her as soon as he figured out how to articulate the words. Inez soon became his second-favorite person, and when Estêvão was busy with other matters, the canine sought her out. They played fetch with a knotted piece of rope, he allowed her to brush the tangles out of his shaggy coat, and now and then, they just sat amicably together, Tubarão chewing on a bone or stick while Inez absentmindedly stroked his wooly head. She had never had a dog, and now she could not imagine being without him.

When they had been at sea for a little less than a week, the water became a perceptibly lighter shade of blue than the dark ultramarine of the deep ocean. There had been random seagulls circling overhead throughout the day, and some of the crew had spotted sea turtles here and there. Though there was no visible landmass in the immediate vicinity, the combined signs of its proximity led Capitán Rey to make the pronouncement that tomorrow they would arrive at their destination. A cheer went up from the crew celebrating the fact that El Rey had, once again, brought them safely home from another voyage. Inez clapped her hands and bounced up and down, caught up in the enthusiasm generated by the news.

That night she lay awake in her bed, contemplating what the morning would bring. Tomorrow they would put into port and from there continue on to the ranch that would someday become her home. She would come face to face with the remarkable woman who had given life to her beloved and with whom she shared so many similarities. She had never had a meeting as important as this, and she fretted a little over the impression she would make. She did not think she would sleep a wink, but as her concentration meandered from one thought to the next, gradually her uncertainty eased and fatigue overtook the worries in her mind.

When Inez awoke in the morning, she was surprised that she had slept at all and happily noted that she felt refreshed and well rested. She surmised that it must be before daybreak, because even her father had not yet stirred, and he was a notoriously early riser. She dressed as noiselessly as she could and tiptoed out of the cabin, glad to have a few quiet moments to prepare herself for the momentous day ahead.

She crept up to the main deck in the pinky half-light of dawn, noticing with awe the quickly changing colors on the undersides of the clouds. A gentle wind ruffled her hair and spritzed her face with a light sea mist, and she shivered, glad she had thought to throw a shawl across her shoulders. She was mesmerized by the serenity of the early morning tableau, and she wondered if there had ever been a more beautiful sunrise in the history of man.

Silently she said a little prayer to thank God for allowing her to witness this glorious display.

Spellbound by the splendor of nature, Inez paid no heed to where her feet were taking her. As she recovered a small measure of her awareness, she found herself standing on the landing just below the helm. She had never really thought about who took responsibility for keeping the ship on course while everyone else was asleep, and she had not previously been up early enough to find out. Out of curiosity she cast an eye up to solve the mystery and froze in her tracks.

By now she had been in Estêvão's company consistently enough to overcome the shyness she sometimes felt in his presence. Perhaps she had also become accustomed to looking upon his striking features and had forgotten the profound impact his physical appearance had on her when she had not seen him for a length of time. This morning she was caught off-guard by the meeting, and the result was reminiscent of that first encounter, so long ago, when she had been a child and sought shelter behind her mother's voluminous skirts. She was struck full force by her emotions, and it shook her to the core.

El Rey stood at the wheel with his legs slightly apart for balance, looking every inch the commander of his ship and of his destiny. His chin jutted slightly forward, and his strong profile thrust into the wind, eager to meet the future head on and conquer whatever it threw his way. The reflection of the rising sun suffused his handsome face with a golden glow, and the wind tossed his glossy hair about, making him look like a god descending to earth. Seeing him here in his natural element was something so beautiful and touching that Inez felt tears prickling at the corners of her eyes. She swallowed hard and bit back the little involuntary cry that threatened to escape her lips.

Estêvão looked directly at her as if he had heard her unuttered call, his dark eyes penetrating the haze of her reverie. He smiled at her, and in that moment his beauty surpassed anything she had ever beheld. Inez actually had to remind herself to breathe. He beckoned her to ascend the few steps to where he stood, and she complied. At her approach Tubarão looked up from where he lay curled at his master's feet, his shaggy black tail beating out a few slow, contented thumps. Inez bent down to caress his silken curls, and when she stood up next to Estêvão, she was close enough to feel the heat from his body. They stood there side by side, not touching, silently facing the coming day together.

Not a single word passed between them, and none was needed.

Chapter 6: Fazenda da Pomba

Terceira derived its name from the fact that it was the third island of the Azorean archipelago to be discovered. In 1450 the Portuguese Infante Henrique, first Duke of Viseu—also known as Henry the Navigator—passed a decree, which named Jacome de Bruges as administrator and began the colonization of the island. De Bruges, a Flemish nobleman, returned to Flanders and recruited fishermen, farmers, and merchants to follow him to the newly founded province of Portugal. He also brought with him animals and provisions that would be necessary to their task. The first people settled in the north and erected the first church, but few of them remained there because of the difficult access.

Eventually the island was divided into two administrative seats, and Angra became the capital in the south. The site was chosen to become a port because of its advantageous geographical location and many topographical attributes. The word 'angra' means cove, and this particular cove was deep enough to provide anchorage for larger vessels. It had the further benefit of being sheltered from strong winds by the ridgeline of Monte Brasil, an extinct volcano directly to the west.

The favorable conditions of its physical location and the changing circumstances of the time contributed to Angra's rapid growth and development of the surrounding areas. New commercial ventures, such as the exportation of wheat and woad to the mainland, added to the importance of the island and thus increased the worth of the port. The town also played an important role on a worldwide scale. With the advent of Vasco da Gama opening trade relations with India, the Portuguese had begun what would be known as the Age of Exploration, and Angra was quickly becoming indispensable as an official port of call.

It was a lively, hectic place, and this was the García family's first introduction to the outside world. Although they were used to the hustle and bustle of the trade industry, their little sheltered port on the northwest coast of Spain serviced mainly local customers and handled distribution of goods mostly to and from nearby Portugal, France, and England. Iñigo's small mercantile could not compare with the sweeping scope of the large emporiums at Angra, which housed many precious metals, gems, and exotic spices. The people who inhabited the town were exotic as well.

It was expected that one would see Portuguese, Terceira being a territory of Portugal. One also expected to encounter a fair population of Flemings, since they were the first to settle on the island, but apart from these more familiar looking people was a mix of cultures not commonly associated with one another. There were colonists from Madeira, slaves from Africa, and many Jews who had sought refuge from the long, self-righteous arm of the Castilian Inquistion. This mélange of peoples translated into a colorful melting pot, the likes of which were unseen in the geographically segregated communities on the mainland. It was different and exciting, and Inez looked forward to experiencing the local flavor firsthand.

When they arrived in Angra, the ship and crew were subjected to the rigors of a customs inspection. Capitán Rey obtained permission for himself and his passengers to go ashore, leaving his first mate, João, to handle all of the paperwork and deal with the inspectors. The dinghy was lowered over the side of the *María Vencedora*, and Estêvão and an enthusiastic Iñigo rowed the smaller craft into the harbor. There the party found their way to a waiting wagon, which Estêvão had summoned seemingly by magic. They mounted their conveyance and began the short trip to the heart of the island and the *Fazenda da Pomba*, Ranch of the Dove.

Estêvão explained that 'Pomba' had been his father's pet name for his mother. When she had first come to Terceira to begin the venture, she had honored his memory by christening the ranch with the name that she still held dear. Their official emblem was also made in the image of a dove, and all commodities produced by the ranch bore the insignia on their shipping crates. Even the brand with which their cattle were marked was a stylized likeness.

Once Estêvão negotiated the streets of the busy town and turned onto the road to the interior, the scenery changed dramatically. The noise of civilization was left behind, and the serenity of the fertile green pastures and wheat fields took over, commanding attention almost as loudly as the dynamic energy of the port. A vast grassy expanse opened before them, mostly flat but for the gently undulating hillocks and patchy stands of trees and scrub. The terrain continued this way to the base of a circular group of eroded hills, which were the remains of an extinct volcano, and from there rose sharply to the top of its once cone-shaped summit. The rolling verdure of the countryside was broken into rectangular swaths of grazing land dotted here and there by herds of browsing cattle and bordered by primitive walls of black lava. As the wagon trundled by, the black and white bovines raised their heads to regard the passing spectacle then placidly lowered them back down to resume their foraging.

Several different varieties of fruit trees began to appear along the roadside. Estêvão explained that some of the first immigrants to the island had brought with them many diverse saplings to ascertain which would best thrive in this new land. The orange trees were the most successful, owing to the warm, subtropical climate. Some of the imports, such as the apple, cherry, and pear trees, were less prosperous for the same reason. These trees needed a certain amount of chill every year to bring on the shedding of leaves, which prompted the period of dormancy necessary to fruit production. Their irregular foliage and random blossoms were a result of the lack of defined seasons and abrupt temperature changes of their native environment. Though the pink and white flowers were pretty and fragrant, they would yield only a sporadic, substandard crop barely good enough for cooking or livestock consumption.

The wagon finally came to a stop in front of a handsome wooden gateway emblazoned with the dove motif of the Fazenda da Pomba. An elderly dark-skinned man in a battered straw hat was waiting to grant them entry. He doffed his *chapéu de palha* in a low bow of respect as the wagon went by then slowly closed the gate behind them. Estêvão nodded his thanks and guided the vehicle up the remainder of the long lane to the main house.

When the house came into view, Joanna visibly stiffened on the wagon seat. In her mind she had envisioned the settlement on Terceira as some backcountry outpost devoid of any culture or refinement and with few amenities. What she saw completely shattered her theory. The large sprawling ranch house was fronted by a tasteful whitewashed façade, adorned here and there with brightly hand-painted ceramic tiles. A wide porch of highly polished laurel wood, cut from the native evergreens cleared to increase pasturelands, ran the length of the house and provided a shaded outdoor seating area for days when the temperature made being indoors unbearable. Each of the mullioned windows had its own planter sown with colorful seasonal flowers cascading naturally over the sides. A profusion of blue, white, and pink hydrangeas, some of them shoulder-high, framed the stately entrance and lent it an air of casual elegance. The effect was impressive.

In the middle of the portico, dispensing with the pomp and stricture of rank and nobility, stood Dona María waiting eagerly to greet her returning son and his guests. She was small and trim with the same glossy black-brown hair as her son pulled up neatly in a loose bun. Her dark birdlike eyes twinkled vibrantly, and her smile was open and friendly. She was dressed richly in a simple but elegant gown of crimson silk, the only embellishments a fichu of black Spanish lace around her neck and matching blackwork borders at her cuffs and hem. The regal set of her head and her graceful posture bore testament to her privileged upbringing.

When Joanna had ascended the few steps to the landing, she began to grasp the fabric of her skirts and inclined her head slightly, fully intending to do homage to the Lady with a deferential curtsey. Estêvão was secretly pleased that his mother was able to shake Joanna's considerable poise, and he brought his hand up to cover the smile that tugged at the corners of his mouth. Dona María realized Joanna's objective and quickly reached for her hand, taking it kindly between her own.

"Please, please," she began in her melodic cultivated accent, "let us not stand on ceremony. I find the traditional rules of the court stuffy and antiquated and lacking in warmth. Out here we are all equals, so let us behave as such. I am very pleased to welcome you to my home."

Joanna straightened, and though her high color betrayed her embarrassment she smiled, taking an immediate liking to this diminutive, compassionate woman. "Thank you. We are grateful for your hospitality," Joanna said, meaning every word.

Dona María then turned to each of her other guests, shaking hands with Iñigo and then Serafina. She held small polite conversation with them both, commenting on Estêvão's high esteem for Iñigo's intelligence and work ethic, and making much of Serafina's golden beauty. Finally she came face to face with Inez.

"And this must be little Inez," María said, putting a gentle hand under the girl's chin, "only not so little now." María's mother had had Gypsy blood, and the Romani people carried the reputation of possessing supernatural abilities. She could not read a person's mind, yet sometimes María could pick up a general but accurate impression of a new acquaintance. She looked into Inez's stunning eyes and perceived much beyond their unusual color. "You are becoming quite a young lady," she finished, satisfied with what she had seen.

Although Inez quaked inside, she maintained a calm exterior. María's friendly attitude had allayed any trepidation she felt, but she still desperately wanted to please this woman. She hoped her voice would not quaver and give away how much this meant to her. She swallowed hard and smiled, her nose twitching ever so slightly.

"I am delighted to finally meet you," she got out, thanking the heavens that her voice sounded normal. "Estêvão has told me so much about you, and it seems we have much in common. I am sure we will be great friends."

María raised her dark eyebrows, admiring the composure it must have taken for Inez to make such a speech. She smiled at the young woman's spirit and said, "Yes, I'm sure you are right. We shall have to compare notes as soon as we get the chance," she added with a conspiratorial wink.

Inez exhaled the breath she was holding, and relief flooded through her. She had made the favorable impression she had striven for without sounding overeager, and the mother of her beloved had more or less accepted her as an equal. Of course she would have to tread carefully and give the proper respect accorded to a Lady of such high rank—it would not do to treat her too familiarly—but that would be comparatively easy. Her heart soared, and her hopes were high.

With the introductions accomplished, María turned back to Joanna, folded her guest's arm into her own, and led her congenially into the house. Estêvão followed the group, shaking his head in mild wonderment. Inez and his mother had taken to each other as readily as he'd known they would, and to top it off, Joanna's usual spikiness had been quickly subdued by María's inherent charm. He didn't know how she did it, but his mother had the same effect on everybody. Her soothing ways had certainly earned her the moniker of 'Dove'. Maybe this wouldn't be so bad after all.

Chapter 7: The Puppy

The García family's first day at the Fazenda da Pomba was mostly one of settling in. They were shown to their rooms and given ample time to wash up before heading down to the veritable feast Dona María had waiting. As the weather was sunny and mild, a large table had been set up outside under some majestic old laurel trees. There was a giant tureen of seafood soup called *caldo de mariscos*, big loaves of bread baked in rustic freeform rounds, every type of fruit one could imagine, and a selection of cheeses made from the milk of the ranch's own cows. Though they had not eaten breakfast, none of them realized how hungry they were until they saw the abundant spread before them.

By the time they had eaten their fill, their luggage had arrived, and they set to the task of unpacking. With their bellies full and the chore of unloading out of the way, the excitement began to wear off, and they felt the effects of the long morning grind. Dona María suggested that they all take a *siesta*, and although Joanna felt that it might be exceedingly rude since they had so recently arrived, María assured her it was as customary a practice in these parts as it was on the mainland. They retired to their respective rooms, thankful for the opportunity to refresh themselves.

A short time later, Inez descended the stairs and found her father deep in conversation with a man she had not seen before. He had dark curly hair and nearly black eyes, and his skin was a deep bronze color, an indication that he spent much time out of doors. He was not quite as tall as Iñigo, but his muscular build and long arms and legs gave the impression of added height. His rolled-up sleeves exposed powerful forearms, and he looked like he could wrestle a wild boar to the death and emerge without a scratch. His clothing was wrinkled and bore the stains of a hard day's work, but he wore it in such a dignified manner that one instantly recognized that he had spent much time in an aristocratic household. Inez was fascinated by his sheer mass and was completely and pleasantly surprised when she heard him laugh.

The giant man and her father were standing companionably by the immense fireplace in the spacious main parlor. They were discussing some point of agricultural interest, and true to Iñigo's insatiable quest for knowledge, he was shooting question after question as fast as the senhor could answer them. So far the man had been extremely tolerant, patiently giving his guest thorough explanations down to the smallest detail. Inez had been the victim of her father's interrogation before, so she had full understanding of the restraint it took not to lose one's temper. The stranger had not quite finished his current oratory when Iñigo began posing another query.

"*Meu Deus*, man! Let me finish!" the senhor roared out, a bit more forcefully than he intended. At the stricken look on Iñigo's face, the man paused for a moment then burst into guffaws of unadulterated laughter, the booming sound filling the room to the farthest corners. His face turned a deep shade of red, and Inez feared that he had suffered some sort of attack or had forgotten to breathe. To her relief he leaned back, inhaling audibly, and then continued laughing, slapping his leg in utter merriment. The hilarity was contagious, and Inez found herself joining in, unable to resist his childlike glee.

When the fit had passed and the senhor had recovered his good humor, he noticed Inez standing at the foot of the stairs. Her face was flushed with the remnants of her own bout of giggles, and the golden lights in her eyes danced with excitement. Iñigo tracked the direction of his new friend's gaze and saw his pretty daughter across the room, noting with a pang how grown up she looked.

"Mynah, you are awake. Come over here and meet Dom Martín," he said, holding out his hand to her.

Inez quickly covered the space between them and curtsied demurely in front of their brawny host. She looked up at him, her mouth falling slightly open in awe. He was even larger up close than he had looked beside her father. He bowed and took her hand in his to bestow a courtly kiss, and she giggled once more, because her hand looked like a baby's swallowed up by his huge bear paw.

"*Encantado*, Senhorita," he said with a gleam in his eye that indicated his appreciation of her female charms.

The trio continued the temporarily suspended discussion, and this time Inez's presence had a mitigating effect on her father's inquisition. She asked some very astute questions, and Dom Martín admired her intelligence as well as her comely appearance. All was going swimmingly until suddenly the conversation came to an abrupt halt. Dom Martín stopped short, his unfinished statement hanging awkwardly in the air, and his eyes were drawn to the top of the stairs. There, like a softly glowing candle, stood Serafina.

The siesta had done her well, and her golden peachy skin was radiant from the short rest. She had taken the time to brush her hair into a shining wheat-colored flow, which framed her heart-shaped face. She had also thought to don a fresh gown, both things in which Inez had been remiss. The dress of teal silk clung to her form, showing off her lithe figure and bringing out the blue-green of her eyes. Serafina smiled slowly, and Inez felt a sharp twinge of jealousy rise within her. This happened all the time, but it was something to which she could never quite become accustomed. Serafina gracefully glided down the steps and across the room to where the others stood and in one fluid movement swept into an elegant curtsey before Dom Martín. He stood there completely charmed, and when he bent to kiss her hand, he lingered a few seconds longer than was necessary.

The discussion resumed, but by now Iñigo had run out of ready questions, and Dom Martín only gave a few distracted, half-hearted answers before the talk completely died out. A few minutes later, Joanna showed up and rekindled the dialogue in a more socially oriented direction. Dom Martín did not seem to mind, but this sort of talk bored Inez to tears because it inevitably turned to the subject of eligible young men, something in which she nor her father had the least bit of interest. The two of them listened politely, but each knew the other would have gladly opted to explore some new territory. They were both extremely relieved when Estêvão entered the room.

He strode over to where the group stood and observed silently until he got the full sense of the conversation. He looked around at the individuals and noticed that Joanna and Serafina were the only ones truly interested in what was being said. His stepfather seemed happy enough to answer Joanna's questions as long as he could look upon Serafina, but he saw the glazed looks in Inez's and Iñigo's eyes and understood that they needed to be rescued. They had probably heard this same line of discourse innumerable times.

Estêvão waited until there was a break in the banter then said, "I hope you'll excuse me, Señora García, but I have a matter outside about which I would like your husband's opinion. You know how much I value his keen business sense. Would you mind if I borrowed him for a moment? Uh ... and Inez too, of course."

Joanna was flattered by his praise of her husband as if it were something she had accomplished herself. She waved her hand in a dismissive gesture, nodded her approval, and then returned to her two remaining captives. Inez and Iñigo happily followed Estêvão out the door, viewing him in the new light of savior as well as host.

"Thank you, Capitán Rey," said Iñigo sincerely when they were out of earshot. "I don't know how much longer I could have stood there. I only hope that Dom Martín will forgive us for abandoning him. I love my wife dearly, and she has honorable intentions, but she can seem a bit overbearing if one does not know her well."

Estêvão smiled, nodding in understanding. "Actually, my stepfather was so taken with *Serafina* that I don't think he even noticed."

Inez saw a strange fleeting look cross his face as he said her sister's name. Was it a look of distaste, or was her imagination running wild? "She has that effect on a lot of men," she said, prodding the slightest bit.

"I suppose she does," Estêvão finished with an edge of cynicism in his voice.

The three of them walked the short distance to the stables, and as they came around the blindside of the building a black and white blur raced up to them, furiously wagging his tail and barking wildly. Estêvão issued a sharp, short whistle, and Tubarão immediately ceased his antics and sat attentively, waiting for his next command. Inez dropped to one knee and lavished affection on the patiently waiting canine, and he licked her face in return. When she stood up, Tubarão barked and ran back toward the barn, stopping and looking back once to make sure they were following before ducking inside.

"I think he wants to show off," Estêvão said, still smiling at the animal's rambunctious display. "He recently became a father, and he's as proud of his brood as any human."

The trio entered the barn and came upon Tubarão keeping watch over a straw nest. It contained an orange and black brindled female nursing five little balls of fur. The bitch was a long-legged, shorthaired cattle dog, and her puppies ran the gamut of possible combinations of the physical traits of their parents. One of the puppies was an exact replica of his sire, two resembled their mother, one had a short black coat, and one had longish, wavy tan hair with black tips. This last heard the humans approach, disengaged himself from his mother's teat, and wobbled over to the section of the enclosure closest to Inez's feet, his chubby belly swinging from side to side. He sat down and gazed up at her intently in a perfect imitation of his father, his brown eyes sparkling with intelligence.

Inez bent down to pick him up, and the female raised her head, protectively keeping an eye on her tiniest whelp. "It's all right, mama dog," Inez said in a pacifying tone. "I will be very careful." Satisfied that the girl meant no harm, the mother lowered her head to the straw and continued nursing her litter. Inez carefully scooped up the hairy little pup and cradled him tenderly against her chest, murmuring non-words of assurance while he nuzzled her neck.

"I think he likes you," said Estêvão, "and so does the bitch. I've never seen her act like that before. She doesn't like anybody," he finished, clearly impressed with Inez's gentle handling of the temperamental animal. "Well shall we go look at the horses?"

Inez knew she could not carry the puppy away from his mother without repercussions, so she lowered him back to the straw and took a few steps to follow the men to the stalls. Immediately the tiny dog began to jump up and down, attempting to scrabble up the side of the hay barrier that blocked his escape. He yipped the entire time, and when Inez came back into view, he rolled onto his back and covered his eyes with his scruffy paws. His mouth hung open, his tongue lolled to one side, and he kicked his back legs energetically in an attempt to get her to pick him up once more. Inez looked apologetically at Estêvão and her father, torn over what to do.

"It looks as if there's nothing for it," said Estêvão. "You will just have to stay here while I introduce your father to Tesouro."

"I suppose you're right," Inez said, sitting down on the hay. "Come here little clown dog," she told the squirming ball of black and tan fur as she settled him onto her lap and began to sing him a song.

Though they were both loath to leave the sweetness of the scene, the two men each gave Inez one last look then started again toward the stalls. After all, they had come out here to look at the horses, and there would be time enough for Inez to join them in other pursuits. They headed down the corridor toward their destination, resuming their friendly chatter while Inez crooned an impromptu melody to her newfound admirer.

Chapter 8: Entertainment

The next morning dawned as mild and sunny as the day before. The members of the García family had fully recovered from their sea voyage and found their rhythm in the new household. They all realized how sorely this vacation was needed and put their hearts into enjoying it to the fullest. The break from the monotony of their everyday lives was a welcome blessing, and all in their own way were grateful to Estêvão for suggesting it.

Joanna bonded quickly with Dona María after sharing a few stories and discovering that they had similar backgrounds. It had been years since Joanna had trusted anyone enough to consider befriending them, and this new relationship was already changing her for the better. She lost the stiff, guarded attitude she had adopted for so much of her adult life and regained some of the lightheartedness of her youth. The rigid lines between her brows and around her mouth relaxed, and the smile, which began to appear more frequently, made her look ten years younger. She was fun and flirtatious, and everyone could see what a beautiful young woman she must have been.

Serafina would never have imagined she would go on a trip that consisted of something so precarious as sea travel. She supposed that since she had lived a life in which someone else had always taken charge, it had been but a further extension of the same concept. She was merely entrusting someone other than her mother with her well-being. Although she had passed the majority of the trip below deck, the day they had sailed into Angra she'd felt well enough to emerge from her cabin. That small amount of time spent in the open had been positively invigorating, and the element of the unknown made her feel like a different person. The idea that she would be in a place where no one knew her past breathed new life into her, and her outlook suddenly looked brighter. Maybe this bold new attitude would encourage her to take more stock in her future. After all, Dona María had been fearless enough to make the same voyage so many years ago, and look how well she had done for herself. Perhaps this trip was just what Serafina needed.

Inez had known that she would have the time of her life, but she had never dared to dream that things would go so smoothly. Spending so much time with Estêvão was heaven, and the way Dona María had accepted her from the first was more than she could have hoped. She had known they would get along, but it appeared as if the esteemed lady was already treating her as a daughter. Even Dom Martín seemed to have come to appreciate her as quickly. Of course, he was particularly partial to a pretty face—he spent much of his time admiring Serafina—but Inez thought that his feelings for herself included a high regard for her intellect. In any event, this trip was yet another treasure Estêvão had given to her, and she would cherish it forever.

Iñigo turned out to be the biggest surprise of all. He was still in a state of shock over how easy it had been to leave his business behind. After boarding the ship, he experienced only a few bouts of niggling guilt over deserting the mercantile at this time of year. He reasoned them away with the logic that, because he was taking a break, he would return refreshed and be able to redouble his efforts. Besides, he could also justify the trip by calling it business. Wasn't he coming out here to see about an investment that would provide extra income? Wouldn't that make it so they could all live a little easier without working so hard? He didn't know if this was merely another attempt to rationalize the vacation, but he found that deep down he really didn't care. This sort of opportunity might never present itself again, and he planned to savor every minute.

After breakfast, Estêvão organized a horseback tour of the property for anyone who was interested. Joanna declined, giving the excuse that she had not ridden for many years and did not want to slow them down. Serafina did not ride, and Dona María could not conscience leaving her guests alone on their second day to the island. Dom Martín was already at work in the fields, and no one had seen João since the day before. That left only Inez and Iñigo, the two Estêvão had assumed would join him from the start. He headed to the stables to have their mounts prepared while father and daughter changed into suitable clothing.

Estêvão was checking Tesouro's rear hooves when the horse began to nicker softly in greeting and bob his head up and down. Estêvão stood up to see who approached and saw Inez walking toward them. She was wearing the old straw hat he had given her over her long thick hair, which was bound at her neck with a leather thong. The silver rabbit at her neck glowed softly in the mid-morning sun. She also had on a man's *camisa* and a pair of funny-looking trousers cinched tightly around her small waist. The legs were tucked into a fine pair of English leather riding boots. It was something he had never seen on a woman, and his eyes betrayed his surprise.

"What's wrong?" Inez asked innocently. She had been dressing this way for her daily rides with her father for some time now, so she was oblivious to the fact that her outfit was a bit out of the norm.

"What are you wearing?" Estêvão blurted out, still in a mild state of shock.

Inez immediately flushed, the hot, pink color slowly spreading back to her ears and partway down her neck. She turned slightly to the side in an effort to minimize her exposure and absently stroked Tesouro's soft muzzle. Her nose crinkled up, and she fought back the tears that threatened at the corners of her eyes. "I do not like to ride sidesaddle, so I made myself these riding trousers because a full-skirted dress is too cumbersome for comfort when riding astride," she said looking up at him, the hurt evident in her face.

Estêvão was sorry he had lost his composure, and he reached for her hand, taking it tenderly in his own. "Forgive me,

Coelhinha. I did not mean to injure your feelings. I was just taken aback."

"Because I look like a boy?" she asked ingenuously.

He burst out in sudden laughter, unable to stop himself. "You most certainly do *not* look like a boy," he choked out, desperately trying to keep his eyes from roaming over her shapely backside where the fabric clung enticingly to the roundness of her hips. The thought occurred to him how curious it was that clothing designed for a man should bring out the most feminine characteristics of a woman. Stranger still was the fact that he was now thinking of Inez as a woman. He shook his head once to clear it and said, "I think it is very practical and rather smart-looking. In fact, my mother will probably be jealous. She is always railing against society's double standards when it comes to the sexes."

This last comment seemed to mollify her, and she beamed a smile at him, his insensitive behavior completely forgotten. They stood there for a few moments, her hand resting comfortably in his, the world around them entirely unheeded until they heard the crunch of boots coming up behind them. Estêvão let her hand slide out of his, and Inez brought it up to her face, self-consciously tucking an errant strand of hair behind her ear.

"I must say, Capitán Rey, your stallion looks even more impressive out in the light of day," said Iñigo as he joined them, totally oblivious of what had just transpired.

Inez moved a short way off to catch her breath as the two men began discussing the advantages of introducing Arabian blood into the native breeds. Estêvão was clearly distracted, giving only one or two-word responses at best, but Iñigo cheerfully prattled on rhetorically, sometimes answering his own questions. Finally the groom appeared leading two other saddled horses out of the stable.

One was a giant Lusitano gelding, which measured at least sixteen hands. It was the biggest of that breed Iñigo had ever seen, and he did not fail to inform the groom of that fact. The stable hand indicated that this would be Iñigo's mount, and stood at attention while the senhor made his way up to his seat. The stirrups had been set at their fullest length to accommodate Iñigo's height, so there was no adjustment necessary.

Inez was to ride a smaller, half-breed mare. This was one of the first generation hybrids Estêvão had attempted, and she was a combination of the best attributes of both breeds. She was sturdy and unflappable like the Lusitano, yet she also possessed the fire and sure-footedness of the Arabian. This had been his intent when he'd first thought to intermingle the bloodlines. He wanted a horse that was durable enough to stand up to the cattle yet nimble enough to cut quickly and avoid the horns of an enraged bull. This little mare was the embodiment of that ideal.

The groom held the mare's head while Inez put her left foot in the stirrup and expertly swung her right leg up over the horse's back. She took the reins, gripping them firmly, and removed her foot from the stirrup, holding it back out of the way while the groom shortened the strap. He did the far side first then came around to the front to adjust that strap. When he had done, he slipped Inez's foot back into the stirrup, unconsciously resting his hand on her knee while she tested the length. Inez smiled down at him from her seat, and Estêvão felt the insidious worm of jealousy writhe within him.

"Fausto!" Estêvão said sharply, his eyebrows drawn down in irritation. "I think you've got the senhorita's stirrups just right. Now you may return to cleaning out the stalls."

The young man looked up at his master, his eyes wide with disbelief. He had been a part of this household for many years, and this was the first time he had ever been the object of El Rey's displeasure. Fausto took his leave, bowing low before the three riders, and headed back toward the stables, racking his brain to figure out what he had done wrong.

"Shall we go?" Estêvão asked, shooting one final peevish look at Inez.

Inez was so excited about the ride that the implication of the look escaped her. The three riders urged their mounts into a comfortable canter and began their tour.

After a few minutes on horseback, Estêvão recovered his good mood. The rhythmic motion of Tesouro galloping beneath him and the gentle warm air rushing past had a calming effect and gave him time to sort out the scene they had just left behind. He realized that the incident had been in no part Inez's doing. She had just been her sweet, considerate self, and Fausto had responded naturally to her kindness. Wasn't that why Estêvão himself had been drawn to her from the start? That was part of it, and the other part he was not willing to examine further right now. He decided to let the whole thing go and enjoy the ride.

The horses flew over the lush green terrain, and the sense of freedom was exhilarating. Estêvão led his guests to one of his favorite vantage spots. The little mesa sat slightly higher than the rolling hills of the basin, and it was topped with a few underdeveloped but tenacious pear trees that had fought the odds and sprouted with a fairly promising display of delicate sweet-smelling blossoms. From here one could see the entire breadth of the fazenda. The northern boundary of the property stretched partway up the base of the extinct Guilherme Moniz volcano where Estêvão's uncle was testing the soil for the prospective vineyard. The southern border reached halfway to the port city of Angra. The view was breathtaking, and Inez and Iñigo could both see why Estêvão felt the need to share his home territory with them.

From there they headed down to where Dom Martín was supervising the plowing under and fertilization of one of last year's wheat fields. He explained that this was necessary to enrich the soil and maintain the high yield of their crops. Some of the other wheat farmers were sowing wheat season after season without allowing the fields to recover. Blinded by the enormous profits they collected from the mainland, they were too shortsighted to acknowledge the danger of the practice. This narrow attitude would soon lead to mineral depletion of the soil, and although they were reaping acceptable harvests at the moment, eventually the rich lands would be exhausted, and the farmers would be left without a source of income or the means to earn one.

This was not a problem for the Fazenda da Pomba. They had diversified enough to sustain themselves through any hardship.

Though Dom Martín had spent the majority of his life attached to a noble household, he had been intelligent enough to pay competitive wages and hire experienced farmers to work the land. He had listened to the good advice they offered about leaving certain fields fallow and rotating crops in others. With his keen wits, he had taken quickly to the running of an efficient business. He had never been averse to hard work, and it showed. The fazenda turned a sizable profit and sustained all who called it home.

From there the trio moved on to the pasturelands. The herds were impressive, and one could tell merely by looking that they were the finest specimens of their breed. The cattle served the triple purpose of supplying milk and dairy products, providing meat for the household, and being sold as fodder for the bullring. The Fazenda da Pomba had the highest reputation for quality livestock, so this was another source of its considerable income.

Iñigo was fascinated by the cattle dogs. Estêvão explained that each dog had been raised to do this job from birth, and from the time that they could walk they were exposed to the sounds and smells of the bovines. From there the young pups were moved out to the fields to watch the older dogs work and learn the whistles and hand gestures of the *vaqueiros* who seemed to share an affinity with their charges. They had been around the cows for so long that they anticipated each move beforehand, and they directed their dogs accordingly.

The tour lasted longer than expected due to Iñigo's perpetual need to learn every nuance of a new subject. He asked about the walls dividing the fields, he investigated the copses of remaining native vegetation, he had questions about the neighboring farms, and he even rode along with the field hands for a time while they moved a group of cows from one section of pasture to another. Inez did not mind, because it gave her more time alone with Estêvão. They waited for Iñigo while he made his side trips, laughing together over his antics and drinking in the loveliness of the scenery.

When Iñigo tried to head toward the northern end of the

property where Estêvão's uncle was assaying the soil, Estêvão tactfully suggested that they save that trip for another day. Although he admired Iñigo's inexhaustible energy, he could tell that Inez was flagging. He had to admit that he too was still recovering from the trip across the Atlantic, and he used that as an excuse to head back to the house for some refreshment and perhaps a siesta. In spite of his disappointment, Iñigo would never dream of being rude, so he agreed to postpone any further explorations to a later date.

After they retired their mounts, Iñigo engaged in a lively conversation with Fausto about the differences in caring for Estêvão's high-spirited Arabian stud as opposed to the maintenance of the even-tempered Lusitano workhorses. As the discussion did not affect Inez directly, she found her way back to the nest of puppies, which she had been dying to visit since the morning. She neared their enclosure as quietly as she could, but there was no sneaking up on the little family within. She supposed that they had perceived her approach with their keen sense of smell or heard her boots crunching on the ground as she drew up to their den, because by the time she peeked over the edge they were all sitting stalwartly at attention. When they saw her, they all began to wiggle frantically and crawl over one another, each of them yipping in a bid for her attention.

She knelt down on her side of the encircling hay barrier, keeping an eye on the bitch to make sure she was not being distressed unduly. The female dog appeared even more unaffected than the day before. She sat close enough to keep watch over her brood but busied herself with washing her belly and gnawing intently at some foreign object between the toes of her right front paw. She seemed to have accepted the human girl as a friend, because when Inez swung her legs over the hay and lowered herself to the straw inside their little refuge, the mother dog did not even look up from her grooming.

As soon as Inez hit the ground, the squirming mass of puppies swarmed over her legs. They jumped and joggled in her lap trying to get at her face, and when she put her head back to laugh, they settled for giving her neck a good, thorough washing. A couple of them lost their footing and tumbled back down into the straw, but in no time they had recovered enough to return to the melee, vigorously attempting to supplant the siblings holding the prime positions. This went on for a few more minutes then, as puppies do, they began tussling with one another, forgetting all about Inez who had been such a novelty just moments before, except for the little clown dog.

The scruffy little black and tan runt stared up at her, his sweet brown eyes sparkling with adoration. His front legs splayed out in front of him with his rear end sticking up in the air and his longhaired tail curled over his back. He barked at her a few times then tore around in a circle at full speed, coming to a stop in the same spot in front of her. He jittered from side to side, growling playfully, then he repeated the entire sequence three more times before plopping down beside Inez and rolling onto his back, his tongue hanging out in exhaustion. When Inez stopped laughing, she picked up the silly little dog and held him close while he lovingly licked any part of her he could reach.

"I guess that is what they call reckless abandon," she said to the hairy little creature as he cocked his shaggy head from one side to the other, trying to understand her. "Someone needs to teach you some tricks and put you in a circus, because you are a natural-born clown. In fact, I think I shall call you *Palhaço*." At this the puppy barked his approval, and Inez squeezed him tight.

"It is a very fitting name," Estêvão said, kneeling down in the hay.

"How long have you been there?" Inez asked, fighting the rising anxiety that she had done something to embarrass herself.

"I have been here long enough to see that Senhor Palhaço is becoming quite attached to you," he said with an unreadable look in his eyes. "What is he going to do when you return home? You've spoiled him for anyone else. "

"That is something I don't want to think about right now," she replied equally as enigmatically. "I just want to enjoy the time we have left here together." She dropped her eyes down to the furry bundle in her lap and caressed his head, the gesture filled with a bittersweet tenderness. Inez and Estêvão sat there silently together, unwilling to elucidate further, each contemplating the underlying meaning of what the other had spoken.

After waking from her siesta, Inez washed meticulously, donned a fresh gown, and brushed her hair, painstakingly pulling the sides back away from her face in a style that was very becoming and drew attention to her eyes. She had made the mistake of being lax with her appearance once. She would not be so careless a second time. She dabbed a few drops of her pear blossom perfume behind her ears and along her hairline, checked her reflection in the mirror, and headed out the door.

She paused at the top of the staircase surprised to see that she was the last to awaken from the midday nap. She supposed the exertion of the morning ride coupled with the restlessness of the previous two nights had made her sleep overlong. As she stood there, her father looked up from the conversation he was holding with Dom Martín and smiled at her. Dom Martín followed his guest's gaze across the room, and his mouth fell open at the sight. The remaining occupants of the room turned to see what all the fuss was about, and soon all eyes had settled on Inez at the top of the stair.

The gown she had chosen was a lilac-colored silk. The color set off the red tints in her hair and turned it into a living thing, framing her face then rippling over her shoulders in a fiery cascade. The dress had been tailored to fit her exactly. It was cut in the Spanish style with a tightly fitted bodice and a square neckline, but instead of the modesty the style conferred on most women who wore it, it had precisely the opposite effect on Inez. Her full bosom was pushed up into a rounded display of creamy female flesh veiled alluringly by an inset of black lace. The clinging fabric below emphasized the smallness of her waist in comparison. The fullness of the skirt was designed for a *verdugado* to be worn underneath, but because their vacation was to be on the informal side, Joanna had decided to leave the hoop skirts at home. As a result, the pastel purple silk spilled fluidly over her shapely hips in a body-skimming sweep to the floor.

She was a bit confused for a moment by the astonished looks the others cast in her direction and actually checked behind her to discover the source of their wonder. Then she realized they were looking at her. She blushed in embarrassment, unaccustomed to the attention, and it added a rosy tinge to her ivory skin. In her consternation she nearly scrunched up her nose in the old habit that was second nature, but she caught herself and lowered her eyes instead, her dusky lashes casting little smudgy shadows across the tops of her cheeks. When she looked up, a lovely slow smile spread over her face exposing her white even teeth and setting the gold lights in her eyes dancing with a sultry flicker. As she descended the stairs, her full hips swayed naturally from side to side, the silk of her skirts swishing softly with each step in a hypnotic motion that added to the dreamlike quality of the moment.

Inez would never have the tall, willowy grace of her sister, but she had something else, something more. Her coloring and the curviness of her figure brought to mind a sensuality, a warm, welcoming earthiness, which even Serafina's golden aura could not rival. There was also an innocence, a complete unawareness of her beauty that only added to her appeal. Even with the lack of polish and artifice that the coquettes of her station were encouraged to employ, there was no doubting the fact that she was a desirable young woman. To punctuate this fact João, ever the connoisseur of the fair sex and their charms, arched his right eyebrow and made a low purring noise in his throat.

Estêvão cut his eyes at his brother in a scathing, sidelong look then strode across the room to meet Inez at the base of the stairs. He bowed low before her in his smooth courtly manner, took her hand, and led her to where the remainder of the group had not yet recovered from the spectacle of her arrival. She took a seat in one of the chairs next to the other ladies and looked up at Estêvão to thank him, gratitude shining in her eyes. In that moment, their mutual adoration of one another was laid bare for any who cared to observe it.

Dona María, who had been watching Estêvão while the others' attention had been concentrated on Inez, was astounded to see such blatant infatuation on her son's handsome face. The feverish sheen in his eyes and bemused half-smile on his lips were things that she had never witnessed in him before, even when he had been a young lad. Oh, he had had his fair share of romantic adventures, it would have been strange for a young man of his looks and status not to have dallied with the opposite sex, but nothing serious had ever developed. Now that he was thirty-one, it was all the more remarkable that this young girl should be the object of such regard. María made note to keep an eye on the situation.

No one else seemed to find anything out of the ordinary, and soon the conversation returned to normal. The men discussed business specifics of the ranch with a bit of politics thrown in, and the women talked about the upcoming social events that would take place during the García family's stay on the island. Joanna, who still held out hope of finding a stellar match for Serafina, was obsessed with the subject and monopolized the conversation, turning it artfully to talk of the local landed gentry and wealthy merchants.

Noticing that their mother was totally engrossed in the discussion with Dona María, Serafina leaned over to Inez and whispered, "Brava, little sister! I could not have made a more dramatic entrance myself if I'd had time to plan one. Your Portuguese appears to be completely smitten. Well done!"

"Shh! Someone will hear," said Inez with an alarmed look in her eyes. She glanced about to make sure no one was listening then she smiled and said, "Thank you, Serafina."

A short time later, all made their way to the table where a sumptuous meal was laid out. The dishes had been prepared to demonstrate the prosperity of the fazenda, and they featured the bounty yielded by the hard work that had gone into the establishment of this successful enterprise. This time the soup was a *caldo verde* made with kale and spicy homemade *chouriço*. The meat was a shank of beef marinated in red wine with carrots and onions then roasted to a dark juicy perfection. There were *bolinhos de bacalhau*, cod mixed with herbs and potatoes, formed into little balls then fried to a crisp golden brown. A salad made from fresh garden vegetables rounded out the selection, and courtesy of the dairy cows there was a sweet creamy butter to slather onto the chewy white bread.

All dug into their plates with relish, and soon the conversation gave way to the contented sounds of the group enjoying their evening repast. The García family was used to good hearty meals, and because Iñigo owned his own mercantile, they had access to many of the same spices and herbs, but the food had a special savory quality on which Iñigo could not put his finger. Perhaps it was the freshness or the exotic combinations of the seasonings, or maybe it was just the uniqueness of the situation, but to him it seemed significant enough for comment.

"Dona María, I must tell you this food is fantastic!" he exclaimed. "I think your cook must have access to some magic ingredients or secret ancient cooking technique, because I have never tasted such excellence."

"Thank you," María said with a smile. "The cook is always telling me that the recipes have been handed down through her family for generations, so maybe that can account for it."

"The only things I have tasted that rival it are some of the creations made by my little Mynah," he said absentmindedly, examining the morsel on his fork.

"Mynah?" María inquired politely.

"Oh, I'm sorry. I meant Inez. Mynah is my pet name for her," Iñigo explained, smiling at his reddening daughter. "I use it more than I use her given name, and sometimes I forget that new friends do not know her by it."

"And she cooks?" María prompted, attempting to get the full story.

"Oh, yes!" he proclaimed proudly. "She makes the most delicious dishes. Pastries are her specialty. Oh, and the bread!" Here he rolled his eyes and rubbed his stomach in pleasure. "I tell her all the time that, based on her bread alone, someday she will make a wonderful wife for some lucky man."

María turned her benevolent gaze on Inez who sat blushing furiously in her seat. Her ears grew hot and turned a violent shade of pink while she fought the urge to crinkle up her nose.

"Well then, Mynah," María said kindly. "Perhaps someday soon you can honor us with your talents."

Inez drew up her head with as much dignity as she could muster and said, "I would consider it a privilege."

When they had finished their meal, they all returned to the parlor where a fire had been lit to chase away the marine chill. The talk resumed in a vein similar to that of the pre-supper conversations, but it soon lulled into an agreeable silence. Recalling that night so long ago when Estêvão had first heard the sweet sound of Inez's voice combined with his own, he pondered the idea of inviting her to duet with him now. She had matured in so many ways, he was sure that her singing must have also been altered and was curious to find out to what extent. He cast his gaze upon her, marveling at the changes time had wrought, and suddenly he could wait no longer.

Clearing his throat to draw attention he said, "Perhaps it is time for a little music." He turned to Inez and holding out his hand he added, "Senhorita Inez, if you would be so kind."

She rose from her chair, blushing the smallest bit, and began to cover the distance between them. When she reached the halfway point, she stopped suddenly, pulled her hand up in front of her as if to avoid his grasp then, without a word, turned and made her way quickly up the stairs to her room. Everyone exchanged baffled looks with each other, mystified by her strange conduct and slightly embarrassed for Estêvão who stood with his hand still extended. His mind labored urgently to discover what he had done to offend her. No one had a clue as to what this meant or what had sparked this bizarre behavior, which was completely out of character for Inez.

The puzzle was solved a few moments later when they heard her descending the stairs again, this time with her lute in her hand.

Estêvão heaved an audible sigh of relief and strode to the corner to retrieve his guitar from its stand. João arranged two chairs next to the fireplace then took his seat with the others and waited for the serenade to begin. Inez and Estêvão took a few moments to tune their instruments and discuss song selection then they were ready to start.

The silence was deafening, and when they struck the first chord, Inez thought how oddly loud it sounded in the spacious room. She had a momentary lapse of confidence concerning her talent, so she let Estêvão take the lead and sing the first verse on his own. He hesitated at first, but ever the consummate showman he forged on, understanding that Inez was probably suffering from a bout of nerves and knowing she would recover enough to harmonize with him at the chorus.

As always his voice had the profound effect of stunning the listeners with its clarity and the ease with which it issued from his throat. No matter how many times anyone had witnessed his performance, they could not help but be affected. The expression with which he sang each note carried its own story and a small piece of his very soul. His signature intonation was like no other and heralded to all the reason he had earned such an excellent reputation for his vocal abilities, throughout Iberia and beyond. They all sat enthralled while Estêvão spilled out his feelings in song.

The sound enveloped Inez like a warm blanket and loosened her inhibitions more effectively than a glass of wine. She forgot all about the others in the room and saw only her beloved pouring out his heart for her in the most precious way he knew how. She ached to meet him on the common ground of their music, and so she reached out to him in like fashion. Her voice rushed forth from her with the bell-like quality he remembered but not in the bright, tinkling tones of the child she had left behind. Her singing was still as true and clear as it had been two and a half years before, but the timbre had mellowed into something rich and sensual and ripe with emotion. Their voices came together and melded in that same exceptional way, and the harmonies they created were like a third voice, distinct and ethereal and a gift for those who heard it.

Their audience sat spellbound by the scene before them, recognizing the singularity of the situation. Inez and Estêvão each had their own particular attractions, but when combined they exuded a brand of irresistible magnetism uncommon in everyday existence. It surrounded the other people in the room and made them feel as if they too played a vital part in this special event. None of them would remain untouched by the extraordinary occurrence that they had just experienced nor would they ever forget it.

When the song ended, all in the room remained silent and a little breathless, and no one dared to break the spell. Finally João cleared his throat and clapped heartily, encouraging the others to join him, in an attempt to take the focus off of his brother. It was his way of giving Estêvão a second of privacy by distracting the rest of the room's occupants with applause.

In that moment Estêvão caught Inez's hand, leaned over and whispered, "Thank you," into her ear. The combination of her body temperature and the heat from the fire had activated the perfume she'd applied earlier, and it wafted up from her hairline in a sweet aromatic cloud that staggered his senses. She too was dazzled by his closeness paired with the thrilling sensation of his warm gentle breath on her ear. They sat there together in their isolated bubble, the only two people in the crowded room.

Again João came to their rescue by suggesting loudly that they play some more lively tunes in which everyone could join. They happily obliged, and no one was the wiser.

María was the only one who realized that her son had fallen in love.

Chapter 9: The Women

The ensuing days passed in much the same fashion. After breakfast, Inez headed out with her father and Estêvão for their morning ride, and each day they explored a different aspect of the fazenda. Dom Martín oversaw most of the work being done and always seemed to have a full schedule. They never visited him in the same place twice. They learned much about the running of such a diverse establishment, and though it was hard work, it seemed that all who had a stake in the venture were utterly satisfied with their lives and viewed each other as members of one big family.

Every day after the horses were returned to their stalls, Inez stopped to visit the puppies in their nest. She played with all of them while they were interested, and unfailingly her little Palhaço remained by her side long after the others had found something else to distract them. She realized how amazingly smart the little dog was and began to train him with a few simple commands, which he picked up in no time. He was already responding to his name when she used it, and he could also sit, stay, and fetch a little stick she gave him as a toy. He was growing at an incredible rate, and she was saddened to know that soon he would be moved out to the fields to begin his assimilation into the ranks of the working cattle dogs. It brought tears to her eyes to think that she would soon have to leave him here when she returned home. She squeezed him tight and wondered if he would remember her after she had gone.

The noonday meal was usually followed by a siesta, which

was observed by workers and owners alike. Even Dona María took advantage of the few hours of down time to recuperate from her busy mornings. Inez found out that although Dona María did a limited amount of physical work, she did all of the bookkeeping herself. When she had arrived on Terceira with only her family and a deed of land ownership, she had had to keep track of every transaction and account for every *real* that changed hands. The first few years had been rough, but eventually she had scrimped and saved enough to turn a profit and build a successful business. Out of habit she had continued to handle the paperwork herself. That was part of the reason she was so down to earth and her wits remained sharp. It was yet another thing that she and Inez had in common and one more thing that would bond them more closely when they became family.

After all had risen from their afternoon naps, they usually dressed and gathered to unwind before supper. On a few occasions they accepted invitations to parties at neighboring properties where they met many of the island's most prominent families. They were even asked by one of Terceira's wealthiest residents to watch the *touradas à corda* from his apartments in Angra. Their prime seating afforded them an excellent view of the festivities. They sat in the balcony above the streets to watch the antics of the brave young men of the village as they attempted to grab a rope tied around the neck of an angry bull. They cheered their favorites and laughed heartily when the infuriated bovine chased his tormentors off the end of the dock into the churning waters of the harbor.

As always at these types of engagements, Serafina was the main focus of attention. Her golden beauty and polished manners transcended any barriers of language or class, and she never lacked for admirers. Joanna was immensely pleased with her reception, and hope blossomed anew that an appropriate match would soon be found. Of course Joanna's ideas had begun to change slightly from what she had originally thought of as a suitable husband.

As Dona María had indicated when she greeted them upon their arrival, the old days when the nobility held precedence were quickly waning. Out here on Terceira there was an entire colony of people who were, one way or another, looked down upon by the traditional society of the mainland. In a reversal of fortunes, it was the merchant class who now possessed the power, and hard work was admired more than mere birthright. Ironically, in this society Serafina's father would be regarded as an asset to her when considering a proposal instead of an impediment.

Inez didn't care one way or another about it. As long as she could spend her days in Estêvão's presence, nothing else mattered. She was having the time of her life, and soon all of her dreams would be realized. When she and Estêvão were married, she would have her own life and her own issues with which to concern herself. She loved her sister and hoped for the best for her, but in the grand scheme of things what did Serafina's future husband have to do with her?

One morning Estêvão arranged for the trip out to the northern edge of the property to see how his uncle was getting along with his assays. This was the entire premise of Iñigo's visit to the island, and there would be much discussion of finances and some things not very interesting to a young woman. The ride would be long and hard, and they would most likely return much later than their regular outing. This was an inordinate amount of time for Inez to spend among all-male company. Some of the men were of a very rough sort and were used to passing time amongst each other. It was a near certainty that a good part of their banter would be unfit for delicate female ears. It was decided that she should stay behind. She began to protest until Dona María reminded her that it was the perfect opportunity for them to get to know each other better.

After the men had gone, Inez returned to the house from seeing them off and visiting the puppies. She entered the parlor where the other women were doing some needlework and chatting amiably. Still pouting, she pulled up a chair, searched in her mother's basket for something to work on, and began to sew, her mind far away with Estêvão and her father. Eventually the repetitive action of her stitching had a calming effect. The tension in her neck relaxed and her resentment began to fade. Soon she started to enjoy her work and pay more attention to the conversation around her. She looked up and noticed María studying her intently with her bright bird eyes. Inez smiled and joined their discussion.

The talk was about the usual subject of social engagements and eligible young men. Joanna had long ago mastered the art of manipulating conversation to any given subject, and this was one of her favorites. It had been her life's work to groom Serafina for an exceptional matrimonial match, so it stood to reason that she would bring it up again now that a new circle of acquaintances had been opened to her. With a long exasperated sigh, Inez tuned in to what her mother was saying.

"... and that striking young blond man with the dark moustache and impeccable manners, he seemed to be enjoying your company, dear."

"Yes," said Serafina with a sigh that matched her sister's. "He was pleasant enough but somewhat boring and completely narcissistic. I fancy he'd spend more time gazing romantically at his own reflection in the mirror than into his wife's eyes."

This brought a little amused grunt from María, and Inez glanced up at her, surprised and utterly pleased that the reaction echoed her own sentiments.

"Yes, but his father owns one of the biggest emporiums down at the harbor. I suppose that would account for his ego," Joanna reasoned.

"As if it were something he accomplished for himself," Serafina answered with a wry smile. "I've heard that his father is quite a notorious profiteer and *that's* why they have such a grand living. Mama, how could you even consider such a scoundrel? Besides, after talking to him, or rather *at* him since he never uttered more than two words in response, I have the sneaking suspicion that he does not have wits enough to come up with as original a way to take advantage of his clientele as successfully as his father. Why, in two years after his taking control of the business, I would probably be begging in the streets for a crust of bread. Surely you could not want that for me."

This entire commentary was made without Serafina ever taking her attention from her embroidery, and her mother was left speechless. Inez looked on with her eyes wide, flicking back and forth between them to see what would happen next. In her entire life she had never heard Serafina speak to her mother with even a hint of disrespect in her voice. Now she was virtually challenging Joanna to an argument. María also glanced up to see what would ensue.

"Serafina," Joanna began in an injured tone with an equally hurt expression on her face, "how could you even say such a thing? I have spent your entire life, and a good portion of my own, attempting to educate you in a manner, which would bring you a match suitable to your station. You can hardly fault your mother for trying to look after your best interests."

Serafina sighed and lowered the piece on which she was working. "I'm not assigning blame, Mama," she said with a determined look in her eyes. "I'm just saying that perhaps I would have been better off if I had learned a *marketable* skill, as opposed to how to make a elegant curtsey. If this trip has taught me anything, it is that times are changing, and some of the social graces at which I excel will soon be obsolete. Who says a female must rely on attracting a husband to have a fulfilling life? It is not as unthinkable as it once was for a woman to possess some sort of business acumen. Dona María and Inez are the best examples I have seen of that."

María saw that things were taking an emotional turn, so she jumped at the opportunity to diffuse the situation. "Serafina," she began gently, "your mother and I were raised in a different culture, so you must be patient with some of our old-fashioned ideas. I did what I had to out of necessity, and it was very hard work to succeed in a man's world. You must also remember that I had my husband beside me through it all. I must thank you for the compliment though. It's nice to know that my efforts have at least *inspired* someone to think a little more progressively."

María was secretly impressed with Serafina's astute

observation. She also recognized the effort it took for the young woman to stand up to her mother in such a manner. When the García family arrived, she had been stunned by the girl's looks— Serafina was one of the most beautiful women María had ever seen—but she had taken her for merely another pampered debutante content to coast through life by virtue of her comely exterior. She was now discovering that there was more under that lovely façade than anyone imagined.

Joanna felt a bit put out at being called old-fashioned, but she accepted the peace María made and let the subject drop. She wondered when Serafina had come around to this new way of thinking then came to the conclusion that she should not have been surprised that any daughter of hers had inherited at least some part of her strong will. Hadn't she rebelled against her own mother's authority in her youth? Maybe Serafina was right. Times were changing. Perhaps this would work out for the best.

After a few tense minutes, the ladies all relaxed a bit, and inevitably Inez began to hum a little tune. Joanna joined in followed shortly thereafter by María then Serafina. This eased the tension further, and soon the mood returned to the companionable sisterhood they had been enjoying before the disagreement occurred.

"So, Mynah," began María, "when are you going to treat us to a demonstration of your marvelous culinary skills?"

"I would be delighted to cook for you any time you decide," Inez answered immediately. "Well, except for tonight. There is some planning involved, which can be time-consuming, and I will probably need a little help with certain preparations."

"Well then, if you will make out a list of the things you need, I'm sure the kitchen staff can have it ready by tomorrow. As for the help," María said with a twinkle in her eye, "I think we will be able to find some willing volunteer to assist you."

"Oh, thank you, Dona María!" Inez gushed, excited by the prospect of impressing her future mother-in-law with her talents.

"Please, dear," María said kindly, "you needn't be so formal. Aren't we nearly family by now?"

"Oh, yes," Inez said, bursting with joy. "Yes we are!"

Estêvão and Iñigo returned just before the evening meal. They were tired and dirty, and they headed straight for their rooms to wash up and change their clothing for supper. When they joined the others in the sitting room, Inez could see the exhaustion written clearly on both of their faces. Estêvão walked over and sank heavily into the chair beside her, but Iñigo was so excited about what he had seen that he chattered on animatedly while all looked on in amazement.

Estêvão leaned over to Inez at his side and said with due admiration, "Your father is indefatigable! He is twenty years my senior, yet when something piques his interest, he has the energy of a man half his age!"

Inez giggled behind her hand, knowing exactly how he felt. There had been innumerable times when her father had worn her out with his unrelenting enthusiasm. In fact, even in his normal unagitated state most people were hard-pressed to keep up with him. She was feeling a bit saucy after the agreeable day passed with Dona María, and Estêvão's presence after the time spent apart made her feel the tiniest bit giddy.

"That must be the reason he needs new shoes so often," she whispered in reply, pointing to where Iñigo sat with his ankle resting on his knee. The sole of his shoe could be seen plainly, and there at the toe was a small round hole where his lighter-colored hose showed through. Estêvão was too tired to exert any restraint over the silliness rising within him and could only attempt to confine it to the two of them. They sat there leaning against each other, shaking uncontrollably in their mirth, praying desperately that nobody else would notice.

The only person who detected their hysterics was María. She sat on the other side of the room wondering how long it was since she had seen her son so carefree. Their laughter was contagious, and she could not help but smile at them. She thought how rare it was to find two people so attuned to one another and how well-matched a pair they made. It was a shame that Inez was only fourteen.

Chapter 10: The Meal

The next morning Inez gave Dona María a detailed list of the items required for that evening's supper. María in turn passed it on to the cook who assured her that everything would be ready by noon. Inez then went out for her daily ride, which they all agreed should be a light one so that she would not be too tired afterward to prepare the meal. They returned after a couple of hours, and after Inez paid a quick visit to the puppies, she headed back to the house to wash up and change out of her riding clothes.

She entered the kitchen to find everything she had asked for washed and laid out on the large center table. The cook handed her an apron and gave her a quick tour of the cabinets and drawers to make sure she would be able to find anything she might have omitted on her list. Inez assured her that the provisioning had been accomplished to her utmost satisfaction, and they began the business of preparing the meal.

The first task was to mix up a batch of bread dough, as it would need a few hours to rise before it could even be baked. This was one of the recipes that Inez had worked hard to perfect, so she kept a scrupulous eye on every ingredient and made sure that all of the measurements were exact. The cook had been skeptical at the outset of this out of the ordinary undertaking, but after watching Inez meticulously perform each step with her practiced hand, the cook relaxed and began to pay attention thinking that perhaps she would learn a new way to treat some of the everyday ingredients.

After the dough had been kneaded and formed into two springy mounds, Inez covered them and set them in a warm corner to rise. She then turned her attention to the two large chickens in the center of the table. They had been plucked and washed, but when she was fixing a meal, Inez felt the compulsive need to wash her hands each time she touched any type of meat. To facilitate the process, the cook moved the fowl closer to the washbasin, so Inez could clean up more easily after massaging the seasoning into the large birds. She did the job quickly and thoroughly, washed her hands a final time, then turned to ask the cook to return the chickens to the table where they could stuff them on a stable surface.

She had expected to find the cook melting butter or chopping the fruits and vegetables for the stuffing, but what she saw stopped her in her tracks. Where the cook had been just moments before, Estêvão now stood in her place tying an apron about his slender hips. He looked up at her with his dark hazel-green eyes, a few strands of his glossy hair falling across his face, and smiled at her obvious surprise.

"What are you doing here?" she blurted out without preamble.

"I am here to help you prepare the meal," he said matter-of-factly with his arms spread wide.

"What happened to the cook?" Inez asked, still having difficulty processing the information.

"I sent her away," he said, crossing over to where she stood. "I think we shall manage quite well without her. I've always found her to be a bit bossy, and things will go more smoothly without an extra person to get in the way. Where do you want these, Coelhinha?" he asked, picking up the cutting board on which the seasoned chickens rested.

"Set them there on the table," she said absently, waving her hand in that direction. She was trying to figure out which were the most uncomplicated jobs she could assign to him now that the cook with her years of experience had been dismissed.

Estêvão set the birds on the table and came over to where she stood wringing her hands in her apron. "Coelhinha," he said, taking her hands in his with infinite tenderness, "everything will be fine. I know you are worried, because you want everything to be perfect, but I am actually quite handy in the kitchen if I do say so myself. What do you want me to do first?"

She let out a long, trembling sigh and set him to task tearing the day-old bread into small pieces while she began to chop some onions. By the time she finished with the onions, Estêvão stood dusting breadcrumbs from his hands, smiling with satisfaction that he had completed his assignment so quickly. She nodded her head in approval, thinking that maybe this wouldn't be so bad after all.

The next step was to cut all of the fruits and vegetables into uniform pieces, so they would cook evenly. She gave him some apples to begin with while she started on the carrots and celery. In no time she had expertly diced the amounts she needed and then turned her attention to see how he was getting along. She put a hand up to cover the smile that spread across her face as she watched him comically attempting to core his third apple. His tongue stuck out the side of his mouth and his eyebrows drew down in concentration while he tried to dig out the last few seeds with the sharp knife, nearly slicing his palm in the process.

"Here, let me show you an easier way to do that," she giggled, taking the apple from his hand. She set it down on the board, cutting off one side, then placed the flat side down and cut carefully around the core in swift downward strokes, tossing the rectangular center of the apple in the refuse pile and dicing the rest of it in a few quick movements. "There! Simple as that!" she exclaimed, pleased with her handiwork.

"Fine," Estêvão said with mock-seriousness. "But next time, no showing off ... and *no* laughing!"

They stuffed the chickens and set them to roasting. Inez then retrieved the risen bread dough from the corner and punched it down to release the air so they could begin to shape it into loaves. Estêvão watched her form the stuff into a long smooth rope and twist it deftly into an evenly coiled pile. She made it look extremely easy, so he decided to try his hand at shaping the other half. He gamely began to fashion a long rope like the one he had seen her make just moments before, but the longer he played with the dough, the stickier it got. When he attempted to shape the dough into the twisted loaf Inez had so easily managed, it wound itself around his hand. Soon it looked like a pasty, floury mitten, and he was at a loss about what to do next.

Inez stood with her hand clamped tightly over her mouth, trying with every fiber of her being not to laugh at him, but when he turned to her for help, the look on his face was so pathetic that she could not hold back any longer. She burst into paroxysms of laughter, her petite body shaking in a manner similar to the evening before. She did not want to make him feel bad, but every time she looked up at him with the bread dough wrapped around his hand, it made her laugh the more. At first Estêvão felt a little hurt until he realized how ridiculous he must have looked. Then he joined in with her until they were both near tears.

When they had calmed enough to continue, Inez floured up her hands and began to pull the doughy mitten from his fist, a few residual giggles sporadically vibrating through her frame. She kneaded the gooey mass a few more times, working in some extra flour, then coiled it into a loaf just like the other one. She did not say a word and avoided his gaze, so they would not begin the scene anew.

They put together the remaining side dishes then moved on to the dessert course. Inez had decided to make some empañadas filled with fruit as opposed to the meat filling used for the savory version. While she cut the butter into the dry ingredients for the pastry, she put Estêvão to work chopping up the remaining apples and mixing them with nuts, dried figs, and apricots she had soaked in some red wine. The pastry was even more temperamental than the bread dough, but when he offered to help her shape the empañadas, she didn't have the heart to refuse.

As they finished the little fruit pies and stood back to survey their work, Inez could not help but notice the dejected look on his face as he compared his work to hers. Because she made them so often, she had formed two to every one of his, and that was not the worst of it. Each of her flawlessly formed pair of pastries was followed by one little misshapen blob of dough with the fruit inside unevenly distributed and the edges imperfectly sealed. She tried to put on a sunny front, but he would not be cheered.

"Well," Inez began, trying to console him, "as they bake the shell will puff up, and they will look fine. Nobody will be able to tell the difference. Besides, they will taste exactly like the others."

"I'm sure that with more practice I will improve. At least we are finished," Estêvão said, wiping his forehead with the back of his floury hand. As he lowered it to his side, Inez put her hands to her mouth in yet another attempt to disguise a chuckle. "What is it *this* time?" he asked in exasperation.

"Come here," she said and stepped toward him with a damp towel in her hand. She leaned forward on her toes and took his chin gently in her left hand as she reached up with the towel in her right to clean the dusty white streak from his brow. She was so close he could smell her warm female scent and feel her moist breath on his skin. He opened his eyes and found himself looking directly at the center of her chest where the silver rabbit glowed softly against her flushed ivory skin. His eyes traveled up to the small hollow at the base of her throat where her pulse beat rhythmically in a delicate blue vein. He felt the sudden urge to brush his lips across it, and his hand reached up of its own accord and clamped onto a fold of her apron. At that moment she came back down to her feet and looked up at him, her silver and gold eyes glittering with excitement. He felt himself drawn by their magnetism, and he began to pull her to him. Her lips parted with a sharp little intake of breath.

Suddenly the kitchen door burst open, and the scullery maid entered, backside first, lugging two heavy buckets of water. Inez and Estêvão jumped apart from each other, and he strode quickly over to shut the door while Inez pretended to wipe her hands on the towel. The woman thanked her master, put down the buckets, and with a little groan, straightened up with her hands on the small of her back to stretch it. She espied the trays of empañadas ready to be baked and smiled widely.

"Looks like you two have been quite busy," she said amiably.

Inez blushed a deep red, and Estêvão's dark eyes flashed in anger. He would not tolerate such impudence from a member of his staff. He opened his mouth to give her a good tongue-lashing then paused, following her gaze to the table, at once realizing what she was talking about.

"Oh the food!" he said, relieved he had not lost his temper.

"Well what did you think I was talking about, Senhor?" she asked, looking confused and a little perturbed.

"Nothing, nothing at all. Yes, we have been very busy."

"I can tell *that* by the state of the floor, Senhor. I think you must have be working over here," she said, indicating a place on the floor dusted with a distinct circle of flour and littered with random bits of chopped fruits and vegetables.

"I'm sorry," Estêvão said apologetically. "I didn't realize I had made such a mess."

"*Nenhum problema*, Senhor. At least you made the effort." She shrugged and smiled at Inez. "Men! What would our lives be without them?"

"Indeed!" Inez said, feeling quite grown up. "Men!"

That night at supper everyone raved about the deliciousness of the food. Each person had his own particular favorite, but all of the dishes seemed to disappear more quickly than usual. The soft, sweet loaves of bread, which had wrought such hilarity in the making, were a hit with all. Inez thought to herself that next time she would be sure to make a double recipe so not to run out. Dom Martín and João filled their plates several times, and Estêvão saw fit to remind them that there was still dessert to be presented and that it would be wise of them to save room in their expanding bellies for it. They each shot him a look that suggested he should mind his own plate and continued the process of clearing theirs. All in all, the meal went off without a hitch, and each diner began to regard Inez with a newfound respect.

"Well, Mynah," began María, "I must tell you that your father's assessment of your culinary expertise was not just an idle boast. The food is delectable. Even the cook, who admits she was reluctant to let you into her personal workplace, has given her grudging stamp of approval on your skillful preparation techniques, although she was very put out about being dismissed from her own kitchen."

She directed this last comment at her son who shrugged his shoulders and said, "Her objections are ridiculous. She treats the kitchen like some sort of shrine. Besides, we left it none the worse for wear."

Inez knew what it was like to have a foreign person intrude upon one's own private territory and quickly came to the cook's defense, "I completely understand her misgivings. I suppose it is sort of a new idea for someone like me to even possess the desire to enter the kitchen. As for leaving it none the worse for wear, I seem to recall that you left quite a mess on the floor," she finished with an impish gleam in her eyes.

"Yes, well," Estêvão said, coloring the slightest bit, "at least I made the effort." This last remark echoed that of the scullery maid who had unwittingly interrupted their intimate moment, and this time it was Inez who blushed.

João looked back and forth at the two of them, his black eyes taking in the amused glances they exchanged as if sharing some private joke. He cleared his throat to draw attention away from the pair and said, "So, where is this famous dessert my brother has been boasting about?"

Just then the serving girls came to clear the remnants of the main course and began to set down the dishes of fruit-filled pies with a lightly spiced almond custard spooned generously over the tops. The aroma was irresistible, and Dom Martín groaned in anticipation. As soon as the plates were set down, all dug into them with gusto. There was a communal clinking of spoons against plates, and then a collective, "Ahhh," rose from the table.

"Inez," said Joanna softly with uncharacteristic appreciation, "you have outdone yourself."

Inez beamed with the compliment. This was high praise indeed. Joanna had never understood her daughter's fascination with the kitchen and always looked upon it as some sort of shortcoming, a sign of a lack of breeding. As Inez had, in the past, used every opening she could as an excuse to defy her mother and assert her own strong will, Joanna had merely tolerated this obsession so not to appear to be losing the contest. She had reluctantly given the odd compliment here and there but never as genuinely as she did tonight. This was the affirmation that Inez had sought, and it made her feel like an adult, more like a peer to everyone at the table instead of a mere child.

"Thank you, Mama," Inez said quietly.

She glanced around the table to see if the others were appreciating the dessert as much as her mother, and her eyes settled on João. Between bites he was intently examining the plates on either side of him. Estêvão noticed him too and wondered what he could be doing.

"What's wrong, Brother?" he asked as João took another bite of his empañada, a curious look on his dark face. "Is the dish not to your liking?"

"No, it is quite delicious," João said, shaking his head in mild befuddlement. "I just don't understand why mine *looks* so different from the others. It's all lumpy and sort of smashed in on one side, like somebody dropped it on the floor before they put it on my plate."

Estêvão let out a small cough, as if he had swallowed his food the wrong way. All eyes turned, expecting him to provide an explanation, and Inez could not suppress a little giggle. She watched him squirm uncomfortably for a few seconds then came to his rescue.

"I think they must have fallen against each other while they were baking," she suggested. "Pastry can be a bit delicate, so the smallest deviation in the process can sometimes cause little differences in the finished product."

"Well," João said doubtfully, taking another bite, "it does *taste* incredible. I just don't understand why mine is the only one that looks so funny."

Estêvão's eyes settled on Inez with gratitude and something more, an undefined softness. Inez smiled back at him and let out a long sigh of satisfaction. The evening was a total success, and it had bound everyone at the table together with a sense of familiarity. They were like one big happy clan complete with sibling squabbles and differences of opinion but in the end, standing together as one. They only lacked union by a marriage of blood, and that would come.

Chapter 11: The Picnic

Time sped by and soon the return to Vigo was foremost in the minds of all. The carefree days that they had enjoyed at the start of this idyllic interlude gave way to a sense of bittersweet poignancy, and the time remaining took on a sentimental quality tinged with melancholy. This had been the experience of a lifetime and, in the years to come, would be idealized and looked back upon nostalgically with fond memories by everyone who had played a part.

Though the García family's tenure on the island was drawing short, there was still business to be addressed. Joanna's long trip out to visit the site of the potential vineyard could no longer be postponed. Of course Iñigo could have just invested in the venture of his own accord, but by now he knew it was best to include his wife's opinion in even the smallest of decisions. It made her feel needed and would make for a more peaceful coexistence in the long run. They made their preparations and left Inez and Estêvão to take their daily ride alone.

Under ordinary circumstances it would have been unheard of for Inez to accompany Estêvão unchaperoned, but Joanna had come to respect his quality of character, and any objection she had voiced in the past now seemed ridiculous. The two of them had never thought to deviate from their daily routine and, in fact, had planned a little picnic to distract themselves from the impending separation. Estêvão asked the cook to put together a simple lunch for them, and she cheerfully packed a bag with bread, fruit, and cheese, and some watered wine for their excursion. He thanked her, slung the sack over his shoulder, and headed out to the stables to look for Inez.

Inez was exactly where he knew he would find her. She was playing with her little clown dog in the puppy nest, which had become increasingly empty as the days passed. The young dogs had grown at an astonishing rate, and the two largest had already been moved out to the fields to study the coordinated movements of their mature counterparts. There were only three left in the nest with their mother, who was daily showing less and less interest and patience with her remaining whelps. Now that her offspring were becoming more independent—they only nursed sporadically and more out of habit than necessity—she was starting to exhibit signs of restlessness and the urge to return to her normal activities.

As Estêvão approached their den, the three puppies heard him coming and ran to greet him, standing in a neat line with their forepaws resting on the hay barrier, their synchronized tail ends swaying back and forth like a furry metronome. He chuckled at their exuberance and bent down to give them each a pat on the head. They stood expectantly at attention for a few moments before losing interest and returning to wrestle with each other, the runt completely ignoring his brothers in favor of Inez's warm lap.

"Looks like he's the smartest one of the bunch," Estêvão said, smiling at the way the little dog looked up adoringly at Inez from his perch.

"Oh, yes. He is very smart," she replied, totally missing Estêvão's implication.

"Well, shall we get started on our excursion?"

Inez nodded her head, put the puppy down, and stood up, brushing some clinging fragments of straw from her backside. She stepped over the side of the enclosure, and as she and Estêvão turned their backs to walk away, they heard a loud, "Roo-roo-roo!" from the nest. They both looked back in surprise to see the little dog sit down prettily, waiting patiently for their return.

Inez smiled and said, "He thinks that if he sits in that manner, we are *obligated* to give him what he wants." Turning back to the dog she said, "Be a good boy, Palhaço. I will be back later."

Again they started out of the stable, hearing a faint whining issue from the dejected canine. The whining became a few hopeful barks, and after a short silence, they heard the patter of furry footsteps on the earth behind them. Inez turned around to see Palhaço racing toward her, his black and tan fur flying back from his face, all of his energies focused on reaching her no matter the cost. When he caught up to her, he bounced around enthusiastically, dancing on his hind legs and trying to scrabble up her front.

"Now that he has learned how to get out, there will be no containing him," Estêvão said with a frown on his face.

Inez nodded in agreement knowing that it could be dangerous for the little dog to be underfoot of the horses. "What should we do now?"

"I think he will have to be guarded closely until we leave. He should be fine when he realizes that he cannot follow us."

They made their way over where Fausto stood with their saddled mounts. Estêvão explained the situation then scooped up the puppy and placed him firmly in Fausto's arms. He held the reins while Inez mounted the little half-breed mare, and he swung himself up onto Tesouro. As they rode out of the yard they heard the little dog crying sorrowfully, and Inez looked back once to see him struggling with every ounce of his small hairy body to escape Fausto's strong grasp. She smiled sadly, trying to squelch the knowledge that in two days she would have to leave him behind.

Estêvão read her thoughts and attempted to put her mind at ease by saying, "Don't fret, Coelhinha. He will be fine. He has a happy home here with everything he needs. He will miss you, but when you return he will be that much happier to see you."

This last comment reminded her that sometimes separation was necessary but was not necessarily a permanent condition. She had endured it before, and she could endure it again. It also assured her that she would soon call Terceira her home.

They rode across the countryside, admiring the beauty of the fine spring day. This morning the lush green hills had a different feel, a different significance than the times when Iñigo had come along. Those other outings had given them a sense of belonging to something larger, as if they existed to attend the land. Today Inez felt like the verdant grassy landscape had been rolled out like a sumptuous carpet just for them, a welcoming playground exclusively for their own personal enjoyment.

There was only one spot they had ever considered for their picnic, and they headed there now. The little stand of defiantly blossoming pear trees greeted them with shade and their sweet aroma, a promise of the fruit to come. They dismounted, and Inez spread out an old blanket for them to sit on while Estêvão removed the bridles from the horses so that they could graze.

"Won't they stray if they are not tethered?" Inez asked.

Estêvão shook his head and replied, "Tesouro always stays close enough to keep me in his sight, and the little mare will not leave his side. Even if they did run off, it would not be such a long walk back to the house," he finished, smiling at her concern.

He sat down on the blanket across from her, and for a few moments they did not speak, silently taking in the magnificent view from their scenic overlook. They sighed in unison like two halves of one whole then began to chat comfortably with each other. They talked about trivial matters, making commentary on mundane everyday occurrences, both of them conspicuously avoiding the subject of her departure. Again they fell into a pensive silence, the pause hanging heavily in the air between them.

Inez was awed by the beauty of the countryside, and the thought struck her that she had never heard the full story of how the Fazenda da Pomba had come into existence. She recalled that long ago conversation when Estêvão had mentioned his father's untimely demise, and she knew that it all had to be connected, but how? At the time he said the story was long and involved and not fit for a young girl's ears, but that seemed ages ago. She was an adult now, and she believed Estêvão regarded her in the same light. Perhaps this would be the perfect time to learn the history. Her curiosity piqued, suddenly she could wait no longer.

"The island is so beautiful," she began. "How did your mother come to settle here?"

Estêvão did not answer immediately. She could see that he

was torn by the way he clenched the muscles in his jaw. Automatically his right hand found the garnet ring on his left. Out of reflex he began to twist the ring—which he never removed— around his little finger. Inez was beginning to doubt that he would respond. Perhaps it was still too painful for him. She was sorry she asked and opened her mouth to tell him to forget about it.

Before she could stop him, he turned to her with a small sad smile and said, "The story is a long one, but I seem to recall a day much like this when I vowed to tell you the entire tale. Now that you are all grown up perhaps it will not be so shocking."

Inez knew that a smile would be inappropriate, but she could not help but be utterly pleased with his statement. He remembered that day they had spent together almost three years before, and he had called her a grown-up all in the same breath. This was further confirmation that his feelings mirrored her own and that he trusted her, both necessary components of a successful relationship. She sat quietly, lending her unspoken emotional support as Estêvão prepared himself to begin his narrative.

BOOK 3: El Rey
1460
Chapter 1: Maria

Throughout history, native populations of a given region have had a fear of foreign cultures they could not understand. Gypsies were the ultimate example. When the Gypsies, or Romani, first came to Spain, they brought with them their nomadic and mysterious way of life. The Romani also had the distinct reputation of possessing supernatural powers, which added to the xenophobic attitudes of the zealously Catholic locals. Although the Moors were the main focus of the effort to eliminate non-Christian groups from the Iberian Peninsula—they held the largest stretches of enviable prime real estate—the campaign soon expanded to include the Jews and eventually Gypsies.

There were specific laws written with the Romani in mind designed to increase prejudice and drive them from Spain. Their settlements were disbanded, they were denied their rituals, and any speaking of their native tongue was a sure way for them to be identified and subjected to further hostilities. They basically had two choices, leave or be assimilated into the general populace. One way to do this and escape persecution was to marry a non-Gypsy. Some of the Romani were forced to do so, but María's mother needed no such coercion.

When her clan arrived in Ciudad Rodrigo, Cassia caught the eye of a nobleman, a minor grandee and distant relative of the royal family of Castile with a considerable estate. The serious-minded young man fell head over heels in love with the exotic young Gypsy, and further seduced by her sensuous dancing,

Emilio Del Rio soon determined he could not live without her. In this case the regulations mandating that the Romani intermarry with Castilian nationals worked in his favor. Because they loved their daughter and knew that this quiet gentleman would cherish her as much as they did, Cassia's parents gave their consent and the pair were married.

They lived an ideal life facilitated by Emilio's substantial fortune and his vast land holdings. The local estate was so large and isolated that there was no need for them to mingle with the township unless they so deigned. A few years into their marriage they were blessed with a healthy son, followed by a beautiful baby girl two years later. Their life was complete, and they were utterly happy.

As the children grew, they came to resemble their parents more and more with each passing day. Francisco followed his father everywhere and seemed to absorb his enterprising nature through association, and María had clearly inherited her mother's physical grace and ability to empathize with people on an emotional level. Each of the children had an ear for music and an ease of movement, which made them seem like creatures from another world.

Although outside their secluded estate the distinctive Romani dances were fast becoming an art to be performed away from the scrutiny of the reproving public, they seemed an entirely appropriate pursuit for the Del Rio children. Dance had always been one of the acceptable forms of expression for the aristocracy, so Cassia reasoned that with her many years of training it would be a terrible waste to allow her knowledge to be squandered. What harm could come from teaching her children a valued skill that would showcase their natural talents and demonstrate their refinement and culture? It would also expose them to their heritage and reinforce her contention that to be part Gypsy was nothing of which to be ashamed. This confident attitude would also become her legacy.

So the dance lessons began. It soon became evident that the children were natural performers. Though reserved and unassuming in their everyday activities—they shared the understated demeanor of their quiet father—once they took the dance floor, their charisma could not be denied. They both had a certain flair to their steps, an inherent flamboyance that could not be taught. The sharp staccato footwork, dramatic gestures, and precise handclaps added a theatrical element that enthralled anyone privy to their performance. Their brown-black coloring was arresting, and a fire burned brightly in those two sets of dark eyes.

Word began to spread among the privileged upper class of the half-Gypsy Del Rio children and their irrefutable talent. Soon, under the guise of business, many of the local nobility of Castile and nearby Portugal found ways to finagle supper invitations from the reclusive family, hoping to catch an impromptu performance and brag that they had witnessed the spectacle. The children enjoyed their art and the attention and obliged on most every occasion.

The estate soon became a popular haunt of an erudite, progressive class of people with liberalist views on immigration and the established hierarchy of the ruling faction. During the quiet times of the evenings—after supper and the recitals by the Del Rio children were done—they discussed the fantastical ways in which they would change the current government if granted the reins of power. This sparked endlessly imaginative discussions in which even María and Francisco participated. The group gained the reputation among the more conservative old Christian crowds as semi-subversive, and although no one truly believed that this mild-mannered *primo* of Queen Isabella was doing anything seditious, it would not hurt to keep a close eye on the situation.

When María was sixteen, there arrived a mysterious visitor to that evening's supper whom nobody could remember inviting. Although this was an odd occurrence and these were suspicious times—the Pope had issued a bull of inquisition just two years before in 1478, so there was always the threat of religious espionage—his refined manners and cultured speech bespoke his nobility, and he was allowed entry along with his two companions. When they removed their traveling capes, the rest of the guests were stunned by their appearance.

The gentleman himself was a good-looking medium-sized man in the prime of life with a curious resemblance to the royal family of Portugal. Nobody commented on this likeness, and he offered no explanation. He was accompanied by a slender youth, who turned out to be his younger brother, and a long-legged, brawny warrior with a military bearing and a fierce black stare. It was assumed that this large man was present in the capacity of protector, and he filled the role well. Upon entering the Del Rio home he scanned the attendees, assessed the staff, and surveyed the layout of the house in one sweeping glance, a habit born of many years spent defending his lord from enemies foreign and domestic. His martial air was disconcerting, and there was no doubt that had he perceived the slightest menace to his charge, it would have been immediately neutralized. He settled himself in a corner of the room where he could observe the proceedings and made himself as inconspicuous as possible.

During the meal María felt her gaze being drawn to the gentleman, and she picked up a strange feeling that with him lay her destiny. She was a level-headed girl and not usually prone to flights of fancy, but she did possess the uncanny ability to assess a person's character or sense an accurate impression of them just from a brief time in their presence. This was a far cry from the supernatural fortune-telling powers popularly attributed to the females who shared her Romani ancestry, but she was extremely attuned to her environment, and her intuition was rarely mistaken. She tried to convince herself that she was simply romanticizing the enigmatic visitor and the way he had arrived—suddenly and of his own accord—but the notion of their entwined fate persisted.

After supper came the inevitable appeal for María and Francisco to demonstrate their polished dance skills. They quickly acceded to the request and took the stage. María's heart pounded in her chest, and nervous energy coursed through her as she stood in position and waited for the music to begin. She had never worried over her performance before and did not care to speculate why the sudden anxiety rose within her now. The guitarist stuck his first chord, and with her opening set of dramatic handclaps, her nerves transformed into a raw sensual energy never before incorporated into her art. She arched her neck and threw back her shoulders, seeming to cast off of the traditional constraints associated with her sex and her race. Her skirts whirled and her dark eyes flashed, and though her brother was equally as graceful and equally as skilled, the audience barely noticed him at her side. She danced as never before, and when the music ended, she stood with her bosom heaving and her cheeks aflame, and no one could deny her womanhood or her regality. A cheer went up from the appreciative crowd, and the mystery guest was smitten.

The usual discussions ensued of the inequality of the classes and the mistreatment of Castilian citizens based on their gender, religion, or personal beliefs. The Portuguese gentleman was further impressed by María's understanding of the plight of the second-class population and her vision of the work and sanctions necessary to remedy the current outdated system. He had never met such a talented, intelligent, and self-assured young woman in his life. Oh, there had been plenty of females who carped and complained about their shabby treatment at the hands of their husbands, employers, or the perpetually evil government, but none of them had even begun to understand how to effect a change. This young woman was fascinating.

After midnight, the crowd began to dwindle, and a steady stream of guests began to leave the Del Rio estate in a slow, reluctant exodus. A few of them lingered, interested to see if the identity of the mystery guest would be revealed. The man himself was deep in conversation with his host, and his younger brother dozed in a comfortable chair by the fire. The guardian in the corner had not moved the entire night and maintained his vigil as alertly as ever. Cassia performed her hostess' duties by cheerfully bidding a good night to her departing guests and offering refreshment to the ones who remained. María was about to ask permission to be excused when she heard her father call to her from his seat.

"María, *mi amor*, come here," Emilio said in his calm assuring way.

She crossed the room in the graceful floating step that accomplished dancers possess and came to rest in front of the two waiting men.

"I would like to present you to Infante Diogo, Duke of Viseu," her father said easily.

María was stunned. She had sensed that the man was a high-ranking member of the Portuguese nobility, but cousin and brother-in-law to the current regent? It had never entered her mind that such an important personage would show up at her home. She quickly regained her composure and curtsied low.

"I am very honored, Your Excellency," she said charmingly.

"No, Señorita," he began sincerely, standing to greet her. "*I* am the one who has been honored to see you dance." He then took her hand and kissed it.

María blushed deeply, lending a deep rose-colored glow to her cheeks and setting her dark eyes sparkling. Emilio recognized the signs of a quickly blossoming romance and excused himself under the pretext of helping his wife with the last of the straggling guests. Diogo, who still held María's hand in his own, guided her to the chair her father had vacated and entered into a conversation with her that would last until dawn. The guardian in the corner grunted to himself, having seen this many times before, and settled more comfortably into his seat, knowing that this would be another long night.

Chapter 2: Estêvão

The passionate feelings between Diogo and María bloomed rapidly, and their courtship developed accordingly. The duke came to visit María as often as he could, but sometimes he was away for long stretches at a time. Though she wished he could be with her every moment of every day, María realized that with his important position came many responsibilities. She resigned herself to the fact that if she were to be a part of his life, she must accustom herself to his long absences and accept that their time together would have to be lived as privately as possible. It would not be a huge adjustment—she had spent most of her life in a like manner—but she couldn't help feeling a twinge of jealousy when he left her to address the duties of his office.

One such evening while preparing himself to attend an official state function, Diogo mused aloud about the things foremost in his mind. This was an unconscious habit he had of thinking through certain private matters with only his most trusted bodyguard present. Though the big hulk of a man was only a *fidalgo*, Dom Martín had been a part of the duke's household now for many years and had become his lord's closest friend and confidante, and Diogo valued his opinion.

"I have been thinking lately that it is very unfair for me to string Señorita María along in a manner to give her false hope," the duke said speculatively while straightening his collar.

The big man grunted and with a wry smile said, "I was wondering how long it would take you to tire of this one. She *is* fascinating, but it could be very dangerous for you to dally with a relative of Isabella of Castile."

"Oh, there has been no *dalliance*," Diogo replied with a dismissive wave of his hand. "I respect her too much for that."

"So she would not give in, eh?" Martín jibed. "She is even more fascinating than I thought."

"No, she would not give in," Diogo smiled rakishly. "But I think I have a plan that will make her acquiesce."

"Oh, do tell," said Martín, rubbing his hands together in perfect imitation of the world's greatest villain.

"I plan to marry her."

Martín sat silently, waiting for the punch line to come. This had to be a joke. Diogo's affections were his own to bestow where he saw fit. He might even sire children if he wished—he had already done so in his youth with a certain Dona Leonor—but to wed was a completely different matter. As an Infante his marriage was a tool of state. His nuptials would be used by his king to strengthen alliances or quell rebellions or bind the royal family more firmly together to maintain their monopoly on the throne. He would not be allowed to make this determination for himself.

When no explanation came forth, Martín shook his head in disbelief. "You are mad," he said, hoping to force his master to admit the hoax.

"Perhaps I am," Diogo smiled to himself, "but I love her and will not give her up."

"I cannot be a part of this," Martín said in an anguished voice. "You know how self-righteous your cousin is, the self-styled 'Perfect Prince'!" he spat out. "You could be jeopardizing your very life."

"Yes but I love her," the duke repeated simply. "The arrangements have already been made. We will be married in a secret ceremony in one month's time, and what my cousin does not know will not hurt him."

His master had already made up his mind, so now Martín could do nothing but support him and attempt to protect him. He recalled that when he had pledged his life to the young Duke of Viseu so many years ago, his oath had been unto death. He realized now that it might well be the way it ended.

The month passed and Diogo and María were married as planned, in secret and without the knowledge or consent of his royal cousin. It was decided that she should remain with her parents so not to draw attention, and Diogo could rest easy in the fact that she would be well cared for during his frequent but necessary absences. Dom Martín, though skeptical at the outset, now saw that there was true love between them and grew to accept the grim reality of the situation. What was done was done, and one day they would have to deal with the consequences, but not today.

This gloomy truth could do nothing to dampen the lovers' spirits. They were supremely happy, and the estate rang with the boisterous bliss of new love, the way it had for María's parents twenty years before. All who beheld the young couple fell victim to their contagious happiness, and when María fell pregnant, everyone from the most humble stable boy to the neighboring landed gentry shared in their wild joy.

Diogo was the most solicitous of expectant fathers. Though María's compact little body had not even shown the slightest sign of the life growing within her, the duke was continually looking out for her comfort. He forced her to use an extra cushion to support her back when she sat in a chair, he made sure she ate the freshest foods, and he was forever covering her with a shawl or blanket, even when she did not feel chill.

"My love," she began patiently, "if you continue to pile blankets upon me, I shall melt into a puddle, and nothing will be left but a soggy pile of clothing."

"I am merely looking out for our son, Pomba," he said seriously, using his pet name for her, 'dove' in Portuguese. "He shall be heir to an important position and title. I don't want to risk his welfare simply because his obstinate mother refused to wear her shawl. Please," he implored, taking her hand, "do it for me."

Unfailingly she gave in, knowing that he was only fussing because he loved her. Eventually her body began to change, and she was grateful for his small courtesies. She had heard many stories of husbands treating their wives as no more than breeding machines. She was reassured to know that Diogo was not one of these.

As María's period of confinement drew near, Diogo spent more and more of his time at her side. His duchy was less than a day's ride away, so he kept his fastest courier at the ready in case something urgent should arise. He made his excuses at court, feigning illness, and settled down to await the birth of his legitimate son. He was so full of grand plans for the child that María could not bring herself to mention the fact that it could in all possibility turn out to be a girl. Instead she said nothing and let him continue dreaming.

It resulted that he was right. María was delivered of a vigorous baby boy with dark hair and eyes and, so the midwife declared, the healthiest pair of lungs she had ever heard. María had a relatively easy labor but was exhausted from the effort of pushing the child from her petite body into the world. The midwife wrapped the newborn tightly, and handed him to his father who proudly carried him to his mother's side.

"You see, Pomba," Diogo said with quiet awe, "I knew he would be a boy. Oh, and he's perfect. Have you ever seen such a perfect child?" he asked the room in general.

Everyone in the room shook their heads to indicate that they had not, and the duke leaned over and kissed his tired wife on the cheek. She had never looked so beautiful in her life with her black-brown hair loosely tumbling down her shoulders, a dark rose flush on her cheeks, and the vibrant glow of motherhood and true love shining in her eyes. Diogo thought that if someday he had to answer for his impetuous decision, this one moment would make it all worthwhile.

They named the child Estêvão, the Portuguese version of Stefan, María's Gypsy grandfather. He was very curious and very active and his parents loved him to distraction. He had a certain knack of attracting affection, and he used it to his every advantage. The entire staff was at the beck and call of their little Infante, and he thrived on their attention.

His father doted on him. As an infant Estêvão enjoyed his position as heir apparent and its benefits, one of which was having every toy under the sun in his possession. His favorite was a beautifully carved set of exotic animals complete with cages. He also liked to play with an oversized wooden chess set, and although he did not understand how the pieces *should* be used, he enjoyed pitting them against each other in mock-battles, which consisted mostly of smacking them together or using one piece to topple the other. This behavior had convinced Diogo that his son was a genius. What child of his age had ever figured out that chess was really just a miniature war? Although Estêvão was too young to understand the official rules, wasn't he wielding the pieces in the true spirit of the game?

Diogo's indulgence continued in the same manner when for Estêvão's first birthday, he gifted his son with a pair of custom-made boots and a little wooden sword with a jeweled leather scabbard. María laughed heartily at her tiny son stomping shakily through the house, waving his toy sword before him, and bellowing at anyone who got in his way. It really was comical, but she felt compelled to reprimand him and remind his father that if he did not curtail his generosity, his son would become spoiled and unruly and would take his noble rights for granted.

"That is the entire point, Pomba," Diogo said seriously. "He needs to learn his position in this world, and the sooner the better."

"I understand," María countered, "but he should not be raised to believe he can treat people as inferiors based simply on some accident of birth. With the fickle state of the crown these days, our fortunes could be overturned on a whim. We have all seen it happen before."

"Pomba," he said, taking her hands in his, "our position is secure. Even if João were to become upset with me, he would never risk offending his wife, my own sister, by taking action against me. For heaven's sake, she is his queen!" This was true. The royal couple had accomplished their official coronation five months earlier.

María let the subject drop, but she still tried to make her tiny son understand that people for whom he cared should not be treated so shabbily. Perhaps he did not grasp the entire meaning of what she said, but he knew she was upset with him for shouting, and he apologized. The current crisis averted, María still could not shake the impression that her son would never inherit his due.

Chapter 3: Braganza

Their life went on in a similar fashion, and Diogo continued to spoil his son at every opportunity. For Estêvão's second birthday he got him a pony, and though the two-year-old could not actually control the horse on his own, he did have a natural affinity for the pursuit and sat steadfastly in the saddle while the groom led the pony around the exercise ring. He soon learned how to use the reins, and a few months later he could gallop his pony swiftly about while the groom monitored them on a lead.

One afternoon in late June 1483, María was watching two-year-old Estêvão demonstrate his new "trick" of riding around the ring with his hands high in the air and his eyes closed. She heard riders fast approaching on the path from the main gate, and she turned to discover their identity. Diogo had been away for two weeks this time and she had not expected his return for another three days, so she was a bit concerned to see him now. Her concern turned to panic when she saw the ashen pallor of his skin and the same sickly green tone echoed in the face of his young brother, Manuel. Dom Martín was as grim as ever, his expression basically unchanged. She tried to wait calmly while her husband made his way out to the exercise ring.

As the duke closed the distance between them, María saw his eyes soften, and he swept her up in a crushing embrace, forgetting all about the spectators around them. He held her that way for a few minutes until he felt a tugging at the tail of his cape. He turned and looked down to see his tiny son and scooped him up in the same manner. The three of them stood unspeaking in a communal hug, a sweet familial tableau. Finally Estêvão broke the silence.

"Father," he began excitedly, "did you see my new trick?"

"I did, Falcão. You are becoming quite the circus performer."

This was the highest of praise as Estêvão worshiped the circus above all else. He beamed smugly at María and said, "See, Mother! I told you Father would like it!" He then turned back to his father and asked, "What did you bring for me this time?"

Diogo reached into his leather travel bag and pulled out a tiny pair of golden spurs and handed them to his son. Estêvão bounced up and down in his father's arms and whooped for joy. "Real spurs!" he shouted in his small voice. "Now I can be a real vaqueiro!" Wranglers were right below circus performers on his list of prospective occupations. "Thank you, Father! Oh, thank you!" he gushed as he squeezed the duke's neck tightly.

"You are very welcome, Falcão," Diogo said as he lowered his son gently to the ground. "Now go and have your Uncle Manuel show you how to mount them. I need to speak to your mother for a moment."

Estêvão nodded then raced off to greet his uncle and Dom Martín, jumping and whooping as he went. Smiling after the tiny figure speeding up the path, Diogo turned to his wife and said, "Let us take a walk, Pomba. I have much to tell you." As they walked the grounds of the Del Rio estate, he recounted the events that had taken place while he was at court. The story he told was horrifying, and it validated all of María's worst fears.

During the reign of King João's father, Afonso V, their cousin Fernando had supported and accompanied the king on his expeditions and had been rewarded with many favors. In 1478 he inherited the Dukedom of Braganza and soon became the richest and most powerful aristocrat in all of Portugal. He believed that he had as much right to the Portuguese crown as his cousin, João, and had let his opinion be publicly known.

The nobles who had increased their riches under King Afonso were now in danger of losing their wealth under João. They formed a conspiracy to back the strong and valid claim of the Duke of Braganza, going so far as to even seek support from Isabella and Ferdinand of Castile. They were so confident in their cause that they became lax about security and were eventually betrayed by royal spies. Braganza was arrested, charged with treason, convicted, and beheaded at Évora on June 20th. His supporters fled to Castile, and his estates were confiscated by the Portuguese crown.

Although Diogo was clearly shaken, he attempted to put on a sunny front. "I assure you, Pomba, the same could never happen to me," he said pulling her close. "I would never be so foolish as to contest the position of my cousin. I am satisfied with my lot, and I would *never* jeopardize my happiness with you and our son." Then he kissed her with feeling to show it was true.

María tried with her whole heart to believe him, but there was something in the back of her head that told her their life together would be short-lived.

Chapter 4: The Summons

Estêvão's birthday came round again, and to celebrate the completion of his third year, Diogo brought him a toy sailboat complete with a tiny crew. The boat came equipped with everything that a full-sized version carried on board down to the miniature banner, which Diogo explained depicted a stylized falcon, a representation of Estêvão's own nickname. It was an extremely fine day for January, so the family took a picnic out to the pond on the estate, and Estêvão splashed about in the frigid water while his parents sat on the shore and laughed at his antics.

After half an hour, María tried to coax her shivering son out of the pond, but Estêvão maintained that if someday he were to become a ship's captain, he would have to prepare himself to withstand the freezing temperatures of the wild open seas. She responded that if he caught a chill at this time of year, he might not survive to adulthood. Then she held a warm blanket open to him while he sulkily exited the pond. He reluctantly let her dry him off, grumbling the entire time that perhaps this was why they did not allow women on board. Diogo laughed at this extremely astute observation, and María grudgingly smiled at his perfect imitation of a disgruntled adult male. These days were typical of their happiness, and there on the secluded estate they could almost believe their lives would go on that way forever.

Diogo spent as much time as he could with his family, only leaving to answer official summonses or attend to matters that required his physical presence. The execution of his cousin, Braganza, had been forgotten immediately after his recounting of the event to his wife and now seemed part of the ancient past. He had maintained limited contact with the court since the incident, and so in September of 1484 when he received a summons from his royal cousin, King João, he was taken completely by surprise.

That night as Diogo and María lay side by side, she pleaded with him not to go. She had the distinct impression that he was in peril, and if he left her, this time he would not return. She clung to him and employed every tactic she knew to get him to ignore the summons or make yet another excuse, but he resolutely refused to give in to her fears.

"Pomba, you are overreacting," he said calmly. "You are frightened because you think that I will suffer the same fate as Braganza, but that will not happen."

"How do you know what will happen?" she asked, the strain evident in her quavering voice. "Sometimes I think your cousin does not know what he will do *himself* until it is done. Can you not indulge me just this once?"

He shook his head in the dark. "I have already disregarded too many of his requests. One time too often and he is sure to become suspicious. He would send spies out to track me down. They would find out about you and our little Falcão, and that would endanger you both." He rolled onto his side and put his arms around his wife. "I could never live with myself if anything happened to either one of you."

When he touched her the impression of danger became even sharper, and she knew that she would not convince him to stay. The tears silently streamed down her face.

"Pomba," he said gently, "It is a simple informal meeting in his apartments. If it were to be an official engagement, he would have made arrangements in a public venue. Besides, Martín will be with me. What harm can come to me while I am under his protection?"

This last comment made her feel a little bit foolish. It would take an army to overcome Martín, and he would die before he allowed a hair on his lord's head to be touched by an unfriendly hand. Perhaps she was overreacting just the smallest bit. She lay there in his arms, warm and secure, and did not speak again until morning. After breakfast, Diogo told her he loved her, kissed her and Estêvão goodbye, and rode away from the estate with Martín by his side. It was the last time she would see her husband alive.

As the duke moved his mount into an easy traveling canter, María's behavior began to have its effect on his mood. He replayed the previous night's scene over in his head, and began to feel an inkling of doubt worm its way into his mind. She had never acted so hysterically at his departure before. In fact, now that he thought about it, he could not remember ever having witnessed her tears. On previous occasions when she'd gathered a strong impression, it had usually turned out to be correct. It would be wise for him to proceed very carefully with his cousin and take all possible precautions. He would do everything in his power to return to his family in one piece. He did not want to run the risk of leaving his beloved wife and precious son at the mercy of the snakes at the Portuguese court.

Chapter 5: Royal Murder

It was a long journey, and after many days of hard riding, Diogo and Martín arrived in Setúbal exhausted and filthy. They immediately headed to the ducal apartments to bathe and nourish their battered bodies. After seeing to the horses, they entered the building and found Manuel waiting in his rooms.

"Little brother!" Diogo exclaimed as Manuel rose from his seat to greet him. "Have you received a summons from our royal cousin as well?"

The younger man said that he had, and Diogo's suspicions receded the slightest bit. If João had asked Manuel to be present at their meeting, then it truly was an unofficial appointment. Manuel had no titles or land in his own name, so it would be completely pointless to view him as a threat and, in turn, expose him to any foul intention. The duke's mind relaxed the more, and he excused himself to take advantage of a hot tub of water that required his attention.

When he had finished his bath and dressed in clean clothing, he ordered a feast and sent a message to his cousin informing the king of his arrival. Diogo, Dom Martín, and Manuel sat around the table and conversed amiably while they ate their meal.

"So, how fare my Lady sister and my precocious little nephew?" Manuel asked with a smile.

"They do well," replied Diogo unconvincingly. His brother looked at him with one eyebrow raised, and Diogo went on to explain. "María seems to believe some sort of ill-fortune will result from this summons. I tried to tell her that her fears are unfounded, but she would not be persuaded."

"Women can be flighty creatures," Manuel said dismissively, returning to his soup.

"Not my wife," the duke said thoughtfully. "She often has these eerily accurate impressions, and this one seemed to affect her quite strongly." He looked up at his brother with his clear green eyes and said seriously, "Manuel, make an oath to me, here and now, that if anything should happen, you will do what you can to look after them."

"Oh, *now* who is the flighty creature?" Manuel asked jokingly.

"I am serious, Brother," Diogo said more urgently.

Manuel wiped the smile from his face and said, "I swear it."

"Good! Now, let's finish this food and have a nice game of cards. I have a purse full of gold and the urge to enrich my trusted bodyguard with its contents!"

Dom Martín grunted a laugh and poured himself a cup of wine. This would be another prosperous night indeed.

The next morning was the day of the fateful meeting. Diogo had slept but fitfully during the night, and his lack of rest had left him in a pessimistic mood. He dressed hurriedly and began to ransack his quarters, searching for various miscellaneous items. He gathered a stack of important documents and articles of jewelry, set the whole heap on the dining table, and began methodically to organize it, writing out meticulous instructions for each pile. When he had done, he called Dom Martín to him and began the explanations.

"My loyal friend," the duke began somberly, "I have asked you here, because you are the one person in the world upon whom I can rely." Martín remained silent, knowing that they were beyond the point of bickering.

Diogo nodded his head and continued. He told Martín that on the table were deeds of ownership, notes of deposit, pieces of jewelry, in short, all of his personal earthly possessions. There were explicit directives on the handling of each portion of his property and sealed letters for every person who had been important to him to be opened only in the event of his death. He indicated that if said demise came to pass, Martín was to handle the distribution of his belongings and carry out the duke's final wishes in a discreet and timely fashion. Finally, he had some verbal instructions for Martín's ears only.

"As you know, old friend," the duke continued, "I am very concerned that my little family not be discovered. If you should need to bear them the news of my passing, you will take all of the usual precautions. Although their security is imperative, there is one who will need your protection more. I want you to promise me right now that you will not lose your head or your life and swear your allegiance to Manuel. He is still but a boy, and he needs a solid attendant to guide him through the pitfalls of the court."

Martín did not answer but crossed the room with four strides of his long legs and knelt before his lord, kissing the ring on that familiar hand with emotion he had never before displayed. When he looked up, his black eyes were shining with unshed tears, and his knees shook as he rose from his deep genuflection. The duke clasped his forearm, uncharacteristically demonstrating the genuine love and respect he felt for this most faithful of companions, and they stood there wordlessly until the bells told them it was time to go.

They made their way to the courtyard of João's royal apartments and were stopped by the guards at the gate. The clearance was given, but when Martín tried to follow his master inside, he was refused entry. He began to lose his temper and jostle about with the watchmen until his master intervened.

"Dom Martín!" Diogo shouted sharply. "A private word, if you please." Martín angrily shrugged off the hold of the guards and strode over to where the duke stood waiting. "This is not what we agreed, my friend," Diogo said pointedly.

"Yes, but they have no right …"

"They are the king's guard. Regardless, there is something I forgot," the duke said as he twisted at a ring on his little finger. He dropped the ring into Martín's bear paw and said, "This belongs to my wife. It was a part of her Gypsy heritage and has no place in this court. The garnet was supposed to ensure that we meet again, so perhaps we will in the afterlife. Make sure it finds its way back to her." With that, he turned and strode through the guard. "Remember your promise," he called back over his shoulder as he disappeared into the building. Martín let out a frustrated roar at the sentries and turned back toward the ducal apartments to look for Manuel.

Martín returned to the apartment and found his new charge sitting at the table staring at the whole of his brother's possessions. Manuel had a confused look on his face, and when he saw the big man enter, he looked to him for enlightenment. "Where is my brother?" he asked expectantly.

"The duke has gone to his meeting with the king," Martín answered evenly.

"But why have I not been sent for as well?" the teenager asked.

"Your royal cousin has his own reasons for what he does. The rest of us will have to wait to find out," the big man replied and sat down to wait.

The time passed with excruciating slowness, and after what seemed like hours, there was a knock at the door. Manuel sprang up from his seat and ran to open it, wondering why his brother would bid entry to his own rooms. "It's about time, Diogo. What took you so ..." The question died on his lips when he saw that a royal courier, and not his brother, stood in the corridor outside.

"Dom Manuel," began the messenger, "your presence is requested by His Most Faithful Majesty, King João II. You are to come with us immediately to the royal residence. The service of your bodyguard is not required."

"Not required, but he will damn sure have it!" snarled Martín.

"As you wish, Senhor," replied the man, completely unruffled.

So Martín made his second trip of the day to the courtyard where he had last seen the duke. As before, he was denied entry and could only watch his young charge disappear the same way his brother had. This time Martín determined to wait outside the building, in case he should be needed. He crossed his powerful arms across his chest, leaned up against the wall, and tried to keep himself from storming the entrance and breaking his oath to his master.

Half an hour passed, and soon after Martín heard footsteps quickly approaching from the interior. He turned to see Manuel hurrying toward him, a stunned look on his blanched face. His glazed eyes stared blankly into the courtyard, and his steps were clumsy and leaden. Martín's heart sank to his feet, and he was hard-pressed to restrain himself. No one tried to stop the youth as he stumbled past the guards, out of the compound, and around the corner into an alley where he promptly doubled over and vomited.

"What happened?" asked Martín in a low, dangerous voice as Manuel gulped for air. The big man took a long controlled breath and exhaled very slowly. "What happened?" he asked again more forcefully. The boy looked up at him, opened his mouth to speak, and slowly crumpled forward in a dead faint.

Martín caught his young charge as he toppled headlong toward the ground. He slung the slender teenager over his shoulder and carried him back to their rooms. He laid the boy on a bed, placed a cold compress on his forehead, and forced some wine between his lips. When Manuel came to, he looked around the room, heaved a huge sigh of relief, and leaned back in the bed with a tired little smile on his lips.

"Thank God it was all a dream," he said, taking the compress from his head.

"It was no dream," Martín said through his teeth. "You fainted in the alley, and I carried you back here. Tell me what happened."

Manuel's face disintegrated into an avalanche of torment. The tears poured down his face, and he tore at his clothing in an expression of utter anguish. Great sobs racked his thin chest with his misery, and he was wild with grief. When the harshest part of his suffering passed and only a few hitching spasms ran through his thin frame, Martín sat beside him on the bed and coaxed him to recount the entire story.

Manuel took a deep shuddering breath and began, "I was escorted to the king's quarters, and after I had knelt to give homage, João bade me rise and led me to an inner chamber. I saw what looked like a pile of bed linens on the floor and thought it strange that my cousin should tolerate such ineptitude from a laundress. And then João requested me to pledge fealty a second time. I did as he asked, and suddenly he whipped the blanket from the pile and there was ..." Manuel broke down into tears once more and could not continue, his entire body trembling at the memory. Martín patted the boy on the shoulder and waited as patiently as he could for him to go on. Finally, Manuel regained control of his emotions and filled in the rest in a quavering voice.

Underneath the bedclothes had lain his brother's murdered corpse. The duke had been stabbed several times in the abdomen, and João defended his actions by accusing Diogo of treason and the heading of a conspiracy to do away with the king and place himself on the throne. He terminated the audience by granting Manuel the ducal titles and estates, insisting that he should now consider the king as his own father. Terrified, the boy agreed then asked to be excused to attend to the responsibilities of his new position. João granted him a month for mourning then said that he expected to see him back at court at the end of that time. Manuel's face dissolved again into a mask of pain as he tried to wake himself from the nightmare.

"That viper!" Dom Martín shouted at the top of his lungs and began to pace the room like a caged beast.

"What will you do?" the boy asked through his tears.

"I will kill him!" Martín hissed venomously through his clenched teeth.

"No, please, Dom Martín," Manuel begged. "If you even try, he will have you executed."

"Then let him!" the fidalgo thundered. "It would be better than allowing him to get away with it, and I swear I will take as many of the bastards with me that I can!"

"Then who will I have to defend me?" Manuel asked simply. The pitiful quality of his weary voice broke through the big man's rage. It echoed the vow his master had exacted from him and reminded him that he still had a job to do.

"Fine, fine," he said, coming to his senses. "There will be no more killing, but I cannot remain here now. Will you be all right for a few hours with the guards outside?"

"I think so," the boy replied. "Where are you going?"

"I have some *business* to take care of," Martín said, grabbing the purse he had won the previous night and hiding a dagger in his boot.

"But you will return?"

"I promise I will return. I swore an oath to your brother, and I am duty-bound to keep it. I will return." With that, Dom Martín exited the apartment for the third time that day.

Chapter 6: Punishment

Martín made his way to the roughest part of town and entered the seediest establishment he could find. Upon closing the door behind him, he surveyed the coarse-looking crowd, nodded his head—satisfied that it would serve his purpose—and elbowed his way to a seat at the gambling table, stepping on several sets of toes in the process. He obnoxiously demanded wine, plunked a pile of gold coins down on the table, and proceeded to get roaringly drunk.

He had a talent for gambling and won nearly every game, leaving some of the mob grumbling that he had cheated. He gloated over his winnings, grabbed the bottoms of the serving wenches, and swore profusely and creatively, taking his pleasure at the expense of others. Over the course of the evening, he managed to offend nearly every person at the inn along with most of their family members who were not present. He invited several of the patrons to perform various lewd acts on certain favorite parts of his anatomy and offered to reciprocate with their mothers or wives. Finally the innkeeper had enough and asked him, none too gently, to leave. Martín cursed him one last time, threw a handful of gold in his direction to cover the bill, and staggered out into the street.

After urinating on the side of the building, he turned around to find that he had been followed out of the dive by several opportunists of an ostensibly violent nature. He rubbed his hands together in anticipation of the inevitable confrontation and continued to insult them in his most colorful language. They fanned out to surround him, careful to stay out of range until they were ready to strike. They were wise to be wary. They had him outnumbered, but he was large and strong and full of rage, and he was only half as drunk as he appeared.

The first would-be criminal struck out at him from behind with a kick that was meant to throw Martín off-balance. He caught the man's foot easily in one hand and held it firmly while he swung with the other and obliterated the man's nose. The man fell to the ground, screaming and writhing in pain as his blood poured through his fingers. There were still five men standing around him, but with the sudden loss of their cohort their courage diminished commensurately. They looked at each other, wide-eyed with fear, trying to decide if the spoils were worth pressing their assault.

"Who's next?" Martín called out and spat on the ground to show his contempt.

The largest of the thugs grabbed a good-sized stick and took a run at him from the shadows. Martín did not see him until the last second, and the man landed a glancing blow on his forehead that split open the skin and dripped blood into his eye. He swiped his hand impatiently across his brow, and the gore smeared over half of his face, making his appearance all the more fearsome. The man came at him again, but this time Martín was ready. Just before the blow landed, he ducked to the side and stuck out his foot as the man ran past. The hoodlum landed full-force on his front, and a loud, "Oof!" was heard as the air rushed out of his lungs. He sat there helplessly gasping for breath as Martín mercilessly approached him, lifted his head with one hand, and punched him soundly on the chin, knocking him out cold.

He turned to the remaining four men, who now cowered together against the building. "I suggest the rest of you come at me all at once to improve your odds of success." He dangled the purse out in front of them to provide a little incentive. "There's still quite a bit of gold left, and now that your friends have *forfeited* their shares, yours are much larger. Come on, ladies. Let's dance," he said and beckoned them forward with the tips of his fingers.

As if in a trance, they advanced as a unit. One of them picked up the stick of his fallen comrade, and another pulled a blade from inside his jacket. Dom Martín licked his lips and nodded his head, his eyes glittering dangerously in the moonlight. All at once they rushed him, and for a moment he did nothing, taking the punishment they dealt, hoping that the physical pain would assuage the ache he felt inside. Suddenly he could hold back his fury no longer, and with an animal growl he threw them off in an Herculean effort and began to attend to them one at a time.

He caught the two smallest men by the hair and bashed their heads together like cymbals punctuating the climax of an overture. They collapsed in a heap on the ground while the melee raged on around them. The man with the stick was landing random blows about Martín's head and shoulders, but these were not much more than an annoyance, so he ignored them. The man with the knife was the one to beware. He focused all of his attention on him while the stick wielder whacked away energetically behind him.

Martín faced off with the knife man, and they circled each other cagily, waiting for an opening. He remembered the dagger in his boot, but harried as he was by the man with the stick, he could not reach for it without exposing himself to the man with the knife. Besides, he did not want to kill the man, he just wanted to make someone, *anyone*, pay.

Martín continued to circle and finally he could take no more. With one swift movement, he half-turned to the man behind him, caught the descending arm in his two strong hands, and flung the man over his shoulder. The man flew through the air in a graceful arc straight toward his partner, who had used the distraction to advance on Martín. Stunned, knife-man instinctively stretched out his arms to catch stick-man, and the full weight of the flying body brought them both crashing to the ground. As they fell, there was a loud "Snap!" and stick-man rolled around in the dirt, howling, his hands clutching at the right cheek of his buttocks. Knife-man looked down at the hilt of his weapon—now minus the blade, which was lodged deep in stick-man's rear end—and in one last effort, flung the piece futilely at his enemy. The hilt bounced harmlessly off of Martín's broad chest and landed at his feet. He picked it up to examine it, and knife-man fled noiselessly into the night.

Martín looked about, surveying the damage that surrounded him, and chuckled tiredly. *A good night's work,* he thought to himself. He walked over to where stick-man lay in the dirt. The man's howls had now quieted to whimpers, and he was employing the new strategy of moving the least amount possible. Martín took out his purse, shook the contents from it, and said, "This should cover the cost of the medic to remove the blade from your backside. Tell your *friend,* if you see him again, that he is a coward!" He then turned and walked wearily back to the apartments.

In the morning Martín awoke to the soft sound of Manuel's anxious voice calling his name. His heavy eyelids had to be pried open, and his mouth felt like someone had stuffed it with wool. He also had a raging headache, and his body was stiff and sore and itchy with dirt and dried blood. The glare from the morning sun was too much to tolerate, and he asked Manuel to draw the curtains to lessen its brightness. With much effort, he pushed himself up to a sitting position and poured himself a cup of wine.

"How are you feeling?" Manuel asked, the concern beginning to fade from his eyes.

"Sore ... and tired," Martín answered in a cracked voice.

"I thought you were dead," the boy said quietly. "Or dying," he corrected himself with a nervous laugh. "I couldn't tell if those were snores or death rattles. It was so loud it woke me from my own sleep." Martín grunted and took another sip of wine. "All that blood," the boy said, shaking his head. "Whose is it?"

"Some of it is mine, and some of it is ... not," the big man said. "I apologize, Excellency. I did not mean to frighten you."

"Excellency?" the boy repeated then turned his head away.

"Yes, I suppose that is my title now, and I suppose I will have to bear the news to my family."

At that moment Martín's gaze landed on the table where sat the garnet ring with which the duke had entrusted him. The last mission with which Diogo had charged him was the delivery of the ring and the report of his death. It was imperative that the information come from him before reaching María from another source. What had he been thinking? Why had he been out picking fights when he still had a job to do? He tossed back the last of the wine, and rose from the bed.

"Dom Martín what are you doing?" the newly made duke asked, startled by his sudden energy.

"I need a bath then we must go," Martín said gruffly.

"But where?"

"To the Del Rio estate. Dona María must not hear this news from anyone else."

When the import of the statement sank in, the young duke drew himself up with sudden dignity. "You are right. I will send for the horses, and we shall depart immediately. Make haste, Dom Martín. I will be waiting for you in the antechamber." He then exited the room and shut the door behind him. Martín looked at the closed door with a small smile. Perhaps the boy would be a worthy successor after all.

Chapter 7: Honor and Dignity

When they arrived at the Del Rio estate, they were informed that the family had made a trip out to the marketplace but were expected back soon. The two men were offered refreshment and made comfortable to wait for the family's return. It wasn't long before they heard the rattling wheels of the wagon outside. Manuel jumped up from his chair, not knowing what else to do, and Martín took a long, ragged breath but remained seated. Neither one of them was looking forward to the task at hand.

Emilio was the first person through the entrance, and when his observant gaze landed on the travelers' careworn faces, he knew that the news was grim. He nodded in understanding and backed out the door, careful not to let Estêvão squeeze through the opening.

"Grandfather, please!" they heard the three-year-old call out. "I must get to my room to rig up these new sails on my ship! Won't Father be surprised when he sees them!"

"Yes, Estêvão," Emilio said as he scooped up his grandson, "but first we must take an apple out to *Siroco*. We have been away a long time, and he must be feeling lonely." He turned to his daughter with a meaningful look and said, "María, you have company." He reached out with his free hand and hugged her close. "Be strong," he whispered in her ear. Then turning to his wife he said, "Grandmama, shall we go out to visit the horses?" and the three of them walked away, leaving María standing on the porch.

She did not know who was waiting inside, but she could tell by her father's actions that all of her worst fears had come true.

223

She brought her shaking hands to her face—unconsciously pressing them together in a gesture of prayer against her forehead—and breathed deeply, trying to slow the nervous pounding of her heart. After a few moments, she was ready. She took one last, deep breath, smoothed the front of her skirts, and entered the house with her head held high.

"Sister," Manuel said gravely as he reached out his hand and guided her to a chair.

Martín rose from his seat and bowed as María walked past. After she had settled herself, he sat back down. He and Manuel had discussed the scenario, and as he had performed this exact duty repeatedly during wartime, Martín offered to deliver the news to save the boy further heartache. Manuel had refused, making the point that if he were to become duke in actuality as well as title, he would have to carry out every obligation, no matter how unpleasant. It was sound reasoning, and they came to the decision that it was the boy's right and privilege to give the report of his brother's passing.

Manuel sat next to his sister-in-law and held her hand as he related the story from start to finish. She sat bolt upright and watched his face the whole while, her expression never changing. She did not interrupt him, and she did not shed a tear. The only time she moved was to pat the young duke's hand in encouragement when his voice faltered as he described the moment of his greatest horror, when his cousin had presented him with his brother's bloody remains on the apartment floor.

When he had finished, the two of them sat silently with their hands clasped and their eyes still locked together. Martín thought that perhaps she was suffering some form of catalepsy from the shock of it all until she lowered her gaze to her lap and sighed. She looked back up at her brother-in-law, squeezed his hands tightly, and said, "I want to thank you, Manuel. That must have been very difficult for you. You handled it beautifully."

Martín's mouth fell open. He was astounded by her strength. In the past when he had delivered news of the death of a loved one, there had been a multitude of different reactions. Some women screamed, some pulled at their hair or faces, some of them rent their clothing, some had even cried silently, but never had any of them accepted the news with such quiet dignity. He was so moved that he rose from his seat and walked over to where she sat. He knelt in front of her and kissed her hand austerely in a manner to convey his respect for both her and her husband.

"My Lady," he began in a voice gravelly with emotion, "your husband bade me to deliver his personal effects. He also charged me with returning this to you," and he pressed the garnet ring into her hand.

"Ah, yes," María said, turning it over in her palm, a faint smile on her lips. "The garnet. It was supposed to protect him. Perhaps he should not have taken it off." She stared at it absentmindedly for a moment then shook her head to clear it. "No matter now. What's done is done, and I shall have to figure out how to live with it."

"Dona María," Martín said, still holding her petite hand in his big bear paw, "please know that I consider it my bounden duty to protect you and young Estêvão. If there is ever a need, no matter how small, send for me and I shall come."

"And I," added Manuel. "I may not be at liberty to come to you personally, but as the new Duke of Viseu, I shall have many resources at my fingertips. Consider them yours, Sister."

María nodded her head in appreciation. "Thank you, gentlemen," she said sincerely. "That is very comforting. Now please make yourselves at home. The staff is yours to command. If you'll excuse me, I have to think of a way to break the news to my son." She rose from her chair, inclined her head, and left the room.

The two men stared after her, at a loss for words. Finally Manuel cleared his throat and said with clear admiration, "What an astonishing woman! Now I see why my brother was willing to incur the wrath of our cousin to marry her. I only hope that one day I find someone who approaches her in character. I swear I will do *everything* in my power to see that she and my nephew are looked after." Martín nodded his head in agreement, and they ascended the stairs to their rooms.

As María made her way out to the stables, her mind processed the news she had just been delivered. Though the full significance of exactly what this meant to her would not settle in for some time, she was not surprised by her husband's murder nor was she fully unprepared for the task ahead. When he had left her nearly a month earlier, in the back of her mind she had known it would be the last time she would see him. Since that day she had tried to compose her part of the conversation, which now loomed before her, but she did not know how Estêvão would react. She would find out soon enough.

She reached the stables and as soon as her son spotted her, he came racing to her side. "Mother!" he cried excitedly. "Who are our visitors? I saw the strange horses in their stalls, and they are very fine-looking specimens. Who did you talk to?"

As she looked down at him, she felt the first pangs of real grief. He was like a miniature version of his father right down to the words he had chosen to describe the horses. He gazed up at her with his hazel-green eyes in an open, expectant manner, and she realized that the true tragedy of the situation would be that this little boy would grow up without his father. She swept him up in her arms and hugged him tightly to her.

He tolerated her embrace for a moment then his curiosity got the better of him. He put his tiny hands on her face, one on each cheek, and brought her gaze around to meet his. "Mother, please, who has come?"

"Dom Martín and your Uncle Manuel have come to visit," she said evenly.

"And my father?" he asked.

"He is not with them, Falcão," she said, unconsciously using his father's pet name for him.

At that moment her parents approached from the interior. "Would you like us to stay, *Hija*?" Cassia asked, gently laying her hand on her daughter's shoulder. María shook her head with a sad smile, and her parents continued walking.

Estêvão, who never missed a thing, saw the look that passed

between them and understood that something was amiss. "Mother, what is it?" he asked in a quiet voice.

"I have some important news that I need to share with you, and I'm afraid it is not good. Let's find a place to sit." She squeezed him again before she lowered him to the ground, and this time he did not fuss.

They sat on an old worn bench, and María held his tiny hands in hers as she stoically informed him of his father's passing. She omitted the graphic details and the accusations of treason, because she deemed it inappropriate subject matter for such a young child. Someday she would tell him the full story if he so wished, but right now the most significant thing to him was that his father would not be coming home. When she had finished, she sat silently, waiting for his reaction.

When María had told him that his father would not return, Estêvão had dropped his gaze to his lap, and she did not know if he was crying or simply processing the information. He looked up at her now, dry-eyed, with another question in his face. "Yes, Falcão, what is it?" she prompted.

"I just wanted to know if my father died with honor and dignity?"

She could not disguise her surprise at the question. He was a precocious child and would be four on his birthday in few months' time, but it seemed too mature a remark to come from a child so young. She took a moment to collect herself before she nodded that he had.

"Good," he said, satisfied. "He told me the day he left that the true measure of a man was the honor with which he lived his life and the dignity with which he died. He said that I should strive to live in that manner, because that was how people would remember me. I shall never forget him."

"Nor shall I, my son," she said sadly. "Nor shall I."

Chapter 8: El Rey

The first few months after Diogo's death were the most difficult. Because they could not attend a funeral or memorial service, it was hard for María and Estêvão to accept that he was really gone. Some special event would occur and one of them would make the off-hand comment that they could not wait to share it with the erstwhile duke, and then they would remember that they could not. Christmas and Estêvão's fourth birthday were sad occasions, made more so by the fact that they should have been celebrations, but as time passed the tenderness of the open wound faded to the faint ache of an old injury. Eventually they could remember him to each other with happiness.

Dom Martín and Manuel kept their promises. With his new title of Duke of Viseu came much responsibility and much obligation to the Portuguese crown. Although his visits were not frequent, Manuel was forever sending gifts and items of interest to both mother and son. Perhaps he felt somewhat guilty for his absence and was trying to make up for it by overindulging them with material possessions. María did not know, but they lacked for nothing.

Dom Martín was completely the opposite. He made many trips out to the Del Rio estates and seldom brought anything other than his person. Although he had promised Diogo that he would be there to help young Manuel navigate the dangers of court life under João, there were times when he was expressly refused entry to engagements that would place him in close proximity to the king. Anyone who knew the full story knew that Dom Martín was a very dangerous man and that he had been devastated by the death of his master. It would be tempting fate to put him in the same vicinity as his nemesis. After one too many humiliations, he declined to accompany Manuel to court, instead fulfilling his obligation by handpicking a new bodyguard for the young duke. This was a clever solution and mutually beneficial for both parties.

Now that Dom Martín had been released from his detestable situation, he seemed like a different person. María was surprised to find that he was funny and charming and actually quite handsome when he smiled. She also discovered that he had been married and had a son only a few months younger than Estêvão. The boy's name was João—an ironic and unfortunate coincidence—and his mother had died of consumption shortly after her son turned two. It was strange that María had never known any of this, but apparently she had not known Dom Martín well at all.

The months turned into years, and Estêvão grew as did the relationship between María and Dom Martín. Though Diogo was the reason they had originally come together, now he was more like a guardian angel than an actual person, and they seldom spoke of him unless it was to recall a fond memory or to remark how like him his son was becoming every day. In Estêvão's mind his father had achieved hero status, and no one around him would dare dispute it.

He was isolated on the Del Rio estate, and the few times he had ventured outside of the gates had not been successful. As news reports were scanty and unreliable and the relationship between Portugal and Castile was tenuous at best, rumors ran rampant and people tended to distort the few facts they heard to fit their own personal beliefs. The talk of treason had been too juicy a tidbit to ignore, and Estêvão became the object of local disdain. Any time he attempted to play with a child outside of the estate he was ostracized and treated like a pariah. The children, egged on by each other, taunted him by calling him 'El Rey', the king, insinuating that had his father succeeded in his traitorous plot, Estêvão would someday have become the King of Portugal. But the father had been executed, and as a result the son was king of nothing.

After one such outing when Estêvão was eight years old, he returned to the house before supper with his clothing torn and dirty. María let out an involuntary cry and ran to kneel in front of him. "What happened, Estêvão?" she asked as she looked him over to make sure he was not severely injured.

"I'm all right, Mother," he said, impatiently brushing her hands away. His bottom lip jutted out and his hands clenched into fists in his aggravation. "Those *children!*" he spat out, as if it were a dirty word. "They said that you ..."

"What did they say?" María urged him gently.

"They said that you and my father were never married. They said you were just another of his mistresses, and I am just another of his bastards. They also said that we are nothing but a pack of Gypsies."

"I see," said María evenly. "So how did you get dirty and how did your clothing get torn?"

"I walked straight up to their leader and punched him right in the nose!"

María stifled an inappropriate giggle behind her hand. "I don't suppose he took that very well."

"No he didn't, but it was a good punch. Father would have been proud."

"Come over here, Falcão," María said, and she led him over to where they could both sit comfortably.

His mother proceeded to explain to him that some people in the world bore grudges against those who were more prosperous. She supposed it was mostly out of frustration. Some of the laws were unfair and discriminatory, and they made it extremely difficult for a person to change his lot for the better. Even though things were beginning to evolve, it would take a long time. As part of the more privileged population it was their responsibility to be patient and do what they could to aid those less fortunate. She knew many families who had lost their estates during the wars. It could happen overnight, so one should never rely on his wealth or family ties. Hadn't the last thing his father told him been to live his life with honor? How honorable was it to add to the local children's miseries by engaging in physical violence with them? Finally, she impressed upon him how important it was never to be ashamed of his origins. She told him that the best way to silence his critics was to prove them wrong.

He took in the information she gave him, and though he did not understand the political implications, his mother was usually right and he trusted her judgement. Most of all he did not want to disgrace his father's memory by acting dishonorably. Just because the other children did not know any better, he should not have allowed himself to be pulled down to their level. He nodded that he understood, and from that day forward he never attempted to make friends with children outside the estate.

Chapter 9: Dom Martín

Dom Martín came to visit not long after mother and son had their conversation about honor and the plight of the less fortunate. The three of them took a picnic lunch up to the pond, and while María and Martín chatted amiably on the shore, Estêvão stood at the side of the pond practicing the trick Martín had just taught him of skipping stones across the water's surface. The adults watched as the eight-year-old repeated the action over and over until he had the technique just right. He threw his arms up in celebration of his last throw when the rock bounced five times before sinking into the pond, a new record.

"He grows more like his father by the day," remarked Martín. "I recall a time when we were *much* younger men. Diogo's elder brother wagered that he could not ride an unbroken colt. It was meant as a joke. The animal was the most foul-tempered creature I have ever come across," here he paused to chuckle, "besides myself I suppose. Every time he approached the beast it would bare its teeth at him. He began to carry apples in his pockets, and eventually when he visited the creature's corral, it walked over to greet him. Soon he could lean on it without consequence, and then he tried to mount it. Well, the horse did not like that, but no matter how many times Diogo got thrown, he always picked himself back up and tried again. His backside was blue from the bruises, but one day the colt allowed him on his back, and in no time he had it trained as well as a circus animal. He won the wager and the horse. He was most persistent person I have ever met, and I see that same tenacity in his son."

María smiled at the recounted memory of her beloved

husband and how well this big man beside her had known him. "Yes, Estêvão shares many qualities with his father, but sometimes I fear that I will not be able to raise him the way a boy should be raised. I'm afraid that I will coddle him too much, but at the same time, I don't want him to get hurt." She then went on to tell Martín about the incident at the gate. "Now he is reduced to finding a playmate among the children of the staff, and there are only one or two of his approximate age."

Suddenly Martín snapped his fingers. "I don't know why I have not thought of this before," he said excitedly. "What do you think about having my João come to Estêvão's birthday celebration next month? He is always asking me why I visit so often, and I think he is curious to finally meet you both."

"I think it is an excellent idea," replied María with a nod. "I would love to meet him as well."

"Good then, it is settled," Martín said. He looked up at the sky and saw some threatening clouds begin to move in from the west. "Shall we head back to the house?" he asked, rising from the blanket and holding his hand out to offer her assistance. She grasped his hand, and he tugged her toward himself a little too forcefully. She stumbled against him, and he held her tight to keep her from falling. The contact sent an unexpected jolt of electricity through them both, and they stood there together for moment before pulling apart in embarrassment.

"Forgive me, Dona María," he said formally, blushing from his surprising reaction to her touch.

Unable to respond verbally, she waved her hand to dismiss his apology. She was rendered momentarily speechless by the impression she had received in the brief moment when he'd held her in his arms. The sudden realization struck her like a thunderbolt. Dom Martín was in love with her! The thing that startled her even more was that she loved him too.

That evening after supper, María and Cassia took up their embroidery while Estêvão fussed with some new rigging for his ship. Emilio and Dom Martín sat playing chess and discussing the current state of affairs, which affected their neighboring homelands. Emilio moved his knight in the L-shaped pattern of attack to threaten his opponent's queen. Martín grunted to himself and stroked his chin as he contemplated his next move.

"My daughter tells me that you plan to bring your son with you on your next visit," Emilio said casually.

Never taking his eyes from the board, Martín nodded his head and said, "I thought it was time for the boys to finally meet each other. It would be good for both of them. Estêvão would have someone to tussle with once in a while, and my boy would definitely benefit from a more cultured companion than his current group of friends has to offer. They are decidedly ... uh ... *unrefined*."

"Yes, and it would be well for them to get used to one another considering the situation between their parents."

Martín stopped the unconscious rubbing of his chin and looked up at Emilio, his black eyes showing his utter surprise. "What *situation*, Señor Del Rio?" he asked formally.

The older man smiled back at him and said easily, "My wife seems to believe that you are harboring some tender feelings toward our daughter. I never would have thought to question the frequency of your visits, but Cassia with her Gypsy ancestry has always been much more perceptive than I. Now that she has brought it to my attention, I see that what she says is true. We are both curious to know how long it will take for the two of you to come to your senses."

Martín dropped his gaze back to the chessboard and said in a low voice, "Even if I were so inclined, I could not act on my emotions. She is ... *was* the wife of my best friend and far above my station. It would be inappropriate."

"If you love her, it would be entirely appropriate," Emilio said simply. "Anyone who knows my daughter knows that she places little value on titles or the classifications of society. She has always formed her own opinions based on a person's character, not on his station. She does not need to be taken care of, your duke left her well provided for, and I dare say that she has a level head for business and is fully capable of making her own wise decisions in that regard. What she needs is a partner who will work side by side with her, encourage her when things get difficult, and above all love her, no matter the circumstances."

"What if she does not share your point of view?" Martín asked, his eyes still glued to the board.

"I have it on good authority that she is merely waiting for you to declare yourself."

Martín took Emilio's knight with a nearby bishop then looked his opponent in the eye, "When do you think I should approach her?"

"How about at the end of our game?" Emilio asked with an impish grin. He then moved his castle in a long straight line to take Martín's queen. "Checkmate!" he exclaimed victoriously and without pause added, "Now go propose to my daughter."

Chapter 10: The Azores

With the proposal out of the way, María and Martín decided to set the date of the wedding tentatively for March of the coming year. Estêvão's ninth birthday celebration would be held at the end of January, so the boys would have a couple of months' time to get to know each other and resolve any issues that might arise before they became a permanent family.

María was concerned about Estêvão's reaction to the news that she would soon be remarried. She fretted that he might feel as if she were attempting to replace his father, but she needn't have worried. Dom Martín had been a part of his life from the very beginning and this was just a formalization of their relationship. Most of all he was excited to meet his future brother.

For the month-long period before the meeting, Estêvão peppered his mother with questions about the unknown personage. What did he look like? Did he like horses? Did he want to be a sailor? María could only repeat some of the general information Dom Martín had given and finally told him he would have to wait and see. At last, the anticipated day arrived.

Estêvão had been up since dawn, waiting at the window for the slightest indication of their appearance. It was a gray, drizzly day, so when the travelers neared the house, they seemed to materialize out of the fog thus adding to the mystique. The two shadowy figures dismounted their horses and stomped up the steps, shaking the water from their capes as they came. They were granted entry, and as they crossed into the parlor all in the Del Rio household were amazed at the striking resemblance between father and son.

João would not be nine for five months, but he was already taller than Estêvão and showing every indication that he would someday be as powerfully built as his father. He had the same long legs and arms and the same piercing black gaze. His carriage and movements were strangely synchronized with those of the older man, and they moved in concert with one another as the introductions were made. He nodded his head, shook hands, and addressed his new acquaintances all in his sire's same gruff manner.

When he had finished with the adults, the meeting came for which everyone had been waiting. The two boys stood there for a moment, each sizing up the other, and the observers could not tell if they would become friends or not. The expressions on their faces were unreadable, and neither boy looked away. Finally, João grunted in exact imitation of his father's trademark habit and stepped forward with his hand held out. Estêvão smiled and grasped it firmly in his own.

"My father tells me that we are to become family," João said sternly. "He has also told me that he served your father for most of his life and that the duke was his closest friend. Let us pledge now to continue the tradition, Brother," and he clapped Estêvão heartily on the back to demonstrate his sincerity. Estêvão nodded his agreement, and from that day forward the boys were inseparable.

The brothers found that they had much in common. They both had a love of horses, ships, and weaponry, and they spent many hours discussing the advantages of the placid Lusitano horse over the larger Andalusian, the fleetness of the caravel as opposed to the less maneuverable *nau*, and the power of a crossbow versus the range of an English longbow. This sparked endless heated debates, neither boy willing to concede, yet in the end they always found a way to remain friends.

María and Martín were married in March as planned, and soon the entire family fell into the pleasant rhythm of domestic life. Nothing changed much for María. As it had seemed to her son, the marriage was just a formalization of the relationship between herself and her new husband. As young boys do, the new brothers discovered some interesting ways to pass their time, and Emilio and Cassia simply enjoyed the new life and ebullience the union brought into their home. The only person not content was Martín.

As a man of action he was used to doing some sort of physical work every day. The first few weeks of their new life were an enjoyable respite from the years spent in constant motion, but soon the novelty wore off, and he began to chafe at the inactivity. He sought out little projects to keep himself occupied. When those were finished, he tried to pass time by teaching fighting techniques to the boys. When that failed, he attempted to take up woodcarving, and soon his mood became testy and unpleasant. He snapped at the staff, lost patience with the boys, and grumbled at María simply because she was not miserable along with him. One day she had finally had enough and vowed to get to the root of the problem.

"Martín, what has come over you?" she asked that evening when they were getting ready for bed.

"What do you mean?" he countered angrily, attempting to goad her into an argument.

"Just that," she answered, refusing to rise to the bait. "You have been *out of sorts* for the past few weeks, and I am beginning to take it personally. What is causing this ... angst?"

He did not answer immediately and continued to stew while removing his boots. When he had done, he sat in his chair with his elbows on his knees and gave a long exasperated exhale. "I'm sorry," he said, still avoiding her gaze. "It has nothing to do with you." He then rose from his seat and began to pace the room. "I just need to have something to do. I have spent my whole life working at one thing or another, and just sitting here doing *nothing* is starting to get to me. My rear end hurts, my head is buzzing with ideas that have no outlet, I eat too much so I have indigestion, and look, look at this!" Here he lifted his shirtfront, grabbed his increasing belly with both hands, and jiggled it up and down for his wife to regard. "I am getting fat! I have never had to worry about that in my life!" María clamped her hand over the lower half of her face, trying to hide her amusement, but her laughing eyes gave her away. "It is not funny!" Martín roared, infuriated by her reaction.

María rose from where she sat, took his hands gently in her own, and led him over to sit beside her on the bed. "Husband," she began patiently, "if you were on your own, without wife or family, how would you resolve this problem?"

"I would drink heavily and pick a fight," he replied without thinking.

María giggled at his childish yet genuine response. "And after, when the fight was over, what would you do then?"

This time he understood her point and thought for a moment before giving an answer. "I suppose I would find a suitable spot to begin my own little farm or ranch. A place where I could work hard everyday, and make a decent living," here he smiled down at her, "for myself, my wife, and my boys."

"Then perhaps that is what you should do."

"My little Gypsy," he said fondly. "How is it you know me so well?"

She shrugged and with a small smile said, "I would have to be practically blind not to know you after more than ten years, my love."

The next morning María and Martín went through the sheaf of papers bequeathed to her by the duke. She had gone over them once with her father a few months after Diogo's death, but for the most part they had remained untouched. She riffled through the stack until she found the one she was looking for. "There," she said with satisfaction. "What do you think of that?"

"The Azores," Martín said, mulling the prospect over in his mind. "I do not know anyone who has been, but I know that much of Portugal's wheat is now imported from that source. I have also seen some fine-looking cattle from Terceira. It would be worth a look," he finished, nodding his head.

"I don't think it would be wise to uproot the boys until it were a sure thing," she said.

"I wouldn't dream of it. I think the wisest thing would be for me to go alone, assess the work to be done, find the right men for the job, and get things under way before you and the boys made the trip." He stopped making his plans for a moment and looked down at her. "What are you smiling at?"

"I see the change in you already," she said, pleased with this new optimistic attitude.

"Yes well, a man with a job to do is a happy one. I will have to book passage, probably the sooner the better. The weather is just now turning and it would be good to get there when ..."

He went on with his preparations and María sighed contentedly, knowing that everything would be just fine.

A few days later, Dom Martín was ready to go. He thanked Emilio and Cassia for their hospitality, admonished the boys to behave and take care of their mother, and kissed his wife heartily before starting off on the journey that would change their lives forever.

María was sad to see him leave, but she knew Martín had many things on his mind already and did not want to further distract him by adding her own worries. She tried to look at things as philosophically as possible. She had endured long absences from a loved one many times in the past, and sometimes it seemed to her that married life consisted mostly of a series of separations and reunions. She also realized that sometimes inconvenience had to be endured in order to better one's circumstances in life, and this was something that would benefit them all. Besides, there was no way she could control the future, so she put on a sunny face and resolved to accept what came her way.

Time passed quickly, and because there was much traffic between the Azores and the mainland, the family received news often. Martín wrote of the bustling port of Angra, which was now becoming a major hub on the stage of world trade, and he also described the fertile green farmlands he had passed on the way out to the little chunk of property deeded to María by the duke. The acreage was extremely promising, as evidenced by the prosperous neighboring establishments, but it would take much hard labor to transform it into something workable. He had already hired men to clear the trees and convert the raw materials into lumber so that they could begin construction on the homestead. The black lava walls to section off the pastures were being built as he wrote. He also said that the days were long and the work was hard, but María could tell by the tone of the letter that it was exactly what he needed.

The months turned into a year, and the family began to look for Martín's return. He had written in his last letter that he would be heading back as soon as sailing conditions were favorable, and so María began to prepare in earnest for his arrival. She began to make lists of business matters that required her attention. She crated up items that were not daily necessities but could not be left behind, and she began to sort through clothing—her own and that of the boys—to decide which items were still useful, which were good enough to donate to the poor, and which would only serve as polishing and dusting rags for the household. She knew that her husband would reserve the right to override some of her decisions, but at least she would have an inventory and a preliminary account of their possessions.

One day while she was in her room absorbed in her organizing, she heard a soft knock at the door. She assumed it was her mother coming to ask if she needed help. Without looking up from her sorting, she bade her to enter. The door opened and she heard a footstep on the floor. "Mama, would you please hand me that fan on the table? It was given to me by Martín, and I cannot leave it behind."

"You know you can get these for a song at Angra, Gypsy," said her husband in his gruff voice.

She was on her feet in a trice, and had crossed the room into his embrace before he could put the ornate piece down. With the fan still in his hand, he lifted her off of the floor, crushing her against him in a passionate bear hug as she threw her arms around his neck and covered his face with kisses.

"Now *this* is the homecoming I have been dreaming of," he

said between pecks. "I missed you sorely, Gypsy."

"And I missed you," she said, meaning every word.

Martín set her gently back on her feet and held her at arm's length to get a good look at her. "You have not changed a bit. Still the sweet little wife I left a year ago."

"But you," she said, opening her eyes wide. "Why Martín, I have never seen you look so fit!" He had shed the protruding belly of which he had complained during their last argument, and the months of hard physical labor had chiseled his body into the lean, bronzed physique of a man ten years his junior. "And you look happy," she smiled up at him, noticing that the vertical furrow between his eyebrows and the frown lines around his mouth had all but disappeared.

"A man cannot help but be happy when he is busy building a future for his family," he answered.

"Oh, the boys will be so happy to see you!"

"And I will be glad to see them too, but right now I am only interested in the company of my wife," he said meaningfully and pulled her to him for another kiss.

Chapter 11: João

The excitement of Martín's return and the prospect of the trip ahead were almost more than the boys could bear. There was much for their parents to do before they left, and Estêvão and João knew that it was best to give their father a wide berth so not to incur his displeasure. They were given stern warning not to get into any trouble but were basically left to their own devices. This was a heady dose of freedom for two mischievous ten-year-olds, but they were relatively good boys and could be trusted to a certain extent.

One day they decided to go into town to watch the blacksmith work. The local smith was a master armorer and a true artist when it came to weaponry. The massive hulk of a man had big bulging arm muscles, and the force with which he wielded his hammer always left the boys' ears ringing for hours after they left the forge. João had always aspired to the trade and was fascinated by the dichotomy embodied in such a man. He was awestruck by the power it took to pound iron and steel into submission and intrigued by the finesse required to make the intricate filigreed guards for the ornate swords popularly commissioned by the military aristocracy.

They watched him for a few hours then agreed it was time to head for home. They had promised to return well before dark and to ride straight to and from town so not to become easy targets for lurking brigands bent on trouble. They were both excellent riders, so for them to fall prey to a common highwayman would have been rare indeed. They made their way out of town and sped along the road toward the sprawling Del Rio estate.

Estêvão and João galloped up to the gate, and as they

approached, they saw a ragtag group of five local boys attempting to bar their entrance. They looked to be a few years older than the brothers, and the leader was a tall, fat preadolescent with uncombed hair and a permanent scowl on his dirty face. He had a malicious air about him, and João disliked him on sight. Without slackening his pace, he guided his horse directly at the malcontent, forcing the boy to leap to safety at the last minute. He laughed heartily and turned to see if Estêvão had witnessed the drama.

His laughter died out immediately. Estêvão had reined in his mount and was rubbing at his forehead. The young delinquents at the gate were jumping up in down in glee, patting each other on the backs in wild congratulations for the humiliation they had wrought. "El Rey! El Rey!" they chanted derisively in unison.

João turned his horse around and rode over to check on Estêvão. "What happened, Brother? Are you injured?" he asked, the concern written plainly on his face.

Estêvão looked up at him, and João could see an angry red splotch in the middle of his forehead where a welt was beginning to form. There were small pieces of apple in his hair and juice ran down his face in little droplets like tears. "I'm okay," he said, his voice quavering ever so slightly. "It was just an apple. Let's get home so I can wash up."

"No," said João resolutely. "They shall pay for this."

"It was just a prank," Estêvão said, having been through this before. "Besides, we are outnumbered," he pointed out logically.

João shook his head, stubbornly refusing to listen. "My father told me it is my duty to serve and protect you. If you are harmed, it is *my* failing."

"Yes, but fighting is pointless," Estêvão said wearily. "Nothing we could do will make them respect me."

"If they will not give you respect, you must *take* it!"

He dismounted his horse, handed Estêvão the reins, and started back toward the small crowd of urchins, all in one quicksilver movement. As he closed on the group, the largest boy flung an apple directly at João's face intending to leave a mark identical to the red lump now rising on his brother's forehead.

With his catlike reflexes, João snatched the apple out of midair with his left hand and, without ever breaking stride, continued his merciless advance on the instigator. "Good!" he said as he drew up in front of him. "Saves me the trouble of finding out who threw the first one! So, *Gordo*, I guess you're the one who needs a lesson."

The boy winced at the spiteful way João had pointed out his distinctly untoned midsection, and the other children looked at the ground, saying nothing, hoping to avoid his wrath. They sneaked a few covert peeks at the standoff, intensely curious to see what would develop. No one had ever stood up to their leader before.

"It seems to me that there are two options left to you," João said coolly examining the apple in his hand, which he noticed was half rotten and home to a big juicy worm. "You can either apologize to my brother then eat this apple of your own accord, *or* ... you can apologize to my brother and I can *make* you eat the apple. The choice is yours," he finished up, matter-of-factly shrugging his shoulders.

"What are you going to do? Fight all of us?" snickered the chubby bully, confident in his size and the support of his cronies.

"No, just *you*," João replied through his clenched teeth, jabbing his long index finger sharply into Gordo's fleshy chest.

The troublemaker was clearly shocked. Nobody had ever dared to confront him like this. As far as he could remember, he had faced down all comers and reigned supreme over his little band of thugs since he was eight. He was now nearly twelve and must have outweighed this new boy by half. João was tall for his ten years, but he still only came up to the bully's nose, yet there was something unnerving about that calm, black, emotionless stare. Gordo felt a cold finger of doubt beginning to poke at his lower belly.

He thought to get the better of his opponent and struck suddenly, his right arm swinging out in a long, arcing haymaker. It was unexpected but not fast enough to catch the smaller boy off-guard. João ducked easily under the punch, hooked the fat boy's ankle with his foot to throw him off-balance, and gave him a small downward shove to help him to the ground. The fat boy landed face first in the dirt with João's knee squarely in the middle of his back. He flailed his arms in a futile attempt to make contact with any part of his tormentor, but it was useless. As a safety measure, João grabbed a handful of Gordo's tangled hair and yanked back hard.

"Let me go, you son of a whore!" the older boy cried, his voice an equal mixture of anger and terror.

"Oh, Gordo, now there is another big mistake," João said, never losing his composure or his seat. "My mother was a saint, and now you have one more apology to make. Perhaps you should get started before the list gets longer."

Gordo screamed to his cohorts to help him out, but the other boys simply stood there, shuffling their feet, secretly pleased that someone had finally given the bully his just desserts. When he realized he would receive no help from that quarter, he refused to utter another word, biting down firmly on his lower lip.

"Apologize!" João said, jerking back on Gordo's hair for emphasis.

"All right! All right! I'm sorry! Now let me go!"

"What are you sorry for?" João prompted.

"I'm sorry for throwing the apple."

"And ..."

"And for calling your mother a whore."

"Excellent!" exclaimed João. "Now there's just one more little piece of business to attend to, and you can be on your merry way!" He held Gordo's hair in one hand and the rotten part of the apple to his lips with the other. "Bite!" he commanded.

Gordo opened his mouth, now rimmed with dirt, and crunched down on the apple, biting the worm in half. He chewed a few times then began to cry, the tears making salty tracks down his dusty face and the saliva, mixed with apple and pieces of worm, oozing out the corners of his mouth. João made a disgusted face, and giving the older boy's hair one last firm tug, he bent over until he could whisper into Gordo's ear.

"You are lucky I have had such a long day," he hissed cruelly. "Now don't *ever* let me see you out here again!" He let Gordo's head fall into the dust and dropped the remainder of the apple next to him in the dirt. He wiped his hand on his trousers, mounted his horse, and he and Estêvão trotted away.

They rode in silence for a few moments, each of them digesting the significance of what had just happened. Estêvão was both repelled by the violence and exhilarated by the demonstration of his brother's fearless nature. He was pleased that João cared for him enough to risk his own bodily harm and thought to himself that he would never want to be on the receiving end of such humiliation. Suddenly, he laughed out loud, and João joined in.

When they had sobered a bit, Estêvão said, "My mother says that to respond to ruffians of that nature is beneath my honor."

"Some people are not worthy of your honor, I'll give her that, but there are ways to deal with them, and I shall teach you how."

Estêvão nodded in agreement then said, "I'll race you the rest of the way home!" Without even acknowledging his brother's challenge, João kicked his horse into high gear, and the boys flew down the path, feeling full of themselves, confident in the invincibility of their young, healthy bodies. Nothing would ever touch them or break the new bond that had been forged.

Chapter 12: Relocation

At last the long-awaited day of departure arrived. The house was a beehive of activity, and María was having difficulty keeping track of things that needed to be done. She sighed heavily and resigned herself to the idea that she could only do so much. Whatever got left behind could be sent for or replaced. The most important thing was that the family get to their destination intact and healthy. Everything else was inconsequential.

With the wagon fully loaded, they said their goodbyes to the staff and climbed up onto their seats. Emilio and Cassia planned to see them to the dock, and so they all set off, chatting companionably to keep their minds off of the coming separation. María's parents had never been overly demonstrative with their affections, but their feelings ran deep, and this would be the first time María had been away from home. Though she was a mature woman and had been a mother for over ten years, she was their youngest child, and Terceira was a long way away. They would also be bidding farewell to their grandson, who had spent his entire life in their home, and Martín and João, whom they had grown to love as well.

At the dock the workers loaded the boxes and trunks onto the ship, and finally it was time to say goodbye. The boys allowed themselves to be hugged and kissed then excitedly tore up the gangplank, taking positions in the foremost part of the ship so they would miss nothing. They were finally going on the sea voyage to which they had looked forward for over a year. María watched as her husband bid a gruff farewell to his in-laws then stood to one side to wait for his wife. María stepped forward with a rising lump in her throat and hugged her father tightly while he squeezed back and kissed her on the top of her head, telling her how proud he was that she would be building a life of her own. Then she turned to her mother.

Cassia stood holding a handkerchief to her face, blotting carefully at the silent tears that slowly seeped out the corners of her eyes. When her daughter turned to her, all pretense of self-control fell quickly to the wayside. She held out her arms and sobbed openly as María walked into her embrace. The two women stood unspeaking, clasped together in a physical expression of the depth of their love for one another. At last, when Cassia could trust her voice she said, "I'm sorry, Hija, for being such a foolish old woman, but I never thought you would leave us."

"Oh, Mama," María replied, wiping at the pesky tears that she could not suppress. "I am not going so far. There are many ships that make the voyage routinely. There will be plenty of opportunity to visit. Besides, if it does not work out, we will be back."

"Everything will work out fine. Your husband is a hard worker, and he will take supreme care of you and the boys. I have seen that you will be very successful with this venture." Here she sniffled a little and shook her head in an attempt to ward off further tears. "But we will visit. Who knows? Perhaps some day we will follow your example." She hugged her daughter one last time then said, "Go now, Hija. Your future awaits."

María reluctantly loosed her hold and allowed her husband to guide her up the gangway. She situated herself at the rail and looked back at her parents, who now looked very small, standing with their arms about each other's waists. The ship cast off from the dock, and María waved until she could no longer make out their shadowy figures.

She experienced a few minor misgivings and then reprimanded herself for her weakness. Even her mother had complete confidence that this was the proper course of action. Hadn't this been the thing for which she had protested her entire life? She had always thought of herself as a progressive woman.

What sort of example would she make if she quailed at the prospect before her now? Hadn't Queen Isabella turned the tide of war by riding out to the battlefield, *while pregnant*, to deliver supplies to her husband in his hour of desperation? This was simply a relocation and not even close to that heroic deed. Surely she would manage.

She set her mind to the task at hand and resolved to conquer each little trial as it came. She would demonstrate to her family, and everyone else, that a woman could do anything a man could do and still remain the nurturing, feminine presence dictated by tradition. She would disprove those who discriminated against her sex and her heritage and bring honor to all of the spirits crushed under the outmoded constraints imposed by society. She heaved a sigh as she realized this was not just her own journey but also a furtherance of that taken by every woman who had gone before. It was a battle and a giant obligation to her gender and her race, and she would do everything in her power to succeed. She *could* do anything, as long as she had her family by her side.

Chapter 13: Under the Pear Trees

The sun shone down hotly from its place in the late spring sky. A gentle breeze swept the little mesa and shook the pear blossoms loose from their anchorage, setting them floating gently to the earth like small fragrant snowflakes. Inez sat munching on a section of orange, her head cocked to one side, as she listened to Estêvão's mellow voice chronicle the story of his childhood. When he stopped at the family's point of departure from the Del Rio estate, she glanced over at him with a question in her face, her crinkled nose a clear indication of her consternation.

"What is it, Coelhinha?" he asked, recognizing the look.

"Well," she started, not wanting to pry but unable to leave the story unfinished, "I just wondered what happened afterward. You said the piece of property in the deed was a small one, but now the fazenda reaches all the way to the base of the volcano."

"Oh, that is all due to my mother," Estêvão said with clear admiration. "It was only due to her meticulous bookkeeping and innovative vision that the fazenda is the success you see today. She reinvested every *real* of income in the form of seed, tools, livestock, and the neighboring land, and in the beginning we often did without items, which most people think of as necessities. There were no coverings for the windows or floors and only the bare minimum of furniture. And although she made sure we had good boots and warm capes, every other item of clothing was darned over and over again until the fabric wore through. For those first lean years, she worked all day and sewed every evening and did not buy herself one new item until we all had all that we needed.

"But things eventually began to look up. The ranch reaped

massive profits, and my mother slowly turned the house into the comfortable home that you see now. It's true that we are well off, but it was hard work, and without her none of it would have ever happened."

He went on to explain that his Uncle Manuel also kept his promise to look after his sister-in-law and nephew and the faithful bodyguard who had done so much to protect his brother and his own person. A few years after the family arrived on Terceira, King João's only legitimate son died, and Manuel was named heir to the Portuguese throne. He assumed the position in 1485, and renewed his offer of assistance soon after. María respectfully declined, stating that now that the fazenda was turning a handsome profit, they lacked for nothing. She did ask that when there arose an opportunity on any future official exploration, if he would kindly remember the two brothers, they would be forever grateful. The boys had always dreamt of a life at sea, and in 1497 when they were sixteen, that dream was realized when they set sail with Vasco da Gama for India.

It was during that voyage that the moniker 'El Rey' began to define Estêvão's person. Being a formally sanctioned expedition of Manuel I, the crew was essentially Portuguese. Although Estêvão bore a Portuguese name, and his father had been their own countryman, the crew teased him relentlessly about his half-Castilian origins. Instead of translating his nickname into the Portuguese version, *O Rei*, they left it as it was in an attempt to alienate him and incite him to anger. João suggested that any time they used the name as an insult his brother should favor each of his antagonists with a good solid punch in the mouth, but Estêvão had another solution.

Because he had had his lesson in humiliation early on, he was able to resist the temptation to strike out at those around him. He remembered what his mother had told him that day when he was eight. The best way to win people over was to work hard and prove them wrong, so that is just what he did. He did more than his fair share of hard work. He learned every job on deck, down to the most menial. He took extra turns at the wheel, and something began to happen that his crewmates did not anticipate. In addition to picking up the knowledge of life at sea more rapidly than he would have ordinarily done, he made himself an invaluable person to have on board. He saw things with a fresh perspective, and so he came up with new and inventive ideas on the efficient management of a vessel. He used his God-given talents of his singing voice and story-telling ability to entertain the men and alleviate homesickness. He resolved disputes with his objective and fair-minded point of view. He slowly won the admiration of the crew, and eventually they called him El Rey as a title of respect.

"The first part of that voyage was sheer torture," Estêvão smiled, shaking his head at the memory. "But a few years later when I purchased the *María Vencedora,* I had no trouble manning her for her maiden voyage."

"And that is when I met you," Inez said, remembering the night she'd first laid eyes on him and fallen in love.

"Well, a few years later," he smiled at her, "but basically, yes."

"I understand your fascination with the sea. I was quite taken with it myself, but a man cannot stay away from home forever."

"You are right. Lately I have been thinking that it's time I considered settling into family life."

A little thrill ran through her, and Inez stretched out her legs to quell the excitement rising inside. She had known all along that this was the reason he had invited her family out here to meet his. The proposal could not be long in coming. She was so happy.

"Looks like it's about time to head back," Estêvão said, raising his head to check the position of the sun. He pushed himself up to standing and extended his hand to help her up. "We don't want your parents to think I kidnapped you," he said with a grin.

Inez returned his smile and let him pull her up beside him. They then began to pack the remains of their picnic in the bag and folded the blanket between them. When they had done, Estêvão whistled to Tesouro and replaced the bridles he had removed earlier. He secured the blanket behind his saddle and slung the sack over his shoulder. He wound the little mare's reins around her pommel once to keep her still while Inez mounted, then he held his hands together in a makeshift stirrup to give Inez a boost up. Inez grasped the leather knob and stepped into Estêvão's hand. As she began to lift her other leg off the ground, the mare shied to the right. Inez lost her grip on the saddle, slid down the equine's sleek belly, and somehow wound up on the ground. Estêvão quickly caught Inez's hand and jerked her up out of range of the horse's sharp hooves. As she fell against him, he found himself looking down into her laughing face, her open mouth just inches from his own. Her sweet breath smelled faintly of the watered wine and the oranges she had just finished eating. The scent of the falling pear blossoms mixed with that of her perfume and wafted up to his nostrils in an intoxicating fusion of sweetness and sensuality. She stopped laughing, but the golden lights in her silver eyes still swirled and danced, hypnotizing him ever so slightly. He broke her gaze, and this time his eyes strayed to her full bottom lip, plump and moist and the delicate pinky-mauve of the hydrangeas so prevalent on the island. His right hand found its way up to cup her jawline, and he ran his thumb along the downy softness of her cheek. His other hand fingered a loose tress of her hair, which had escaped from the thick coppery braid hanging down her back. He bent his head down and drew her chin up, fully intending to cover her lips with his own. He took in the warmth of her exhale, their two breaths commingling as one.

He caught himself just in time. What was he doing? He was appalled at his behavior and repelled by the feelings she evoked in him, feelings he could only describe as lust. Was he really about to take advantage of this fourteen-year-old girl with whose welfare her parents had charged him? He was supposed to be a gentleman, not some uncouth teenager overrun by his hormones and pressing his affections on an innocent young girl who looked up to him. What was he thinking? He had not been thinking, and *that* was the problem.

He turned her chin to the side and pretended to remove

something from behind her ear. "There," he said lamely. "You had a leaf in your hair." He then put her firmly from him and asked, "Are you all right? I thought you had been hurt."

"I'm not hurt," Inez answered, a bit confused, wondering what had just happened. She was sure he had been about to deliver her first kiss. What had she done wrong?

"Good. Your parents trusted me to keep you safe. I wouldn't want to disappoint them. Let's get back before they start to worry."

Ah, there it is, she thought to herself. He did not want to abuse her parents' confidence. No matter. There was time.

She mounted her horse, and he mounted his, and soon they were galloping back toward the house, each going over what had just happened. They both made their resolutions to wait but for completely different reasons.

Chapter 14: Departure

During the ride back to the house, Estêvão was desperate to come up with a way to avoid Inez or at least not to be alone with her for the remaining two days of the García family's vacation. He was having difficulty coming to terms with his feelings for her. It was an awkward place for him. He could not decide if he regarded her as woman or child, if he felt protective or desirous of her person. He needed time to himself and a quiet place to examine the situation and sort things out.

When they arrived at the stables, Inez went to play with Palhaço. Estêvão made an excuse and headed directly to the house, mumbling about some matter he had left unattended. To his surprise when he got to his room, there was a letter waiting for him. He inspected the seal and saw that it was from his uncle, King Manuel. He read the letter and let out a huge sigh of relief. His uncle was summoning him to court on a matter of some importance. Manuel requested his nephew's presence at the earliest possible instant.

Estêvão dispatched a message to his crew to ready the ship for departure, but he said nothing to anyone at the house except João. He needed to distance himself from the situation with Inez and did not want to confuse things with a sad and protracted goodbye. He would leave late tonight and make his excuses in the form of a letter. Typically he would never resort to such boorish behavior, but he did not feel like himself due to the conflict raging inside. He consoled himself by reasoning that the quicker he figured this out, the quicker he would return to normal, and that would be best for all the parties involved.

That evening at supper, Estêvão uncharacteristically steered clear of any direct contact with Inez. Any time she attempted to engage him in conversation, he uttered a terse, distracted response and avoided her inquiring gaze. His behavior bordered on rude, and María wondered what had happened to make him act this way. Inez soon got the idea and stopped trying to attract his attention. Though it was painful to experience, she thought perhaps she was making more of it than she should. Maybe he had some important matter on his mind. He might even be thinking about how to best manage the proposal.

Joanna was extremely excited and talked nonstop about the trip out to the site of the vineyard. They had nothing but positive things to say about María's brother, Don Francisco, and his handsome young son, Christophe. Both of the men had been very polite and very knowledgeable, and they knew their business so well that this venture could not help but thrive. Though it had made for a long and tiring day, it had been well worth the effort. Joanna thanked Estêvão sincerely for having thought of her husband when considering investors, and she suggested a toast to celebrate the partnership.

"Here's to the beginning of a successful relationship. May our families be united as one, and may the union bring happiness and prosperity to us all."

Everyone at the table heartily cheered their approval, and Inez's spirits soared to note that Estêvão also joined in the revelry. She knew her reasoning could not be far off the mark.

The next morning at breakfast, Inez noticed that the two places where João and Estêvão usually sat were unoccupied. She did not think much of it. There had been several occasions when they missed a meal because they had business obligations. She continued eating, only half paying attention to the conversations taking place around her. She was buttering her second roll when she heard Dom Martín make an off-hand comment about the brothers. She tuned in to what he was saying as she chewed the bite she had just taken.

"This is not unusual," their big host said. "King Manuel has always kept an eye out for the boys. He does throw them some prime assignments, but he knows they are both extremely hard workers and will always succeed."

"What is this latest mission?" Iñigo asked with enthusiasm.

"I don't know. João was very vague when they left last night. I don't think even Estêvão was given advanced knowledge. Sometimes these summonses from Manuel can be very hush-hush. There's always the threat that the messenger will be intercepted. They probably won't get the full story until they arrive at court."

Inez stopped in mid-chew and swallowed her mouthful of bread. "They left last night? For Portugal?" she asked in panicky voice.

Dom Martín nodded in confirmation. "But don't you worry, Senhorita Inez. I will escort you on your ride today. There are some young calves out in the fields that are just beginning to find their legs, and they are very entertaining to watch."

Inez nodded her head slowly and tried to muster a convincing smile, but her heart was not in it, and the corner of her mouth trembled threateningly. Serafina grasped her hand under the table in a gesture of sympathy, and Inez turned to her sister with a look of gratitude, fighting the urge to break down and cry. María was the only person at the table to witness the exchange.

"My son did leave a letter apologizing for his unceremonious departure," María said kindly. "You may read it if you like."

Inez nodded her head, a look of hope leaping into her eyes. Perhaps he had left a special goodbye to her or a mention of something shared exclusively by the two of them. Even if it were just a general farewell, she at least would know he had thought of her at all.

After breakfast, María produced the letter for Inez to analyze. Inez scanned it eagerly, looking for any sign that Estêvão had spared her the least consideration. She went through it line by line, interpreting each word, looking for the smallest indication that she had occupied any place in his mind or heart while he'd been preparing to set sail. Finding none, she sighed bereftly and handed the note back to María.

"You may keep it if you wish, Mynah," the older woman said gently. "Sometimes the most trivial things can make us feel closer to the ones we love."

"Thank you, Dona María," she said. She folded the piece of paper and sadly tucked it into her bosom.

María sensed the despondency in the gesture and could not tolerate the fact that her own son's thoughtlessness had contributed to it. She felt moved to assuage, at least in part, the girl's heartache, so she reached out and patted her forearm in a token of understanding. "You know, when I was married to Estêvão's father, he frequently had to leave at a moment's notice. Often times he would wait until the last second to tell me in hopes that the parting would not become a long, drawn-out affair. I think men simply want to spare us any sorrow and, in doing so, overlook a woman's strength. But you and I know we can bear much more than they imagine."

What she said made much sense. Inez contemplated this bit of wisdom and accepted it as a compliment. After all, Dona María had just categorized the two of them as strong women. She had also made the comparison of Inez and Estêvão to the marriage she'd shared with his father. Inez decided that she was acting immature and chastised herself for her childish behavior. Estêvão could hardly keep the King of Portugal waiting simply because he had to bid farewell to his guests. She determined to bear this little upset like the strong woman Dona María knew she had inside and look forward to his return instead.

"Thank you, Dona María," Inez said with a smile. "You always know just the right thing to say." She excused herself to get ready for the ride out to visit the calves.

María looked after her with a sense of dread. What had her son gotten himself into? She was genuinely fond of the girl and could see the potential within. It was too bad she was so young. Every woman was destined to suffer some form of heartbreak during her lifetime, but it was especially devastating when it happened so early. She said a little prayer that things would work out all right.

For the remainder of the day, Inez was her normal cheerful self, and she enjoyed the last bit of her time on Terceira. After looking at the situation with Estêvão with a different perspective, her only sadness was the fact that she would be leaving Palhaço behind. She spent extra time with the little hairy dog and tried to console herself that she would soon return to be with him permanently. She knew that if she moped, he would sense her unhappiness. She did not want to cause him undue distress, so she tried to forget the coming separation and take pleasure in the time they had left together. It occurred to her that perhaps this is what Estêvão had felt before his trip, and hope sprang back into her heart, and her spirit soared.

Finally, the day arrived for their departure and the García family's belongings were loaded onto the wagon for the ride down to the harbor. María's brother, Don Francisco, was heading back to his vineyard in Soutomaior. Before he'd gone, Estêvão had made arrangements with his uncle to carry the family back to Vigo as the town was on the way. Dona María and Dom Martín forwent their daily responsibilities to see the family to the ship, and now it was time for all to take their seats so they could begin the ride into Angra.

That morning Inez had not been able to work up the courage to visit Palhaço for the last time, and now she sat in the back of the wagon trying not to cry for the loss of her furry companion. She lowered her head to her knees attempting to hide the signs of her grief as she felt the wagon start forward with a jolt. She felt the tingle inside her nose and the prickle in the corners of her eyes that signified that tears were not far behind, and she scrunched up her face in an effort to hold her emotions in check.

Suddenly, there was a shouting behind the wagon, and she looked up to see what was happening. She saw Fausto come around the corner of the house, waving his one free hand in a bid to stop the wagon. In his other hand he held the end of a taut leather lead. At the front end of the strap, Palhaço pulled and strained with every ounce of strength in his small shaggy body, dragging his human anchor behind him. When he saw Inez, he let out a loud, "Roo-roo-roo!" and redoubled his exertions, his front legs rising off the ground and pawing the air ferociously. Inez yelled for Dom Martín to stop the wagon and jumped out the back, meeting the bouncing bundle of fur halfway and dropping to her knees to hug him. Palhaço jumped up and down on his hind legs, licking her cheeks and chin as the tears streamed unchecked down her laughing face.

"Oh, my little clown dog, I could not bear to say goodbye," she sobbed between his enthusiastic wet kisses.

"Capitán Rey left specific instructions for the dog to go with you, Senhorita Inez," Fausto said, breathing hard from the struggle. "He said that the little dog would not be happy without you."

"Nor I without him," Inez agreed, sniffling.

Her father approached from behind her, and the canine barked a cheerful greeting. "What's going on, Mynah?" he asked, his concern written plainly on his face.

"Oh, Papa," she began, looking up at him. "Estêvão left orders that Palhaço should come home with me. Please, Papa, please may I keep him?"

Iñigo heard the urgency in her voice, saw it unmistakably in her eyes, and he immediately sensed how important this was to her. Normally he would have sought his wife's approval before giving his own—this would be one of those things which would most likely cause friction in his marriage—but this time he did not care. He did not have the heart to refuse his daughter her earnest and not unreasonable request. Besides, the little dog was very cute. Perhaps Joanna would not object too much.

"Yes, Mynah, you may bring him home with us, but remember that he is your responsibility. You will have to look after him, feed him, and keep him out of trouble," he added, thinking of his wife's limited patience.

"Oh, Papa, I will. I will do all of that," and she stood up to squeeze him tightly while the small hairy dog bounced boisterously around the two of them. "Thank you, Papa. Thank you so much."

"You are welcome. Now get your dog, and let's get moving. We have kept everyone waiting long enough."

Inez nodded her head and wiped the tears from her face. She turned to Fausto to thank him then led the puppy the rest of the way to the wagon. They took their seats and resumed the ride to the harbor. She heard her mother say something in a harsh whisper to her father, but he shushed his wife, and surprisingly that was the end of it.

Inez sat overjoyed in her seat with Palhaço held firmly in her arms. He eventually settled down next to her with his head resting warmly in her lap, only raising it now and then when they came to a rough patch of road. The gentle pressure of the furry head on her leg was comforting, and she smoothed the silky tan curls back away from his face while he looked up at her adoringly. Her heart overflowed with love for the little animal, and she allowed her mind to mull over the meaning behind the gift.

If Estêvão had thought to send the puppy with her, then she *had* been in his mind before he left. Also, there had been a few times when Inez sensed that he'd expressed his feelings vicariously through the little dog. Could that have been what he'd meant when he'd told the stable hand that *Palhaço* would not be happy without her? It was entirely possible and she believed it to be so. She had never been so happy in her life. Now all that remained was to go home and wait for her beloved to declare himself.

At the harbor the García family thanked their hosts for their hospitality and offered to reciprocate at any time. They bid them a fond farewell, saying that they hoped to return someday in the not too distant future, while Palhaço bounced around the entire group. Dom Martín shook hands with Iñigo, slapping him on the back with his large bear paw and rattling his teeth one final time. María hugged Joanna and Serafina then turned to Inez with a special smile.

"Well, Mynah," she began, taking the girl's hand warmly in her own, "it has been a pleasure getting to know you. I have become very fond of you, and I see clearly why my son holds you in such high regard."

"Yes, well, you set a lofty standard," Inez answered, beaming with the praise. "I only hope that one day I can live up to it."

"You will do just fine," María said and pulled the girl close. "Have a safe trip, and I will see you soon."

"Thank you, Dona María," Inez whispered with emotion, "for everything."

With that, the family boarded the waiting ship with the dog in tow then turned back and waved until they pulled away from the dock. María and Martín walked hand in hand back to the wagon, and the Garcías were greeted by their benefactor.

"Don Francisco," Iñigo said. "It is a pleasure to see you again. I'd like to thank you for your generosity. We appreciate it to no end."

"It is nothing," said the dapper man, waving his hand. "Vigo is on our way, and I am in no rush."

Don Francisco was a male version of his sister. He was of medium height with a slender frame, and he moved with the same graceful confidence of the physically adept. The black-brown hair and flashing intelligent eyes gave away his Gyspy heritage, and his voice had the same cultured intonation as his sibling.

"You remember my wife, Joanna," Iñigo said, presenting his family. "And these are my two daughters, Serafina and Inez."

"Ah, Señor García, you have been blessed to be surrounded by so much beauty," Don Francisco said suavely. Joanna giggled behind her hand, and Serafina blushed prettily.

"Where is your handsome son?" Joanna asked.

"Christophe has stayed behind to supervise the work to be done before the vineyard can be started in earnest. I'm sure he will be very disappointed to learn he has missed out on such attractive company."

"Isn't he a little young to be overseeing such an intricate

operation?" Iñigo asked, having acquired enough knowledge to understand the specifics.

"He is sixteen. I suppose that is young, but he has grown up in the vineyard at Soutomaior, and he knows every detail. He is also a very hard worker and can make sure things get done correctly. The men all respect him a great deal," the man said with evident pride. "Now, let me show you to your quarters," and he indicated that they should follow.

The trip back to Vigo was tinged with melancholy. The García family would be returning to the mundane everyday existence they had lived before taking their exciting vacation to the previously unknown land. The voyage did not hold the excitement of that first expedition by sea, but the family soon found ways to keep from getting bored. Iñigo lent a helping hand on deck, Joanna was charming and maintained a good humor for most of the trip, and to everyone's surprise, Serafina spent more time above board and, as a result, did not suffer as acutely from the seasickness that had plagued her during her first trip across the Atlantic.

Inez kept herself busy with her dog. They found ways to stay out from under foot, and although Palhaço did not possess the same confidence on a ship as his sire, he loved Inez so much that he would tolerate anything to be near her. They did not play the energetic games of fetch that had passed the time so well on the journey to Terceira, but it was enough for them to sit quietly and watch the ocean speed by, simply enjoying the companionship each had to offer the other.

At mealtimes the family shared the company of Don Francisco, who was as excited about this joint venture as Joanna and Iñigo. He had spent his life becoming a successful vintner with his current home base at Soutomaior. The town was about twelve miles inland of Vigo, and its location had been part of the original circumstances that brought Estêvão into their lives.

"I travel routinely to France, Belgium, and Italy," he explained one evening at supper, "but I have never attempted to raise grapes in such proximity to the ocean. The soil is fertile and the climate is right, but the salt carried inland by the winds will be a major challenge." Here he smiled then went on with evident pride in his son, "If there is a way to make it work, Christophe will find it!"

The days passed quickly, and soon the rocky blue outline of the mainland could be seen in the distance. The family had enjoyed their little getaway, but now it was over and home life loomed before them. It was time to return to the everyday grind, but that familiarity did have its benefits. Iñigo craved the excitement provided by the demanding pace of his mercantile, Joanna longed to resume control of her own household again, and Serafina yearned for a break from the constant pressure of perpetuating the illusion of her gracious perfection.

Inez was the only one indifferent to their homecoming. Her head was filled with dreams of revisiting the peaceful life that the Fazenda da Pomba had to offer and making it her permanent home. To her it did not matter how she spent this last, temporary period of waiting at her childhood residence. It would be only a short while before Estêvão came to claim her as his bride, and then she would be leaving for good. In the meantime, she had Palhaço to keep her company, a reminder of her beloved's promise. Everything else was unimportant. Soon her life would be complete.

Chapter 15: Back in Vigo

It took no time at all for the García family to fall back into the rhythm of home life. Iñigo found that as soon as he stepped foot into his mercantile, he realized how much he had missed it. Though the month-long hiatus and the hopeful dreaming about the new vineyard on Terceira had been a pleasant diversion and it seemed like a sound investment, he wondered now if he would ever really be able to get the trade business out of his blood. It had been a part of his family tradition for generations and seemed as synonymous with his identity as his name. He was still relatively young and enjoyed the robust health of a man half his age. He could imagine himself doing the same type of work well into his sixties like Dom Martín. Joanna was always after him to slow down and take better care of himself, but he had made a good job of it so far. Only time would tell.

Joanna was happy to again be in charge of her own home. The Fazenda da Pomba had been as well-run a household as she had ever visited, but that was just it. She had been a visitor. There had been little things here and there that she would have liked to change to suit her own personal tastes, but she had been there in a guest capacity. It would have been exceedingly rude for her to suggest anything directly to the staff. Instead she kept her opinion to herself and looked forward to her return home. Although the vacation had done her well and she had loosened up considerably—her staff noticed the change and jumped to oblige her in hopes that this new mood would persist—she still liked to give orders as she saw fit and have them followed exactly. Like her husband, she felt that her work ethic had served her well up to now. Why bother to change it?

The girls were the ones most affected by their time away from home. It seemed that a reversal had occurred in their attitudes. Serafina had been so inspired by Dona María's forward thinking that she now spent much of her time trying to inventory her God-given gifts and come up with a way to put them to work for herself and others. She attempted to evaluate the depth of her natural talents in a sort of self-appraisal, but she had not been raised in a progressive, encouraging atmosphere like that of the Del Rio household. She tried again and again to put a value on her self-worth, but lacking guidance and someone by which to gauge it, she found herself coming up short. She grew frustrated and unsatisfied and longed to be back under Dona María's extremely able tutelage. She knew there was something more out there for her than just becoming a wife and mother. She just needed to figure out how to achieve it.

Whereas before the trip Serafina was the one most likely to idle away her time—daydreaming about the man who would soon appear to whisk her away to a new, romantic life, fulfilling all of her childhood aspirations—now it was Inez who could not keep her mind off of her future husband. The exciting memories of Terceira were still too fresh in her mind to give way to the more commonplace realities of her everyday existence. She had her duties at the mercantile, but often she found herself making mistakes, or her mind wandered away from the paperwork before her. She also now had Palhaço.

Many times she had taken the little dog with her to keep her company while she worked. He was very well behaved, and for the most part he sat quietly chewing a bone or sleeping while she organized her receipts. Sometimes though, he did something cute or just his presence reminded her that he was a symbol of Estêvão's affection, and that would be the end of her concentration. Iñigo noticed but did not mind. Don Pedro's son had decided that he liked the extra income so he stayed on, and Inez found herself spending more and more of her time at home. After all, she was still only fourteen. She should be enjoying her youth not spending it slaving away behind a desk.

The moment Inez set foot back in her childhood home she made her way to her room and placed Estêvão's letter of departure in her maple box with her other treasures. She also returned her vial of pear blossom perfume to its place. It had served her well. There was very little left, and she decided to save it for the time when she would be reunited with her beloved for good. She also found herself falling into the same routine she had established before Estêvão had returned from Ceuta. Every morning she and Palhaço made the pilgrimage to the olive tree on the knoll and scoured the harbor below. She looked for the *María Vencedora* and her blue falcon banner because if *she* were there, Estêvão would be coming to Inez in person. In all reality, *any* of the ships down in the port of Vigo could be carrying the proposal. All Inez had to do was wait.

One day in June after returning from their morning lookout, Inez and Palhaço made their way to the kitchen. The long heart-to-heart conversations with Paulina were one of the things Inez had missed most during the time she had been away. Things had been so hectic since the family's return she had not found an opportunity to share the latest news with the older woman, and she sought her out now. Inez pulled a chair up to the big center table and dropped little trimmings of meat to the puppy at her feet while Paulina chopped some carrots for that evening's supper.

There had been a time when Joanna had strictly forbidden the little dog's presence inside the house. She had banished him to the stables, assuming that because he'd been a whelp in similar accommodations, the familiarity would soothe him and ease his transition. She had not realized the strength of his attachment to Inez.

That first night after everyone went to bed, there began a scratching at the kitchen door. Joanna had raised two daughters and reasoned that, like a child, as soon as the little dog realized that he would not get his way, he would return to his nest and go to sleep. The scratching persisted and gradually grew louder. Then it stopped. Joanna smiled to herself in the dark, satisfied that her logic was sound. She had almost drifted off to sleep when the howling began.

She thought that the noise would soon lessen and employed the same method of ignoring Palhaço's attempts to get into the house. Instead of fading though, the howls grew in volume until they resembled those of a full-grown wolf, baying from a place next to her very bed. She tried to put her pillow over her head, and stop her ears with her fingers, but it was no use. The dog awakened everyone in the house, and finally even Iñigo stirred from his sound slumber beside her.

"What is that noise?" he asked, sleepily blinking his eyes.

"It is your daughter's *cute little* dog," she retorted nastily. When something was amiss, Inez was always his daughter.

Iñigo listened for a moment as if to verify the truth of his wife's words. He then turned to her and said, "I don't see why you will not allow him into the house, Reina. He is a small scrap of a dog. He could not possibly make enough mess to matter. Besides, at least we'd all be able to sleep."

"Fine then, but *you* go tell her," Joanna said testily and threw herself back into a recumbent position.

"Ay, mi reina," Iñigo said, kissing his pouting wife on the cheek and getting out of bed, "you always know best." He left the room to tell Inez that Palhaço could sleep in her room, and everyone had a peaceful night's rest.

The next morning Joanna handed Inez a few old blankets and said they would make a nice warm bed for the puppy. She told her daughter that the dog could stay in her room but not on her bed. She did not want the expensive bed linens to be ruined by Palhaço's dirty fur or his sharp nails. Inez nodded her agreement, kissed and hugged her mother enthusiastically, and promised to obey the rules. And although sometimes *she* slipped out of bed to sleep on the floor with the puppy, she never broke her vow to her mother.

Joanna soon came to accept the little dog as part of the family. She reluctantly admitted that he was extraordinarily smart, and she even made the comment that sometimes he looked like a little man in a dog suit when he listened to the conversations going on around him, his lively brown eyes passing from one speaker to the next. He stayed out from under foot, he never begged for food from the table, he never made a mess in the house, and he was *very* cute. Eventually she grew fond of him and occasionally patted him on the head and told him he was a good boy.

Paulina developed a soft spot for the dog as well. Once she got past her aversion to having a furred creature in close proximity to food preparations, she rarely even noticed his presence. He usually found his place at the foot of whichever chair Inez chose to sit in then made himself inconspicuous, satisfied just to be near the object of his affection. Paulina had even gotten into the habit of leaving extra morsels of meat on the bones and scraps, which she put aside for the scruffy little creature. She smiled down at him now while he gnawed away at one with gusto.

"I never had a pet when I was growing up," she began, regarding the canine while he pulled at a piece of sinew held fast to the bone between his curly front paws. "I am only now coming to appreciate what good companions they make."

Inez grinned and said, "Yes, Palhaço always listens to what I have to say, no matter how banal, and he never interrupts me. He is the *best* companion."

"I'll bet he kept you from being bored while you were on vacation."

"I could have never been bored on Terceira," Inez said excitedly. "Oh, Paulina, I have so much to tell you."

Paulina chuckled to herself as Inez launched into a detailed account of her voyage from the hour she left the snug García home to the moment of her return. She left out nothing as she animatedly chattered on like the mynah after which she had been named. Where she had been somewhat guarded with others about expressing her feelings for Estêvão, with Paulina she was candid and her words flowed free. The quiet intelligent housekeeper had known of the infatuation from the very beginning, and Inez trusted her implicitly and valued her opinion.

"And so now I am merely waiting for him to come declare himself or send someone with his proposal," Inez finished up, her eyes sparkling with anticipation.

"Perhaps you should not take this proposal for granted, Baixinha," Paulina said with a cautioning tone. "You could be interpreting his fondness for you as something more. Even if he *is* romantically inclined, there are often other considerations that factor into an offer of marriage, especially with his relationship to the court," here she hesitated, not wanting to completely extinguish Inez's high hopes, "and you are very young."

"I am nearly fifteen," Inez said, drawing herself up with as much dignity as she could muster. "Our own Princess Catalina of Aragon was only fifteen when she wed Prince Arthur of England."

"Two weeks after which she turned sixteen. And that union was never consummated." Paulina saw the muscles in Inez's jaw twitch and a stubborn look come into her face. She patted the girl's hand and said gently, "There is a vast disparity between almost fifteen and nearly sixteen. Sixteen months makes a world of difference at your age, particularly when a man needs to get an heir."

"Yes, but he promised me," Inez said petulantly, "and I know he is a man of his word."

A poignant smile spread across Paulina's lips at the girl's childish reaction. She remembered what it was like to be so in love only to have her entire world come crashing down. It had nearly been the end of her. She could not bear for it to happen to Inez. "Sometimes outside circumstances can cause even a man of his word to break his promise," she said insistently. "I just don't want you to set your heart on this, Baixinha. Many things can happen to alter a man's intentions."

"Not Estêvão," Inez said, her faith in him completely unshaken. "He will come."

Chapter 16: The Decision

While Inez was having her heartfelt conversation with Paulina about Estêvão's prospective marriage proposal, a very different discussion was taking place in the parlor of the Fazenda da Pomba. Estêvão and João had returned from their summons to the Portuguese court and were now relating the visit to their parents. María stitched on a piece of needlework while Dom Martín smoked his pipe. In a corner João slouched bonelessly in a heavy oaken chair with its front legs off the floor, lazily cutting an apple into slices with a deadly looking pocketknife. Estêvão filled their parents in with information about the current state of the crown and the proposition Manuel had laid before them.

"My royal uncle says that some of the explorers currently stationed in India are becoming restless," he recounted as he paced the floor. "He has received communications that a small group of them wish to set out in search of the land to the east. Rumors have said that it abounds with riches never before imagined, and Manuel wishes to be the first to befriend this new country and establish a trade relationship that will be mutually beneficial for both parties."

"Beneficial for both parties," grunted Dom Martín. "I can't believe I ever doubted that the boy had the makings of a suitable duke. He certainly turned out to be a shrewd ruler," he said with grudging admiration.

María smiled at her husband's cynical attitude. Never looking up from her embroidery she asked, "So why did he call you two to court?"

"He wanted to know if João and I cared to make the trip out

to join them," her son answered.

"And what did you respond?" she prompted, beginning to feel that he was hiding something.

Estêvão took a deep breath and reluctantly pronounced his decision. "I told him that João could command my ship and crew if he wished to go, but I am planning to marry and begin a family, so I must respectfully decline."

"Are you out of your mind, boy?" Dom Martín blurted out. "Do you understand the magnitude of the opportunity you are giving up?"

Estêvão fixed his stepfather gravely with his dark eyes that were so much like those of the deceased duke and nodded. "I do," he said solemnly then continued. "Although my uncle assures me that nothing much would change in the event of my death, I worry that everything you and my mother have worked so hard to achieve would be forfeit if I do not leave an heir. Since we cannot rely on João to produce a *legitimate* son, the entire estate would be bombarded by claims from innumerable women of questionable origins and intentions, asserting that their offspring were entitled to a fair portion. Many of their claims would be valid, and we would be hard-pressed to keep the fazenda together as a cohesive unit."

"Even if no such claims came forth, João would probably lose the entire ranch in a poker game," María remarked truthfully. "No offense. You know I love you, João," she said, casting her gaze in his direction, "but you are profligate." He shrugged his shoulders and continued to munch his apple in a placid manner, completely unaffected by his stepmother's honest observation.

"So what will you do?" asked Dom Martín.

"I will forgo this expedition and marry at the first possible juncture."

"Brother, you are an incurable romantic," João interjected sarcastically from his seat in the corner. "What about the courtship? You can't just jump into a relationship because you deign to do so. These things take time, you know," he finished up innocently with a wicked gleam in his black eyes.

Estêvão shot his sibling a murderous look. María was used to these little spats between the brothers and knew exactly how to defuse them. "Although João lacks diplomacy, he has a point. As far as I know, you have not expressed an interest in a female of marriageable age," she said carefully.

"What is your opinion of the García girls?" Estêvão asked a little too casually.

João burst out in guffaws of laughter from his place in the corner and would have tipped the chair over backward had it not been braced against the wall. Estêvão colored immediately, but attempting to maintain his façade of composure, he restrained himself from striding over to throttle his brother. Instead he ignored João's bad manners and waited for a reaction from his mother.

"Well," she began thoughtfully, "the girls are certainly intelligent and have excellent manners. Their mother has claim to a noble English lineage, and their father is a very successful, hardworking type. I heard something about a Jewish background, but with my Gypsy blood, who am I to even mention it?" she smiled self-deprecatingly. "Which one were you considering?"

"I hoped you would all help me with that decision."

"There he goes again, losing himself to his passion," came the inevitable derision from the corner.

"João, I don't think you're helping the situation," María said in an effort to silence him. "Perhaps you have some useful commentary."

"My only useful comment would be for my brother not to complicate his life with matrimony, but I don't think that's what you mean." João paused for a moment, tapping his forehead with his index finger. "Hmm. Well the older one is unquestionably beautiful, but she strikes me as a little contrived."

"She is a beauty," agreed Dom Martín.

"And she is not as contrived as she first appears," added María. "I have held conversations with her away from her mother, and she seems much more natural and very willing to please. I think with some guidance she could become a very accommodating partner. She is also much more intelligent than she lets on."

"But not as intelligent as Inez," Estêvão said with a look in his eyes that bordered on dreamy.

"No, not as intelligent as Inez," María agreed. She knew her son believed himself to be in love with the younger of the two sisters, but Inez was only fourteen. Estêvão was sensitive about his feelings for the girl. María would not dream of exposing him to his brother's ridicule. This issue would have to be brought up in private. She would let the family debate continue for now, but she resolved to speak to her son confidentially afterward.

"And besides being more intelligent, the little one certainly can cook," João said. Then with a confused expression on his face he added, "I'll still never understand why my dessert looked so funny that night, but it was delicious." He shook his head and continued with a wolfish grin, "She also shows promise of future talents."

"That's enough, boy," Dom Martín growled dangerously. João could push a saint to violence and was now testing the patience of the entire family.

"I think what João is *trying* to say is that Inez has a body shape more conducive to childbearing," María said.

"Yes, that's *exactly* what I meant," he nodded energetically, adopting her explanation as his own.

"It is true," Dom Martín added. "Out in the field sometimes the narrow-hipped cows have a devil of a time trying to calve. I had to put a few of them down before I learned they were no good for breeding. Lost the cows *and* the calves. What a waste."

"Well, you have all given me much to think about," Estêvão said, tired of the banter and disappointed that he had not heard a definitive confirmation of his own thoughts. His family had all made some valid points that had not occurred to him, but no obvious course of action had been revealed. He was just as confused as he'd been before the conversation. He would have to weigh all of the information and come to his own conclusion. A decision would have to be made very soon.

A short time later, Estêvão was in his study going through a stack of business papers that had accumulated during his trip to the mainland. There was a knock at his door, and he absently gave permission to enter. His mother came in, closed the door behind her, and made her way to the table, setting down a tray of tea and cookies. He looked up from his work and smiled as the neat little woman dragged a chair over and sat down. He leaned back in his seat and stretched out his legs while María poured out two cups of tea.

They said nothing for a few moments, simply enjoying each other's company and the comforting warmth emanating from the cups in their hands. Estêvão took a bite from one of the cookies then sipped some of the steaming liquid to wash it down. He set his cup back on the table and regarded the remarkable woman at his side. How could this small, gentle female have been so strong and accomplished so much? She never ceased to amaze him.

"Well, Mother, what is on your mind?" he asked, sensing her need to more thoroughly examine his proposition in private.

"I came to find out what you intend to do," she said without preamble.

"That is a good question," he said, nodding his head. "I thought the family discussion would help, but things were mentioned that I had not even thought of and it confused me all the more."

"Well this is not a group decision. This is something you have to determine on your own. You will be the one who has to live with the result."

"Yes, but I value your opinion, and perhaps hearing it would help things to fall into place. What do *you* suggest?"

"First, you need to be honest with yourself about your feelings before you can make any choice at all." He opened his mouth to object, but she held up her hand to silence him. "There is no need for you to pretend with your mother," she said gently. "You are a part of my flesh, and I know you as I know myself. I fear when you are in danger. I suffer when you are distraught. I rejoice when you are happy. I will support you whatever you decide, but I want you to choose well."

Estêvão looked up at her, the unshed tears in his hazel-green eyes a clear indication of the conflict churning inside him. "I want that too," he said quietly. "I am just having difficulty discerning how to do it."

"I think I know why. I suffered a similar dilemma when I discovered my feelings for Martín," she said, smiling at the memory. "I found myself attracted to a man who, according to convention, should have been unsuitable for me. I have preached my entire life against the traditional restrictions of society, but it is a difficult thing to overcome. It becomes engrained in us without our knowing and sets up barriers in our conscience. You are wrestling with yours because society has dictated that a man of your age should not be attracted to a girl of fourteen, but the heart knows nothing of boundaries."

"She is half my age," he said stubbornly.

"Now, but in a few years the disparity will have diminished considerably. There was a similar age difference between your father and myself, and it was never an issue. I can honestly say that I have never witnessed you as happy as you are with Inez. You are well-matched on every level, but it would be best to wait until she is at least sixteen before you try for a child. The question is whether you are willing to postpone your plans for that long. Even if you decide to marry the sister this year, it is no guarantee that she will conceive immediately. These are the things you need to contemplate before you make your final decision."

As she rose from her chair, he got to his feet with her. She started to clear the table, but he grasped her two delicate hands in his own. "Thank you, Mother," he said sincerely. "I know now what I need to do. I should have spoken to you at the very beginning. It would have been much less trouble." He hugged her tightly to him, happy to have made his decision at last.

After María left the room, Estêvão sat back down at the table with a fresh sheet of paper before him and a quill in his hand. He thought for a moment about appropriate phrasing, took a deep breath then busily began to scratch away before he lost his nerve. He sanded the note to blot up the excess ink then read the whole thing from start to finish. Satisfied with the content and the tone, he folded it closed and sealed it with wax. His future and that of the entire fazenda depended on this one letter. He said a little prayer that he had done the right thing then called a servant to post the missive.

BOOK 4: Marriage
1512
Chapter 1: The Proposal

On a warm evening at the end of June Iñigo arrived home from the mercantile in an extraordinarily good mood. The girls were too absorbed in their own affairs to notice the playful twinkle in his eyes, but Joanna had seen this mischievous light many times before and knew that he was keeping a secret. She was itching to discover what it was but reasoned that eventually he would have to tell her, so she tried to restrain her curiosity.

When they retired to their room to ready for bed, Joanna could stand it no longer. The relaxed demeanor that she had acquired on Terceira had stayed with her, and this time instead of being perturbed at the little mystery, she was as excited as her husband. She closed the door then whirled on him with girlish exuberance and tried to coax it out of him.

"So, Señor García," she began in high spirits, "what has brought on this whimsical mood that has you so smug?"

Iñigo looked at his wife appraisingly and smiled at her still-lovely face made even more appealing by the animated expression she wore. Her bountiful hair tumbled down alluringly from the pins that had held it securely in the severe bun she preferred for everyday duties. It had once been the color of honey and, though now streaked with gray, still had the body and bounce of youth. It framed her face and softened the little lines around her striking blue-green eyes, and he glimpsed the angelic young woman who had stolen his heart. Had it really been over twenty years ago? He waxed nostalgic and pulled his wife firmly to him.

"Oh, Reina," he said huskily. "What did I ever do to deserve such a beautiful wife?" He kissed her tenderly and ran his fingers through her abundant tresses.

"You are full of surprises this evening," she remarked, wide-eyed at his amorous behavior. "What has come over you?"

"It seems that love is in the air," he said, making a mental note to resume his attentions to his wife when they had done with the matter at hand.

He proceeded to tell her about an interesting communication he had received at the mercantile that afternoon, which contained a sensible and intriguing suggestion that they had never thought to ponder. She listened intently as he thoroughly gave the details of the letter and laid out the proposal before her. Capitán Rey was seeking to solidify their business partnership and secure the future of the Fazenda da Pomba by a marriage to one of their daughters. Eventually, the child produced by the union stood to inherit the entire enterprise and all of its holdings, from the ranch to the vineyard, all the way down to the *María Vencedora*. It was a reasonable and generous offer, and they would be foolish to refuse without proper consideration.

"I know you have personal reasons for not wanting to associate with Portuguese on any level," Iñigo began, watching his wife carefully for her reaction, "but I hoped that after spending time with the family, you have realized that they are of the highest caliber and very prosperous."

Joanna nodded her head in agreement. "It seems that everything they touch succeeds."

"How could it not? They work very hard to bring it about. I think you have also seen that Capitán Rey is a man of honor and well respected. He would never treat his wife shabbily, so we know that our daughter would be well taken care of and have everything she needs. Even if this proposal was not romantically motivated, I think you and I would agree that love and affection can spring out of the most unlikely of circumstances."

Joanna looked up at him with a genuine smile of admiration. This tall, awkward man was her rock and had seen value in her when it seemed that even God had forsaken her. He took her as his wife, knowing full well that she might never overcome the disillusionment caused by the tragedies suffered before she met him. He loved her and had provided her with every creature comfort she could ever desire. Through his persistence and gentle, caring nature, after many patient years, he had helped her to abandon the bitterness and hate that hardened her heart and become a loving mother and a devoted wife. She owed him much.

"Then there is the other matter," Iñigo ventured a bit uncomfortably.

"What other matter?" Joanna asked, her brows drawing together in confusion.

Iñigo took a long breath and uttered the words that had wrought so much turmoil in his life. "The reason that Serafina has had such difficulty finding a husband is because I am a Jew."

Joanna took in a sharp little gasp. This was a subject about which her husband was extremely sensitive. Though an accident of birth and no fault of his own, it had caused him much remorse during his lifetime, and through tacit understanding it was a fact rarely mentioned.

"You needn't act so shocked, Reina," he said with a weary smile. "I know it never even crosses your mind and does not present a problem in our everyday lives, but that does not mean I am naïve enough to believe it is a nonissue. The people of our little town have never treated me any differently than anyone else, and they happily purchase their tea and yard goods from their local Jewish merchant, but it is another matter to invite a Jew into one's family. Not very long ago that simple action could have brought a death sentence for all involved. It has diminished Serafina's marriage prospects substantially, regardless of her outstanding beauty, and Inez will most probably suffer the same difficulty."

Iñigo paused for a moment from his musings and noted with surprise that his wife had begun to cry, the tears coursing slowly down her cheeks. It always amazed him that Joanna could display her emotions in a manner, which did not detract from her beauty but added to it. Where most women turned red in the face, their eyes bloodshot and their features contorted by their exertions, his wife's stunning aquamarine eyes simply filled with tears and overflowed.

He walked over to her and took her lovely face in his hands. "Do not be sad, Reina. I am far beyond lamenting my lot in life. I would not change any part of the path that brought us together. If I had not suffered these trials, fate would have never led me to you, and my life would have been a far worse tragedy than simply being a Jew."

Chapter 2: Iñigo

The history of Jews in Castile is a long and turbulent affair. At times they represented a desirable economic presence and source of valuable state income. During other periods they were erroneously accused of exerting their purportedly sinister influence over old Christians and their erstwhile brethren newly converted to Catholicism. They were often blamed and punished for their so-called crimes against Christianity. These misguided and narrow-minded views no doubt contributed to the fanatical massacres of several Jewish populations throughout Europe during the Crusades of the Middle Ages.

After the *Reconquista*, the taking back of Iberia from the Muslim invaders, the new Christian kings faced the problem of how to colonize the region and keep it from slipping back under Moorish control. They set out to attract colonists to the area by cleverly offering them special privileges and freedoms in exchange for their loyalty to the crown. Included in this burgeoning group of new patriots were large numbers of Jews in quest of the same autonomy offered to Christian settlers.

They established separate communities under aegis of the king, and the region flourished as a result of their able management. They took jobs as treasurers, lawyers, and administrators, and eventually found their way to court. Their communities became independent legislative entities and paid taxes directly to the royal treasury. They also gained a peaceful reputation and ceased to be an object of fear to Christians.

In the early 13th century however, the tolerant attitude and harmonious coexistence with the Catholic ruling body began to change. Several papal bulls were issued during that interval, which could have been interpreted as anti-Semetic, and they set in motion a steady downward spiral of Judeo-Christian relations. The emergence of the Black Death in the 1350's sparked anti-Jewish riots, and the mass exterminations of entire Jewish communities resumed. After much vacillation by the crown, in 1390 when Enrique III succeeded to the throne at eleven years of age, the church reigned unchecked and violence ran rampant. In 1391 mass conversions were instituted. Some Jews were compelled to renounce their beliefs while others were forcibly converted. Many Jews acquiesced to escape persecution.

Among these new Christians, or *conversos,* was a tall, slender bookkeeper who had held the position of treasurer in the administrative council of an *aljama,* a Jewish quarter outside of Seville. His name was Benjamin Ha-Levi, and he had a six-year-old daughter named Rachel with long black hair and clear gray eyes. She was his entire world, and he converted to save her from the overzealous, anti-Semitic frenzy that had played a hand in the death of her mother.

In due course, Rachel married a merchant in the same *judería* where she had grown up and gave birth to a daughter of her own who inherited her mother's coloring. They took a Castilian surname to prove the sincerity of their conversion and their fervor for the newly adopted religion. These were Iñigo's paternal grandparents, and he could still remember being a child sitting in his grandmother's lap, gazing up at the old woman's odd storm-colored eyes.

One of the major objectives of the pogroms instituted by the Catholic hierarchy was to break up the self-governed Hebraic districts. These ambitions were never fully realized, and many of the Jewish quarters remained largely intact. Some conversos quickly evacuated and broke all association with their former lives. They did this to demonstrate to themselves and others that they were truly converted and had completely forsaken their old beliefs for the new. Others sought out the comfort and familiarity of their long-standing homesteads and everyday relations. These people returned to their native environs looking to assess the condition of their property and reestablish a sense of normalcy.

Among the many shops and businesses still standing after razings in the judería outside of Seville was the García mercantile. There had always been talk of relocating to a more welcoming climate on the outskirts of Castile, but the store had been in the family for generations and was now considered more an institution than a mere means of support. Although the García clan whole-heartedly threw themselves into their new faith, they remained in the same location mostly due to the clientele they had worked for so many years to build. Some of their neighbors thought them foolish to be so trusting of the current period of peace, but Aarón García staunchly maintained that God would protect them now that they had repented for the error of their ways. Besides, his family had been Christians for nearly one hundred years, and anyone who knew them could plainly see the truth of their devotion.

The Garcías loved the regimen of attending mass and the ceremony of taking communion every Sunday. It was a weekly reaffirmation of their conversion and a rededication of their souls to God's will. It showed their true commitment and allayed any occasional doubts they experienced about their tenuous position with the crown or forsaking their Jewish heritage. Aarón had made a pilgrimage to Compostela in his youth to prove his own devotion, and to further solidify his stance he sent both of his sons to be educated by the Church in order to better serve God.

Iñigo and Alejandro García were the first of their family to bear completely non-Jewish names. The boys were very similar in age, temperament, and appearance. Their birthdays were only fourteen months apart, Alejandro enjoying the honor of preceding his brother into the world. They were both serious, reserved lads, highly intelligent and well versed in reading and mathematics, and they looked almost like twins with tall, dark forms similar to their father's. Aarón thought them utterly suited to a cleric's life and so placed them under the capable guidance of a kind old scholar, Father Gabriel Alvarez, who also had converso blood.

The brothers were like sponges and soaked up every bit of knowledge Father Gabriel put before them. He soon ascertained that, while Alejandro was more disciplined and worked harder at his lessons, Iñigo was the cleverer of the two and had a raw artistic talent as well. Father Gabriel also began to suspect that the younger boy had a natural gift, which went beyond mere intelligence.

One day while at their lessons, Father Gabriel was looking for a piece of text he had gone over the day before. He searched his worktable, checking the books stacked here and there and shuffling piles of papers from one place to another. Finally he threw his hands up in frustration and cried, "Where could I have put the blessed thing? I had it out just yesterday. It could not have grown legs and walked away."

Without looking up from the page he was illuminating, in an offhand manner Iñigo said, "You placed the book on the shelf behind your desk, third from the end on the left-hand side. I think we left off on page 178, the paragraph that begins with the sentence, 'The scourge rapidly spread northward and westward, eventually crossing the channel from France and making its way to the shores of England.' If that's what you are looking for."

The good Father followed the boy's directions, quickly located the book, and riffled through the pages until he found the section Iñigo had so accurately quoted. Stunned, he stood there with his mouth hanging open. This had to be some sort of trick. "Can you continue the passage, boy?" he asked.

"I think so," Iñigo replied looking up from his painting. "Let's see," he began and finished the paragraph to the end.

Satisfied, the priest allowed the boy to go back to the illustration that he loved so well and sat down to mull over the new development. It was entirely possible that the child had memorized this section of the book. Heaven knew they had gone over it often enough. If this were the case, it would be futile to bid him to continue his recitation. But what if it was some amazing power of recall that the boy possessed? In all his years spent instructing the youth of the community, he had never come across something so extraordinary. He would have to devise a way to assess the lad's capability.

The next day Father Gabriel spent a good portion of their time together testing Iñigo's newly discovered gift by quizzing him about the content of materials they had used in the course of their lessons. The priest would arbitrarily pull down a book, read the title to the boy, begin a sentence from a random page, and see if the child could continue it. In nearly every instance Iñigo persisted until the old man bid him to stop. The few times when the boy could not do it, the cleric questioned his own memory as to whether or not they had covered it as he'd thought.

When he asked the youth how he could perform such an amazing feat, Iñigo shrugged his shoulders and said that he just could. He explained that it was like a picture in his mind, and once he had visualized *anything*, be it text, receipts at his father's mercantile, stacks of merchandise, even a collection of everyday objects, he could recall it exactly as he'd seen it.

The priest was astounded, and his mind pondered the possibilities. This boy could be extremely useful for the order. He could do accounting, make copies of important documents, organize libraries, and locate books in an instant. He could go so far as to work in the royal treasury, and all the gratitude would fall to Father Gabriel. His unearthing of such an incredible talent would bring him the praise he had desired his entire career. He lost himself for a moment thinking about the glory he would reap by exploiting the lad's uncanny ability.

Then he looked over at the brothers. Alejandro was busy scanning and making notes from the material they had parsed earlier that day. He fervently scoured the manuscript, smiling and nodding when he found the information for which he searched, and occasionally he kissed the crucifix about his neck or pressed his hands together in prayer as a gesture of thanks. The boy was certainly endowed with a passion for the Lord without having to instill it. This was rare indeed. He also had a keen mathematical ability, nearly as sharp as his brother's, and his skills of communication far surpassed the younger lad's halting manner of speaking whenever he had to talk to anyone outside of his normal sphere of acquaintances.

In turn he observed Iñigo. The younger sibling was staring out the window watching the traffic on the street below. His eyes eagerly followed the goings-on of the village as if projecting himself to be among them. Come to think of it, the old priest had never seen him really enthused about any part of his education inside the classroom. Only when he was engrossed in his illuminations was he truly present. Even with all of the excitement about his remarkable powers of recollection, Iñigo himself had remained unimpressed and unmoved. If he spent his life in the order, he would be miserable and feel like some sort of captive or circus freak.

Father Gabriel shook his head with a little chuckle, realizing he could never conscience being responsible for the lad's imprisonment. What a fool he was searching for accolades at this late stage of his life. He had had his chance to attract royal notice and had forgone it all to become a humble educator. What made him think that this shy, awkward, brilliant young man would enjoy it when he himself had not? Perhaps the Church could make due with just one of the García boys after all.

The next day the correctness of his actions was confirmed when only Alejandro showed up for lessons. He had a distracted, moody air about him, certainly not the outgoing eager pupil the priest had come to expect. Father Gabriel pulled a chair over alongside Alejandro's, and asked the lad about his troubles. To his surprise, a few quiet tears ran down the boy's face. When he had recovered enough to speak, he recounted the events of the evening before.

The boys had returned home from school to find their father in bed and their mother overwhelmed in the shop. She hurriedly explained to them that Aarón had not felt well and had lain down at midday. The brothers pitched in, and Iñigo soon had things running smoothly. He told his mother she should use the opportunity to check on her husband. He was sleeping soundly, so she left him, assuming that he just needed some rest.

In the morning she had wakened the boys in a panic and sent Alejandro out to fetch the doctor. Iñigo ran to his father's side, and a shock ran through him at what he saw. Aarón lay in the bed on his side with his limbs curled, unmoving beneath him. Half of his face was a frozen mask, and he could not speak. Only his open eye showed any sign of expression, following his wife and son about the room, seemingly disconnected from the rest of his body. Iñigo sat down next to his father and covered him with the blanket, holding his left hand to provide him succor.

The doctor finally arrived and ushered the boys out of the room while he examined their father and interviewed his wife. When he emerged from the room, his countenance was grim. He explained that Aarón had suffered an apoplexy and would need special care. In some cases the patients recovered much of their bodily functions, in some they required constant attendance, and in others they simply died. Aarón was not the worst case he had ever seen, and with much rest and special exercises he could expect to regain much of his former self. For the meantime, someone else would have to run the business.

Iñigo jumped at the opportunity, and though only thirteen years of age, he soon had the mercantile running as efficiently as ever. Alejandro continued his instruction under Father Gabriel, and because of the old priest's fondness for the brothers and the guilt he felt over his intention to exploit Iñigo's gift, he made it his special mission to advance his young protégé every chance he could. Alejandro's gregarious personality made him a natural candidate for promotion, and he soon found himself working in the same royal household as Tomás de Torquemada, another descendent of conversos in the Church's employ and Queen Isabella's personal confessor. Father Gabriel died a few years later without ever receiving the official recognition he so desired but at peace with his conscience, knowing beyond a shadow of a doubt that he had done the right thing.

With Iñigo in charge of the family business, it gained a new reputation for being better organized and providing quicker service than it ever had in the past. With his amazing memory, it took him only a short while to inventory outstanding orders, get the receipt books up to date, and lay in the stock they would need for the coming season. Of course there were many small details, little particulars, which would have escaped Iñigo's notice had it not been for Don Pedro.

Pedro Torres was a twenty-year-old Sevillian who had been a part of the García family mercantile since he was a boy. Aarón had noticed him one day loitering outside the storefront. The eight-year-old Pedro was dressed in filthy rags, his hair long and greasy, and his face and neck covered in grime. Aarón thought nothing of it. There were many such children wandering the streets of the city. One could not help them all.

The next day Aarón was occupied with a customer when he heard the bells on the door signal a new arrival. He looked around just in time to see the grubby little urchin streak into the store, grab two sausages from a bin, and attempt escape through the closing door. He would have made good his getaway had another shopper not been entering the mercantile at that very moment. The lad bounced off the customer's considerable belly and landed smack on his rear end, never losing hold of his precious, ill-gotten goods. Aarón quickly collared the raggedy would-be thief and locked him in a storeroom to await judgement.

When Aarón closed up his shop for the midday siesta, he opened the door to the storeroom and found the offender asleep on the dusty floor. He gently awakened the boy so not to frighten him and guided him to the García living quarters behind the store. His dutiful wife had lunch waiting for him and said nothing as her husband steered the unfamiliar child to a chair at the table and pushed his own bowl to a spot in front of him. The boy looked from one adult to the other with wide-eyed wonder, and suddenly the aroma of the soup was too much to resist. He dove into the meal with voracity, sipping then slurping and sopping up the broth with a piece of bread. When he finished, Señora García silently refilled his bowl and sliced him another slab of bread before returning to her chores.

When the child could hold no more, he pushed himself back in his chair and belched loudly. Aarón smiled kindly at the boy's contented reaction then proceeded to inquire about his circumstances. At first the eight-year-old was reluctant to give any information, but when he espied a cake the Señora was preparing to cut into servings, his story came spilling out of him.

His name was Pedro Torres, and he was eight years old. His mother had once been a fine lady admired by all for her beauty. She had fallen in love with a high-ranking nobleman, and they had married and produced little Pedro, who would one day become a great *caballero* and inherit the whole of his father's estate. Tragically, his father had been killed in a duel with an evil duke. The heir apparent and the hapless widow had fallen on hard times, and Pedro often had to fend for himself while his mother looked for work. Royalty dressed in rags.

It was a very sad story and could not have been sadder...had it been true. The mother was a notorious liar and a woman of ill repute. It very well could have been that Pedro's father had been a nobleman, but considering the volume of business the woman regularly handled, she would have been hard-pressed to determine which of her customers had sired the child. The boy sat uncomfortably, regarding the shopkeeper with anxious eyes, waiting for the man's reaction and an offer of dessert. Aarón nodded to his wife and she placed the warm square of cake in front of the lad with a cup of milk. The boy seemed to have recovered his appetite and fell on the treat with gusto.

"Well, Don Pedro," began the merchant, using the title the boy would have been granted had his story been fact, "it just so happens that I am in need of an assistant for my store. As you can see my wife is very busy. She has a new baby to look after, and she is also caring for our first-born who is only a toddler. She cannot possibly help me out. I know that nobles do not regularly do trade work, but if you would not consider it beneath your dignity, do you think you could deign to help me out?"

Pedro puffed his chest out with pride and said, "I suppose I could find the time to lend a hand in your hour of need."

"Excellent, Don Pedro. Then if you are finished with your lunch, let's go see if we can find a uniform to fit you. This is a position of great importance, and a uniform is necessary to reflect your standing."

Aarón led the boy to the storeroom where they found a full suit of clothing in just his size. The merchant also gave him hose and shoes and a cape to complete the ensemble. He included some soap and a comb—Don Pedro would certainly want to wash every evening after leaving the dusty shop—and a cap to keep his hair out of his face while he worked. Aarón wrapped the parcel securely and scooted the boy out the door, telling him he would see him in the morning. No mention was made of the attempted theft or of the boy's neglected physical state.

When he returned to his wife at the end of the day, he recounted the scene while she prepared his supper. "He will probably sell the items the first chance he gets, and you will never see him again," she commented cynically. "You are too decent for your own good, Aarón García," and she kissed him on top of his head.

He shrugged his shoulders and smiled at his wife's pragmatic attitude. "We shall see. It is a small cost for us to absorb, and it may change his entire life. At the very least, he will have gotten a hot meal and some practical use from the clothing."

The next morning Pedro was waiting at the front door when Aarón arrived to unlock it. He was clean and neatly dressed, and he greeted the shopkeeper with a hearty handshake. "So, Señor

García, what is the first task that requires my attention?" he asked readily.

"Well, Don Pedro, I was wondering if you could help me out with this," Aarón said, presenting a large empanada wrapped in a napkin. "I was not very hungry this morning, and I did not want to upset my wife. Perhaps you could finish it off before she finds out," he whispered conspiratorially. The lad nodded his head and eagerly bit into the savory meat pie.

When he had done, Aarón assigned him chore after chore, which he quickly and efficiently accomplished, and by the end of the first day, the merchant knew he had made a wise investment. When he locked up shop that evening, he dropped a few coins into Pedro's small hand, thanked him for his hard work, and told him he would see him the next day. He had been a loyal employee ever since.

The Señores García had gone beyond charity when they took Pedro Torres off of the streets and gave him a livelihood and sense of self-worth, so now he did everything in his power to repay the debt. With Don Pedro's knowledgeable guidance, Iñigo soon learned everything about his father's business down to the tiniest nuance. The two men worked long hard hours and increased the store's income until the family was the envy of the neighborhood. The business grew so much that they were able to hire a clerk to assist customers and tidy up. These had been part of Señora García's duties before Aarón had fallen ill. Now, most of her time was spent caring for her husband. She always had hot meals waiting for the men at midday and in the evening, but the rest of her day belonged to her spouse.

Aarón surprised the doctor and recuperated more quickly than anyone had imagined. The paralysis brought on by the attack mostly affected the right side of his body. As luck would have it,

Aarón was left-handed so was able to communicate his needs quite clearly through written messages. After a few weeks, he recovered his speech, though he was difficult to understand at first because of the uncooperative muscles on the largely motionless half of his face. With massage and exercise, the parts of his body that had seized up with the event began to relax, and he could get around reasonably well with the help of his wife. Though eventually he could make his way around the house with only a cane to steady him, he never regained the whole of his former vigor.

Alejandro was busy with his new position in the royal household. He came to visit as often as he could but not as often as his parents would have liked. Though sometimes he missed the coziness of his childhood home and the warm company of his family, he had grown accustomed to the luxuries of his office. He did not earn a regular income, but he lived in considerable comfort and received many expensive gifts and contributions. The other members of the residence respected and enjoyed this charming, hard-working cleric and went out of their way to garner his favor.

Their lives went on in this uneventful fashion, and for a few years the García family had a serene, secure existence. They all seemed happy with their lot and looked forward to living out their days in harmony then passing on the family business to a future generation. Their most recent troubles felt like a bad memory and part of the distant past, and the new prosperity and unity under Queen Isabella and Ferdinand of Aragon showed promise of a lasting peace. Then the letter arrived that would change their lives forever.

When the García brothers were very young—but old enough to understand the impact of religious devotions—they began to attend mass every Sunday with the rest of their family. Iñigo tolerated the service, because he sensed that it was important to his parents. He behaved himself, because he knew that it was expected of him, and sometimes he gleaned a valuable lesson out of the stories taken from the extensive text of the Holy Scriptures. After a while though, because of his extraordinary gift, the repetitive nature of the Catholic mass became a droning sameness, a mind-numbing litany too monotonous to bear. He continued to attend out of respect, but he usually found his mind wandering to matters of more personal significance.

Alejandro, on the other hand, was struck by a sort of divine fervor. The first time he entered the church he felt like he had truly come home. The alabaster crucifix with the beautifully wrought body of Christ depicted in His act of ultimate sacrifice, the stained-glass windows illustrating the devoutness of various influential saints, and the comforting ceremony and ritual of the mass itself—all convinced him that herein lie his destiny. The rest of his week became just a period of time between Sundays when he could return to the place where he felt he truly belonged.

Now that Alejandro was a fully ordained brother of the Dominican Order, the belief that his fate was intertwined with that of the Church had been confirmed, and his passion for the Lord burned brighter than ever. He took his vows very seriously and threw himself unreservedly into his duties. His position as a minor secretary, though sounding inconsequential, was actually a very vital one. Every communication addressed to any of the members in his household had to first pass through his hands. As a result, he was continually abreast of the news and developments of the whole of Castile.

In November of 1478, Alejandro learned of a development that he feared might have an affect on his family. He heard rumors of a papal bull, which might have the power to dredge up the old menace of inquisition. This time though, it was not to be directed against the Jews so much as conversos who had slipped back into their old system of beliefs. Because his father had chosen to remain in a section of Seville that was predominantly Jewish, he worried that it might appear that Aarón fell into this category. The part that made him uneasy was that no proof was necessary to bring a person to trial. All that was needed was the testimony of a disgruntled neighbor or an envious rival and a person could be held indefinitely. Alejandro did not think there was an immediate threat, but it would not hurt to apprise his family of the situation.

When he told his father of the development, Aarón pooh-poohed him and told him he was overreacting. How could anyone possibly suppose that this devout family of Christians were secretly adhering to the old ways, which they had discovered were so misguided? Just because they had stayed in their ancestral home did not mean they were rejecting the true faith. They had given one of their own boys to the Church, for heaven's sake. Besides, he had complete conviction that God would take care of them. All they had to do was believe.

Alejandro returned to his residence that evening dejected and disconcerted. He was pleased that his father was such an avid disciple, but he had a troubled feeling about this. If Aarón failed to see the urgency of the situation, the whole family could be in jeopardy. He had to figure out a way to get through to them. Perhaps he should concentrate on Iñigo.

Alejandro corresponded with his brother, and they agreed that it was imperative to convince their father to leave. It would be a difficult task and would take much effort, but between the two of them they could handle one little old man. Iñigo suggested that they enlist their mother's help, as she would shoulder the responsibility of Aarón's care. Starting off slowly, winning one small victory after another, nearly a year later they had obtained their mother's approval. Now they would just have to convince Aarón.

The family gathered just after the New Year in 1480. It was the first break Alejandro had enjoyed from his hectic schedule of duties for the Season of Advent and the Nativity. The Garcías sat around the supper table and caught themselves up on current events from around the neighborhood and news of the mercantile. Alejandro threw them tidbits of insignificant gossip from the royal household, and then there was an obvious pause in the conversation. He took a deep breath and reluctantly divulged the real reason behind his visit.

"Papa," he began carefully, "I know we have covered this subject before, but I feel compelled to bring it up again. There is rumor that Queen Isabella is preparing to sign the order enforcing the papal bull of inquisition. She is reluctant to do so, because she does not believe in the persecution of any particular group, especially Christians, but Brother Torquemada says that this is an indication that she has become complacent in her faith. She is a just and determined ruler who prides herself on her clemency, but he makes the point that pride is one of the seven deadly sins. He almost has her convinced that she must take action now to save her soul. I think it would be prudent for you to consider relocating."

Aarón was silent for a moment, and his family wondered if he understood the situation clearly. There were occasions since his attack when he had difficulty comprehending large amounts of information at one time. He looked at each of them in turn, fixing them with his dark gray eyes, then his gaze returned to his eldest child.

"No," he said resolutely. "I will not go."

"But, Papa," Alejandro cried out, "you could be killed!"

"If it is God's will, then so be it!"

Alejandro could stand it no longer and got up to pace the room. "Do you want to be made an example by the Church? Do you want to be a martyr? Is that it?" he ranted as he walked back and forth in front of his father's chair.

"No, I don't want to be *made* a martyr or an example by the Church. I just want to *be* an example of a good Christian," Aarón said simply.

Alejandro stopped pacing and dropped to one knee before his father. He grasped his father's hand and kissed it with much tenderness. When he looked up at Aarón, there were tears shining in his eyes. "Then why, Papa, why? What is this obsession with dying to glorify the name of God?"

Aarón lovingly regarded his son, and a smile of infinite patience spread across his face. Then deliberately, as if speaking to a small child, he explained, "I do not *want* to die. I would much rather *live* to glorify God's name, but when I do finally stand before Him, I want to do it with a clear conscience, knowing that my faith in Him never wavered." He paused for a moment letting his declaration sink in. "Can you understand that, son?"

Alejandro nodded his head, a defeated posture settling over his lanky frame. His father's faith was ever a source of wonder to him. He reasoned that it must be how he had come by his own devotion. It was too bad his faith in human nature was not such an easy thing in which to trust. He sat back down in his seat and tried to enjoy the remainder of the evening.

He returned to his duties, and though his father had rejected the idea of relocation, Alejandro continued to monitor the situation. He resumed his correspondence with his brother and sent him regular updates on the tenuous state of affairs. In the months that followed, Queen Isabella maintained her staunch attitude against instituting the order, which would be equivalent to a witch-hunt, but Tomás de Torquemada would not let it go so easily. He insisted that it was her duty as a Christian and implacably exhorted the monarch to root out the heretics and expel them from the motherland. His tenacity was part of the reason he had risen so high, and soon all resistance began to weaken.

When Alejandro returned to the García home in August for Iñigo's twentieth birthday, he brought with him some bad news. He knew it was futile to continue the debate with his father, so he concentrated on Iñigo and his mother. When Aarón lay down for his daily nap, the three of them had a hushed discussion about the pressing situation, which was quickly approaching critical status.

"It seems that Queen Isabella is beginning to give in under Brother Torquemada's demands," Alejandro said gravely. "I heard just the other day that it will not be long before she signs the official order for the Castilian Inquisition."

"God save us," said his mother and crossed herself.

Iñigo put a supporting arm about his mother's shoulders. He turned to Alejandro and asked, "Do you really believe this could mean danger for us? Speak frankly, Brother. We need to know exactly where we stand."

Alejandro looked into Iñigo's face, so like his own, and nodded. "Anyone who knows our family knows we are above all else Christians. I am just worried that our success may have caused resentment among people not as fortunate. There will be some who do not understand the dire consequences of an accusation. Once made, *it cannot be withdrawn*, and the Church is obligated to investigate, no matter how ridiculous. I am afraid our father is no longer strong enough to survive even the detention. Iñigo, would you subject our mother to such a fate?"

Iñigo shook his head. He looked down at his mother's sweet familiar face and could not fathom being separated from her. He pulled her to his chest, squeezing his eyes tightly to fight back the tears. When he recovered, he cleared his throat and asked, "What should we do?"

Alejandro had thought often about the present conversation and had long ago formulated a sensible plan. He laid it out for his brother and mother now in a methodical manner and made sure they all understood precisely what to do and what to say so not to become suspect. They had just finished outlining their conspiracy when Aarón entered the room.

"I just had the strangest dream," he said, limping into the room on his cane. "I was standing on a hill looking out at the sea. I looked above me and saw the leaves of an olive tree, and when I turned, I saw Iñigo and a beautiful girl with golden hair. She looked like an angel. There were two little girls, and as far as the eye could see the land was green. The sun shone warmly on my face, and a feeling of utter peace settled over me. I wonder what it means," he finished, the glazed look of the dreamlike state still evident on his features.

"Perhaps it means that Iñigo is not completely beyond hope," Alejandro said, pulling the chair out for his father to sit.

The whole family laughed at this including Iñigo. He did not mind being the butt of a joke if it eased the tension. He was used to it. His social awkwardness had long been a source of amusement to them all. "Well at least I still have hope," he shot back.

"I think we all do now," said the Señora quietly, and the men all nodded their agreement.

A month later, Queen Isabella enacted the papal bull issued two years previously and signed the royal order for the Castilian Inquisition. It authorized the use of torture and confiscation of property to elicit confessions from suspected dissemblers. Soon after passage of the order, Sevillian conversos panicked and abandoned the city to seek refuge in distant parts of the Iberian Peninsula. Businesses established in that quarter for decades were boarded up and abandoned as family after family fled to the countryside.

The Inquisition was based on an anonymous testimonial

system, which required no burden of proof against the accused. Even courageous citizens who dared to speak out against the injustice of the process risked falling under suspicion themselves. Members of the old Christian nobility turned over many conversos, having been compelled to do so by their priests on pain of excommunication. They were told that failure to do so would result in disqualification of oneself from salvation in the afterlife.

Many of the first defendants summoned by the Holy Office were released after their initial hearings with no further investigation required, but as the Inquisition spread northward, it grew beyond the Church's ability to accommodate its victims. Prisoners were often housed in monasteries and castles. The conditions were better than those of ordinary prisoners in municipal jails, but instead of receiving speedy trial like their counterparts, they often languished behind bars for months. This was exactly what Alejandro had feared, and he prayed that something would happen to change his father's mind.

The García family watched helplessly while the chaos raged on about them. Many of their oldest friends and neighbors packed up and left the city, some taking only the necessities fundamental to their survival. Seeing the devastation happening all around, Iñigo and his mother hoped that Aarón would finally agree to evacuate the premises, but he steadfastly refused maintaining that God would protect them. They could not force him to change his mind, so they continued with the original strategy laid out by Alejandro months before.

By the New Year, Iñigo had done everything required to put the plan into action. The stock in the store was down to a bare minimum, and the accounts were completely up to date. He sold or exchanged much of their valuables for cash and disguised the reserves in bags to look like sacks of grain. He packed their essentials in crates and loaded them into a large wagon purchased months before. A team of horses he procured was housed in a nearby stable and kept at the ready. The only thing left to do was wait.

One evening in January of 1481, a prominent Sevillian named Diego de Susan called a meeting of the conversos who remained in the sector. Aarón had been waiting for some sign to tell him how to proceed, and this seemed like an answer to his prayers. He readied himself to go to the assembly, and when he stepped into the room, his wife and son were both surprised to see him dressed in his church clothes. He made his intentions clear to the two of them, and when he started for the door, Iñigo stepped in front of him to block his path.

"Papa, you cannot go to this gathering. This man is nothing but a troublemaker, and he will not be satisfied until the crown brings armed forces against us. This is not something in which you want to involve yourself."

"Son," began Aarón patiently, "the man merely wants to organize a system of defense. It is just a practical preventive measure, and it is an action on which the community should come to a consensus. I am going merely to listen and give my opinion."

"I'm sorry, husband," his wife said from her chair. "I think this is wrong, and I will not be a part of it. I will not take you."

"You must act as your conscience dictates, mi amor. If must needs, I will go alone." He turned toward the door and limped the length of the room on his cane.

"Papa, wait," Iñigo said, reaching for his cape.

"Iñigo, I forbid you!" his mother cried in an anguished voice. She knew he was far past the age she could prohibit him to do anything, but she was terrified of losing her son to this madness.

"Mama," he said, gently taking her hand, "I do not condone this dissention, but how can I condemn it if I don't know what they are planning? If I do not hear what they have to say, how can I form an opinion as to whether this is the right or wrong thing to do? Besides, I can keep my father out of trouble and make sure he arrives home unharmed. Don't worry. We will be fine." He kissed her on the cheek then guided his father through the open door.

Señora García said a small silent prayer to keep them safe, crossed herself, then laid her head on her forearms and cried.

A couple of hours later, Aarón and Iñigo arrived home from the meeting. Both of their faces were grave, and Aarón looked as if he carried the weight of the world on his shoulders. He leaned heavily against his rangy son, and when his wife looked at him, for the first time the realization struck her that he was an old man. She hurried to his side and lent him her arm for support.

"You were *all* right," Aarón said wearily, falling into a chair. "We need to defend ourselves but not this way." He looked up at his wife with eyes reddened by tears. "They are stockpiling arms, mi amor, saying that it is merely a means of defending ourselves. This *defense* will cost the lives of many innocent people. When I go to the Father, I do not want my shining white robe stained with the blood of blameless women and children. I have been a fool. I intended to fight for what I believe and live out the rest of my life here, but not this way. Not this way."

"Mama," Iñigo said quietly, "I think Papa should get some rest. He is overly tired, and it is late." He helped his father up from the chair and supported him while Aarón hobbled to his bed, a broken man. The Señora pulled back the blankets and knelt down to remove her husband's shoes. Iñigo made his way back to the dining room and sat down to wait for his mother.

A few minutes later, she entered the room and took a seat next to her worn-out son. She slid her hand over and lovingly squeezed Iñigo's long artist's fingers, which now bore the calluses of much hard physical labor. What a good son he was. When he'd been a boy, she and Aarón had done everything in their power to take care of him and protect him, and for many years now their roles had been reversed. She smiled at him lovingly and asked him how they should proceed.

"Well, I think my father is finally ready to concede," he said, pulling his hair back from his face. "We will sleep tonight, and in the morning we will head out."

"Where will we go?" his mother asked.

"I don't know. I would like to get as far from this place as we can. I suppose that means north, but we need to distance ourselves from these *objectors*, and we need to do it quickly."

"What about Don Pedro?" his mother asked. "We cannot just leave without speaking to him first."

"Leave that to me, Mama," Iñigo smiled down at her. Even in a crisis she thought of others first. "He is always here before dawn. I will speak to him then. Don't you worry. Everything will be fine." He kissed her familiar cheek then said, "Now go try to get some sleep. Tomorrow will be a very long day."

She rose from the table and leaned over to kiss her son on the top of his head. "You are a good son, Iñigo," his mother said, giving voice to the thoughts that had run through her head just moments before.

"Good night, Mama. I'll see you in the morning."

Iñigo did not sleep that night. He tossed and turned, mentally going over and over the things that needed to be done the next morning. He finally rose from his bed, realizing that he could not allow himself to rest until they were all safe. He busied himself filling a crate with the last few items they could not leave behind while he tried to plan what he would say to Don Pedro when he showed up for work. The man had been a loyal employee and so much more. He was like a brother, and without him the mercantile would have never survived. They owed him much, and Iñigo could not imagine starting over without him. This was a sad occasion indeed, and he dreaded the conversation that now loomed ahead.

There was a knock at the door, and Iñigo knew Don Pedro had arrived. He got up from the crate he was packing, took a deep breath, and crossed the room with a heavy heart. He still had not figured out how to break the news. He dispiritedly opened the door and was astonished at what he saw. Don Pedro was standing there with all of his earthly possessions loaded in a rickety handcart, and Elena, the plump little store clerk, stood smiling at his side.

"Good morning, Master Iñigo," Pedro said cheerfully. "It looks to be a nice day for a trip. I figured you might need a bit of help along the way, safety in numbers and all that. Is there enough room left in the wagon for my paltry pile of baggage and my new wife?"

"Don Pedro," Iñigo choked out, "this is too much to ask. You are not obligated to do this. It will be a long and difficult journey, and we do not even have a destination."

"All the more exciting," he said with a smile. Then in a more serious tone he continued. "As for being obligated, your parents were not obligated to help me when I was a young thief and tried to steal from them. They could have had me arrested and put away or sent to a workhouse. The way I look at it, they saved my life that day when they gave me a job, and this is my chance to repay them for that act, which went far beyond simple compassion. Please allow me to do this."

Iñigo was now weeping openly, touched by the reminder of his parents' generosity and the appreciation expressed so forthrightly by the simple, hardworking man in front of him. He wiped his eyes, led the newly married couple to the waiting wagon, and helped them to situate their cartful of humble belongings. The three of them returned to the kitchen and prepared their last meal in the place that had been a home to them all for so many years. A little while later Iñigo's parents joined them, and just after dawn the family set out to find a new place they could call home far away from the storm that would bring terror into so many lives.

A few weeks later, three Sevillians were burned at the stake for heresy. Among them was Diego de Susan, the man who had sent out the call to arms such a short time before in an attempt to spark a rebellion. He was betrayed by his daughter, Suzanna, who was in love with a soldier. He was condemned for his part in the conspiracy and sentenced to death in the first *auto de fé* of the Castilian Inquisition. The exodus of conversos and Jews alike continued, and the García family's decision to vacate the mercantile that had been home for generations proved to be a wise one.

The first few days of the trip had a sort of carefree air about them as if the little group had simply elected to take a vacation and were touring the countryside. As the days dragged on though, the jauntiness wore off and the grind set in. The going was difficult, and the days were long. Aarón's compromised health plagued him in the form of reduced vitality and stamina, and there were many times when the family had to postpone their progress because it was just too painful for him to endure more. Iñigo was glad for Don Pedro's company, and Elena did more than her share to ease the burden. They were a blessing and the trip could not have proceeded without them.

Despite their hardships, eventually the weary travelers settled in the farthest reaches of the Kingdom of Castile along the northern border of Portugal. When Aarón had made his pilgrimage to Santiago de Compostela in his youth, he had stopped on the shores of the Ria de Vigo, fascinated by the greenness of the land and the advantageous position of the harbor. He had often thought about the possibility of building a business in this remote outpost, but he had grown too comfortable and complacent in Seville. As that was no longer at issue, he now sought to fulfill that long ago ambition. Even if his son would be the one to make the venture succeed, at least he would finally realize his dream.

They bought two lots, one for the mercantile on the waterline and a separate one on a hill overlooking the town below. Here they would build their new home. One of Aarón's favorite things to do while their house was under construction was to make his way up to an old olive tree on the knoll and visualize the port below full of traders lined up to unload their cargos in the García family store. He would stand there for long periods of time, and sometimes he sat on the ground. He usually returned to his wife tired and with an aching back but content, because he finally felt at peace with God.

One day his son accompanied him on his daily vigil. They chatted along the way, and as they neared the olive tree, Iñigo bade his father to close his eyes. He had been working on something special for Aarón, and he wanted it to be a surprise. His father obliged, and Iñigo led him up to his favorite spot, stopping under the cool shade of the lone arboreal sentinel. When Aarón opened his eyes, he was touched by his son's thoughtfulness and his beautifully demonstrated artistry.

"Son, it is a masterpiece!" he said clearly impressed.

"Sit down, Papa. That's what it's for."

Aarón sat down on the bench his son had so lovingly crafted and ran his hand over the smooth polished surface. He looked up at Iñigo with infinite tenderness and patted the place next to him, indicating that his son should sit beside him. Iñigo smiled down at him, a boyish look coming into his face, and lowered his tall frame next to the older man. They sat for a moment in silence, simply enjoying the view.

"Thank you for this, son," Aarón said sincerely.

"It was nothing, Papa," Iñigo said, looking out at the sea. "This is a very lovely spot, and I thought you needed a comfortable seat from which to appreciate it. Don't tell Mama, but I get tired of hearing her tell you that sitting on the ground is bad for your back."

Aarón grunted a little laugh. "She is just watching out for my health, but I agree. It is a bit tedious. That is not what I meant though." Iñigo looked at his father with a question in his eyes. "Well, not *only* what I meant." Aarón went on to explain that it was only because of Iñigo's patience and perseverance that the family was still alive and now had a chance to prosper in this breathtaking new land. He was the one who had kept the business going for all the years between, and now he would be the one to build the new business from the ground up. Aarón would be forever grateful.

"Do you remember the dream I had the night of your twentieth birthday?" he continued.

"How could I forget," Iñigo said with a smile. "I have thought of the golden-haired angel often."

"I believe it was more a vision than a dream. We are sitting on the same hill overlooking the water. Here is the olive tree, and green surrounds us for as far as the eye can see. I believe that God led us to this place to give us a small taste of heaven before we leave this earth." He turned to his son and covered Iñigo's hand with his own. "Son, I want you to promise me one more thing."

"Anything, Papa."

"When I die, take my heart to Compostela. It is my final request. I want to show the world that my faith in God never wavered, and I placed my heart and soul firmly in His hands. I want people to know that though human nature may succumb to suspicion and temptation and fear, God will never fail us."

Iñigo could do nothing but agree.

The house and mercantile were finally finished, and it seemed that Aarón was merely waiting to see his vision complete. He died a few months later. He passed away in his sleep, peacefully and with a smile on his lips. No one doubted that he had gone to the Father with a clear conscience unstained by the blood of the innocent. They would all miss him, but they were happy for the time they had been given.

All was proceeding well at the mercantile. Iñigo and Don Pedro were building their clientele slowly but steadily, and they sensed from the start that the venture would be a success. It would take a while for word to spread about the new outpost in this remote corner of Castile, but eventually it would become the booming business it had been in Seville. At the moment there was only enough work for two people, so Iñigo decided to take advantage of the respite to fulfill Aarón's final request. He left the store in Pedro and Elena's capable hands and set out for Santiago de Compostela.

Upon arriving in the town of Compostela, Iñigo procured a room then headed straight for the shrine itself. He made his way through the crowds of pilgrims, searching for a quiet spot in the vast cathedral to pay personal homage to his father's memory. He passed through the massive vaulted nave and finally found a small peaceful chapel just off of the main altar in the impressively lit choir. As he stepped into the room, he looked down into his leather travel bag to remove the wooden box that contained his father's heart. When he looked up, he stopped in his tracks and his mouth fell open.

There, lighting a votive candle before the statue of the Virgin Mary, was the most beautiful woman he had ever seen. She was of medium height, not quite as tall as his mother, and curvy though extremely slender. Her long honey-gold hair fell in a shining mass of ripples to her waist, and when she turned her lovely heart-shaped face to him—her dewy, pink mouth an 'O' of surprise—her startled aquamarine eyes pierced him to his core. She quickly lowered her gaze, said, *"Perdón*, Señor," and returned to her candle, kneeling before it in prayer.

Iñigo tried to return to the task at hand, but he was too excited to concentrate. With shaking hands he put the hand-carved box back in his satchel, silently backed out of the chapel, and walked quickly to the inn where he was staying. He paced his room, grinning uncontrollably, while the thoughts swirled in his head. It was amazing. It was unbelievable. It was impossible. Was it luck? Destiny? God's will? How could Aarón have seen this so long ago? Iñigo had just met the girl with the golden hair from his father's vision, now where should he go from there?

Chapter 3: The Announcement

The next morning at the breakfast table Joanna was in an extremely chipper mood. On her way past her husband she leaned over and kissed him on the cheek then continued to her chair with a satisfied look on her face. Inez and Serafina looked at each other and smiled in mild surprise. This outward display of affection was rare, especially in the company of others. Their parents could not exactly be said to be passionately *in love*, but from time to time it was reassuring to know that after all they had been through, they still loved each other very much.

Everyone turned their attention to the food before them, and before long the meal was finished. Inez asked to be excused so she could take Palhaço for his morning jaunt, but Joanna said that her father had some important news to share first. Both of the girls looked up expectantly while Iñigo finished the wine in his cup, wiped his mouth with his napkin, and cleared his throat to speak.

"I received a letter at the mercantile yesterday that contained a very interesting proposition," he began. "It came from the Fazenda da Pomba. It is something that your mother and I had not considered, but it is actually a very sensible and generous offer."

Inez sat stock-still in her seat, her unblinking eyes glued to her father's face. She felt breathless and light-headed, and her heart pounded so hard in her chest that she thought it might burst. Here it was. The long-awaited proposal from her beloved had finally arrived, and all of her hopes and dreams would be fulfilled with the next words that issued from her father's mouth. She felt Serafina's hand squeeze her own under the table in a gesture of support, and she turned to her sister with a look of gratitude, the corner of her mouth trembling the slightest bit. With their hands locked together, the sisters turned back to hear the official announcement.

"It seems that Capitán Rey is planning to settle down and take a wife. He is looking to produce an heir to secure the future of his vast business holdings, and he has done us the honor of choosing his bride from our family." Here he paused and looked at his daughters. He loved them so much, and he was happy that their luck was beginning to look up. He would be sad to say goodbye, but he knew that the coming separation was inevitable. He took a deep breath then said, "Congratulations, Serafina. You will become a bride in a few weeks' time."

"What?" Serafina asked in confusion, assuming that she had not heard correctly. She felt her sister's hand first grow cold then slip lifelessly from her own. She looked over at Inez whose attention had never left their father's face. Her skin had a pasty gray pallor, and her eyes were wide and shiny with unshed tears. Serafina saw Inez drop her gaze to her lap and swallow hard. "Papa," Serafina pleaded, "there must be some kind of mistake!"

"I know it's unexpected, dear," he said, misinterpreting her alarm for astonishment at her good fortune, "but there is no mistake. Capitán Rey has asked for your hand in marriage."

They all sat in silence for a few moments. Then without looking up from her lap, in a voice choked with tears Inez asked, "May I be excused, please?"

"Yes you may, but don't you want to congratulate your sister first?" Joanna asked, oblivious to her daughter's state of shock.

"Congratulations, Serafina," Inez said in a quavering voice

and headed toward the door before anyone could notice her distress. Palhaço trotted devotedly behind her.

"Well, dear," Joanna said turning back to Serafina, "there is so much to plan and very little time to do it. It's a good thing we did not skimp on your trousseau. We don't want Dona María to think that we do not have the means to dower you properly, even if they are not seeking a formal dowry of property or ..."

Joanna went on with plans for her daughter's upcoming wedding, which would be the social event of the season. None of the local girls of marriageable age had made such a stellar match. Serafina should have been happy to have landed such a desirable husband from such a prestigious family, but all she could think about was the misery it would bring to her little sister.

As soon as Inez got clear of the house, she could hold back her tears no longer. They came of their own volition, brimmed her eyes, and flooded down her cheeks in torrents of sorrow. The scenery swam before her, her vision blurred, and she stumbled up the path to the olive tree where she fell to her knees before the bench, her head in her hands. Palhaço followed behind her whining his commiseration. When his mistress sat on the ground, he gently nudged her with his cool damp nose and licked her arm, attempting to draw her out of her suffering. She pulled the puppy to her and buried her face in his silky tan curls. She wept until she could weep no more then sat there with her head pounding, feeling empty and alone.

When she realized she would not die of heartbreak, she took a deep, cleansing breath and turned around to look at the sea, her back resting against the bench. Palhaço quietly laid down next to her with his furry head in her lap, sensing her need of his comforting presence. She absently stroked his unruly mane, repeating the motion over and over while the thoughts whirled in her mind. Eventually it had a calming effect, and she began to breath normally. When she finally thought she could examine the situation without further breaking down into hysterics, she allowed herself to go over the reality and let it truly sink in.

Serafina was stunned. Poor Inez! How could this have happened? When she'd met Estêvão nearly three years ago, she had tried to make herself appealing to him with a little harmless flirtation. She had never been on the receiving end of a rejection before then, but he had firmly rebuffed her coy coquetry, refusing to engage himself in anything more than polite conversation. Even while on Terceira, he had not made any effort to solicit her favor. It seemed to Serafina that he and Inez shared a unique connection and were compatible on every level. So why had he proposed to her instead of her sister? She didn't know, but she was determined to find out.

She made her way to Iñigo's study where her parents had withdrawn to discuss wedding plans after making the announcement. Serafina knocked on the door, resolutely making up her mind not to be turned away. When she entered, her parents were not surprised to see her, and Joanna welcomed her in, fussing over her every step.

"Sit down, sit down, sweetheart! We are just composing the acceptance letter, so we can begin arranging for the nuptials. You must be anxious to get things in motion. I completely understand. We have been waiting for this moment for so long."

"Yes, Mama," Serafina said slowly. Her mother was so excited, and what Joanna said was true. She had been waiting for this for a long time. Serafina would have to proceed very carefully. "I have a few questions if you don't mind?"

"Of course, darling," Joanna gushed. "It would be unnatural for a girl not to be interested in her own wedding. What do you want to know?"

Serafina swallowed hard and asked, "Did Capitán Rey say why he wanted to marry me?"

"Serafina, why would he *not* want to marry you? You are a beautiful, intelligent, charming girl. What man would not want to marry you?"

"That is not exactly what I meant," Serafina said, frustrated at her ineptitude. She took a deep breath and tried again. "It always seemed to me that he was more interested in Inez. They have much in common, and I think they would make a far more successful match."

"Inez?" Joanna blurted out. "Your sister is not much more than a child. She cannot possibly marry at her age and most definitely not before you."

"Yes," Iñigo said joining in, "Capitán Rey would have had to wait another two years if we had decided on your sister."

"If you had decided on my sister?" Serafina asked, her startled eyes flicking back and forth from one parent to the other. "You mean the two of *you* made this decision?"

"Well, I suppose in a manner of speaking we did, but it was the only decision that could be made. You are the eldest, therefore you must marry first," Joanna finished up logically.

"Mama, you cannot do this!" Serafina said frantically. "I have nothing in common with this man. We have never said more than a handful of words to each other in nearly three years' time. How could I possibly live with him as his wife? I do not love him!"

"Serafina," began Joanna patiently, kneeling in front of her and taking her daughter's hands in her own, "your nervousness is understandable, but many marriages begin in this manner. Even though you may feel like you can never love him, in time that may change. He is a courteous, respectful, successful man. Give him a chance. Love has bloomed out of stranger circumstances than these."

"But what about Inez?" Serafina asked.

"Your sister is young. Of course she will be sad to be without you, but eventually she will get over the loss of her elder sister. She knew this day would come. Perhaps she can even visit you from time to time."

"Mama, you don't understand," Serafina said urgently. "Inez …"

Joanna knelt in front of her daughter, waiting for her to finish her thought, but Serafina could not bring herself to divulge her sister's secret. There had been many times when the sisters had quarreled or teased or tattled on one another, but never, *never* had one of them betrayed the trust of the other. Serafina could not bring herself to do it now. She sat there, feeling wretched, hating herself for losing her nerve.

She shook her head and chastised herself for being weak. How could she let something so important go so easily? How could she stand up for her sister if she couldn't even stand up for herself? Maybe there was another way. Maybe she could convince Inez to fight for her own cause. She slowly got up from the chair and excused herself. She left the room and went to look for her sister.

Serafina found Inez exactly where she knew she would be, under the olive tree. She moved toward her quietly, knowing that her state of mind would be fragile. Serafina had had her heart broken once while spending time with her Aunt Margaret, and she would not wish that terrible hollow feeling on anyone, least of all her baby sister. Palhaço lifted his eyes at her approach and his tail thumped a slow familiar greeting. Serafina patted his head and sat down next to her sister. Neither of them said anything for a while. Finally Inez broke the silence.

"So, when is the wedding?" she asked, still looking out at the sea.

"It doesn't matter," Serafina said, taking hold of her sister's hand. "Inez, it doesn't have to be this way. You don't have to take this decision as final. Why don't you go and tell Mama how you feel about him?"

"What good would that do? She would never take me seriously. She would laugh and say something about me being a silly child then tell me that one day I will get over this ridiculous infatuation. That would be worse than doing nothing at all. At least this way I can keep my love to myself and not have someone belittle it by calling it silly."

"Inez, look at me," Serafina said, turning her sister's face to hers. "I *know* that your love is not just a silly infatuation. You love your Portuguese, and I believe he loves you too. You cannot give up this easily!"

"If he loves me, then why did he propose to you?" Inez asked simply, her silver eyes turning dark and stormy. "Can you tell me that?"

Serafina was on the verge of telling her sister that Estêvão had not specifically proposed to her, but would it help or hinder the situation? There were too many what-ifs, too many uncertainties, too many secrets, which were not hers to reveal. She decided to try another tack.

"Inez, what happened to the little sister who did not care about other peoples' opinions? That maddening, independent, self-confident little sister who would not let anything stand in her way? Where is that little girl now?"

Without pause Inez said, "Nearly three years ago that little girl began to reform herself for the sake of someone else, and now the last bit that remained is gone forever. We will not be seeing her again," she finished, and a single, heartrending tear slid down her face leaving a glistening track of grief in its wake.

Chapter 4: Resolution

The days passed with agonizing slowness as the arrangements for Serafina's wedding to Capitán Rey got under way. The menu had been decided, the bride's gown was being made, and invitations had gone out to all the proper people. Every local in the area with any social standing whatsoever received notice. This marriage of the firstborn daughter of the house had been anticipated for many years now, and it would be the most memorable thing that had ever taken place there. The house was buzzing with excitement, and the staff went about their tasks in a cheerful manner. The only two people immune to the gaiety were Inez and the bride-to-be.

Serafina was miserable. She went through the motions of being excited, because this meant so much to Joanna, but she could not get past feeling guilty for her sister's sorrow. A sense of self-loathing set in, and she began to blame herself for the whole affair. If she had not been so self-centered, if she had not set all of her hopes for her future on getting married, if she had been a little more independent and concentrated on making herself a stronger woman, perhaps none of this would have happened.

Serafina tried to ease her guilty conscience by focusing her energies on Inez. She attempted several times to encourage her sister to investigate, hinting that perhaps there had been some sort of misunderstanding. She implored Inez to go to their parents and confess her love for Estêvão, saying that the situation could not get any more desperate than it was now. Such a declaration could only help matters, but Inez steadfastly refused. She insisted that had she been so important to Estêvão, he would have stated his intentions clearly. Inez had had many years to perfect her obstinacy and easily defeated Serafina who finally let the subject drop and continued to feel responsible for the fiasco.

For Inez the first few days after the proposal were a blank. She could not remember a single detail after the conversation with her sister under the olive tree. She only vaguely recalled going about her days in a wooden, mechanical manner doing all of the things she regularly did out of habit more than any conscious effort. She had not cried again. It was as if she had shut off the part of herself that had once been human in an attempt to stifle the anguish that was now her constant companion. Her capacity for emotion had been replaced by an apathy for life in general, and she felt like an empty shell, a ghost of her former self. The only thing that mattered to her now was Palhaço.

The little black and tan mutt was her salvation through it all. He remained staunchly by her side providing solace and silent sympathy by virtue of his presence. He still required attention, exercise, and care, and it forced Inez to think about something other than her personal tragedy. He kept her too busy to dwell on her misfortune, and he was so silly that he could even make her laugh. He was endearing, and she loved him so much that sometimes she forgot he had been a gift from the person who had wrought this devastation.

Aside from the few confrontations with her sister, Inez was almost able to remain unaffected. She found that as long as she kept herself occupied with Palhaço and stayed away from the preparations, she could almost pretend that none of it had ever happened. What her mother said did have a ring of truth to it. Even

Paulina, who usually took Inez's side, had tried to tell her that she was too young to be married. Maybe it *had* just been a one-sided infatuation fabricated by a young girl's imagination all along. Perhaps Estêvão had simply been polite to her, and she had misinterpreted his affection for love. She had almost convinced herself of that fact when he showed up to take his bride.

Despite the fact that Inez was no longer waiting for the proposal from Estêvão, she still visited the knoll every morning. The view of the harbor was calming, and the invigorating walk up to the summit had become routine for Palhaço and herself. The weather was turning warm, and the shade of the olive tree was a welcome spot to play or read or just sit quietly and enjoy each other's company. It was the busiest time of the year for the trade industry, and the port of Vigo was crowded with vessels on a daily basis. These days Inez did not go out of her way to distinguish the blue falcon banner of the *María Vencedora*, so when the ship slipped into the harbor on a cloudy day in July, it completely escaped her notice.

The day dawned hot and muggy with the sharp ozone smell of a storm in the air. The stifling heat and deep rolling rumble of distant thunder put Inez in an irritable mood, so she headed up to the hill directly after breakfast to escape the last-minute preparations for the wedding. She tried to read but had difficulty absorbing the content, so she shut her book to play with Palhaço. After chasing her around the tree a few times and retrieving a stick, the puppy found a cool spot under the bench and panted to cool himself down. Inez followed his example and sat in the swing to catch the breeze.

There was the crunch of a footstep on the path behind them, and Palhaço lifted his head to see who approached. Inez ignored the intrusion, assuming that it was Serafina coming to apologize again or to tell Inez how much she regretted that things had worked out this way. It didn't matter. Inez had already forgiven her sister. In fact, she felt quite sorry for her. Serafina had not had any say in the decision. She was just an unwitting bystander caught up in the debacle. She had no cause to feel guilty. Inez sighed and waited for her sister to appear.

"Bom dia, Coelhinha," came a familiar mellow voice from behind. "I thought I might find you here," said Estêvão as he stepped into view in front of her.

The thunder reverberated through the sky, and the wet, earthy smell of approaching rain wafted in on the breeze. Inez sat ramrod straight in the swing. Her eyes stared at the man before her, unblinking, and her face took on a rigid, pinched look. Her hands gripped the ropes on either side of her until her knuckles stood out, white from the tension, and her jaws clenched tightly in an attempt to maintain her composure. She could think of nothing to say. Her capacity for rational thought had deserted her at the sound of his voice.

"I don't blame you for not wanting to speak to me," he went on with a sad smile. "I don't like myself much these days either."

"Why have you come here?" she was finally able to force out.

"That is a good question," he said, dropping his gaze to the ground. "I suppose I wanted to explain." The wind began to blow more insistently now, rustling the leaves of the tree above them.

"There is no explanation required. You needed a wife who could produce an heir for you, so you asked for my sister's hand in marriage. It's as easy as that."

"But it's not, Coelhinha," he said with a pleading look in his dark eyes, taking a tentative step toward her.

"Please, do not call me that," she snapped in the voice of a stranger. Estêvão stopped short and looked into her face, searching for some trace of familiarity. He was surprised to find that her silver eyes, which had always danced with a warm, golden fire for him, were now cold and hard as steel.

"You must yet feel some affection for me. I see you still wear the necklace that I gave you."

She put her hand up and touched the rabbit on her chest. It had become such a part of her that she had forgotten all about it. With a resolution born of self-preservation, she reached behind her neck and untied the leather thong from which the rabbit pended. She brought it down to her lap and set it on the cloth of her dress. It was her way of telling him that she was through with him, symbolic of the fact that he was the cause of her misery. A gust of wind ruffled the bottom edge of her skirt, this time bringing with it a few fat drops of warm rain. Inez looked up at the dark threatening clouds above then turned her attention back to Estêvão.

"My sister has tried to make excuses for your behavior," she said with a wry smile. "She swears to me that this must have been some sort of misunderstanding. I think perhaps she is trying to assuage her own guilty conscience. I told her that this is none of her doing, that if you had cared for me you would have made your feelings clear."

She was right. He was to blame. If he had been a man and stated his intention plainly instead of leaving the decision in someone else's hands, none of this would have ever happened. He stood there feeling sick at heart. He ached to take Inez in his arms and tell her that he now knew, irrevocably, it was she he loved, but he knew to do so would make himself reprehensible and alienate her from her parents, whom she now needed more than she needed him. He could not accomplish anything by voicing these thoughts, so he said nothing.

"Be kind to my sister," Inez went on. "She is a good person and will make a dutiful wife. She will do all that is required of her, but she will never love you." *Not as I do*, she added silently to herself, her heart breaking anew. She rose from the swing and called to Palhaço. He trotted to her side, and they took a few steps in the direction of the house. The rain was beginning to fall in earnest now, but Inez stopped and turned back to face Estêvão a final time. "I beg of you. If you ever bore me any affection whatsoever, do not seek me out again. I cannot bear this particular brand of cruelty," and she walked away with her dog, leaving Estêvão under the olive tree alone.

Estêvão watched her walk down the path until she disappeared from his sight. He dragged himself over to the seat she had just vacated and sat down in an unconscious attempt to feel close to her. The rain fell harder, some of it making its way through the leaves of the tree and dripping onto his head then down the neck of his shirt. He stared out at the sea and let the pain wash over him in waves, welcoming the sting of her words just to recall the sound of her voice. What had he done?

He had thought he was being so clever when he composed the letter of proposal. He should have just listened to his mother in the first place and come to terms with his feelings instead of patting himself on the back for his clever solution. Now he had ruined at least three lives, and he would have to live with the result. Not that he disliked his bride-to-be, he was indifferent to her. She could have been anyone else. No one would ever be Inez.

"What have I done?" he whispered to himself. "Oh, Coelhinha, will you ever be able to forgive me?" He dropped his head to his hands, and his gaze was drawn to the ground. He saw the little silver rabbit glowing up at him from the dirt where it had fallen from Inez's skirt. He reached down and closed his fist around it in frustration. "Someday I will make this right. Someday, Coelhinha, I will prove myself worthy to love you again," he said as the storm broke upon him. To seal the vow, he brought the little rabbit to his lips, consecrating it with the kiss he would now never be able to bestow upon his true love. He then placed the necklace in the little pouch he carried close to his heart, and with a hope that would never quite burn out, he made his way to the house to face the consequences of his foolish, thoughtless actions.

The rain continued to fall.

Upon reaching the house, Inez silently made her way up to her room. Now that the groom had arrived, the wedding could proceed as planned, and everyone rushed about in a frantic attempt to put the finishing touches on the preparations for the momentous occasion. With all of the commotion over the final details, no one noticed the sister of the bride ascend to her room with her dog in tow. She was relieved to have escaped their attention and leaned heavily against the door after closing it behind her.

The confrontation with Estêvão had left Inez mentally and emotionally drained. It had taken every ounce of her resolve not to rush into his arms and beg him to change his mind. Had tears still been a possibility for her, she would have laid on her bed and cried, but her suffering had surpassed weeping's ability to diminish it weeks ago. Besides, she had already made up her mind that she would never allow another person to have that kind of power over her again. She had learned her lesson well, and she would not be made a slave to her emotions. It was a treacherous path, and she dared not tread it a second time.

Her eyes alighted on the lute in the corner. That cherished instrument had seen so much life in its time on earth. The ribbons tied gaily to the tuning pegs represented the hopes of the little girl who had so passionately desired to express the love that had blossomed from an unexpected meeting mere weeks before her twelfth birthday. It had brought with it so much hope and so much joy. Now those things were gone, and the little girl had been replaced by a young woman who had had her first taste of life's disappointment.

Inez could no longer feel what the little girl had felt and could not imagine ever experiencing those sentiments again. Suddenly it was all too much to bear, and she crossed the room with a determined step, pulling up in front of the lute on its stand. She took a deep breath, gently removed the revered instrument from its place in the corner, and carefully packed it into the box where it had resided before finding its way into her hands. She felt a pang of remorse at its loss, but it was a symbol of the painful memories she so desperately wished to forget. Perhaps one day she would feel the urge to play again, but that day would not be soon.

It was the last time she would touch the lute for many years to come.

Chapter 5: The Wedding

The ceremony took place the next afternoon. Although the squall of the day before could have been interpreted as a bad omen, by comparison the wedding day seemed all the more sunny and cheerful. Everyone took this as a sign of God's blessing and maintained high hopes that the union would prove fruitful and harmonious. The bride and groom played their parts perfectly, and none in attendance had the slightest suspicion that the marriage was not a love match. Serafina and Estêvão were attentive and gracious, and only they knew that their façade of happiness just barely disguised the fact that their alliance was one of expediency and filial duty.

Not one of the guests failed to comment on the combined beauty of the newly wed couple. This much was true. Estêvão stood straight and tall in his signature cobalt blue captain's clothes with his head held high and his shining black-brown hair falling in a silky mane past his shoulders. His regal bearing made him seem the master of all that surrounded him, and none could doubt that he was nephew of the King of Portugal. Those who had scoffed at him before now understood a part of how he had come by the moniker of 'El Rey', and converted by his charisma, they vowed never to mock him again.

In complement to her groom's blue attire, the bride wore a persimmon silk gown trimmed with honey-gold lace. Joanna had taken pains to match the lace to her daughter's hair color exactly, and the effect was impressive. The warm metallic accents flickered and flashed with every small movement, and Serafina looked like a pillar of dancing fire topped by a brightly burning flame. Her natural grace and delicate beauty left no one uncharmed, and all could see the reason she had married so well. It was what she had been groomed for from the time she was a child, and all of the hard work had finally paid off.

The celebration was a complete success, and all of the staff's efforts were well worth the trouble. As mother of the bride, Joanna was completely in her element. She accepted congratulations on her daughter's good fortune as if it were something she had managed herself. She overcame her aversion to the Portuguese half of her new son-in-law's heritage by simply ignoring it, and in her eyes the idea that she could boast about his relation to the royal houses of not only Portugal and Castile but England as well, more than made up for that little shortcoming. One had to make sacrifices to enrich the lives of one's children, and this was just an example of the many she had made for hers.

There were so many people present and so much excitement that the bride and groom were the only two who noticed the absence of a certain fourteen-year-old girl. That morning while preparing to head to the church, Inez made the excuse of not feeling well. Having been through harrowing experiences with ill children in the past, Joanna was now supersensitive concerning their health. She took in her daughter's flushed face and listless nature and recalled that Inez had not been herself for a few weeks' time. She was sad that Inez would miss the festivities, but she did not want to risk worsening her condition. She kissed her daughter on the forehead and left Paulina to attend her.

Inez moped around the house looking for ways to pass the time. She did not want to face Paulina so soon after her rejection.

She knew the older woman would try to comfort and console her, and *that* she could not bear. She wished that she could simply jump ahead to a time when her suffering was over and the rest would be just a memory. She thought that if she did not attend the wedding she could escape her thoughts, but being alone with herself was almost worse. She decided to get out of the house.

It was late afternoon, and the revel should have been nearly concluded by now. Inez and Palhaço headed to the olive tree to see what they could from there. She espied the *María Vencedora* at the dock, her gangplank down, her crew at the ready. Inez felt a pang of jealousy that they were not waiting for her, but she pushed it aside, determined to stay strong. She moved her gaze up the road and saw the wedding procession as the guests accompanied the new husband and wife to their transport.

When they arrived at the dock, Estêvão swept Serafina off of her feet and carried her up the ramp to the ship. He set her down gently, and they walked to the rail to bid farewell to the crowd. A crewmember went down to cast off from their moorage then returned to the deck, pulling the gangway up behind him. As the caravel headed out to sea, the well-wishers dispersed, and Serafina turned from the rail to head below. Inez stood on the hill unable to take her eyes off of the man who had broken her heart, the man whom she still thought of as her beloved. Estêvão stood for a moment, unmoving, his glossy dark hair tossed about by the breeze. Then he looked straight up at the top of the knoll and bade her a final goodbye. Inez turned from the sea and made her way down the path to the house.

After leaving the deck, Estêvão headed straight to his quarters and knocked on the door. A pleasant female voice invited him to enter, so he opened the door and strode into the chamber. He found Serafina standing at his worktable holding a large tiger's eye gemstone, a memento of his first trip to India. He used the stone as a paperweight, and the letters that it usually held securely in a neat stack were now in an untidy spread across one corner of the table. Estêvão walked briskly over to his new wife, took the weight from her hand, straightened the correspondence, and firmly placed the tiger's eye on top.

"I'm sorry," Serafina said, blushing from the brusque manner with which he had removed the stone from her hand. "It's just that I have always been fascinated with these since I was a child."

"Yes well, these papers are very important, and I cannot afford to lose one. I trust that you've found everything to your liking?" he asked, not looking at her.

"Oh, yes," she replied. "The quarters are quite comfortable."

Estêvão nodded his head then raised it to look at her, taking a deep breath. "I have taken the liberty of hiring an attendant to see to your every need. He will be posted outside your door, so if you lack for anything, all you have to do is call. Even if it is the middle of the night, do not hesitate to wake him. This is his only job, so you will not be interrupting the running of the ship in any way. You must be very tired after the long day, so you may retire as soon as you'd like. I will not disturb you further." He bowed low and turned toward the door.

Serafina stood with her mouth hanging open in shock. Did he hate her so much? He had just let her know in no uncertain terms that she was of no significance to him, and he did not take pleasure from the fact that she was now his wife. This was not the marriage she had dreamt of her entire life. She fought back the tears and decided to give it one more try.

"Husband," she said, putting on her most radiant smile. Estêvão looked at her over his shoulder, one eyebrow raised and his hand on the door. "I suppose being married will take some getting used to, but I will do my best to please you," Serafina said hopefully. "Thank-you for being so considerate."

"It is nothing," he said, his expression unchanged. He then exited the chamber closing the door behind him.

Serafina, who had always been a much more emotional creature than her sister, burst into tears and threw herself onto the bed. "What have I done?" she cried to the empty room. "Oh, Inez, I'm so sorry! Little sister, will you ever be able to forgive me?"

Chapter 6: Broken Hearts

When the newlyweds arrived at the Fazenda da Pomba, they were greeted by a surprise homecoming celebration. The family had not accompanied Estêvão to retrieve his bride for different reasons. João was planning to head for India and had many business arrangements to make before he commandeered the *María Vencedora* and her crew for that purpose. Dom Martín never liked to leave the everyday operations of the ranch for very long, and María suffered from a chronic ailment that periodically rendered her unable to go about her usual activities. Sea travel always seemed to exacerbate her condition, so she had stayed behind to organize the festivities in honor of their newest family member. Serafina was touched by the warmth of her welcome, and sudden tears sprang to her eyes as she clung to her mother-in-law on the porch.

"Oh, Dona María," she said with feeling. "Thank you so, so much!"

"You are very welcome, dear," the older woman said, surprised by the fierceness of her new daughter's embrace. "But now you shall have to call me Mother," she added, pulling back to look her in the eye. "Welcome to your new home, Serafina."

"Thank you, Mother María," said the bride, trying out the new title. The family entered the house while the staff went about the task of unloading the personal effects of the new mistress.

The rest of the day was spent getting reacquainted, and Serafina began to relax and settle into her place within the family dynamic. She chatted with María, filling her mother-in-law in on the details of the wedding while Estêvão conversed with Dom Martín and João about the upcoming expedition. João would be leaving in two days, and Estêvão was feeling a pang of regret over having to remain behind while his crew set out for the new adventure to lands unknown.

"I envy you, Brother," Estêvão said, forgetting the reason he had elected to forego the current mission.

"You envy *me?*" João asked, confused at the comment. "You're the one who gets to relax here at home with your new bride, who looks like the Queen of Heaven I might add, with only one very delectable job to perform. How could you possibly envy me?"

"It's far more complicated than that," said Estêvão with a frustrated sigh.

"I would not find it complicated at all," João said with a salacious grin. "With a wife like that, *I* might even consider becoming a family man."

"Easy, boy," Dom Martín growled. "You are speaking of your brother's wife not some hussy hanging about by the docks." He looked over to where his wife sat with the subject of their discussion. "She is very beautiful though. I can't imagine you'd need much more incentive than that."

Estêvão shrugged his shoulders and turned the conversation back to João's upcoming voyage, trying to put his predicament out of his mind for the time being. The evening proceeded accordingly and soon it was time to retire. The family bid goodnight to one another and headed upstairs to their respective bedrooms. María had converted the largest guest room into a bridal chamber, and Estêvão led his new wife there now. He held the door open for her to enter, and as she crossed into the room a little delighted gasp escaped her lips.

Along with arranging the homecoming celebration, María had given instructions for the room to be made over for the newest member of the household. The giant four-poster bed had been appointed with a white lace coverlet embroidered with a flowering vine motif featuring the married couple's initials entwined in the center medallion and each of the four corners. The tester and draperies were done in the same clean linens, and new rugs lay scattered about the floor. Fresh flowers had been brought in and occupied every corner of the room. Garlands of hydrangeas, in a range of colors from the purest white to a deep blue that was nearly indigo, hung gracefully from every high point in the room, dripping down in fragrant cascades of floral splendor. Candles flickered from every surface, and the effect was dreamlike and exceedingly romantic. This was the wedding night that Serafina had always envisioned.

She had the fleeting thought that she was glad her husband had not touched her on the voyage over to her new home. It would make tonight all the more idyllic and memorable. She turned to him now, her face flushed with excitement and anticipation, and gushed, "Oh, Estêvão, it is beautiful!"

He perceptibly stiffened at the sound of his name issuing from her lips. It was the first time that she'd used it, and it would be the last. She saw his hands roll up into fists and his jaw muscles flex as he unconsciously ground his teeth together. Serafina knew she had offended him deeply, but she did not know how. She brought her hands together in a pleading gesture and opened her mouth to apologize, but the damage was done.

"I shall relay your gratitude to my mother," he said in a clipped, formal manner. "She will be pleased to know that you appreciate her efforts. I trust that you have everything you need. I shall see you in the morning. Good night." Then without waiting for an answer he turned and strode down the hall to his own room. Serafina stood at the open door, staring down the empty corridor after her husband. Again the tears came, but this time they flowed more silently than before. She knew that this union would not be without obstacles, but this, this was beyond difficult. This bordered on cruelty. She closed the door, and retreated into her bridal chamber alone.

A few days later, João sailed the *María Vencedora* out of the harbor at Angra. Serafina thought that with his brother gone, perhaps Estêvão might resign himself to the idea of settling into life at home. She reasoned that without the constant prospect of the expedition before him, he would realize his duties as a husband were as important a pursuit as any for the future of the fazenda, but this was not the case. Instead of seeking out his wife's company, Estêvão left her to her own devices and spent his time helping Dom Martín with the everyday operations of the ranch. He worked himself to exhaustion, and in the evenings he was withdrawn and untalkative. The bedtime ritual was repeated night after night, and eventually Serafina got accustomed to his rejection. She no longer cried when he abandoned her to go to his own room, and soon she ceased to care.

One morning after breakfast, Estêvão and Dom Martín left for the fields, and Serafina sat with her mother-in-law mending some work clothing. The women stitched and chatted pleasantly, comparing childhoods and making observations about how much times had changed. No matter how much things progressed though, many notions stayed the same. Here they were in the sixteenth century, yet they were still sewing clothing for their husbands. They laughed together over the idea then were quiet for a moment.

"Well before you know it, you will be sewing clothing for another little man," María said with a smile. Serafina blushed a little in response but did not say anything. "You know, dear, carrying a child can sometimes be a complicated and daunting responsibility. I would like you to feel that you can come to me if you have any questions."

"Thank you, Mother María," Serafina began, "but I don't think I will be needing advice anytime soon."

"Sometimes these things happen more quickly than you could imagine," María said with a smile.

"Yes, but so far it is not possible that I have conceived a child."

María lowered the shirt on which she was working. "What do you mean?" she asked, observing her daughter-in-law with her sharp Gypsy eyes.

"I mean my husband has not touched me," Serafina said simply.

"But it has been over a month since you were married," María said, stunned at the revelation.

Serafina nodded her golden head and continued sewing. María looked at the girl, and though no one would ever think to pity a creature as beautiful and fortunate as her daughter-in-law, she could not help but feel a wave of compassion rise in her heart for the child. This was not normal. She knew that her son had thought himself in love with the younger sister, but this union was a result of his own actions. It was heartless of him to punish his wife, who was innocent of any wrongdoing, simply because *he* had made a foolish decision. María could not tolerate or condone this behavior, and she determined to speak to him about it at the next opportunity.

The opportunity for María's conversation with her son arose

the next afternoon. Some business correspondence that required his attention arrived in the morning, and Estêvão stayed behind while Dom Martín rode out to oversee the branding of the spring calves. After doing some of her own accounting, María made her way up to her son's study and knocked on the door. Estêvão distractedly bade her to enter. She opened the door, quietly crossed the floor to an empty chair, and waited for him to finish the letter he was composing. He signed the document, placed his pen back in its stand, and sanded the note to absorb the excess ink. He pushed back in his chair, folded his hands behind his head, and smiled at his mother with a loving look in his eyes.

"What brings you here at this hour, Mother? I thought you'd be resting. I know you haven't felt yourself for a while."

She waved off his observation as if it were of no importance and said, "*I* am fine. It is *you* that I am concerned about."

He raised his eyebrows, sat forward a bit, and brought his arms down, crossing them over his chest. "What is it that concerns you, Mother?" he asked warily, cocking his head to one side and lifting his chin in an unconscious posture of defiance.

"There is no need for you to become defensive, Falcão," she said gently. Whenever she began one of these heart-to-heart conversations with her son, she automatically used his father's pet name for him, instinctively slipping back to a time when they had only each other. He visibly relaxed, and she continued. "I want to know how your marriage is proceeding. Living with a new person takes some adjusting, and you have the added task of accustoming yourself to life at home. It will take a while before you truly feel comfortable, but with a wife as willing to please as Serafina, it should not be a difficult transition."

He shifted uncomfortably in his seat and let what she said sink in. His mother always knew how to get to the bottom of a situation without mincing words. He struggled with how to formulate a reply. Finally he looked directly at her and sighed, "I think I have made a huge mistake."

María nodded her head, never taking her eyes from his, her expression never changing. "So how do you plan to fix it?"

"I don't know," Estêvão said, folding forward and placing his elbows on his knees. "I don't know that it can ever be fixed."

"You could get an annulment," María suggested. "Serafina says that you have not yet consummated your marriage."

"No, we have not, but the damage cannot be repaired that easily."

"To what damage are you referring?" she asked, knowing what he meant but wanting to hear him confirm it.

He sighed again and resigned himself to her inquiry. "I have involved myself in a loveless union that I will never see as a true one, I have trapped an innocent girl in it and stolen any dreams that she may have harbored of a real marriage, and ..." here he paused, looking up into his mother's eyes, laying bare the conflict within him, "and I have broken the heart of the person whom I suspect I truly love." He looked at his mother with a smile that was more a grimace of pain. "It is the betrayal with which I really struggle. Not only of her love for me but of the standard of truth and honor I have striven my entire life to uphold. Each time that I try to forget it, I feel I am belittling her emotions and abusing her trust all over again." He sat back in his chair and dropped his gaze to his lap. "If I sought an annulment, I would lose all credibility with the family, and Inez would be as far out of my grasp as she is now. How could this ever be right?"

María seized his hands in her own and looked directly at him. "You must make it right. You must accomplish what you set out to do from the start."

"Get an heir," he said.

María nodded solemnly. "You have broken Inez's heart, and

you admit that nothing you can do will remedy the situation, so you must at least make it worth the pain you have caused her."

"But I cannot bring myself to do it."

"You must find a way," María finished, rising from her chair. "It should not be so difficult," she said with a smile. "Serafina is a beautiful girl, and she wants very much to please you. I think you will find that once you make up your mind to do your conjugal duty, the rest will come more naturally than you imagine. Once you begin a family, perhaps you will find love with your wife after all. Stranger things have happened."

She bent down and kissed her son on the top of his head then walked across the room. She opened the door and turned to regard him one last time. "Inez is very young, Falcão. I'm sure in a few years she will find someone else to love, and you will become merely her brother-in-law and her feelings for you a distant, cherished memory." She then exited the room, pulling the door closed behind her.

"That's what I'm afraid of," he said quietly to the empty room. His mother had meant this final comment as a salve for his aching soul, but it had precisely the opposite effect on him. His hands clenched into fists at the thought of someone else, unfettered by the bonds of matrimony, pursuing Inez and winning his place in her heart.

Chapter 7: Husband and Wife

A few days later, Estêvão thought he had come up with a way to get through his connubial obligation without an attack of conscience. There had been a few times in his youth when he had taken a little too much wine and awakened in a strange place the next morning without a clue as to how he got there. It seemed a solution tailor-made for his dilemma, so that evening at supper he downed cup after cup of wine until he felt pleasantly warm and completely uninhibited. He participated in the conversation more than he had since bringing home his bride. He related amusing little anecdotes for the entertainment of all. He even looked directly at his beautiful wife, smiling and winking for a change instead of treating her as if she were not present. Serafina was surprised and pleased at the attention, and she was more radiant than anyone had seen her since her arrival. Martín was glad that his stepson had finally stopped moping, and the staff jumped to refill his cup as often as he drained it, happy that he had ceased to be so snappish. María was the only one perturbed by his behavior.

María understood what he was trying to accomplish, but it seemed to her that instead of facing up to his problems, he had simply found another way to run from them. She felt bad that things had not worked out the way he planned, but she felt worse for Serafina, who would probably wind up being more deeply hurt when she realized what her husband intended. He was a grown man and at the moment too drunk to be reasonable, so María held her peace and prayed for the best.

The evening progressed more or less in the usual manner, and Estêvão was not intoxicated to the point of slurring his speech or any other telltale sign of acute inebriation. Perhaps everything would come right after all. The family all bid each other goodnight, and his parents headed down the hall to their room. Estêvão walked Serafina to the bridal chamber as he did every night, but this time instead of leaving his wife to go to his own quarters, to her surprise he followed her into the room and closed the door behind them. She was astonished by his sudden change of heart and thought to herself that finally tonight they would become husband and wife in truth. Her beautiful aquamarine eyes opened wide and sparkled with anticipation as her husband crossed the room, swept her up in his arms, and carried her to the bed.

He set her down gently and removed his shirt while she watched him. She marveled at his lean, well-developed physique, fascinated by the way his wide shoulders and broad chest tapered down to his trim narrow hips. The clearly defined male musculature was something she had never seen before, and she longed to run her hands over its surface. Estêvão approached the bed and took his wife in his embrace, one arm encircling her tiny waist and the other sliding up her neck into her abundant, golden tresses. He pulled her close and kissed her deeply as she closed her eyes and let herself enjoy the softness of his lips and the pleasant, heady taste of the wine on his breath. He ran his hand down the length of her body and it came to rest on her hip, clutching a handful of her full skirt as he began to trail warm, gentle kisses up her jaw toward her ear. She made a little purring noise in her throat and arched her head to one side to afford him better access, and suddenly she felt him stiffen and pull away from her. She looked up into his face, and saw that his eyes had returned to the cold hard gaze to which she had become accustomed.

"What's wrong?" she asked in a pleading voice, desperate to know how she had failed him this time.

"Your perfume," he said curtly. "What scent is it?"

"It is pear blossom," she replied. "If you don't like it, I can scrub it off. It will only take a moment," she said, rising from the bed and hurrying toward the basin. She picked up a cloth and dipped it in the water.

"Don't trouble yourself," he said, grabbing his shirt and heading for the door. "I have just realized how exhausted I am. I'm sorry to have kept you awake so late. I will see you in the morning. Goodnight," and he left the room, closing the door behind him.

Serafina stood at the basin with the wet cloth in her hand. She had thought she was beyond caring, but her husband's sudden interest then abrupt repudiation was more than she could bear. She dropped the cloth into the basin and walked dejectedly to her bed as silent tears coursed down her face.

Estêvão entered his quarters and with all his strength flung his shirt across the room and began to pace. What had he been thinking? How could he have possibly thought it would be that easy? It had taken a complicated and convoluted chain of events to get him into his predicament, how could he have thought a few cups of wine would solve all of his problems? He had underestimated how firmly Inez had made her place in his heart and in his psyche. Would he ever be able to forget her?

The first part of the evening had gone according to plan. He had drunk enough wine to loosen up and let down his barriers, and he found himself attracted to the exquisitely stunning creature across the table from him who just happened to be his wife. What man would not feel blessed to be married to such a woman? He began to think that perhaps what his mother said made sense. Serafina did seem very eager to please him. Maybe in time love could bloom between them, if not at least a friendly and comfortable partnership. He told himself that he was being ridiculous and made up his mind to be a true husband. His wife had suffered enough at his hands through no fault of her own.

After the first kiss, he decided that María was right. Once initiated his overtures came more naturally, and he found himself getting caught up in the heat of the moment, physically responding to his wife's warmth and willingness to yield to him. He thought that he could finally put Inez behind him and move into the role of family man, securing the future of the fazenda in the process. But alas, it was not to be. He had fully committed himself to his duty when he caught a whiff of the scent that he associated with Inez, thought of as hers alone. Suddenly the thoughts of betrayal and guilt came rushing back, and his desire deserted him, leaving a bitter, empty feeling in its place.

He was a far more complex animal than he ever imagined. It seemed that once given, his heart could not be so easily deterred from its path. At the same time though, he realized that his marriage could not continue in this same fraudulent fashion. Serafina was his wife, and he was bound, not just legally but by honor, to do right by her. He could not continue to subject her to this cruelty. He could do nothing to remedy the situation with Inez, but he could at least attempt to make amends with her sister. Even if his heart would not allow him to love her, he could at least live in harmony with her. With his decision made, a sense of peace settled over him, and he climbed into bed exhausted but with a new hope. He hoped that one day Inez could find it in her heart to forgive him, and in turn he could forgive himself.

The next day Estêvão got up early and rode into Angra. When he returned from his errand, it was mid-morning, and he was surprised to note that his wife was nowhere to be found. He was told that she had not felt well at breakfast and had retired to her room to get some more rest. He made his way upstairs and knocked quietly at the door, not wanting to wake her if she were sleeping. Serafina bade him enter, and when he caught his first glimpse of her, he was shocked to note how truly ill she looked.

Instead of the healthy peachy tone with which her skin usually glowed, it appeared sallow and drawn, with a waxy, gray cast to it. Her golden hair looked dingy and washed out, and her eyes seemed dull and listless with exaggerated dark circles beneath them. Estêvão was immediately alarmed, and the thought struck him that this was all his doing. He walked quickly to her side and sat down on the bed.

"What is it that ails you, wife?" he asked. He was concerned for her well-being, but he still could not bring himself to use her name.

"I was just a little tired this morning. I did not sleep well last night. Do I look so terrible?" she asked, seeing the anxiety clearly reflected in his eyes.

"You look somewhat pallid is all." He sat there for a moment then became self-conscious of their proximity. He stood up and pulled a small package from his satchel. "I brought you something," he said, handing it to her.

Serafina took the proffered parcel and undid the wrapping. A perfume bottle lay in the center of the paper. She pulled the stopper from the vial and brought it to her nose. "Ambergris," she said with wonder. "My mother never allowed us to wear such an exotic scent. She always said it was too mature for a young girl. I think it was just an excuse, because it is so costly."

"Yes well, you are a married woman now, and I can well afford to buy you a little gift from time to time."

"Thank you," she said, smiling up at him. Her face brightened immediately, and suddenly he realized that it was the color of the robe that was making her look so sickly.

"Where did you get that dressing gown?" he asked, picking up her shawl from a nearby chair.

"I think it is something that Ine ..." Serafina stopped herself short. She knew of Estêvão's feelings for her sister. Maybe it was not such a good idea to mention her name now that things were starting to feel more normal between husband and wife. "It was part of my trousseau," she finished up lamely.

"Well it does not suit you. Here, give it to me," he said, holding out his hand to receive the garment. Serafina had tried to keep from revealing that Inez had made the piece, but Estêvão picked up on the slip, and his mood quickly soured. When his wife removed the robe and handed it to him, he awkwardly dropped her shawl about her shoulders and excused himself without looking at her again. He exited her room and made his way to his own.

Once in the privacy of his own chamber he allowed himself to relax. He sat down in a chair and meticulously inspected the dressing gown made by the hands of the young girl who had stolen his heart. He marveled at the tiny, perfect stitches that held the garment together, impressed by the flawless embroidery that adorned the borders and matching sash. She had used his favorite cobalt blue set off by a deep wine red, and in one corner he was surprised to find a miniscule 'E' entwined with an 'I' so skillfully hidden that at first glance no one would know it was there. He sat unmoving for a few minutes, holding the robe in his hands. Then, resolutely he rose from his seat, lovingly folded the piece, and placed it on a high shelf in his wardrobe. Perhaps in some way it would keep her close to him, and from time to time he could look up at it and remember that there was a time when Inez had truly loved him.

Eventually Estêvão and Serafina consummated their marriage

and were able to peacefully coexist with one another. The original purpose of their marriage had been to produce an heir, and their infrequent attempts were performed perfunctorily and out of a sense of duty. After these procreative sessions, Estêvão never lingered in the bridal chamber, which he now thought of as his wife's personal room. He always headed straight to his own quarters so he could sleep alone in the manner to which he was accustomed. They remained virtual strangers and never felt quite comfortable enough to call each other by their first names, addressing each other only as 'husband' and 'wife'. They were polite and civil, and he no longer held a grudge against her for not being Inez. This was not the fairy tale marriage that Serafina had dreamt of as a child, but it was tolerable. She never used the pear blossom perfume again.

Chapter 8: Confession

After the marriage and departure of the eldest daughter of the house, the García household returned to normal. Iñigo resumed working his regular hours at the mercantile, and Joanna now set about the task of assembling a trousseau for her remaining daughter. It would be a few years before Inez would be of marriageable age, but there was no reason to wait. If they started now, by the time the first proposals came in there would be a substantial and respectable dowry for Inez to take to her new home.

Because Serafina had married so favorably, Joanna's hopes for an auspicious match for Inez were high. Of course Inez did not possess her sister's dazzling looks, but she was very pretty with her masses of coppery hair and those stunning silver and gold eyes. She also had other outstanding attributes. She was intelligent and hardworking, she could prepare the most amazing delicacies, and she could play the lute and sing more beautifully than anyone Joanna had ever heard. The curious observation struck her that she had not heard Inez play her lute since they returned from Terceira, but she brushed it away reasoning that they had been far too busy planning Serafina's wedding for her to notice.

In the evenings after supper, the family removed to the sitting room to unwind before bed. Iñigo usually read a book while the two women sat stitching, and Palhaço lay curled at the foot of whichever chair Inez chose to occupy. Joanna chattered on with the latest bits of gossip and had already begun assessing the available local men in terms of prospective suitors for her remaining daughter. Inez did not mind. The embroidery was relaxing, and she had long ago learned to listen for key phrases, which required her response. She usually kept her mother happy with a series of nods or grunts with an occasional 'Yes, Mama' or 'No, Mama' thrown in.

As far as her marriage was concerned, Inez did not care a fig about it. She had convinced herself that with her one true love already married to her sister it made no difference whatsoever whom her parents selected for her. They could have married her into the notorious House of Borgia, and it would not have mattered. If she wound up a wizened old spinster, that was fine too. She had made up her mind to never let her emotions rule her again, and if that meant having to spend the rest of her life alone, then so be it. This attitude helped her get through the long evenings with her parents, but it did nothing to fill the emptiness in her heart.

She had trouble sleeping, and all food had lost its savor. She occasionally helped Paulina out in the kitchen, but even that brought back memories of the meal she had prepared with Estêvão on Terceira. When she tried to read, she lost her concentration, and she was no longer needed at the mercantile. The only thing that brought her any pleasure was Palhaço.

The puppy grew quickly and was nearly unrecognizable as the same little black and tan runt he had been on Terceira. Most of his black hair had fallen out, leaving only a silky black fringe along the bottom edges of his ears and a peppering of black down the center of his back and curly tail. Inez got into the habit of taking him for long walks to previously unexplored locations of the surrounding countryside. He was always eager for activity and watching him sniffing and snorting and marking his territory always brought a smile to her face. A few times he flushed out random wildlife, a squirrel or bird or other small creature, and she laughed at his antics and admired his athleticism as he ran and leapt over hill and dale in close pursuit of his quarry. The little animal always seemed to dart to safety at the last moment, but Inez doubted that Palhaço would even know what to do with it had he actually caught the thing.

Joanna had noticed the difference in her daughter the day of Serafina's wedding. Though she did not associate it with the event itself, she felt that something had happened around that time to bring on the alteration in Inez's personality. At first she thought Inez was upset at the lack of attention, but weeks after Serafina had gone, Inez was still mopey and listless in nature. Joanna then assumed that Inez was missing her sister. They had argued and annoyed each other, the way that all siblings did, but they had loved each other very much. Joanna was not very concerned. She missed Serafina too, but in time they would both recover. She did not notice the extent of change in Inez until an evening nearly six months later.

The family was invited to a New Year celebration at the home of one of Iñigo's wealthiest customers. The man was the owner of a sizeable estate a few miles up the Ria de Vigo. He had a tall, dashing son who was just three years older than Inez, and the man always joked that someday it might be profitable for the families to link their fortunes by marriage. Joanna opined that perhaps this was more a hint than a joke, so when the invitation arrived, she fussed and clucked over Inez, planning what her daughter would wear on the night of the party. She recalled the time at the Fazenda da Pomba when Inez had entertained with Estêvão. She had looked beautiful in the lilac silk gown, and all of the men had gazed upon her in clear admiration. Estêvão had even offered his arm at the foot of the stairs and guided her solicitously to her seat. Maybe the dress would have the same mesmerizing effect on their current host's son.

This meeting between the two young people would be very important, so they could not leave anything to chance. Joanna made Inez try on the gown to make sure it was still suitable and to make any small alterations that it might need. When Inez put on the dress and returned to her mother for the assessment, Joanna let out an audible gasp of shock.

The gown had originally been made to fit Inez exactly, and when she'd worn it in Terceira, it had hugged her as closely as a second skin. The tight square neckline still fit reasonably well, but from there the fabric fell loosely to the floor only flaring out slightly over Inez's wider hips, which stood out sharply, their outline showing plainly through the silk. Joanna could see her daughter's prominent collarbones and the ridged skeletal structure of her chest. The sleeves of the garment draped like curtains from the flat planes of her bony shoulders. Suddenly Joanna took in the shadows under her daughter's eyes, her narrow face with its newly revealed cheekbones, and the slender corded neck, all of which had once been covered with a healthy layer of plump adolescent flesh. How did she not notice this sooner?

Knowing that Inez would most likely refuse to discuss the cause of this transformation if she made too big a fuss over it, Joanna tactfully resisted the urge to fly into hysterics and make a dramatic scene. Instead, she put her hand up to cover her gaping mouth and walked around her daughter as if gauging the work to be done.

"Well," she began carefully, "it is a little loose around the middle. If you wear the verdugado underneath, it will take up some of the slack. I am sure I have a length of this black lace left. Perhaps we can make a sash. It will be very flattering and show off your tiny waist. Yes, that is what we will do."

To Inez it did not matter one way or another. She shrugged her fleshless shoulders and turned to exit the room. Joanna watched her daughter's thin frame shuffle listlessly across the floor, and she could not stand it one second more. Inez had been the independent child about whom Joanna had never had to worry. She had been the self-confident, defiant little hoyden who never thought twice about speaking her opinion or standing up for what she believed. This person before her was only a shadow of her former self. What had happened to extinguish the fire that had burned so brightly inside her?

"Inez," Joanna said softly. Her daughter slowly turned to face her with a questioning look in her eyes. "Is there anything you'd like to talk about?"

"No, Mama," said Inez, shaking her head.

"I have noticed that you are not quite yourself since your sister got married," Joanna said. She thought she saw a slight crinkling of her daughter's freckled nose. Inez had tried very hard to master the habit, but that one little twitch was enough to give her away. Joanna knew she had discovered the source of her misery, and so she pressed forward. "I miss Serafina too. I know sometimes you annoyed each other, but all siblings do. Deep inside you love her very much, and to have her leave is a big adjustment, but your sadness will pass."

Inez looked straight into her mother's face with tears shimmering in her silver eyes. She tried to smile, but the corners of her mouth trembled and pulled down into a frown. "It is true that I love my sister," she began in a quavering voice, "and I have been heartbroken since she married, but the source of my suffering is not what you think." She was crying openly now, her fragile frame shaking with the force of her sobs.

Joanna could bear her daughter's torment no longer. She got

up from her chair and strode across the room. She put her arm about Inez's slight body and quietly led her to the window seat where she hugged her child to her and held her while she wept. She rocked her gently, making little clucking noises until her sorrowful spasms subsided. She let her sit quietly for a few minutes, and when she believed she would not cause her further pain Joanna said, "If you do not tell me what ails you, I cannot help."

"You cannot help me, anyway," Inez said dejectedly.

"There is nothing in this world that cannot be fixed. Tell me, hija. Tell me what happened."

Inez was reluctant to reveal the source of her heartache. Her mother had let it be known time after time that Inez was not old enough to be married. She would never understand how Inez had fallen in love before she had even turned twelve. This love was so precious to her, something so very treasured, cherished. It would destroy her for Joanna to trivialize it by calling it an infatuation. Inez was torn over what to do, but she had already gone too far to refuse an answer. She took a deep, shuddering breath and said, "You married my sister to the man I love."

Suddenly everything clicked into place for Joanna. The sweet, stolen glances, Estêvão's solicitous manner, the way they had seemed to be singing for each other, all of it now made sense. No wonder Inez had been so affected. It would have been one thing for him to marry another girl from a different family, but they had married Inez's own sister to the man she had chosen for herself. A wave of guilt washed over Joanna, and tears flooded down her cheeks.

"Oh, mi *hijita!*" Joanna cried. "Why did you not say something?"

Inez was astounded at her mother's reaction. Both women were sobbing freely, clinging to one another for support. "I thought you would think me foolish and too young, that you would view it as an infatuation."

Joanna pulled back a little and looked into her daughter's red-rimmed eyes. "I know you think of me as an old woman, but I was fifteen once and in love. I have lived enough of life to know that to love is never foolish, and age rarely enters into the equation. I have experienced tragedy and heartbreak, and what I would not have given to have spared you your own."

Chapter 9: Joanna

Catalina of Lancaster was born in 1373 in Hertfordshire, England to the Infanta Constanza of Castile and John of Gaunt, Duke of Lancaster. Constanza believed herself to be the rightful heir to the throne of Castile and was obsessed with the idea of returning to her homeland in that capacity. It was widely rumored that her husband had married her precisely for this reason—he was possessed of his own kingly aspirations—and he was an eager accomplice in her schemes. In 1386, the couple took an English army to Castile to press their claim and had limited success, capturing the cities of Santiago de Compostela, Vigo, and Pontevedra. But after a failed invasion of Leon, they were forced to withdraw to Portugal.

Shortly thereafter, the Duke and Duchess accepted the proposal of the king regnant of Castile, Juan I, to marry their daughter to his son under the condition that Constanza renounce all claim to the throne. It was a compromise aimed at bringing peace to the region and ending the conflict between the warring provinces of Castile and Leon, and Aragon. The agreement would realize their ambitions to rule by setting their daughter on the throne, and it would help imbue the Trastamara line with at least a small measure of legitimacy. In 1388, Catalina was married to the future Enrique III of Castile. Eventually an armistice was reached, and the kingdoms were united as modern-day Spain.

Among Catalina's English ladies-in-waiting was a golden-haired beauty named Joanna. She was wife of one of the men John of Gaunt brought with him to fight for the Castilian crown. Sir Thomas Newenden elected to stay in Castile and was granted estates near Valladolid so that his wife could continue to serve the future queen. Joanna was an accomplished musician with a voice like an angel. Her musical talents and soothing manner won favor with Catalina, and though the queen was reputedly virtuous and reserved—she banished many women from her household for their perceived looseness of character—she kept Joanna by her side.

In the years before Queen Catalina died in in June of 1418, her life began a downward spiral that left her disheartened and without hope for the future. After suffering a stroke and continued poor health, her royal authority was reduced, and she was forced to cede custody of her son. In spite of these unfortunate circumstances, even when things were at their bleakest, Joanna was able to cheer her by playing her lute and serenading the queen with her enchanting voice.

The Newenden family enjoyed their new home in this exciting foreign land. Sir Thomas had been a wool merchant before he joined his liege lord's army. He now returned to that profession and continued to prosper. The wool from the Merino sheep of Castile was an extremely sought-after commodity, and Sir Thomas was able to keep his Joanna and their two daughters in the comfort to which they were accustomed. They moved in the most exclusive social circles, mostly keeping company with their fellow expatriates and a few well-to-do Castilian Anglophiles. They learned the Castilian language out of necessity but continued to speak English among each other and their friends. Their daughters, along with the offspring of the rest of their distinguished group, were raised in the manner of their erstwhile homeland and developed an elitist attitude in regard to the superiority of all things English. Their homes were styled after the manors in which they had lived before bidding farewell to their native land, their furniture was imported from overseas, their clothing was fashioned to follow the *mode du jour* adopted by the English aristocracy, and even their gardens were planted with roses that originated from the same soil.

Another of the traditions that Joanna and Thomas tried to keep alive was the naming of their daughters after family members in the particular order of their birth. Their firstborn was Joanna for her mother, and her sister was Margaret after their grandmother. Instead of translating the names into the Castilian versions—Juana and Margarita—they insisted upon using the Anglo pronunciation. These customs persisted for three subsequent generations. The lute that had made the journey with the original Joanna when she accompanied Catalina was also passed from mother to daughter, as much a family trait as her golden hair and aquamarine eyes.

In 1461, another Joanna came into being. Her parents had tried for many years to conceive a child, and at the advanced age of forty, her mother found herself unexpectedly pregnant. The angelic baby girl followed in the footsteps of the previous three women who shared her namesake. She had the same ethereal coloring, and her parents soon discovered that she was blessed with as much, if not more, musical talent than that of her forebears. She learned to play the beautiful antique lute at the early age of six, and her parents thought her an angel come to earth.

Because she was an answer to many years of prayer, they doted on the child, showering her with her every desire. She grew used to getting her own way, and as there were no other children in the household, there was no need for her parents to temper their indulgence. She soon grew spoiled and demanding, and instead of attempting to curtail her bad behavior, they fed into it by acceding to her every whim. By the time she was ten years old, she was headstrong and thought she knew much better than her middle-aged, old-fashioned parents. She continued to do as she wished, and no one did anything to rein her in.

In April of 1475, when Joanna was fourteen years old, King Afonso V of Portugal and his son, João, began an invasion of Castile. Afonso's niece, Juana la Beltraneja, had been overlooked in the succession of the Castilian crown, and he and many others believed her to be the rightful heir. Joanna's father felt duty-bound by the Treaty of Windsor—which in 1386 had established an Anglo-Portuguese Alliance—to support Afonso and rally to his cause. He had always been a staunch loyalist, and along with many other prominent Castilian nobles he left to join Afonso's army.

In addition to the erstwhile English nobles who now made their residence in Castile, there were many with similar histories who had chosen to make their homes in Portugal. When these men were united with their one-time countrymen, they came together, striking up friendships with one another as people who share a common background often do. Among the men Joanna's father brought home with him during the long months of Portugal's occupation of Castile was a seventeen-year-old stripling named Robert Crowle. His family was originally from Lincolnshire, England and had also come over with John of Gaunt in his bid for the Castilian crown.

Young Robert had been dubbed Robin not only to distinguish him from his father, Robert senior, but because he had a thick thatch of bright red hair that stood up from his scalp in an unruly explosion of curls too springy ever to be tamed with comb or cap. He was tall and wiry with milk-white skin covered with a profusion of freckles. His appearance would have been comical if he had not been blessed with the chiseled face of a Greek God dominated by pair of nearly black eyes. His brooding eyes, which sparkled with intelligence, were topped by intense dark brows, and his quick, perfect smile captured Joanna's heart the first time it flashed.

Robin was smitten by the angelic looks of his host's beautiful young daughter as well. Her golden hair, peachy skin, and blue-green eyes were delicate and rare, features seldom seen in the population of women surrounding the Crowle estate in Portugal. It was also difficult to believe she was only fourteen years of age. She had the fully developed body of a mature woman, and her confidence and imperiousness were characteristic of a much more experienced adult. The young people were naturally drawn to each other and soon discovered that they had much in common.

After their first meeting, Robin and Joanna became inseparable. While their fathers and their companions discussed strategies of attack and the righteousness of their cause, the two young lovers would take long rides on the grounds, walk in the English gardens, or find an out-of-the-way location to talk or sing. Robin was an accomplished flute player and was never without some version of the instrument on his person. Though most of their concerts took place in private, on occasion they deigned to entertain some of the men gathered for an evening meal. For those few odd performances, their audience knew that they were witnessing something rare and magical, and they were left feeling privileged to have attended such an event.

The months passed and the relationship between Robin and Joanna became more and more serious. Both sets of parents could see the love developing between the two young people and decided to unite the families by marriage. The couple was engaged and a date was set for a time after Joanna's fifteenth birthday and when the war would be at an end. When the official betrothal was celebrated, the pair were ecstatic and put on a concert that evening that no one present would ever forget. They poured out their love for one another in song, and their emotion was palpable. It was such a display that some of the attendees found themselves flushing with embarrassment to have been privy to such an intimate moment.

Robin and Joanna were sad to learn that their days together would be short-lived. The lull in Afonso's invasion was rumored to be nearing an end, and Robin's return to the battlefield soon loomed before them. Ferdinand and Isabella had finally assembled enough troops to begin a counteroffensive, and they cunningly harassed Portuguese border towns far away from the amassed forces of their rival's legion, attempting to draw attention from his stronghold at Toro. The stratagem worked, and thousands of Portuguese soldiers returned to their homeland to defend it. Afonso began to reassess the judiciousness of his decision to enter into the conflict and proposed a settlement, but *Los Reyes Católicos* would have none of it. The offer was rejected and after much skirmishing back and forth, both sides began preparations for a final confrontation at Toro.

In mid-February 1476, Joanna celebrated her fifteenth birthday. It was a momentous occasion for her, because she had just fulfilled half of the conditions set forth by her parents as requisites for her marriage to Robin. The young people danced and sang and rejoiced for hours, and as the evening wore on, Joanna's parents retired leaving the teenagers under supervision of the staff. As soon as the old couple ascended the stairs, Robin turned to his betrothed with a conspiratorial whisper.

"I have a special surprise for you, mi amor," he said, kissing her insistently on her pink rosebud mouth.

Joanna pulled back and giggled nervously. "Robin, not in front of the servants," she said. They had kissed often before, and much more intensely than this but, out of propriety, never in front of other people. "They are sure to gossip," she added to lend weight to her objection.

"What do I care if they gossip? Besides, whose business is it but my own if I kiss my wife?"

"We are not yet married," she reminded him, waggling her finger in front of his handsome face. "Only one of the requirements has been satisfied."

"To the devil with the requirements! I have made other plans!" he replied. Then he told her about the arrangements he had made for them to be married that very night. He laid it all out so methodically and logically, that she could not formulate the slightest objection. "We are in love and have been officially betrothed with our parents' blessings. What difference will a few months make anyway? Besides, why should our union be delayed by a disagreement rooted in events that occurred long before either of us was even born? There will always be wars and rumors of wars, should our lives be put on hold because of it?" he asked rhetorically.

Joanna began to see the reason behind Robin's side of the argument so when he urged her upstairs to pack a bag, she did so without further protest. She came back down in her traveling clothes, and they composed a letter of explanation for her parents, bribing a servant to deliver the note no sooner than the following morning. They made their way quietly to the stables and mounted his horse, riding off into the night, laughing and singing as they went.

When they arrived at the little church where Robin had made an agreement with the priest just two days before, they found it locked up tight with no one in attendance. It was late, this much was true, but with the amount of the donation Robin had contributed, he expected to find someone waiting to receive them, no matter the hour. He pounded on the solid oak doors in a frustrated attempt to rouse someone within, but his efforts were in vain. The place was deserted. The young couple reluctantly turned away and remounted their horse.

It was very late now, and they were far from home. They were both tired and cold, and a thick mist began to move in dampening their spirits and their clothing. This was to have been their wedding night, and nothing but the best would do for Señor Crowle and his beautiful new wife. Robin had paid a large price to reserve the most elegant room at the most expensive inn in the town, so they headed there now to escape the dreary weather.

Contrary to their reception at the church, the innkeeper had eagerly awaited their coming, insisting that his wife stay up with him to welcome their distinguished guests when they arrived. "Ah, los Señores Crowle," he said enthusiastically, taking Robin's hand in his and motioning for his wife to help Joanna with her cape and belongings, all of which were soaked through. "What a miserable night for such a happy occasion," the innkeeper continued. "It seems that love does not feel the need to wait for a sunny day! It is a good thing we were expecting you. We have hot food and wine at the ready and a roaring fire warming your room. I suppose being newlyweds you are impervious to any of life's little discomforts, but at least you will have a place to dry your traveling clothes!" He said this last with a short bark and a salacious wink, utterly pleased with his joke.

The young people were too tired and wet to correct him in regard to their marital status and followed him up the stairs to the chamber he had readied for them. His wife disappeared to the kitchen to prepare a generous platter of victuals and quickly reappeared to bring up the rear of the procession. Joanna had not paid enough attention to her surroundings to pass judgement upon them—when Robin had procured the room two days prior he only noted that the premises was neat and well-kept—but when the innkeeper stood aside for her to enter the room, her beautiful face lit up, and she clapped her hands together in pleasure.

The interior was typical of any Spanish bedchamber with heavy oak furniture and dark tapestries distributed liberally about the room. There was a blazing fire crackling cheerfully in the hearth, and the bed was made up with crisp, clean linens and a deep, luxurious feather mattress. There were vases filled with lavender and roses, and rosemary and thyme provided fragrant sprigs of greenery in contrast to the rainbow colors of the floral bouquets. Candles had been lit around the room and lent a fairytale air to the heavenly scene, elevating it to an apartment fit for a queen.

"I'm thrilled that you are pleased, Señora Crowle," said the innkeeper. "If you require anything else, do not hesitate to ring for it. I hope you will enjoy your stay." He bowed smoothly and waved at his wife to move her along. She placed the food-laden tray down on the table and hurried to his side, dropping a quick curtsey before closing the door behind her.

"Oh, Robin!" exclaimed Joanna. "It is perfect, just perfect!"

"The only problem being that we are not married," he said moodily, his dark brows drawing together in consternation. "I cannot believe that the church was closed when we got there. I was sure there would be someone waiting."

"Perhaps there was some sort of emergency," said Joanna, settling herself in his lap and playfully nuzzling his freckled neck with her nose. "It does not mean that we can't enjoy this romantic little love nest."

"Don't start that, mi amor," he said, looking down at her with his intense black gaze. "You may initiate something for which you are not ready."

"I have been *ready* for this night since the moment I met you," she said with meaning, her eyes glittering with desire.

"Besides, we are already married in our hearts. What difference would a few words uttered by a priest make?"

"None at all, mi amor. None at all." Robin stood up with her in his arms and carried her over to the bed, setting her down in the deep feather mattress. He pulled his shirt off over his head and bent down to kiss her tenderly. "I promise you, Joanna," he began with emotion, "that tomorrow at first light, I will take you to the church and make us husband and wife in the eyes of God." He kissed her again, and they gave themselves to each other fully, consummating the marriage that they intended to take place the next morning.

Robin would never fulfill his vow.

The next day they rose with the sun and headed to the church to pledge their love to one another. They were greeted by an altar boy who looked as if he had not slept for a week. His eyes were puffy and bloodshot, and his hair was greasy and unwashed. When Robin asked the lad what had happened to the priest to whom he had spoken three days prior, the child broke down into a pathetic outpouring of grief and could not speak. When he could finally give an explanation, Joanna and Robin were aghast at the implications.

Father Miguel had suffered an attack the previous afternoon and now lay hovering near death in his bed. Because of the war communications were delayed, and there would not be another priest to take his place or even to read him his last rites for an unspecified period of time. The young altar boy was terrified to be alone with the priest. He did not want the padre to succumb on his watch thus leaving him accountable for the good priest's descent into purgatory. Joanna and Robin felt bad for the child but could not do a thing to help him. They mentioned nothing of their own predicament and trudged dejectedly from the church, leaving the altar boy crying in a pew.

"What are we going to do now?" Joanna asked, wide-eyed with worry.

"I suppose the best thing to do would be to go home and say nothing of this until we can remedy the situation," Robin replied, chewing on his lower lip. Joanna nodded her assent and they mounted his horse and headed for home.

When they arrived back at Joanna's home, the entire manor was in a state of upheaval. A steady stream of armored men rode past them, grim-faced and battle-ready, heading for the staging grounds to receive their orders. The young people barely managed to stop an escudero to find out what the activity meant.

It seemed that Afonso V was tired of the long drawn-out engagement and the fickle whims and capitulation of the nobility. He wanted to make a final effort to end the conflict and return the land to a peaceful coexistence that would benefit Portugal and Castile alike. He had marshaled his forces to explain his objective and request their cooperation in this last heroic attempt aimed at bringing the war to an end. The men were tired of waiting and happily rushed to comply with this demand.

Joanna and Robin proceeded to the house with heavy hearts and heavy minds. They were greeted at the door by the same maidservant with whom they had left the message for Joanna's parents, and she quickly explained that the Señores had been so busy that she had not had a chance to deliver the letter. She had no sooner handed the note back than Joanna's mother appeared behind her.

"Joanna," she said, clearly relieved to have found her daughter. "I have been looking all over for you, dear. I wanted to make sure you didn't get trampled in all this furor. I know that you are anxious to spend your last few moments alone with your betrothed, but be careful! The men have a lot on their minds, and you could easily be injured. I will leave you two to say your goodbyes. Good luck, Robin," she finished and made her way back into the house.

Joanna was close to tears, so Robin led her to a peaceful spot in the garden where they could talk uninterrupted. He held her to him until she recovered her composure then pulled back a little to look her in the eye. He marveled again at her beauty and thought to himself that if anything happened to him, at least they had had last night. It was something he could not bring himself to voice to her, so instead he said, "Well, mi amor, it looks as if the wedding will have to wait."

"I don't care, Robin. I only want you." She looked away from him out at the serenity of the garden, finding it ironic that preparations for war were taking place not a hundred feet in the opposite direction. "Isn't there a way you could hide? Some way we could sneak away and leave all of this chaos behind?"

"I could never live with the shame of it, Joanna."

"To the devil with the shame!" she cried out. Finally it was too much, and her beautiful aquamarine eyes filled up and overflowed with tears. "I could live with the shame and whatever else I had to endure as long as I had you by my side."

"Shhh," he said and held her to him, rocking her like a baby in his arms, trying to still the hitching sobs that quaked through her grieving body. When she stopped shaking, he put his long fingers under her chin and lifted her face so he could look into her eyes. "There's my girl," he said, smiling down at her. "Be brave and give me that angelic smile that I love so well. It will be the first thing I see in the morning and the last thing I see at night. The memory will keep me going for the short time that I am away. When I return we will be united, and nothing will ever come between us again. Nothing."

Joanna did not feel like smiling but did so because her love had asked it. He smiled back at her then took her in his arms, crushing her lips with his own. They sat there, locked together, tears streaming down Joanna's face, and finally, swiftly, he turned and was gone.

The final battle of Toro was fought on March 1, 1476. When the Portuguese crown prince, João, could not break through the Castilian lines with reinforcements, Afonso V left the battlefield to take refuge in Castronuño. His forces broke and his army fell apart. Ferdinand and Afonso both declared victory, but the Portuguese monarch's integrity was permanently compromised. He left Castile soon thereafter, and Juana la Beltraneja retired to a convent in Lisbon to live out her days. There were heavy casualties of Castilian and Portuguese soldiers, and both Joanna's father and Robin were among them.

When news of the Portuguese defeat arrived at the estate, Joanna and her mother were frantic with worry. Neither one of them could eat or sleep, knowing deep in their hearts that their men stood only a slim chance of survival. Joanna spent many of her waking hours railing against the Portuguese, king and countrymen alike, condemning them for their cowardice, cursing their schemes and overreaching ambitions, blaming them all for her personal distress. If they had just been satisfied with the territory they had and not tried to conquer every bit of land in sight, she would have been married to her betrothed and happily settled on a quiet English manor somewhere in the Portuguese countryside. These rants helped to keep her mind off of the tenuous state of affairs, but it did nothing to prepare her for the inevitable.

Finally the courier came with confirmation of the women's worst fears. Both Joanna's father and her betrothed had been killed on the field of battle. Robin and his father would be lionized because they had died in brave service to their sovereign, but her father's estate would be treated in a much different manner. Because he had enjoined in acts of sedition against the anointed rulers of his country, his property was now subject to confiscation. Not only had Joanna and her mother lost their beloved male counterparts, now they would lose their home.

The truth of the situation was much worse than either of the women imagined. Both of them were plunged into a morass of mourning and took to their rooms shunning solace and sustenance. They were so inconsolable that they did not even attempt to comfort each other. They simply retired to their own quarters and did not emerge for the length of their bereavement.

A few weeks later, Joanna made the decision to rejoin the human race. She was tired of the same four walls and made up her mind to enjoy the lavish grounds of her childhood home before being banished from them forever. As she descended the stairs, a wave of nausea washed over her, and she had to clutch at the banister to steady herself. She was not really surprised by her lightheadedness. She had not consumed a substantial meal since the night she and Robin sneaked away to be married, and for the weeks since the courier arrived bearing the news of his death, she had rarely been out of her bed at all. She waited for the spell to pass then continued her downward progress.

As she approached the dining table, she was happy to see that her mother had also dispensed with her lamentations. When her mother looked up from the breakfast in front of her, Joanna let out a little cry of shock at her haggard appearance. She had always thought of her mother as an old woman, but now she certainly looked it. The elder Joanna's once beautiful eyes were now dull and sunken into their sockets. Her face was gaunt, and her cheekbones stood out sharply under the paper-thin skin. She labored to breathe, and her lips were tinged a pale shade of blue. Joanna forgot her own sorrows for a moment and bent down to hug her mother tightly. Neither woman said anything as the tears flooded down both of their faces, and they clung to one another for support.

When the moment had passed, the elder Joanna patted her lovely daughter on the cheek and waved her on to her chair. The servants brought out a breakfast of fruit and bread, and the younger woman loaded her plate with the delicacies she had eschewed for the previous few weeks. The food was exceptionally appetizing and she tore into it with relish. She was just pushing her plate away from her when she was assaulted by another attack of queasiness. She abruptly rose from the table, stumbled out to the gardens, and expelled every morsel she had ingested. She wiped her delicate mouth with the back of her hand and reentered the dining room where her mother sat with a concerned look on her sallow face.

"Are you all right, dear?"

"Yes, Mama. I'm fine," Joanna replied, patting the beads of sweat on her forehead with the napkin from the table. "I guess I ate just a little too quickly, and my stomach was not used to the food," she reasoned, setting the napkin down. "I feel much better now."

"I don't feel much like eating either, dear, but I suppose like all things, it will pass."

Joanna nodded her agreement, and in the days that followed she was more careful with her delicate stomach, usually only drinking watered wine and nibbling on a biscuit or some toasted bread.

As the weeks wore on, the two Joannas began to pack their personal belongings to ready for the inevitable eviction. They had not received official word yet, but several families in similar situations had already been ushered unceremoniously out of their homes. The elder Joanna had already written to her sister Margaret, the Vizcondesa de San Marcos, to beg shelter for herself and her daughter. Margaret did not think twice about taking the ladies in and looked forward to having some female companions who were more straightforwardly seeking her favor as opposed to the roundabout way the pretentious society women went about it. Besides, they were family and she loved them dearly.

One day when the Joannas were supervising the crating of some artifacts that had made the original journey from England, the elder noticed her daughter tugging at the fabric of her bodice. The younger woman wore an irritated grimace, and she could not seem to get her dress adjusted to her satisfaction. The material across her bosom did look as if it was stretched more tightly than usual, and Joanna the elder wondered how it had arrived in that condition.

"What is wrong, dear?" she asked as her daughter pulled at the neckline of her gown one more time.

"I don't know, Mama. This dress is just so uncomfortable," the younger woman replied, frustrated with her inability to keep the dress from binding.

The elder Joanna looked appraisingly at her daughter, wondering if what she was thinking could be true. There had been the nausea in the mornings, her daughter's unusual moodiness, and now this unexpected swelling of her bosom. She would have to keep a close eye on her to see if any other symptoms developed.

Two weeks later, mother noticed that her daughter was still fussing with her necklines. She had worn every one of the most recently made gowns from her wardrobe and the fit was the same. Joanna was too shrewd to pretend any longer and set out to have a serious talk with the younger woman. She ascended to her daughter's room and knocked resolutely on the door. Her daughter bade her to come in, and she entered the room, closing the door behind her.

"Joanna, we must talk," she said seriously, sitting down next to her daughter on the bed.

"What do you want to talk about, Mama?" Joanna asked, looking innocently up at her.

"Your condition, dear," her mother said, smiling kindly. Joanna looked up at her with a confused look on her face, and her mother began to explain what she believed to be affecting the state of her daughter's health. Joanna listened, wide-eyed with shock, unable to recall a time when her mother had been so open with her. She answered all of her mother's questions as honestly and accurately as she could and sat anxiously awaiting her verdict.

"Well, Joanna, it seems that you have resulted with child."

"But Mama," Joanna said with wonderment, "it was only that one night."

"With some women it only takes one night."

Joanna crinkled up her nose and looked up at her mother out of the corner of her eye. "And you're not mad at me?" she asked, more childlike than her mother had ever seen her.

The older woman took ahold of her daughter's hands and smiled widely, looking happier than Joanna had seen her for a very long time. "No, dear. I am not mad at you. What would that accomplish? The deed is already done. Besides, I always wanted a house filled with children, if not my own then yours, and I was not sure I would live to see them. This way I stand a very good chance."

Over the course of the next few weeks, the household was packed and a wagon loaded with all of the items too precious to leave behind. The two Joannas had procrastinated over their departure trying to postpone the quitting of their lifelong home as long as they could, but because of the younger woman's newly discovered condition, her mother decided they should make the journey before her daughter grew ungainly and uncomfortable. They were scheduled to leave in two days' time, and the younger Joanna was in her room packing up the last of her personal effects.

There were many small items that she determined she could not live without. She had placed every gift Robin had ever given her in a small box at the back of her wardrobe. She removed the box now and carried it to her bed to review the mementos within. She lifted the lid and the combined aromas of cedar and flowers wafted up to her nose. Unbidden tears sprang to her eyes as she handled the physical evidence of the love that had come to such a tragic demise.

There was an ornate comb Robin had given her for her lovely golden locks, a dried posy of wildflowers they had picked during one of their long strolls together, a small book of romantic poetry, and several letters in which he had expressed his love for her. All of these little objects brought the memories flooding back, but none so much as a flute he had given her to mark their betrothal. She took it out now and held it lovingly in her hands.

When a young couple was officially betrothed, it was customary to present the future bride with a ring or some such piece of jewelry to represent the groom's good faith and seal the contract. The ring that would have eventually become Joanna's was deemed too costly a family heirloom to be trusted to a fourteen-year-old girl. Robin's mother said she would happily bestow the ring upon her daughter-in-law at the wedding ceremony, but until then she preferred to keep it in her own possession to avoid any chance of its being misplaced. Robin was embarrassed by his mother's preemptory attitude, so he sealed the contract in his own fashion with a gift much more precious to him than any piece of old jewelry.

After supper that evening, he led Joanna out to the garden seat to plight his troth in their own private ceremony. He got down on one knee and took her delicate hand in his long freckled one and promised her that he would never love another. After resting his lips on the back of her hand, he gently turned it over and placed in her palm a long object wrapped in a length of fabric. His dark eyes glowed with anticipation as Joanna carefully unwrapped her betrothal present.

"This flute has been in my family for generations, years before we made the trip from England," he explained. "It is as much an heirloom as the ring my mother so stingily withheld, and it means much, much more to me than that. It is my most prized possession, and I entrust you with it now as faithfully as I entrust you with my heart. I have placed my lips on it so often that I am sure my essence lingers on the mouthpiece. When you miss me, you can press your mouth to the same spot and feel like your lips are kissing mine."

Joanna smiled at the memory. It was the first time she had thought of her Robin since his death and had not broken down in tears. She held the flute to her lips and kissed the mouthpiece tenderly before placing the instrument back in the box with care. She put the box in a larger crate and brought her hands to her barely protruding belly. Perhaps someday the child growing in her womb would follow in his father's musical steps and desire to play the flute of his own accord. Until that time, she would guard the instrument and her memories, preserving them for the day when she would tell their child all about the father he would never know.

When the last crate had been packed, the two Joannas made the trek to their new home with the Vizcondesa de San Marcos, a few miles to the east of Santiago de Compostela. When the Vizcondesa was informed of her niece's delicate condition, she made the very wise suggestion that the girl should be presented as a widow whose young husband had been killed in the war. This was not so far from the truth and exactly how young Joanna viewed herself, but she still felt uncomfortable with the deception. She could not help but feel that one day she would be called to pay a penalty for her dishonesty. She only hoped that the price would not be too dear. Despite her uneasiness, the modified history was adopted and became the accepted explanation of her circumstances.

Joanna experienced no further complications with her pregnancy, and at the end of her term she was delivered of a beautiful healthy boy with a thatch of reddish-gold hair and somber grey eyes. Joanna named him after his father and adopted the same fitting nickname to denote his coloring. The women were all thrilled at the prospect of a male in the home—the Vizconde had passed on shortly after taking his second wife, leaving no children behind—and little Robin was pampered and treated like a crown prince.

As Joanna had speculated before his birth, little Robin showed promise of musical talent. No one was surprised. After all, both of his parents had possessed substantial aptitude in this area, it stood to reason that he should inherit at least an inclination toward music. At the age of three he would sing or hum to keep himself company, and for his fourth birthday, Joanna purchased a little rudimentary flute for him to carry on his person and play when he wished. Little Robin marched around the house, his carrot-colored curls bouncing up and down around his ears, toodle-ooing on his flute, bringing smiles to everyone in the household.

After the initial performances of largely unorganized pipings, he began to pay attention and make a conscious effort to work out little songs on his flute. Some of the tunes he played were bits and snatches of pieces he heard, but some of the melodies were of his own composition. He developed a respect for his instrument and began to treat it with care instead of as just another of his toys. Joanna thought it was time to introduce him to his father's revered heirloom, so one day she sat him down and brought out the box.

She lifted the flute out of the box and unwrapped the cloth that protected it from the elements. When the highly polished, deep red rosewood of the flute was revealed, little Robin sucked in his breath and looked up at his beautiful mother, his solemn gray eyes open wide with awe. She offered him the instrument so he could examine the intricate engravings, but he shook his head nervously, refusing to handle it.

"What's wrong, little Robin?" she asked her son, tenderly tucking a coppery curl behind his ear.

"I don't want to ruin it, Mama. It's just too special," he replied.

"Then come over and sit in my lap," Joanna said, patting the space in front of her. "I will hold it while you look at the decorations." Robin scooted over to the place she indicated and turned the flute carefully, oohing and aahing at each new discovery.

"Would you like to play it?" she asked him when he had finished with his thorough inspection. He shook his head again, daunted by the prospect. "I'll tell you what then," she began, caressing his silken curls. "When you change your mind we can bring down the box, and I will sit quietly while you try it out. Does that sound all right?"

Robin nodded cheerfully, his sunny smile breaking across his freckled face. Joanna took his chin in her hand and placed a kiss on top of his crinkled up nose. He hopped down from his seat and streaked across the floor, stopping at the open door. He turned back to regard her with his dark gray eyes and said, "Thank you, Mama. Thank you so much!"

Joanna nodded, tears springing to her eyes, "You are very

welcome, little Robin. I love you," she managed to squeak out before her emotions overtook her.

"I love you, too!" he shouted then turned and raced down the hall.

Eventually, Robin built up enough courage to play his father's flute. He never took it out of his mother's rooms, and he always returned it so she could wrap it back up securely and return it to the protection of the cedar box. The instrument served as a catalyst, and being introduced to this part of his father only fueled Robin's desire to know everything about him. On days when the weather was bad or when there was nothing else to do, he sat and listened while Joanna told him all she knew about the man she loved.

Robin's grandmother often sat in on these sessions as well. She was now confined to the house where there were enough people present to keep constant watch. Since her husband had been killed in the war nearly seven years before, her health had steadily declined, and now she could not be left alone for fear she might slip and fall or need some other form of assistance. She knew her days were nearing their end, and her greatest joy was to spend time with her daughter and six-year-old grandson, listening to them play their instruments together or recalling stories of the halcyon pre-war days of Castile.

One morning she could not rise from her bed and called her daughter to her side. Joanna immediately dropped what she was doing and hurried to her mother's room. She looked down at the frail, shrunken woman, her beloved mother who had always given her everything she needed and desired, and she could not accept that she would soon be without her. She took her mother's fragile, birdlike hand in her own and placed a warm loving kiss upon it.

The elder Joanna opened her rheumy eyes and regarded her

daughter's angelic face, the face nearly identical to her own in her youth. She smiled weakly and tried to speak. Joanna lowered her ear to her mother's mouth to hear what she had to say. The older woman proceeded to tell her daughter how proud she was of how she had handled the circumstances, which would have brought a weaker woman to despair. She had done a marvelous job with her son, regardless of the fact that she had borne him at such an early age, and she was a wonderful, loving mother. She thanked her daughter for having brought so much joy to her during her final days, and she told her not to worry. She had lived much longer than she had ever expected and would go to the Father in peace.

The old woman held on for a few more days, long enough to say goodbye to her sister and her grandson, but finally she succumbed, simply going to sleep and slipping away. Joanna was devastated. The thought occurred to her that everyone she had ever loved—except for her son—had died, but she resolutely pushed it out of her head. She had other business to take care of now. She put on a brave face for Robin, explaining to him that death was just a natural part of life and that his grandmother had gone to heaven to be with God. They still had each other and Joanna would never leave him.

Time wore on and Joanna's pain at the loss of her mother faded. She had Robin to take care of and devoted all of her time to that purpose. He was now seven years old, and every day he grew more and more like his father in body and in mind. He was tall for his age and had the long, lanky build of his sire. He had the same milky white skin peppered liberally with freckles. His hair was not the exact shade or coarse texture of his father's, but it was still remarkable for its shining copper hue and the abundance of its curls. Although he was a reserved child, the intelligence shone plainly in his dark gray eyes. He had a thirst for knowledge that his mother did not have the background to satisfy, so the Vizcondesa hired the most esteemed tutor her substantial fortune could afford to take charge of her grandnephew's education. The man was a highly reputed friar of the Franciscan Order at Compostela.

When Father Bartolomeu was not treating pilgrims, in special cases, like that of the Vizcondesa's not inconsiderable donation to the Church, he took on a select group of pupils to whom he could pass on his enlightened views. Besides healing people in the Name of the Father, it was the one ability he prized above all others. He had the distinct talent of exemplifying the Church's principles by applying them to situations of everyday life. This always demonstrated his daily tutorials in a crystal clear manner, and Robin eagerly looked forward to each new sitting.

It bothered Joanna that the priest was of Portuguese descent. She had lost everyone whom she had ever loved, either directly or indirectly, as a result of their dealings with the Portuguese. In addition, this man daily came into contact with pilgrims at the shrine of Santiago de Compostela, not merely a passing association but sometimes actually treating them. She was afraid he might inadvertently expose her son to some incurable contagious disease, but her Aunt Margaret assured her that everything would be fine. The lessons continued, and Joanna's fears gradually subsided.

One day the priest arrived late for Robin's lesson. He was clearly nonplussed, and he distractedly explained the reason for his tardiness. When he had been on his way out of his cell, a group of supplicants had carried an ailing companion to his quarters and settled him on the cleric's bed. Father Bartolomeu tried to explain to them that he did not treat patients in his room, but the men were insistent and he finally acceded to their requests to examine their friend.

The patient had a high fever and was for the most part

unresponsive. He had an inflamed rash that looked oddly like freckles, and his companions said that he had suffered from nausea and vomiting during the night. Father Bartolomeu called for a litter and supervised the move to the infirmary. He prescribed a treatment of fluids and compresses, but he feared that the man was beyond saving. He advised the companions to pray. When Robin's lesson was concluded, the priest hurried back to the infirmary to learn the fate of his patient.

The next day he arrived for the lesson tired and gray. He informed the women that his patient had succumbed during the night, only after prolonged treatment and prayer. Father Bartolomeu looked drained and moved with the lethargy of a man twice his age, but he explained it by saying he had stayed awake with the man for most of the night. He attempted to forge ahead with a lecture he had prepared but wound up cutting the session short and headed back to his room to rest.

The following day Father Bartolomeu did not come. No messenger was sent to provide explanation, so the Vizcondesa dispatched one of her own to find out what had become of the teacher. The courier had no sooner closed the door behind him than young Robin appeared in the room complaining of a headache. Joanna flew to his side and pressed her cool hand to his forehead. She drew it back in shock, and she felt her heart rise to her throat. He was burning up! She immediately sent him to bed and ordered compresses applied to lower his fever.

The messenger finally returned looking tired and shaken. When he had arrived at the church, he'd encountered a panic of epic proportions. The infirmary was filled to capacity, and he had been unable to flag anyone down to ask about Father Bartolomeu. Finally he pulled one of the nurses aside and extracted the terrible news. The priest had died during the night along with several other people, clergy and pilgrims alike. The worst news of all was that the sickness bore a striking resemblance to the Black Death.

When Robin began to expel even the clear broth and watered wine his mother tried to force into his body, Joanna knew that her worst fears had come true.

The funeral took place two days later. Robin's illness had progressed rapidly, and he expired before the next morning's dawn. Everyone else had been mercifully spared, and even Joanna, who had never left her young son's side, had not come down with so much as a headache. The house was plunged into a pall of mourning, everyone saddened to have lost the little master who had brought so much sunshine into their everyday lives.

Strangely enough, Joanna was the only one who did not cry. She mechanically went about the task of preparing her seven-year-old son's remains for burial. She washed his little body with care then rubbed the traditional unguents and spices into his skin to keep him smelling sweet. She dressed him in his best suit of clothing and folded his arms serenely across his chest. She combed his hair, arranging it neatly on the white satin pillow beneath his head. Then the thought occurred to her that she had left something out.

She made her way upstairs to her room and took the cedar box from its place in her wardrobe. She set it down on her table and removed the rosewood flute for the last time, unheeding of the protective cloth that fluttered gracefully to the floor. She turned the lovely old instrument in her hands, smiling faintly at the rabbits and deer engraved on its surface. She nodded her head once and went back downstairs to the parlor.

Joanna was taken aback as she viewed her beautiful little boy in the coffin that would be his final resting place. The full import of the situation assaulted her senses, and her courage almost faltered. She swallowed hard and approached the bier, determined to perform this ultimate act of a mother's love. She slipped the flute into his delicate white hands and placed a kiss on his cold alabaster nose with its sprinkling of freckles that would never again crinkle under the touch of her lips. Then, she ascended to her room, closed the door, climbed into her bed, and waited for death to effect the reunion she so desperately desired.

For the second time in her twenty-three years on earth, Joanna returned to the ranks of the living. This time she had spent nearly two months trying to figure out why God had deigned to deprive her of every person, excluding her Aunt Margaret, whom she had ever loved. When she did not perish during the weeks of her self-imposed exile, she concluded that He must have some other design for her existence and made it her new mission to find out what it was.

She was weak and weary, her body wasted away to the very edge of expiration, but she made no effort to repair it. She reasoned that being so close to the gates of heaven would enable her to hear God's reply more clearly when it came. She limited her intake to the least amount of sustenance to keep her alive only long enough to complete her objective. She shunned the luxurious gowns in which she had once taken such pleasure, only donning the plainest of wool frocks not even good enough for the Vizcondesa's servants. It was her version of a hair shirt, which her aunt would absolutely not permit her to wear.

She began to make a daily pilgrimage to the cathedral at Santiago de Compostela, always taking with her Robin's little toy flute, which she now carried wherever she went. Once she tried to walk the few miles to the church but had nearly collapsed in the road. From that day forward, her aunt insisted she be driven, logically pointing out that she could not receive an answer to her petition if she were lying unconscious in the dirt. Joanna accepted the assistance and continued with her quest.

She lit votive candles to the Blessed Virgin Mary. She prayed for hours, reciting the rosary, eschewing the padded kneelers to prove her devotion. Her knees were swollen and purple with bruises, but she welcomed every little ache and every little pain because it afforded her the opportunity to feel something other than the emptiness where her heart had once resided. Each day she returned to her room depressed and downtrodden, devoid of emotion.

One day, at the end of her patience after not receiving a reply for months on end, she hurled her prayer book across her room in a fit of despair. It hit the floor spine first and opened to a page where she had used a sprig of rosemary as a bookmark. She slowly walked over and retrieved the book, pulling the rosemary from its pages. She held the fragrant herb to her nose recalling whence it originated.

She had pressed it there the morning her betrothed rode off to perform his patriotic duty. It was part of a flower arrangement from the room where she and Robin had consummated the marriage that had never taken place. She also recalled all the lies and deception in which she had engaged to avoid the shame of her sin. Suddenly everything became crystal clear, and the guilt and remorse brought her to her cracked and throbbing knees. She crumpled to the floor, weeping for the punishment she had unwittingly wrought upon her child, and she begged God to forgive her so at least she could go to her grave without the burden of little Robin's death on her conscience. She beseeched Him to send her a sign, any sign, so she would know how to proceed from there. She fell asleep on the boards of her bedroom floor, her hands still clasped together in prayer.

The next morning she awoke cold and sore but with a

lightness in her soul that she had not felt for a very long time. She slowly rose to her feet and hobbled to her wardrobe, picking out a fresh gown to replace the wrinkled one in which she had slept. Then she began to brush her hair. During the length of her penance she had never bothered to brush it, merely covering it with a mantilla to avoid the added sin of vanity. Today though, she felt in her heart that God had finally forgiven her, and she shrugged off the lace shawl, which had shrouded her golden tresses, hoping to lighten her burden of guilt by the action. She went down to breakfast, nibbled her customary biscuit, and set off on her daily trek to the church.

She made her way through the crowds of pilgrims, speculating about the reasons for their presence here. Had any of them suffered as she had, or was it merely the carnival aspect of the journey that drew them? She knew that tragedies similar to her own, and sometimes much worse, happened every day, and some people went an entire lifetime without receiving an answer. She considered herself lucky. She had the distinct feeling that today she would receive some indication of her absolution.

She reached the little chapel off of the choir that had become as familiar to her as her room at home. It always seemed to be deserted, and this was the original reason she had chosen it. She took out Robin's little toy flute and her donation for the day and proceeded to the bank of candles at the front of the room. She looked up at the effigy of the Virgin Mary and crossed herself before settling down to pray. She took the already lit taper from its holder to light her own votive, and suddenly she heard a shuffling at the chapel's entry. She turned to see who approached.

There in the doorway stood a tall, lanky man with the same build and mannerisms as her beloved Robin. He did not have the curly red hair or the freckled white skin of her betrothed—it was clear that he was of Mediterranean descent—but when her eyes locked with his, she was amazed at the resemblance. The intelligent dark gaze and intense black brow were nearly identical in the sharp angular plains of his handsome face. Her mouth fell open and her heart began to pound quickly in her chest.

Joanna recovered her composure and was able to utter a weak, "Perdón, Señor," before returning to light her candle and kneeling to begin her prayers. She heard some more rustling behind her, and when she mustered enough courage to peek at the doorway, the man was gone. She was too excited to concentrate on her prayers so she rose from her knees, dusting off the front of her dress, and made her way out of the cathedral. She scanned the crowd, casually looking for the dark head that would tower above the rest of the patrons, but he seemed to have disappeared. She shrugged her shoulders, got into the cart, and let her mind wander as the driver headed for home.

Joanna had prayed for months for any sign to show that God had forgiven her. There had not been anything to signify even the smallest hint of His clemency, and it had been because out of ignorance and human failing Joanna had not completely confessed her sin. Last night her revelation had come, and she had poured out the confidences of her very soul, and today she had received her sign. What else could it be? Aside from his coloring and the texture of his hair, the man was a replica of her Robin. She was not concerned that he had disappeared almost as suddenly as he had shown up. If this were meant to be, he would be at the shrine tomorrow. All she had to do was wait.

The next morning Joanna's mood was as light as the day before. Her Aunt Margaret noticed the change and marveled at the resilience of youth, but she did not say anything. She also noticed that her niece ate less this morning than the bird's meal that she normally ate, but again she withheld comment. Joanna could sometimes be a fickle creature, and the Vizcondesa did not want to spoil this new peace by bringing attention to it. She went on with her breakfast, only making conversation about topics they had established as 'safe' months ago.

Joanna felt the excitement rise within her. She had thought of nothing but the tall, slender stranger since he had stumbled into the chapel the day before. She could not concentrate, and she had no appetite. She finished half of a biscuit, patted her lips, and rose from the table. As she headed for the church, she had to think about something else to keep from jumping out of her skin.

When Joanna got to the chapel, she did all of the things that had become routine to ready herself for prayer. When she took the taper to light her own candle, the flame flickered and danced and almost went out because her hand was shaking so much. As she crossed herself and prepared to kneel, she heard the swift, staccato footsteps, recognizing them from the day before. She lowered her head with a little smile and tried to concentrate on her devotions.

When she finished her prayers, she crossed herself again and rose slowly from the floor. She brushed off the front of her gown, and when she lifted her gaze from it, she discovered the tall, dark man regarding her openly and unabashedly with a question in his look and an innocence she had never seen in the eyes of a grown man. She nodded and gave him a little half-smile then made her way out of the chapel.

She wended a path among the pilgrims crowding the cathedral and stepped out into the courtyard. A slight breeze ruffled her golden hair, and she filled her lungs with fresh air, looking up to behold the clarity of the sky. A pair of doves flew across her line of vision, brilliant white against the azure background, and she tracked them until they disappeared, certain that this was another sign of God's forgiveness. These were all things that had gone unnoticed during the months of her mourning, and now they were spread out before her like a feast before a starving man. All she'd had to do was look. This was the sign for which she had been waiting.

She nearly skipped the rest of the way to the waiting driver. She hopped into the cart and pulled out Robin's toy flute, which was now ever present on her person. She pressed it gently to her cheek, enjoying the shock of its cool smooth surface against her sun-warmed skin. She held it to her as she would have held her precious boy, and she smiled at the thought of how much she loved him.

"Oh, little Robin, you will *always* be with me," she said aloud, pressing the flute to her bosom, and a single tear slid down her face. The driver snapped his reins, and the cart started forward with a jolt. The last thing she saw as she wiped the tear away was the talk, dark stranger from the chapel.

The next few days passed in the same fashion. Each day when Joanna settled herself to pray, the man entered the chapel to attend to devotions of his own. He never said anything, only regarded her openly and returned the nods she directed at him.

One day when she was lighting her votive, her hand shook more than usual. She was over the worst of her nerves, and she wondered what was the matter. She had had no appetite of late and had eaten less than usual. Perhaps that was it. She shrugged it off and continued with her prayers, smiling when she heard the man enter the chapel behind her. She finished her rosary, crossed herself, and began to rise from her knees. As she straightened to her full height, her vision swam before her and began to dim. She clutched at the rail to steady herself, but the action was in vain. She sank to the floor in a graceful heap, mercifully avoiding injury in the process.

When she came to, the dark man was kneeling over her

fanning her face with a square of cloth. He wore a concerned look on his handsome face, and when she opened her eyes, he heaved a sigh of relief. He helped her to sit up and held a bottle of watered wine to her lips, insisting that she drink from it. When she was ready, he helped her to stand and supported her as they made their way outside. Not a single word was uttered between them, and finally she broke the silence.

"Thank you, Señor ... ah ..."

"Iñigo," he offered in a pleasantly modulated voice.

"Thank you, Iñigo," she said, trying out the name. She did not know anyone by that name, but it felt familiar and comfortable. "I am Joanna."

"A beautiful name for a beautiful girl ... um, woman ... uh," he stammered clumsily, blushing at his incompetence. His social awkwardness had long been a source of embarrassment for him and a family joke, but with this girl it seemed not to matter. She laughed out loud at his stumbling tongue, and he thought it the sweetest sound he had ever heard. He escorted her to the waiting cart and held her hand as she climbed up to take her seat.

"Thank you, Iñigo," Joanna said sincerely, "for all of your assistance. I don't know what I would have done if you had not been there."

"It was nothing, Reina. I was happy to help. Have a safe trip, and I will see you tomorrow."

The driver urged the horses forward, and Joanna smiled back at her new acquaintance, raising her hand in a wave of farewell. Iñigo immediately looked down at the ground. He was dazzled by her beauty, her smile too radiant to bear. Without looking up, he raised his hand in answer and headed for his rooms at the inn.

Joanna watched him walk away from the church with his head pointed down at his feet. *What an odd man*, she thought to herself. Odd, but strangely enough she was drawn to him as she had not been drawn to any other man, even Robin. Perhaps it was his innocence and his bumbling, endearing manner of speaking. He seemed intelligent enough, even though he had gotten her name wrong, but there was something about him that soothed her, like a balm for her aching soul.

Joanna knew she had reached a turning point. For the first time since the death of her son, she had ceased to dwell upon the past.

The days progressed in a like manner. Joanna kept up with her daily devotions, and like clockwork Iñigo appeared at the chapel. They never said anything during their prayers, but afterward they began to linger, longer and longer with each day that passed, making small talk and simply enjoying each other's company. They finally reached the point where they trusted one another enough to reveal the reasons for their own pilgrimages to Compostela. They were both awed at the power of faith and amazed by the way in which it had brought them together. They each began to believe that their meeting was destined to be, but they kept their suspicions to themselves, reluctant to be the first to openly acknowledge the blossoming relationship between them.

Eventually Iñigo ceased to feel discomfited by her presence, but each day when he walked her to her transport at the end of their time, he always said the same thing. "Farewell, Reina. Have a safe trip, and I will see you tomorrow." Joanna thought this a curious and incongruent idiosyncrasy of his personality. She had gotten to know him well enough to have some idea of his intelligence, which to her appeared remarkable, yet he did not seem able to get her name right. She had told him many stories about her history in which she had referred to herself by name, but he continued to call her 'Reina'. She vowed to ask him about it the next day.

The following afternoon when they had done with their chat, Iñigo walked Joanna to the cart and handed her up to her seat. He made a short bow and said, "Farewell, Reina. Have a safe trip, and I will see you tomorrow."

This time instead of overlooking the slip Joanna asked, "Why do you call me Reina? It seems strange to me that we have become such close friends, yet you still do not know my name."

Iñigo smiled up at her as if she were a child in need of explanation. For his entire life he had been socially awkward, only finding himself at ease when speaking with repeat customers at the mercantile about business affairs. He had never been able to achieve the facility with language that he had with numbers, but his love for this exquisite and ethereal creature had emboldened him and lent him the silvered tongue of a poet.

"Yes, Señorita Joanna, I know your name well. You are the subject of my dreams every night. How could I fail to know everything about you? I call you 'Reina', because you have become the queen of my world. Every breath I take, every moment I live, every aspiration I have, are all in the hopes that one day you could deign to grace me with even the smallest hint of your love. I live for you, Reina, and I am yours to command."

Joanna sat there with her mouth hanging open. No one had ever made such an eloquent speech to her in her life, and coming from Iñigo, it was doubly surprising. It was so unexpected from this usually artless and plain-speaking man, and with his reticent nature she knew what it must have cost him to make this declaration. She also knew that he was sincere and that he would do everything in his power to take care of her and try to make her happy.

As the cart started its forward progress Joanna locked eyes with her admirer, and he did not look away, simply stared after her in his honest, innocent way. Unbelievably she realized that she had begun to look forward to her future, and she felt in the depths of her heart that her future lay with him.

Chapter 10: Laying the Past to Rest

Inez sat curled up against Joanna's side. She held a handkerchief in her hand, dabbing at the tears that seeped out the corners of her eyes. Her mother's tale had explained much, from the faraway looks she got when she held her lute to her mistrust of the Portuguese, right down to her irritation at her daughter's habit of crinkling her nose and the exasperation with her sassy tongue. Inez would never have believed her mother had lived such an eventful life filled with so many tragedies, any *one* of which would have broken a weaker woman. She began to look at Joanna with a new respect and view her own problems with a more realistic perspective. Although it did not feel like it now, her pain would eventually subside and someday become nothing but a distant memory.

Their shared stories of mutual despair bound the two women more closely together, now more confidantes than mother and daughter. "Mama," Inez began quietly, reluctant to break the spell, "what happened next? When did you and my father get married?" Joanna proceeded to fill in the requested information.

After Iñigo's astounding pronouncement, there was nothing left between them with the potential to be embarrassing or a source of chagrin. It only served to make them more comfortable with one another and more open. Joanna related all of the most shameful details of her trials, and in turn Iñigo told her all about the promise to his father that had brought him to Compostela and about Aarón's dream, which turned out to be more vision than mere reverie. They held nothing back and their relationship grew stronger.

Iñigo was invited to dine with the Vizcondesa. Joanna had, for the most part, already made up her mind that she would accept a marriage proposal from Iñigo the moment it was put forward, but it would be nice to have her Aunt Margaret's approval. In addition to her sanctioning of their union, Joanna could count on the Vizcondesa giving her unbiased assessment of his person. Joanna's aunt had always been a shrewd judge of character and was a very useful protector for someone who had grown up in as sheltered an environment as her niece.

Iñigo arrived for lunch one afternoon, and over the meal the Vizcondesa peppered him with a non-stop line of questions that covered everything from his familial lineage to the reasons for his pilgrimage to Santiago de Compostela. There were several points during the interrogation when Joanna had to lower her head in humiliation for her suitor, but to his credit he never batted an eye. He simply answered the questions as they came in his open, honest way, and his gaze never faltered. The Vizcondesa paused for a moment, and Joanna heaved a sigh of relief, believing the assault to be at an end. But her aunt was not finished.

"So, Señor García," she began with a malicious little smile, "basically you are a Jew who has fled the Inquisition, and now you expect me to give my approval for you to marry my niece, who is like a daughter to me I might add. She is descended from a noble English lineage that once served the Queen of Castile, yet you think you are worthy of her affections. Is that right, Señor García?"

Joanna was mortified! What was her aunt doing? It was bad

enough that the Vizcondesa had been so discourteous as to barrage this shy sensitive man with questions throughout the entire meal, but to call him a Jew and tell him that he was beneath any consideration! Inconceivable! Joanna sat miserably waiting for her beloved to answer.

Iñigo pondered the question as if someone had asked him which soup he preferred before the main course of his meal. Then he looked directly at his hostess, and in the most unaffected voice Joanna had ever heard him use he said, "I can understand why you would call me a Jew, but if I may correct you, Vizcondesa, my family have been Christians for nearly one hundred years. While it is true that we fled the Inquisition, it was not out of any sense of wrongdoing or feelings of guilt. Though human nature fell short of my father's expectations, his faith in God never wavered. And it renewed my own convictions, because it led me to Joanna." Here he looked at his golden-haired angel and took her hand gently atop the linen tablecloth. He turned back to the Vizcondesa with a serious look. "You ask if I believe myself worthy of her affections and the honest answer is no—how could anybody be worthy of the affections of such an exquisite creature?—but I assure you, I will spend every minute that remains to me working toward that end."

To Joanna's surprise, the Vizcondesa began to clap loudly. "Bravo, Señor García! Bravo! Well done! Intelligent, courageous, honest, and Joanna," she said turning to her niece, "he loves you! I apologize for my methods, Señor García, but I had to be certain of your devotion to my niece. If you can stand up to me, the terror of the society ladies of this region, I know you will do everything in your power to give Joanna the life she deserves. I heartily give my consent! We will hold the wedding as soon as possible. Oh, it gives me untold pleasure to welcome you to our little family, Iñigo."

Shortly afterward the young lovers were married, but before Iñigo took his beautiful new wife home to his family, there was one last task to complete. He had finally received permission for the interment of his father's heart at Compostela. When he told his new wife of the observance, which would take place the next morning, she began to reflect upon her own part in the circumstances that had brought them together.

Joanna brought out little Robin's toy flute and held it in her hands, caressing it as if it were the soft downy cheek of her precious copper-headed boy. The tears flowed freely down her face at the thought of someday allowing another child to fill the place in her heart left ravaged by her firstborn's death. The thought of having another child terrified her. What would she do if a second child were to succumb to a fatal illness? Then the revelation struck her that to live in terror would be no life at all. That was how she had existed during the two months of her seclusion. She had awakened every morning terrified at the thought of facing another day. When she had accepted the fact that she had nothing left to lose and finally trusted God, He'd brought her Iñigo and the promise of a new life. She now understood that she would have to lay the remnants of her old life to rest and continue to trust.

After much meditation, she approached her new husband to present her petition. She wanted him to allow her to place Robin's toy flute in the box containing Aarón's heart. She explained that it seemed only meet for the two to be buried together as they had provided the catalyst resulting in Joanna and Iñigo's own union. Didn't it stand to reason that their loved ones be bound for eternity as the families would now be joined? Iñigo nodded his approval, and the next day the husband and wife sealed their pact, completed their pilgrimages, and headed for their new life in Vigo.

When Iñigo presented Joanna to his family, they were

awestruck by her beauty and the realization of Aarón's vision. Although the part of his dream about the hilltop overlooking the sea surrounded by a field of green had come true, they had often joked among each other of the golden-haired angel who had played such a prominent role. They never imagined that such an ethereal woman existed, and for her to be interested in their lovable, awkward Iñigo, well, that was even more fantastic! Yet here she stood among them, married to the man who had never dared speak to a woman outside of the family or mercantile. Certainly this was the hand of God.

When Joanna was delivered of her first child with Iñigo, it was further proof of Aarón's vision. The baby girl was a tiny replica of her mother, and they named her Serafina, 'angel', to commemorate the vision of her grandfather who had enabled her existence but whom she would never know. It was breaking with Joanna's family tradition of Joannas and Margarets, but she had already forged ahead with her life, it was good to continue her forward progress.

When she gave birth to the second little girl of the vision, they named her for Iñigo's mother, Inez. He had always maintained that his mother was the bravest woman with whom he had ever come into contact, aside from his wife, and he hoped that his daughter would carry on not only her name but also her admirable traits of quiet fortitude and determination. In this Inez had succeeded beyond his wildest expectations. Her silver eyes reminded Iñigo of the times he had sat in his grandmother's lap when he was a child, so fascinated by the odd misty coloring of her loving gaze. They reminded her mother of someone else.

Inez's coloring was very similar to her deceased half-brother's coloring, only slightly deeper and more dramatic. At first Joanna had found it difficult to bond with her baby daughter because every time she looked into those solemn, silver eyes she saw Robin's soft gray ones looking back at her. It dredged up all the old pain of loss she had thought long forgotten—loss of the child as well as the father—but eventually, she began to see her baby girl as just Inez, and she reveled in her cleverness and her independent ways.

Joanna experienced a bit of misgiving at her daughter's impertinence and her unconventional stubbornness as she approached adolescence. Perhaps she feared Inez would fall into the same trouble of which she had become victim, but she soon realized that her daughter was far too intelligent to repeat her mistakes. She accepted Inez for herself. Once she did that, she discovered that they had much in common. A mature relationship began to bloom, and mother and daughter developed at least a respect for one another, if not a friendship. It was what had enabled the confidence to grow between them and allowed them to comfort each other.

The story Joanna recounted to her daughter made her parents seem more relatable and much more human to Inez. "I never knew my father was such a romantic," Inez said, voicing one of the more surprising revelations that occurred to her.

"Yes," Joanna nodded, smiling at the recollection, "and so much more. Your father has been my rock, my stability, in a very large part my strength. Sometimes I get irritated by little things he does, but I would have never survived without him. I love him more than I have ever loved anybody, even Robin, who was my first love and the passion of my youth." She paused a moment to let the significance settle into her daughter's mind. "When I was your age, I thought that my grief would never wane, but in time it becomes bearable. Now that you have come to terms with it, it will lessen even more. In time, perhaps you will even be able to love again." She lifted Inez's chin with her hand and looked her in the eye. "Maybe this upset was simply preparation so that you will recognize your true love when it arrives, like I did."

Joanna kissed Inez on the forehead and squeezed her daughter to her as her silver eyes began to fill with tears. She held her as she cried, knowing how impossible it was to let go of one's first love, Inez's only love. She knew it caused the heart to break anew.

Joanna was experiencing her own heartbreak at that moment, her own struggle to come to terms with the role she had played in the catastrophe that had caused her daughter such pain. She felt for her, but Joanna could not bring herself to divulge the rest, of how the decision to separate Inez from her beloved had been left up to her. The marriage could not be undone, so what good could come from that admission? Inez was already past the most difficult part of her grief, why restore her false hope? Tears began to flow down her own cheeks as well.

Chapter 11: Someone to Care For

As Joanna had done so many years before, Inez put aside her grief and returned to the world to face what the future would bring. After the long months of mourning, it seemed that their mother-daughter talk had provided the necessary boost to bring Inez out of her shroud of misery. Inez got over the worst part of her grief and her broken heart began to mend. Her body began to transform as well.

Inez was still very slender, but her weight was no longer a source of concern. The once protruding bones were softened by a layer of healthy new flesh, and some of the wholesome pink color returned to her skin. Her magnificent eyes, which had appeared so dull and listless during her bout of depression, began to take interest in her surroundings. Her smile began to show itself more often, and she again started to take pleasure in things other than just the long walks with Palhaço, even helping Paulina out in the kitchen from time to time.

The temporary diffidence Inez had experienced as a result of Paulina's accurate assessment of the marriage proposal was a thing of the past. The women resumed their relationship where they had left off. Inez's heartbreak actually drew them closer together because now she understood more fully the ordeal Paulina had survived in her youth. It made the quiet housekeeper seem all the more courageous and more the romantic heroine than ever.

True to Inez's curious nature, she began to wonder how her mother and Paulina, who had suffered similar tragedies in their youth—the loss of husband and child—could have continued their lives in such dissimilar manners. Her mother said that one day she would be able to love again, but this had not happened for Paulina. Inez took a mental inventory of the housekeeper's outstanding attributes and concluded that any man would consider himself lucky to win the admiration of such a woman. The decision must have been Paulina's own.

One day Inez was helping Paulina make bread. The two women stood side by side, kneading their loaves and chatting comfortably as they worked. When the dough had reached a satiny smoothness and a springy elastic consistency, they each patted the excess flour from the rounded mounds and covered them with towels to let them rise. They sat and enjoyed a cup of tea while Palhaço gnawed on a bone under the worktable.

"He certainly has grown," Paulina said with a smile, peeking under the table to note the dog's progress with his treat. "It would be difficult to recognize him as the same little black and tan runt he was when he arrived."

"Yes," Inez added, "that was over a year ago. I can't believe time has passed so quickly."

"And it only moves faster as life goes on, Baixinha."

"Paulina," Inez began tentatively, crinkling her nose and looking up out of the corner of her eye, "why have you never remarried? You are still quite beautiful and relatively young. I'm sure there are plenty of men who would be happy to take you as a wife."

The housekeeper laughed out loud at Inez's rudimentary assessment of her virtues. "Thank you for not relegating me to the graveyard yet," she said, her dark eyes sparkling with amusement.

"That is not exactly what I meant," Inez answered, blushing at her inadvertent blunder. "It's just that my mother found love a second time, even with her, um … *complex* personality. She says my father is the greatest love of her life and that her first love was just preparation for the one that followed. Perhaps you could find love again."

"Your father *is* an exceptional man," Paulina said, pondering the younger woman's supposition. "It's not that I have not found love again. I had not really thought about it but now that I do, I suppose it's more accurate to say that I have not sought it out. As I explained to you before, Nuno was more an extension of myself than a separate person. How does one go about finding a replacement for that?"

Inez shrugged her shoulders and looked down at her lap. "I wish I knew. It seems like for the three years before Estêvão married Serafina, I built my entire world around him." It was the first time since the wedding she had used her beloved's name in conversation with someone else. She swallowed hard and looked up at Paulina, tears shining in her eyes. "It turned out to be just the ill-advised folly of a little girl, but how do I stop loving him? How do I move on? I guess what I really want to know is how do I lessen the ache inside of me?"

Paulina put her arms about Inez's shoulders and hugged her tight. She could not stand to see the naked pain in the younger woman's eyes. It reminded her too much of her own loss. She thought about the questions and examined how she had remedied her own predicament after the tragic death of her husband and unborn child. Then it came to her. She *had* found love again, just not in the same way. Finally she knew how to answer.

"You must care for someone else," she said gently, squeezing Inez then pulling back just far enough to look into her eyes. "It was what mended my broken heart. As you know, I was planning to retire to a convent, but I did not do so because I was needed here. Through caring for you I found a new reason to live my life. I did find love again, the love of a child, and that is what healed me. You must care for someone else, Baixinha," she repeated.

Inez understood what Paulina was suggesting. It dawned on her that a part of what had sustained her during the worst of her grief was caring for Palhaço. If she had not had the scruffy little bundle of fur to look after, she would have probably done what her mother had done, simply shut herself in and wasted away. Taking care of someone else left little time for one to dwell on her own problems and forced a person to concern herself with other issues. Inez knew this was the answer, but for whom could she care?

Inez occasionally pondered the question, but as it was not an immediate concern she did not distress herself over coming up with a solution. Because she had bared her feelings to the two women who had had the most impact on her short life, it acted as a sort of temporary emotional catharsis. It did not fully resolve the last of her sadness but diminished it enough not to be the foremost thought in her mind. She carried on with her daily routine. Time continued to march on and soon her sixteenth birthday came to pass.

Now that Joanna understood her daughter's situation clearly, she did her best to avoid anything that would cause Inez undue hardship. A young woman's sixteenth birthday was the accepted benchmark to designate her as eligible for marriage, and because Joanna knew it was not possible for Inez to make a marriage of the heart, she deemed it an unnecessary cruelness to attribute too much importance to the occasion by celebrating it excessively. The family marked it with as little ceremony as possible. They had a quiet family dinner with all of Inez's favorite dishes, and Paulina made a special cake for dessert.

Far away at the Fazenda da Pomba, Estêvão also noted the

occasion of Inez's sixteenth birthday. The girl he should have waited to wed had finally reached marriageable age, and he could not overlook the bitter irony of the situation. He had married the elder sister to expedite the process of getting an heir, and his wife had still not shown any sign of producing a child. It would just serve him right if she turned out to be barren. He had brought this on himself.

Chapter 12: Happy News

In the first week of November, Serafina confided in her mother-in-law that she believed herself to be with child. Dom Martín and Estêvão had already left for the fields that morning, so María sent for the doctor to examine her daughter-in-law before the men returned from their work. There was no reason to excite the household if it were a false alarm, and Serafina agreed that it was a good idea to be sure before raising her husband's hopes. The doctor arrived, asked many pertinent questions, did a short physical evaluation of his patient, and said he would return in two weeks to give his verdict. He advised the women not to say anything until that time, but it appeared to him that, yes, the young senhora was expecting.

It was almost too big a task to keep the secret. Every time Estêvão glanced in her direction Serafina was tempted to exclaim that she had finally accomplished her purpose, and they could now look forward to becoming a family. She prayed fervently that her pregnancy would effect the change in his attitude that she had hoped for since his first rejection of her on the *María Vencedora*. She could not really complain of his treatment. He had never gone out of his way to be deliberately cruel but neither had he treated her like a wife or friend or even a partner. He maintained his cool demeanor toward her and treated her in an aloof, courteous manner like a casual acquaintance, never allowing her sway over his emotions. Deep inside she understood why he did it, but the knowledge did not ease her suffering.

The two weeks passed and the doctor returned for the decisive visit. He ran through the same process he had before then expressed his hearty congratulations and gave his approval to inform the rest of the family. The two women were overjoyed and set about planning the perfect meal over which to make the announcement. They asked the cook to prepare all of Estêvão's favorite foods and made sure the table was set with the best linens and tableware. This was the most important event that had happened since the fazenda came into being. It stood to reason that a celebration was in order.

When the men came in from the fields, they made their way up to their rooms to wash and change for supper. Neither one of them noticed the elaborate table setting, and when they were finally called in for the meal, they looked at each other in bewilderment and then at María for some sort of explanation. María returned their looks with an impish grin, her dark Gypsy eyes sparkling with mischief, and merely motioned them to take their seats. The wine was poured, and before anyone could take a sip, María cleared her throat to draw their attention.

"It seems that a celebration is in order. We have received some long-awaited information, and it is only fitting that my beautiful daughter-in-law deliver it." She chuckled to herself at her pun then continued, "Serafina, please tell the men your news."

"Well," she began, blushing prettily, her aquamarine eyes aglitter with high hopes, "it seems that I have finally resulted with child." She shifted her gaze to her husband in order to better survey his reaction and direct a final comment his way. "Next spring you will have your son."

"Has the doctor confirmed it?" Estêvão asked, arching his right eyebrow and reserving his judgement until the news was definitive.

"He has already made examinations on two separate occasions, and today he gave his official endorsement," Serafina said breathlessly. The anticipation was too much to bear. Would this communal anticipation of the child they had created be the thing that finally bound them together as husband and wife?

Estêvão's face broke into a genuine and unrestrained grin. His white teeth flashed brilliantly, and his hazel-green eyes danced with pleasure. It was the first smile directed at her that Serafina had witnessed during their time together, and she thought it the most beautiful smile she had ever seen. In that moment she understood her sister's attraction to him and could not deny his appeal. She let her breath out and returned his expression with a radiant look of her own. It seemed as though things would finally be set to rights.

"That is excellent news!" he exclaimed, clearly pleased with the prospect of impending fatherhood. "Well done, wife!"

"Well I didn't exactly manage it on my own," Serafina said, coloring at the implication.

Estêvão did not even notice. He was accepting congratulations from Dom Martín, the smile still in evidence on his handsome face. He then turned back to his wife and mother and said, "Oh, I have been waiting for this for so long! It has felt an eternity. Now I can finally get back to my ship and her crew!"

"Your ship?" Serafina asked uncomprehendingly.

"Yes," Estêvão said, still smiling. "Now that my job here is done I can get back to the East and take a look at this new land they have discovered."

"But our child," Serafina blurted out on the verge of tears. "Don't you want to be here when he arrives?"

"I should be back in plenty of time to greet him. Well if not in time for his birth then shortly thereafter. There is no longer any reason for me to remain here. My mother has been through this process before. She will know better than I how to handle any situation that should arise. You will have everything you need and the finest doctor that money can afford. I would only be in the way. Besides, my crew have had a vacation long enough. It is time for them to do some real work again." He then turned to his stepfather and excitedly began to make plans.

Crestfallen, Serafina dropped her gaze to her lap in an attempt to recover her composure. Her cheeks stung with his rebuke as if he had physically reached across the table and slapped her. She had convinced herself that when she finally conceived his heir— providing the security that had been the objective of their union— things would magically repair themselves, and she and her husband would attain the ideal marriage she had envisioned from childhood. This had not happened, and after having her dreams dashed in such a manner, she was more dejected than before. Would she ever cease having to pay for breaking her sister's heart?

María reached across the table and squeezed Serafina's hand in a gesture of support. She knew that the girl's heart was breaking but could do nothing except support her emotionally and impart the wisdom she had gleaned from her own wealth of experience. She knew her son, and she knew that if she approached him now in an authoritative capacity, it would only serve to make him more distant and more determined to have his own way. She could only do what little she could to make up for his insensitive behavior and pray for the safe delivery of her grandchild.

Over the course of the next few days, Serafina seldom saw her husband at all. Estêvão was so busy planning his departure that he did not even join the family at supper. Three days later when all of the arrangements were finally accomplished, he said his goodbyes before retiring to bed and was gone the next morning. He did not reserve a special farewell for his wife, not even a note of encouragement or well wishes for her pregnancy. He was simply no longer there.

A short time after, Serafina and María sat amiably sewing baby clothes for the eagerly anticipated addition. They chatted while they worked, and they happened upon the subject of Serafina's family. María wondered if her daughter-in-law had informed the García clan of her condition, and Serafina replied that she had not. She had been so busy moping over her husband's departure that she had not been in the mood to send the joyful notice the news required.

"I suppose it is natural for you to be a little upset," María said kindly, "but you must try to maintain good spirits for the child. If you fret overmuch, it could have lasting effects on his health." She looked at the defeated posture of her daughter-in-law and decided to change the subject to a more neutral one. "How is your mother doing now that she has only one daughter left over whom to fuss?"

Serafina looked up at her mother-in-law with a guarded look in her eyes. She knew that María had some inkling of the feelings between Inez and Estêvão, but nothing had ever been openly stated. She could not bring herself to betray her sister's trust so she said, "The last letter my mother wrote to me said that they have begun putting together a trousseau for Inez, but my sister has not been very interested in social functions since I married her … ah … my husband." María's sharp eyes took in the little slip, and Serafina did what she could to cover it. "She has spent most of her time taking care of her little dog."

"I would think that although it is an honorable pursuit, it could become a bit tedious."

Serafina shrugged her shoulders and continued to stitch on the tiny garment in her hands. "Marriage is probably the furthest thing from her mind right now. Besides, Inez has always loved animals. When she was very young I think she actually preferred the company of the livestock to human companionship. I can't remember how many times I found her singing to Neblina or just the chickens in the yard." She smiled at the memory. "I would give anything to have that sweet, carefree little sister back again." Serafina wiped at a remorseful tear that seeped out the corner of her eye.

"Well then why shouldn't you?" María asked cheerfully. "What do you think about bringing Inez out to keep you company for the length of your pregnancy?"

"I'm not sure that would be such a good idea," Serafina said hesitantly.

"Why not? Your husband will probably not return for a long while. You should have a young person around to keep you company instead of just us old folks, and maybe," here María paused for a moment and Serafina thought she saw the characteristic impish gleam in her mother-in-law's vivacious Gypsy eyes, "she could occasionally ride out with Dom Martín to check on the progress at the vineyard. After all your parents are partners in the venture. It would be the perfect excuse."

"Excuse for what?" Serafina asked, intrigued by the wording.

María waved her hand. "Oh, just an excuse to get her to Terceira," she said, pleased at the logical concealment of her little slip. The idea was a stroke of genius. She didn't know why she had not thought of it before, but in order for it to work it would have to seem as if everything had come about naturally. Inez was so independent that she would not allow herself to be open to something if she felt like she were being pushed or as if things had been arranged. "When you compose the letter to your parents I will extend the invitation to Inez. Yes, that is what we'll do."

Chapter 13: Saying Goodbye

Since her conversation with Inez about finding love a second time, Paulina had thought hard about how to approach Joanna with her opinion on the matter. The two women had never really gotten along and maintained a strict business relationship. Paulina was just the housekeeper. What right did she have to approach the Señora and tell her what she believed to be the best course of action to heal Inez's broken heart? She finally reasoned that her love for the young girl gave her the right. She pushed aside her reservations and waited for the opportunity to broach the subject.

One afternoon Joanna was in an exceptionally good humor. She had received a communication from Terceira earlier in the day, and it seemed to be happy news. She walked through the house with an extra bounce in her step and a smile on her face, humming a little tune. The staff all looked at each other in amusement then returned to their chores, hoping to sustain the Señora's buoyant mood. Paulina overcame her apprehension and decided that there would be no more auspicious time than this. She waited for Joanna to settle down in the parlor then put together a tray with some tea and freshly baked cookies.

"Paulina, how thoughtful of you!" Joanna said as she looked up at the housekeeper's entrance. "Those cookies smell marvelous!"

The Señora was undeniably in an excellent frame of mind. Paulina set the tray down on a little side table and poured out a cup of the steaming amber liquid. She then stood up straight, wiped her hands on her apron, and waited for the mistress to address her.

Joanna looked up at her, surprised that the housekeeper had lingered. There had always been a mild tension between them and a sort of tacit understanding that they only endure each other's presence when absolutely necessary. "Is there something you wish to discuss?" Joanna asked a bit warily.

"Yes, Señora, if I may have a moment of your time," Paulina said quietly.

"This must be important indeed. By all means continue."

Paulina swallowed hard and chided herself for her reticence. She needed to speak out now. "Recently I noticed that Señorita Inez is not her normal cheerful self." Paulina saw Joanna stiffen and knew she needed to proceed in a delicate manner. "She told me a bit about her situation, and it brings to mind a similar experience from my own youth. As I have always tried to do my best to look out for her welfare, I felt compelled to speak to you."

"Did you think my daughter's melancholy had escaped my notice?" Joanna asked, imperiously arching her eyebrow.

"No, Señora. I know that you miss nothing," Paulina said placatingly. Joanna seemed to accept this and settled back in her chair. "I know you must have already come up with several ideas on how to assuage her pain, but if I may make a suggestion." Joanna nodded her head and Paulina continued more carefully. "When I suffered my loss, the only thing that kept me from entering the convent at Santiago de Compostela was to come here and care for your daughters. It allowed my wounded soul to heal and made it possible for me to love again. I know it is not my place, but perhaps if Inez could care for someone else, it would speed the healing of her heart."

Joanna sat silently in her chair, appearing to mull over Paulina's submission. After what seemed like an eternity, she sat forward and said, "You are right. It is not your place." The words hung in the air between them and Paulina felt her spirits plunge to the pit of her stomach. How could she have thought the Señora would listen to her? She stood there waiting to be discharged but finally, unbelievably, Joanna added, "It just so happens that I have received a letter from Dona María that suggests the very same thing. I will discuss the proposition with my husband this evening, and we will come to a decision then."

Paulina looked up at her mistress and could not suppress the smile that spread across her face. "Thank you for listening, Señora," she said, overjoyed. Joanna simply waved her hand in dismissal. Paulina crossed the room and opened the door to leave.

"Paulina," came Joanna's voice from behind her. The housekeeper turned to face her mistress. "You must love Inez very much to confront me in such a manner."

Paulina nodded her head in agreement. "As if she were my own," she said sincerely then left the room.

The García family was delighted at the news of Serafina's long anticipated pregnancy. The subject of Inez leaving for Terceira to attend her was discussed, and it was decided that she should go. Although winter was fast approaching and the Atlantic could be treacherous and unpredictable, one of the sea captains with whom Iñigo did repeat business made the run from the mainland to the Azores on a regular basis. He was held in high regard by his fellow mariners and was reputed to possess the uncanny ability to sniff out bad weather and skirt it without disrupting his schedule. He assured Iñigo that even if his ship were to encounter a storm, the sturdy vessel would withstand it, and Inez would reach her destination unharmed and no worse for wear. The arrangements were made and Inez set about packing her things for her trip.

Inez had always felt in her heart that she would return to the Fazenda da Pomba, just not in this capacity. She had wholeheartedly believed she would be taken back as Estêvão's bride, not as his sister-in-law. She had mixed feelings about going, but she had felt a sense of belonging on Terceira that she had experienced nowhere else, not even in Vigo. She longed to again ride out on that rolling green carpet in the fresh island air, the fragrance of hydrangeas, laurel wood, and pear trees, mixed with the honest animal scent of wildlife and livestock.

Was it the land that she missed, or did Inez simply yearn to be close to the man she loved and the things she associated with him? After close introspection she decided that this was something else that she needed to discover. She knew Estêvão would not be there for the first few months of her presence, but sooner or later he would come. How would they respond to one another? Would he feel awkward around her, or would he pretend as if nothing had ever happened between them? Eventually they would be required to come into contact with one another, after all they were now family, but could she do it? She would have to find out.

These thoughts ran through her mind as she packed her belongings for departure. She opened her wardrobe to take out her latest supply of gowns. Although she had regained a small amount of the weight she lost after the wedding, her old dresses were no longer suitable. Some of them were able to be salvaged by being restyled and taken in, but Joanna had ordered new ones made, and Inez could not leave them behind. She took them down one by one and folded them carefully before placing them in the crate.

When she had done, she espied the two boxes in the top of the cabinet. She had stowed them there because she could not stand to look at them every day. They reminded her too much of her loss, but she took them down now to assess what should be done. The larger of the boxes was the ancient grayed oaken case that held her heirloom lute. Since the day of the wedding announcement, she had not had the least desire to play it. She didn't know if she ever would again, but she could not bear to leave it behind. Perhaps one day she could pass it on to a child of her own. It had made the journey from England over a hundred years ago and now it would go to Terceira. She settled the instrument among her dresses and reached for the other box.

She took down the hand-carved maple box so lovingly crafted by her father's artistic hands. She ran her fingers over its glassy finish, but she could not bring herself to open the lock and review its contents. It had once represented her hopes for the future, but now it only stood for the heartache that had resulted. Still, the items inside had played a large part in making her the person she was. She did not think she could ever bring herself to dispose of them. They had meant so much to her and still did. It would be wise to keep them close along with the lessons she had learned. Besides, she did not want to leave anything behind that might one day be of some importance.

For some reason Inez could not shake the feeling that she would not be returning to Vigo. She had the distinct impression that Terceira would become her permanent home. She didn't know why or how this would come about, but life frequently offered up little twists and turns that one did not anticipate. It had happened to her mother, Paulina, even Dona María. Each of them had experienced a major event that had changed the course of their lives. One could not control the things that life brought her way, she could only accept it with grace and dignity then move on. Inez shrugged her shoulders and continued with her chore. She dug down the side of the crate, wedged the maple box between the layers of fabric, and tucked the edges of her gowns down around it for protection. Her packing was finally done.

A few days later, the crates that held all of Inez's earthly belongings were loaded onto the wagon in preparation for her voyage. Paulina stood looking down into Inez's somber silver eyes, holding the younger woman's hands in her own. Sometimes it was hard for her to believe this was the same little red scrap of humanity she had helped to deliver over sixteen years ago, but no matter how adult Inez looked or acted she would always be that little baby girl, as precious to her as a child of her own flesh. She felt tears prickle at the corners of her eyes, and she hugged Inez to her.

"Well, Baixinha," Paulina said, pulling back slightly, "I will miss you every day of our separation, but your sister will need you. Besides, this is just the thing you need to renew your spirits. Perhaps in time you will love again."

"Thank you, Paulina," Inez said, wiping at her eyes, "for everything. You have been like a second mother to me. I will miss our conversations and all of your good advice. I know sometimes I seemed not to listen, but I heard every word and I keep them right here in my heart," she said, patting her chest with her open hand.

Paulina nodded and said, "I know it. I hope one day it will serve you well. Go now," she said giving Inez a gentle push. "Your parents are waiting."

Inez squeezed the housekeeper one last time then turned toward the waiting wagon. "Let's go, Palhaço," she said to her curly tan mutt, and the two of them jumped up to their seats and settled themselves for the short ride to town.

The wagon started forward, and Inez waved to the staff, all of which had assembled to see her off. The younger daughter of the house had brought much joy to each of them over the years, and it had pained them all to see her in such obvious despair. They wished her the best in this new enterprise, hoping that some day she would be restored to the lighthearted little girl with the sunny disposition they all remembered and loved so well.

It didn't take long to get to the dock, and the captain and crew were waiting for their lone passenger. In no time at all the baggage was stowed and it was time to cast off. The captain shook Iñigo's hand, bowed low to Joanna, and said, "When you are ready, Señorita," to Inez. He strode up the gangplank to prepare the ship for sail, and Inez turned to her parents to say her goodbyes while Palhaço sat waiting patiently.

"Well, Mynah," Iñigo said brightly. "I know you are in good hands, both at sea and when you arrive on Terceira, so I will not bother to wish you a safe crossing. I will only say that I hope you find what you are seeking."

"Oh, Papa," Inez said, throwing herself into his arms. "I didn't realize you knew there was anything wrong."

He held his young daughter tightly, the beloved daughter he had named for his revered mother. He kissed her on the top of the head and said, "How could I fail to see the sadness etched so clearly on the face of one I love so well? Of course I knew, Mynah. I just felt that your mother could help you more ... that you could help each other." He took her chin in his hand so he could get a good look at her face. "And you did, Mynah, more than you know. We will see you soon." He kissed her on the forehead then released her so she could bid farewell to her mother.

"Well," began Joanna with her arms spread wide, "I suppose this is goodbye for now."

Inez nodded her head and walked into her mother's embrace. The two women stood there silently, neither one of them trusting her voice not to betray the poignancy of the moment. Finally Joanna believed she could speak without crying. "Take good care of your sister," she ventured. "I know you will be tempted to be envious of her position, but you may find that she needs your sympathy and support much more than you need hers."

Inez was stung by her mother's comment and drew back a little at the words. She thought her mother had begun to see her side, yet here she was favoring Serafina again. "What do you mean?" she blurted out.

Joanna's eyes softened at her daughter's obvious bewilderment. "Don't you understand, mi hija?" she asked gently. "I have *always* known that you are the stronger of the two, and you are more like me than I ever cared to admit. Perhaps that is why I was so hard on you and seemed to dote more on your sister, but," she distractedly smoothed an errant tress of Inez's wiry copper mane, "Serafina is not to blame for this misunderstanding, and she is more delicate than you imagine. Inez, you are a remarkable young woman with your whole life ahead of you. Don't spoil your future by carrying this burden of resentment. Learn from my mistake. I carried my hatred for far too long and it turned me into a bitter old woman. Do not let that be your fate."

"Oh, Mama," Inez said, clinging to Joanna as her intention became clear. "Why is it that we only begin to appreciate each other now that we are to be separated?"

"Such is life," Joanna said, smiling at the irony. "We will not be apart long. Your father and I plan to be there for the birth of our grandchild. Make sure your sister follows the doctor's orders so the child grows healthy and strong. I love you, Inez."

"I love you, too," Inez managed to squeak out, giving her mother one last squeeze.

With that she turned and called Palhaço to her. The two of them scrambled up the gangplank, and Inez made her way to the rail to wave a final goodbye. Her parents stood on the dock returning the gesture, and Inez saw Joanna suddenly turn and bury her face in Iñigo's wiry chest. The ship began to exit the port, and the last glimpse Inez had of her parents was her mother sobbing into her father's side as he led her back to the wagon. In that moment she realized how much they loved her, and she vowed to put her personal feelings aside and do her very best to take care of her sister and the child she carried.

BOOK 5: Life and Death
1513
Chapter 1: Moving On

Inez's second crossing to Terceira turned out to be as uneventful as the first. The ship made the trip in good time, and two weeks after she left Vigo, Inez was unpacking her belongings in her room at the Fazenda da Pomba. It was the same chamber she had occupied on her previous visit. It had been hers for a mere month of her life, but strangely enough Inez felt like she had come home. She bent over the crate, shaking out each gown and smoothing out the wrinkles before hanging it in the wardrobe. Palhaço lay on his bed in the corner following her movements with his eyes.

When Palhaço and Inez had first arrived, the staff had tried to bar the dog's entry by blocking the doorway and refusing to move. He had responded by sitting prettily and waiting for an invitation to enter. When he had not been invited in, he attempted to explain the situation by issuing a loud, "Roo-roo-roo!" When that did not work, he simply bulled through the human blockade and sniffed his way after his mistress. The servants banded together to chase him and shoo him outside, and for a while Palhaço thought it a merry game. He had never had so many people to play with at once! Finally though, after nearly overturning two costly end tables and upsetting a vase of flowers, he was apprehended and unceremoniously tossed out into the yard.

After ten minutes of his mournful baying, Dona María came out to see what wild animal had been mortally wounded so near the front door. When Inez explained the misunderstanding and showed Dona María how well behaved her dog actually was, the mistress of the house gave permission for him to have the run of it. Palhaço thanked her by wagging his tail and placing a sloppy wet kiss on her hand. He then peaceably followed Inez up to their room as if nothing out of the ordinary had happened. Palhaço would feel at home anywhere as long as he could be near Inez, and although the rest of his surroundings were different and smelled strange, his bed was familiar and comforting. He laid down in his corner and waited patiently for her to finish her task so they could go explore their new environment.

Inez had done hanging her dresses and placed the lute in the top of the wardrobe. She was trying to decide whether to stow the maple box alongside the lute or leave it out when there was a light knock on the door. She bade her visitor to enter and was not surprised to see her sister's golden head peek around the edge of the door. Palhaço got to his feet and trotted across the room to greet the new arrival. He sat down in front of Serafina and waited for her to tell him what a good dog he was. She patted his shaggy tan head and smiled with amusement.

"So this is the ferocious beast that had the entire staff up in arms," she chuckled. "I can't believe this is the same little dog you took to Vigo with you a year ago! He is so tall! Time certainly passes quickly." Serafina made her way to where her sister stood by the wardrobe. She embraced her tightly and Inez could feel her body quivering with emotion. "Oh, little sister, I am so happy to see you!" Serafina cried, unwilling to release her.

"And I you," Inez replied sincerely.

"It seems an age since we were last together," Serafina said, finally letting her go and holding her at arm's length. "Let me look at you." She walked around her little sister with her hand on her chin, openly appraising her. "You are *very* slender," she said with a little frown on her face, "but Inez, you are beautiful!"

Inez blushed deeply, taking the compliment as simply the overenthusiastic praise of the loving sister who had not seen her in over a year, but it was true. Because Inez had lost weight, the high cheekbones formerly hidden by the awkward flesh of adolescence stood out regally, and the dusky shadows under her silver and gold eyes merely made the magnificent orbs appear larger and more luminous. Because Inez had spent much time indoors and had worn a hat on her long hillside explorations with Palhaço, her skin was a creamy ivory expanse with a rose-colored blush across her cheeks and a sprinkling of tiny delicate freckles over the bridge of her nose. Her hair was no longer the brassy orangey tint it had been in her childhood but a deep wine color with small glints of copper where the sun had kissed it. There was no denying her allure.

"And to think I always regarded myself as the great beauty of the family," Serafina said with quiet wonder. "I shall have to revise my opinion. Inez, you have surpassed me."

"Nonsense, Serafina," Inez said, embarrassed in the extreme. "You look even more like an angel with the glow of motherhood about you." This time it was Serafina's turn to blush. Though her pregnancy was not advanced enough to have noticeably changed her body, there was a special aura about her that enhanced her already exceptional beauty. Even after combatting the nausea that assailed her every morning and the fatigue, which had become her constant companion, Serafina was more radiant than Inez had ever seen her. "It seems that married life agrees with you," Inez said without resentment, simply stating the truth.

Serafina swallowed hard, lowering her eyes to the floor. This conversation was inevitable. She had known from the moment the proposal was announced that one day she and Inez would have to come to terms. She had just not imagined that it would arise in such a casual manner. "Inez, you must believe me. I ..."

Inez shook her head and took ahold of her sister's hands. "I know it was not your doing, and I have forgiven you long since. That I am here is testament to the fact that I am over the disappointment," here she grunted a little, smiling at the half-truth. "Well, *mostly* over it. I have made up my mind to move on and the best way to do it is to be the best sister and aunt that I can."

"Oh, little sister, I am so happy!" Serafina exclaimed and embraced Inez again in a fierce, interminable hug.

Good, Inez thought to herself, *I have convinced my sister. Now all that remains is to convince myself.*

Inez quickly settled in and basically took up where she left off. In the mornings she rode out with Dom Martín to check on the happenings in the fields. Palhaço was now big enough to keep up with the horses, so he went along too, always keeping close to Inez and staying out of the way of the work being done. Dom Martín was glad for the company. He had gotten used to having a companion, and when Estêvão had sailed for the East, Dom Martín had been left with only the field hands to pass the time. They were good men and hard workers but a bit coarse and unrefined. Sometimes Dom Martín longed to discuss business or share his wealth of knowledge with someone who would appreciate the information, so now Inez filled that void. She was always desirous of acquiring new knowledge, so she listened carefully and asked many astute questions. Dom Martín began to see her intelligence and value her judgement, and he soon realized that she had been struck from the same mold as his resolute, opinionated wife.

In the afternoons before supper, Inez spent time with the

ladies. The three of them sat and did needlework together, working on the various items that would be necessary for the eagerly awaited heir. Although they all understood the strangeness of the situation that brought them together and its potential to create discord among them, they tacitly avoided mention of the one name that would be the undoing of the harmonious atmosphere that enveloped them. Instead they talked about the time spent apart and how it had affected them all. Dona María asked about Iñigo and Joanna, and Inez told her that they were doing fine and planned to arrive for the birth of their grandchild. All of the conversation was pleasantly banal, an agreeable way to pass the time, but there was another more intimate discussion that María itched to initiate. She did not have to wait long for the chance.

One day Serafina did not join the other two women for their afternoon gathering. She had not slept well the night before and took advantage of the cool weather to replenish the few extra hours of sleep she had lost. María and Inez sat together, each of them waiting for the other to begin the conversation they had both desired to have for over a year. They were both hesitant. Neither of them wanted to risk Serafina's interruption. They did not want to have to suddenly drop the subject once it was opened or accidentally hurt Serafina's feelings if she were to overhear. Finally Dona María broached the subject.

"So, Mynah," she began in a serious tone, "how have *you* been?"

Inez lowered the piece on which she was working and looked over at the woman she had believed would one day be her mother-in-law. She understood the implication behind the innocuous question and pondered how she should answer. She recalled the peace of mind that had settled over her after her heart-to-heart conversations with the two other women she so respected and loved, and it occurred to her that perhaps here was another opportunity to glean even more useful advice on how to move on with her life. She made a conscious decision to be open and honest, took a deep breath, and let out a long, cleansing sigh.

"I suppose I am well," she began tentatively. She knew that from the beginning Dona María had sensed the love Inez felt for her son, but there had never been an open declaration of her feelings. This was tantamount to a confession. Inez swallowed her anxiety and continued. "At least I am better than I was a year ago."

María nodded her shiny dark head knowingly. "People try to comfort you by telling you that your heart will mend. They mean well, but I don't believe that the pain ever truly goes away. It merely lessens enough for you to move on."

"Was that how it was with your first husband ..." Inez hesitated, not wanting to say anything to upset the bond that was forming between them, "Estêvão's father?"

María looked up at Inez with her bright bird eyes, impressed by her dauntless nature. Most people would not have dared to ask the question. The young woman deserved an answer. "Yes it was," María said plainly. "At the time I did not believe that I would ever love again. My mother was sensible enough not to insist that I would. She merely pointed out the fact that the most important thing was for me to care for my son. Caring for Estêvão made it difficult to dwell on my own misery, and I suppose that speeded the healing process."

"I know it is not quite the same thing, but I don't know what I would have done if I had not had to care for Palhaço," Inez said with a smile. "Paulina said the same thing, that I must care for someone. That is in part why I came to help my sister."

"Paulina sounds like a wise woman." María reached over and patted Inez's hand. She looked directly into her eyes and said, "You were very brave to come here."

Inez shrugged her shoulders. "I knew my sister would need

help and companionship. I have never blamed her." She looked up at Dona María with a wry smile and said, "Oh, I was very angry with her for a while, but now I understand why it had to be her, and I do want to move on." Here she paused and wiped at the pesky tears that formed in the corners of her stunning eyes. "Besides, I have always felt that one day Terceira would be my home."

This is exactly what Dona María had hoped Inez would say. She had just heard the very thing that would make her plan a success. She squeezed the girl's hand with affection. "That's the spirit, Mynah. You can count on me to do whatever I can to help you to that end." She smiled to herself. Now all she had to do was wait for the right opportunity.

Chapter 2: María's Plan

The last days of December passed without incident, and soon the New Year was upon them. There were many invitations to celebrate the occasion, and Dona María could think of no better way to reintroduce Inez to some of the younger population of Terceira society. It had been over two and a half years since her last visit, and much had changed in that time. Many of the awkward adolescents had transformed into strapping young men, and some of the pretty little girls had gotten fat or become aware of their charms, growing unbearably conceited in the process. It was interesting and entertaining to see the differences, and though Inez captivated many of the male attendees—young and old alike—and left them enamored of her beauty and astounded by her intellect, she did not seem to have found anyone who appealed to her.

During the second week of January, Dom Martín and the ladies had just arrived home from a luncheon given by an important business associate. Dom Martín always begrudged the time spent away from the fields, but he had not been able to wriggle out of this appointment. The entire family had donned their very best clothing and suffered their boring old host in order to maintain good relations.

Inez looked especially beautiful in a jade-colored silk gown trimmed in black lace. She had tied a matching green ribbon around her long graceful neck and piled her abundant curls on top of her head in a style that drew attention to her face. The green of her gown showed off her wine-colored hair and creamy pink skin to perfection, and her silver and gold eyes reflected the hue and glittered like opalescent jewels. The cut of the dress clung to her superb figure, and the lascivious old philanderer who hosted the party spent the entire afternoon trying to get a better look at her ample bosom. Dom Martín had acted as her protector and placed himself strategically enough to impede the degenerate without his being offended. It had been a necessary but exhausting engagement, and now Serafina was in sore need of an afternoon nap. Inez moved to help her sister up the staircase when there was a firm knock on the door.

"I wonder who that could be?" Dona María asked innocently. "Inez, dear, I gave the staff the afternoon off. Could you go see who it is? Dom Martín will see your sister to her room."

Inez shrugged her shoulders and headed for the front door as Dom Martín took her place beside Serafina. She smoothed the front of her gown and brushed a fallen auburn curl out of her face before she reached for the handle to open the door. She pulled it open and emitted an audible hiss as a sharp intake of breath caught in her throat. Her hand came up to the ribbon about her neck, and she ran a finger along the inside to loosen it because she suddenly felt that she could not breathe. Her heart pounded in her chest, and she blinked her eyes a few times to make sure they were not playing tricks on her. She stood there frozen for what seemed like an eternity until slowly her senses began to return.

The young man on the porch was not Estêvão as Inez had first imagined. After the initial shock passed, upon closer inspection she began to register the differences. She realized that he was much younger, perhaps only a few years older than herself. He was of a similar height and build as Estêvão only slightly broader and more heavily muscled. He shared the same strong features with her beloved—the same high cheekbones and strong jawline, the same prominent Roman nose and exotic almond-shaped eyes— and he had the same glossy hair and olive complexion but in a more uniform version. Instead of the striking contrasts that were so prevalent in Estêvão's physical presence—the long nearly black hair and dark hazel-green eyes against his pale skin—the youth's short brown hair and sun-darkened skin were more monotone in color. The most outstanding thing about him was the color of his eyes. Leonine in appearance, their tawny color was more a deep amber than light brown.

The young man seemed similarly affected by Inez. Though she had begun to feel a bit self-conscious over her prolonged silent observation of him, he had not attempted to break the uncomfortable pause between them. He simply stood on the porch returning her gaze with a slightly dazed look on his face, his mouth open the smallest bit.

Finally Inez cleared her throat and asked, "May I help you?" Her voice shook a little and sounded strange to her ears, but the young man seemed not to notice.

He blinked his unusual yellow eyes a few times, and realizing the absurdity of the situation, a slow smile lifted the corners of his full lips and they parted to convey his amusement. His dazzling white teeth were startling in his dark face, and Inez, who thought she had gained control over her senses, felt her heart leap in her chest and begin to pound anew. "Yes, *Chérie*," he began in a mellow voice much like Estêvão's, "I received a communiqué from my Aunt María. I am here to deliver the papers she requested."

"Oh," said Inez, recalling the vineyard and finally making the connection. "You must be Christophe."

"I am," he replied, bowing low. "And you are?"

"How rude of me!" she said, flustered by his courtliness. "I am Inez."

"*Enchanté, Mademoiselle* Inez," Christophe said, taking her hand and grazing it with his lips. "Now, shall we go find my aunt?" Inez blushed a little at her lack of manners and stepped aside for him to enter. She closed the door and led him to the parlor where Dona María was waiting.

On their way there, they were intercepted by Palhaço who had come to investigate the source of the unfamiliar voice. He trotted directly up to the newcomer and barked once, attempting to ascertain whether the stranger was friend or foe. To Christophe's credit he did not flinch, pull away, or ignore the large shaggy dog. He dropped to one knee and held out his hand, patiently waiting for the canine to make his decision. When Christophe had passed the test, Palhaço gave his final stamp of approval by slurping him wetly on the hand then turning to escort him the rest of the way to the sitting room. The two young people smiled after him and followed him through the entrance.

"Christophe!" María said as she glided over the floor to greet him. "I am so pleased to see you!" she added as if his presence were a complete surprise to her. Her dark Gypsy eyes flicked back and forth between the two young people, taking in the blushes and the bemused looks on both of their faces. "You have met Inez."

"I have, Aunt María," he replied, nodding his head. "She is as beautiful as you described."

"Come, come," said María, waving them into the parlor. "I have just ordered some tea. It will be ready shortly." Inez glanced at Dona María with a question in her eyes, and María conveniently ignored the look, ushering her handsome nephew to a chair.

"I brought the papers you asked for," Christophe said, pulling them from his satchel.

"The papers?" María asked, momentarily bewildered. "Oh, of

course!" She took them from his hand and tossed them onto a side table as if they were unimportant. "I will see to them later. First tell me how things are going at the vineyard." She sat down in her seat and motioned for Inez to do the same.

Christophe again flashed his astonishing smile and began an account of the current state of the enterprise. As Inez listened to his pleasant melodic voice, so much like that of his cousin, she began to piece together the seemingly unrelated events that had culminated in their meeting. She finally came to the conclusion that María had planned the whole thing, and she idly wondered how long the scheme had been in the works. With a wry smile, she returned her attention to the conversation at hand.

When Inez looked up at Christophe, she was not surprised to see that, although he directed his comments to his aunt, his gaze had settled on her. She felt herself blush and lowered her eyes to her lap. When she had worked up the courage to glance at him a second time, he was still openly regarding her, and this time he cast a quick little wink in her direction. She could not help but smile in return. She began to pay attention to the discussion, and she found that not only was he handsome and charming, he was extremely knowledgeable and well-spoken. She recalled the positive comments her mother had made upon returning from the vineyard during the last days of their previous stay and the surprise Iñigo had professed when Don Francisco mentioned that sixteen-year-old Christophe had been left in charge of the entire operation. She thought to herself that his father's trust had not been unwarranted.

A little while later, Dom Martín descended the stairs, grumbling to himself about the day he had lost just to maintain his business relations. He had changed out of his finery and needed a cup of wine to wind down before supper. When he espied Christophe in the sitting room, Dom Martín strode across the floor, holding out his hand to greet the young man. "Christophe!" he boomed as he yanked the lad out of his chair and pounded him on the back. "How are you, boy? I'm surprised to see you. You are usually knee-deep in grapevines and fertilizer. What brings you here?"

"I came to bring my aunt some papers she requested."

Dom Martín looked at his wife with one eyebrow raised. "Strange," he mumbled to himself, shaking his head. "Well now that you are here, you must stay for supper, unless of course you have to get back to the vineyard."

"I would be delighted to dine with you," Christophe said, looking at Inez with a twinkle in his amber lion's eyes. "I believe the grapevines will manage quite well without me for a few more hours."

Because there were additional demands on his attention at supper, Inez had the chance to observe Christophe more openly without his notice. In this relaxed environment, she marveled even further at his similarities to Estêvão. He had a sharp mind and witty sense of humor. He had the same quick laugh and effortless, casual mien. He exuded charisma and feeling of bonhomie toward all. He was respectful and listened intently to whomever was speaking, and he was especially solicitous of Inez. During the lapses in conversation, his eyes would return to gaze at her and he would either smile, wink, or nod in her direction. Each time he did, it sent a little thrill through her, and she would feel herself blush and return his smile or demurely lower her eyes.

As the meal progressed, Inez began to feel more comfortable and not so self-conscious. She listened to the conversation about the vineyard, and true to her insatiable desire for knowledge she began to participate, delving more and more deeply into Christophe's field of expertise. He was impressed by her insightful observations, and he offered to give her a complete tour of the grounds whenever she had the time. She agreed that she would enjoy it. It would be new and exciting, a welcome break from her everyday routine. Besides, her parents were part owners of the venture. It would be a good idea for her to learn more about it.

María and Serafina shot little knowing looks at each other, both pleased to note that something special was blooming between the two young people. Even Dom Martín, who normally only noticed anything out of the ordinary when it pertained to the fazenda or its holdings, seemed positively affected by the romance in the air and offered to escort Inez to the vineyard the next morning. María smiled to herself, smug because her little intrigue had succeeded so easily. She had known from the start that Inez and Christophe would be well-suited to one another. They had just needed the opportunity to discover it for themselves.

When the meal was concluded and dark was beginning to fall outside, Christophe rose from his seat and reluctantly admitted that it was time for him to go. "I would like to get back before nightfall. Besides, I don't want to return to a Bacchanalian revel with the men having drunk up all of the profits we've labored so hard to produce. I must thank you, Aunt María," he continued, placing a warm kiss on her cheek. "I have not had such a delightful and relaxing evening for a very long time. It was wonderful to escape from the grapevines and be surrounded by such beauty, even if only for a few hours."

"You are welcome anytime, Christophe," María replied sincerely. "In fact, your birthday is quickly approaching. How would you like to celebrate it here with us? Inez is quite an excellent cook. Perhaps we can persuade her to make a special meal for you," she suggested casually.

Christophe raised his eyebrows in surprise. "Is there anything Inez cannot do?" he asked with a laugh. Inez felt herself flush yet again and lowered her eyes to the floor. Christophe proceeded to bid goodnight to Dom Martín and Serafina, thanking them for the lovely evening, and then he turned to Inez. "Will you see me to the door?" he asked plainly. She nodded her head and followed him out of the parlor.

At the door he turned to her, his amber eyes glowing with warmth, and said, "I wanted to thank you especially for your part in this most pleasurable evening. I know my aunt must have been planning this for quite some time, but I must say that I find myself very willing to play my part in her little intrigue. I hope you will also be open to her matchmaking. I look forward to giving you the tour of the vineyard tomorrow, and I wish you the sweetest of dreams. With any luck, I will make an appearance there. Goodnight, Cherie."

He took her hand gently in his and placed a kiss on it, his lips lingering a bit longer than was necessary. He flashed his brilliant smile at her one last time, descended the steps, and strode to the stables, whistling to himself as he went. Inez held the back of her hand to her cheek, dreamily closing the door when she could no longer see his retreating figure. She leaned back against the door, a little breathless at his clear admiration and honest declaration.

No one had ever said anything that romantic to Inez in her life. She smiled to herself and made her way back to the parlor, her hand still held to her cheek and an extra bounce in her step. She did not see the secret looks that passed between the other people in the room as she flounced down in her chair and took up her embroidery, humming a little tune all the while. She let herself go back over the evening from the time she had opened the door to the moment Christophe had let go her hand and walked whistling across the yard.

Inez realized with some satisfaction that for the first time in the four and a half years since she had met him, Estêvão had not dominated her thoughts. She didn't know how or when it had happened, but at some time during the evening she had ceased to think of Christophe in terms of his comparison to Estêvão and had begun to assess him on his own merit. There had been the obvious similarities to his cousin, which had most likely been the initial source of Inez's attraction to Christophe, but there had also been many differences.

Christophe had frankly expressed his interest in her as opposed to trying to disguise it, as had been the case with Estêvão. Inez knew that the less pronounced age difference had much to do with this more open attitude, but it seemed to her that it would not have mattered to Christophe. He appeared to know exactly what he wanted and did not feel any compunction about declaring it and doing what he needed to get it. In this first meeting, he had made her feel like the center of attention, like he was there to attend her alone. For a young woman who had spent her entire life in the shadow of her beautiful elder sister, it was a novel and exhilarating experience. It was flattering and exciting, and she could not wait for their next meeting.

Perhaps Paulina and her mother were right after all. Maybe she would someday love again.

Chapter 3: Christophe

As Christophe rode home that night, he could not suppress the smile that played about his lips. He thought about the fickle hand of fate and the strangeness of life's twists and turns. The evening had been genuinely enjoyable and a nice break from the never-ending toil he had engaged in since coming to Terceira. He felt as if he had finally received a reward for all of his hard work, for being a respectful son and fulfilling his father's wishes. It was just odd that the reward had come in the form of a veritable Venus and not in a bounty of the grapevines, as he would have supposed.

When his father had asked him to oversee the operation here in this far outpost of Portugal, he had not known what to expect. The long hours of drudgery were a given, but he was no stranger to intense labor. He had grown up in a vineyard and performed every task, starting with the most menial and working his way up to the ones that required the most finesse. By his fourteenth birthday, he was expert at every job. He had been the obvious choice to manage the new venture, and he was well enough equipped to do it. The thing that surprised him was the personal change that had happened in his attitude.

Although he relished the challenge of hard physical labor and the satisfaction of mastering new skills and adding them to his already extensive repertoire, he had never really taken ownership in his father's considerable holdings. He knew in an offhand manner that one day the properties would fall to him, but in his youth he had only been interested in the pleasures that such a position could afford him. He enjoyed the celebrity of being heir to the prestigious Don Francisco Winery and the recognition it brought him. When he was not working, he dressed in the finest clothing, wore expensive jewelry, surrounded himself with cheerful, good-looking company—both of male and female persuasion. It did not bother him that the majority of his 'friends' were sycophants, and he eagerly provided food and drink to all just to ensure a revel. In short he had been a fop, happily squandering his father's hard-earned fortune in the name of dissipation. After a month in Terceira, all that had changed.

During the first few weeks assaying the soil, his father had mentored him personally, astonishing Christophe with his wealth of knowledge. Because Don Francisco had grown up in a privileged household with a claim of kinship to the royal house of Castile, Christophe had assumed that the vineyard was just a hobby and that his father had simply given financial backing and his seal of approval when it was required. He soon found out how wrong this perception was. It turned out that the grapes were his father's passion and, in fact, had been how his parents had met and fallen in love. Christophe listened and learned and began to care more than he ever imagined.

At the end of a month's time, his father had returned to the main vineyard at Soutomaior leaving Christophe in charge of the offshoot enterprise. He also left some of his most reliable employees behind to ensure a reasonable chance of success. Of course when Don Francisco chose the workers, he had sensibly opted for single men. It would be unfair to ask the men with families to be separated from their loved ones for an extended period of time or to ask the families to relocate to the primitive conditions to which the men would be subjected until proper housing could be built. The men were all of a good hard-working sort, but they were coarse, single, and hard living as well. It would be ridiculous to presume for them to live like monks.

On their days off the men all went into Angra and spent their hard-earned salaries on gambling, drink, and women, all once believed by Christophe to be worthwhile pursuits. For some reason though, his mindset began to change. He went along on a few of the first expeditions into town but quickly curtailed his participation, finding himself inexplicably repulsed by his old habits. The establishments seemed seedier, the women more wanton, and the senseless waste of the fruit of their labors suddenly infuriated him. He began to eschew the regular jaunts, instead spending his time making plans for a house of his own.

In the beginning he simply viewed the carousals as an annoying but perhaps necessary release for the men. He was patient with their sluggish return to work after a full night of drinking and fighting. He brought in the doctor to attend to their more serious afflictions. On some occasions he even went so far as to provide transport back to town for their female companions, but he soon began to tire of these little distractions and laid down a new set of rules.

Although the men could do as they wished away from the grounds, the vineyard was to be considered sacrosanct. It was the source of their income, their livelihood, their very existence, and should be treated as such. The men could follow his example and build their own dwellings in their free time if they wished—what they did in the privacy of their own homes was their own business as long as it did not affect their work—but the common area of the vineyard would no longer be treated as a flophouse. The men grumbled and carped about how Christophe saw the vineyard as some sort of shrine and how like his inflexible father the young man was becoming—and he used to be such a merry sort!—but they grudgingly gave him their respect, even christening him with the new nickname of 'Chief'. It was something he had never thought to accomplish, and it pleased him to no end.

He had also never expected to find one of the most beautiful women he had ever seen in such a backwoods settlement as Terceira, a world away from the high society in which he had grown up. His aunt first mentioned Inez after Estêvão had married the girl's sister. He remembered her parents coming to tour the grounds just before his father had set sail to return to the mainland. They were old, but he recalled that they made a very handsome couple. The gentleman was an extremely intelligent man and quickly grasped the task before them, and the woman, though stout and a bit overbearing, had a certain vibrance about her. Christophe imagined that she must have been a beauty in her youth, and he idly wondered what the daughters looked like.

A few months later, he met his cousin's bride. It was no surprise that she was exquisite. He had been told as much by his father after Francisco had shuttled the family to the mainland. Estêvão could have chosen anyone in Iberia. It stood to reason that his wife should look like an angel. Oddly enough, it had only increased Christophe's curiosity about the younger girl. Did she look like her sister? Would she be dark like her father? Would she be intelligent like her father or bossy like her mother? Then a few months ago his Aunt María had begun to extoll her virtues. He didn't know why his aunt had decided to play matchmaker, but it was entertaining to imagine the possibilities. It was not like he was being betrothed to the girl. If she did not live up to his expectations, he could simply make his excuses and choose not to associate with her again. What harm would it do to meet her? Nothing he could have done would have prepared him for that meeting.

When Christophe raised his fist to knock on the door at the

Fazenda da Pomba, he noticed that his hand shook the slightest bit in anticipation. This was out of character for him. He was usually very self-assured and rarely got nervous. He tried to rationalize to himself that it was most likely the build-up his aunt had given the girl, but he couldn't shake the feeling that this meeting would somehow be a life-changing event. He had never placed very much importance on female companionship. Oh, he had indulged in his share of amours, but he had never been in love and did not expect to be. All of that changed the moment Inez opened the door.

The creature before him was like nothing he could have concocted on his own. Even if he had been told to dream up the most beautiful woman he could imagine, his expectations would have fallen short. She stood there, a perfect incarnation of Demeter, the Greek goddess of the harvest, complete with her russet red curls piled on her head and her flowing green gown. Her magnificent eyes sparkled like jewels, whirling with a kaleidoscope of colors, and a delicate pink flush spread across her creamy ivory skin. Christophe's mouth fell open at the sight, and his wits deserted him, leaving him incapable of breaking the silence between them.

Their first words of conversation and the walk to the parlor passed in a dream. Only when his Aunt María began the line of questioning about the vineyard did he truly recover his powers of speech and begin to feel himself. Even then he could not stop his eyes from straying to Inez, though his comments were directed at his aunt.

Throughout the evening Christophe realized with some surprise that she was unaware and unaffected by her beauty. Every time he smiled or winked in her direction, she lowered her eyes demurely as if unaccustomed to the attention. She was polite and interested in his work, and she was extremely intelligent. She also showed all the signs of being attracted to him. He found himself hoping for this to be the case.

As Christophe drew up to his almost finished house, the thought occurred to him that perhaps his whole perception of the evening was thrown off by the shock of seeing such a startling contradiction to what he supposed he would find. Maybe he was ascribing qualities to Inez she did not possess. Maybe she was not nearly as attractive as he remembered. Her gown had been elegant and her hairstyle becoming, but with the right amount of grooming and attention to her appearance even a homely girl could be transformed. Perhaps tomorrow when she showed up for her tour of the vineyard he would find that she was missing one leg, her magnificent eyes were cunningly painted fakes, and her glorious hair was a wig. Instead of the goddess he had compared her to, she would turn out to be more akin to a Gorgon without a single eye of her own and only one tooth. He laughed out loud as he dismounted his horse and led the animal to its stall.

Chapter 4: At The Vineyard

The next morning Christophe arose in an excellent mood. Today would be the day he would see the truth of Inez's appearance. Gorgon or goddess, there would be no means for her to hide her flaws in the open sunlight. Either way he would be able to put his mind at ease. He dressed in his work clothes and went to find some breakfast.

As soon as he finished his morning rounds, Christophe was summoned to the dwelling of one of his most reliable men. The day before a large splinter from one of the oaken storage casks had penetrated Arnoldo's work gloves and had lodged deeply in his index finger. The splinter was removed, but now the finger was hot and swollen with an angry red discoloration reaching all the way to the middle of his palm. The man was not one to complain, so when he screamed as Christophe took hold of his hand to get a better look, a courier was dispatched immediately to call the doctor. Christophe also ordered a cool compress made to bring down the swelling, and he sat down to wait with Arnoldo until it arrived.

When the man delivered the compress, he also delivered news of visitors who had shown up for a tour. Dom Martín was a familiar enough figure, but when the man mentioned the young woman who accompanied him, he wiggled his eyebrows in a meaningful manner and made a lewd, smacking noise with his mouth. It was comical and Christophe nearly made the mistake of laughing at the gesture, but he recovered himself enough to issue a firm reprimand. Apparently the impression he had retained of Inez's beauty had been more or less an accurate one, and he did not want to set a precedent of disrespect toward her. He would not suffer his men to treat her in such a discourteous, lecherous way, especially if she should turn out to be as important to him as he believed. He rose from his seat, his disapproval evident on his scowling face, and went to greet his guests.

Upon exiting Arnoldo's house, Christophe was assaulted by a furry tan missile, jumping and barking in joyous greeting. He issued a firm, "Sit!" and Palhaço immediately responded to the command, dropping his rump and waiting for further instruction. Christophe patted him on the head and said, "Good boy," then strode over to greet his human visitors with the dog trotting docilely beside him. The sun shone directly into his eyes, and as he approached the party he had to squint to make out their figures. Suddenly he was upon them, and as his vision adjusted to the change in the light, he stopped in his tracks.

He wondered how had he ever doubted Inez's beauty. She was even more a goddess in her natural state than dressed in all her finery. Her garnet-colored hair was bound at the nape of her neck by a leather thong, but a few of the unruly tresses escaped their restraints and blew wildly about her lovely face. The golden light of the morning sun revealed the extraordinary nuances of her coloring—the true silver and gold of her eyes edged by her dusky charcoal lashes, the pinky mauve of her plump lips, and the subtle tinge of rose on her translucent porcelain skin. Everything about her suggested an earthiness and the promise of abundant fecundity. In that moment, he did not care what he had to do to win her heart. If he had to make a deal with the devil, she would one day be his.

"I'm sorry, Christophe," Inez smiled in apology, breaking

into his thoughts. "Sometimes Palhaço is so happy to see a person that he forgets his manners."

It took a moment for Christophe to respond. He was momentarily dumbstruck by her vivacious smile and the propriety with which his name fell from her lips. "I ... um ... had a dog when I was a child," he stammered, hoping it would be enough to cover his lapse.

"Yes, well," she giggled, making her even more enchanting, "he certainly seems to have taken to you."

"Perhaps he senses my honorable intentions," Christophe countered with a brilliant smile of his own.

Dom Martín sighed loudly, beginning to lose patience with the young couple's flirtations. "Well then, shall we begin the tour?"

"Of course," Christophe said cheerfully. He turned to Inez, intending to offer his arm for support. As he did he took in her appearance, and a little grimace flitted across his handsome face.

She was dressed modestly enough, if a bit unusually, in a man's long-sleeved camisa and a pair of man's breeches cut down to fit her petite frame. Her recent weight loss had left her curvy figure even more pronounced, and her still full bosom and rounded hips made her slender waist seem impossibly tiny in comparison. She had thrown her cape back over her shoulders inadvertently exposing her feminine charms to anyone who cared to behold them. Christophe racked his brain for a tactful way to urge her to cover herself. Finally he came up with a solution.

"Perhaps it would be a good idea for you to wrap your cape a little more snugly around you. Although the weather outside feels warm with the sun shining down on us, it can get quite chilly in the shade of the volcano."

"Thank you," Inez said, flattered by his concern for her comfort, and she pulled her cape down over her figure and took the arm he offered. Dom Martín fell in behind them, and Palhaço jauntily brought up the rear.

The vineyard was fascinating, and Inez could see why her father had been so enthusiastic about being a part of the new enterprise. She was also impressed by the amount of work that had been accomplished. She found herself marveling at Christophe's work ethic and was astounded how someone who would be only eighteen on his birthday the following week had done so much in less than two years. She shook her head in amazement and admired him all the more. She also wondered what other hidden talents he had to offer.

At the conclusion of the tour, Christophe guided Inez and Dom Martín back to where they had tethered their horses. It was plain that he was reluctant to let them leave, and he attempted to draw out the conversation as long as he could. When there was nothing left to prolong the discussion, he held his hands out in a defeated gesture and said, "I would ask you to stay for a meal, but I'm afraid I don't have anything to offer but some leftover pieces of roasted chicken and some wine. The wine is quite excellent though, if I do say so myself," he added with a little wink at Inez.

"Dom Martín and I always carry a little bit of food with us," Inez said, getting an idea. "If you have a few staples, I could probably throw something together. Oh," she said, her face falling with the realization, "but you probably have to get back to work."

"Actually this time of year there is not that much work to do. Besides, one of my most reliable men had a mishap yesterday and will not be able to do much more than supervise for the new few weeks. It seems I will have a bit more free time than I am accustomed to. What sort of staples do you need?"

"Let's see," she said taking a mental inventory. "Perhaps an onion and a little bit of olive oil?"

"I'm sure I could rustle that up for you. Well then," he said with a twinkle in his amber eyes, "I would be delighted for you to dine with me. After you, Mademoiselle," he said, making a sweeping courtly flourish with his arm. Inez giggled, and Dom Martín rolled his eyes and went to retrieve the sack containing their victuals.

The human trio plus Palhaço walked the short distance to Christophe's house. The dwelling was very basic with only the barest of necessities, but it was close enough to completion that one could see the open spacious floor plan and tasteful lines of the structure. Christophe showed Inez to the kitchen and gathered the items she required to put the meal together. He left to help Dom Martín collect enough furniture for them to sit comfortably, and Inez set about preparing the food.

She picked the meat from the carcass of the chicken and cut it into small cubes. She took the onion and an apple from Dom Martín's sack and diced them too. She threw in a handful of raisins and nuts, and tossed the mixture with a drizzle of olive oil and a splash of wine. While the concoction was marinating, Inez cut the crusty edges off of a rounded loaf of bread and slit them lengthwise to form pockets. She shaved some cheese into very thin slices and lined the bread pockets before stuffing them with the chicken mixture. Satisfied with the finished product, she placed the food on a small board and carried it out to the table where the men were talking.

"*Mon Dieu!* Would you look at that!" exclaimed Christophe, clearly impressed. "These look fantastic! Where did you get this recipe?"

"I didn't follow a recipe," Inez answered with a little moue. "I hope they taste all right. I just thought the ingredients would go nicely together."

The men were not even listening to her any longer. Suddenly

famished at the appearance of the food before them, they each grabbed ahold of one of the stuffed chunks of bread and immediately bit into them. Dom Martín rolled his eyes and groaned his approval, and Christophe chewed his bite thoughtfully, savoring the subtle blend of flavors coalescing on his tongue. He swallowed his mouthful and looked up at Inez without even a hint of a joke in his tawny eyes.

"My aunt was right," he said sincerely. "Inez, you are an excellent cook."

"A magician is what she is," came the hearty agreement from Dom Martín.

Inez smiled broadly and sat down, taking a dainty bite from the portion that was left. "They are quite good," she said, nodding her head.

The three of them ate and chatted amiably. Inez dropped little pieces of bread and cheese to Palhaço who was situated strategically on the floor between her chair and Christophe's. Dom Martín asked questions regarding the fabrication of the house, interested to see how much the methods had changed since he had built his own. Christophe happily gave them a tour when they finished their meal. Dom Martín grunted his appreciation of each room, admiring the sound construction and the sensible architecture.

"It is not quite finished," Christophe said proudly, "but I hope to have it completed within the next few months. Then comes the task of furnishing it. I have the means, but I must admit the process is a bit tedious to me."

"Yes, and the women are never really satisfied with a home until they can put their own touches on it," Dom Martín added, sharing the knowledge gleaned from years of experience. "You've made a thorough job of it so far. Maybe you should consider marrying so your wife can tackle the task of turning it into a cozy family home," he finished with a chuckle.

"I have been thinking about that a great deal lately," Christophe replied seriously, his deep yellow eyes straying to Inez a few feet away. "More with each day that passes."

He escorted his visitors back to their horses and gave Inez a leg up while Dom Martín swung onto his mount. Christophe placed Inez's boot firmly in the stirrup and rested his hand on it, absently caressing the leather with his thumb as he thanked them for their interest. He was still reluctant to let them leave, but they had toured the entire property and there was no justification left to keep them any longer. He sighed deeply and looked up at Inez from his place at her feet.

"I suppose I shall see you in a week's time, if that is still the plan."

"Oh, yes," Inez smiled down at him. "I have a very special supper planned for you."

"I will count the days until then."

"Well, son," began Dom Martín, sensing the young couple's unwillingness to part, "I would ask you to join us tomorrow, but you will probably want to spend your free time working on your house. We will be in the northernmost pasture separating the pregnant cows from the rest of the herd, and we can always use as much help as we can get."

Inez almost leapt at the chance to urge Christophe to join them, but she knew the house was his priority. He had already expressed his eagerness to be finished with the project. They had only just met the evening before. What right did she have to distract him from his plans? Besides, he might consider it far too forward of her.

Her spirits sank even further when he said, "You are right, Dom Martín. I really should use the time off to my advantage. Besides, I will see you in a week."

He let go of Inez's boot, and ruffled Palhaço's silky tan mane. The dog barked one last time and looked up at his mistress, waiting for the trip home to get under way. Inez and Dom Martín kicked their horses into a trot, waving back over their shoulders as they guided their mounts up the lane. Christophe stood in the courtyard returning the farewell until they disappeared around the bend.

He slowly turned and made his way back to Arnoldo's house to check on the man's condition. He hoped that the injury was not serious, but he was secretly thrilled at the prospect that he could use the excuse to put Arnoldo in charge of operations for a few weeks. It would give him the time to ... what?

There were so many matters that required his attention. The last thing Christophe needed right now was to complicate his life with a woman. Inez was an exceptional example of the fair sex, but he barely knew her. She was bound to have her flaws just like everybody else. Why was he already putting her on a pedestal? He shook his head to clear it and took a deep breath. He was thankful that he had not obligated himself to help with the cows the next day. What he needed was some time alone to sort things out, to honestly assess his feelings. Using the opportunity tomorrow to work on his house would give him a chance to take a step back from the situation and think about in which direction he really wanted to take his life. Yes, it would be best to go slowly. He would see her soon enough.

The next morning Inez and Dom Martín rode out to the north end of the property to tend to the task of separating the cows. Inez had been a bit sulky since they had parted ways with Christophe the day before. Everything had gone so well up until the end of their visit. She went over and over the scene in her mind, trying to figure out what she had done to effect such a turnabout in

Christophe's attitude toward her. He had not done or said anything negative, but she had sensed a sudden restraint in him. She tried to console herself with the fact that she would see him in less than a week. Perhaps he would return to the attentive, solicitous young man he had been the night they first met. She tried to put it out of her thoughts and concentrate on the chore at hand.

Dom Martín stationed Inez to one side of the open gate in the paddock where they were working. Her job was to make sure the bovines stayed headed in the right direction so the farmhands could easily pick out the pregnant cows and reroute them to a separate pasture. Palhaço stayed close enough to her to stay out of harm's way, but she did her best to keep an eye on him and make sure he remained behind the safety of the gate.

Though Palhaço was untrained at the job, he did have the natural instincts of his cattle dog ancestors. He stayed out of reach of the cows' sharp hooves, and if any of them began to veer off in the wrong direction, he barked loudly and nipped at their heels. He was uncharacteristically focused, and Inez began to relax, feeling comfortable enough to take her eyes off of him for short lengths of time. She was caught completely off-guard when he suddenly sprinted away from his place at her side, streaking off across the open fields before she could shout out to stop him.

Inez turned in her saddle to ascertain what had prompted the dog's sudden flight and was surprised to see a dark figure galloping toward them across the rolling green countryside. Upon reaching his target, Palhaço made a wide circle around Christophe then bounded along beside him, barking and leaping, heralding the new arrival to all. Inez's face broke into a radiant smile as Christophe reined in his mount and pulled up beside her.

"Good morning," he said with a wide-open smile. "Can you still use some help?"

"I'm sure we can, but you'll have to ask Dom Martín what he

wants you to do. I thought you were going to work on your house today," Inez said, scrunching up her nose.

"The weather is too nice. It would be a shame to be indoors on a day like today. Besides, I can work on my house any time."

"It is lovely out here," Inez agreed with a sigh.

"Beautiful," Christophe said meaningfully.

There was much to do, and the day passed quickly. At the end of their time together, Dom Martín thanked Christophe for his help, everyone said goodbye, and they all headed to their respective homes. There was never any verbal agreement made for Christophe to show up in the days that followed, but each morning he rode across the fields to join them in their labors. The two young people worked well together, anticipating what needed to be done and accomplishing the tasks before Dom Martín had a chance to issue the order. They were very attuned to one another, and he speculated that if they ever married, their union would be very successful and harmonious.

Unable to resist his attraction to Inez, Christophe stopped looking for reasons to maintain his distance. It was futile to fight it, so he gave himself up to his emotions. He found his thoughts straying to her at the oddest of times, even when he should have been concentrating on the vineyard or his house. He had never witnessed anything as lovely and graceful as Inez on horseback. He would often flash back to a moment during the day when she was unaware of his observation. His recollection of her unrestrained laughter at some silly antic of Palhaço's or the way she tucked little wayward strands of escaped hair under her battered old straw hat always brought a smile to Christophe's face.

He compensated for his inattention to his obligations by assigning Arnoldo to oversee the small amount of work to be done at the winery. As far as his house was concerned, there was not much else to be completed apart from installation of the windows and some interior finish work. He could not take care of the windows until they arrived, and the finish work could be done anytime. In regard to the décor, perhaps he would ask Inez to help him make those decisions. This thought utterly surprised him because it implied that she would one day come to live in the house. Was he really beginning to contemplate matrimony?

Inez was overjoyed at the burgeoning relationship between them. She took pride in the fact that, aside from the way he looked at her and the intimate conversation they shared between tasks, Christophe treated her no differently than he treated any of the other men. He admired her skillful management of her mount and her ability to complete her part of the job at hand. He respected her judgement and trusted her instincts. It was yet another acclamation of her strong character and a further step toward liberation from the heartbreak that had oppressed her for the previous year and a half. She tried to truthfully assess her feelings and came to the conclusion that she was at least infatuated with him, if not well on her way to falling in love.

Chapter 5: Canelle

The day of Christophe's birthday celebration was at hand, and there was much for Inez to do. The pork roast she planned to serve as the main course would take most of the day to cook, so she rose early and did not accompany Dom Martín to the fields. She felt a little nervous as she made her way to the kitchen. In her mind this meal was even more important than the first one she had fixed here. Even though she had been cooking for twice as many people that first time and she had been trying to impress those who she had been certain would one day be her family, expectations had not been nearly as high as they were now. The meal this evening would have to surpass the previous ones to uphold her reputation.

When Inez crossed the threshhold into the kitchen, the memories of the meal prepared with Estêvão came flooding back, assaulting her with a bittersweet nostalgia that nearly brought her to tears. After the first night she had met Christophe, she had rarely thought about Estêvão at all, even when she spent time with her sister. Of course she knew obliquely that Serafina was carrying his child, but these days Inez regarded it more as her sister's child. Perhaps it was because Estêvão was not present, but analyzing her feelings for Christophe had taken priority over the unresolved emotions toward Estêvão that lingered on the periphery of her conscious mind. Now was not the time to address the issue. It would take much serious contemplation and most likely a painful and unsettling self-examination. She shook her head to chase away the memories and brought her attention back to the task at hand.

The cook had all the requested foodstuffs washed and waiting to be treated. Inez had won her over after that first meal prepared in her kitchen, and she now stood smiling and ready to lend assistance where it was needed. As Inez tied on her apron her anxiety dissipated, and she respectfully asked the cook to begin coring and slicing the apples into rings while she turned her attention to seasoning the roast. A short time later, the pork had been set on the spit, and the apple rings were simmering away in a heavily spiced mixture of wine, honey, and raisins. Inez then began to prepare the dessert.

She had the cook dice some more apples and chop some nuts while she mixed up a sweet brown cake batter, again using generous quantities of cinnamon, cloves, and ginger. She folded in the fruit and nuts, and poured the mixture into small individual tins to bake. Inez then set about making a syrup reduced from the liquid of the stewing apple rings while the rich little cakes filled the house with their delicious spicy aroma, a promise of the mouth-watering feast to come. When they had done baking, Inez removed them from their tins and saturated them with the reduction. It would require a good amount of time for the cakes to absorb the syrup, so she put them to one side. Then she and the cook set about putting together the soup and side dishes.

Occupied with the preparations, time slipped quickly away. Soon the hour approached for Inez to ready herself for the celebration. She gave the cook some last-minute instructions and thanked her for her help and the use of her kitchen. Inez then removed her apron and headed to her room to wash and dress.

The kitchen had been warm and her exertions energetic, so she took the opportunity to thoroughly scrub her sticky body and wash her grubby face. She donned a midnight blue satin gown trimmed with blackwork at the square neckline, cuffs, and hem. It was one of the new dresses Joanna had ordered after Inez's weight loss, and it fit her like a second skin. She tied a matching ribbon around her neck then pondered what to do with her hair.

She undid the heavy single plait, which had held her hair back out of her face while she worked at the supper, and brushed it out with quick, impatient strokes. Still damp from the humid atmosphere of the kitchen, the mass tumbled down around her shoulders in a cascade of loose auburn curls. She feared that it yet carried the aromas of the food preparations, and she wished she had planned enough time to wash it. Instead she smoothed it up and back away from her face and pinned it closely to her head. The effect was like that of a horse's mane with the ringlets pushed up toward the center of her head and trailing freely down her back. Satisfied with her reflection in the mirror, she went down to the parlor to wait.

As Inez descended the last few stairs, all eyes turned to regard her and simultaneously opened wide to show their surprise. Dom Martín quickly strode over to offer his arm while Serafina and Dona María looked on, beaming with approval.

"Oh, Mynah!" Dona María cried. "You look just beautiful!"

"It's true, Senhorita Inez," rumbled Dom Martín at her side. "You will knock your young gentleman off of his feet."

Tears sprang to her eyes, and Inez opened her mouth to thank him, but no words came out. Dom Martín had always shown his appreciation of her horsemanship and his respect for her intelligence, but he had never openly acknowledged any part of her feminine appeal.

"Now, now, little lady," he said quietly. "Don't go spoiling your appearance by crying. Christophe will be here too soon for you to fix your face."

"Thank you, Dom Martín," she choked out and squeezed his

massive bicep.

Inez settled herself in a chair next to her sister's. Serafina leaned over to her and whispered, "If Christophe does not fall dead when he sees you, he is either blind or not worthy of your attentions. You are the most beautiful woman I have ever seen, Inez. I can hardly believe you are the same little hoyden I grew up with!"

Inez reached over and pinched Serafina on the arm, and as they laughed together over the old familiar gesture, there was a firm knock on the door. Here was the moment for which they had all been waiting. There was a collective intake of breath, and they all listened with anticipation as the guest of honor entered the house, gave his cape to the servant, and made his way to the parlor. Everyone sat stock still as he strode into the room, scanned its occupants with his tawny leonine eyes, and began his salutations.

He first greeted Dom Martín with a firm handshake, moving on to plant a warm kiss on his Aunt María's cheek. Then he stopped in front of Serafina, bowing low to graze the back of her hand with his lips, the whole while keeping his left hand hidden conspicuously behind his back. He finally turned to Inez, his deep yellow eyes blazing with obvious appreciation, and he repeated the action, bending over her hand, his lips lingering ever so slightly longer. He straightened up to his full height and pulled a massive bouquet of flowers from behind him, laying them in Inez's open arms.

"My compliments to the cook," he said with his brilliant white smile.

"Oh, Christophe," Inez began, breathing in deeply of their scent, "they are beautiful!"

"Not nearly as beautiful as you," he answered in his self-assured manner.

"Thank you," she said, blushing a little but clearly dazzled by his open admiration. Again she marveled at his directness. He always seemed to state exactly what he felt and did not care who witnessed it. She rose from her seat and started across the floor. "I will have someone put these in a vase with water. They are too lovely to let wilt," and she left the room, Christophe's amber eyes following her progress.

"Well, son," began Dom Martín in his booming voice, "did you get anything done at your house today?"

"I did," replied Christophe, his eyes never leaving the door through which Inez had exited.

The supper was a smashing success. The pork roast was tender enough to be cut with a fork, and the spiced apple rings provided the perfect complement to the salty, smoky flavor of the meat. Everything turned out just as Inez planned, and the diners issued their verbal appreciation between bites, Dom Martín grunting and groaning his in a continual flow throughout the meal. The supper plates were cleared from the table, and everyone eagerly awaited the special birthday dessert.

As the dishes were set before them, all showed considerable restraint until the others were served. The fragrant brown cakes were each topped with a generous dollop of fluffy whipped cream, and Dom Martín licked his lips in boyish expectation. When he saw that the others had been presented with their portions, he dug his spoon into the creamy, sticky concoction and rolled his eyes back into his head as the delightful fusion of flavors assailed his tongue. Inez giggled under her hand. She saw that Dona María and Serafina were also enjoying their cakes, and her eyes strayed to the birthday guest to regard his reaction.

The smile quickly faded from her lips when she saw that Christophe was still contemplating the dish before him and had not yet taken ahold of his spoon. Inez's face fell immediately, thinking that perhaps he did not care for the ingredients or the look of the dessert, and she chastised herself for not having inquired about his preferences. She had so wanted to please him. She swallowed her wounded pride and mustered up the courage to find out what was wrong.

"Is the dessert not to your liking, Christophe? You have not even taken a bite."

He directed his dark yellow gaze at her, as if he had been awakened from a dream. "I'm sorry," he said with a smile, shaking his head slowly. "I did not mean to alarm you. The cake smells and looks heavenly. I was just thinking that no one has ever taken the time or effort to make my birthday as special as you have tonight. Perhaps it is silly of me, but I just wanted to draw out the feeling of anticipation and savor it as long as I could. I suppose it is my little way of showing reverence and preserving the moment."

He then picked up his spoon and took a tiny slice off of one corner. He brought the bite to his mouth and slowly removed the utensil from his lips, chewing thoughtfully and nodding his head in approval. He swallowed the mouthful and turned back to her. "It is superb, Inez," he said plainly. "Not only are you beautiful and intelligent, you are undeniably the most talented woman I have ever known."

She blushed again at his straightforward praise, and she heard Serafina let out a little sigh at his romantic declaration. Inez thanked him for his flattering comments, and Dona María smiled smugly to herself.

Everything was proceeding exactly as María had foreseen. All she'd had to do was introduce the pair. They had gotten on as well as she had known they would, and they were extremely well-suited to one another. She would not have to do anything more than sit back and watch. The two young people were falling in love all by themselves.

The rest of the evening was enjoyably spent, and Christophe stayed much later than the curfew of dusk that he had previously imposed upon himself. It was clear that he was reluctant to go, and María asked him if he would like to stay the night. He seriously considered it for a moment and then politely refused claiming his responsibilities at the vineyard. His aunt's invitation made him realize the lateness of the hour, and soon afterward he rose to leave. He bid his farewells, and just as he had before, he asked Inez to see him to the door. The two young people exited the room leaving the three older persons nodding and smiling and exchanging knowing looks with one another.

At the door Inez stood with her hands clasped together as Christophe donned his cape and retrieved a flat, medium-sized box from a chair. He turned and presented the box to her and smiled, satisfied by her surprised reaction.

"What is it?" she asked, amused by the irony that he should be giving her a gift at his own birthday celebration.

"I suppose you will have to open it to find out," he said, still smiling.

Inez sat down in the chair with the package on her lap. With shaking hands she struggled to untie the twine that held the box closed. Christophe came to her aid with his pocketknife. Inez gently removed the lid, pulled out the packing paper, and let out a soft melodic chuckle at what lay inside.

"A new hat," she said, smiling up at him.

"Yes. I noticed that the one you wear in the field is a bit … ah … worn," he said, finding an inoffensive word to describe the shabby old chapéu de palha. "It would be a shame for the tip of your funny little nose to get burned by the sun."

"Thank you," she said, rising from the chair. She crinkled up her nose in the old habit that was so difficult to rid herself of completely, and Christophe laughed that she had just proven his point.

"Oh, Inez," he said affectionately. "I have the sudden urge to embrace you. May I? Please say yes. Certainly you would not deny me such a small happiness on my birthday."

Inez nodded her head in acquiescence, and Christophe stepped forward, gently enfolding her in his arms. He held her to him and pressed his lips into the abundance of curls pinned on the top of her head. He inhaled the lingering aroma of the spices she had used so liberally in her cooking and whispered, "*Canelle*," without thinking.

She pulled back slightly and looked up at him, the lovely golden lights in her eyes flickering with pleasure. "What is that?" she asked.

"It means 'cinnamon'," he explained, dropping his arms from about her but clasping her hands in his. "Your hair smells like cinnamon."

"I'm sorry," she said, coloring in embarrassment. "I didn't have time to wash it."

"Do not be sorry. It is one of my favorite scents," he said, smiling down at her. "Even more so now. Besides, it suits you." Christophe reluctantly let go of her hands and opened the door. He turned back to her a final time, reached his brown hand up to cup her cheek, and ran his thumb softly over its downy surface. "Thank you, Canelle, for everything. I shall see you tomorrow." Then he turned and walked off into the night.

The rest of the evening passed like a dream, and soon it was time for bed. Everyone bid each other goodnight and made their way to their respective chambers. Inez carried the box containing the hat to her room and set it down on the table next to the vase with the flowers Christophe had brought her. She pushed her face into the arrangement and took a deep breath of their sweet floral fragrance. She sighed contentedly then turned to the unavoidable task before her.

Christophe had presented her with the new hat, because the old one was tattered and shabby. The gift from Estêvão had served its purpose, but now it was time to put away this last vestige of her heart's first venture into the realm of love. Her experience had not turned out the way she wished, but contrary to her belief that she would never care for another, she had found a man who was thoughtful and attentive, and he very clearly admired her. It was time to stop dwelling in the past and begin looking toward her future.

She gently took the battered, floppy chapéu de palha and carefully folded it flat, running her fingers along the gaily colored ribbons she had sewn on it to keep the hat in its place on her head. She tenderly caressed the frayed ends of the straw that had worn loose around the edges, and an unexpected tear ran down her cheek. She wiped the tear away and resolutely crossed the room to the wardrobe where she relegated the hat to the top shelf along with the other items that caused her too much pain to behold on a regular basis.

She took a long, cleansing breath and closed the doors of the wardrobe on her old memories. The significance struck her suddenly, and she nodded her head in silent assent. Making up her mind to put her old life behind her, she was now ready to move forward with the new.

Chapter 6: Revelations

The days flew quickly past and soon turned into a month. The vineyard still had only a minimal amount of work to be attended, and Arnoldo's hand needed a few more weeks to completely heal. Every morning Christophe did a quick run through of operations and saw to any pressing business that required his attention. Afterward, he left a list of duties to be accomplished then set off to visit Inez. The workers all gave each other meaningful looks and chuckled behind their hands at their obviously smitten Chief, but they understood, having been through the situation themselves— some of them multiple times. Besides, the young master had devoted his life thus far to the vineyard and worked harder than any to make it succeed. He had earned this time away and deserved a little female diversion.

Inez and Christophe were all but inseparable, spending every spare moment with each other. They happily helped out when Dom Martín needed extra hands in the fields, but occasionally there was naught to do but oversee the work of the day. On those instances, he cheerfully dismissed them, sagely acknowledging that love needed freedom and a certain amount of privacy in which to bloom. He had grown very fond of Inez and viewed her as the daughter he never had. He trusted Christophe and knew the young man's intentions were honorable, so he felt no compunction about sending them off unchaperoned except by Palhaço.

They spent their time together in a variety of ways. Some days they went back to Christophe's house and worked on the little jobs that were yet unfinished. Inez knew nothing about the carpentry trade except for the names of a few basic tools that she had seen her father use in his woodworking. Christophe patiently tutored her on the names and uses of the implements, and she quickly became an eager and able assistant. Many times her opinion determined the outcome of a certain detail, and the project began to feel like a true collaboration. Little by little, the house neared completion.

Other days were spent exploring the interior of the island. Though Inez and Christophe had both lived on Terceira for a substantial length of time, neither one of them had ventured very far out of their isolated environments. Much of the island was still pristine and densely wooded, and as they both had a keen appreciation of nature, they spent hours on horseback discovering delightful little displays of floral splendor or laughing while Palhaço chased the native wildlife.

On these outings Inez always packed plenty of small individual treats that could be munched while they rode in addition to a sumptuous lunch. They usually stopped when they got hungry and found a suitable clearing to spread out the old blanket that they carried with them. Over lunch they would share stories with one another about their childhoods or noteworthy events in their lives. They found that they had more in common than they ever dreamed, and their conversations bound them even closer together. Soon they knew nearly everything there was to know about the other.

On one such juncture they sat swapping anecdotes. They had laid out their blanket in a sunny spot next to a little stream that trickled down from the heights of the nearby volcano. Inez sat with her back leaning against a tree, and Christophe stretched out his legs and propped himself up on one elbow. He had just finished telling her about his frivolous adolescence spent reveling in his position and devising ways to further enhance his celebrity. He shook his head at his youthful folly and wasteful ways. It seemed a lifetime ago, and it was hard for him to believe that he had ever been that person.

"I have had embarrassments of my own," Inez began tentatively.

"I would have never guessed. You seem much more mature than I ever was. What sort of embarrassment could you possibly have suffered, Canelle?"

He had been so open with her about his own foolishness, and his honesty inspired her in a like manner. She speculated that this was just one more step in the process of healing and furthering their relationship, and so hesitantly she said, "I was in love with your cousin."

Instead of laughing or acting surprised as she had predicted he might, Christophe simply said, "I can see how a young girl could easily believe herself to be in love with Estêvão. He is charming, good-looking, and very charismatic. Love is nothing to feel embarrassed about," he finished, looking up at her.

"That is not the embarrassing part so much as I was convinced he would propose to me," Inez said, swallowing hard and dropping her gaze to her lap.

"But he has been married to your sister for nearly two years. You were still just a child."

"That is the general opinion, but I believed he had feelings for me that went beyond mere affection, and my sister did too. Of course the purpose of the marriage was to get an heir, and he would have had to wait for my sixteenth birthday to actually make me his wife, but Serafina was as shocked as I was when it was announced that he would take her as his bride," here she looked up at Christophe, her eyes welling with tears. She wiped at them impatiently then continued, "My sister insisted that perhaps there was some sort of terrible misunderstanding, and she urged me to investigate, but if he cared, he would have made his objectives clear."

Christophe took her hand tenderly in his and squeezed it in silent support. "The only thing I will say," he began in his quiet mellow voice, "is that if I ever had the opportunity to make you my own, I would never forgive myself for letting it pass me by. I would declare my intentions openly and not let there be any doubt as to whom I wished to take for a bride. That being said, I am grateful for my cousin's carelessness, because without it I would not have the opportunity before me now." He rolled over on his stomach and looked directly up into her face, never letting go of her hand. "Do you still harbor feelings for him?" he asked in his direct manner.

She pondered his question for a moment in order to make sure she gave Christophe the honest answer he deserved. "I believe I have recovered from my heartbreak, but I don't know how I will react when I see him again. I suppose I will not know for sure until we come face to face with one another."

Christophe nodded, satisfied with her truthful confession. Suddenly his face broke into the flashing white smile that was still so startling every time she saw it. "Then perhaps we should take things very slowly, just so you can be certain of your feelings for me." He raised her hand to his lips and placed a warm kiss on the back of it before pushing himself up to his feet. He brushed himself off and pulled her up from her seated position. When she was standing beside him, he did not let go of her hand instead keeping it within his own warm grasp. "Shall we go find Palhaço?" he asked, gazing down at her. She nodded her approval, and they walked off, hands clasped together, to look for her dog.

As the relationship between Inez and Christophe grew, it was a source of happiness for all who cared for the couple. Dom Martín was amused by their silly behavior. When they worked for him, they were as reliable as any of his seasoned hands. They paid attention to the tasks of the day and always did a fine job, but they spent the moments between making cow eyes at one another and giggling at little personal jokes. He was oblivious to the drama that had taken place between Inez and Estêvão, but he was happy that two such competent young people, about whom he was genuinely fond, had found each other.

Dona María was overjoyed that her little scheme had succeeded so effectively. She had originally set out to bring Inez and Christophe together to assuage the pain of the young woman's heartbreak. She supposed that she felt partially responsible for the way things had turned out. If she had just voiced her opinion a little more strongly and suggested outright that Estêvão propose to the younger sister, perhaps it would have saved everyone the distress they had suffered. María knew her son should never have considered taking Serafina as his bride, but was it really her burden? Ultimately he had made his own decision. María knew that Estêvão now recognized his mistake—he was in love with Inez, and he would probably never find anyone as perfectly suited to him—but she did not see why Inez should also have to be miserable because of it.

Serafina was also thrilled to see Inez finally getting over her heartbreak. It had torn at her spirit to not only witness the anguish of her baby sister and to be helpless to stop it but to have been a party to it. That had nearly destroyed her. She and Estêvão were both unhappy with the way things had worked out, but in her eyes they were deserving of their fate. Inez had been innocent and trusting of them both. It was a much greater wrong to inflict that sort of torment on someone whom you professed to love. Now that Inez finally had a man who treated her as she deserved, everybody could put the past behind them and move forward with their lives.

One morning Dona María could feel a bout coming on of the mysterious ailment with which she was periodically afflicted. It rendered her incapable of performing her usual duties, and the only thing that eased the condition was sleep. After breakfast, she headed back up to her bedchamber, and Inez deemed it a wise idea to stay at home in case she should be needed. After all, she had made the trip to Terceira to be of assistance to Serafina, and so far all she had done was entertain herself. She asked Dom Martín to relay the message to Christophe, and she settled down to spend the day with her sister.

Since the day of the proposal announcement, there had been an understandable strain between the sisters, but now that Inez had found a new male interest, that tension had eased. The two young women sat in the parlor stitching the tiny items necessary for the new baby who would arrive in a few months' time. The situation was familiar and reminiscent of the way they had spent a good portion of their childhood. It had been an age since they had passed time in this manner, but they quickly fell back into their old patterns, as close as they had ever been.

"I'm glad you decided to stay home this morning," Serafina said sincerely. "It seems a lifetime since we last spent a day together."

"I feel like I've been shirking my responsibilities," began Inez with a wry smile on her face. "I was supposed to come out here to help you, and all I have been doing is running off to explore the island with Christophe."

Serafina grunted a little laugh and turned her lovely aquamarine gaze upon her sister, "You should not feel bad. Right now the baby is in the early stages, and I can still do things for myself. It will be a couple more months before I become fat and unwieldy. That is when I will really need your help. Besides," she said sincerely, "it makes me happy to see you in love. You are nearly back to that annoying little sister that I missed so much."

Inez blushed at the mention of her state of heart. It was true that she was falling in love, but it was a bit embarrassing to hear it acknowledged so plainly. "It is so strange that Christophe and Estêvão should be so much alike," she mused. "They are cousins but they look more like brothers."

"The resemblance *is* quite shocking," Serafina agreed. "I was taken aback too, the first time I saw Christophe. And those eyes! They remind me of the tiger's eyes I was so drawn to as a child." Here she paused, recalling the disenchantment of her wedding night so long ago, which was supposed to have been such a joyous occasion. Things had certainly not turned out the way she'd expected. She shook off her momentary sadness and continued in grudging approbation. "I must admit, I'm a little jealous. Christophe treats you like a princess."

It was true. Christophe admired Inez and did not care who knew it. It was precisely the opposite of her relationship with Estêvão. Christophe's world revolved around her instead of the other way around. Inez suddenly felt sorry for her sister and opened her mouth to object, but Serafina waved her hand in dismissal.

"We all know my marriage was not a love match, and I've accepted that," here she looked up from her sewing with a wistful smile on her lips, "but sometimes I wish I had married that sheep farmer that we always joked about with such disdain. As long as he had loved me the way that Christophe does you, I believe I would have led a happy life."

Inez was struck with the sudden realization that her sister was discontented with her position. It was something that she had never thought to contemplate, because if Estêvão had taken her as his bride, she would have been the most ecstatic woman in the world. "Serafina," she began unbelievingly, "are you not happy with your marriage?"

Serafina sighed heavily and tried to smile, but Inez knew it was forced. "There are some parts of it that are pleasing to me," she began carefully. "I enjoy being here with Dona María, and the staff treat me well. I am also very excited to become a mother, but my husband's treatment of me is ..." she paused for a moment, trying to find words that would not cast Estêvão in an unflattering light, "disappointing."

"How so?" Inez asked before she could stop herself. "Certainly there have to be some good things. What about the physical part?" she asked, remembering Paulina's description of the merging of body and spirit and her mother's inability to wait until marriage. "*That* has to at least be pleasurable."

Serafina blushed uncomfortably and Inez was sorry she had blurted out such an insensitive question. "The physical part is ... not intolerable," she replied.

"Not intolerable?" Inez knew she was entering dangerous territory and should not go down this path, but she could not help it. It was like when she had been a child and had a loose tooth. Though the flesh was sore and bleeding, she could not keep from pressing on the spot until she felt the exquisite pain at the threshhold of her tolerance. Once the tooth came out, the torture subsided and the compulsion ceased. She hoped the same would happen now.

Serafina nodded. "My husband is always polite and considerate and finishes his duties quickly." She looked up at her sister, her face still red from the embarrassment. "Inez, please, can't we talk about something else?" she begged.

Inez nodded slowly, still in a state of shock over the revelation at the words her sister had chosen to describe her connubial relations. Duties, not intolerable, polite, considerate? Where was the passion and excitement, the bonding of heart and soul? Christophe had not even kissed her yet, but the physical contact they had shared had been much more than just tolerable. The warm touch of his hand grasping hers, the affectionate manner in which he embraced her before they parted for the day, the comfortable way they sometimes sat close together with their arms about each other's waists—all of this had gone further than polite, considerate, or even merely pleasurable. It was not the fiery, ardent affair that categorized the greatest love affairs of all time, but Christophe had certainly swept her off of her feet, and there was at least mutual desire and a warm, smoldering promise of something more. She fiercely hoped that her own marriage would be much, much more than just an obligation.

A few days later, everything was back to normal and Inez was able to spend the day with Christophe. There was a spot on the volcano overlooking the vineyard that he thought of as his own, and he longed to share it with Inez. They prepared for one of their outings in the usual manner and made their way on horseback as far as their mounts could carry them. They dismounted, tied the horses securely, and took down the old blanket and their lunch. Hand in hand, they set out on foot with Palhaço following close behind. They walked for a few minutes, chatting away in a compatible fashion, and finally came to a little flat ledge that was just large enough to accommodate them. Christophe spread out the blanket, and the two humans sat down to enjoy the scenery while Palhaço went off to sniff a short distance away.

"What a magnificent view!" Inez exclaimed. From their vantage point they could see the whole of the rolling green plain below all the way down to the ships in the harbor at Angra. It was an even more comprehensive view than the little mesa with its stand of pear trees that was Estêvão's favorite spot.

"Now you know why I wished to share it with you," Christophe said, pleased with her reaction.

They sat down next to each other and enjoyed the beautiful spring day. The sun shone warmly down on them, and soon they were lying flat on their backs with their heads nearly touching. They squinted to find familiar shapes in the puffy white clouds that passed overhead and pointed them out to each other, racing to see who could make out the next one first. They laughed when Palhaço returned to give them each a smacking wet kiss on their faces, which were now readily accessible, and they generally enjoyed the other's company. A short time later, they sat up to partake of the lunch Inez had packed.

They talked as they ate, and Inez asked him how long it had taken to adjust to the more rural life on the island as opposed to the metropolitan areas in which he had been raised. She had grown up in a like environment—Vigo was smaller than Angra, but most port cities were for the most part similar—but Christophe had spent time in some of the largest cities in Castile, Naples, and the south of France. Surely he must have had a difficult time getting used to the slower pace at which things moved and the primitive conditions at the vineyard. He pondered the question thoughtfully, as he did with everything he deemed worthwhile, and finally he answered.

"When my father asked me to start this operation here in this far outpost of Portugal, I did not know what to expect. When he left, I was determined to work hard and make this venture succeed. I found that the more I concentrated on the job at hand, the more I began to feel that Terceira was my home," he paused for a moment, a small surprised smile spreading across his face. "You know, Canelle, I never realized it until this moment."

"I didn't know what to expect either," Inez said, recalling her first glimpse of the island, "but the moment I set foot on Terceira, I had a strange feeling that this was where I belonged."

"I certainly never expected to find one of the most beautiful women I have ever seen."

"That is not a difficult feat on such a small island," she answered, self-deprecatingly.

"You forget that I have traveled widely. I have been in the company of some of the most sophisticated women in the world," he said, chucking her under the chin.

"My sister is the beautiful one," Inez said stubbornly.

"She is beautiful but perhaps a bit too perfect. She is like a work of art, some artist's conception of perfection. Her features are completely symmetrical, her coloring is the accepted standard of beauty, she has the long willowy figure of an angel, and she never has a hair out of place." He looked over at Inez and saw that she was beginning to sulk. He laughed softly at her pique then added, "I think I would become bored very quickly with such perfection. I much prefer my Canelle, my spicy little wild-haired adventuress at whom I never tire of looking. It is much more interesting to note the way your eyes can go from welcoming to stormy with the slightest change in your mood. I love the way your dusky grey lashes elongate the shape of your eyes and make them exotic and so much more alluring. Your funny little nose puts me in the mind to place a kiss on the tip every time you crinkle it, and your bottom lip is much wider and fuller than it should be, and I cannot resist it one second longer."

He lifted his warm brown hand to her cheek, tenderly taking hold of her earlobe with his finger and thumb. He gently pulled her to him and lowered his lips to hers, finally bestowing upon Inez her first kiss. She closed her eyes and melted into him, and they lingered there for a few moments, savoring the closeness and the warm pressure of the other's mouth on their own. When they finally pulled apart, Inez let out a small, breathy sigh of contentment.

"I was wondering when you were going to do that," she said with a little dreamy smile.

Christophe grinned at her for a moment, and then his tawny amber eyes turned speculative and serious. "I never thought I would fall in love or even contemplate getting married, until now. I only know that if you should ever agree to be my wife, I would never let you go." Then he kissed her again.

Chapter 7: Birth of the Heir

The months passed and as Serafina had predicted, her figure became swollen and cumbersome. The stress on her slender frame was considerable, and she was extremely prone to backaches and edema. The doctor came to examine her six weeks before she was scheduled to deliver her child and proclaimed that the expectant mother should be restricted to her bed. Inez reflected that it was a good thing she had come out to aid her sister, and Serafina was grateful for her ministrations.

A few weeks later, Joanna and Iñigo arrived, making the trip across the open seas to be present for the birth of their first grandchild. As Joanna did in most every situation, she immediately took charge of her pregnant daughter's care, and Inez was released from her responsibility and left to do as she pleased. Each morning after she checked on Serafina's condition, Inez joined the men in the fields, as was her wont, and things basically took up where they had left off two years prior. The only difference was that Christophe now filled the role previously occupied by Estêvão.

Iñigo was delighted to find that his favorite daughter had returned to her old cheerful self. He, like Dom Martín, was unaware of the situation that had taken place between Inez and Estêvão. He had noticed that the two got on well and had much in common, but because of the pronounced age difference, he never suspected that their feelings had run much deeper. When Inez had turned mopey after the proposal announcement, he did not think to connect the two incidents, assuming as everyone else had that Inez would simply be sad to lose her sister. He only knew that whatever had been afflicting his little Mynah had been resolved, and she had moved forward with her life.

Iñigo was extremely pleased with Inez's choice of young man. He had been impressed with Christophe at their meeting two years before. Even at that time he had drawn the comparison between the younger man and Capitán Rey. They were both hardworking, respectful, and very knowledgeable and capable in their respective fields. Christophe was the example of how Iñigo would have liked a son of his own to turn out, and if he had to one day give his daughter up to a husband, he would be content that she should marry someone of this young man's caliber.

Joanna also approved of the romance between the two young people. Because she knew the entire story, it was even more touching to her that Inez had found happiness with Christophe. When Inez had made her second trip to Terceira, Joanna had hoped something like this would happen to restore her daughter's broken spirit. She also esteemed the young man's character. The thoughtful, loving way in which Christophe treated her daughter reminded her much of how Iñigo had won her own heart so many years ago. She would unreservedly welcome him into the family when that day came.

Serafina's time of confinement drew near, and everyone began to look for El Rey's return. There had been no complications during the pregnancy—except for the fact that the size of her protruding abdomen had caused the expectant mother so much discomfort—and everything was proceeding according to schedule. It was surprising that Estêvão had left his wife's side at all, but it was unthinkable that he would not be present for the birth of his son. All of the necessary preparations were put into place for the blessed event, and everybody settled in to await the arrival of both the child and El Rey.

It was now June, and still there had been no communication or any other sign to indicate that Capitán Rey was on his way home. Serafina's due date was fast approaching, and the restlessness that most women experienced in the final stages of pregnancy unsettled the expectant mother. There were little aches and pains in her lower belly and back, her breathing was labored, and no matter how she situated herself in her bed, she could not get comfortable. Against the orders of the doctor, many hours of her day were spent pacing her bedchamber or shifting her position between sitting erect or lying back against her pillows.

One sunny morning when Inez came to visit her, she was alarmed at the ashen pallor of her sister's skin. Serafina complained of cramps low on the underside of her enormous belly. She had felt them off and on during the night, but now they seemed to be coming more frequently and for a longer duration. Inez recognized this as a symptom of the onset of labor and left to call her mother.

Joanna came quickly and, after a few perfunctory questions, sent a servant to summon the doctor. By the time the doctor arrived with the midwife, the entire family had assembled in the parlor to await the imminent birth of Serafina's child. The doctor informed them that it could be days before the child was finally born, but no one was deterred. They all tried to act as normal as they could, but it was clear that everyone was nervous. The men paced the floor, and the women chattered among themselves, but when Serafina's first agonized scream broke through the façade of calm, real panic set in.

The men all headed outside, knowing that the best thing they could do to assist was to stay out of the way. Dona María went to harry the staff to make sure they were busy supplying everything the doctor requested. Joanna and Inez headed up to Serafina's room to see if they could provide any assistance.

Upon opening the door, Inez was staggered at the chaos that had taken over in the previously tranquil, well-ordered chamber. Her sister writhed on the bed emitting animal shrieks of agony one moment and panting heavily in the next. The doctor and midwife both looked terrified and confused, and there was a pile of bed linens in the corner soaked with gore. Inez had never seen so much blood in her life, and she wondered how Serafina could still be alive. Joanna assessed the situation and began issuing commands in her brisk, authoritative manner.

"Inez!" Joanna snapped, calling her daughter back from her state of shock. "Take that pile of linens out of here and bring back fresh ones. Doctor, hand me that compress on the side table! Señora, please pay attention! My daughter's life is in your hands!"

As Inez descended the stairs to take out the soiled linens, she was never so glad of her mother's domineering character. She deposited her load, collected the pile of clean sheets, and headed back up the stairs. This time when she opened the door, she saw that some semblance of organization had returned to the room. Her sister was still laboring to give birth, and Inez could tell by her mother's attitude that something was not right, but the doctor and midwife now wore expressions of grim determination as opposed to the fright that had been evident in their faces ten minutes before.

"Inez," said Joanna softly, petting Serafina's sweat-soaked hair back from her face, "set those down on the table then please wait outside. It will be a while, but your sister may need your help again. Perhaps you could find yourself a chair."

"Yes, Mama," Inez said quietly and went to look for a chair.

Inez sat outside the door for hours, but eventually she heard one last tortured howl. There was a pause and an audible sigh, and Inez heard a female voice say, "Finally," under her breath. She heard a few slapping noises, a feeble mewling like that of a hungry kitten, and the sound of footsteps purposefully moving about the room. About half an hour later, her mother exited the room carrying another load of blood-soaked linens. She called Inez over to her.

"Your sister would like to speak to you," Joanna said, wiping her hand across her tired face. "The doctor has given her a sedative, so she may say some things that do not make sense. She is very weak. Keep your conversation brief, and Inez," her mother took her chin gently in her hand and looked directly into her eyes with meaning and said, "be strong. Tell her what you think she would like to hear."

The doctor emerged from the room and bumped into Joanna on his way to the stairs. "Forgive me, Señora," he said clearly flustered. "I was on my way to send for a priest." Joanna merely nodded her head, and the doctor all but ran down the stairs.

Inez looked at her mother, her eyes wide with alarm, and Joanna took ahold of her hand, squeezing it gently. "I will go down and inform the others. Be strong," she repeated and wearily followed the doctor down the stairs.

Inez entered the birthing chamber with a heavy sense of trepidation. She didn't know what she would find, but when she looked about the room, the only thing out of the ordinary was that the cradle in the corner now held a tightly swaddled, newborn baby. The midwife fussed over the child, and Inez turned her attention to her sister on the bed.

"Inez," Serafina said in a nearly inaudible whisper, "come over where I can see you clearly."

Inez walked over to sit beside her sister on the bed and had to stifle a gasp. Serafina was whiter than the sheet that covered her, and the thought struck Inez that she looked like a marble effigy of herself. Joanna had washed her elder daughter's face and combed her hair, arranging it neatly in a rippling golden mass about her shoulders. Inez thought about Christophe's comment regarding Serafina's perfection, and she marveled that even now, after the horrible ordeal she had just experienced, her sister should resemble an angel. She reached down and took her sister's cold, bloodless hand in her own.

"Did you see my son?" Serafina asked proudly. Even though Inez had not yet inspected the child, she nodded that she had. Serafina smiled wanly then continued, "My husband will finally be pleased with me. I was finally able to give him what he wanted."

Inez was suddenly furious with Estêvão. He was the one responsible for this tragedy, but he did not even have the consideration to be here. He had treated her sister poorly, yet even now Serafina only thought about giving him the heir he desired. All of the feelings Inez had suppressed and harbored inside of her came bubbling up to the surface, and in a righteous rage she spat out, "That bastard! He could not even deign to be here for the birth of the heir he so desperately desired! Why should it still matter what he wants?"

Because they were the only source of color in her face, Serafina's eyes burned brightly, blazing with a blue-green fire. "Inez do not be so hard on him. None of this is as it appears. I have kept this secret inside of me for nearly two years, and I cannot die with it on my conscience. Little sister, Estêvão did not ask specifically for *my* hand in marriage. Our mother was the person who made that decision and his honor would not allow him to gainsay her. Don't you see? Part of the reason that he could not love me was because he blamed me for not being you. Inez, Estêvão still loves you!"

Her head reeled and Inez struggled to breathe. For a very long time she had believed this information to be the one thing that would release her from her torment, but now it had the exact opposite effect. Her heart again plunged into the depths of despair, and she realized that she had never stopped loving Estêvão at all. She thought quickly and said the only thing she could. "Nonsense, Serafina. Your thinking is clouded because of the medicine the doctor gave you. You will recover and all will be as it should."

Serafina shook her head, refusing to accept this rationalization. She staunchly maintained her stance. "Promise me that you will make amends with Estêvão and take care of my son. Promise me!"

Inez could do nothing else, so she swore she would do all that her sister demanded. This seemed to pacify Serafina, and she let go of Inez's hand and shut her eyes. "I think I should like to rest now. I am so tired." She opened her eyes one last time and said, "Do not forget your promise. My son will need you," then she drifted off to sleep, the only distinction between life and death the barely perceptible rising and falling of her chest.

Inez stood motionless for a few moments, trying to digest the information revealed by her sister. It was too much. Later, she would have to find a quiet place to sit down and sort everything out. Right now she would tend to the tasks at hand. She placed a kiss on Serafina's cold porcelain forehead then walked over to examine her nephew in his cradle. Again she had to stifle her reaction.

The pitiable little newborn lay silently in his bed gasping for breath. His skin was a deep purple color instead of the healthy pink tone Inez had expected to see. His poor little misshapen head was too long for his proportions, and his temples were slightly concave where the midwife had attempted to seize him to assist his debut into the world.

"The poor unfortunate babe," the midwife said sadly. "The Senhora's narrow hips were not wide enough to accommodate him. He'll most likely not survive the night." Inez shot her a scathing look, and the woman merely shrugged her shoulders. She had done this for long enough to know. Some people just could not face the truth.

Inez returned her gaze to her nephew and espied his tiny little fingers. She reached down to touch the perfect replicas of her own hands, and the baby opened his eyes. They rolled unseeingly in their sockets, but to her surprise he gripped her finger tightly with much more strength than she would have expected. Maybe he had a chance after all. She ran her thumb over the velvety soft skin on the back of his hand, and her eyes filled with tears over the fate of such an innocent little creature. She knew that life was unfair, but this was beyond comprehension. She finally eased her finger from her nephew's grasp, cast one last concerned look at her sister now sleeping peacefully on her bed, and went to find her mother.

Joanna was waiting outside the chamber, sitting on the chair that Inez had occupied for so many hours. When Inez opened the door, her mother rose to meet her. "How is your sister?" she asked quietly.

"She is sleeping now."

"And the child?"

Inez did not know how to answer the question so she simply stared at her mother at a loss for words, tears springing to her eyes at the image of the little boy in his cradle, fighting for his life. Joanna hugged Inez to her as her daughter cried, stroking her hair and making little clucking noises in an attempt to comfort her.

When her sobs had finally abated, Joanna pulled back and looked her daughter in the face. "You should go get some rest now," she said. "I will stay by your sister's bedside tonight to keep watch over her and the child."

"But, Mama, you must be exhausted!" Inez exclaimed, astounded by her mother's fortitude. "Let me stay up with them."

Joanna shook her head resolutely. "A situation might arise that you are not equipped to handle. Besides, I will not sleep tonight, anyway." She looked at stubborn set of her daughter's chin and smiled. "You may look after them in the morning. That is when I will need a break."

Inez nodded reluctantly. Joanna squeezed her one last time and placed a loving kiss on her cheek before entering Serafina's chamber. Inez stared absently at the door for a moment then made her way to her own room. She knew that she would get very little sleep that night. Her head was too full of the events of the day to allow for any peace.

As Inez lay in her bed, her mind kept returning to the conversation that had taken place after Serafina had given birth to her son. She recalled her sister's last words to her and the solemn promise she had made. Inez tried to convince herself that her sister had been under the influence of the sedative and had not known what she was saying, but deep in her heart she knew it was the truth. Eventually she drifted off into a fitful sleep and awoke before dawn, filled with a sense of dread.

In the dark she tiptoed to Serafina's room and knocked quietly on the door. If the people inside were sleeping, she did not want to wake them. All of them had had a harrowing experience. They deserved as much sleep as they could get. The midwife opened the door, still wiping the sleep from her eyes, and stepped aside for Inez to enter.

"How does my nephew?" Inez asked in a whisper.

"The poor little soul is still fighting for life," the midwife replied. "He has lasted longer than I expected. I suppose today we shall have to find him a wet nurse."

"But what about my sister?" Inez asked frantically. The

midwife merely shook her head sorrowfully and went back to monitor her charge. Inez turned her attention to where her sister lay on the bed and slowly approached, her panic increasing with every step.

In the candlelight Inez could see Joanna bent over her sister's recumbent figure. She was massaging Serafina's arms with some sort of unguent, and Inez thought that perhaps Joanna was trying to restore her sister's circulation. Oddly though, Serafina was able to remain asleep during their mother's vigorous exertions. She wore the same serene expression as she had the evening before when they'd finished their conversation. Her golden hair was still perfect, and not even her eyelids twitched when Joanna pulled the sheet back to rub more of the balm into her naked flesh. Inez gently touched her mother on the shoulder, and Joanna turned her red-rimmed eyes from her task to regard her younger daughter.

"Mama," Inez began quietly, "I came to watch over Serafina so that you could get some sleep."

"That will not be necessary. Your sister is past needing any earthly attendance, and I will soon be finished with my final maternal obligations."

Inez stood there with her mouth gaping open, trying to comprehend the gist of what Joanna was saying. "But she just wanted to sleep," she said lamely.

Joanna nodded silently, letting her surviving daughter process the information. "She simply did not wake up. She stopped breathing a few hours later, and now she is done with the troubles of this world."

"But, Mama," Inez objected, her voice rising toward hysteria, "how can you be so calm?"

"It is a mother's duty to do what is necessary, even if the task may tear at her soul. This is the last thing I can do for your sister, and I have made up my mind to do it correctly. I will mourn later."

Then she turned back to Serafina on the bed and continued with her ministrations.

Fortunately, the wife of one of the field hands had given birth two months earlier, and she happily agreed to nurse the heir. Her new position would elevate her family's status. If the master's son should be milk brother to her own child, the family could look forward to all sorts of little advantages in the years to come. But it was not to be.

She arrived at the main house with high hopes, looking forward to the attention and new celebrity that would come with the responsibility, but to her dismay, the newborn heir refused to nurse. She continued her attempts to suckle the child, but again and again he shunned the proffered meal. Finally the woman returned to her own home, her dreams of fame and fortune crushed by the baby boy's refusal to partake of the sustenance she had presented.

Dom Martín had seen this sort of thing in newborn calves. Sometimes they could be coaxed to drink from a bottle when all else failed. Everybody congratulated him on his excellent idea then set about devising a makeshift apparatus small enough for the heir's tiny mouth. After a few minutes, it was apparent that the baby would have none of this either, and they all sat about feeling dejected and helpless to do anything to save him.

He died the next day, silently slipping away in the same manner as his mother.

Chapter 8: Confrontation

After Estêvão's initial excitement following his arrival in the new land had worn off, he had had much time to dwell on his dishonorable treatment of his wife. He had come to the conclusion that he could not continue to punish Serafina for his mistake and had set out from the East with every intention of making amends, beginning with being present for the birth of his son. Perhaps his family could find happiness after all. Revitalized by the thought of his impending fatherhood and his determination to redress the situation with his wife, he sailed for home with many gifts and a new sense of optimism. But plagued by unseasonable squalls and unfavorable winds, the trip had taken much longer than originally expected.

Just after rounding the Cape of Good Hope, another ship intercepted his and delivered the tragic news of the death of his wife and his heir. Estêvão's aspirations for a fresh start were crushed, and he was plunged into a morass of mourning and self-recrimination. He eventually overcame the shock of his loss, but the guilt remained paired with an overwhelming sense of despair. Now he would never be able to atone for his reprehensible behavior. He could only pray for forgiveness and attempt to move on.

On a hot day in July, the *María Vencedora* sailed into the harbor at Angra. Leaving João in charge of the port inspection,

Estêvão rowed himself to shore, hired a horse, and set out for the Fazenda da Pomba. He rode straight into the stable and dismounted. Fausto appeared at once, pleased to see the young master home but saddened by the circumstances. He offered his condolences and made small talk, asking about Capitán Rey's recent exploits and the discovery of the new land in the East. While they were chatting, Palhaço trotted around the corner eager to investigate the new arrival. Estêvão patted the strange dog on the head and struggled to place him. The canine looked familiar and acted as if he knew him, but Estêvão did not grasp his identity until the furry mutt sat at attention and barked a loud, "Roo-roo-roo!"

"Palhaço?" he asked, astounded by the size of the dog who had once been the runt of his litter. The dog instantly responded by licking Estêvão's hand and enthusiastically dancing around on his hind legs. "Is the Senhorita Inez here?" Estêvão asked the stable hand, his resolutions deserting him and hope leaping wildly into his heart.

"She is," Fausto replied, "but the Senhora is ..."

Estêvão was not listening any longer, having turned his full attention to the dog. "Let's go, Palhaço! Where is Inez?"

The canine barked his acknowledgement of the question and took off toward a small shaded meadow a short distance from the main house. It was the place the family had considered for a cemetery, so Estêvão knew he was headed in the right direction. His heart quickened its pace, and his mouth went dry as he followed Palhaço's lead. Upon reaching the little green clearing, he stopped short and had to catch his breath.

Inez knelt in the freshly turned soil of the new graves. She was wearing her riding clothes, a new straw hat, and protective work gloves. A pair of garnet earrings twisted and swung against her slender, graceful neck, and they looked strangely fitting with her casual clothing. She was planting flowers around the grave markers, and she smiled at Palhaço as he bounded up to her, wagging his tail furiously at the completion of his task. Her smile wrenched at Estêvão's heart, and he was touched by its loveliness. Despite his desire to repair his relationship with Serafina, he had missed Inez sorely and fantasized about this moment for two years. Palhaço turned back to Estêvão to receive his accolade from that quarter, and Inez's gaze followed the dog's attention. Her smile fell immediately, as did her heart.

Estêvão's prior thoughts of repentance fell by the wayside replaced by the vision before him. "Bom dia, Coelhinha," he said easily as if naught had ever transpired between them.

Inez said nothing and lowered her head in order to collect her thoughts. She had known this day would come. She had believed herself prepared to handle the situation, but being away from Estêvão had given her a false sense of immunity to his charm. It took everything inside of her not to respond to his warmth.

"What's the matter, Coelhinha? Aren't you happy to see me?"

"Please," Inez replied, her eyes turning steely, "I asked you not to call me that."

"But the situation has changed completely from when we last met," he said, making his way across the little glade. He came to a spot close to her and squatted down by her side, tucking a strand of hair behind her ear and fingering the elegant jewelry. "I will finally have the chance to put things right."

"You had that chance two years ago," she said, brushing his hand away. "If you had spoken then, maybe none of *this* would have happened," she said, indicating the graves before them.

"I am sorry about them. It is a tragedy. I never meant for this to happen. It was all a big misunderstanding."

"I know. Your *wife* told me the truth before she died," Inez said dryly, taking off the work gloves. "She also extracted a promise from me that I would make amends with you."

"Don't you see then? We would be righting a terrible wrong and fulfilling your vow to your sister. Please Inez," Estêvão said, taking her hands in his. "Please marry me."

She looked at him, her silver eyes wide with disbelief. His wife and child lay dead in the ground before them. How could he even imagine that she would consider his proposal? Was he really that selfish? A small bitter smile lifted the corners of her lips. "You have no idea how long I waited to hear those words from you."

"Then say yes," he pleaded.

"Did you care for my sister so little?" she asked, pulling her hands from his grasp.

"Inez, that is not fair. It affected me deeply to hear the news of their passing." He lowered his eyes, and Inez saw the agitated twitching of his jaw muscles. After a few moments, he let out a long, shuddering sigh, and when he looked up at her, his eyes glinted with unshed tears. "But your sister understood that our marriage was not a love match. Only after I sent the proposal, did I admit to myself that I love you, and I will never love another."

"That is all very well, but it doesn't make a whit of difference," she said, rising from her knees and dusting off her trousers. "What you ask is impossible."

"Do you hate me so much?" he asked, standing beside her and taking her hand again, this time bringing it to his lips.

"I could never hate you," she said in a low voice, her resistance softening the slightest bit, "but we cannot be married."

"If you love me, there is no impediment. We will wait the required year, and then we will make this right."

At that moment they heard a quiet cough behind them. They both turned to ascertain the source of the intrusion and saw Christophe leaning against a tree, placidly regarding them. "So, cousin, you are finally home," he said, stepping forward.

"Hello, Christophe," Estêvão said irritably. "Yes, I am home, but if you'll excuse me, I am discussing a personal matter with Inez at the moment. Perhaps you could give us some privacy."

"I will give you the privacy you ask if Inez also desires it," Christophe replied, his amber eyes flicking back and forth between them. "Although I do not know what sort of personal matter you would have to discuss with my wife."

His cousin's words hit Estêvão like a physical blow. He was stunned and his mouth gaped open in astonishment. "Wife?" he asked incredulously. "Is this some sort of joke? Inez, please tell me. Is this true?"

She took her hands from his grasp again and wiped them on her trousers. She looked up into the hazel-green eyes that she dreamed about so often and slowly nodded her head. "It is true," she said simply. "Christophe and I have been married for two months."

Christophe smiled at his little victory and moved to a position between them. He put his hand on his wife's shoulder and gently aimed her toward the house. He looked directly into Estêvão's angry green eyes to make sure his rival had received the message. "Now, if you'll excuse *me*, cousin," he said pointedly, "my mother-in-law is looking for her daughter."

Inez lingered a moment longer, reluctant to break eye contact with Estêvão, then she tore her gaze away and headed toward the house. Christophe turned to follow his wife, but his cousin caught his arm and pulled him close.

"You are a lucky man, Christophe," Estêvão hissed dangerously. "Inez is a treasure and should be treated as such. There are those who would jump at the chance to make her their own. Make sure you guard her, *and yourself*, well."

The two men stood locked together, their eyes never leaving

the other's face. Inez stopped to regard them, her hands clasped together in a gesture of pleading. They were so similar, like mirror images of each other. It was like watching a man struggling with himself. The tension between them was palpable and could have quickly escalated to violence. Finally Christophe came back to his senses and backed down from the confrontation for the sake of his wife.

"I know full well my good fortune," he said calmly, unfazed by his cousin's threatening stance. "Be assured that I cherish Inez as the treasure to which you liken her and treat her accordingly. Perhaps if you had heeded your own advice, she would still be yours. Now, if you'll excuse me," he said, looking meaningfully down at Estêvão's hand on his sleeve, "I have to see my wife to her mother. You are clearly overwrought and not your usual chivalrous self. I will leave you to your grief."

Estêvão released him with a jolt. Christophe brushed off his sleeve and strode briskly over to where Inez stood waiting. He put his arm possessively about her shoulders, and they walked toward the house with Palhaço trailing behind.

When they were well away from Estêvão, Christophe turned his attention to his wife, his tawny eyes full of concern for this beautiful woman he loved so much. She was clearly shaken. He knew this was the meeting she had dreaded for so long, and he surmised what it must have cost her.

"Are you all right?" he asked, holding her close and patiently waiting for her reply.

Inez thought about his question for a moment, trying to objectively assess what she was feeling. Her husband was so caring and understanding. He deserved an honest answer. Suddenly she looked up at him, surprising him with an unexpected smile. "I think I will be fine," she said, amazed at her own response.

"That means that *we* will be fine," he said, satisfied with her reaction. He flashed his brilliant smile at her then added, "Let's go, Canelle. Your mother is waiting," and hand in hand they continued their progress to the house.

Inez and Christophe tried to beg off of the evening meal, but the cook had prepared a special supper in honor of the young couple and would have been upset had they not stayed to enjoy it. The evening was awkward and the conversation strained. Only Iñigo and Dom Martín were unaware of the drama between the young people, and they peppered Estêvão with a constant flow of questions about his expedition, undeterred by the short, snippy manner in which he answered them. Joanna and Dona María noticed that the newlyweds did not join in the banter and guessed the reason why.

After the table was cleared, Christophe and Inez gave their thanks to the cook, bade their goodnights, and headed off to the house they had built together. Estêvão claimed his weariness as a pretext to stomp off to his room to brood. Dona María waited an inconspicuous amount of time then also made her excuses. She knew Estêvão would need to talk, and she ascended the stairs to oblige him.

María knocked softly at her son's door. When he did not answer, she opened it anyway, knowing that he would not admit his need. He was seated at his worktable, riffling furiously through the papers accrued during his absence, muttering to himself in his frustration. María walked over and gently placed her hand on his shoulder, attempting to get his attention without startling him. He slowly turned his gaze around to regard her, and she almost did not recognize him so transformed was his face by rage.

María let out an involuntary cry and hugged her child to her. In all of their thirty-three years together she had never seen him in such an anguished state. She slowly smoothed his silky black-brown hair until she felt the telltale tremor of his despair and his breathing returned to normal. After a few minutes, she released him and busied herself finding a chair while he composed himself and tried to erase the signs of his grief. María dragged her chair over to sit beside the man who had changed back into the son she knew and loved so well.

"Mother, why did you not tell me of their marriage?" he asked, still wiping at his face.

"I did not think it was information that should be conveyed through a letter," she said logically. "Besides, I did not deem it as pressing as the news of the passing of your wife and child."

Estêvão let the comment sink in, welcoming his mother's scorn. He felt like the most despicable person in the world. He should be treated as such. "You are right," he said in a defeated tone. "You have been right all along. Why did I not listen to you? You tried to tell me that I should wait for Inez, but I thought I had come up with such a clever solution."

"You could have cleared up the confusion when you arrived for your wedding, Falcão. Serafina would have understood. She always knew you loved Inez, even when you would not admit it to yourself."

"Inez said the same thing," he laughed mirthlessly. "But Mother, she knew I loved her. If she loved me, why did she not wait?"

María took her son's hands in her own, piercing him with her dark Gypsy stare. "How long did you expect her to wait?" she asked simply. "Did you think she would put her entire life on hold while you went on with yours? With her sister?" She shook her head, surprised that he still did not understand. "We women are strange creatures," she went on with mild sarcasm. "We like to feel that we are unique and special and not just a replacement commodity in case the current one does not work out. Christophe treats Inez like a princess. He worships her. Even you could not begrudge her happiness after what she has suffered at your hands."

Estêvão opened his mouth to object then snapped it shut, knowing that his mother was right. "I will never love anyone else," he said stubbornly. "If it takes a lifetime, I will prove it."

"You should not make such vows so thoughtlessly," María said ominously. "A lifetime can turn out to be much longer than you think."

After his mother had headed off to her bed, Estêvão mulled over his predicament. In retrospect, he was appalled by his disregard for his dead wife and son and his misbehavior toward Christophe. He was consumed by his love for Inez and knew that if he remained on Terceira, he would not be able to contain his impulses during subsequent encounters. The best thing for him to do was to return to the East where he could do something productive. There was nothing left to keep him here. He realized that what his mother said was correct. He had no right to further impede Inez's chance for happiness. He knew that Christophe would treat her much better than he had ever treated his own wife. If he truly loved Inez, he would let her go. He made up his mind to leave the next morning.

Chapter 9: Married Life

That night Inez tossed and turned in her bed while Christophe lay sleeping peacefully at her side. She always marveled at the way he drifted off so quickly, reasoning that it must be the product of having a completely clear conscience. In the short time she had known her husband, he had never done anything objectionable. He was the most honest person she had ever met, admitting the truth even if there was a chance it might injure her feelings. For this reason she had believed him when he'd declared his undying love for her, and she'd agreed to marry him.

Among his many positive characteristics, Christophe was patient, caring, and kind. He was considerate and deliberate, never making rash decisions and seldom losing his temper. Inez had fully apprised him of her state of heart, and he had accepted the situation and taken her as his bride anyway. He was completely understanding and unflappable, two qualities that he would need to maintain his equilibrium in his dealings with his cousin. No one had realized how soon he would have to call on his remarkable reserve.

When Joanna and Iñigo had arrived on Terceira for the birth of their grandson, they were both pleased to see that Inez had recovered most of her former exuberance. When they found out that Christophe was the source of her transformation, they were ecstatic. They both approved of the handsome, hardworking young man and thought that their daughter's choice in suitor could not be more fortuitous. If the two young people married, it would bind the families more firmly together, and the sisters would stay in close proximity to each other in case they should need assistance. Joanna even began to ponder the possibility that one day she and Iñigo might relocate to the island. With their entire family across the ocean, what was left to keep them in Vigo? Iñigo could start a mercantile anywhere—he had already done it once before—or perhaps he would consider learning something different, like helping out with the vineyard. It was an exciting new prospect, and she let it be known that if Christophe were to propose to her daughter, she and Iñigo would give their wholehearted consent.

Two weeks after the Señores García settled into life at the Fazenda da Pomba, Christophe requested an interview with his beloved's parents. He solemnly declared his love for Inez and detailed his plan to provide for her future. He expressed his desire to make his life with their daughter and asked for her hand in marriage. That evening Iñigo and Joanna discussed it, and the next day they gave permission for Christophe to proceed with his proposal.

Being the thoughtful, romantic person that he was, Christophe meticulously went about setting the scene for the proposal. He told Inez that he had planned a special lunch for her—sadly Palhaço was not invited—and she would be required to do nothing but show up. He made all of his arrangements the day before, even preparing the meal, and the next afternoon he took Inez up to the spot on the volcano that had become their own.

For the last few steps of the hike up to the secluded spot, Christophe held his hands over her eyes to make sure his surprise carried the impact he intended. When they reached the little flat niche in the side of the volcano, he removed his hands and allowed her to look. Inez opened her eyes, and to his extreme satisfaction, she gasped and let out a cry of pleasure at the sight.

"Oh, Christophe!" she exclaimed. "It is beautiful! Just beautiful! And so, so perfect!" She turned to him and threw her arms around his neck, showering his face with kisses.

Christophe had spent the evening before gathering loads of wildflowers and transporting them up to their ledge. As soon as he laid down one armful, he headed back down the slope to gather another. He continued his work until the entire space was carpeted with flowers, and not a single square inch of soil showed through. It looked and smelled like a dream, and he deemed it well worth his aching legs and back just for the smile on her face.

When she had finished demonstrating her appreciation, Christophe dropped to one knee and held her hand to his lips. He looked up at her with his tawny lion's eyes and flashed his brilliant white smile. "Inez, my love, my sweet little Canelle," he began, his voice quavering the slightest bit. "I have come to the conclusion that I cannot be happy … that I cannot *live* without you. Yours is the face that I imagine before I sleep, the one I see in my dreams, and crave when I wake. I promise to do my utmost to keep you happy, safe, and adored. I treasure you above all others. Will you do me the honor of becoming my wife?"

Tears of happiness streamed down her face and she could not speak, so she merely nodded her assent, sat down on his knee, and let him hold her close. When she finally stopped crying, they spread out their blanket, sat down amongst the flowers, and enjoyed the lunch Christophe had fixed with his own hands. They devoured the paella, which was quite excellent. He had even made a bread pudding with nuts and raisins, heavily spiced with the cinnamon he loved so much, and topped with a fresh berry sauce.

To seal the contract, he gifted her with a pair of elegant garnet earrings that went perfectly with her natural coloring. Inez commented that they resembled a ring Estêvão always wore, and

Christophe explained that they came from a set his Gypsy grandmother had inherited from her parents. Cassia had distributed the pieces to her children to be given as wedding presents to their spouses. Francisco had put the earrings into safekeeping when Christophe's mother died five years before, and he had sent to his father for them two months prior. Inez was thrilled with the earrings and the sentiment. It was the first time she had been bestowed with a bit of adult jewelry, and it marked the occasion in a thoroughly memorable manner.

When the newly engaged couple shared their happy news with the rest of the family, everyone was extremely pleased. Christophe and Inez had discussed tentative wedding dates before they made the announcement and were content to wait until after Serafina gave birth and her child was christened. Joanna brought up the point that it was just as easy to have a small family ceremony earlier as opposed to later, and Serafina, whose restlessness had begun to unsettle her, opined that preparations for a wedding celebration would help keep her mind off of her coming trial. So a few days later, they were married.

It seemed that all were destined to have their own little piece of joy. Of course nobody had foreseen the events that would bring Estêvão home and release him from his marriage vows in such a dramatic fashion.

Inez awoke the next morning with a new sense of hope. The confrontation between Christophe and Estêvão the day before had been stressful but had passed without further incident. Christophe had shown that he would always choose to do what was right for her, even though he might lose face because of it. He forever surprised her with his devotion and selflessness, and she would do her best to be the partner he deserved.

After breakfast, they headed out to the fields to help with the branding of the new calves. Dom Martín and Iñigo were already there, and they were discussing how strange it was for Estêvão to make the trip all the way back to Terceira for day-long visit with his family only to head back to the East the next morning. Christophe asked if they knew why he had gone, and the older men shook their heads. It seemed that all were shocked at his mysterious departure.

Inez tried to act sufficiently surprised, but she had a very good idea why Estêvão had left. She tried to feign disappointment about his leaving, but deep inside she was enormously relieved. Yesterday she had felt so vulnerable to him, and if Christophe had not interrupted them, she didn't know what might have happened. Oh, things would not have progressed too far. She would have quickly come to her senses, but she might have done something impulsive and regrettable. Her attraction to him was still as strong as ever, even if she would not admit it.

With Estêvão far away from Terceira, Inez and Christophe settled easily into a happy marriage. They were young and fortunate and had their entire lives ahead of them. They were utterly compatible, and the very best of friends. They enjoyed each other's company, and rarely spent time apart. Inez never regretted her marriage, and not a day went by that she was not grateful for her loving spouse.

Christophe was an ideal husband. He always seemed to intuit exactly what Inez needed when she needed it. He was forever bringing her little surprises, and Inez never understood how he accomplished it. When she was feeling blue, he brought her flowers. When she was frustrated with the events of the day, he brought her perfume. When she was bored with the same old suppers, he brought her new spices or some other exotic ingredient. When her sorrow overwhelmed her, he held her close and let her cry—never questioning her reasons, only providing her support. He made her feel safe and secure, and these were the moments she cherished the most.

She knew she had a wonderful life. Most women would be envious of her contentment, and she realized that she should be thankful to be so blessed. The only area in which she felt unfulfilled was in their marriage bed. She knew that some women did not enjoy this aspect of being a wife. Although Inez did not think she fell into this category, it seemed that her sister had been one of these.

When Serafina had described the physical act of love, she had used words that suggested a distasteful obligation. Though Inez did not feel the passionate release she had built up in her mind as the epitome of connubial bliss, she found her conjugal encounters with her husband enjoyable and a pleasant expression of their love for one another, even if the bonding did not seem to extend to a spiritual level as it had for Paulina. She delighted in the closeness, and her husband seemed to desire it regularly. She never denied Christophe his rights as a husband and maintained hope that one day she would experience the gratification that was proving so elusive.

She still struggled with her feelings for Estêvão. She alternated between relief that he had chosen to go and upset that he stayed away so long. Her attitude toward him had softened, now having some idea of what he had gone through in his own marriage. She loved her husband dearly, but she began to suspect that he had simply been the man of the moment. These ideas made her feel extremely disloyal, and she always tried to reason them away as quickly as she could. The thought occurred to Inez that if she had never met Estêvão, she could have spent her life with Christophe blissfully happy and blithely unaware that there existed an emotion called heartache.

Time flew by, months turned into years, and still there was no news of Estêvão's return. Inez and Christophe had been married for seven years, and she began to feel a restlessness of spirit for which there seemed to be no cure. She chided herself for her inquietude—she really had no right to be dissatisfied with her life—but still the feeling persisted. She finally came to the conclusion that she needed something more to occupy her time. When she really analyzed the situation, she realized that the times when she was happiest were when she was fussing over somebody else. She needed to care for somebody again.

She had originally come to Terceira to care for her sister, and though she had been dispirited and sick of heart, she had enjoyed the evenings passed with Serafina and Dona María, busily stitching the tiny items necessary for the eagerly anticipated baby. Inez had been nearly as excited for the arrival of the child as the expectant mother. She had pictured herself as a doting aunt, giving her nephew a bath or rocking him to sleep, much as she had done with Palhaço. Suddenly it seemed curious to her that she had not conceived a child of her own. Maybe that was the source of her discontent.

One morning in late summer of 1521, Inez experienced one of the classic symptoms of the onset of pregnancy, and the fleeting thought ran through her head that she might be with child. She did not say anything—she did not want to get Christophe's hopes up should it turn out to be a false alarm—but she fervently prayed that it might be the case. A few weeks later, she was sure of her condition, and she let her husband in on her secret. As she might have expected, Christophe was ecstatic that he would finally become a father, and a sense of excitement ran through her. Maybe this would be the thing to make her happiness complete.

The news of Inez's impending motherhood was shared among the families. In less than a year the child would arrive who would finally bind their lineages together by blood. Everyone was elated, but the specter of the last such happy occasion haunted the recesses of their minds. Joanna was especially disturbed by the situation.

Logically she understood the reason Serafina had not been able to give birth as easily as most women. Because of her elder daughter's delicate frame and narrow hips, the birth had been all but impossible. Inez's body was more capacious, more suggestive of fecundity. There was no rational cause for Joanna to worry, but deep in her psyche lingered the slightest inkling of fear. It seemed that she was destined to lose her loved ones, and she racked her brain for a plan that would help Inez avoid her sister's tragic fate.

Finally she recalled the reason that Paulina had originally been sent to the family. The tall, quiet, Portuguese woman had been housekeeper for so long that Joanna had forgotten her substantial healing skills. Although the last time Paulina had attended a birth was to bring Inez into the world nearly twenty-four years before, Joanna was certain the woman would still be more knowledgeable and competent than the midwife, or even the doctor, who had been present for Serafina's ill-fated confinement. She sent for the woman, pleased with her inspired idea.

Paulina arrived quickly and stood before Joanna with expectant attention in her serene black eyes. Joanna took her time in addressing the housekeeper. Although she had overcome many of her irrationalities, she could not get past her uneasiness when dealing with someone of Portuguese descent. Eventually she looked up from her correspondence and cleared her throat.

"I suppose by now you have heard the news of my daughter's happy condition," Joanna began.

"I have, Señora," Paulina respectfully replied.

"And you know the circumstances of her sister's passing."

Paulina simply nodded her head.

"I was present at the travesty, and it is my conclusion that had there been someone in the room who knew what they were doing, my eldest daughter would still be alive. I do not think it very likely, but I want every precaution taken to ensure that Inez does not suffer a similar fate." Joanna paused here and took a deep breath to calm herself. "I admit there were times when I was jealous, because you could be all the things to Inez that I could not, but I never doubted your love for her or your abilities. I know I have been overly harsh with you, but now I realize that I must put my personal feelings aside and humbly beg you to safeguard my daughter and do everything in your power to bring my grandchild into the world. Paulina," Joanna looked up at her with tears shimmering in her aquamarine eyes, "will you go to Terceira?"

"Of course, Señora," the housekeeper said simply, pretending not to notice the desperation in Joanna's face.

"Good," Joanna said briskly, lowering her gaze to her lap. "I will make the necessary arrangements. Please be ready to leave in three days' time. You may go now."

"Thank you, Señora," Paulina said and left the room to pack her belongings for the trip to Terceira.

Chapter 10: The Storm

In December of 1521, Manuel I of Portugal died. During his reign the beloved king had done much for his country. He was a staunch supporter of the exploration and foreign trade that had expanded the Portuguese Empire and made it a world power. He established trade treaties and diplomatic relations in the Orient. He was a religious man and had sought to enlighten the people of the new Portuguese colonies through the work of missionaries. He reformed the courts and modernized taxes. He used the country's wealth to attract the attention of illustrious scholars and artists to his court, even inspiring the Manueline style of architecture. The second half of his reign was considered the most prosperous period in Portuguese history. He would be missed by his subjects, and a pall of mourning swept the nation.

When the news of his uncle's demise reached Estêvão in China, he made the decision to immediately sail for home. He had spent the seven and a half years since the death of his wife and child struggling to open up commerce with the rich new land. In the beginning things had looked promising, but lately the relations had soured. There were reports of misconduct by some of his countrymen, and the native rulers were seeking alliance with each other in an attempt to rid themselves of the Portuguese. Estêvão's existence in the East had become very precarious, and so he decided to avoid further exposure to danger and head to Lisbon to pay his final respects to his uncle. From there he would proceed to Terceira.

In the time he had been away he had had much opportunity to dwell on his last visit home. The scene in the cemetery ate at him every time he thought about it. His cousin had been right about his boorish behavior. In Estêvão's youth he had vowed to live his life with dignity and honor, and on that occasion he had exhibited neither quality. He could only justify it by telling himself he had not been in his right mind. His love for Inez had made him irrational, and he wanted to set things right by apologizing to Christophe man-to-man.

Inez. How would he react when he saw her again? He was more convinced now than ever that he loved her and would never love another. He dreamed about her almost every night and thought about her many times during the day. He would always regret not clearing up the confusion over his proposal when he'd had the chance. If he could do it all over again, he would not care who he offended as long as in the end Inez would agree to be his.

He laughed at his boyish folly. It did no good to live in the past. He would do better to look to the future. He would make his peace with Inez and Christophe then concentrate on things at the fazenda. It would be wonderful to see his mother again. He missed her calm, gentle manner and her wise, pragmatic advice. It would even be good to see Dom Martín. He knew his stepfather would welcome the help and the company, and Estêvão would be more than happy to oblige. The hard physical labor would keep his mind occupied, and maybe, just maybe, this time he would find peace on the island.

Inez sat in a sunny clearing a short distance away from the house she and Christophe had built together. She watched Palhaço as he romped and sniffed, snapping at insects and generally enjoying the lovely spring day. She never ceased to be amused by his antics. He was her constant companion, and her life would have been very different without him. Although he was not quite as spry as he once was, he still showed his puppyish enthusiasm when it was time for their daily walks.

Paulina held the belief that walking was the best exercise to prepare Inez for giving birth. Of course she should not engage in strenuous hiking or walk on uneven trails where there was a chance she might fall, but a long, gentle walk everyday would help to alleviate some of the more insidious complaints of late pregnancy. Paulina had also advised Inez to expose her skin to sunlight for a short length of time each day. She did not know the scientific reasons behind this little bit of wisdom, but it was said that the practice would ensure a healthy baby. Inez listened intently to Paulina, and did all that she advised. After Serafina's tragedy, she did not want to take any chances.

She rose from her spot in the grass and called Palhaço to her. It was getting time for them to return to the house to welcome Christophe from his day of hard work at the vineyard. The grapevines were at a very sensitive point in their growth, and they required constant monitoring. Along with that delicate task was the rotation of the wine casks and the supervision of the shipping. It was much responsibility, and Inez tried to make her husband's home life as carefree as possible.

She and Palhaço covered the remaining stretch of the path, and upon their arrival at the house, Inez recognized the courier from the Fazenda da Pomba. He had just dismounted, and something about the set of his face suggested that the message he bore was a sad one. Inez's heart rose into her throat, and she quickened her pace. *Please let it not be Estêvão,* she silently prayed to herself, and she stood there terrified, waiting to receive the news.

"I bring you sad tidings, Senhora," the messenger said formally. "The Fazenda da Pomba is a house of mourning this afternoon. I regret to inform you that the Dona María has passed on."

Inez was stunned. Deep inside she was relieved that Estêvão was safe, but she had never expected this. For whatever reason she had thought of Dona María as a sort of eternal being. Rationally she knew that everyone would eventually die, but Dona María had always been so strong, so vital. Inez sat down on the steps of the veranda to digest the information.

Christophe was just coming from the vineyard, and when he saw the courier and Inez sitting dazed on the steps, he knew there was something amiss. He hurried over to his wife's side to discover the reason for her distress. The courier repeated his message, and Christophe sat down next to Inez placing his arm protectively about her shoulders for support.

"Are you all right, Canelle?" he asked gently.

"It's just such a shock," Inez replied. "The last time we visited she was fine. How could this have happened?"

The courier explained that when her brother-in-law, King Manuel, had departed this world to receive his eternal reward, Dona María had felt it her bounden duty to sail for Lisbon to pay her respects. Although she knew that the trip might induce a painful bout of the periodic ailment from which she suffered, she felt her mission was far more important than her discomfort. Manuel had done so much for the family. Without him they would never have had any of the things that they held so precious, and they owed him homage. She deemed it unconscionable that she should not make the voyage, so she went.

When she returned, Dona María was incapacitated by her malady, and she took to her bed. This had long been her way of healing herself, and she believed it to be the best course of action.

This time instead of improving, her condition worsened. She lay in her bed while the illness laid waste to her body, ravaging the vivacious little woman until her health had deteriorated far past the point of possible recovery. She had finally succumbed a short while ago.

"How is Dom Martín taking it?" Inez asked, knowing how much the gruff old warrior had loved his wife.

"He is inconsolable. He has taken to his chamber in his grief. It is a good thing Capitán Rey has come home. I think he will have to run things for a while."

At the mention of Estêvão's name, Inez stiffened in her seat. Christophe looked at his wife to monitor her reaction to the news. In her delicate condition it was not a good idea for her to be exposed to such a stressful situation. He rubbed her shoulder soothingly to calm her anxiety.

"My father will be devastated," Christophe said mostly to himself. "He cannot be allowed to receive this report in a letter." He looked up at the courier. "Has Capitán Rey dispatched the news to the mainland yet?"

"No, Senhor. He wanted you and the Senhora to be the first informed."

"Good. Please tell him to hold off. I will go in person to relay the news." He looked down lovingly at Inez. "Will you be all right if I go?"

"I think so," she replied, nodding her head slowly. "Paulina says the baby will not come for another month or so."

"I will be back well before then. Canelle," he said tenderly, his dark yellow eyes very serious, "you know that I would not risk missing the birth of our son if this were not so important."

"I know it," she said simply.

"Then it is decided. I will pack my things and leave tomorrow."

Then next morning Christophe rose early and quietly set about getting dressed so not to wake his wife. In this late stage of pregnancy she needed all the rest she could get. He wanted to take no chances with her health or the development of his son. He tiptoed out of the room with his boots in his hand.

Christophe sat at the table eating his breakfast, meticulously going over the list of things he needed to accomplish. He was nearly finished with his meal when Inez entered the room, dressed and ready for the outdoors.

"I did not mean to wake you," he said, rising from his seat and kissing her on the cheek. "I thought I was being quiet."

"You were quiet," Inez said, "but I was already awake. I decided that I want to go with you at least as far as the Fazenda da Pomba. I talked it over with Paulina last night, and she said that the short ride there and back should not pose a problem. I just feel so terrible for Dom Martín. I feel that perhaps I can do something to lessen his grief."

"And Estêvão?" Christophe asked plainly.

"I know how much he adored his mother," she began thoughtfully, "but his welfare is none of my concern. I put you before him many years ago, and I don't intend to change my loyalties. Besides, I am sure he has moved on."

Christophe nodded, satisfied with her response, and they continued their preparations.

The first drops of rain began to fall just as husband and wife arrived at the Fazenda da Pomba. Christophe hopped down from the wagon and reached up to help Inez down from her seat. When she was firmly on the ground, he held his cloak over her head to shield her from the precipitation, and they made their way carefully to the door.

They were greeted by a red-eyed servant and led into the parlor. When Estêvão saw his visitors, he rose from his chair and hurried over to them, his arm held out to Christophe in greeting. Christophe gripped his cousin's extended hand and shook it firmly, grasping his shoulder with the other, a look of sincere sympathy on his face. "I am so sorry, cousin," he began. "My aunt was an extraordinary woman. I loved her very much, and I will miss her."

"Thank you, Christophe, for your sentiments and for your willingness to carry the news to the mainland. Every time I began a message it sounded cold and impersonal."

"I did not want my father to be alone when he received this news. He and your mother shared a connection that went beyond merely being siblings. Maybe it was their Gypsy blood, but they seemed to be almost a part of each other."

"I know what you mean," Estêvão said. His gaze strayed to his cousin's wife. "Hello, Inez. Where are my manners? Please come sit down by the fire," he said easily, taking her hand and leading her over to a comfortable seat.

"Thank you," she said and self-consciously fussed with some damp strands of hair around her face.

Estêvão looked at her speculatively for a few moments then turned to include his cousin in his next comment. "There is something that has gnawed at me for nearly eight years now, and I would like to clear my conscience. The last time the three of us were together, I was … um … a little less than cordial. I was not in my right mind, and only after much reflection have I come to realize how deplorable my actions must have seemed. I apologize and humbly beg your forgiveness."

"There is no apology necessary," Christophe said earnestly. "You were understandably distraught. It has been long forgotten and forgiven. As a family we must stand united. We cannot afford to hold grudges against each other."

"You are right. Ah, here comes the tea," Estêvão said as a servant carried in a tray. At that moment a gust of wind shook the house and blew raindrops against the windows so hard that they sounded like pellets. The woman let out a little shriek of surprise and nearly dropped the tray on the ground.

"If you'll excuse me, cousin, I think I should be going before it is impossible to leave port."

"Again, you are right. João is awaiting your arrival at the docks."

"Then if you don't mind keeping an eye on Inez until the wagon returns, I will be off." Christophe grasped Estêvão's forearm and squeezed his shoulder one last time then turned and held out his hand to his wife. "Canelle, would you see me out please?" Inez rose from her chair, and the couple walked to the door.

Estêvão tried very hard to give the pair some privacy so they could say their goodbyes, but he could not help his curiosity. He was itching to see if there was true love between the couple, or if Inez remained with Christophe out of obligation. He positioned himself just out of their sightline and cocked an ear toward the entry.

"I will be back as quickly as the seas allow," Christophe said. "I am sorely tempted to send João with the message for my father, but I would not ask another to make a journey I would not." He knelt down in front of Inez and tenderly placed his gentle brown hands on her protruding belly. "My son," he began, leaning close, his lips nearly touching his wife's thickened midsection, "I command you to wait for my return. I know you are eager to make your debut, but you will have to delay a few more weeks. Do as you are told, and we will meet when I am safely home." He rose from his knees, crushed his wife's lips with his own, and was out the door before Inez could formulate a reply.

Estêvão felt a twinge of jealousy at the touching scene and immediately regretted that he had intruded on them. He did a quick about face and resumed his place in front of the fire.

Inez returned to the room and sat back down in her seat. The distant rumble of thunder reverberated through the house, and she gripped the arms of her chair tightly. She had never minded storms in the past—she had experienced many savage squalls as a child in Vigo—but the fact that her husband was about to make a sea voyage in this one paired with the tension between herself and her host was unnerving.

"Would you like some tea, Inez?" Estêvão asked attentively.

"Thank you," she said, smiling at his attempt to be coolly polite with her. "How is Dom Martín?"

"He is as well as can be expected. My mother and he were together a very long time. They were married shortly after my ninth birthday."

"I remember," Inez said wistfully. "You told me the story once many years ago."

"So I did," he said, shaking his head at the bittersweet memory. "So I did."

The storm continued to worsen. The wind howled through the trees, there were the frightening sounds of branches being torn from their arboreal anchorage, and the thunder growled at closer intervals. Though it was still early morning, it was dark and murky outside giving the illusion of dusk. One could just barely make out the reflections of the increasing puddles of water, which were beginning to merge, lending the house the isolated feel of an island in a shallow sea. The wagon had still not returned from Angra to carry Inez to the safety of her home, and she prayed silently to herself that nothing had gone wrong. Finally the driver entered the parlor by way of the kitchen and gave his account of his tribulation.

"Did the Senhor get off safely?" Inez asked, wringing her hands together.

"Yes, Senhora. No sooner had the Chief boarded the ship, than the crew put to sail in the blink of an eye. They were well ahead of the worst part of it, and the winds were in their favor. It was the trip back that was the struggle. The road was a raging torrent, and the horses were having none of it. I had to get down and lead them the last hundred feet before we reached the gate. Almost got washed away myself, but it would have been just as dangerous to turn around and head back to town."

"How will we get home?" Inez asked, her voice rising in her panic.

"Oh, there will be no getting home tonight, Senhora. Even if the horses were willing, the water is only going to rise."

"There is no question," Estêvão interjected, "you will stay here until the storm passes and the waters drop. I told your husband that I would keep watch over you, and I mean to do it," he said, taking her hand and looking into her eyes. "I would never forgive myself if anything unfortunate were to befall you." A hot, pink flush spread up her neck to her hairline at his touch, and Estêvão gently released her hand. "It is settled. You will stay."

"Yes, you must stay," said Dom Martín in a gravelly voice as he made his way down the stairs.

Inez looked up at the big gruff man she had come to love so much and was moved by his disheveled appearance. His eyes were red from his grieving, his hair was uncombed and stood out wildly from his head, his clothing was wrinkled, and on his face was an expression of pure anguish. She hurried over as fast as her condition would allow to meet him at the foot of the stairs.

"Oh, Dom Martín!" she cried, holding her arms out to him. "I am so, so sorry!"

The old fidalgo said nothing, simply enfolded her in his powerful arms, and they stood there weeping together. After a few moments, he gently released her and swiped at his tear-stained face.

"Now, now, little lady, you mustn't upset yourself too much. You must think of your child."

"The child will be fine," Inez said, smiling through her tears at his concern for her well-being. "It is *you* that I worry about."

He waved away her comment and walked across the floor. He dropped heavily into his chair, running his giant bear paw around his face and up through his wild hair. Another rolling rumble of thunder shook the house, and he turned his attention to the fire in the hearth, which flickered and danced in the powerful drafts that blew down the chimney.

"This is a devil of a storm," Dom Martín said, his distaste written clearly on his tortured features. "María would have sat in her chair, calmly stitching or reading a book, and told me that it was necessary to shake the deadwood from the trees and clear the moss from the waters."

"Yes," Estêvão said with a smile, "she was unshakeable. It was a quality that served her, and everyone around her, well. She was so quiet and gentle that as a child I never realized that it was she who ran things. She had the patience of a saint," he said, recalling the innumerable conversations when his mother had impassively listened to his problems and placidly pointed out the obvious course of action.

"She had to be a saint to live with me," Dom Martín added with an amused grunt. "I am not the easiest person to get along with."

Inez smiled at his self-deprecating admission. She was surprised and pleased with the direction of the conversation. The fact that the men could talk about the trim little woman without further breaking down was a step toward recovery from their grief and would speed the healing process. "I remember the first time my family came to Terceira," she began. "I could tell that my mother was determined to remain aloof, but Dona María quickly put an end to *that* notion. She was so sweet and genial. My mother could not help but respond."

"She had that way with everybody. That is why my father named her Pomba," Estêvão replied, and the exchange of their fond recollections went on in the same vein for the remainder of the morning.

A short time after noon, a servant came in to declare that lunch was ready, and the three mourners eagerly fell on the food, seeking comfort for their bereaved spirits in the form of nourishment. They quickly finished the meal then returned to their seats in the warmth of the parlor. The food had a soporific effect, and the three were soon nodding in their chairs. Estêvão kept a close watch on Inez, and when she jolted herself awake for the third time, he suggested that she head upstairs to take a nap.

"I suppose I should," she said with an embarrassed smile. "I did not sleep well last night and was up early this morning. Paulina says I should take as much rest as I can get." She rose from her chair, and took a candle from a side table. "I will see you two in a few hours then."

"Shall I see you to your room?" Estêvão asked solicitously and made to rise from his chair.

"That's not necessary," Inez said, waving him off. "I know the way." They were doing fine with one another, and she believed that it would be best if things did not become too personal between them.

Inez slowly crossed the floor, holding the candle in front of her to light her way. The storm had blotted out all sunlight, and her progress would have been tricky going even if she were not large with child. At the foot of the stairs she stifled a yawn with her hand before beginning her climb. Yes, a nap was a very good idea. She put her foot on the bottom step and started her ascent, reaching for the banister to assist her upward motion. She pulled herself up another step and eased her hold on the rail to slide her hand to a spot a bit higher up. Just as she lifted her foot to move up to the third step, a bolt of lightning illuminated the entire house with a blinding flash of white light, and the simultaneous crash of thunder sent a terrifying tremor through the structure. Inez let out a frightened shriek as she missed the step with her foot. Her candle fell from her hand, and she lost her balance. She instinctively grabbed for the banister, but she had already teetered back too far. Her fingertips slid helplessly down the polished wood surface as she fell the three steps, slamming heavily to her side on the floor. The breath was knocked out of her, and a sharp pain ripped through her abdomen from the lowest spot under the front, up and around the right side of her ribcage.

Estêvão saw the entire scene unfold and was at her side before the thunder died away. He knew it was unwise to move a person when they had experienced such trauma, so he held her hand and waited for her to catch her breath. Those few agonizing minutes before she could speak and communicate her state of being were the longest of his life. Finally Inez looked up at him and nodded her head.

"I think I am all right," she said breathily. "I'd like to sit up."

Estêvão tried to ease her very gently to a sitting position, but as soon as her body contorted about the middle, sharp burning pains assaulted her again, and they had to cease their efforts.

"Well, she cannot remain there!" Dom Martín bellowed in his frustration. "She must be moved to a bed!"

"He is right, Coelhinha ... I'm sorry ... Inez," Estêvão corrected himself. "Do you think you could bear it if I carried you upstairs."

She looked at him grimly, knowing it would have to be done. She bit her lip and nodded her head.

"I will be as gentle as I can," he said then slipped one arm around her back and the other under her knees. Dom Martín helped him bear her weight to a standing position then followed them up the stairs, making sure another fall would not take place. The house had seen enough tragedy in the last twenty-four hours, and the drama was not over yet.

Inez let out a cry of pain as Estêvão set her carefully in the bed. "What is it?" he burst out in his concern.

She had borne her discomfort the whole way, but now another source of agony assailed her. "I know it sounds unreasonable," Inez panted out, "but I think the birth pains have begun."

Dom Martín nodded his head and touched Estêvão's shoulder to get his attention. "I don't know if you noticed, son, but Inez is bleeding," he growled in a low voice. "There is a trail of blood all the way up to the room from the foot of the stairs. Someone must go for Paulina."

"So be it! Dispatch Fausto right away!"

"*I* will go," Dom Martín said. Estêvão opened his mouth to object, but his stepfather glared at him with a look that would brook no objection. "The road is washed out, and I know the backwoods and shortcuts better than anybody. Besides, I cannot stand here and do nothing, *again*, while someone I love is suffering. I will go."

On his way out of the house, Dom Martín apprised the servants of the situation. The women had been through the process before, and they immediately set about readying the necessary items. They, like Dom Martín, were glad to have something to keep them busy instead of weeping around the house over the loss of Dona María. Besides, Senhora Inez had been kind to them all, and they would be very sad if the same terrible fate were to befall her as had her sister.

Estêvão never left Inez's side. He pulled a chair up to her bed and kept her occupied during the wait, holding her hand and letting her squeeze his when the pains were upon her. He allayed all of her fears while masking his own, telling her that he was sure João had gotten Christophe well ahead of the storm by now and how happy her husband would be when he returned to his healthy new son. They both let their guards down, neither one of them worried any longer about proving that they were over the other, only concerned about getting through the ordeal before them.

Hours passed and finally Dom Martín returned with Paulina. They were both shaken by their frightening ride and soaked to the skin but basically unharmed. They were each provided with dry clothing and a cup of mulled wine, and after a short while, Paulina made her way up to her patient's room. She knocked softly then entered without waiting for a reply. Estêvão heaved a giant sigh of relief at the sight of her and obligingly stepped outside to pace the hall while she interviewed her charge. A few minutes later, Paulina exited the room and called him over to her.

"Capitán Rey," she began tentatively. "You were very wise to send for me. It seems that the shock from the fall has precipitated the onset of childbirth. Because the child is coming four weeks before its time, there are certain manipulations I must perform to improve the child's chances for survival. I will need an assistant, someone who can keep Inez calm and focused and carry out my instructions quickly and without question. Can you do it?"

"I would sell my soul to save her," he stated plainly, not caring that Paulina should see his love for Inez written clearly on his face.

"Good," she replied. "With any luck it will not come to that."

Sometime later, the storm abated and left behind an eerie silence that was almost worse than the constant howling of the winds. The entire household waited nervously for news of Senhora Inez's confinement, praying that all would be well. Paulina emerged from the room, her body exhausted and her emotions numb. She mopped a cloth across her sweaty face and headed for the stairs. She had never been through anything so grueling in her life, and she was relieved it was finally over. As she descended the stairs, she wondered how she would tell them.

Dom Martín was the first to see her, and he immediately discontinued his pacing and hurried over to her. "Well?" he asked anxiously. "Is she all right?"

"Inez is fine," Paulina smiled up at him wearily, "but the child ..."

"Oh, Meu Deus! Curse this house!" he cried loudly, at the end of his patience. "It should be burned to the ground! So much grief!"

"Dom Martín!" Paulina said forcefully, gripping his massive arm firmly and giving it a stern shake. "Calm yourself!"

He turned to her with a stunned look on his face. No woman had ever joggled him with such force! When he had brought her over from the vineyard, she had seemed so quiet and serene.

Paulina released his arm and smoothed her apron before looking back up at him, as if she had done nothing out of character. "I was merely going to say that the little boy is very small and will need to be kept very warm for a while, but he is healthy, and he will be ..."

Dom Martín let out a loud whoop of relief and swept Paulina up and swung her around in a circle. This was the first bit of good news he'd had in a long time, and in comparison with the previous calamities, it was joyous. He forgot about his grief for the moment and was almost restored to his former boisterous self. The household was exultant. There was finally a new baby. Even if he was not directly part of their establishment, he was related, and Senhora Inez would be fine. This was a happy day indeed.

Estêvão heard the commotion downstairs and smiled at Inez in her bed. No one but his stepfather could make such an uproar. He brushed a deep red ringlet back from her pale face and felt a sense of peace warm his heart at the look she bestowed upon him. She was heartbreakingly beautiful, even more precious to him now after what they had just come through together. He did not know what he would have done had he lost her.

Inez held the tiny little boy in her arms, and the thought crossed Estêvão's mind that this was what it felt like to be a father. As he looked at the sleeping baby he had helped to bring into the world, he felt a distant twinge of grief at the memory of his lost wife and child. The new baby looked enough like him that it could have been his son, should have been his son, but the child was not his. The boy belonged to his cousin as did the woman before him, the woman he loved. He shooed his bitterness away and let himself be content that at least they had this. Not even Christophe could ever take this away from them.

Chapter 11: The Little Prince

The days that followed the storm were mild and sunny with puffy white clouds floating in a cornflower sky. It seemed that the storm, frustrated with its inability to wreak further devastation on the Fazenda da Pomba, blew off in a huff leaving only minor misfortune behind. There had been no human fatalities, and the crops would recover when the waters receded. The worst of their losses were a few cows that had been spooked by lightning and run off and drowned in a swollen creek. All in all, they had been lucky.

Inez and Christophe had long since discussed baby names and decided that if the child were a boy, he should be named Cristian. Everyone agreed that it would be best for Paulina, Inez, and Cristian to stay put instead of trying to get home, exposing the vulnerable new mother and child to unnecessary risk. There was still much cleaning up to be done. Many large boulders and uprooted trees had washed into the road, and it would take a long while to remove them. The fazenda had everything they needed, so they stayed.

Inez was still very weak from the premature appearance of her son. She had lost a lot of blood, and the kneading of her abdomen and repositioning of the unborn child had been painful and exhausting. Paulina had known how risky the procedure was, but in her eyes the benefit had far outweighed the hazard. She had heard of cases in which the child was born deformed or dead. Some women were left unable to have subsequent children, and some died from hemorrhage or secondary infections. It had been a near thing, but Inez was young and strong and Paulina kept constant watch over her ward.

Because the new mother needed much rest and was confined to her bed, it was necessary for others to help with the care of the new baby. It seemed that the staff had claimed the child as their own. They were all amazed by the fact that a healthy new baby had been born just a day after Dona María passed on. It was especially astounding because he had not been due to arrive for at least another month. It had to be some sort of omen. What the omen meant, no one could tell, but in their eyes it was a miracle. They began to call Cristian *o Pequeno Príncipe*, the Little Prince.

There was never a shortage of arms or laps in which the Little Prince could nap. Even when he slept, he did it within someone's embrace. The beautifully wrought cradle that Iñigo had crafted for Serafina's ill-fated baby years ago was rarely put to use except at night. The child was often passed from one pair of hands to the next, and surprisingly, Dom Martín turned out to be the biggest offender of them all.

Any time the big old warrior caught one of the staff regarding him in a peculiar manner while he held the child, he stared back at her rudely and proclaimed that it was the Senhora Paulina who stated that the child needed to be kept warm. What warmer place was there in the house than his strong embrace? He was simply doing his part. He would then hug the child more tightly to him and guard him jealously like his own personal treasure. Eventually the women stopped teasing him for fear that he might crush the Little Prince by protecting him too fiercely.

Estêvão was also guilty of doting on the child. Most of his time was spent at Inez's bedside, but whenever she was ordered to rest, he would take the child to some comfortable out-of-the-way spot and talk to him of anything that came to mind. He chronicled the story of his childhood. He described the many virtues of the Dona María and the circumstances that had brought the baby into the world so soon. He recounted the tale of how he had met the infant's mother and divulged how much he loved her still. Cristian listened intently to the sound of Estêvão's voice and never cried when he was in his presence. By the end of a week, the baby knew even more about Estêvão than his mother did, though he would never remember.

One afternoon Paulina was sitting with the child on the veranda in the warm spring sunshine. Estêvão exited the house and stretched out in a chair alongside them. The two adults sat in companionable silence for a spell, but eventually the baby began to fuss. Paulina rocked him and made little cooing noises, but the Little Prince would not be satisfied. Estêvão offered to take him, and as soon as the baby was in his uncle's arms he quieted, mesmerized by the familiar face and voice. Paulina had not seen this phenomenon yet and was astonished by how quickly the child had settled.

"I believe he prefers your company to mine," she said with a chuckle.

"Oh, yes," Estêvão said, directing a soothing tone at the baby. "O Principe and I are old friends."

"It is a good thing to have such an easy way with you nephew. It will come in handy."

"Nephew?" Estêvão asked. After a few moments, the relationship fell into place. Inez was his sister-in-law, and her child would be his nephew. "Yes, I suppose he is," he said with a broad grin, pleased with his new promotion.

"You know, loving a child is a life-changing experience," Paulina began, looking out at the grass, which was just beginning to absorb the excess water from the recent deluge. "One gets the privilege of seeing the child grow and learn. You can contribute to the formation of the child and provide him with a good example, influence his entire world. It also changes you."

Estêvão noticed that she had begun speaking in generalities, and now it felt like she was addressing him personally. "I did not have that opportunity with my own child," he said sadly. "I failed to be present for his debut into this life or his departure from it. It is something that I will never cease to regret."

Paulina looked over at the baby, now resting peacefully in his arms. "A child whom you choose to love can be just as precious as one of your own flesh," she said, "especially one whom you have helped bring into the world. If you'll forgive me for speaking plainly, Capitán Rey, in my youth I suffered a tragedy similar to your own. The circumstances were slightly different. My husband and I did not marry to get an heir. We were very much in love."

Estêvão was surprised that she had ventured to speak to him in such a manner. No one on his staff would have dared such a comment, but more curiously, he was not offended. He didn't know if it was her imperturbable, quiet manner, or perhaps her intelligent black eyes, but she reminded him of his mother. He simply nodded his head, and she went on.

"My husband contracted typhus a few months before I was due to give birth, and I was helpless to save him or my child, but God works in mysterious ways. He led me to the García home, and I was able to save Serafina from the same illness and bring Inez safely into the world." She paused for a moment to let the significance sink in. "Many times we do not understand why it's necessary to experience certain painful trials in our lives, but sometimes in hindsight we can see that we would not be the person that we are if not for those heartbreaking moments. I know that you love Inez. Perhaps you now have the opportunity to prove to her how much. I love her as my own, and I want what is best for her."

He did not answer for a few moments, and Paulina feared that she had overstepped her bounds. She had not meant to preach overmuch. Sometimes when that happened, the subject ceased to listen, and she desperately desired that he absorb the lesson. Finally he let out a deep breath and regarded her with a smile.

"I suppose that binds us together then," he said and turned his attention back to his nephew.

Eventually Inez recuperated enough to leave her bed. The weather continued to improve, and the new baby and mother were able to spend more time out of doors. Estêvão was their constant companion. He considered himself their guardian, and he never let them out of his sight. Because he had promised his cousin to look after Inez and the child—and partially to atone for his callus behavior toward Serafina and the lost opportunity to attain her forgiveness—he did everything in his power to see to their well-being.

Inez and Estêvão easily fell into their old relationship. They laughed together over Dom Martín's possessiveness of the Little Prince. They reminisced and traded stories about Dona María. He told her all about the time he had spent away in China and India, and she teased him with some of the new recipes she had concocted during his absence. By tacit understanding, neither one of them mentioned Christophe or Serafina. They were both determined to enjoy the time they had together and not to let anything damper the joy of these precious carefree days.

After his talk with Paulina, Estêvão threw himself wholeheartedly into his role as uncle, and Inez was surprised to see how eagerly her tiny son responded to his affections. The thought crossed her mind that he would have been a wonderful father, but she pushed it away, viewing any such idea as disloyal to her husband. Her husband loved her and worked hard to give her a secure life. She at least owed him her allegiance. Christophe was a good man and competent at most everything he did. He was hardworking and thoughtful. He was strong and athletic and quickly mastered anything requiring physical prowess with ease. He was intelligent and well-spoken, and people were drawn to his pleasant personality. He even played the guitar and sang well. She should have been grateful to marry such a man. He simply was not Estêvão.

One day Inez and Estêvão were sitting side by side on a blanket in a sunny spot not far from the house. A gentle breeze rustled through the leaves above them, and the flowering fruit trees and ever-present hydrangeas filled the air with their sweet fragrance. The Little Prince napped in the shade at the head of the blanket, and all in all it was a lovely day.

Estêvão was in a whimsical mood. Having Inez and the child in his house had given him a taste of what it would be like to spend his life with them. It would be sheer delight, and sometimes he let himself imagine it to be reality. He was carried away by the ideal conditions and the poignant realization that their private time together in the secluded little fantasy they had created would soon be at an end, nothing more than a beautiful memory.

"Oh, Coelhinha," he said, taking her hand, "the only thing that would make this day more perfect is for you to tell me that you love me." He had meant it to be a joke, but as the statement left his lips, he realized that he was voicing his innermost feelings. He cringed inwardly, fully expecting his spontaneous outburst to sour the mood of the day, but when he ventured a look up at Inez, he saw that she had not been offended. She looked as if she were actually contemplating his words and trying to formulate a reply.

Inez was torn. She hated the thought of being unfaithful to her husband, but she could not bring herself to deny Estêvão his due. Paulina had deemed his assistance in the birthing room crucial to the survival of both mother and child, so in small degree he was their savior. She and her son owed him their lives. He at least deserved the truth. She turned to him—her silver eyes very serious—took a deep breath, and confessed.

"I have never stopped loving you," she said solemnly. Her eyes immediately filled with tears, and she had to look away.

Estêvão put his arms around her and pulled her to him, her cool cheek coming to rest against his sun-warmed chest. He held her while she cried, stroking her hair and murmuring little words of endearment. Her hot tears streamed down her face then dripped onto his skin, leaving a ticklish liquid trail in their wake. When she ceased to weep, he put his fingers under her chin and lifted her face to his.

"I never meant to cause you such pain," he said, finally getting his chance to apologize to her after so many years. "In fact, it is the one thing I would have given anything to avoid. Now that I know you still love me, I can wait as long as it takes to make the rest of it right."

She was so close and warm in his arms. He longed to kiss away every trace of her sorrow, but to do so would violate the vow he had made to his cousin and his own personal code. Instead he ran his thumb softly across her bottom lip, trying to memorize every detail of the moment, and placed a warm, lingering kiss on her forehead.

"I love you, Inez," he whispered into her hair, "and I will love you until the day I die."

Two days later, her husband returned.

Christophe was overwhelmed by the meeting with his beautiful new son. Though the Little Prince had made his appearance a month early, no trace remained of his low birth weight or his delicate condition. He was now a healthy, exuberant baby as robust as any other infant of the same age. He was still a bit small, but he was alert and active, and he nursed with gusto. Paulina offered the opinion that in another month or so, no one would be able to tell that he had come early.

His grandparents were also very impressed. Of course Cristian was the most perfect baby ever born. He was quiet and happy and beautifully formed, and he was certainly far more intelligent than a normal child. They all had high hopes for him. He carried the combined blood of the families, and one day all of the most impressive qualities of both lineages would unite in him. They all opined that the staff could not have been more perceptive when they had dubbed him the Little Prince.

When Inez and Christophe discussed the christening, he was a bit concerned that his wife put forth Estêvão to be the child's godfather. He raised his eyebrows a little skeptically at her suggestion, but after hearing the dire circumstances of his son's birth, he was more than happy to accede to her wishes. Christophe even went one step further with his gratitude by suggesting that they add 'Estêvão' as the baby's second name. Inez readily agreed, and the christening was accomplished.

Having the double responsibility of uncle and godfather, Estêvão lavished the Little Prince with everything the child could possibly need. He paid regular visits to the family, always bringing with him some new item of clothing, toys, or food said to be beneficial for the development of his nephew. Dom Martín also came along on these visits and did his best to monopolize the child's attention. The men from the Fazenda da Pomba were present for many of the child's milestones—crawling, standing, his first words, and his first steps—and they took almost as much pleasure in his accomplishments as did his parents.

Time flew by and Estêvão began to understand what Paulina meant about the love for a child being a life-changing experience. He found himself caring less and less about his own desires, instead spending his time thinking of ways to please his nephew. He daydreamed about the child's future and the things he would teach him. He would show him to ride and sail, how to play the guitar and sing. He would educate him about how to be a gentleman and conduct himself with honor, all the things he would have shown his own son. Then the crushing realization hit him that Cristian was not his son, and he was plunged into despair.

He also tried to suppress his feelings for Inez. He looked forward to every moment in her presence, and the time he spent with her was enjoyable, but it was not enough. Though he had believed he could live with his decision, the knowledge that she still loved him made it increasingly difficult to uphold his vow to be patient. After nearly two years of fighting his instincts, one day he woke and knew he could not tolerate the situation any longer. He decided that it was time for him to leave again, and he began to make his plans.

In the first week of April 1524, Estêvão paid a visit to his cousin's family to inform them of his impending journey. He pulled up to the vineyard and dismounted Tesouro, tethering him to a nearby hitching post. He carefully removed the canvas sack he wore slung over his shoulder and hung it on Tesouro's pommel. His nephew usually greeted him in his most energetic manner, and Estêvão did not want his precious cargo to be harmed.

At the sound of the hoof beats in the yard, his nephew came tearing around the corner of the house as fast as his chubby little legs could carry him. "Uncle Estêvão!" the nearly two-year-old shouted in glee at the sight of him. He made a beeline for his uncle and barreled recklessly into Estêvão's knees where he jumped up and down until his uncle lifted him up for a hug. Cristian squeezed Estêvão's neck as hard as he could and planted a smacking kiss on his cheek. "What did you bring me today?" he asked.

"Cristian, that is very rude," said Inez with a smile, coming to a stop in front of them. "Besides, a visit from your uncle should be enough. Hello, Estêvão," she said giving him a one-armed hug. "You'll have to forgive my son. He spends so much time outside he believes he is a wild animal with no need for manners."

"We were planting flowers on Palhaço's grave," Cristian said sadly, shaking his head in a perfect imitation of a grieving adult. "Poor, poor Palhaço. I will miss him."

"Yes, I was very sorry to hear the news," Estêvão said to Inez. He knew how much she had loved the scruffy old dog.

"He was very old, and he had a good life," she said, attempting to console herself, "but I miss him every day."

"Well, I may have something that will lift your spirits," Estêvão said with a smile.

"I knew you brought me something!" Cristian shouted excitedly, clapping his hands together.

"You will have to be very quiet and gentle, young man. Do you think you can do that?"

Cristian nodded his head and pinched his lips together with his dirty little fingers, and Estêvão lowered him to the ground. The child tiptoed behind his uncle, and Inez had to put a hand over her mouth to stifle her laughter at the ridiculousness of her son's exaggerated attempt at stealth. They made their way over to Tesouro, and Estêvão unhooked the bag from the pommel, holding his finger to his lips one last time to ensure that his nephew remembered the lesson. Cristian repeated the gesture then squatted down—his hands on his knees and his rosy-cheeked face alight with expectation—to wait for the surprise.

Estêvão placed the bag on the ground and motioned for the

boy to open it. Cristian carefully reached for the cloth and slowly pulled back one corner. The prize inside made a sudden movement, and the boy jumped back and tittered a little nervous giggle, his gray-brown eyes shining with anticipation. He quickly reached forward pinching the flap between his thumb and index finger and flung it back, opening the bag. A small black ball of silky curls popped out of the sack and yipped happily as Cristian jumped up and down with his hands in the air, rejoicing over his new companion.

"Mama, Mama! A new puppy!" he shouted in his loudest whisper. He ran silently around in a little circle while the puppy chased him and nipped at his heels. He finally fell down and rolled in the grass, the puppy thoroughly washing his laughing face. After a few minutes, Cristian sat up, stroking the puppy on his lap with a serious expression on his face.

"What is it, nephew?" Estêvão asked.

"Does he have a name? I can't just call him 'puppy' or 'dog'," the child said with a frown.

"Well, as his new master, it is your privilege to name him."

"I can name him anything I want? Anything?" His uncle nodded that he could. Cristian sat deep in thought for a few moments then looked up at his uncle and shook his head. "I would like to name him after you, but Estêvão is ..." he struggled with how to express himself with the appropriate vocabulary.

"Not a very suitable name for a dog," Estêvão offered. "Yes, I see your dilemma," he said, tapping his forehead in thought. "How about 'Falcão'. It is my nickname, and with all that black curly hair, he does resemble the falcon on my standard."

"Falcão is perfect!" the boy exclaimed. "Falcão, Falcão, Falcão!" he cawed, and the tiny black puppy cocked his head at the sound. "See!" Cristian cried. "He knows his name already! Falcão, Falcão, Falcão!" and he ran off, flapping his arms like wings, the puppy merrily chasing after him.

Inez watched her little son race across the grass, continually amazed by his abundance of energy. She turned back to Estêvão and smiled up at him. Since their reconciliation after the birth of her son, the warm golden lights in her eyes had returned and glowed brightly every time she looked at him.

"That was a very thoughtful thing to do," she said appreciatively. "You have been very good to him ... us, and I am grateful to no end. Would you like some tea or wine?"

Estêvão shook his head. "Inez, I came to bring the puppy, but there is something else I have to tell you." He took a deep breath and continued. "In a short time I will be going back to India. Vasco da Gama is being sent back to restore order, and he needs a reliable crew. I will be leaving to join him in three days."

Inez stood looking up at him, the smile gone from her face and her mouth gaping open. "Why?" she asked uncomprehendingly. "I thought we had reached an understanding. Things were going so well. Why have you decided to leave?"

"Inez," Estêvão said, taking her hand, "I thought I could do it, that I could live this charade, but I can't. I know I told you I would be patient and wait for you if it took a lifetime, but I cannot do it here. Don't you see? Every time I see you, I want to take you in my arms. Every time I see your son, I rail against God that he should have been mine. Every time I see my cousin, I curse him for his good fortune and myself because I did not treat you better. I love you, but if I stay here, I cannot trust myself to uphold the promise that I made. Can you understand, Coelhinha?"

She nodded her head and wiped at her tears with her free hand. "You should have kissed me that day under the pear trees," she said with a bitter smile, "then kidnapped me and blamed it on pirates."

Estêvão laughed at the idea. "My entire life since I met you has been one long string of should-haves," he said tenderly. "I cannot afford another misstep. That is why I must leave."

At that moment they heard Cristian come crowing back accompanied by his father and a barking Falcão. Estêvão discreetly let go Inez's hand, and she turned away and wiped at her eyes. Christophe greeted his cousin heartily as if he noticed nothing amiss and thanked him for the gift of the puppy. Cristian looked up at his mother and saw the telltale signs of her tears.

"Mama," he said, pulling at her skirt to get her attention, "why have you been crying?"

She scooped him up in her arms and hugged him tightly to her. "Your new puppy reminded me a bit of Palhaço when he was little, and it made me sad," she lied, the hot, pink color spreading up her neck, flooding her face, and coloring her ears at the deception.

"Don't be sad," Cristian said, hugging her tightly. "Falcão will not die for a very long time."

She managed a small laugh at his earnestness and his little boy's logic, and she put him back down to play with his puppy.

"Well, cousin," Inez heard her husband say to the man she loved, "if you are leaving us, you must stay for supper. I know you must have many preparations to make, but I will not take no for an answer." Estêvão agreed, and the entire group entered the house. It was the last time they would all be together.

Estêvão left for India three days later.

Chapter 12: Tragedy Strikes

After Estêvão's departure from Terceira, Inez's life acquired a new rhythm. Eventually the wrenching of her soul subsided to a dull ache, and though constant, it was bearable. Her son's perpetual need of attention combined with the responsibility of the new puppy left her no time to dwell on her sadness, and she threw herself into her duties hoping the activity would keep her mind off her loss. The distraction helped, but in the quiet moments between her thoughts returned again and again to the man who had played such a major role in her life.

Christophe knew the reason for the flagging of his wife's spirits, and though it saddened him to know that he could do nothing to change the situation, he had accepted this possibility long ago. He could do no more than be patient and support her and wait for her mood to lift. Inez was his world, and he did know that she truly loved him if not quite in the same way as she loved his cousin. He could only bolster his own morale with the fact that she had chosen to make her life with him and that things would soon return to normal.

Dom Martín continued his regular visits, and he regularly brought news of his sons' progress in India. He was still oblivious of the relationship between Inez and Estêvão, and he never noticed the tension between the married couple as he related the latest events. What concerned him most was the entertainment of his grandnephew. He would take Cristian on his lap and render the most dramatic version of the facts as he could, taking pleasure every time the boy's eyes grew large with interest or he cringed with fright. His deep voice rumbled through the house like thunder as he described the skirmishes between the valiant Portuguese and the wily natives. Cristian viewed Estêvão and João as demigods, and he was always proud to hear that his relations had saved the day.

Inez also had the added happiness of her parents' comforting presence. Iñigo and Joanna had begun to consider the prospect of moving to Terceira when their daughter married, and with the added incentive of the birth of their grandson, there was nothing but the mercantile to keep them in Vigo. Iñigo sold his share to his partner for a very reasonable price—Don Pedro would not accept the entire enterprise as a gift—and the house on the hill brought in more than enough to recoup the value. The Señores García arrived on the island with more money than they would ever need. With his phenomenal memory, Iñigo quickly picked up the running of the vineyard, and after two years, he was as knowledgeable as the men who had spent their entire lives in the field.

Time flew by with astounding rapidity, and each new year that came brought to Inez a sense of settling, a sort of peace with her surroundings and an assuredness that she had made the right decision. The family was extremely happy and the vineyard prosperous. She began to view Estêvão as she had when she was twelve, a shining white example of chivalry and virtue. Why else would he have made such a sacrifice? And the love they shared was the yearning unrealized romance of novels, in a different class than the practical, steadfast love she shared with her spouse. Now she understood that Estêvão had made the right choice to go away. The hero always did.

In March of 1530, Inez was in her kitchen making preparations for that evening's supper. Paulina expertly chopped vegetables for the soup, and Cristian rolled tiny balls of dough for a special dessert. Even Joanna helped out, having overcome her differences with Paulina after the Portuguese woman had saved her daughter and grandson. She sorted through berries in a large wooden bowl, picking out the ones that had been pecked by birds or showed signs of mildew. Falcão chewed on a bone under the table as Palhaço had used to do so many years ago.

The four of them chatted while they worked discussing the local gossip and Cristian's birthday the next month. He would be eight years old, and none of the ladies could understand how he had reached that age without their noticing. He was as handsome and intelligent as everyone had predicted, and he was every inch a young gentleman. He was very mature for his age and was reaching a point in his development where he desired to exert his independence. He itched for a little more freedom from the women in the house. He loved them all dearly, but they were always clucking and fussing over him like a baby. There was only so much a man could take.

"Dom Martín says that I will be able to help with the branding this year," Cristian said, expectantly looking up at his mother. "He said that I had to get your permission first, but he is already counting on my assistance."

"It is just so dangerous out there," Inez said. "You could get hurt."

"Mama," he said exasperated with the same old argument, "I could get hurt anywhere, doing anything. I could step off of the porch wrong and break my leg. I'm not a child anymore. Someday you will have to let me *live*."

"That sounds very familiar," Joanna said with a chuckle. "Your mother used to run off and do the most appalling things when she was a child. And I seem to recall that she was not much older than you the first time she rode out to the fields with Dom Martín."

"I was fourteen," Inez said, shooting a peevish look at her mother. "There is a very big difference between eight and fourteen."

"Yes, but I am a man," Cristian said importantly, "and it's time you started treating me like one."

"Perhaps if you removed your apron and washed the sugar and cinnamon from you hands, your mother would take that statement more seriously," said Paulina.

Cristian looked down at himself then back at Paulina. "I suppose she would," he said with a grin. "But seriously, will you at least discuss it with my papa?"

"Yes, Cristian," Inez said with a sigh.

She knew her son and her mother were right. It was just so difficult to think of him as a young man. He would always be her baby. She loved him so much, and she would never forgive herself if something unfortunate were to happen to him. There were so many dangers out in the world—accidents, disease, evil people bent on doing harm. Her own mother had lost two children.

At the time Inez had thought Joanna's story to be very sad, but now that she had her own child, her mother's tragedies took on a new significance. She gained a new respect for Joanna and marveled at her strength. She was sure she would die of heartbreak if anything were to happen to her son. She did not know how her mother had survived it.

She admitted that she was a little overprotective of Cristian. Perhaps it *was* time to give him a bit more freedom. She remembered how close a watch Dom Martín had kept on her whenever she worked in the fields, and she knew he would never allow her son to get hurt. The old fidalgo loved the boy almost as much as she did, and he would not assign him a job beyond his capabilities or a task that would expose him to risk.

Inez opened her mouth to tell Cristian that she would not need to discuss the matter with his father, and there began a faint rattling of the windows in their frames. After a few seconds it stopped, and although Inez was left with a subtle feeling of uneasiness, she rationalized the noise by attributing it to the wind.

Falcão began to whine under the table, and Cristian squatted down to see what was the matter. "What's wrong, boy?" he asked, stroking the dog's curly head in an attempt to soothe him.

"He probably bit himself while he was working on that bone," Paulina said. "He'll be fine."

"I don't know," Cristian said skeptically. "He's all curled up under there, like he's afraid."

"He probably got spooked by that gust of wind," Joanna added logically, also having noticed the rattling windows. "Animals don't do well with changes in the weather."

Falcão abandoned his comfortable spot under the table and slinked over to the door, and the four humans continued their banter. Paulina put the vegetables into a pot of boiling water, and Joanna rose from her seat to wash the bowl of culled berries. Inez was just basting the meat for the final time when the stack of dirty dishes began to clatter in earnest. The floor beneath them began to shake, and the heavy worktable jittered sideways, creeping slowly from its place in the middle of the room. A vase of flowers crashed to the floor, and Falcão howled loudly, scratching frantically at the base of the door.

Inez grabbed her son's hand in terror and raced for the door, shouting, "Outside!" to Paulina and her mother over her back. She threw the door open, and the four of them spilled out of the house into the large open clearing where they had buried Palhaço. They squatted, huddled together—Inez clutching her son while he hugged his dog, the two older women clinging to each shoulder—and waited for the earth to stop its trembling.

Living so close to the volcano, they felt little rumblings and vibrations all the time but nothing of this magnitude. The year of Cristian's birth the neighboring island of São Miguel had experienced a violent upheaval that nearly obliterated the capital. The earthquake shook the soil loose from the hills above Vila Franca do Campo causing a mudslide that inundated the town, bringing down official buildings and destroying many homes. Major damage had also occurred in the town of Maia. It was an assumed risk of life on a volcanic island, but that did not make the event any less frightening.

Finally the shaking abated, and Falcão ceased to cower. Inez took this as a sign that things had returned to normal, and the group made their way back to the house to assess the damage. When she reached the door to the kitchen, her spirits dropped at the wreckage that greeted her. The floor was littered with shards of glass and pottery from all the bowls and dishes that had been flung to the ground, and the window had a long jagged crack in it diagonally across one pane. She blocked the entrance to keep Falcão from running into the dangerous debris field and asked her son to keep him occupied outside until the women could restore some semblance of order to the chaos within. She bent over and began picking up the larger pieces while Joanna went to investigate the rest of the house. Paulina grabbed a broom and started to sweep.

Most of the cooking vessels were replaceable and the window would serve its purpose until a new one was installed, but Inez was crushed when she came across some pieces of the brightly colored serving platters she used at almost every meal. Christophe had spent years of birthdays, Christmases, and anniversaries gifting her with the collection, because he thought his wife's cooking was too special to be served in the same old plain dishes every night. He knew that she took pains to make the food look beautiful, and he wanted her to be able to present it in style. Inez's eyes welled with tears at the thought of telling him, and she wiped them away with the back of her hand.

"Don't worry, Baixinha," Paulina said with a sad smile. "It will give him a new excuse to bring you a present."

"I suppose you're right," she said. Her thoughtful husband often brought her little surprises unjustified by a special occasion, and Inez reasoned that by this point he must be running out of ideas. She dropped the shiny red remnant into the trash and reached for another. At that moment there was an urgent pounding at the door. Inez rose from her task and brushed off the front of her apron. What did Cristian need so badly that he should hammer on the door in such a manner? She carefully picked her way over to open it and was surprised to see one of the men from the vineyard, twisting his hat in his hands with a look of bona fide panic on his face.

"Tristão, what is it?" she asked, her stomach somersaulting at his darting eyes, which refused to rise to her face.

"Senhora ... I ... you ... Ay, Meu Deus! Senhora, come quick! The Chief ... he is ..." and he began to sob.

Inez immediately hitched up her skirts and ran for the vineyard, leaving the distraught man crying on the porch. Cristian and Falcão made to cross the yard to join her, but she stopped and commanded them to stay where they were. If something terrible had happened to his father, she did not want her son to witness it. She resumed her desperate flight, petitioning God with every step to let everything turn out all right. She reached the door of the storage room where she knew her husband and father had planned to spend the day rotating the giant barrels of aging wine. With a heavy sense of trepidation, she entered the cellar.

Inez paused to let her eyes adjust to the dim light, and the strong alcoholic bite of wine fumes assaulted her nostrils. When she could see enough to make her way safely down the steps, she noticed several broken casks that had been tossed to the ground by the strong temblor and spilled their contents into the dirt. When she stood on solid ground, she looked left and right and chided herself for not having thought to bring a candle. Finally she made out a group of men in a far corner and rushed over to ask about her husband. The workers turned at her approach and moved aside to allow her access, avoiding her gaze as Tristão had at the house. Just as she reached the end of the line of men, her father stepped in front of her and gripped her shoulders.

"Mynah," he began gravely, "it is very serious. Christophe is badly injured. It is a miracle he is still alive. I think he was hanging on just for you. Do not let him see your sorrow. Be strong, and try to make his final moments as pleasant as possible."

Her father's comment struck terror into her heart, but she nodded her head, bit her trembling bottom lip, and tried to prepare herself for what she would find. Iñigo hugged her to him then stepped out of her way, gently pushing her forward. Inez choked back the cry of anguish that threatened to escape her throat.

Her husband lay in the dirt of the cellar with all four limbs flung wide, as if trying to cover the largest area possible. His normally brown skin looked waxy and pale, and his eyes were clenched tightly closed, concentrating all of his faculties to stave off the inevitable. Where his work shirt should have been filled out by his well-muscled chest, it lay flattened and crumpled, and spots of spreading blood discolored its creamy linen fibers. He labored to breathe, and Inez could hear the audible gurgle of fluid in his lungs.

His deep amber eyes flew open as soon as she moved forward, and a tired version of his brilliant white smile spread across his face, this time the corners stained with bloody flecks of foam. She threw herself down on her knees at her husband's side and found his hand with her own. The hand that was always so strong and vital was now cold and lifeless, and she held it to her bosom in an unconscious effort to warm it.

"This is not a very good place to take a nap, husband," Inez said, her voice quavering with emotion. "You might catch a chill."

He laughed at her pitiful attempt to lighten the mood, and it brought on a weak fit of coughing. She was immediately sorry for her mindless blunder and waited helplessly for the spasm to subside. After a few agonizing moments, his wheezing lessened, and he cleared his throat to speak.

"Canelle," he rasped, his usually mellow voice unrecognizable, "is everyone all right? Cristian?"

"Yes, yes, Christophe," she answered quickly, sensing that their time was short. "Everyone is fine."

"Good," he said and closed his eyes. A few seconds later, he opened them again and took as deep a breath as he dared. "From the moment I met you I felt the luckiest man in the world," he began, racing to convey the depth of his love for her before his time ran out. "I never thought to find such a treasure as you, and I thank God for every moment. You gave me clarity and focus and a son to carry on my name. I know you never loved me with your whole heart. How could you when you had already given it to my cousin? But you loved me the best you could, and that was enough for me."

Inez sat shaking her head, the tears streaming down her face, trying to deny the reality of what he had known for so long. He had not meant it reprovingly, but having struck a chord of truth so close to her guilty conscience, Inez felt it as such. She tried to tell him that he held a place in her heart that not even Estêvão had been able to touch, but each time she opened her mouth to begin, her sentiments overwhelmed her and choked back her attempts.

"It does not matter now," he said, his voice very faint, the life beginning to fade from his dark yellow eyes. "I love you, Canelle. Know that I love you." His eyes closed and his head lolled to one side, and the distinctive prolonged exhale of death issued from his lungs in a final sigh.

"Nooo!" Inez cried out, her voice rising in a long mournful keen. "Not like this! I never meant it to happen like this! Christophe, please, please don't go! Nooo!"

The men had all moved away in order to avoid the intimacy of their Chief's final moments with the woman he loved, and now they turned their backs, unnerved by Inez's naked display of grief. She sat with her dead husband's hand still clutched to her chest, smoothing his silky brown hair back from his face with the other. She rocked herself back and forth in her misery, and the tears flooded down her cheeks.

Iñigo knelt behind her and placed his hands gently on his bereaved daughter's shoulders. "Mynah, we have to get him out of here. If there is another tremor, more people could get hurt."

"But Papa, I cannot leave him," she said, looking up at him frantically. The manic light in her silver eyes bordered on hysterical. "I have to prove to him how much he means to me. He doesn't know how much I love him."

Iñigo saw that his daughter was beyond rational thought so he said, "Why don't you go wait for him outside. You can resume your watch there. He should be moved from this cold, dark cellar."

Inez nodded her head eagerly. "You are right, Papa," she said. "He should be out in the sunshine. Maybe that will warm him up. He is so very cold." She reluctantly let go her husband's hand, rose from her knees, and allowed her father to lead her out of the musty darkness of the storage room.

Later that evening, Iñigo divulged the details of Christophe's final heroic moments before being mortally injured in the wine cellar. The men were finished rotating the barrels and had determined to stop for the day when Tristão came down with an order in his hand. The order necessitated the removal of one of the topmost casks, and it was a big job to fill. As the equipment was already in place and the crew were already grimy from the day's work, Christophe made the decision to take down the barrel then, rather than wait until the next morning. It would complete their work in the storage room, and they could move on to something else the following day. The men all saw the logic of this and quickly set about to complete the task.

They nearly had the heavy tun secured when the shaking began. Off-balance and terrified, the man working to hook the last strap into place missed his target. The load swung free of the intricate system of ropes and pulleys and spilled from the sling, which was meant to bring it safely to the dirt floor. Christophe saw the barrel fall in a deadly arc toward Arnoldo, and he sprinted to his loyal worker's rescue, shoving him out of harm's way and taking the full brunt of the force on his own torso. His body had been crushed under the weight, precluding any hope of survival. Up to the end, he had been true to his selfless nature, and his men would always remember his ultimate sacrifice so that one of them could live. The bravery of Christophe's final act in the wine cellar had enabled Arnoldo to enjoy the continued gift of life but had left his wife more convinced than ever of her guilt.

Inez was beyond reason. The trauma of losing her husband in such a horrific manner combined with her inability to communicate her love for him while he lay dying had rendered her unreasonable with a slight madness in her eyes. Paulina brewed up a sedative and saw Inez to her bed, but even after the drug had begun to work, the widow rambled on about how the accident was her fault and how she had brought this curse onto the family. In her eyes, Christophe was yet one more innocent victim claimed to pay for the all-consuming love she bore Estêvão. She held herself responsible, and she was paralyzed by the irrational fear that her son would be next.

Though each of her family members did their best to draw Inez out of her self-imposed exile, she thwarted their efforts, stubbornly refusing to listen to reason. She continued to reproach herself for Christophe's death and insisted that she was doomed to lose everyone for whom she cared. The only time she ceased her disturbing maunderings was when her son made his daily visit. Her chatter then took on a different but equally unsettling tone, fawning over Cristian, telling him that she would never let anything hurt him, and making him promise to stay out of danger. As a result, he kept his visits short and looked forward to the day when his mother would return to normal.

When Dom Martín heard the news, he was overwrought. It was a completely unforeseen tragedy, something that he'd never thought to witness in his lifetime. He had been there from the very beginning and had thought to pass on long before either of the two young people whom he had come to regard as his own children. They had brought him much pleasure, and Christophe had been a fine, honorable young man. To show his love for him, Dom Martín offered to bury him in the cemetery with Dona María, Serafina, and baby Estêvão. After all, they were a family and should remain united in death as they had in life. Everyone agreed that it was an excellent idea, and the arrangements were made.

The day of the funeral arrived, and the mourners made their way to the Fazenda da Pomba. It was a lovely sunny day and except for the solemn tone of the attendees, a passerby might have thought they had gathered in the grassy little clearing for a celebratory spring picnic. All of the workers from the vineyard and the fazenda were dressed in their finest attire to show their respect for the gracious young senhor who had always seemed to have a kind word for them all. They considered him one of their own, and they were very saddened by the senselessness of his untimely death. They were also troubled by the affect it had brought to bear on his wife.

Inez had spent the time since her husband's accident isolated in the room they had shared in the house they built together. She had spent many days and sleepless nights in mourning and self-recrimination, and now she was incapable of further display of emotion. She stood at the graveside shored up on either side by her father and Paulina. She was pale and drawn, oddly beautiful in her russet brown mourning gown, her silver eyes larger and more luminous than ever. She accepted condolences in a subdued, dry-eyed fashion, and all were amazed by her illusion of strength. No one but Paulina and Joanna suspected how truly fragile she was.

After the interment, the mourners all headed for the outdoor dining area to partake of the feast Dom Martín had ordered prepared in honor of Christophe. Inez insisted that she could tolerate no more, and Paulina volunteered to see her back to the house. Iñigo and Joanna would stay and act in her place, and Inez implored her parents to keep a watchful eye on her son to make sure no harm would befall him. They both swore that they would, and satisfied, the widow allowed Paulina to drive her home.

That evening Inez and her family sat in the parlor and talked about what a fitting sendoff Dom Martín had arranged for Christophe. Iñigo and Cristian played chess, and the ladies worked on baby clothing for the wife of one of the men at the vineyard who was expecting. The fact that Inez did not run off at the first mention of her husband's name was a definite sign of improvement, and they were all encouraged and continued the exchange. They moved on to little anecdotes and tender moments they had shared with the deceased, and they secretly speculated that perhaps, Inez would finally move past her bout of depression and get on with her life. The conversation slowed, and Cristian decided to relate another interesting event that had transpired.

"My Uncle Estêvão is back from India," he said excitedly, "and he says that he has something special for my birthday."

At the mention of Estêvão's name, Inez blanched and her face returned to the drawn mask of tension she had worn since the day of her husband's tragedy. Paulina and Joanna both shot her concerned looks and attempted to change the subject, but Iñigo's insatiable curiosity had already been piqued, and Cristian would not be deterred.

"Yes, I wanted to speak to him myself," Iñigo replied, "but I was besieged by well-wishers and questions regarding the fate of the vineyard. How long has he been back?"

"He and João returned after the first of the year, but my uncle says he has not come to visit because he is just now recuperating from his wound."

"He was wounded?" Inez asked breathlessly. Her heart pounded in her chest, and her voice quavered. Even now, after so many people had suffered because of their love, she could not feign indifference.

"Oh, yes," Cristian said, his grey-brown eyes alight with enthusiasm. "Last year Nuno da Cunha sent an expedition to sack the city of Damão. The objective was accomplished, but the *María Vencedora* was hit with flaming arrows and the fire spread too quickly to extinguish. My uncle made sure that his entire crew reached safety then he turned to make his own escape and took a musket ball in the hip. He said it was nothing, but he almost died from his wound. João says that my Uncle Estêvão is a hero, and if not for him, the *whole crew* would have died. He has already commissioned a new ship, and he said that when it is finished, he will take me out and teach me to sail."

When she heard about Estêvão's close brush with death, Inez stiffened in her seat. It seemed the curse had now extended to include even him. The fear for her son's welfare took hold again, and she could not shake her terror. "Do not even *think* about going out on a ship!" she snapped unreasonably.

"But, Mama, everyone in this room came over to the island on a ship," Cristian pointed out logically. "Besides, Uncle Estêvão is one of the most experienced and respected sea captains in all of Portugal *and* the East. I could not be safer."

"I forbid this discussion!" Inez retorted. "You will not go, and that is final!" She folded the piece she was working on with angry, jerky little movements, stuffed it in her bag, and stomped up the stairs to her room.

Cristian stared after her with an open mouth. He had never seen his mother so irrational. Even during her seclusion after his father's death, she had not acted so incensed. Overprotective, yes, coddling, to the point of frustration, maudlin, to excess, but this outright vehemence was something he had never seen.

"What did I do wrong?" he asked the adults in the room. "All I did was state the obvious, and she exploded."

"You did nothing wrong," said Paulina, rising from her seat. "Your mother is having a difficult time dealing with your father's passing."

"I loved my father too, but life must go on," Cristian said with a soulful look in his big brown eyes. "She cannot spend her entire life locked away in her room."

"Not everybody is as philosophical as you are," said Paulina, crossing the room and placing a kiss on the top of his head. "You must understand that your mother and father were married for twice as long as you have been alive. It is a horrible shock. She will recover, but it will take time." Then she proceeded up the steps to speak to Inez.

At the door to the bedroom Paulina listened to Inez's frenzied pacing inside. She knocked lightly and when she did not receive an answer, she entered anyway. She stood silently near the entry and waited for Inez to calm down. Inez eventually looked up from her pacing and launched into a tirade against Estêvão.

"Three months! He has been home three months and did not bother to call! He nearly died, he lost his ship, and now he wants to take my son out on the open sea! Without asking! He acts so *entitled*! He has no right! He had no right to be there!"

Paulina saw the torture in Inez's eyes. Her disorganized outcries were simply reflections of her scattered thoughts. This woman, whom she still thought of as her own little girl, was being torn in two directions. Her love and anxiety for Estêvão pulled her in one, but her perceived guilt over the death of her husband and concern for her son pulled in another. It cut Paulina to her core to see Inez like this, and she did all she could to remain calm and attempt to reason with her.

"Baixinha, he had every right to be there. It would have been improper for him not to make an appearance."

"Yes, but half the burden of guilt for Christophe's death is his to bear," Inez insisted.

"There is no burden of guilt. It was an accident."

"It was no accident!" Inez exclaimed. "It was retribution, and now he wants to risk my son to the same fate! I will not allow it!"

She was livid, but tears of vulnerability shimmered in her angry eyes. Paulina saw that Inez was at her breaking point, and she pulled the younger woman to her and held her while she cried. The barrier that Inez had built up finally came crashing down, and she let Paulina soothe her like a child with a grazed knee. She let go of all the resentment and culpability and cried until nothing remained. She allowed Paulina to put her to bed, and as soon as her head hit the pillow she fell into a deep, exhausted sleep. It had taken much out of her to get to this point, but now that she had moved past it, everything else would fall into place. Paulina kissed Inez on the cheek and closed the door gently behind her.

Chapter 13: Hope and the Heart

After Inez's breakdown, she was able to sort through her emotions and put her life back into a semblance of order. Her new perspective helped to speed her recovery, and things eventually returned to normal. She still grieved the fact that during his final moments she had not been able to voice to Christophe how much she had truly loved him. Her regret was not that she had been unable to absolve herself of any wrongdoing but that she had been helpless to assure him that he had not failed her in any way. He had exceeded her expectation for marriage on every level, and she had loved him far more than just second best. Testimony from several different sources told her that he knew, but the lost opportunity still gnawed at her conscience. She realized she would never attain a full sense of closure, but she learned how to cope with it and began to move forward, yet again.

As for her love of Estêvão, that had been the most constant thing in her life outside of her relationship with her family. She had known since the day she met him that he was the only man who would ever complete her, but now she was unsure whether she could allow herself the happiness that she had always thought to realize with him. She had moved past her guilt, but there were other reasons she believed she deserved to remain unfulfilled. Her desire for him had been the obstacle to absolute satisfaction with her husband. Wasn't it restitution to deny herself a full measure of happiness as she had deprived Christophe of his? How would she answer when Estêvão came to propose? She laughed at her presumption. He had been home for many months and never sought her out. Maybe he was not interested in her any more. Perhaps he had even married. She shooed the thought to the back of her mind and continued with her life.

Inez maintained her focus and concentrated on the family she had left. She relented her iron-fisted control over her son. Her mother pointed out that this tactic had never worked on Inez as a child, and Cristian was even more obstinate than she had been. Joanna reasoned that Inez's unfounded authoritative attitude would lead Cristian to rebel or be deceptive with her, and wouldn't it be better to know what he was doing instead of him sneaking out to do the things she forbade? Inez finally saw the logic of this and allowed her son a liberal amount of freedom. As long as he told her the details and did not ride off alone, he was permitted to do nearly everything he asked.

Cristian spent most of his time between the vineyard and the Fazenda da Pomba. On some days an extra pair of hands was needed attending the grapevines, and on others Dom Martín needed help in the fields. Although Cristian was only eight, he was persistent and very intelligent. He listened to instructions intently, his gray-brown eyes taking in every bit of information, and he performed his chores quickly with a minimum of fuss. There were days when Inez watched him work, and she was struck by his resemblance to his father. A twinge of sadness would twist inside her and then be gone, replaced by her love for her son.

On the days when he rode out to the fields, Cristian always brought back news of happenings at the fazenda. There were tales of João's never-ending exploits, which now encompassed the lands in the East, and amusing anecdotes of Dom Martín's dissatisfaction with the current government or impatience with his aging body. There was always news of the building of Estêvão's new ship but never any mention of a new Senhora or even a prospective one. Estêvão always sent his regards specifically for Inez, but still, he did not come. She resigned herself to the fact that he had lost interest and went on with her life.

By the New Year in 1531, Martin Luther had issued his Augsburg Confession officially establishing Protestantism as an alternative to the monopoly on Christianity held by the Catholic Church. King Henry VIII had repudiated his queen, the Castilian princess Katherine of Aragon, and was hammering Pope Clemens VII to grant him a divorce so that he could marry the notorious Anne Boleyn. Frustrated with the pope's refusal, later in the year Henry would have himself appointed head of the Church of England. Queen Katherine's nephew, Spain's Carlos I, would be crowned Holy Roman Emperor and King of Italy. Lisbon would be hit by an earthquake killing 30,000 Portuguese. The conflict in which Estêvão had been wounded continued in the East, and the Portuguese under Nuno da Cunha would be forced into retreat. It seemed that the world around Terceira was in a state of constant flux, but life on the island continued in the same uneventful fashion.

In the second week of January, the courier from the Fazenda da Pomba arrived to deliver an invitation. In honor of Capitán Rey's fiftieth birthday there was to be a large celebration, and all of the members of the vineyard, family and workers alike, were expected to take part. Iñigo offered to provide the wine, and the vineyard was abuzz with the preparations. Everyone was excited about the revel and looked forward to a happy excuse to come together. Joanna clucked over her daughter saying that this would be a very important meeting, so she should take pains to look perfect. Inez let her fuss, but when the time came to go, she could not bring herself to do it.

"After all that preparation?" Joanna asked, dismayed that her efforts had come to naught.

"Really, Mama," Cristian said, exasperated by his mother's fickle behavior. "I hate to say it, but Grandmother is right. My uncle will be very disappointed."

"Your uncle will not even notice," Inez said, kissing her precious son on the cheek. "If he asks, tell him I was not feeling well, but I wish him the very best."

"All right," Cristian said dubiously, "but he *will* be disappointed. He talks about you all the time."

"I'm sure he does, in a fond, nostalgic sort of way," she said with a faraway look on her face. "Anyway," she continued, shaking her head to clear it, "go, and have a good time. Tell me all about it when you get home," and she shooed her parents and son out the door.

Paulina had decided to stay home with Inez, and they sat by the fire in compatible silence. Paulina sensed that the younger woman wanted to talk—she knew Inez almost better than Inez knew herself—but it was always easier to get to the root of the problem if she let her broach the subject, so Paulina waited. Eventually Inez let out a long, wistful sigh and began to speak.

"I suppose I should have gone just to get this meeting over and done with. I don't see how we can possibly continue to avoid each other, knowing how much he loves my son." She paused for a moment then let out another long sigh, this one shaky and full of emotion. "And I guess it would be better to know for sure that he does not love me anymore. At least then I could stop hoping." She sniffed wearily, and a single, silent tear slid out of the corner of her eye and down her cheek.

Paulina reached over and patted her on the arm. "One should never stop hoping, Baixinha. When everything else is gone, there is always still hope."

In March the vineyard marked a year since their Chief's passing. They closed down all operations for the day, and each of the workers and their families made an appearance at the house to show their respect. Inez received them graciously, and they were all happy to see that the Senhora had now fully recovered. It was a bittersweet occasion—joyful because Christophe was loved by so many people but sad because he was not there to see the positive affect he had brought to bear on so many lives. It left Inez with a warm feeling of affection for her husband and satisfaction at the knowledge that he was now at peace.

A few days later, the women of the house were sitting in the parlor repairing work shirts for the men. Cristian and Iñigo were laboring among the grapevines, fertilizing and inspecting them for any sort of blight that might affect their development. It was delicate work that required much focus, so Falcão had been left at the house to keep him out of trouble. He lay drowsing by the fire while the women chatted.

All of a sudden the dog snapped to attention and sat up. Inez was startled at his unexpected action. Since the day of the earthquake, she had learned to trust the dog's instincts, but he was not showing any signs of distress or impending danger. Falcão was simply sitting expectantly at attention with his curly black tail wagging slowly, the way he did when Cristian and Iñigo returned from the vineyard. It was too early for the workday to be over, and they would never use the front door after a hard day's toil. Any time a stranger approached the house the dog sent up a loud warning bark, so she could not fathom who it could be.

There was a firm knock at the door. Paulina rose from her chair to answer it, and Falcão trotted out of the room behind her. The mystery would soon be solved. Inez continued with her darning, but when Paulina reentered the room followed by the heavy tread of a man's boots, she looked up to see who had come to visit. Her needle stopped in midair, she made a little choked noise in her throat, and her head began to spin. Joanna sensed her daughter's upset and also looked up to discover the source. A little smile spread across her face, and she rose from her chair.

"Estêvão!" Joanna said warmly, giving him a quick hug. "What a wonderful surprise! We were not expecting you. To what do we owe the pleasure of your company?"

"Hello, Joanna," he said never taking his eyes from her daughter's face. "Actually, I came to speak to Inez."

"Oh!" she replied with feigned surprise. "Then we will give you some privacy. Paulina, let's go check on supper." Paulina nodded her head, and the two women left the room.

Estêvão turned to watch them go, an amused smile on his handsome face. "I will never get over the change in your mother," he said, shaking his head. "She is a completely different person from the one I met so long ago."

"We all are," said Inez quietly.

"I suppose we are," he answered thoughtfully, "but some things never change. May I sit down?"

Inez nodded her head. He leaned on his walking stick and lowered himself into the chair next to her, wincing with the effort. When he had settled himself, he caught her staring at him, a look of concern evident on her face.

"My little souvenir from the East," he said with a wry smile.

"I was sorry to hear about the *María Vencedora*. I know how much she meant to you."

"Yes, but other things are more important," he said, taking her hand and looking into her eyes. "Inez, can we please dispense with all the polite chit-chat. You know why I've come."

She stiffened in her seat and pulled her hand away, her eyes turning steely. "No. I have no idea why you've come. You have been home for over a year, and this is the first opportunity you have had to call?"

"I was in no shape to do anything but lay in my bed and moan for the first three months, and then your husband was killed. Was I supposed to show up the next day, like a vulture, to pick over the scraps he left behind? Inez, I may have made mistakes, but even I am not without my honor."

"Honor!" she spat out. "It was your honor that wrought this … this disaster! If only I had meant more to you than your honor."

"You do," he said tenderly. "That is why I am here. Inez, look at me." He took her chin in his hand and turned her to face him. "This past year has been the hardest of my life, even more difficult than the two years I spent playing the devoted cousin to you husband and much worse than my time away. Knowing that you were here, a short ride up the road, and no longer obligated to someone else. I had to remind myself every day of my vow to do things right this time, to *make* everything right. I could do no less. Ours is an enduring love that has survived every tragedy that life could throw at it, and it deserves to be fulfilled in the proper manner."

She sat gazing up into his hazel-green eyes, the eyes that she had loved for so long and dreamed about so often. She was torn. If only it could be that simple! She forced her eyes away from his and looked down at her lap. She had no right to desire this.

"Why is it that this *enduring love* has brought nothing but suffering to all who have come into contact with it? Can you answer that, Estêvão?" she asked, looking up at him defiantly, the threat of tears shimmering in her eyes. "Why does someone always have to die for us to be together?"

She was intent upon punishing herself. He could see the hurt and the guilt she carried inside her. *Oh, my sweet love, what have I done to you?* he thought to himself. *If only I could have spared you this anguish.* He knew that to voice this would drive her further away from him, so instead he tried to reason with her.

"Inez," he began, patiently taking her hand again, "if I have learned anything from my years of regret, it is that love without complication is impossible. It never waits for a convenient time to present itself. I know I have caused you a lifetime of heartache. Please allow me the chance to prove that it was all worthwhile." He got down on one knee in front of her, wincing again at the pain in his hip. "I am nothing but a useless old man, but I have loved you since the day we met, and nothing would make me happier than if you'd consent to be my wife."

She sat there for a long moment, unspeaking, and Estêvão thought he had finally been able to break through her defenses. Then, to his utter disbelief, she slowly shook her head and said, "I'm sorry. I cannot."

"All right," he said quietly, trying to restrain himself. "I will accept that if you can look me in the eye and tell me that you do not love me."

She looked up at him with a challenging set to her head and mechanically said, "I do not love you." Slowly a hot, pink flush spread up from her chest, coloring her neck then face, and ultimately making its way to her ears. Estêvão had seen this reaction to her attempt at deception only a handful of times, but it was as telling as if she had admitted her lie. There was still hope. She still loved him. She just needed time.

"Fine. I suppose I deserve that, but know that this does not end here."

Estêvão rose shakily from his knee, leaning heavily on his walking stick for support. He brushed off the front of his clothing, turned to exit the room, then paused and reached for the little pocket that held his most valued possessions next to his heart. He took out an old yellowed piece of linen and unfolded it. Inez recognized it immediately and let out a little gasp, bringing her hand up to cover her reaction. It was the embroidery sampler she had given him when she was eleven. He had told her that he would cherish it, and here it was, still with him nearly twenty-two years later, but that was not what he was after.

From the center of the cloth he pulled up a leather thong and, like a magician, slowly drew it out to its full length. He paused for a moment and regarded the object that lay in his hand with a look of affection. Then he let the pendant swing free from his palm and dangle before her. Inez nearly broke her resolve, but she stifled the urge to cry out and snatch the necklace from him. Instead she sat there trembling, waiting to see what he would do next.

"You dropped this under the swing that day in Vigo," he said, refusing to mention the events that had precipitated its loss. "I kept it in hopes that one day I would be able to return it to you. That day has finally arrived, and it seems that some hopes can still be realized." He dropped the rabbit into her hand and leaned over to kiss her cheek. "I love you, Coelhinha," he whispered into her ear. "I will always love you." Then he turned and walked stiffly to the door, exited, and closed it behind him.

Inez sat gazing down at the familiar piece she had thought gone forever, now returned to her after so many years. Its soft silver patina winked up at her from its place in her hand, and she stroked its satiny smoothness with the tip of her finger. So many years he had kept it. So much time lost between them. At that moment Paulina and Joanna entered from the kitchen, both smiling with anticipation.

"So when is the happy day?" Joanna asked, ecstatic that her daughter would finally find the contentment that she had sought for so long.

"I refused him," Inez said, unable to meet her mother's gaze.

"What?" Joanna cried unbelievingly. "After all this time? This is what you have wanted since you were twelve! Why did you refuse him?"

"Eleven, I have waited for this since I was eleven."

"Then why? Why did you refuse?"

Inez looked back and forth between the two women. Suddenly the tears she had supressed during her conversation with Estêvão came pouring forth, and Paulina rushed over to comfort her. Inez wept for a few minutes, her sobs racking her body with a heartrending sorrow. Eventually her tears subsided, and she blotted the moisture from her eyes and sniffled in her misery. When she could finally breathe without shuddering, she revealed her reasons.

"I simply cannot get past the tragedy it has taken to get to this point. Serafina, baby Estêvão, Christophe. It just seems so disloyal to their memories."

"Mi hijita, everyone has had tragedy in their lives," Joanna pointed out logically, "but you must move past it, as Paulina and I did."

"Your mother is right, Baixinha. You cannot stay loyal to a memory for the rest of your life."

"Why not? You did," Inez said accusatorily.

"Nuno was the completion of my spirit, the other half of my soul. *That* is what you will be missing out on if you do not marry Capitán Rey."

"My head cannot get past it," Inez said stubbornly.

"What does your heart tell you?" Paulina asked, gently squeezing her hand.

"My heart?" Inez repeated. She looked back down at the silver rabbit, and a bitter little smile lifted the corners of her mouth, more an expression of torment than anything else. "My heart cries out for him every moment of every day, and when I go to sleep at night, he makes his appearance in my dreams. My heart has ached so much this past year that I feared it would break simply because he did not come. When he finally came, I sent him away, because I am terrified that my heart will burst with happiness if we are united, and if I should lose him, my heart will shrivel and die. That is what my heart tells me."

"That is why you must not waste a minute of the time you have left," Paulina said with a sagacious smile. "That is why you must go to him."

Inez knew Paulina was right. With a cry she tore herself from her chair and ran across the room. What if this had been the last straw? What if he was finally tired of pursuing her only to be rejected? What if she had forced him to change his mind? She did not care. She would do anything to win him back, even if she had to beg him on her knees.

She had to get to the stable as fast as she could. She reached for the door, jerked it open, and without looking up stepped hurriedly outside. She bumped hard into a warm body and fell onto her backside with a surprised shout. The silver rabbit bounced away from her, and she scrambled on her knees to regain it before it could be lost again. When it was safely in her grasp, she held it to her bosom with her eyes closed, thanking God that it had not been ruined. Then she rose quickly, intent on resuming her pursuit.

"Perdon, Senhor," she said absentmindedly without looking up. "My mother will see to your needs. I have urgent business to attend," and she made to go around him.

The man stepped in her way, irritating her the slightest bit until she noticed the walking stick. "If you'll forgive me, Senhora, my needs can only be satisfied by the daughter," said Estêvão in his familiar mellow voice. She looked up into his laughing green eyes, her mouth dropping open in surprise.

"I thought you had gone," she said in a choked little whisper.

"I had," he admitted, "but I could not leave things so

unfinished. What is this urgent business of which you speak?"

"I ... uh ..." she stammered, searching for a way to maintain her dignity. Suddenly she realized that her dignity meant nothing in the face of losing him. She dropped every defense she had erected and grabbed the front of his jacket, beseechingly looking up into his eyes as the tears streamed down her cheeks. "Please, I beg of you, forget everything I ever said about not loving you. God forgive me, I love you, and I cannot live without you. If I have to spend an eternity condemned because of that love, then so be it. Please don't ever leave me again."

Estêvão put his arms around her and pulled her to him, his hands catching in the coarse masses of her deep red curls. His cheek came to rest on top of her head, and he said nothing, content just to hold her. After a few moments, he pulled her face up to look at him, his right hand coming up to cup her jawline, his thumb tracing the length of her cheekbone. She closed her eyes and leaned into his hand, turning her face into its warmth to place a tender kiss in his palm. He looked down at her dusky gray lashes resting against the subtle rose blush of her cheek, and he brushed his lips gently across her temple, overwhelmed by the unbelievable softness of her skin. He rested his lips on her forehead, placed a playful little kiss on the end of her nose then raised her chin with his fingers. Her eyes opened and Estêvão could see their silver irises smoldering with golden lights of anticipation. He teased her mouth with a couple of quick little pecks then lowered his lips to hers and kissed her in earnest. Her lips parted beneath his, and they were both jolted to the core. Neither of them had ever experienced such a reaction nor felt so moved by just one kiss. When they pulled apart, Inez let out a dreamy sigh of satisfaction, and they came to rest forehead-to-forehead, nose-to-nose.

"Now that I have you, I will never let you go," he promised her, his voice husky with emotion. "I love you and would forfeit everything I have to spend the rest of my life with you. If we should be condemned, then we shall be condemned together. At least we will have had our little piece of heaven here on earth."

Chapter 14: Homecoming

Inez and Estêvão were married on the first day of April. The day dawned sunny and warm, more akin to summer than spring. The ceremony was held at the vineyard and the reception at the Fazenda da Pomba. Both households were ecstatic. Aside from the birth of the Little Prince, this was the most joyous event that had ever come to pass in the history of either establishment, and it would firmly cement the future of the two families and the businesses.

Estêvão was fifty years old, but the contentment that had settled over him with his beloved's acceptance of his marriage proposal subtracted years from his countenance and lent him a boyish air. He was dressed in a wine-colored jacket, a near perfect match to his new wife's hair color. His gleaming brown-black hair, now frosted at the temples with gray, was still as abundant and silky as ever, and he stood before the crowd as proud and majestic as the falcon for which his father had named him. Though his injury necessitated the use of his walking stick, it endowed him with a certain dignity and an aura of heroism.

Inez was the most beautiful bride that any of them had ever seen. She wore a cobalt blue gown of moiré silk that glowed with an iridescent shimmer when any chance motion rippled its surface. The whole of it was embroidered with seed pearls, and the sun gleamed off of them like water dripping from a fish's scales. Her deep red hair fell in a riot of curls to her waist, and she looked like a mythical creature emerging from the sea, a mermaid or Venus come to earth. The smile never faded from her lips, and her mood was contagious, infecting everyone present with her jubilation.

After the couple was officially married, they jumped into Estêvão's custom-made trap and led the bridal procession to the reception at the Fazenda da Pomba. They sat arm in arm, chatting and laughing along the way. Inez had not been down the road for over a year—the last time being to bury Christophe—and when they passed the line that marked the division of the two properties, Inez began to see pear trees at regular intervals. They were in full bloom, their long limbs, loaded with delicate white blossoms, bobbing in the breeze. Their sweet aromatic fragrance enveloped the newlyweds as they drove past and completed the fairytale quality of the occasion. They were a new addition, and Inez asked Estêvão when this had been accomplished.

"I had them planted last year when I knew I would finally have the chance to fulfill the promise I made to you when you were not yet twelve," he said, chuckling at the memory. "I thought they would be a nice surprise for you if you accepted and a fitting reminder of my foolishness if you refused. I'm glad I did not have to spend the *remainder* of my life being mocked by my own folly. The past twenty years have been quite enough."

Inez was touched by the sentiment, and she scooted closer to him on the seat, squeezing his arm and reaching up to kiss his warm cheek. "It would have been much more than foolish on my part to refuse you," she said laying her head on his shoulder. "I'm glad you did not believe it."

"You are a terrible liar," he said with a smile, and they both laughed at her capricious rejection of his advances.

When they reached the Fazenda da Pomba, Fausto greeted them at the stable and reached up to hand the new Senhora down from the vehicle. When she was on the ground, the stable hand swept her a low bow and placed a quick kiss on her hand. Inez graciously accepted his tribute, and Estêvão thought to himself how strange it was that it had taken so long for her to finally come to the place where she belonged. She had been here so many times as a guest, why hadn't he seen that this should have been her home from the start? He shook his head, again struck by his foolhardiness, and they proceeded to the house.

Dom Martín was waiting for them, and he stood grinning ear-to-ear at their approach. "Welcome home, little lady," he rumbled in his deep, gruff voice. "I always felt that this was where you belonged," and he lifted her off of her feet in a crushing bear hug. He set her back down, and Inez had to pause to catch her breath. Dom Martín apologized for being so rough. "I'm just so happy," he said sheepishly. "María would have been overjoyed at your homecoming." He sniffed and wiped at his eyes, and Inez was moved by his display of emotion.

The wedding guests began to arrive, and the celebration got under way. The wine flowed freely, and the food was excellent. The cook, who had felt a kinship and a deep affection for Inez since the first day the girl had used her kitchen, went all out to create a feast, which would be talked about for years to come. She had used many of the techniques gleaned from working with the new Senhora and created new signature dishes specifically for the day. Inez was extremely appreciative and lavished compliments on the cook who glowed with the praise.

The food ran out and the festivities began to wind down. The attendees filed past the newlyweds to wish them well before heading for home. There were many ribald jokes to the groom and vicarious, romantic sighs directed at the bride. Eventually Inez's family came to stand beaming before her. Joanna hugged them both tightly and uncharacteristically said nothing. Iñigo embraced his daughter and warmly shook Estêvão's hand, clapping him on the shoulder. Paulina squeezed Inez and then moved on to Estêvão, taking his hands in hers, regarding him with those serene dark eyes so much like his mother's.

"Capitán Rey," she began with a smile, "perhaps now you more fully understand the point I was trying to make that day on the porch. It is not often that I feel the need to speak my mind, and perhaps I had no right, but I felt it was my duty."

"You have earned the right," he said sincerely. "Without your medical skills Inez may have never survived her ordeal, and without your wise counsel I may have never reached this moment of happiness. You have every right," he repeated. She smiled and thanked him and moved aside to let Cristian say his goodbyes.

"Well I suppose I shall see you in a week," the boy said happily. "Just think, now I will have to call you 'Father'."

"You don't have to call me Father," Estêvão said. "Uncle Estêvão has served fine thus far."

"No, I *want* to call you Father," Cristian insisted, looking up at him, his gray-brown eyes shining with admiration. "My papa told me long ago that if anything ever happened to him, you would make sure that my mother and I were taken care of. He said that you had helped bring me into the world, and he believed you loved me as your own son." Inez gasped at this eerie message from the grave, but Cristian simply shrugged his shoulders and continued. "The way I see it, your marriage to my mother honors my papa's wishes and makes our relationship official."

"It seems your papa was a very wise man," Estêvão said, squeezing his new son's shoulder. "Well then, Son, we shall see you in a week," and he pulled the boy to him for a hug.

Cristian squeezed his father's waist with every ounce of strength he possessed then turned and did the same to his mother. He hopped down from the porch and ran to where his grandparents and Paulina were waiting for him in the wagon. They drove off into the night, and Inez and Estêvão waved until they disappeared from view. The newlyweds turned and entered the house, *their house*, and closed the door behind them.

"This has been a very long day, Wife," the groom said with a meaningful smile. "Shall we retire?"

His look sent a shiver of expectation through her, and Inez blushed to the roots of her hair. She lowered her eyes demurely and nodded her agreement, taking the arm that he offered. They silently made their way up the stairs, their progress slowed slightly by his compromised left hip, and Inez felt her anticipation increase with every step. He directed her toward the room that had always been hers, and he waited while she reached her shaking hand forward and fumbled with the knob. When she finally opened the door, her little surprised intake of breath sent a warm feeling of pleasure straight to his heart.

Since the beginning of their time together, Estêvão had thought of the scent of pear blossoms as Inez's alone. In preparation for their wedding night, he had ordered an abundance of the budding boughs brought into the room and used in various applications. Some of the limbs hung above the windows, and others had been woven into a floral canopy over the bed. Some loose petals were strewn across the coverlet, all of which gave the space the appearance of an arbor. The cheerfully winking candles lent the bridal chamber the charming atmosphere of an enchanted cottage, and the redolence of the flowers hit the newlyweds like a heady, sweet-smelling wave, the whispered promise of the bliss to come.

"Do you recognize the bedding?" Estêvão asked her with a mischievous look in his eyes.

Inez walked over to get a better look and again came the delighted little gasp that pleased him so much. She ran her hand over the sage green silk, lovingly caressing the arabesque border embroidered in the same blue and red of their wedding clothes. A large medallion of their entwined initials decorated the center of the counterpane, and she turned to him with tears in her eyes.

"How did you know?" she asked, overwhelmed by his sentimentality.

"I kept the robe that you made," he replied, indicating the garment draped over a chair, omitting how he had come by it. "I had the bedding made in the same pattern. I hope you don't mind."

"How could I mind?" she asked, turning to embrace him.

Inez brought her arms up and hooked them around his waist, her lips coming to rest against his warm neck. The masculine musk of his skin combined with their closeness sparked an instinctual response in her, and she felt her hunger for him rise inside. Her nervousness forgotten, she feathered soft little kisses down to his chest, and he made a low, growling purr deep in his throat. He swept her up off of her feet and onto the bed, gritting his teeth at the sharp stab of pain in his hip.

"Your wound," Inez said with concern.

"To the devil with my wound!" he answered, tearing the jacket from his shoulders and coming to rest beside her on the bed. "It is our wedding night, and if I had one foot in the grave, it would not keep me from proving my love to you."

He cupped his hand firmly around the back of her head and brought her mouth to his, kissing her ardently. His other hand came up behind her back and loosened the laces of her gown. He trailed a line of tender, sensual nibbles down her neck to her shoulder and pushed her sleeve down to expose a pale expanse of creamy velvet skin. He laid a warm, lingering kiss on the rise of flesh just below her collarbone, and Inez brought her hands up to clutch his silky hair, pulling him more closely to her and letting out a little moan of desire. He was thoroughly aroused by her passionate display, and he raised his head to smile at her one last time.

"I love you, Coelhinha," he whispered in her ear. "I have always loved you," and he kissed her deeply. His touch kindled a warm fire of lust low in her belly, and she let herself be carried away on a cloud of euphoria.

The next morning Inez woke late and stretched languorously in her bed, luxuriating in the type of divine contentedness written about in romantic novels. Her husband lay beside her, his hands folded behind his head, a satisfied smile on his lips. She rolled over and carefully threw her leg over his, her head coming to rest on his shoulder, her hand on his chest. He brought his arm down to encircle her, and pulled her more tightly to him, kissing her tenderly on the forehead. After a few moments, their bodies melded together, and Inez had to concentrate hard to delineate the two. She was amazed at the phenomenon and thought back over the extraordinary night she had just shared with her new husband.

When they had consummated their union, it had been the most moving experience of Inez's life. Though it had lacked some of the vigor and urgency of youth, it lacked none of the passion. It was slow and sweet and simple, everything Inez had ever dreamed of but so much more than she ever imagined. She thought back to Paulina's description of the physical expression of love, and she was grateful the woman had communicated it so genuinely. Without Paulina's standard, Inez might never have known to search for more. After the first few moments, she had abandoned her sense of self and surrendered her spirit to Estêvão, and in doing so finally found the fulfillment that had eluded her for so long.

Now she lay beside her husband, her soul mate, the very heart that beat within her. She was sublimely happy and amazed how an act so invariable could render such a different result when performed with the person of one's heart's desire. "How could I have ever believed I could live without you?" she asked, giving voice to the thoughts in her head. She placed a warm, teasing kiss on his neck then playfully nipped at the sensitive area where his arm connected to his chest.

"You should not start something that your poor old husband cannot finish," he said with an amused smile. "Besides, I have something to show you."

He kissed her lovingly then rolled out of the bed, donning his dressing robe and tossing her the one she had made so many years ago. He paused to watch as Inez slipped it around her shoulders and sat up in the bed, her masses of auburn curls tumbling down to frame her face. The sage green silk made her tresses blaze even brighter by comparison and infused her ivory skin with a rosy healthful glow. He fleetingly thought of Serafina and how the color of the robe had sapped the golden peachy tone from her, leaving her sallow and drawn. Then he shook his head and proceeded with his task.

He hobbled over to the bureau, picked up a black velvet bag from its surface, and limped back to the bed. He resumed his place at his wife's side, handed the bag to her, and looked on while she turned it thoughtfully over in her hands.

"What is it?" she asked, the curiosity shining in her eyes.

"You will have to open it to find out," he replied.

Inez loosened the cord around the mouth of the bag and slid the contents out onto the bed. The red stones spilled out onto the pale green silk of the coverlet like a sparkling cascade of live embers. She neatened the jumble of garnets and silver and caught her breath at the beautiful necklace laid out before her. Estêvão smiled at the radiant look on her face and began to explain.

"I know you already have the earrings, and yesterday I placed the ring on your finger myself. This is the remaining piece of the set." He paused and took a deep breath to calm himself then continued. "When my mother was ill, she reached a point when she understood she would not survive her suffering. She called me to her and gave this to me. She said, 'I saved this piece for the day when you would marry. Its proper place is around the neck of the woman you take for your wife. When you give it to Inez, please tell her I always knew that it belonged with her and that I will be proud to have her as a daughter to carry on the tradition of strong-willed women in our family.' She loved you very much," he said, wiping the moisture from his eyes.

"How did she know?" Inez asked, shaking her head over Dona María's astounding gift of perception.

"She knew many things that I, myself, was too stubborn or too blind to admit."

Inez and Estêvão spent that first week of their life together in a carefree manner, doing whatever struck their fancy. The weather maintained it's warm summerlike feel, and they took advantage of every moment. On days when Estêvão's wound did not trouble him, they rode up to the mesa to picnic under the little stand of pear trees that had come to mean so much to them. Estêvão rooted the ancient English lute out of the top of Inez's wardrobe, and she carried it along on these outings, playing it to accompany the songs of love and joy that now sprang from her soul with alacrity. Sometimes the husband and wife made up silly ditties with nonsensical words or fragments of improvised absurdity, but inevitably their laughter bound them closer than ever, and they considered these ridiculous escapades worthwhile pursuits.

One day he took her down to the marina where his new ship was being built. It was now nearly completed, and Inez was particulary impressed by the size. It was much larger than the

María Venecedora. Estêvão explained to her that it was not a caravel but a galleon, and he launched into a detailed inventory of the differences. This ship would be used primarily for trade, following established routes as opposed to exploration into unknown territories, therefore the increased stability and cargo room of the vessel would compensate for its reduced speed and maneuverability. Inez seemed satisfied with this, because it indicated that the days of his long absences from home were drawing to a close.

She asked him what he intended to name the ship, but he did not answer. Instead, he led her to the workshop of a master carver in town, and with an impish gleam in his hazel-green eyes he asked the man to show Inez the figurehead he was crafting. The man swept the protective canvas covering from his work, and Inez clapped in childlike enthusiasm at what stood beneath. It was a large lifelike depiction of a rabbit stretched out full-length at the apogee of a leap. The figurehead was meant to distinguish the ship from a distance, and she guessed correctly that Estêvão had named the ship for her. He told her that the *Coelhinha* would someday belong to Cristian, and would continue the tradition of ships named after the strong women of his family. She was touched by the sentiment and overwhelmed again by how much he loved her.

On occasions when his hip was too painful to do anything strenuous, Estêvão and Inez stayed close to the house. Sometimes he joined her in the kitchen to keep her company while she kneaded bread, or he did little preparatory tasks if she was making a larger meal. The cook never let him forget his sullying of her shrine on his first foray into her domain, and her treatment of him became a point of teasing for Inez. Other times they were content to idle away their time chatting by the fire, playing chess, or Inez doing needlework while Estêvão attended to his business concerns. She did not chastise him for working when they should have been enjoying their time together. She knew that if he left things undone, his mind would stray when she sought his full attention, and that was something she could not bear to risk.

Though their days were passed in easy, pleasing companionship, their nights together were spent making up for twenty years of lost opportunity. Estêvão's love for Inez proved to be a potent restorative, and he exuded the virility of a man half his age. Discovering each other's proclivities proved to be a ticklish undertaking, often resulting in attacks of laughter or playful tussling, but this merely served to strengthen the bond between them. Sometimes, the next day she would think back to these intimate moments and blush over her lack of inhibition during their connubial relations. Occasionally this prudishness would carry over into the next session, but as soon as she felt the warmth of his touch, her modesty disappeared, and she gave herself to him unreservedly. She felt like a young girl experiencing the thrilling titillation of first infatuation, and long after that first week of their marriage came to an end, her desire for him never ebbed.

One of the things she loved most was waking in the morning with her husband's face pressed to the back of her neck and his arm draped casually over her waist, her body nestled warmly against his. She was always struck anew by the feeling of oneness, the miracle of their merging into one body, one heart, and one spirit. The configuration never mattered. Whether they lay side-by-side, front-to-back, or back-to-back, she never ceased to be amazed at how their bodies fit so perfectly together. It was as if God had designed them specifically for each other.

Their life was not perfect, far from it. Estêvão's hip often plagued him, and he would rage in frustration at his reduced mobility and the constant nagging pain, but any time Inez grew exasperated with his foul mood and found herself tempted to react to his embittered tantrums, she thought about how empty her life would be without him. She would say a little prayer for patience, do all that she could to soothe his discomfort, and wait for the change in attitude and the apology that inevitably followed.

They were supremely happy and lived every second to its fullest, knowing that no matter how much time they had left together, it would never seem enough. Sometimes Inez would catch herself gazing at him, touched by his handsomeness, wondering how in a world so vast she had ever been fortunate enough to find the man who completed her the way he did. His sobriquet took on a new meaning to her, and she too often thought of him as El Rey. He was the unrivaled king of her heart, her world, her life. El Rey was her one true love, and she would never cease to pay him homage.

EPILOGUE
1581

Inez sat in her chair next to the fire, the cheerful silver rabbit resting in her palm and her great-granddaughter at her feet reverentially turning over the items in the maple wood box—the square of silk Estêvão had used to dry her tears the night of their first meeting, the red and blue tassel from Tesouro's bridle, the remainder of her first bottle of pear blossom perfume, and the two notes written in her beloved's own hand. Her treasures. They were things that would be meaningless to anyone else but priceless to her, because they evoked memories of him.

The little girl looked up at her, crinkled her nose, and smiled, the enchantment of the fairytale still evident in her eyes. Inez bent to return her cherished rabbit to its place in the box, and suddenly it struck her that it did not belong there but around the neck of a young girl. She leaned forward, dropped the leather thong around the child's neck, then sat back in her chair.

The girl looked up at her great-grandmother, her mouth gaping open, the surprise showing clearly in her dark gray eyes. "It is yours now, Inez," the old woman said, patting the child on the cheek, "and the box. I know you will treasure them as I do."

"Oh yes, Grandmama!" she said, rising to her feet. She

carefully hugged her namesake and kissed her on the cheek. "I promise to take good care of them. Thank you. Thank you so much!"

Their tender moment was interrupted by the heavy tread of a man's boots descending the stairs. Inez looked up to see her grandson hurriedly donning his cobalt blue captain's jacket. His beautiful wife, Yesenia, followed a few steps behind him, carrying their three-year-old boy, a look of anguish on her face.

"I just don't understand why you are so determined to fight," she said. "You have so many responsibilities here. Can't this be left to men who do not have as much to risk?" she pleaded.

"We *all* risk our freedom if we do not stand up for what is right," he said, his gray-brown eyes determined on his present course of action.

"Yes, but would it really be so terrible to be under Spanish rule? Would anything really change?"

"That is not the point. It's the principle. The *honor*," he retorted stubbornly.

Inez slowly shook her head. Honor. The word and concept had wrought far too much heartache in her own life. How could she keep it from doing the same to these young people who still had so much of their lives ahead of them? Why could he not understand that there were many things that were of much greater consequence than honor?

Her grandson was extremely obstinate, but he came by it honestly. It had long been impossible to convince the men of her family of the best course of action. Inez was certain that deep inside he knew what was right. Sometimes he just needed a gentle reminder.

"Cristóvão," Inez called from her place next to the fire, "before you rush off to do your duty, would you do me a small favor?"

"Of course, Grandmother," he said with a slightly put out look on his face. "What is it?"

"I would like to go out to sit with your grandfather for a while. Will you take me?" she asked innocently.

"Certainly," he said, his irritation immediately vanishing from his features. He crossed the room and helped her from her chair, once again the caring, solicitous young man that she knew and loved. Inez had known this little distraction would work. Cristóvão revered his grandfather above anyone else. When he was a toddler, Estêvão had seen fit to spoil him at every turn. He would sit his grandson on his knee and sing to him or tell him stories of his years in the East. The boy never tired of the attention and bragged to anyone who cared to listen that his grandfather was the great El Rey. Although he was now a grown man, his adulation had still not diminished. He had even named his son for his hero.

As they neared the stairs on the way outside, her great-grandson reached out to kiss Inez as she passed. She squeezed the child to her and let him lay a smacking wet baby kiss on her cheek. He hugged her neck fiercely and rubbed his cheek against hers, closing his eyes to better enjoy the sensation.

"Gentle, Estêvão," his mother said, worried that his exuberance might throw the old woman off-balance.

"That's all right, Jessi. I am not quite as delicate as you think." The younger woman blushed, staining her fine white skin with a pretty pink glow and making the blue-green of her eyes even brighter.

Baby Estêvão had not noticed any of the exchange. He was still busy rubbing Inez's cheek with his own. "Grandmama, your cheek is very soft," he said, his green eyes wide with appreciation, "and you smell like flowers."

Inez chuckled to herself. She supposed that after the long years of using pear blossom perfume, everything she owned smelled like flowers. She kissed her great-grandson one last time then exited the house, resuming her progress toward her meeting with her husband. Cristóvão patiently slowed his pace to match hers, and she took her time, enjoying the opportunity to have him to herself.

"You know, Cristóvão," she began thoughtfully, "even your grandfather reached a point when he understood that some things were more important than honor."

He turned to regard her with his gray-brown eyes, the surprise showing plainly on his handsome face. "That is something I did not know," he said.

Inez nodded her head then continued. "That is part of the reason he gave up the running of a ship. When your father was old enough and capable of handling the *Coelhinha* on his own, your grandfather only went along on the first few voyages to make sure things went smoothly. He said that although he loved the sea and the honor of exploring and claiming new territories in the name of his country, he realized that love and family were far more meaningful pursuits."

A little smile came to Cristóvão's face at the recollection of the love that his grandparents had always exuded toward one another. They were forever holding hands and kissing each other on the cheek when they thought no one else was watching. Even long after they had reached old age, they were inseparable, taking long walks together or simply sitting on a bench in the sun if his grandfather's hip was troubling him.

Inez saw from her grandson's expression that he was beginning to understand. She went on to drive her point home. "It became even more clear to him after you were born. He never stopped telling me how sorry he would be to miss out on any part of your childhood."

Cristóvão looked directly into her silver and gold eyes, smiling at her gentle wisdom. He affectionately patted the familiar old hand resting on his sleeve, and they walked on in silence, nothing further needing to be said. They reached their destination, and Cristóvão settled his beloved grandmother on the bench, making himself comfortable beside her. They enjoyed each other's company and the beautiful summer day, the earlier urgency of the morning momentarily forgotten.

Inez looked down at her hands in her lap and regarded the ring on her finger, the gift bestowed upon her by her husband on her wedding day. The garnet shone with a deep red fire, and the silver reflected the rays of the summer sun above. Jessi already had the earrings and the necklace, and it seemed utterly fitting that Cristóvão should have the ring. Knowing it to be the correct course of action, Inez twisted it free and handed it to her grandson.

Cristóvão looked at her in astonishment, his heavy black eyebrows drawn up in surprise. "Grandmother, what are you doing?" he asked. "I have never known you to take off your wedding ring."

"Your grandfather wore this ring for most of his life. The garnet is fabled to be a stone of protection. You should have had it long ago." He opened his mouth to object, but Inez simply raised her hand and shook her head. "He would have wanted you to have it."

Cristóvão closed his mouth, nodded his head, and graciously took the treasure from his grandmother's hand. "Thank you," he said and slipped the ring onto the pinky of his left hand. "It is a perfect fit," and he held his hand out, turning the ring from side to side, the garnet flashing its fiery approval. Inez smiled at his obviously pleased, childlike reaction.

Suddenly a crewmember from the *Coelhinha II* came running up behind them, cutting short the heartwarming scene. "Capitán Pereira," the man began. Because of the pear trees lining the road on the border of the fazenda, locals had begun to refer colloquially to it as the Fazenda Pereira, and so the family had adopted the surname as its own.

"One moment, Álvaro," Cristóvão said, turning to Inez on the bench. "Grandmother, I must attend to this business. It will take only a few minutes. I will be back to take you to the house when you are ready. Do you mind?" he asked. She shook her head. Her grandson kissed her on the cheek then walked off with his first mate to discuss what was to be done with the *Coelhinha II*.

Inez sat on the beautifully crafted bench her father had carved as a wedding present for her and Estêvão. Was it really fifty years ago? It had originally stood on the mesa underneath their little stand of pear trees. When her husband could no longer make the trip because of his injury, the bench had been moved here. It was a lovely spot and not far from the house. They had spent many peaceful hours enjoying it.

She sat taking pleasure in the sunshine and vivid green beauty of the quiet clearing. The dappled shade of the trees, the buzzing insects, and the scent of hydrangeas were common things, seemingly trivial, but somehow they had a larger significance in this place. They became sacred. She looked out at the family cemetery, mulling over how important a role each one of these people had played in her life. Dom Martín, Paulina, her parents, she had even outlived her son and his wife. The only member of the family not accounted for was João.

It was said that João had incurred the wrath of a powerful Chinese lord by stealing away the man's favorite and most beautiful wife. The woman had eventually been returned, but months later she had given birth to a child who was clearly *not* Oriental. She and her child were disgraced and tossed out of the lord's palace to fend for themselves, and a few days later, João disappeared. No one had any idea what had happened to him, but the rest of the family was here, and Inez would soon join them.

Earlier this year Inez had marked the one hundredth anniversary of her beloved's birth. She had begun to feel his loss keenly of late, and an emptiness grew inside her. The only thing that brought her any comfort was to dream about her past. She found herself living more and more in that world and less in the one around her. It was a welcome escape and the only thing that seemed to stem the bleeding of her spirit where the other half had been torn away. She loved her grandson and his beautiful wife, and her great grandchildren were a never-ending source of pleasure, but nothing could fill her heart the way Estêvão had. She felt only half alive and was always tired and cold, so cold.

I will just lie down in the sunshine here, next to my husband, she thought to herself. She slowly rose from the bench and situated her wizened old body on the grass next to his grave, running her hand lovingly over the spot where he lay under several feet of earth. *Soon, mi Rey, very soon we will be together.* Then she laid on her back and closed her eyes, welcoming the warmth of the sun shining on her face. She reflected back on how she had always felt that Terceira would be her home, and now it would be her final resting place. A peaceful smile came to her face, and she slipped into a dream.

Cristóvão and his family came out to take his grandmother back to the house. Inez and little Estêvão raced ahead while a smiling Jessi walked comfortably at his side. His first mate had come to inform him that the Spaniards had already been defeated, and there was no longer any need for Capitán Pereira to make the trip down to the *Coelhinha II*. It would not have mattered. After the conversation with his grandmother, he had already decided not to go. It was uncanny the way she was able to provide the simplest solutions to life's most complicated dilemmas. She was a wise old woman, and he was grateful for her counsel.

Cristóvão put his arm around his wife's shoulders and pulled her tightly to his side. He watched his children skipping and shouting back and forth to one another, delighting in the sunshine of the fine summer day. These were the things that were important. Everything he needed to live was right here. He was overwhelmed by the blessings in his life, and again, thankful that his grandmother had been there to point them out. He kissed his wife on the cheek and let the cares of the world fall by the wayside.

When they reached the cemetery, they stopped short and Jessi let out a little gasp, bringing her hands up to cover her mouth. Inez walked toward them with silent tears streaming down her face, her nose crinkling in her grief. Little Estêvão ran up to his parents, a look of concern in his big green eyes, and tugged at his father's free hand.

"Papa, Grandmama is sleeping, and she won't wake up."

Cristóvão bent down to scoop up his worried little son and embrace his crying daughter. The four of them stood there in a communal hug, united in their sorrow and drawing comfort from each other. After a few minutes, he lifted his head, dried his eyes, and pulled them more closely together.

"Do not be sad," he said to his little family. "She has finally gone to join her love, and we will always have the lessons that she taught us. As long as we have each other, everything else will be all right."

The End

Author's Note

First of all, thank you for downloading this book. I heartily appreciate your support. Without readers, there would be no point. I hope you enjoyed the complete version of EL REY with all of the fascinating history intact. I trust that the backstories of Paulina, María, Iñigo, and Joanna did not prove distracting. They were meant to provide an incisive look at a two hundred year period in the turbulent shared history of Portugal and Castile and give a well-rounded perspective of the events leading up to the state of early 16th century Iberia. I would here like to provide some additional information.

The earliest records of religious expeditions to Santiago de Compostela, or the Way of Saint James, date back to the 9th century. James is regarded to have been one of the first disciples to follow Jesus and one of only three whom Jesus selected to bear witness to His Transfiguration. He is also said to be the first apostle executed for his Christianity. His death by the sword mandated by Herod is the only martyrdom of an apostle recorded in the New Testament. He is the Patron Saint of Spain, and tradition holds that his remains were transported by boat from Jerusalem and enshrined at the place now called Santiago de Compostela to commemorate his sacrifice.

During the Middle Ages the religious procession to Galicia became one of the most important and popular pilgrimages along with those to Rome and Jerusalem. Traditionally these journeys began at one's home and ended at the chosen site. Many Christians made the arduous treks as penance or atonement for grave error rather than pass from this world with the stain of grievous sin on one's soul. Some were bidden by the Church to do so, others by their conscience. The characters in this story are fictional but representative of the vast numbers of visitors to the shrine seeking to find answers, comfort, and redemption through their faith.

As in all of my writing, the basis for Joanna's story is also firmly rooted in historical events. Catalina and Constanza of Lancaster, John of Gaunt, and the rest of the personages and circumstances surrounding the struggle for the throne of Castile are documented in English, Spanish, and Portuguese resources. The resulting Treaty of Windsor is the longest standing diplomatic alliance in the world and is still in force today.

Likewise, the war for control of Castile between Afonso V and Queen Isabella and Ferdinand of Aragon took place and happened, more or less, as I have related. Although there were undoubtedly many families who served their sovereigns and suffered similar fates, the Newendens and Crowles are merely products of my imagination.

Similarly, the Castilian Inquisition and its precipitating factors are all documented by various reliable resources. The dates and papal bulls were accurately cited to the best of my ability, and the fate of Diego de Susan—betrayed by his daughter and subsequently condemned and sentenced to death in the first *auto de fé* of the Castilian Inquisition—is also documented. Although there were many real people who faced the same decisions and consequences, the García family is purely fictional.

In addition, the members of the Portuguese court who appear in María's story actually existed. Their familial relationships and events surrounding the throne are also recognized historical occurrences reported to have transpired in the manner described. Fernando, Duke of Braganza, was executed for treason, and the shocking murder of Diogo, Duke of Viseu, did indeed occur at the hands of his cousin and brother-in-law, King João II of Portugal. The future Manuel I was witness after the fact, and the conversation between him and the King immediately following the act also took place.

It is recorded, too, that as a young man Diogo visited the kingdom of Castile and had a love affair with Doña Leonor de Sotomaior y Portugal resulting in a natural son, Afonso de Portugal. After ascending to the throne, Manuel granted Afonso an exalted position as Constable of Portugal, and eventually his descendants were assimilated into the legitimate ranks of the royal family.

Diogo never officially married, and the rest of Maria's story and the characters therein are purely fictional, merely a product of my imagination. But weddings performed in secret were not unheard of among the aristocracy of the era, so it is not beyond the realm of possibility that Diogo might have had an undisclosed family. And it makes a very entertaining story ... wouldn't you agree?

Thank you for purchasing this book. If you enjoyed

El Rey: A Novel of Renaissance Iberia

you might also like these other books by

Ginger Myrick:

But for the Grace of God: A Novel of Compassion in a Time of War

Insatiable: A Macabre History of France ~ L'Amour: Marie Antoinette

The Welsh Healer: A Novel of 15th Century England

Work of Art: Love & Murder in 19th Century New York

ABOUT THE AUTHOR

Winner of the Rosetta Literary Contest 2012, Ginger Myrick was born and raised in Southern California. She is a self-described wife, mother, animal lover, and avid reader. Along with the promotion for her five novels,

BUT FOR THE GRACE OF GOD: A NOVEL OF COMPASSION IN A TIME OF WAR,
EL REY: A NOVEL OF RENAISSANCE IBERIA,
INSATIABLE: A MACABRE HISTORY OF FRANCE ~ L'AMOUR: MARIE ANTOINETTE,
THE WELSH HEALER: A NOVEL OF 15th CENTURY ENGLAND,
and
WORK OF ART: LOVE & MURDER IN 19TH CENTURY NEW YORK,

she is currently crafting her sixth. A Christian who writes meticulously researched historical fiction with a 'clean' love story at the core, she hopes to show the reading community that a romance need not include graphic details to convey deep love and passion. If you have any questions or comments, she would love to hear from you! You can learn more at

GingerMyrick.com

44449675R00353